The G

THE GOD'S WIFE

First edition. February 1, 2019.

Written by Sarah Holz.

For Alex, dancing in the Field of Reeds

Ismene, sister, mine own dear sister, knowest thou
what ill there is, of all bequeathed by our father,
that Zeus fulfills not for us twain while we live?
Nothing painful is there, nothing fraught with ruin,
no shame, no dishonor, that I have not seen in
Thy woes and mine.
- Sophocles, *Antigone*

Most of all, however, large numbers of persons are led to lose sight of justice by the craving for military commands, civic honors, and fame. The saying of Ennius, 'Where kingship is concerned, no social bond or covenant is sacred,' has a much broader application; for as to whatever is of such a nature that but few can be foremost in it, there is generally so keen a rivalry that it is exceedingly difficult to keep social duty inviolate.
- Marcus Tullius Cicero, *de Officiis*

I remember the first time the Lord of the Red Land came to me and whispered in my dreams with the breath of an airless desert wind pressing against the waters of the Nile. I remember the rumble of his voice in the back of his throat, reminding me that he is also the lord of thunder and of the wild desert storms. He was so unknowable, though I knew enough to recognize him for who he was — young as I was. Though even now, so many years later, I struggle to put it into words. As with many things that happen in dreams, the harder one works to pin them into place, the more they scatter. Perhaps that is why I have struggled so to make the plans I began in my haunted nights bear fruit in the Waking World.

The ancients likewise struggled to name his aspect: this mighty being who refused to come to them in a form they could understand. This warrior prince who did not take the forms of the animals they knew like the other gods, who claimed half of Egypt as his own. Priests argued amongst themselves as to whether he was a donkey or an aardvark, a fennec fox or a giraffe. Finally, a priest of Lord Ra serving in the reign of Djer is said to have ended the argument in the religious ranks with the pronouncement that since he was the Arbiter of Chaos, he assumed any and all forms to proclaim his superiority over mankind.

The priesthood was satisfied, but common folk will always try to put a name to their fears. They are the ones who invented the word they needed, free from the dictates of rulers and scribes. Thus this creature of fantasy and nightmare was branded the sha. *Everything under the sun and nothing ever seen all in one. Ganymedes taught me about the chimera of Greece, the monster Bellerophon slew with the help of the flying horse Pegasus. He always said the* sha *was a chimera, or some other demon born out of the old gods that came before the Olympians imprisoned chaos and darkness. As if it were all that simple.*

My Lord is so very old, he laughs when he hears talk of Zeus (or Jupiter for that matter), or their squabbling progeny. Family turmoil is terribly outmoded to him, though he has always been sympathetic to my concerns, for he knows the importance of vigilance in one's own house. For in a world where brothers and sisters and uncles and aunts are all spouses and rivals, blood lives too close to hide much. We strive to be godly and in the end we are nothing but ugly grotesques of the holy ones. We insist on imitating them in the very things that cause them grief and expect to rise above consequence. Perhaps that is the only kind of immortality we are capable of.

I should perhaps begin by saying I did not want any of this. Many in turn will say I was clearly ill-equipped and out-classed by the other players on the gaming board we made of our lives. I have made so many mistakes and the damage — the damage wakes me in the darkest hours of night with sobs in my throat. I have never enjoyed games of chance and have not my sister's love of risk. Or power. I had to answer the call of my Lord or be taken at the flood. Often I have found myself with little else to cling to other than the will to see another sunrise bathe itself on the river's edge. I was born a girl in shadows and I have struggled all my life to escape. In those longest ago days my greatest desire was to see my mother again. My nurse Baktka used to tell me that she had turned into a skylark and had flown away chasing the jeweled butterflies she wished to put in my hair. How I would have to be as swift as a kite if I wanted to catch her. I ran until my feet bled, though I was never fast enough to meet her. I had survival callouses on my soles by the time I learned that some things can never be recaptured. And yet I still find myself hoping her ka is as bold as the skylarks I hear singing in the reeds.

When my Lord speaks, I listen and he hears my voice when I answer, the voice of the invisible daughter. The youngest, the most insignificant. He came to me because I am the daughter of Egypt, I am Tjesiib Arsinoë Philoaígyptos, and I would fight for him and his people. Even if they had long turned away from him as a fratricide and usurper, a god whose name must never be spoken, and who must be exiled from the Black Land of his nephew by the power of a million burning wadjets. Even if I was only a half-native, raised to emulate a foreign conqueror and his worshipped liege-lord. My Lord came to me because he knew that even if my lips were white with fear, I would jump from the top of the lighthouse in Alexandria if it would save Egypt from its enemies.

Or itself.

Chapter One

My father used to curse his fate, saying he grew in the wrong womb. He made himself Pharaoh despite his illegitimacy, though it remained a lodestone around the neck of his reign until the day he died, spent of his strength and demanding tributes of love from the treacherous children he left in his wake. It was Cleopatra who had the foresight to give her and Ptolemy the epithet *Philopator* — "Father-Loving" — to prove she had been sincere with her deathbed prostrations. Ptolemy, for his part, always thought it was laying it on a bit thick. However, my sister was always difficult to read — maybe she had truly loved our father. With all the positions one could take in our family dramas, it stands to reason that possibly someone had ended up on the old pharaoh's side.

It must be said, for they would beg the clarification of me, that Cleopatra and Ptolemy were only my half-siblings. They, and their older sister Berenice, were the children of my father's first wife, Cleopatra called Tryphaena, who was in her turn another bastard sired by my grandfather. In the tangled web of half-siblings and bastards every Ptolemy seemed to leave scattered about the throne of Egypt, even my father and stepmother were probably not sure if they were full siblings or not. Not that a small detail such as incest had ever concerned our House.

The Ptolemies had arrived in Egypt bearing the corpse of Alexander the Great with magnificent pomp and promptly took up the consanguineous practices of the ancient rulers of this land with an ease that scandalized their neighbors and made the tongues of their enemies wag. Like the old dynasties, their justification was to maintain the purity of their blood. The Egyptian royals meant to preserve the blood they believed they shared with Father Ra himself. The Ptolemies meant to sequester their Greek blood from the foreign blood of the Egyptians. Either way, the pharaoh and his family were to remain a breed apart. Numerous illegitimate children conceived with other Greek gentlewomen saved the Ptolemies from some of the more freakish physical deformities that plagued other Egyptian dynasties (though enough familial coupling resulted in all full-blooded members looking rather alike), but it could

5

not save them from the special type of power struggles that occur when everyone is double or triple-related and everyone's claim is as good as anyone else's. The history of my family is not only written in the blood of kin-slain uncles, cousins, mothers, and children: it blots out the book until nothing remains apart from the damning red evidence that stains our fingers even as we seek to turn the page. To hold true to all that had come before, when my father gained the throne of his ancestors by the sword and by animal cunning, his first act was to marry one of his remaining sisters, my stepmother. They had their three blooded children and my father dallied with numerous other ladies and all was well until Cleopatra Tryphaena decided she could rule the kingdom just as easily as the brother-husband she had grown bored of. Indeed she thought she might do a touch better, so she watched and waited for a Ptolemyesque opportunity to be rid him.

My father, while not a great king, did have some gifts of perception, and had realized earlier on than many that the rising power in our world was not a Greek city-state, but that of an upstart Etruscan replacement situated among seven hills that rose up on the banks of the Tiber River. The Republic of Rome had been gaining in prestige for several centuries, though that was nothing more than the blink of an eye to kingdoms that had invented writing and men whose ancestors had conquered the world with Alexander. My father understood that it was with Rome that he should breed friendships and did so with exemplary alacrity. Perhaps he succeed in this endeavor too well, for it was not long before his Rome-love provided the catalyst for revolution his sister-wife had been looking for. She rallied national discontent over the pharaoh seemingly bending his knee to a foreign land and swept him from power, placing Berenice on the throne in her father's stead. I believe my indolent, vain father never saw the betrayal coming.

My mother had been a second wife in name to the pharaoh at the same time, though in truth she was little more than a highly placed concubine in his palace. She had cleverly been sent to the pharaoh once upon a time as girl in the first blush of womanhood by the lingering Egyptian aristocracy, being that she was the daughter of one of the old ruling families clinging to relevance ever since the Macedonians had arrived and ground the remnants of the ancient kingdoms into the desert sand. And my father, drunk on his power, had forgone the general revulsion the Greek lords had for women with native blood and found himself taken for a little while by the slender maiden with the liquid sable eyes. I was born to her during the last few years before my father's Roman sympathies led to the rebellion that ousted him from his throne.

When my father fled to Rome following his deposition, he was able to take very few people with him. Among a handful of loyal retainers, he grabbed my half-sister Cleopatra so that he would have control of a Ptolemy heir and a queen of the blood upon his return. Naturally his only son at the time, Ptolemy, was too well guarded. He also brought my mother so that she would speak to her Egyptian kin on his behalf. I went with them all into exile because my mother refused to leave me behind.

It took several hard, rootless years, but my mother did as she was bidden and some well-placed funds from the coffers of Alexandria helped the exiled pharaoh rally the additional Roman support he needed for his invasion. These lords had no great love of my father, but they loved my gentle mother for her lineage. In the end, they were conservative enough to gamble on the evil they knew rather than the growing uncertainty of a land ruled solely by Greek queens.

It is true that these same lords had no doubt fanned the flames of revolt with Cleopatra Tryphaena that had deposed my father three years prior, though three years under Berenice, who showed both an inclination towards fiscal irresponsibility, and a disinclination to marry and produce an heir, had apparently given them second thoughts. Or least, those were the reasons my father gave out for his fickle people's change of heart. The alleys of Alexandria whispered the accusation of madness and quietly laid it at the feet of Berenice's unmarked grave, an accusation no one dared to utter aloud while my father still breathed. It is a terrible thing to accuse the blood of the king with taint. Indeed, Berenice's name was banished from the halls of the palace and the servants only spoke in the dead of night about the insanity of those three years. Of what had happened to my stepmother.

So my father sat upon the falcon throne once more, by the consent of Rome, as that flinty land stuck its hand deeper into the affairs of our kingdom. He was already tired of the Egyptian woman whom he had promised the native lords to marry upon his second coronation. He ignored my mother and made Cleopatra his co-ruler, though mercifully not his wife. This may seem like a shred of Greek restraint against a custom his Macedonian ancestors would have detested, but truthfully the failed rebellion of Cleopatra Tryphaena and Berenice robbed my father of more than his throne. He became a twisted, angry old man who loved nothing and trusted no one. He held to his new maxim until he died four years later, a bitter husk, and left his throne to Cleopatra and Ptolemy to hold together.

I also suspect that many of our troubles in those red years that followed the death of Ptolemy the Twelfth of His Name, who gave himself the deceptively lighthearted epithet *Auletes* — The Flute-Player — stemmed from Cleopatra's resentment at our father for making her only a joint heir with our brother Ptolemy. She had ruled by the old pharaoh's side as his co-ruler since the age of fourteen and thought she had earned the right to the throne of Egypt in her own name alone. As the funeral ceremonies were carried out and we all awaited news from Rome that my father's will had been ratified by the Roman Senate, Cleopatra kept her own counsel in this matter. Though during this time, I saw several of her maids quietly disposing of a basket of elegant trinkets that had all been viciously smashed.

I was eleven when my father died and my mother had been dead since the spring after we had come home to Egypt, sick and full of grief. As I alluded to before, she departed my world suddenly, and left in her place my only full brother, also named Ptolemy to honor my father, born to her during our exile abroad. When a nurse brought him before us for the first time, Cleopatra had looked into his face full of babyish seriousness wrapped tightly in his swaddles and laughingly proclaimed he was the spitting image of Ptah, the Egyptians' sculptor god who was depicted similarly mummy-wrapped. The name stuck and my beloved brother was Ptah to all of us ever from that day forth. Such things are essential in a world where so many people share names.

Ptah stood with me as we watched Cleopatra and Ptolemy crowned as co-regents, the Seventh and the Thirteenth of the Their Names respectively. My tutor Ganymedes stood on my other side, serving as a chaperon for both of us amidst the the throngs of lords and priests crowded into the greatest of the receiving rooms in the glittering royal palace of the Ptolemies, perched like the rest of the city of Alexandria on the back of the sea.

"Do you think we'll be named princes and princesses, too?" asked Ptah, craning to see past all the adults' heads, his short curls bobbing back and forth as his head weaved around elbows.

"Silly goose," I replied, smiling, "you are already a prince!"

"But I want to be a *bigger* prince!"

I knew what he meant, but changes in royal title are a bit beyond the comprehension of such a young child, so I scooped him up and promised him one day he would indeed be a bigger prince than he was at the moment.

Ganymedes frowned slightly. "I would sleep more restfully at night for Your Highnesses' sakes if I thought your Most Blessed siblings were on better terms at this the most glorious beginning of their reign."

"Do you think there will be trouble?" I asked him. A foolish question. With Ptolemies, one must always anticipate trouble.

He quickly shook his head. "This is not the time for such questions, Your Highness. All rests in the hands of the gods."

Chapter Two

When my siblings ascended the throne of Egypt, I was as ordinary as one would expect the youngest princess born into a family that had ruled a foreign land by blood and in blood to be. Oh, we Ptolemies were deep-swimming Titans whose sins were as infamous as those found in any Greek legend. We seemed destined to prove warty old Plato correct that those who attended to stories of the Olympians would only sow moral decay in their children. Yet there was that brief sliver of time where the crimes of the past lay far behind us gathering dust and our own fangs were clean. I was eleven years old and so was the Pharaoh of Egypt, and my deepest worry was that I had a secret.

It was a secret I carried close to my heart, for as long as I had possessed memory. It was a secret I dared not tell Baktka or even Mudjet, who ostensibly was my maid but in the sheltered upbringing of a royal had been my oldest companion. Ganymedes would have scolded me for being fanciful, though I was in deadly earnest.

The truth was that in every dream I could remember, all my life, there was one constant. In all my dreams there dwelt a creature, one so unlike anything I had seen in life I believed I had cobbled him together from my imagination. He was a dog-like animal, as black as a starless night, and when he moved he walked on long legs that tapered to small, neat paws. His forked tail always stood perfectly straight like a pike, as did his sharply pointed ears. He stared at me in the chaos of my sleeping mind with almond-shaped emerald eyes. The creature never interfered, only endlessly watched. As if it were waiting for some unknown thing.

I was still very young when I first understood who my creature was. Ganymedes had brought some Egyptian scrolls from the Great Library to show Ptolemy and me, even if Pothinus, my brother's tutor, thought it was local rubbish. My teacher unrolled the long sheets of papyrus and let us pore over the pictures inked with bright dyes that smelled of the artists' quarter.

"It is not rubbish, Brother Pothinus," Ganymedes said mildly. "Any ruler of this House that wishes to hold the love of the people must understand something of their gods."

"A thousand score monsters, most of whom are dead even in this land," Pothinus scoffed. "My lord here need only pay some trifling service to Amun, Horus, and that witch Isis, and he will be fine."

The eunuchs continued their debate as Ptolemy and I examined the scrolls with the deep concentration of children absorbed in rapt contemplations beyond the mundane reach of adults.

My brother and I were born in the same year, several months apart, to our respective mothers. We were twins born in different wombs, joined by an invisible chain that bound us to the other even as our differences of status and temperament ensured we would never cleave to one another without friction. When Ptolemy was born, he was the longed-for first son of a line that had carefully distilled its blood against itself to keep alive a connection to a heroic past. I was born the burdensome daughter of a second wife, taken to bargain for the loyalty of men whose own lineage my father despised.

Ptolemy was born during *Shemu*, the dry time of the Egyptian year, and his arid personality, thirsty for warmth, seemed to reflect that, while my birth during *Akhet*, the flood season, seemed to rule my nature. After all, I found it so easy to drown in my own thoughts. Here in this moment though, we managed to simply be curious children.

The Egyptian gods were strange, with their animal heads and rigid poses, and yet, there was something in them that made them feel more accessible to me than the Greek deities who populated my lessons. Their heads were those of animals, but they were the animals I saw every day along the Nile. Crocodiles, hippopotamuses, jackals, ibises, falcons — these were more familiar to me than the sea beasts of Poseidon or the bears that frolicked with Artemis. It was looking among this celestial menagerie that I saw my dream creature and my heart skipped a beat.

"Teacher, what beast is this?" I asked, hoping my finger did not tremble as I indicated the animal on the page in front of me.

Ganymedes took up the scroll and frowned. "This creature is not spoken of, *nedjet*. It is the *sha*, the animal of Set, the god of the desert."

"A god reviled even among the Egyptians for slaying his own brother," Pothinus added. "And Brother Ganymedes, please refrain from using such terms of familiarity with your charge, especially Egyptian ones. She is a Greek princess of a noble dynasty and needs to remember to act like it."

"A brother-slaying god?" remarked a breezy voice behind us, whose clear ring was immediately recognizable to everyone in Alexandria. "That practically makes him the patron deity of the House of Ptolemy, does it not?"

We all turned to see our sister Cleopatra emerge from under a billowy silk awning, accompanied by Damianus, her tutor, and Theodotus, our collective tutor of rhetoric. She was nearly as young as us, the little Queen of Egypt at our father's side, yet she was our older sister and starting to grow womanly in appearance. This pleased our subjects, who relied on the female co-rulers to connect them to the earth fed by the Nile that in turn nourished Egypt. Her chestnut colored hair glinted gold in the sunlight, wrapped up in the white band of a Hellene ruler with pearl pins peeking out through the strands. Her unpredictable hazel eyes chose to appear light brown that day. Her lilting golden voice and pleasant expression as usual hid whatever she might be actually thinking.

Our tutors bowed deferentially as she glided over to us, her eyes shifting thoughtfully as her light fingers fondled the scroll. "Oh, Set is like Hades," she said meditatively. "You need him around, yet no one wants to invite him to dinner or speak his name too loudly." She passed her finger over the *sha* as if casting a spell, before lifting her head abruptly and resuming her lighter tone. "Though I would not worry about him too much, either. He might have killed Osiris and maimed Horus, but they won out in the end. Those are the gods our subjects hold in their hearts."

Everyone else chuckled and fell into easy chatter amongst themselves, though I felt divided from their company, still wracked by fear that my dreams were haunted by the most dreaded of all Egyptian gods. The one whose form was spectacular rather than earthly and whose name was never invoked except in terror.

Despite these misgivings, I could not banish the watchful *sha* from my dreams any more than I could find a way to fit pleasingly among my fractured family. My world revolved on in this way until the night following my brother and sister's crowning, a night filled with great rejoicing and feasting that I spent sneaking out of to play games with Ptah and Mudjet in empty, echoing rooms. A night where I would eventually slip into a sleep that would change my life forever.

I am walking through an abandoned palace I do not recognize. The columns are tumbledown and the entire structure is slowly being reclaimed by the desert. I pad across sandstone steps that lead to nowhere and stare at art I know to be Egyptian, and yet is so different from that with which I am familiar. The figures are not slender human reeds, nor are their faces geometric perfection. They have sloping features and fleshy mouths, the men have potbellies and wide hips. Compared to the willowy figures that fill the temples of Alexandria, these people are practically grotesque. And yet I cannot help but notice how happy they appear. They play with their children, they embrace one another, they lift their strange faces to the rays of the sun. I find myself wondering what it would be like to be a part of this loving, misshapen family when I see the *sha* sitting opposite me at the far expanse of the foundation.

In my dreams since I had put a name to my creature, I had attempted to communicate with it in any way I could think of. I had spoken to it only to be met by staring silence. I had chased it only to have it dart out of reach. So as I step towards it once more, I expect it to skitter away from me again, with the same unnerving hint of laughter in its green eyes. This time as I move closer, it remains stock still, its forked tail twitching back and forth. I am only inches away from its smooth, shining face and as I reach out to touch its nose, the *sha* transforms.

In its place stands a man. A tall man with the same glossy skin of obsidian black, the same laughing green eyes. His whole frame, spare and muscular at same time, is crossed at points with golden scars that trail this way and that, speaking of battle. On his head he wears a hood with the form of the *sha's* head. Underneath the hood, his clever face grins at me.

"*Hai*, Arsinoë," he says to me in a luring voice full of the dark suggestion of thunder.

The change is so unexpected, I falter briefly. How should I proceed?

"*Hai*, Lord Set," I at last respond.

His grin deepens, his white teeth sharp. "Do not be afraid, sweet one. I have been summoned by the gods of the Black Land to be your protector. You have been beloved in my eyes since the day you were born."

"Why me, my Lord? I am a Greek princess encroaching upon the lands of the Egyptian gods."

"You are being raised as a Greek princess, *nedjet*, but you have your mother's blood in you as well and that is the blood of our cherished people. As she prepared to enter the *Duat*, your mother prayed to us to keep you safe. The prayers of a queen of Egypt are always heard."

"Perhaps not always answered, though."

Lord Set laughs, a deep sound that flares like fire in a cauldron. "Indeed nimble one, that is true. All we may do is attempt to influence events in the Waking World, nothing is set in stone."

"Why do you speak to me now, my Lord?"

"Because no one knows better than the Lord of Storms when one is coming, *nedjet*. We need you to be strong, for great tests are ahead of you. The time is coming when the people will look to you, and if you are not Egypt's champion in that moment, all will be undone."

I tremble at the weight of the dark god's words. What calamity lies before us that the gods should come to me, and send the Prince of Destruction as my guide? I repress a shudder of foreboding born of the deepest part of my *ka*. "Your words frighten me, my Lord," I reply slowly, "but if I do not fight for Egypt, I know not what I have in my life worth fighting for."

He leans down and places a black hand against my cheek. I find myself surprised at his palm's smoothness and warmth. "You entered this life with the courage of a goddess in your *ka*, my beloved. I have come simply to reveal it to heaven and earth."

And then I wake up.

I sat up in bed, the desert air cold as it blew through my room and rifled amongst the mosquito nets that looked more like prison bars than cotton gauze.

Mudjet slept on deeply, so I rose and tiptoed down the hall to my nurse's room. Baktka was old and she had been sick for many months now, our father permitting her to spend her final days being cared for in the opulent palace as a reward for her service. In spite of this honor, I was only allowed to see her occasionally, for he had at the end of his own life begun to perceive he had let too many native elements seep into our sphere through my mother. I must be kept more closely amongst those he considered our own kind, the transplanted Macedonians and Greeks, to correct any Eastern faults in my blood. Though if my dreams were any indication, it was already far too late for that.

Mudjet had been my great victory in this struggle. They had once tried to send her away too, yet in the only time I could remember, I stood up to my father and demanded to keep her. Faced with a hysterical child, my father acquiesced. Perhaps because he had more pressing concerns than a third daughter's tantrum.

I needed Mudjet in my life because she was the only person I knew besides Ptah who was like me, part Egyptian and part Greek. Her father had been a Macedonian diplomat who kept a second family in Alexandria and she was one of the products of that arrangement. Eventually he died back home, and her mother, a drifting woman with no support and too many mouths to feed, had begged a place for her youngest daughter at court. My mother heard her plea and perhaps saw her own infant daughter in the half-breed toddler, another rare artifact that proved de-spite their protestations, the Greek elite had not fully sequestered them-selves from their supposedly barbarian subjects.

So for the first years of my life, I lived in the company of my Egyptian mother, her Egyptian nurse who became my nurse, and the sunny com-panionship of the half-Egyptian Mudjet. I can recall only snatches of that time, though what I have are happy memories. We were mostly left to ourselves as my mother's marriage was nothing but a failing political arrangement which required blessedly little time in my father's presence on her part, even after we had returned to Egypt and the death of my stepmother meant he had no other living spouse. Later, I could search this time and see that my mother was already ill with the seeds of her death, though she never showed that face to us children. With us, she was as eternal as the desert sand.

I entered Baktka's room quietly, in case she was sleeping, but I had never been able to outfox her sharp ears.

"Is that you, *nedjet*?" she whispered, raising her head from its position facing the wall next to her bed.

"Yes, Baktka," I answered guiltily. "I am sorry if I woke you."

"For you, my star, I am always awake. Why are you up at this late hour? Do the young Pharaohs know you are here?"

"No, I came on my own. I had a dream."

My nurse shifted herself to face me, her eyes beetle-bright in the low light and the canyons of wrinkles on her face lifting up until her chapped lips peeled into a smile riddled with worn teeth. "Well then, we must be very quiet while you tell me of this dream."

I stole to her bedside and curled myself next to her on the floor, as I had done a thousand times before. I told her of my encounter with Lord Set and about the *sha,* and she listened seriously until I was finished.

"*Nedjet,*" she sighed gently, running her hand over the tousled mess of my curls as she always did. "I told your lady mother when you were born that the gods would bless you as the first Egyptian princess born in over five hundred years. That sustained her through her last illness when she wept for your future alone in this cruel family. Now I too can now pass into the *Duat* knowing the gods heard the sound of her tears."

"You believe this was real and not a dream, then?"

She smiled wearily. "The line between the Waking World and the Dream World is blurrier than your tutors would have you believe, my jewel. If the gods believe that your best help for what is to come is Lord Set, events will be dire, but they have sent you their greatest warrior."

"I do not understand," I said, frowning. "Why Lord Set? They hate him, he is a murderer. The people abandon his altars and dare not speak of him."

Baktka shook her head. "You are thinking like a Greek. He is not Hades, a lord of gloom. What task does Lord Set accomplish every night for the love of the gods and men?"

I thought back to my nurse's stories. "He fights the snake demon Apep to keep it from killing the sun on its journey beneath the horizon."

"Exactly. He is a deceptive god, yet none of us can survive without him. The wise learn to embrace his duality. He and the gods have placed a heavy burden on your slight shoulders, though I know you will be equal to it."

"I do not want things to change," I protested, hating the petulant tone of my voice even as I meant what I said.

Baktka patted my arm affectionately. "It is the way of all things, *ned-jet*. Even the pyramids are shaped by the wind, not even stone can last. So too will you be shaped by the winds of the future. Listen to your *ka* and see that your choices are pleasing to it. Then you need not fear what outcomes may result."

"You will stay and help me?" I asked, already knowing the answer.

She sighed again, more audibly this time. "You know that my days in this world are ending, *imi-ib*. Soon I will join the Happy Dead. This is a path you must walk alone. The gods have decreed it."

She motioned to a small cask on the table beside her. I reached over and lifted the lid. Inside lay a thin ivory bangle inlaid with gold, ebony, and lapis lazuli in a lotus pattern. I picked up the bracelet and the gold shimmered in the dim light of the lamps. "This was your mother's, dearest. Do you remember it?"

I nodded mutely. I had never seen my mother without it, even as the wife of the Pharaoh.

"It was her mother's. And her mother's mother's mother's. It is an heirloom of the women of your bloodline. We were saving it to give you on your wedding day, though now it seems that neither of us will see that shining hour. I said to you that you must walk this path alone, child. But you will not be forgotten by those of us who love you. Walk with a firm step and know we will sing of you in the Field of Reeds."

I slipped the bracelet on my wrist and leaned down to embrace my nurse. I felt her arms loosen as she began to slip back into sleep. I padded back out of the room and as I crossed the threshold into the hallway, I leapt half out of my skin as a figure loomed from the corner of my eye.

"Sorry, my lady. I did not mean to frighten you," said Mudjet clutching a robe over her shift with one hand and a lamp in the other.

My Mudjet was the same age as my sister, though my dear companion had always been taller and thinner than Cleopatra. Her tanned skin and black hair gave her a more classical Egyptian appearance than myself, but her sparkling violet eyes betrayed her dead Greek father as much as my own gray ones did.

"It is all right. I thought you were still asleep."

"I awoke and you were not there. I thought you might be with Bakt-ka."

Presently I recalled that my nurse was not the only person I knew with sharp ears. "Did you hear of what we were speaking?"

Mudjet and I might omit details to one another if forced, but we never lied to one another. "I did, my lady."

"I am sorry I kept these dreams from you. I was afraid I was going a little mad in some corner of my mind. The stain of insanity is not unknown to this House and I did not want you to worry."

"I understand. Dreams are difficult to fathom even for the adept. If I had these dreams, I would have been unsure, too."

I placed a hand on the one that held her robe. "Am I mad?"

She smiled. "I think not, my lady. I think you have been blessed by these dreams." Her smile faded. "Besides, it does not take the omnipotence of the holy gods to sense there may be troubling times ahead."

Chapter Three

I believed then I would have more time before all of these terrible prophecies would come to pass. Surely if the wise gods had come to one such as me for help, they would see to it that I was older when the storm broke. I did not yet grasp the words Lord Set had spoken to me in that first dream, that there are things beyond the control of even the gods, and that the fiery *kas* of the Ptolemies were among them.

When I look back at beginning of my siblings' reign, I can only stare in astonishment at how fast everything fell apart. At how blind we all were to think that there could have ever been any other outcome. How foolish in hindsight it was for our father to have them share the throne, how ill-suited their respective personalities were for the task. In his last days, did he see himself and his sister Cleopatra Tryphaena when they were young? Did he think my brother and sister would become true sibling-spouses as he and she had been? Had he somehow forgotten my stepmother stole his throne for their firstborn daughter and fought to keep him in exile? Did he remember none of the hideous stories of our family of which his was only another entry?

Perhaps he could only see Cleopatra's intelligence that sang through the air like a marksman's arrow, and her sugared tongue that could smooth over the roughest of feathers. Or Ptolemy's long limbs and spare build in a line of stocky forebearers, or his copper-colored eyes that were the same as those of his grandfather: the distant, adored man whose love my father never had. Lulled by death, he forgot my sister's fiendish temper and my brother's petty indolence. Her relentless ambition and his malicious streak of cruelty. How cold she could be and how selfish he often was. And aside from any of these flaws, how terribly young they both were. How young we all were. Surrounded by men clawing for their own position and the power it could give them, could we have ever been anything except our worst selves?

Certainly the situation we stepped into was not ideal. As our father retched out his final breaths, already the rains were late. Without them, the Nile's banks remained dry. Without the floods, our home was quickly reclaimed by the forces of the desert, the holdings of the god who riddled with me in my dreams.

For there have always been two Egypts, that is why the pharaohs wear a double crown. The one is Lower Egypt, the Black Land: the silty lush oasis whose patron god is Lord Horus, the *Wadjet*-Eyed, whose symbols are the cobra goddess Iaret and the red *deshret* crown. The older is Upper Egypt, the Red Land, the primordial desert from which Egypt springs and will no doubt return at the end of the world. This is the land of my Lord Set, symbolized by the vulture goddess Nekhbet and the white *hedjet* crown. Though in a time and place where Lord Horus has chased Lord Set nearly out of memory, the *deshret* is said to also symbolize Horus' victory over the Red Land. Alas, it is difficult to explain to foreigners and plain folk alike how a red crown may not represent the land called Red. Such are the intricacies of this unusual kingdom and its oldest stories, spread down to even one such as me in this late year.

Even as we fêted the coronation of the next generation of Ptolemies, the terrified rumors of famine were slipping under the doorways of every home like the plague. Soon the whispers of divine disfavor followed on their heels and the various factions at court began choosing sides between the joint pharaohs. Our father had wanted them both to rule, but the Black Land and the gods appeared to disagree with his wishes. All that was left for our crafty lords to do was to figure out which of my siblings was the bringer of these disasters.

As the tenuous coalition of Ptolemy and Cleopatra's rule splintered into the first summer months of their reign, the older lords generally backed my brother both because he was the male child, and as the younger, he was more easily controlled. Pothinus became their de facto leader, with older retainers of my father's such as Dioscorides and Serapion providing a check for the other nobles against the eunuch growing too powerful. The only thing my brother's tutor and his loyal lords agreed on other than the necessity of bridling Cleopatra's influence at court was doing the same in regards to the younger men who surrounded the Pharaoh. Chief among that clique was his childhood companion Salvius; along with Achillas, the head of the palace guards; and Lucius Septimus, a young Roman military tribune who had served my father.

Bold and ambitious, these men were a worry to all other factions who understood that even this in-fighting must be handled delicately.

My sister's supporters were ultimately fewer in number, yet on the whole, more reliably loyal to her. She too had her tutor, the eunuch Damianus, who she used to work behind the scenes at court and out in the town rather than the more public role Pothinus had assumed. Her greatest supporter amongst the older nobles was Origenes, who I think saw her as a steadier hand in which to place the kingdom than my occasionally explosive brother and his volatile friends. Less exalted in lineage, but also indispensable to my sister's cause was her Sicilian retainer Apollodorus. Fearless and calculating, he knew his best chance of advancement in our world was single-minded devotion to Cleopatra's star, so he quickly made himself her man of all deeds. He was able to go places and hear things that a queen in a palace would never have access to, and his partner in much of this was my sister's equally devoted maid, Kharmion.

What my sister lacked in retainers she made up for in wits and organization. She had already been installed as our father's co-ruler for several years and though the harsh lessons of the past had made him obsessively watchful of any power she was given, she had still been his deputy and had paid attention during her apprenticeship. She was able to maneuver the wheels of government to suit her interests and slowly, the established courtiers began to migrate to her camp as the center of true authority in the kingdom. Even the careful tutelage of Pothinus and the swaggering intimidation of his royal cohorts could not prepare my brother for that. He and his supporters were swiftly shunted to the wings and by the end of summer Cleopatra was affixing her seal as if she were the only pharaoh in Egypt. Furiously impotent, Pothinus retreated to construct a new battle plan and Ptolemy took to beating any servant who was unfortunate enough to get in his way, having Salvius take over that bloodsport when he became too frustrated for it. Ptah and I learned to avoid him ourselves since he had never been above lashing out at us, either.

If events had continued in this vein, my sister's singular reign might have continued unabated and the black prophecies of the gods might have sank to bottom of the Nile, never to be unleashed upon a weary world. When I am feeling playful, I engage those around me in a game of speculation as to what my life would have been like if Cleopatra had grasped the throne of Egypt and ruled in security for the rest of her days. The scenarios become quite amusing with the benefit of hindsight, though the common thread amongst them all is their unshakable banality. So in those times I raise a cup to my sister and my treacherous family for at least never allowing my life to be a dull one.

The troubles truly began for my sister a year and a half into her reign. Perhaps unsurprisingly in this chapter of the book of the world, the problem came from Rome, that razor-blade land that was always both the cause of and the solution to the problems of the House of Ptolemy.

My father was able to regain his kingdom from Berenice only with the assistance of Roman military intervention to overwhelm our eldest sister's native forces. Once the conflict was over, most of the troops went home, except the soldiers belonging to one of the generals, Aulus Gabinius. They stayed ostensibly to help maintain order, though Alexandria had always suspected their true assignment was to keep a watchful eye on the Pharaoh and the kingdom for the Roman Senate. Gabinius was a former consul, after all, they muttered sidelong into their cups. By this time, though, the so-called Gabiniani had been a part of Egyptian life long enough that one rarely gave them special thought anymore, just as Lucius Septimus and the half-Roman Salvius were never treated as foreigners at court. The soldiers often intermarried with local girls from all lands and attempts by Rome to recall them had been unsuccessful, leading my siblings to believe we had them in our collective pockets. The once-suspicious Gabiniani had assimilated into Egypt and all was well.

Yet, the Gabiniani were still Roman soldiers and Rome still tried from time to time to remind them of the oaths they had sworn to Latium. The Roman governor of Syria was having border difficulties with the kingdom of Parthia, a perennial thorn in the republic's paw, so he sent two of his sons in a delegation to the Gabiniani to request their help in repulsing the foreign incursions into Roman territory.

"Stop pulling such a sour face!" Cleopatra snapped at me despairingly as she directed some slaves as to where to place table vases. "You will attend this banquet and you will be present the whole time. I am placing Kharmion in the wings. Her sole duty this evening is to watch you as a mongoose watches a snake."

"The Bibuliani are not even here to see us, they came looking for the Gabiniani. Why do we have to do anything for them? If they succeed, you will lose your best fighting men," I replied sulkily, fingering the edge of a table runner.

She rolled her eyes at me. "We do things for them because they are the sons of the proconsul of Syria, who is an ally. When the Gabiniani turn down their suit — which they will — we do not want it to appear that we encouraged them to do so. Therefore, we will throw them a party to soften their disappointment. This is diplomacy, Arsinoë. Pay attention!"

"I doubt they will be so easily distracted," I retorted with a huff.

"They are men, little sister, and this is Egypt. Distraction will not be difficult." She gave an impatient swipe at the tendrils of my hair escaping my headbands. "The difficulty will be making you look more like a princess and less like a Gorgon."

I waggled my tongue at her and made a grotesque face before flouncing off down the hall. I had not made it very far when I nearly collided with a frantic messenger looking for the queen. I sighed at losing my escape to what was undoubtedly some small matter built up by a jumpy captain in the city, and reluctantly led him back to her in the dining hall.

"Your Majesty, a fight has broken out in the Soma among the Gabiniani!" he cried out hurriedly, pushing past me roughly as soon as my sister was in sight.

Cleopatra motioned to the nearest slave. "Find Achillas. Have him take a contingent of the palace guards out and get the situation under control."

While she conferred with the messenger, I slipped out of the room once more and found Mudjet trotting down a corridor searching for me.

"Do you know what is going on?" I asked.

"No, my lady. Only that they have sealed the gate and no one is to leave. Perhaps if we find Ganymedes he will have heard more."

We found my tutor speaking with Pothinus as Ptolemy and Salvius stood listening. The latter was kicking at a stone by his foot as my brother appeared to be concentrating on what was being said, his arms crossed over his chest and his eyes narrowed.

"Teacher! What has happened?" I called out to Ganymedes as we ran up to the group. Ponthius, as usual, looked displeased to see me, though the sound of my voice drew Salvius' attention from the ground towards us. I was often at odds with my brother, but it was mostly harmless back-biting. On the other hand, I loathed the beastly Salvius, whose coarse manners and mean eyes made me wish to flee whatever room we happened to be sharing. He had a way of watching people that suggested he was planning something for them somewhere in his ox-brained mind, something those people were not likely to enjoy. The look he gave me as we joined them was no exception.

"It is very bad, *nedjet*. The reports from the city say that several of the Gabiniani have slain the governor's sons and now the people fear the soldiers will run riot through the streets."

"Why would they do such a thing?" I said, aghast.

"It is probably a drunken brawl over some whores," snorted Salvius, leering at Mudjet and me with his thick, oily lips.

"Because apparently the Gabiniani have grown smug enough that they think the laws of Alexander do not apply to them," answered Pothinus with a frown. The fastidious eunuch also disdained his pupil's dearest friend, though not enough to rise openly to my defense.

"Alexander killed a man while drunk too," I blurted out before I could catch myself.

Pothinus peered at me disapprovingly. I had definitely squandered my chance for his support against Salvius' mouth. "It is hardly a moment for your witticisms, Your Highness."

"I'm sure everything will be fine," said Ptolemy in that prim and pompous way he had adopted the moment the double crown had touched his brow. He intended to sound imposing but in reality came off as little more than childish. "Achillas will sort it out."

"Which is perhaps unfortunate for us, Your Majesty," remarked Pothinus. "It would be better if it looked as though your sister cannot control the Gabiniani."

"The more important question is how she will handle them if they have in truth killed the Bibuliani," countered Ganymedes with a pensive twitch of his large nose. "It will be difficult to mete out justice without alienating one Roman faction or another."

Pothinus glanced at my brother significantly. "Indeed. Your Majesty should stay vigilant. We may be presented with an opportunity here."

My teacher, Mudjet, and I said nothing as we all quavered at the ominous weight of the other eunuch's words. Salvius chuckled obliviously at the beetle he had just crushed under his sandal.

We in the palace waited, suspended in amber, as the hours crawled by and screams could still be heard in the streets. I read out lessons to Ptah, who didn't attend to a single word I said, while Mudjet sat beside me winding wool and inadvertently answering the questions meant for my distracted brother. Ganymedes was too busy conferring with Damianus to scold Ptah for his lapses and Ptolemy paced the floor maddeningly, trailing Salvius behind him like a bulgy hound. The lords moved amongst themselves in despondent little shoals from one side of the hall to the other, apparently finding each side as uncomfortable as the other.

Only my sister seemed unconcerned, balanced elegantly on her dais and eating with her usual good appetite any delicacy brought out from the kitchens. At last, as the day drew to a close and I started to despair of any release, Achillas at last returned and knelt before Cleopatra.

"I have taken care of the disturbance, Your Majesty. Aulus Gabinius has released the bodies of the Bibulani to us so that you may preside over the funerary rites. He has also turned over those responsible for the murders to our custody."

"Excellent," she responded crisply. "Thank you, General."

Damianus stepped forward. "My lady, we must deal with the perpetrators swiftly, but carefully. We cannot afford to anger the Gabiniani."

My sister's serenity melted into her sardonic sneer. "They are not gods in the flesh, teacher. We cannot allow them to think they are so indispensable to us that they can do as they please. They believe they can hide behind the largesse of palace law. Let us see how they fare in a Roman tribunal in Syria."

The eunuch blanched. "My lady, I do not think it is wise to leave this to the Romans. The people will also expect their Pharaoh to dispense justice for crimes in her own kingdom. It may be seen as weakness."

"I am a living goddess!" Cleopatra gestured impatiently. "I should not have to settle petty rivalries between Roman riffraff! No, I will write to Marcus Bibulus and assure him he may do with these ruffians as he wishes."

She stood up angrily, and we all bowed as she stalked out of the throne room, trailing servants and slaves in her wake.

"Your queen is a fool, Damianus," said Pothinus, smirking. "She runs boasting to Rome, and it will cost her Egypt."

Chapter Four

I am in a passage somewhere in the palace, but it is dark and I cannot find my way. I grope slowly along a wall as my fingertips pass over sandstone carved in hieroglyphics.

Suddenly, I hear the faint sound of breathing in the darkness, though I cannot pinpoint where it is coming from. It is so slight that for a moment, I think it is my own breath, fluttering this way and that. A moth of life in the gloom, looking for a flare of light. I have just arrived at this conclusion when something furry brushes against my leg, causing me to yelp in surprise. The unseen animal chatters at me in response, in a manner that suggests I should be the one to watch where I am treading, rather than the other way around. Its distinctive call also tells me what it is, as does the bristly fur and catlike size I could ascertain when it touched me.

"I am sorry, little mongoose, but I cannot see a thing in this black hall," I say apologetically.

"Perhaps you must simply ask for light for it to appear, *nedjet*," answers the storm cloud voice of Lord Set, who appears at my side holding a lamp.

In the spluttering glow, I see that the creature who had been my companion in the darkness was indeed a pert little mongoose. It chitters again good-naturedly, sitting up on its haunches as if it were a tiny hairy person dressed in its brindled coat.

"This hall seems rather forbidding, even with the light, my Lord," I answer him.

"The past and the future exist in pools of ebony ink, Beloved. That is why we cannot know them as we know the present."

"If we even know that."

He grins, his sharp teeth standing out in relief in the low light. "This is certainly so."

I glance about me, though I still cannot see beyond the small halo we are standing in. "So which do we visit tonight, my Lord? The past or the future?"

"The past, of course. I must have you look backwards so that we may guide you forwards."

"That sounds very dangerous. The past is a sticky place, easy to be caught in."

He chuckles. "Indeed, that is why you must stay close, my princess." He holds out his free hand to me, and I clasp it as the mongoose leaps up onto my shoulders and arranges itself there like an attractive collar. I reach up and stroke its small head, which makes it snort in a way that sounds a great deal like purring.

I cannot help but walk a half-pace behind the step of Lord Set. Part of it is his long stride and part is that I cannot bring myself to walk at his side as an equal. I catch sight of our shadows as they move along the worn walls and I am struck at how I appear as every painting I have ever seen of the dead, led along the halls of the *Duat* by some god or another. I silently wonder what it means that my guiding deity is the Lord of the Bloodied Hands. I also think of Persephone, stolen from the meadows of spring by the Lord of the Underworld. The world is full of darkened paths for young women lured by the gods.

We walk slowly through the gloom towards a light that appears far in front of us. It seems an innocuous enough destination, and even though the light should be welcome after all my fumbling about in the dark, I find myself very afraid indeed.

"What troubles you, *nedjet*?" my Lord asks, his voice like a wild undercurrent beneath a fish pond.

"I am a good Ptolemy, Lord Set," I reply haltingly. "In that I am frightened of the past. Always do I know what lurks in its shadows."

"And yet my shivering princess obeys my command to follow me into the shadows."

"Better to have the help of a god in the harsh light than to be left alone in the dark."

He gives a bark of a laugh. "There is the wit of my Arsinoë. Do not be afraid and stay close. Where we are going is already in your memory, it is simply hidden from you by time."

We meet the light and enter into another passage in the palace, lit by a flushed sunset and decked with raised voices. The sound of many precisioned feet stomping along the hard stone comes toward us and I turn to see the stony face of my father approaching with a contingent of palace guards. He leads them into a suite of rooms, where they all storm in upon a graceful young woman bending over Baktka and a very small child. My heart stammers because it now knows what it is my Lord wishes to show me.

I twist in the grip of his hand in panic. "No, my Lord! Please! I cannot see this!"

He looks at me and his expression is surprisingly kind. "But you have already seen this, Beloved. And you must remember it now. You can no longer lock it away, for your siblings remember it well and it informs all they do." He touches one of the golden scars on his chest with a long black finger borrowed from his lamp-holding hand. "You cannot do what we need of you, what I need of you, without accepting the scars of the past."

I am trembling now, but I do not let go of the Lord of Many Battles' hand. The mongoose presses its nose against my cheek and gives a tiny squeak. I watch the young woman continue to attend to the baby without acknowledging the soldiers until my father stalks over and angrily grabs her by the hair, yanking her to her knees with a crack against the stone floor.

"You ignore my summons and then have the gall not to grovel before me, whore?!" my father bellows, digging his blunt fingers into her scalp. "I am your husband, your king, your GOD! I lifted you out of the Egyptian mud and I will fling you back there without a second thought!"

The young woman, my mother, looks up at my enraged father quietly, sadly. She has a dignified air about her person, though deep purple circles under her large eyes betray many sleepless nights.

"My Pharaoh has wiped my family from the land since our return, and has ordered me from his sight. I dared not leave my rooms," she replies softly, a tightness around her delicate jaw the only indication of how much pain she is in.

"I order your presence now!" barks my father, jerking her head to one side. "You and your children will come with us."

My mother's large eyes fill with racing thoughts. She is frantically attempting to discover a way out of this. "Please, my lord. I will come, but let the children stay. Ptah is sleeping and I do not know where Arsinoë is."

I feel my eyes flicker over to where I know I am in the room. In spite of knowing exactly where this is leading I find myself praying that the little princess will not be found.

With his free hand, my father smacks her across the face. "Do not call him that!" he roars at her. "He is a Ptolemy, and no prince of mine will hailed as though he is a filthy Egyptian brat!"

My father tightens his grip on my mother's hair, causing her to at last release a tiny whimper. He drags her close enough for him to wrench the baby out of Baktka's arms, pushing the old woman to the floor in the process. He hands my brother off to one of the soldiers and says to the others, "Find her."

Like an armored whirlwind, the men pull apart the room, flipping over couches, tearing down curtains, and ransacking chests of clothes until they finally overturn the one I am in. I watch my younger self pried out of the debris, wide-eyed and pale. Her eyes and those of my mother's meet for the briefest of moments, but my mother's instructions to me are clear. *Do as he says. Do not cry. Be brave, my love.*

My father breaks us apart as he hauls my mother back to her feet unceremoniously. "There now, that was not so difficult, was it?"

He shoves her into the custody of a guard and we all are marched out of the room, back down the corridor. Lord Set and I follow, as I see the terrified eyes of servants and slaves peeking out from behind columns and curtains. We hurry through the winding halls until we reach the very outer steps of the palace, where guards hold Cleopatra and Ptolemy in place.

My father's army mills about below us and curious locals from the city gather around the far gates. My other siblings also look afraid, but say nothing as we approach. My father plucks Ptah out of the arms of his guard and thrusts him into Cleopatra's as my soldier pushes me towards Ptolemy's. The man grabs each of us by a shoulder and we exchange terrified stares.

My father, finally satisfied for the moment, sweeps around to pull the attention of the people below us to him, his square face beaming with too much merriment. "Hear me well, O Egypt, for today is a glorious day! We have returned to you, your rightful King will shelter you under his munificence once more!"

The army makes a few scattered sounds of approval, though the people and those of us on the steps are eerily silent. We are like caged animals that smell the butcher before we see him arrive.

My father continues, unheeding the reception of his words. "Yes, my people, today is a glorious day. The gods of my fathers, Zeus and Ares and Poseidon, have smiled on us!" His cheerful expression crumbles like plaster, revealing a hideous snarl of rage. "They have smashed your filthy gods and drowned them in the Nile..."

The people at the gate quiver as if someone had run a finger along their collective spines. I see Ptolemy tense up next to me, though none of us children nor my mother lift our lowered heads. Watching my younger self, my mouth is dry and hangs open like a panting dog's. I hear my father give a command to a guard, and it is all I can do from moaning aloud as I feel my Lord press my palm gently.

Two soldiers come out of the entrance columns dragging a young woman between them. She is about the same age as my mother, who even in her distress maintains her calm exterior. Meanwhile, this young lady kicks and claws at her captors. Her reddish hair flies wildly out of a few inadequate pinnings and her disheveled *chiton* is so torn one of her breasts is actually exposed before us like an Amazon.

Her guards fling her in front of our father, and once she sees him, her face twists into an unfocused leer.

"Hello, my lord father and King of all the Egypts," she cackles while making an exaggerated bow from her kneeling position. "How may I serve the heir of Ptolemy Soter?"

My father glares. I watch him labor to maintain his royal composure before the audience at the gate. "Hold your flapping tongue, wench. How dare you even speak to me?"

My sister Berenice waggles her head as if she were drunk. "Calls me 'wench' he does," she says in a singsong voice to no one. "My own father, how does one treat that?"

The pharaoh grabs her shoulders to pull her to her feet, his mouth twitching with anger. "You have nearly destroyed us all, you little bitch! All your schemes nearly burned Egypt to the ground!"

Berenice twirls out of my father's hold and flings out her arms, spinning as if she were a maiden in a dance. "Scheming, scheming, scheming. Such a silly word. Sounds like skimming cream and sipping glass."

My mother speaks, low and with a tremor clinging to the end of each word, "My lord, the princess is unwell. She does not know what she says."

"She knows damned well!" screams my father, reaching out to slap my mother across the face again. Rather than calming his anger, my mother seems to have ignited it. He turns and knocks Berenice to the ground and proceeds to kick at her viciously. My sister's limbs flail a little in her defense, but their actions are uncoordinated. Feeling my gorge rise, I cannot help but think she looks like a child learning how to swim.

"Why did you kill her?!" shrieks my father in between kicks. "Why!? I need her, I — she is my only... Cleopatra!"

At the sound of her name, my sister's head flies up, her expression attentive in spite of the horrific scene we are witnessing. Though as soon as her eyes find our father, her face colors in embarrassment and the almost hopeful look she wears crumples into despair. She had thought he was talking to her.

"Does he speak of Mother or Little Sister?" murmurs Berenice distractedly into the blood filling her mouth. "Mother will be so angry that I let Father back into the palace, I was supposed to keep the doors locked..." Her bruised eyes find Cleopatra. "Sister, you have grown big. Did you see Rome? I would have liked to have seen Rome... I have heard that wolves walk on their hindlegs there and make speeches..."

My father is still beating her, but he is not as young as he once was. Along with his sagging weight, he is quickly wearing himself out. That is why my sister continues to breathe. Furious at her unending babbling, he wrenches a sword out the nearest guard's scabbard and raises it over his head. I watch all of our screams catch in our throats, my mother continuing to stand only because her captor holds her up. Berenice stops talking and glances up at our father distantly. She watches him as if he were a fascinating play, moving her head slightly from one side to the other.

Her darting eyes find those of my younger self, green with fear. Her broken lips part into what now passes for a smile. "Littlest Sister," she gurgles. "Mother calls you a bastard because you are not her daughter, only Father's. But I do not see how this is bad. Everyone knows Father is a bas—"

Berenice does not finish her thought because our father brings down the sword on her neck, severing her head in a violent jet of blood, making a single shocked cry go up from the crowd at the gate. He is drenched in scarlet streams as he continues to hack at the corpse screaming curses in Greek.

And we all simply stand there, unable to move, unable to do more than blink at the scene slowly. At last my father tires himself out completely and he holds the sword downward, gasping for breath, his eyes bloodshot. He lets the sword drop to the ground as he crouches low to dip his fingers into the blood oozing from one of the dozen slashing wounds on Berenice's chest. He paints his hands red as if he is initiating a complicated ritual and then rubs the blood between his palms like an alchemist before leaping to his feet with unexpected energy. He rushes at us, his remaining children, and brushes a bloody palm across each of our faces.

"Behold my little vipers, your birthright," he rasps as if he has given us a precious jewel. It was impossible to ignore the fact that he and Berenice had the same eyes. Now his had inherited the flash of madness while hers stared vacantly at the steps of the palace.

The edges of the scene grow hazy like a mirage as I lower my head. "I can still taste the blood," I say to my Lord softly.

"I know, Beloved."

"He was correct, though, my father. We have no birthright other than our blood. We are strangers in an old land." I lift my gaze to his. "I cannot stop the destruction my blood brings upon Egypt."

"Perhaps, perhaps not," he answers gently. "There will always be destruction, because there is always creation. It is a mighty task we ask of you, my sweet, to harness the wild horses of your family. But we do not need you to win outright."

I am confused. "Then what is required of me?"

The mongoose breezily descends from my shoulder and transforms into a young woman with old eyes, her long hair crowned by a net of draped gold chains hung with lapis beads in the shape of cats and mongooses. "We need you to preserve the Two Egypts, little Ptolemy-daughter."

I give an inclination of my head to Lady Mafdet, goddess of both protection and the legal ways of the kingdoms of men. "Preserve us all from the king's justice, my lady?"

Her rain on tin laughter rings out. "Perhaps, child. Ma'at burns with the brightness of the northern star. Let us see if you can lift her heavy feather."

"I am Lord of Upper Egypt," adds Lord Set, "yet if your house burns the land of my nephew to the ground in its ferocity, the duality of our lands is lost and then we are without hope. Dual are the ways of this kingdom, but your father bound us in a tandem that will rip apart our world and yours. We need you to save us all from the Ptolemies."

"So I only need to save heaven and earth, my Lord?" I ask, half in resignation and half in jest.

His carnivorous laugh echoes in this world of dream and memory. "Do not worry, we will make you a warrior queen, Beloved."

And then I wake up.

I sat up in bed as sleep deserted me in the low purple hours just before dawn. My tossing and turning roused Mudjet who rolled over to me.

"What is it, my lady?" she whispered, her eyes alert against the dull linen.

"The Lord of the Red Land returned to me. We spoke of the day Berenice died."

This caused her to sit up and drape her arms around me. "I did not even see what you saw, and yet I could not turn my mind from it for weeks. There was so much blood." She paused. "I remember being consumed by the fear that I would not be able get all of it off of you."

I sighed and leaned against her. "I did not wish to remember any of it, but my Lord said it was necessary for our days to come."

"I suppose it stands to reason," Mudjet answered in her pragmatic way. "We were brought to that day by the hand of Rome. Now that the wheels of Fate bring Latium back into our affairs, invited by the lavish friendship of your sister. It seems your Lord thinks war is coming because we are repeating the past."

I unconsciously touched my lips that had kissed the blood of my oldest sister. "I suppose we shall also see if I am able to profit from the lessons of history."

It did not take long for General Gabinius to catch wind of my sister's decision. For all of her bravado, she had attempted to keep the information that she was sending soldiers to Syria under wraps to avoid unpleasantries with the Roman commander. There was much dicing at court among the nobles as they tried to decide which of her many enemies had tipped him off.

"How dare you send men of my command to Syria for judgement?!" the general roared at her as he burst in upon her hearing hour in the main throne room.

Apollodorus stepped up and barred his way. "Careful how you address the Pharaoh of Egypt, sir," he said dangerously to the furious Roman.

"I don't take orders from you, Apollodorus," Gabinius spat back.

"But you do take them from me, Gabinius," said Cleopatra, speaking up for the first time.

The general leered at her. "We're mercenaries, Your Majesty. We are free to leave any time we wish."

"Not quite, sir," she answered smoothly. "Your men love Egypt so much they ignore Rome to stay in our kingdom. And you, you are in exile for extortion by order of the Roman Senate. Yes, you can leave Egypt, but you cannot go back to Rome and complain of mistreatment."

Gabinius seethed, though he tried to regain his composure. "Your Majesty, you are right. My men love Egypt as they love their Egyptian wives. Let them have Egyptian justice by your merciful hand. The Bibuliani insulted their honor and they simply got carried away. We are a proud people, my Queen, and even *milites* have their *dignitas*. Don't send them to Syria."

My sister remained adamant. "I cannot do this, General. I cannot afford to alienate my support in Rome by overlooking the murder of noble Roman citizens in my lands. You can appeal to Bibulus for amnesty, but my mind is made up."

We waited for Gabinius to explode again, but he was completely still. "If this is your final word on the matter, woman, so be it," he said quietly. "You will regret this for the rest of your life. That I can promise you."

Apollodorus made a move to grab the general, but the Roman shrugged him off and stormed out of the room.

Soon after, the murderers of the Bibuliani were shipped off to Syria, where they arrived before Marcus Bibulus in chains courtesy of Pharaoh Cleopatra of Egypt. The governor, equally as eager to maintain helpful relations with the Senate as my sister was in spite of whatever grief he might have had, sent the prisoners to Rome to be dealt with.

We heard no more of them. However, Gabinius remained true to his word. He and his men abandoned my sister to offer any aid they could to Pothinus and Ptolemy. With the muscle of the Gabiniani, my brother and his faction were able to regain their seat at court and Cleopatra found herself back in a tandem rule with our brother.

Chapter Five

"I think you are angling up at the last minute, Your Highness," said Ganymedes to Ptah as we stood twenty paces back from the line of targets.

"Here, *nedjes*," I offered, straightening his shoulders. "Keep your arm straight as you move the arrow back. It will follow through of its own accord."

"If I'm worrying about my arms, I lose track of the target!" my brother protested.

"That is all right," answered our tutor. "You should be relaxing your gaze so you feel the target more with your mind than with your eyes."

Ptah screwed up his face in concentration as he aimed his bow at the target once more. He pulled back on the string, took a deep breath, and released the arrow. It landed above the middle of the target, but closer than his last attempt.

"Excellent!" I cried with a clap of my hands. "That was much better!"

Ptah looked up at me with a happy grin in spite of himself. "Still not dead center, though."

"You do not have to hit an animal or enemy soldier perfectly to bring him down," replied Ganymedes. "Her Highness is correct, my Prince. That was much improved."

A servant approached our teacher and spoke something in his ear. He gave the servant a curt nod and then turned to us. "Pardon me, Your Highnesses, Theodotus has some matter or another he must speak with me about. I will return shortly. *Nedjet*, perhaps you would help His Highness through a few more practice shots?"

I nodded a he followed the servant off the field. Ptah wandered over to the rack and picked up a sword. "I wish I could spend more time on sword training. It's easier than aiming a bow."

I smiled at him indulgently. "Soon, little brother. I think that sword is too heavy for you yet, anyway."

He swung the sword up in a wobbly arc. "No, see! I can do it!"

"Careful!" I said with a laugh. "Stand with your feet apart so you do not tip over!"

He did as he was told, but gave me a mischievous look. "Pothinus would say you know far too much about military matters than is seemly for a lady."

"Well, Pothinus can think whatever he wants. I have no love of weapons, yet all the classics spend a great deal of time detailing battle. It is impossible not to absorb some instruction."

"He also says you read too much, like our sister."

"That is certainly true. Though I do not know what else he wishes me to do to pass the hours."

"You could try learning to sit quietly and not run about like a hoyden," another voice interjected. We turned to see Salvius sauntering towards us, tossing a pomegranate lazily into the air and catching it in the same hand.

I stiffened at his approach, though I kept my tone casual. "And you could make yourself useful rather than beating up on the servants, but alas, sir, we are all slaves to our natures."

He eyed me in sour amusement, as I felt Ptah shrink behind me. "You have always been a strange little cat, Arsinoë. All quiet watchfulness until someone backs you into a corner. Then your tiny claws come out. Though it is unlucky for you that you've grown so snappish. It is such an unfortunate defect in a woman."

"I could say I am sorry that I so displease your sensibilities, Salvius, but I think we both know that would be a lie."

He arrested the progress of the pomegranate and, in the same motion, grabbed my wrist with his other hand. I could feel Ptah's fist ball up a corner of the back of my *chiton*. "It's true. However, if you know what's good for you, you'll learn to be a little kinder to me. Your brother has promised you to me if I please. You should be grateful for such an advantageous marriage despite your mongrel blood."

"What a good friend you are to accept a prospective engagement to me and my dirty blood, Salvius," I sneered. "Will you hold your nose throughout our marriage or just through the ceremony?"

He tightened his grip and scowled. "I will take my rightful place in this House as a prince and you will learn to cleave to me if I have to school you every hour. You will obey me or I will break every bone in your body until you do. And there will be no one for you to run to."

"Be careful, sir," I replied evenly. "This is a dangerous family to join. Few of us die of old age... and you will have to sleep sometime..."

Salvius glared, but released my wrist and turned to leave. "Say your peace now, Princess. I will save every word and brand them on you letter by letter," he called over his shoulder as he strolled back towards the palace.

I waited until he was around a wall and out of sight before sinking down to my knees. Ptah clung to me from behind, his arms clammy around my neck. I patted him gently with my own sweaty palms. "It is all right, Ptah. Shh, he is gone."

"He can't have you," Ptah said in a frightened whisper. "I won't let him."

I smiled involuntarily. "I know, *nedjes*. You will protect me."

"If it comes to that, we'll run away."

"Where will we go?" I asked dreamily, my mind retreating from the dagger-edged future Salvius had shown me.

"We'll go to India, like Alexander did. We'll ride elephants and you will be a great queen."

"And what will you be, *nedjes*?"

Ptah met my gaze seriously. "I'll be your little brother, of course."

I tousled his curly hair fondly. "You will be my grand vizier. And when you have grown up, you will be the *raaja* and I will help you."

He rested his head against mine. "It is a good dream, Arsinoë."

"Yes. A good dream."

I am curled up in my bed, asleep. I know not what I have been dreaming of, except that I unexpectedly feel the smooth, rhythmic lap of a tongue against my cheek. I open my eyes and see the *sha* resting its front paws on the edge of my bed, its burning emerald eyes lighting the darkness. And then I realize that this too is a dream. Seeing me awake, the *sha* transforms into my Lord who sits on the floor next to the bed, leaning one arm on the edge and the other on his knee.

"Stubborn child," he admonishes me. His voice authoritative, though devoid of anger.

I lay with my head on the dream pillow, looking at him. "My Lord knows me as perhaps no other, he knows this is one of my numerous faults. But what have I been obstinate about recently that summons the Lord of Confusion to me?"

"I — who shapes the thunder in the palm of my hand, who brings the sandstorm and the mirage, who slays Apep with the sword and the spear — I have come out of the Red Land and called you my beloved, Arsinoë Ptolemy-daughter. Do you doubt me?"

"No, my Lord. You have called me this and shown me great honor with your attention."

Now his face contorts in anger. Somehow I know his rage is not with me, so I am not afraid. "Then why does the Princess of Egypt not call upon me to smite the worm that dares threaten her with such blasphemies against her person, which the gods themselves have placed their mantle upon!"

I nearly laugh. In this moment I begin to truly understand the stories I have heard of the gods, both of Egypt and Olympus and elsewhere. I see that the foibles the sages decry as beneath their dignity are real, and to see the frustration in my Lord's eyes fills me with love, not pity. These flaws do not smear the gods and make them unworthy of our adoration, they make them beings whom we can touch and draw close into our hearts. I may be able to teach him as much as he sought to instruct me; not as equals, but rather as a relationship I already understand well, as that between a learned teacher and a cherished pupil.

I reach over and lightly place my hand upon Lord Set's. "Forgive me, my Lord. You must remember that I have lived all my life among dangerous people. Threats, however vile, are not novelties. I have long made my way believing I must protect myself and Ptah without anyone else's aid. I am not used to asking for help."

His expression softens. "I know this, *nedjet*. This is what makes you braver than you hold yourself out to be. I was carried away in my anger at the whelp who thinks he is worthy of being your bridegroom. Do not fear him, I will protect you."

"I know you will do what you can, though I also know the gods cannot always stand against the will of a Ptolemy. My brother desires this union."

"Unique *ka*s can challenge the will of the gods," he answers meditatively. "Even your brother, *Taui*-Pharaoh, can sometimes do this because he has been hailed as king. But he is not as strong as you or your sister. His only hopes for success stem from the aid you or she give him. If you oppose his designs, he cannot carry the day. Certainly someone as lowly as a servant of his stands no chance. I simply desire you not to worry about this."

"With the word of Lord Set, I will not." I look at him dreamily. "Would you have truly smote Salvius where he stood, like in the old days?"

He smiles. "Perhaps, Beloved. I was most wroth. Only the gentle hand of my lady prevented me."

This was the first time my Lord had spoken of his wife, Lady Nephthys, goddess of the night and the ways of the dead. "I hope the Lady of the Darkened Hall is not uneasy about the kindly service her lord heaps upon this humble one."

He gives an elegant shrug. "Do not worry, she is as fond of you as I." Part of me does not take my Lord at his word, as I am not sure her displeasure has ever prevented him from much. He seems not to notice my discomfiture and continues on. "She said the time was not ripe and was correct as usual. So instead I come to you and rage at your self-possession." This last part is delivered with a self-deprecating grin.

I sigh. "I do not feel self-possessed. I feel pulled in every direction as if the wind blew in all ways at once."

His face grows serious. "That is the storm that is to come, *nedjet*. Ever does it come closer. Be prepared for its arrival."

"Do you mean a war between my brother and sister? Every day their enmity grows, I cannot feel this joint rule will last."

"Eventually, Beloved. But first war will blow in from across the sea. Look for its sails on the horizon."

And then I wake up.

Chapter Six

"Teacher, what news is there from the port?" my brother asked Theodotus lazily, leaning back on his couch. We were all together again, maneuvering our separate ways through another shared meal.

"Ah, our traders say there is trouble in Rome, Your Majesty," answered Theodotus as he picked flesh off of the fish bones in front of him.

"There is always trouble in Rome," scoffed Pothinus. "Has there ever been a more turbulent people than the Latins?"

I watched Cleopatra grow very still. She continued to place fruit on her plate, but I could see how quietly alert she was to the conversation. I tried to imitate her as I took fish off of the platter offered to me by a waiting slave and placed it on Ptah's plate. Noticing our distraction, Ptah stopped swinging his feet and looked at me carefully.

"It is all that freedom they are always going on about, if you ask me," remarked Origenes as the steward refilled his wine. "The Romans need their precious Senate like they need a tail. Put a king in charge of them and maybe they would have some order."

"There is nothing more odious to a Roman than a king," said Lucius Septimus. "Present company excepted, Your Majesty," he added with a twist of a grin in Ptolemy's direction.

My brother laughed. "Yes, clearly all Romans hate kings, seeing how you and I are such old friends, Lucius. And then there's the Gabiniani, who would rather murder Roman citizens than leave my kingdom!" he continued, pointing at Aulus Gabinius. In good grace, Gabinius gave a small acknowledgement to my brother's tasteless joke while Salvius slapped the general's back, cackling.

Cleopatra gave a twitch of impatience at this reminder of her less-than-glorious episode with the Roman mercenaries in our midst.

"Actually it is a matter of kingship that is at the heart of the unrest," said Theodotus, pulling the conversation back to himself as he dipped his fingers in the water bowl in front of him. "Or rather what the Senate fears could become a matter of kingship."

"What do they say, sir?" asked Ganymedes, glancing at me as he did so.

"Well, it seems that the plebeians are giving their support to Gaius Caesar again for consulship, but the Senate refuses to allow this without challenge. He has been flouting their authority ever since he became pro-consul of Gaul through the assemblies instead of through the Senate. Pompey Magnus and the senators have demanded that he disband his army and return to Rome privately, which he refuses to do, knowing his enemies there will have him tried for treason."

"Why does he have to disband the army?" Ptah asked me through a mouthful of food.

"Because Roman law forbids a standing army within the city limits," our teacher answered him. "To bring an army into Rome is a declaration of war. And do not speak as you chew, Your Highness."

"Surely Caesar would not risk war against Pompey?" said Origenes with disdain. "He has but a handful of legions. All the other armed forces of the Republic will oppose him."

"But what other choice does he have?" interrupted Lucius. "His supporters have fled Rome to join whatever protection he can give them, so if he forfeits his army, they'll clap him in irons before he can put both feet in the city."

"He should entrench himself in Gaul and dare Pompey to come and move him out," observed Pothinus. "Gaul is where he has the broadest support anyhow."

"No, no. He will not do that," said a quiet voice from down the table. Everyone turned as General Gabinius spoke for the first time. He met our gazes with a ruefully sardonic expression. "You do not know Caesar. His heart burns with ambitions too large to be contented in Gaul. He would rather die trying to harness the world like Alexander than accept quiet obscurity."

"So you agree with the Senate? Caesar wishes to be a king?" asked Pothinus as Ptolemy made a frowning face at the thought.

"It is not so much the title, I think," answered the general slowly. "He wants the power and the authority; if it is by the name of dictator or king, it is little consequence."

Salvius chortled again. "This is what comes of Roman liberty! The Julii haven't been of any consequence in centuries and now the whole city cowers like mice because they let an obscure patrician work his foot back through their door!"

Lucius frowned. "It is unwise to speak of your ancestors with such contempt, Salvius."

The young man made an impatient gesture. "Oh, don't be so pompous! My father never did any so well as to leave his pissant little patrimony in Toscana and rent himself out to the late Pharaoh. And even then, I count his foresight in marrying a Greek heiress here as much more helpful to my current enjoyments than any drop of Latin blood in my veins."

"Careful, Salvius," said Achillas with his usual breezy drawl, wandering into the room from the guards' quarters, "you'll scandalize Lucius by being so completely native." He smirked as he plucked several grapes from one of the plates and sauntered to his place. "After all, the infantry can do what they will, but he and Gabinius have their positions to maintain."

Cleopatra's glass-edged voice cut through the chatter. "Brother-Husband, if there is to be war in Rome, we should be prepared to offer any aid Pompey Magnus may require of us."

Everyone whipped around to face her as Ptolemy let his wine cup hang in midair.

"I think you are being premature, Your Majesty," replied Pothinus with the little note of mockery he added to his voice whenever he referred to my sister by title. "As has been stated, the forces of Caesar are small. This so-called war will be over in a month."

"Less if the patricians of Rome send out their wives instead of their soldiers," snickered Salvius, which earned a few guffaws from the lords.

"If that were so, why is Rome so afraid?" she asked simply.

No one had a response to her question, so after a few uncomfortable moments of silence, Ptolemy coughed and gave an indulgent wave of the hand. "I will think on your position, Sister-Wife, and I will make a decision if Pompey asks for our help."

I saw Cleopatra grit her teeth at his use of "I," but she wisely lowered her head without reply. The general conversation moved on to the chariot races that were to be held the next day.

I made my escape after Mudjet had come to collect Ptah for bed, as Ptolemy and his cabal sank further into their cups. My sister had evaporated like fog during one course or the other. I assumed Cleopatra was in her quarters listening to musicians or brewing medicinals with Kharmion, so I was surprised to come across her standing on one of the verandas that faced the royal harbor.

The white tails of her silk diadem fluttered in the breeze like wisps of cloud. The setting sun moved behind her head in a fiery halo of light, its glow not strong enough to blot out her physiognomy. I found myself lost in one of those moments of contemplation where one sees all that is numbingly familiar with new eyes. It was how I had felt when the *sha* became my Lord in the Dream World. Now, that moment of transformation bled out of my dreams into the Waking World, like a shadow seen out of the corner of one's eye. I looked at Cleopatra and I stepped outside of my head to look at myself and our world.

In truth, my sister was not beautiful. That said, I do not claim she was ill-favored, either. I know as the years fall in upon themselves her critics speak of her as either Aphrodite incarnate or as a monstrous hag, but as is usual, the way of the truth is the path somewhere in between.

Her features were too sharp to be considered conventionally lovely, her eyes rather too large for the face they were set into. She was of a paler cast than I, though still considered a bit too dark to be an entirely respectable Greek woman. Much as she might swat at my own flyaway curls, she too had to work long hours to subdue hair inclined to be wild if left to its own will. Despite this, people rarely commented on these imperfections once they had met her face to face. She had learned to let enough of those glossy curls fall loose against her cheeks to soften her Ptolemy nose; to allow daring sweeps of makeup deepen the positioning of her fascinating, changeable eyes; to have her dresses cut to fall elegantly on her inviting curves so it appeared that she floated into a room like goddess rather than treading the ground like a mere mortal. Next to her I usually felt akimbo in my skinny limbs and gawkish frame, even if the traces of my mother had smoothed out the more forward features of the Ptolemies.

Beyond these little sleights of hand, however, she had taught herself to wrap an invisible mantle of confidence about her, one that she never removed, one that drew the world to her as the beach calls the tide. Never, in even my most daring moments, have I ever managed to command such breathtaking armor. I have wondered whether my stepmother glimpsed its shimmer when she first held her second-born daughter. This cloak of audacity gave my sister the presence of ten ordinary beauties. Her teeming mind laughed at the doe-eyed bleating of girls whose heads had never held a single stimulating thought. These are the things that made her beautiful to behold when the gods did not bestir themselves to make her a new Helen.

"I remember the first time I met General Pompey," she said to me, looking out at the water as if, with a strain of her eyes just so, the general would appear on the horizon. "He seemed so strong and handsome, and he carried himself in a way that made you believe anything was possible. I was probably half in love with him then; a silly, childish love, but my first. When he met with Father and me, I knew we would reclaim our kingdom if he was by our side."

"Are you looking to the past to chart the future?" I asked.

She smiled at sea. "Maybe. We cannot know the future, so perhaps all we can do is learn from the past. I learned many lessons at the feet of our father, the most important being that I cannot hope to sit on the throne of Egypt without a Roman alliance. Ptolemy and his provincial cronies apparently cannot see this. They do not see that we must be quick with friendship and not wait to be asked for help."

I twisted my mother's bracelet fitfully around my wrist. "That seems wise, sister, though there are two sides in every war."

"Oh, it is no question of where we cast our nets," Cleopatra replied firmly, shaking her head. "I am Pharaoh, whatever Pothinus and our brother think, and I am a queen. Royalty does not lend support to rebels.

I have risked enough of our people's mewling by helping Rome as it is; it would be suicide to support Caesar."

"Even though you know it will not be the easy victory Pothinus thinks it will be?"

My words turn her probing eyes from the sea to my face and win the favor of her smile for me. "You noticed that? You are growing astute, little sister. I shall have to remember that... Yes, it may not be a swift fight, though that does not mean we change our alliances thoughtlessly. Pompey has long been an ally of Egypt and besides, we do not know how Caesar will treat us. When one is in doubt, it is always more suitable to deal with a known quantity."

The clash with the Gabiniani had forced my sister to accept Ptolemy's return to relevance, but she was still the more experienced hand. Her grasp of the situation concerning Rome was yet another proof of this. She had lived with risk and uncertainty long enough to lose a lesser person's fear of them, and in that lay her great advantage.

In his heart Pothinus may have also understood the events unfolding all around us, yet he was hampered by the sinews of his own nature. He was a calculating, cautious sort of man whose dearest wish was to wield tremendous power in Egypt through my brother, but the Egypt he dreamed of ruling was a lofty, aloof empire in the clouds. An airy confection that did not have to dirty its own shining light by dealing with lands outside of those that came groveling with tribute. He may have known that collision with Rome was unavoidable, but he could not bring himself to meet it head on. By the time he lowered himself to admitting this, it was too late.

My brother, even when he managed an independent thought or two away from his courtly comrades or scolding tutor, was also chained to his character. A character nurtured from the cradle on the narrative that he was a glorious prince of an exalted bloodline, anointed as a god incarnate who did not have to negotiate with a toad-spittle world full of little men and useless women. Cleopatra had been told many of the same things, but she had also been granted enough insight to realize she and Egypt could not always act as if the rules that govern the world did not apply to them.

So as Gaius Caesar crossed the Rubicon, to cast his lots against tradition, and, as some held, against the gods themselves, those of us sitting on the banks of the Nile watched these three different personalities wrestled for our future. We had the boy who was not yet a man, the girl very nearly a woman, and the boy-king's scheming eunuch-advisor clawing for the throne. None were the perfect fit we needed in those imperfect times. Cleopatra had experience without caution, Ptolemy had pride without experience, and Pothinus had caution without courage. Together, they might have warded off the cataclysm that would engulf us all. Apart, they could only curse the darkness and each other.

As soon as she was able, my sister sent Apollodorus the Sicilian across the kingdom to round up whatever corn could be gleaned from the farmers short of starving them, while southern traders were bullied into selling other raw materials of war to the crown at discounted rates. She sent these and envoys to Pompey, assuring him of their lasting friendship and Egypt's support in the face of Rome's unrest. Of course, talk is so much chatter on the wind when war is imminent, so she also sent a fleet of ships and several armed battalions. And she of course was scrupulous in making note of which of the monarchs Philopator had given so generously to his cause.

As the war raged across the Roman territories, Pompey began to request more troops from his allies in Egypt. Cleopatra cleverly saw an opportunity to lessen the strength of her most recalcitrant opponents among the royal factions.

"You can't send Pompey the Gabiniani!" fumed Ptolemy. Ptah and I had been sitting off to one side on a couch in the corner, only half-listening as we rolled a pair of dice between ourselves until our brother's outburst sliced through the hall.

"Of course *we* can, dear Brother-Husband," Cleopatra answered smoothly as the council erupted into a cascade of low noise. "What could be a more princely gift to send to our greatest ally?"

"But I — we need them here!" barked Ptolemy, whipping himself around to his right. "Aulus! Swear you won't go!"

The flinty general made no acknowledgement of our brother's rising panic as he stared coldly into Cleopatra's polite and waiting smile. "We are men, Your Majesty. Not a few barrels of wheat to be bartered."

"Oh, I am well aware of your value as bits of humanity, sir," she said unhurriedly.

"What if we refuse to go?"

"You will have no recourse but to do so. General Pompey is your old friend as surely as he is mine. Who else could have convinced golden-tongued Cicero who disdains you so much to only seek your banishment when he and his prickly friend Cato howled for your execution from the Senate floor? You owe him, my sweet general."

Gabinius curled his lips back. "If you think the game of politics in Rome is that simple, my lady, you have much to learn. Pompey requires no such showing from me."

She shrugged. "That is your own decision, but it is not the only debt in play here. The pharaoh," she nodded in Ptolemy's direction, "also owes much to the general. His throne, among other favors."

"That doesn't mean I have to send the damned fool my army!" squeaked our brother indignantly.

"No," said our sister, speaking slowly to him as if he were a small child, "though it is right to give him gestures of our appreciation, as I have been doing since the war broke out. You should be thanking me for preserving your good standing with Rome in spite of your obstinacy."

"It is against our own security to send the general all of the Gabiniani," said Pothinus, reluctantly wading into the discussion.

Cleopatra flashed him a triumphant smile. "Perhaps, sir," she conceded with false humility, her cheeks brightening. She knew she was winning. "I would never suggest endangering... *our* ...security."

Aulus Gabinius sucked in his teeth like a man with a lemon. "How many do you want?"

"A thousand."

He shook his head. "Two hundred."

"Eight hundred and fifty."

"Five hundred. And not a man more."

"Done."

The general glared grimly. "Four hundred infantry, one hundred cavalry, and I stay here."

"As you wish, General," our sister said demurely. "Let it not be we who deny you the shores of the heavenly Nile."

Ptolemy impotently smacked his fists on the table, mute with anger.

Cleopatra preened at him. "Oh, do not fret, Ptolemy. It is only five hundred men. You will have plenty of thugs left to send roving through our fair streets."

Chapter Seven

Mudjet and I spread our *himations* on the ground in one of the easterly courtyards so we might enjoy some of the afternoon sun without the heat being too fierce. We laid on our stomachs with our arms folded under our chins as we talked.

"Do you think the Red Lord can truly protect you from Salvius?" she asked abruptly, her eyes troubled under their long lashes.

"I do not know. He certainly seems willing to try, which is more than I have on my own."

Mudjet shuddered. "We or he must do something. Wedding nights can be brutal enough without the groom being a terror to everything that breathes. Have you spoken to Ganymedes of this?"

"Yes, though all he can do is work to rally the other eunuchs to our point of view. And I doubt Pothinus is overly worried about my future."

"He should be. A princess has currency in the wider world, you would be much more valuable as a treaty bride than one practically given away to a local retainer."

She was right, though in my heart I longed for neither option. I knew I could not live with Salvius in Egypt, but I dreaded in a different way a marriage that would send me away from the Black Land. I was already half a foreigner here. Yet this was my home. My ties were here, the light of my *ka* danced here, where the legendary river cut through the desert until it touched the glittering sea. I loved the Egyptian people, as well as those who traveled to this land to dwell because they too were drawn by its ancient song. Restless days came upon me, yes, and I would dream of traveling all over the world and seeing all that the gods had fashioned, but never did those daydreams not end with my return to this land of warmth and magic. This was where I belonged.

Aloud I answered, "Pothinus wants little to do with other lands. Perhaps he will not care."

"But he loathes Salvius as well, and he would not like anything that gives the young lord more influence or power. We might be able to persuade him to bar this plan out of spite if nothing else."

Suddenly, the sound of approaching voices came from our left. They were not many, but I quickly picked out my sister's glittering cadence among them. "Quickly, over here," I said motioning to the large, squat date palms massed in the opposite corner of this courtyard garden.

We grabbed our *himations* and hid ourselves amongst the sticky fronds, waiting for the voices to move on. However, instead of passing, they emerged into the courtyard and arranged themselves beneath the awning we had just vacated.

"I have received a letter from Pompey the Younger requesting more grain to be delivered to his father's armies in the east," Cleopatra said to Damianus as they sat down, enjoying a rare afternoon breeze as it blew by. Lord Origenes was also there, and had absentmindedly been fanning himself until my sister started speaking.

The eunuch paled. "We have none to give, Your Majesty. We have no surplus this year and already we have taken bread from the tables of the people to feed Rome. Any more and there will be riots."

"Riots will strengthen Your Majesty's brother's position," added Origenes, frowning.

"I know," replied my sister. "But if I lose Rome I will lose to Ptolemy anyway. I have no choice."

"I do not believe that to be true, my lady. The people will stand behind you if you defend their bellies."

She tossed her head angrily. "For a day or two until their bellies are full. Then they will be full of adoration for their male pharaoh. Egypt always returns to its king while there is a king to return to."

Damianus' eyes narrowed at these dark words. "We have spoke of this, my shining pupil." His voice dropped carefully. "You cannot be rid of Ptolemy as events unfold now. You have tried once and failed, they will be on their guard now."

My sister's eyes flashed bitterly. "I know this also, but I will not be lured into the mistakes of the past. I have combed the Library for the buried records of Egypt's lost Pharaoh-Queen. Her greatest mistake was to allow her male rival to survive to desecrate her memory. It is not a mistake I intend to repeat."

Mudjet and I exchanged frightened glances. Cleopatra's anger with Ptolemy ran deeper than I realized if she was seriously contemplating his removal. A part of my heart clung to the hope that it was simply our brother's removal from power that she sought. Surely we had not broken apart from one another so irretrievably that we would follow in the bloody footprints of our House. The acrid taste of blood slipped across my tongue and my mind began to drift towards the memory of the mad ogre and the maiden in the torn *chiton* from my dreams... *No, do not think on that. It was not real. It could not have happened that way. We are modern, civilized people. Not wild barbarians.*

"You know the love I bear your person, my Queen," began Origenes, trying to disguise the anxiety I could see breaking out in a thin film of sweat along his hairline. "I will do anything to see you secure on the throne of your fathers, but you must be wary as you walk this path. I am aware that desperate measures may someday be our only course, but do not seek them out eagerly. The man who ascended the falcon throne the second time, the late king, your exalted father, was not the same man who had sat on it upon his first coronation. Spilling blood changes us all; how much more so when the blood we spill is our own."

Even from where we were I could see impatience in the heart of Cleopatra's face, though she smoothed it out for her companions. "These are wise counsels, my friends. Do not think I ignore their advice; I only pray I might be granted enough time to heed them, though I fear time is luxury I may not possess the coin to purchase."

Damianus sighed, resigned. "What will Your Majesty do?"

"I will find the corn Pompey needs, even if Apollodorus must beat it out of the peasants. Does my teacher think I wish for them to die of starvation? We will all die if we alienate Rome."

"Some say it goes ill for Pompey," said Origenes quietly. "Maybe he is an eclipsed star."

"He is not as young as he once was, but there is no one held in higher esteem in Latium among the largest number of people. Not even the fiend Caesar. And he has ever been our friend. I require true allies, sir. I am already tied into one marriage of convenience."

At that time a slave appeared with wine and refreshments, which was a distraction we used to make our escape from the courtyard. We hurried down the long corridor until we could at last turn a corner facing away from the direction we had come.

"The Queen is foolhardy in her course. The people will not stand for this," whispered Mudjet fiercely.

I stared at the ground, still feeling the force of my sister's words. "She feels she has no choice. She wants Rome's help deposing our brother, she must then build a foundation for that ambition made of correct friend-ships and shows of strength. The Romans help those who help them-selves. If she bends to Ptolemy even a little, she thinks they will do noth-ing."

"Are you going to tell the Pharaoh what you heard?"

I hesitated. "Although I do not love Ptolemy, I would if I thought he was in immediate danger. We are still blood and unlike my sister appar-ently, I have no desire to have his blood on my hands. But I think Dami-anus will keep her from doing something so rash."

"I think that is good, my lady. If only as to not make an enemy of the Queen."

"I was surprised that even Origenes balked at her plans. He is usually completely her creature."

"She will bring Lord Origenes around, she always does, but Dami-anus is worried."

"I think his heart harbors genuine affection for Cleopatra. He is afraid for her," I answered abstractly.

"He should be," returned Mudjet. "We should all be afraid."

My sister always kept the promises she made to herself, so she reached out her hand to Egypt and squeezed the land until the parched earth surrendered enough grain to send the legions of Rome. But it was the last stalk of wheat that broke the camel's back. Undulating waves of vi-olence swept through the provincial cities of Upper Egypt as our des-perately hungry farmers burned down buildings bearing the royal cartouches and dragged levy officials out into the street to be murdered by frenzied mobs. In Alexandria, the merchants and traders pounded on the gates of the palace screaming to the stoic guards that the pharaohs meant to ruin them, first by setting the exorbitant tariffs that had meant they could not compete with the crown for the business of Rome, and then by taking all the material goods of Egypt so they had nothing to sell at all.

As the panic that had barely been contained in the face of the drought broke through the dam of public opinion, Pothinus was quick to tell anyone who came complaining who in the royal co-rulership had brought mighty Egypt to such a pass. It did not take long for the tide to turn against Cleopatra even more vehemently than I believe she had anticipated. My brother and his camp stealthily fed our starving people tales of the greedy Romans and other foreign barbarians — their brats growing sleek on the wheat Lord Geb and the other gods had meant for the children of their soil. How the queen was always plotting with her spells and herbs, denying the people the protection of their pharaoh-father. That if only Ptolemy could rule his subjects alone, as a firstborn prince should do, Egypt would right itself and the days of plenty would return. And the people began to listen.

Even in the teeth of more hostility than perhaps was expected, my sister placed her unwavering faith in Pompey and the Senate. She believed they would protect her from what was rapidly evolving from a power struggle within the royal house to a full-blown civil war. I am sure she wrote many elegant letters to both, reminding them of their obligations and requesting their aid, all the while disguising her tone to hide her growing dismay at their silence.

The crisis made my brother bolder and he delighted in finding petty ways to exercise his growing authority over the rest of us. One of his favorites was to demand that we take cruises on the barge upon Lake Mareotis at the edge of the city, enjoying a captive audience while he and his cronies lolled about making snide comments, mostly about Cleopatra.

One of these excursions had us boating in the heat of a seemingly endless afternoon, the sun just beginning its descent towards the horizon. The hour was unusual in that we often waited until the sun was setting to entice a breeze to find us, though Ptolemy did not give us a voice in the matter. He expressed a desire to hunt fish and waterfowl and said he wanted higher light to see by. This was a relatively small party: the four royal siblings and Salvius making up the whole of those present. I actually found myself thinking that perhaps we would enjoy some relative peace that day as the brutal young lord was not much of a conversationalist without brighter lights such as Lucius Septimus or Achillas around, and even my brother might deign to be pleasant without Pothinus there to stoke the fires of discontent.

"Ptah!" barked Ptolemy.

My younger brother and I were leaning over the side of the barge, trailing our fingers through the water.

"Stop clinging to Arsinoë's skirts like a girl and come fish with with us!"

Ptah reluctantly left my side and accepted a spear from our brother, who ruffled his hair with a heavy fondness. "Salvius is going to try to get us some ducks!" he added with a forced attempt at jocularity.

My littlest brother avoided the young lord's beady eyes and gave Ptolemy a wan smile before dropping his head to focus on the lake's surface.

"Oh, don't be timid around Salvius, little brother!" cajoled Ptolemy. "You've known him all your life!"

"I would say such familiarity has bred the correct response," said Cleopatra pointedly from under the barge's awning, her eyes dark with distaste.

Ptolemy glared at her. "Not everyone shares your taste for mincing eunuchs, sister-wife. Ptah needs older lords like ourselves to show him how a real prince should be. Besides," he paused as he turned his attention back to Ptah, "I should like it that you and Salvius become closer, because I have plans for us all to be brothers in truth someday soon."

I flinched as Ptolemy's gaze as it met mine. I turned my head out towards the lake, pretending to be engrossed by the scenery.

Cleopatra's brows contracted sharply as I saw her survey us all in surprise out of the corner of my eye. "You cannot be serious, Ptolemy!" she said with a dry laugh. "Marry Arsinoë to Salvius? What a joke!"

I could feel her gaze demanding the attention of the back of my head, so I turned back to her. Her hazel eyes swept over me, searching for understanding until I saw her give a satisfied little nod that seemed to say: *Ah, you had already heard of this. That is why you are not jumping out of your very skin at this moment.*

Ptolemy's frown deepened into a scowl. "And why not? Salvius has been my loyal friend since infancy and I would like to reward him with an official place in our household."

"Then make him Lord of the Pharaoh's Wine Cup or some other nonsense. This marriage is beneath a princess of the blood royal."

I watched Salvius ball up his fists around his fishing spear until the knuckles went white, while my sister continued to defend me against our brother's wishes.

"No it isn't!" argued Ptolemy. "Salvius comes from a noble family and his bloodline is certainly purer than our sister's!"

"She is still a Ptolemy and she cannot be married to just anyone, brother," Cleopatra countered calmly. "I doubt the lords will find it proper, either."

Salvius suddenly exploded into the conversation. "Who cares what those old fogeys think! He is Pharaoh! He can do as he wishes!"

My sister studied him briefly as if he was an especially clever frog. "The Pharaoh remains a child and as such, in fact must discuss matters of state with his lords during his minority. And the marriage of a princess is a matter of state, Salvius. Not that I expect you to grasp the intricacies of kingship."

"You little—"

"Careful, my lord," she said, glancing at her nails. "I am also Pharaoh, no matter what you and my little brother believe. I would guard your tongue."

Salvius lapsed into a murderous silence, as Ptolemy sought to bring him back around. "Don't listen to her, my friend. Pothinus has already agreed to support us in this, we simply must be patient."

Cleopatra snickered. "If I did not know better, I would say this must be true love indeed to bring our dear Salvius to such a pass. Fortunately, we all know he thinks this will make him a prince of Egypt. Perhaps it is good for the simple to have little illusions to cling to."

Salvius stared at her stonily. "I will be a prince here, *my lady*. You can't stop us."

She shrugged. "We shall see, Salvius. There are many threads in this plot. I certainly do not hear your supposed betrothed leaping to your defense."

He turned to me. I stiffened so as not to quail under his suppressed fury. "She will learn to."

My sister raised an eyebrow. "If you want to believe that, sir, that is your prerogative. Clearly all of the royal wives of this house are very handily controlled."

At this, we all fell into a bitter silence that lasted another half hour until Ptolemy ordered the barge back to shore. We disembarked and were carried back to the palace by chair in the same black mood, the early evening crowds parting for us as we went. Arriving home, Ptolemy and Salvius flung themselves out of their chairs and stalked off down one of the wings, no doubt seeking out Pothinus with this new tale of my sister's too liberal tongue. I helped Ptah down and was about to retreat to our rooms when Cleopatra stopped us.

"Ptah darling, would you excuse your sister and me for a time? There are some things I wish to discuss with her."

Ptah looked to me and I gave him a nod, so he released my hand, scampering off in the opposite direction from the one our brother had taken. Cleopatra motioned for me to follow her down the parallel portico.

"Why did you not tell me of this monstrous thing?" she asked as we walked.

"I was not sure how serious they were. Salvius told me of it, but he could have been making up tales to frighten me." I paused. "Also, I did not think you would care."

She tutted. "That is unfair, little sister. I know we have our differences, but I am not so cruel as to want to see you bound to that pig. Nothing could be worse for you or for Egypt."

"So what are we to do?"

"We shall figure out some plan or another, but this will not stand. I want to talk this over with Damianus. We shall marry you off to Ptah or a foreign prince before Salvius shall be allowed to paw at you."

We turned into the hall where the eunuchs' quarters were. Most of them shared rooms with one another as our other servants did, though high-ranking eunuchs such as our tutors had their own accommodations. Damianus, as the tutor of the eldest of Ptolemy Auletes' heirs, had the largest and most private of suites. As we headed towards his rooms, we met Ganymedes in the hallway. Though clearly surprised to see us, he made the usual gestures of respect appropriate to each of us in succession.

"Teacher, have you seen Damianus?" I asked.

"No, my lady. Not since midday." He glanced at my sister. "Would Your Majesty like my assistance in locating him?"

"Thank you, Ganymedes," said Cleopatra. "I am certain we will find him in his quarters. However, you may come with us if you wish. We are going to discuss the future of your pupil here." She gestured towards me.

My tutor bowed and took the opportunity of my sister's goodwill to fall in at my side. We reached Damianus' rooms. A slight odor I could not place wafted out to us as Cleopatra parted the curtain and we three stepped inside.

"Gods defend us!" said Ganymedes, inhaling sharply.

The room was in total disarray, with furniture overturned everywhere and wall hangings torn so that the shreds barely clung to their hooks. All of it was covered in dark streaks of something that looked like dye until my mind finally understood it to be blood. Damianus himself lay sprawled in the middle of this whirlwind, stripped of his robes and covered in at least a dozen stab wounds.

My tutor held out an arm to block both me and Cleopatra. "Stay here," he admonished as he strode over to kneel beside Damianus' prone form.

"Is he dead?" asked my sister.

"Yes, Your Majesty," he answered heavily. "And for several hours, I suspect. He is quite cold."

"Who could have done this?" I blurted out, trying not to stare at the naked corpse. Damianus' solid, wrinkled flesh gave him such a look of finality in that space. His inertness was like that of a stone or a block of wood. His eyes had rolled back in his head and his mouth hung open slackly, giving him a gaping expression I had never seen him wear in life.

In short, I had trouble processing the scene before me. It was as if I was watching a tableau with a very poor actor in the role of Damianus. I had seen violent death before, but somehow this had an insidious level of intimacy I had not encountered. Perhaps because we stood in the comfort of Damianus' quarters. This was less an execution than a personal screed. Someone had wanted to send a very specific message.

Cleopatra stepped over to Ganymedes' side as my teacher covered up the dead man with a curtain piled up on the floor. "This a warning for me. Ptolemy and Pothinus must have arranged this." Her voice had no depth and I could see the jump of her pulse against her neck.

"I suspect Achillas and Lucius Septimus took care of this for them while you were all out this afternoon," said Ganymedes.

I looked around the room desperately wishing to flee, when I saw the message scrawled in the eunuch's blood on the wall over the doorway. "I believe that message is for you also, sister," I said softly.

Poisoners can also die by the sword

She read it impassively. "I must hear from Pompey soon. Without him, I cannot defend myself against these jackals." She bent down and gently closed Damianus' eyes. "I told you we had no more time left, Teacher. Our enemies are not at the gate, they are in our very beds."

Chapter Eight

I step onto an athletic training field. At first I assume this is an ordinary dream because the arena is so Greek in appearance. There is various equipment strewn about and several eastern horses graze unconcernedly near the perimeter. Two raise their heads and flick their tails at my appearance, but they soon return to the grass. I walk over to a rack of weapons: bows, swords, spears, shields, and a basket full of military daggers. I pick up one of the bows and pull the string back tight across my chest. It is taut and the bow springy.

I try to envision a target and one manifests a hundred paces away. I string an arrow, and relax my eye until the target is barely even a consideration anymore. The arrow sings through the air and lands slightly to the left of the bullseye.

"Tolerable, but what will you do if there is no bow to be had, Ptolemy-daughter?"

I turn my head eastward and watch a lithe figure approaching with a hunting hawk perched on its outstretched arm and a black saluki trotting on its heels. Upon seeing me, the saluki breaks into a run. As it reaches me, I can see it is not a dog but the *sha*, and in one fluid motion mid-stride the beast transforms into my Lord. He grins and embraces me as his companion reaches us.

She is slender, yet every fiber of her being emanates raw power. Her proud, high cheekbones are offset by burning amber eyes that flash under a mantle of long dark hair. She wears the head of a lioness skin as a hooded cloak like Heracles. She does not wear the long sheath dress of the goddesses, but a scarlet man's kilt and short-sleeved shirt piece, covered by an armored breastplate, with Roman-style military sandals rather than bare feet.

She needs no introduction, but Lord Set gives one anyway. "Arsinoë, this is Lady Sekhmet."

Her lips curl back enough to show the gleam of sharp white teeth, her voice as black as a panther's growl. "I am here to give you a warrior's training, Ptolemy-daughter. If you can be taught," she adds with a slightly doubtful air.

"She is young, but she possesses great strength of will, Sekhmet," Set defends me chidingly.

The lion goddess circles me closely. I can feel her catching my scent. I try not think of her terrible epithets and hope I smell braver than I feel. Finally, the long inspection ends.

"I have worked with less in full-grown pharaohs," she concedes, taking a few steps back. "Much less a girl-child princess. She has a supple build for one raised in a palace," she pauses to glance at my torso, "and her breasts are not so large as to be a hindrance."

I blush at this, but neither god takes any notice.

She continues. "I have been told you can ride, child, and I can see you have some facility with a bow. But the enemy has many more weapons at their disposal. I will show you how the spear glides through the air, even if you never throw one. How to wield a sword as if it were simply another part of your arm. How to protect yourself in close combat with hardened soldiers."

"I give thanks for your instruction, my lady," I murmur.

Lady Sekhmet shrugs her arm and the hawk takes flight with a piercing screech as it soars off into the blazing sun. The goddess stalks over to me and holds her hands on my shoulders. "These are the preliminaries. I will also teach you to think like a general. To find your advantages and how to press them. To understand how the wind fills the sails of ships in a battle. To speak to troops so that they will attend to your voice. To lead, Ptolemy-daughter."

I feel the strength of her arms and I find my courage. "Where do we begin, my lady?"

"At the beginning, child. Let us see how easily you hit those bow targets at a gallop."

I jog over to the horses and vault onto the back of the closest one by grabbing a fistful of its mane with my free hand. I kick it into a canter as I ride past the weapons rack and reach down for another arrow as we pass. I notch the arrow to the bow as my heels ask the stallion for a gallop. We surge forward and I steady my arm as we fly to pass the target. I keep Ganymedes' voice in my head, telling me to wait for my moment. Just as we start to go by the target, I twist and take my aim. I exhale as the arrow leaves my hand.

And then I wake up.

I went out to the stables, looking for a way to duck the venom-tinged atmosphere inside the palace walls where my brother and his friends whispered in corners amongst themselves and Cleopatra shut herself up in her rooms after the murder of Damianus, speaking to no one. My horse, Erebus, stuck his head out of his stall testily, though he relaxed when he caught my scent in his flaring nostrils. I reached up and rubbed his forehead affectionately. Without warning his ears flattened back and he made an angry squeal deep in his throat. I moved my hand away, thinking he was in one of his moods, when a hand appeared over my mouth and a blade was at my throat.

"If you cry out, I swear on the bones of my ancestors I will cut you from ear to ear."

I jerked my head away from the blade and met the calm gaze of Apollodorus. Erebus screamed with rage and slammed his heavy body into the stall door. Apollodorus lifted the dagger from my throat and in one practiced move swung his arm up slicing open the windpipe of my horse. The black stallion shrieked, blood spraying from the gash until he fell thickly against the wall. I moaned from behind his hand and struggled to get away. The Sicilian tightened his grip and shoved the now bloody weapon back to my throat.

"In case you thought I wasn't serious. Now stop squirming and start walking."

He half dragged me away to the other part of the stables where the camels were kept. I was weeping and trying to think of a way to break

Apollodorus' hold on me when we rounded a corner, nearly colliding with Mudjet.

"My lady!" she cried, looking wildly between my captor and me.

"Hush, Mudjet," said Apollodorus pointing the dripping dagger at her. "Keep quiet and follow us, or I'll flay open our little princess right here."

I begged Mudjet with my eyes to run for help, though hers answered mine back she was too afraid to call the Sicilian's bluff.

We were hurried along until we found my sister packing up camels and horses with Kharmion and a small contingent of soldiers. Cleopatra surveyed our terrified faces and clicked her tongue coolly. "Really, Apollodorus. She will be useless until gods know when now that you have frightened her half to death."

"You wanted her compliant, Your Majesty, and that is what you have received. The princess is headstrong when it pleases her and she has always required reminding of her place."

I glared at Apollodorus, then turned to my sister. "What is going on?"

"We are leaving, little sister. I have to get out of Alexandria before Ptolemy throws me in a dungeon somewhere."

"That does not explain why we are here," I retorted, gesturing to Mudjet and myself as Kharmion and a slave swathed us in Bedouin traveling clothes.

"Do you want the pretty answer or the ugly one?"

"Is there a difference?" I asked, adjusting the headscarf.

She ignored me. "The pretty answer is that of the siblings remaining to me you are the cleverest and that means you know that a kingdom ruled by Ptolemy and his minions alone will make dearly departed Berenice's reign look like a golden age. You know I am the better choice and you will help me convince our allies of that. We will help one another and I will look out for you and Ptah."

"And the ugly answer?"

"Ptolemy has Ptah and I need leverage as well. If Pothinus means to get rid of me, they will need you because the people will demand another royal sister-wife in my place. Or if they choose to ignore tradition, they will need you to trade for a foreign bride. Ptolemy thinks if he has Ptah, I will be lost. But he forgets how much he needs you."

"What if I refuse?" I spat out defiantly.

"How quickly you forget poor Apollodorus. You have no choice, Arsinoë. You are coming with us. Now at the very least I cannot risk you running off to alert our brother."

Two soldiers stepped behind me and each took one of my arms. I sulkily shook them off and grabbed the reins of the nearest camel. I guided it to kneel down and helped Mudjet climb aboard. Having mounted my own camel, I continued to glare at Cleopatra.

"Do not be so put out, sister," she said breezily as she leapt onto her horse. "Traveling to distant lands is an adventure. You might even enjoy yourself."

She gave a signal and we galloped off across the racegrounds towards the Jewish quarter and the eastern cemeteries. We passed through the Gate of the Sun, following the road east towards Canopus and to the banks of the Nile. From there, we would meet the endless desert and my sister's desperate gambit to recover her kingdom, of which I was now an accomplice. I would have to do as she said or I might never see Ptah or Alexandria again. I pulled the loose cloth of my headwrap around my face and gripped the pommel of my saddle tighter as I called to my camel to quicken its pace.

At first we merely crossed through the delta lands, which while not the barren desert, were hardly the succulent paradise they should have been at this time of year. The drought still bit into the marrow of our kingdom. The children we passed on the trade roads were thinner than they should have been as well, the oxen's hides not as glossy. In the farmlands the people were not quite starving — not yet — though the normally generous peasants were slow to offer us food, even in exchange for coin. And my sister's position was too tenuous to demand more by revealing herself to them.

As we rested at a well we had been grudgingly allowed to drink from, I walked over to Cleopatra. She sat seemingly lost in thought, dandling an empty copper ladle from her hand.

"So where are we going anyway?" I asked, settling myself on the wall next to her.

"Heliopolis," she answered in a distracted voice.

"Not exactly a military hub, sister."

Her eyes came into sharper focus. They appeared a gold-flecked brown that day. "One must plan before one rides out with an army. And not all armies are made of men."

"Do you plan to raise a ghost army in a ghost town?" I returned skeptically.

"Tut, little sister. You of all people should know the value of a good library. We go to Heliopolis for information."

"I thought all of the manuscripts were moved to Alexandria a century ago."

"There are always bits that get left behind. We go to see what has been left in the field after the harvest."

Chapter Nine

Heliopolis was once a great city. The Egyptians called it Iunu, the Place of Pillars, because of its many, many temples that all orbited around the oldest and most magnificent of them all, the Per-Tem. In the common tongue, it meant the House of Atum, the form Father Ra takes in this part of the kingdom. For this is Lord Ra's home, which is why when Alexander galloped into its ancient streets with their rough brick walls he named it Heliopolis, the City of the Sun.

Even the name of the Per-Tem was for the benefit of foreigners, the Egyptians simply call it Per-Aat. The Great House. Its other temples were dedicated to the sun god's immediate family, the Ennead, Egypt's most powerful gods. His children, airy Shu and dewy Tefnut; his grandchildren, solid Geb and heavenly Nut; and his great-grandchildren, kingly Osiris and clever Isis, enigmatic Nephthys and my shadowy Lord Set. Though naturally, when Lord Horus began his meteoric rise, he too entered the sacred spaces of this city as an uncounted tenth god. He dwells as a child in the temples of his parents, and rules in the Per-Aat alongside his great-great-grandfather.

As the seat of the lord of all the gods of the Black Land, Heliopolis had been for much of its history a vast royal archive for the pharaohs and an unrivaled center of learning. It was said that Orpheus and Homer walked in its inner sanctums, and less fantastically, that Pythagoras and Plato had consulted with its philosophers and stargazers. When the first Ptolemies arrived in these parts, they traveled to Heliopolis to learn from the ancients how to rule this unruly land. They sat among the stone works of Ramses and they listened to the wisdom of the priests.

But eventually, the Ptolemies grew bored of Egyptian stories. Like the homesick armies of Alexander, they longed to be among the Greek world again. Heliopolis was too far away from the coast, too close to Memphis and its Egyptian-ness. Too full of the strange Egyptian gods and their beastly forms. So they gathered up the old archives, gutted the temple treasuries, and returned to the north, to the city that they had named in honor of their dead lord. Alexandria's rise came at the expense of Heliopolis, and the latter was eclipsed and forgotten by the wayward Ptolemies. The Place of Pillars began a long, embarrassing slide into decrepitude.

This was my sister's thinking. No one would look for living Ptolemies in its ruined walls.

We entered Heliopolis and made our way to the Per-Aat through empty houses and neglected streets. Merchants half-heartedly tried to sell us animal mummies to offer at the temples, though one merchant's wife wailed at our party until Kharmion paid for an ibis mummy to quiet her. Listless children sat in many of the doorways and the old people sported contemptuous looks, as if we deserved their scorn for bothering to come to their city. Thebes and Memphis might hold proudly to the old ways, but Heliopolis had never recovered from the shame of being discarded by our House. I wondered if it was wise to show one's face as a Ptolemy here at all. Cities like this one have long memories for slights.

We dismounted before the still imposing stone pillars of the main temple, as Cleopatra and Apollodorus entered in search of the high priest. We waited in the baking sun as sweat soaked through the lower layers of my clothes. Eventually, even the camels sat down and rested their heads against the worn pillars. The horses twitched their withers and stamped their feet. The minutes trickled by until Kharmion made a huffing noise of impatience.

"I am going to find some supplies to load the bags with," she said sharply to me, shoving the ibis mummy into my arms. "Do not wander off!"

I watched her storm off back in the direction of the market and waited several beats. Mudjet slunk in front of the nearest shadowy recess between the buildings to block it from view of the soldiers and animal drivers, who were ignoring us anyway.

"Be careful, my lady," she whispered as I slipped behind her and off into the temple avenues.

I had no specific destination in mind as I weaved in and out of the pillar-lined halls and courtyards. I thought briefly of escape, losing myself in this dying city, maybe trying to claim sanctuary in one of the temples but I quickly dismissed such plans. How would I live here? Would I beg with a bowl in the streets where no one had any coin to give and no travelers passed? Could I become a slave to a precariously surviving household, eating less than nothing and waiting passively for death to claim me? Kharmion would be furious that I had disobeyed her. She chose always to forget that she and I were not equals, though I doubted my sister would be overly angry. She knew I was alone in this crumbling place, away from all I knew and at her mercy.

The temples of the Ennead were in various states of disrepair, evidence of the priesthood having to make do in these times. The Per-Aat was still grand like an elder of dignity, though as I pushed out to the houses of Lord Ra's family, the facades became more cracked, the altars dustier. The steps of the House of Shu were swept, though the fires of his sanctum were unattended. His mate Lady Tefnut's altar was clean and littered with offerings, but that was to be expected in a drought year. A priest tended the fires of the House of Geb, though with the resignation of one who knows the Lord of Earth can give nothing without rain. Lady Nut's house had been mostly left to its own devices like her father's, and her daughter Lady Nephthys' fire was maintained only by the fear of those facing so much starvation and death. The houses of Osiris and Isis were lacking the grandeur of temples I had seen in Alexandria and in the other great cities, but here they endured in their genteel poverty as best they could, like a smaller shadow of the Per-Aat itself. It was only as I passed their doorways that I understood where my feet were taking me. I was alone and more afraid in my heart than I dared to let on. My feet were taking me to the house of my Lord to seek protection.

I was not surprised by the state of Lord Set's temple when I reached its doorway. While not literally falling down where it stood, it was as abandoned as the house of a god could dare to be in a land where the people might still fear that god's wrath. Even though I knew this could only be his house, I rubbed away the dirt from the hieroglyphs on the right pillar to reveal the familiar pattern of the *sha* beast seated before the crouched male deity symbol with its pharaoh's false beard. I lifted my skirts as I stepped over the bits of debris scattered in the mouth of the sanctum and made my way through the interior, lit only by the trickle of light from the late afternoon sun.

In the gloom, I could faintly make out carvings on the wall. My Lord leading the royal armies in battle; riding in Lord Ra's boat, spearing the serpent Apep with his pike; standing with Lady Nephthys, his hand outstretched in blessing to his son, Lord Anubis. In one old mural, a pharaoh gave offerings to the *sha* seated on a throne. I squinted to make out the inscription, for it was unusual to see even the old pharaohs pay such homage to my Lord. I found the cartouche, trying to remember the rudiments of their meaning, when the delicately wrought feathers of homage gave way to a seated figure with a *sha* head. Of course. He Who Belongs to Set. Pharaoh Manmaatre Seti. I gazed at his elegant profile and wondered if he and I were the only royal people who had recently made a pilgrimage to this lonely place.

I put the ibis off to the side and began unwrapping the cloth from around my face and head. I took it in hand and cleaned off the altar in sweeping strokes. Normally even one as highborn as I would not be allowed to penetrate this far into the temple without special authorization. I was certainly not permitted to touch my Lord's altar, but there was no one to register a complaint.

Once the altar was free of sand and dust, I shook out my head wrap and replaced it over my hair quickly. I found a few bits of straw on the ground and darted back towards the House of Nephthys. Seeing no one around, I lit the straw in her fire and left as hurriedly as I had come, murmuring words of thanks to her. I placed the burning straw in a bowl I discovered in a corner and with it tossed the straw into the fire pit, praying there would be oil enough for it to catch. The flames that rose up were feeble enough, yet the fact they were there at all felt like a miracle.

I placed the ibis before the sacred fire and closed my eyes.

My Lord, I give you this offering so that you might protect us as we cross your kingdom in the coming days. I know that by lighting the fires of the God of War I probably hasten the doom of which you and the gods have warned me. If this is so, give me the strength I need to stand when the dreaded time comes, if you have spoken true that I am your Beloved.

I did not linger in my Lord's house, for I assumed I had already been missed. In spite of the heat, I sprinted back to the Per-Aat where I promptly received a cuff about the ears from Kharmion for my disobedience.

Mudjet was furious. "You forget yourself, Kharmion, by laying hands upon the princess!"

"What will you do about it, Mudjet?" growled my sister's servant in response. "You are both at my lady's mercy. Who is she going to believe?"

Our argument was cut short by the reemergence of Cleopatra. "It is too late to start anything today, the light is already dying," she said. "We will arrange ourselves in the guest houses of the temple, and tomorrow we will gather up the resources we will need here and in future."

"I have made arrangements with several merchants for our immediate needs, my lady," Kharmion answered.

"Thank you, my dear. That will help a great deal." She turned to Apollodorus. "I need you to organize the men so we have them on guard shifts. I do not know if we are pursued by Ptolemy. And you must keep your ear to the ground for information coming from Alexandria."

The Sicilian nodded and went over to start pulling the soldiers off the ground. My sister reached out for my hand, which I offered up to her, and she led us down the avenue on the other side of the complex from the one I had taken. We entered a small dwelling and began setting up the few possessions we had arrived with. There was only one couch to be had, which meant the we arrayed ourselves on the floor while Cleopatra collapsed with a huff on it. I studied my toes in my sandals and wondered what Ptah was doing at this moment.

My sister's voice interrupted my musings. "This feels just like Rome again." She was staring up at the ceiling, lost in her own thoughts.

"It is hotter here, though, my lady," remarked Kharmion as she sat sorting cloth.

Cleopatra gave a cough of amusement. "True, but the air is less humid." She relapsed into silence again and frowned. "I cannot believe I have to suffer through the same trials as my father. Truly the gods lack imagination."

Kharmion made an anxious noise and clutched an amulet around her neck, but did not challenge her mistress' assessment. I looked up from my feet. "But you have advantages over our father's situation, sister," I countered. "We have not been driven from Egypt, for a start."

"Not yet, though we will have to leave our borders to recruit an army and allies," Cleopatra answered.

"Naturally. But you are much more popular with our Roman allies than our father was, and you are much more adept at persuasion. I doubt our exile will be as long this time." I was in truth unsure about any of the claims I made, but I knew as long as I was forced to be on this journey with my sister, I needed her protection. That meant I needed the wily Cleopatra, not one mired in the debacles of the past.

She looked at me with a rueful smile. "I hope that is the case, little sister. It is kind of you to show such faith even though I know you are unhappy about being here."

I shrugged. "Besides, Ptolemy is not half as canny as Berenice. And his lords may be even more divided."

"That is certainly true," she said, the wistfulness in her tone dispersing. "You are right. I am getting despondent because we are sitting here at loose ends. Tomorrow we shall find what we need, then we will head out into the desert to create our revolution. So we must sleep well tonight."

I am in the Great Library in Alexandria. The scrolls and manuscripts are nestled in their shelves, the lamps hang motionless from the ceiling on their slowly rusting iron chains, caked with sea salt gleaned from the air. I wish this was real, just as much as I wish I was home with Ptah and Ganymedes in my teeming, shatterglass city. And that is when I see the baboon.

Its shaggy coat looks as dusty as the library shelves, its hornet eyes shine sharply against the uncertain light. I freeze under its menacing gaze; I remember the baboons that the entertainers brought to the palace, they could be amusing with their smart hands and sweet little dances, but I also knew of their dagger teeth and roiling tempers.

I carefully back away when I see the bright eyes of a dozen others peeking out from the rows, squatting on top of the high shelves, and from underneath the furniture. I see one path through an unguarded set of shelves, and I edge slowly towards it. I slip into the row and walk as silently as I can, keeping my panting breath as low as possible. The row seems to stretch endlessly before me as I listen for the skittering sound that means I am being followed. I reach the end of the row at last and I throw myself against its wooden end as I round the corner, closing my eyes and letting out a huff of relief.

"There is no need to be so dramatic, Ptolemy-daughter. The monkeys are harmless," a calm voice remarks before me.

My eyes fly open and I see a figure, scribbling away with an ink reed, seated at one of the tables scattered about this open space in the library. He is a man, older in appearance than my Lord, yet not an old man. He has the tanned skin of an Egyptian, but it is paled, like a person who has spent a good deal of time indoors. He glances up from beneath his blue hood, meeting my gaze with the glittering black eyes of an emerald ibis. For it is Lord Thoth, the Self-Made. Lord of All Knowledge.

I incline my head. "My lord."

He gestures for me to join him at the table as another stool materializes. His every movement has both the elegance of a wading bird and an economy of motion that intimates his understanding of how every bone and fiber relate to one another. Nothing is lost or wasted, all is thought of and utilized. Lord Thoth is called the Self-Made because he was not born of another god, but created himself out of the matter of the universe. The Greeks understand wisdom in a similar way, hence the strange birth of Athena.

I take my seat and with a wave of his hand, the papers before Thoth disappear and are replaced by a *senet* board.

"I am told you know how to play, Princess."

"Yes my lord, though I doubt I shall look like it before the game's inventor."

He chuckles. "*Senet* is not really about winning and losing. It is about opposing forces." He holds up one of the cone-shaped pieces and one of the drum-shaped ones. "Day and Night. Man and Woman. Good and Evil. All are present, all are necessary. The trick is holding them in balance." He returns the pieces to the board and makes his first move.

I then make my move. "Horus and Set," I answer.

He nods. "It is so. Egypt has long been out of balance because it has forgotten that it needs the *sha* Lord as much as the Falcon King. To turn one's face from the former is to deny the existence of darkness. And the world needs darkness as much as light, just as mortals bodies need sleep as much as activity." He swaps his piece in place of where I had placed mine.

I frown in concentration as I make my next move. "I do not know if I can restore balance to the Black Land, even if your lordship were to teach me every night for the rest of my life."

"You have wisdom enough for a mortal that you recognize this, Ptolemy-daughter. I am here to explain to you what your elder sister is planning so you might understand what you are facing." He tosses the gaming sticks and advances his piece.

I jump one of my pieces over his. "She is going to go ask Marcus Bibulus for help to regain her throne from our brother. It is not that mysterious."

"Then why are you in Iunu?" he queries shrewdly. "Surely she does not have time to dally anywhere unnecessarily?"

"Enlighten me, Lord of Invention."

He passes his first piece through the Field of Reeds space. "How much do you know of *heka*?"

I have heard the word before, though I cannot remember where. Like so many Egyptian words, it appears to be a compound word, so I break it down in my mind. The second part is easy; the *ka* was a person's life force, their soul. I think on the word *he*. It could have many meanings, so I roll them all over in my head.

At length, I look back at Thoth. "To bring forth the soul?"

He is pleased with my deduction. "After a fashion, Ptolemy-daughter. *Heka* is also a general term for magic, but all magic stems from the will of a being's *ka*. All gods use *heka*, some mortals can use their *ka*s to unlock this potential. It can also be the will in one's *ka* to wield great power."

I place one of my pieces on the *ankh* space. "How does one do this?"

"To unleash one's *heka*, one must perform *seshaw*, the rituals, found in the sacred *rws*."

I start. "That is why we are in Heliopolis. Cleopatra seeks *rw* texts."

"Yes, Princess. It is so."

I feel my body contract with fear. "How can I protect Egypt as the gods have commanded if my sister can use magic? Surely she is the stronger choice?"

"Your sister's will is strong, she will undoubtedly be able to wield *heka*. But she will use it to make worldly alliances with the northern wolves, she will not preserve our Egypt. We have come to you, child, because you are of the land and you carry Egypt's *ka* in your *ib*."

"Can you teach me *heka*, my lord?" I ask, already knowing the answer.

"No, it is not your destiny to wield your own *heka*. Your *ka*'s power is what you see before you," he says expansively.

"The power to miserably lose at *senet*?"

This makes Lord Thoth smile. "The other Ptolemy-daughter has been given the rare ability to use *heka* through her own force of will. Your gift is even rarer — your *ka* can draw on the *ka*s of the gods and thus you can speak with us even in this late time."

"My sister is strong, I do not know if I am enough. Even with the help of the gods."

"Perhaps not, but do not despair. Life is a great deal like *senet*."

And then I wake up.

Chapter Ten

Apollodorus came upon us as we breakfasted the next morning, his face typically grim. "I've had a report from Origenes. Gabinius has left Egypt."

My sister looked up from the apricot she was pitting. "Has Ptolemy sent him after us?"

The Sicilian shook his head. "No, it is not about us. Apparently, Gaius Caesar has summoned the Gabiniani to fight for him and they have answered his call."

I felt my heart quail at this news. In spite of our animosity, Kharmion and I exchanged worried glances. The Gabiniani answered to no one, they had killed to maintain their autonomy from Rome, their general had barely been convinced to send any of them to Pompey — a man he held as an ally. What kind of man could demand their allegiance and receive it as if it were a tin coin and not a ruby?

The only person who seemed unruffled by this intelligence was Cleopatra. "Perhaps we should ride back to Alexandria now that our dear boy-pharaoh does not have his goons anymore as opposed to riding on to Pelusium. I doubt I would even require an army to reclaim my throne."

"That would not be wise, my lady," answered Apollodorus. "Origenes says the general took only several hundred of his men with him. The rest of the Gabiniani remain in Egypt in service to your brother."

"General Pompey is Aulus Gabinius' patron as surely as he is our own, why would he agree to take up arms for Gaius Caesar?" asked Kharmion, finding her voice.

Cleopatra frowned thoughtfully. "This is so, but Pompey did not prevent Gabinius' exile in the Senate. Caesar must have promised to lift his banishment in exchange for his services."

"It is also rumored that Caesar told the general he would not have to fight Pompey directly in battle to exonerate him for oath-breaking," added Apollodorus.

My sister tossed aside the pit she had finished extracting. "I should have found a way to send Pompey all the Gabiniani when I had the

78

chance," she muttered. "I have reaped nothing except trouble from the lot. I hope Aulus Gabinius chokes on his own treachery."

"Do not worry, my lady," soothed Kharmion. "The gods will see his traitorous conduct for what it is."

Cleopatra took a ferocious bite into the fruit in her hand and chewed at the pulp until she felt inclined to respond. "It all matters not. Let us see to this day and the tasks that lay before us in this corpse city. Sister, come with me."

We spent all of the next day and the three that followed it digging through the tattered remains of the royal archives. Because she needed my help finding what she needed, my sister disclosed that we were indeed searching for *rw* pages. We sifted among texts copied into Greek and held up old hieroglyph papyri for priestly interpretation. It reminded me of my sister's potion books, bundled up somewhere in all of our baggage. The Egyptians believe intent is one of the silent ingredients in any concoction and a skilled practitioner knows how to work that to their advantage. Cleopatra had always had this skill. I had no doubt the *seshaws* of *heka* would be no difficulty for her.

I sat perched on a stool reading through documents stacked next to me, thinking of all of this when she interrupted my thoughts.

"Do you think this is foolish?"

I looked up from my work and met her intense gaze. Her eyes looked like dark topazes that day.

I paused before I answered. "There is much that is unknowable in the world. Magic is just another one of those things. If you think it will help, it seems prudent to explore all avenues."

"Do you believe in *heka*, little sister?"

"I know that Egypt is full of lost knowledge," I said. "I know I could not attempt what you are doing. If anyone can revive *heka* as a power in the world, I suspect it is you."

She tilted her head as she scrutinized me. "Sometimes I wonder where you go, little sister, when you speak like this. You find your courtly tongue, but your eyes are looking somewhere else, somewhere very far away."

"I am sorry, sister," I answered, feigning innocence as I thumbed the corner of the papyrus in my hand. "I mean nothing by it. Forgive me if it appears rude."

"No, no. It is something else. I thought —" She pondered her next words carefully. "— it is almost as if you can see something that is not there. Hear a voice that cannot be heard."

I felt myself tense in fear. I had wondered, as she began to explore this idea of using her *ka* as a source of power, if my dreams with the gods would leave traces she could see.

I realized I stood like Oedipus at the crossroads. Here was the one chance I had to tell my sister of my dreams. To tell her the gods spoke to me, with their ancient voices full of love and warning. Did I dare?

Something had told me from the beginning that I should be wary with whom I shared my dreams, but as I dwelled in this singular moment, I was filled with a deadly certainty that I should never tell Cleopatra. At the start of everything I would have done so to avoid being locked away as a madwoman. Now, I saw it was to avoid being seen as a rival, a position I had never seen myself in in all my life.

Had Fate drawn us into these tracks because it had opened its eyes upon the world and seen that there were still two Ptolemy daughters? Two *ka*s destined somehow to always be as we were in this moment, as two girls looking across a room at each other, forever trying to truly see the other and forever prevented by some distortion of nature?

I accepted the warning of my heart and sacrificed the chance for us to draw the other into our bosom and chase away the shadows that lurked between us. I answered her in some noncommittal way and we returned to our books.

I sacrificed our love for the chance of survival. I had felt the brush of the future from the words of Lord Thoth, I had felt the coming power of the *heka*. It would pierce Egypt through — stone, skin, and fire. The true gift the gods were offering me was not their divine intervention, but the gift of being able to veil myself, even partially, from its gaze. So that when

THE GOD'S WIFE

81

the *heka* of my sister saw through everything else, there would be a part of me she could not touch.

I should have been relieved, and yet I also understood the dark side of this gift. The burning anger of my sister when she perceived her destiny might be unable to discern mine.

At last Cleopatra exhausted the library of the Per-Aat and announced we would leave at dawn the following morning. The success of our days in the bowels of Heliopolis I can only measure in hindsight. I know we found several scrolls that appeared to recount the *seshaw*s of *heka* and that Lord Thoth had spoken to me as if my sister would achieve her purpose in these matters. Just as I know my dreams are open to skepticism, so too do I understand not all will look on my sister's life and observe the touch of the mystical. Both opinions have their merits, though I have always believed that neither diminishes the remarkable guiding star that the gods placed over her head when she was born.

And so we turned north then east, towards the coast. For several days, we rode at night, out of the heat of the sun. Cleopatra had sent word to Origenes, meant to be intercepted by Pothinus, that we were traveling south towards our Nubian borders. In truth we were riding for Pelusium, the last sea garrison of our kingdom, sitting on the coast as a beacon between the Black Land of Egypt and the desert of Sinai.

Here there were soldiers stationed far from the politics of Alexandria, our dependable men who were Egypt's wall against the border raiders of the east. My sister intended to raise the garrison to her defense, certain that its stalwart troops followed her rule as the successor of our father.

We rode for several days past the flax fields and the salt marshes until the tall red-bricked towers of the fort at Pelusium came into view. The guards posted at the causeway that crossed the marsh let us pass and we galloped towards the rust-colored outer perimeter of the fort. We halted at the gate and Apollodorus hollered at the men holding the wall to make way for the Pharaoh. The gate was pulled open enough to allow Lucius Septimus to slip out of them before us.

"I see no Pharaoh here, Apollodorus," he commented in a bored tone. "Just two runaway princesses and a rabble of retainers."

Cleopatra and Apollodorus were temporarily made speechless by the Roman's appearance, which caused him to cock an eyebrow. "Oh, you weren't expecting anyone of your brother's here. Well, I am sorry to disappoint you, Your Highness. If it is any consolation, Pothinus did send Salvius to Nubia to make sure you weren't actually going there."

Cleopatra recovered herself. "I still outrank you, Lucius. Stand aside and let me speak with my troops. It is up to them whether they want to follow the misrule of my brother."

"That I cannot allow, my lady. Pothinus has decreed you are both rebels and I will not have you taking over this fort. If you continue on into the desert, I have orders to let you go. But if you set one foot inside these walls, you'll all be arrested."

"But that is not fair!" I cried out impulsively. "I am not a rebel! I was forced to go with them!" As I gestured out, I knew I had made a costly mistake. Cleopatra gave me an icy look.

"Pothinus figured as much, my lady," Lucius answered me, ignoring my sister's anger. "If you wish to stay here, I shall take you back to Alexandria within the week. It is your choice."

I did not have time to answer before I was grabbed off my camel by Apollodorus, who put a knife to my throat once more. I glanced up to where the archers had drawn their bows at us until Lucius signaled them to put their weapons down.

My sister, who had made no visible movement through the scuffle, continued to eye the garrison appraisingly. "Arsinoë will stay with me. If she is so dear to my brother, I will trade her to him for the throne."

Lucius laughed coldly. "Well, then, you had all better be on your way before I change my mind and put you in chains."

With not enough men to take on the garrison, my sister had no other option but to lead us past Pelusium and into the long deserts of the Sinai peninsula.

She turned to Apollodorus. "We will go to Syria and get Roman re-inforcements as we planned. We will simply have to take the garrison on our way back instead of having it as a base of operations. It is done easily enough."

The Sicilian nodded and whistled for my camel, which he roughly deposited me on as Cleopatra grabbed its reins.

"I might be green in *heka* now, little sister, but you should mind me carefully so I do not remember days like today later on," she said in a low, dangerous tone.

"It was the truth. You would have said the same if our places were switched," I retorted. I knew I should not argue, yet I knew she must still have need of me to prevent me from going with Lucius Septimus. So I decided to gamble.

She gave me a penetrating look. "It may be so, yet I would be wary of it all the same. I do not think you are ready yet to play my games." She let go of the reins and kicked her own mount forward. I was about to let out my breath when Apollodorus grabbed my arm.

"You are a silly little girl, Your Highness. You are not your sister's equal, and you will die a messy death if you persist in acting like it," he growled in my ear.

My own anger at failing to escape made me braver with the Sicilian than I normally was. "You do not know the first thing about me, Apollodorus, so do not presume to lecture me." I drew myself up and glared at him imperiously. "Now, you will release my arm."

He did so, but gave me such a dark look as he went to join Cleopatra's side that I nearly lost my nerve. I heard a quick succession of hooves as Mudjet pulled her camel up next to mine.

"My lady! Are you all right? Apollodorus' ruffians were holding me at the back of the train and would not permit me to come to you."

"I am fine, though I have made him and my sister quite angry with me. They did not hurt you, did they?"

She shook her head. "No, they tried to intimidate me, but I am made of stronger thread than that."

"Good. I think we shall both need to be in the coming weeks."

Eventually, my sister's anger towards me softened, and we crossed through the horizonless desert on what passed for amicable terms. Even if she had wished to continue in her rage against me, she could not afford such an emotional luxury. She was short on allies and could not risk alienating me completely. Not yet, at least.

"Was General Gabinius correct, sister?" I asked her one afternoon, as we sat under our tent waiting out the afternoon heat.

"About what?"

"Do you regret the way you treated the Gabiniani?"

She looked thoughtful, then resolute. "No. My choice was either to anger Marcus Bibulus and most likely estrange myself from his friend and ours, General Pompey, the greatest man in Rome; or anger Aulus Gabinius, an exile out of power and his men who love anyone who gives them enough coin. The choice was obvious."

"Even though it led us to this?" I gestured at the barren landscape.

"This is just a temporary setback, little sister. Even Alexander had to deal with little rebellions. Soon we shall be in Antioch and I can collect on the debt Marcus Bibulus owes me for sending him justice for his sons at such great personal cost. Remember that, Arsinoë. All accounts balance in the end."

Chapter Eleven

Denied the speed of travel by sea, we nonetheless clung to the coast until we crossed the Syrian border. There we could join the Orontes River and hire a boat to carry us against the current towards Antioch. The great seat of the Seleucids was a city much like our own Alexandria: the capital of a glorious empire founded by a general of Alexander's, complete with a feuding royal family that eventually sacrificed part of its autonomy to Rome in order to staunch the endless blood wars. The largest difference was that Syria's last king, Philip, was dead. Murdered, they say, by our own Aulus Gabinius to prevent him from marrying our sister Berenice and creating an Egyptian-Seleucid alliance that would have crushed my father's chances of regaining his throne.

And now we traveled to Philip's old palace to bargain with his Roman replacement. The chilling whispers of history sang through my veins and made me shiver with a dark sense of foreboding in spite of the heat. I glanced at Cleopatra and wondered if she felt the warning tug of the past as well, though her face betrayed nothing.

We sailed past the genteel suburb of Daphne with its beautiful laurel trees and graceful shrines to Apollo, into the looming shadow of Mount Silpius to our right. The rugged peaks laced with border walls and citadels as old as the city itself.

This was Antioch in a nutshell, a sophisticated metropolis in love with luxury that danced on the edge of its own destruction. The city was fair and the climate inviting, but it was plagued by unpredictable earthquakes and was virtually indefensible. The mountains were a mirage of protection from the world without, riddled with easy passes open to invading armies. Seleucus, being a military man, recognized this and spent much of his reign vacillating between lovely Antioch and the much more strategic city of Selucia on the coast. But like my ancestor Ptolemy, this flinty man had perhaps wearied of a brutal life of endless warfare and surrendered to the silken chains of the place rightly called Antioch the Golden.

Seleucus' other concession to the security of his city was placing his golden palace on the island district, a piece of the city marooned out in the fork of the river. We disembarked at the quay of the *agora* and crossed over the southern bridge to the island, sending Apollodorus ahead to the palace to announce our wishes for an audience with the governor while we waited in one of the flanking decorative gardens' shady courtyards. The palm trees stirred occasionally in the erratic breeze that came from over the mountains behind us.

Mudjet took her spindle out of her saddlebag and sat winding wool to keep her hands busy, as Kharmion fussily arranged Cleopatra's hair after unwrapping her headscarf. My sister, for her part, sat so perfectly still that she seemed to be made of marble, only the slight motion caused by her steady breathing showed that she was indeed a living thing.

I sat listening to the murmur of the Orontes as it wound around us on either side in a long-armed embrace, and dreamt of our own river. My heart longed to hear the water reverse its direction and tumble south to north like our contrary, stubborn Nile. But it was not to be. The Orontes was a tame river, suited to courtly Antioch, nothing like my wild, dangerous Nilus. I released a sigh of desire I could not contain and tried to push thoughts of home from my mind.

Apollodorus eventually returned to us, his face glum. "Bibulus is gone," he said in irritation. "He left last year to join up with some force or another of Pompey's. The news from the west is he died of a fever months ago."

A crease formed in my sister's forehead, though she remained calm. "Who is his replacement?"

"One Metellus Scipio."

"Well, at least it is not some honor-loving paragon we must treat with," Cleopatra said with amusement. "Scipio is a pig, but he is also an opportunist. I can work with that. Did you get us an audience?"

"I did better than that, my Queen. We will have a private audience with the governor with a banquet in your honor, the price of which is we will have to wait until tomorrow night."

She rolled her eyes. "Very well. If that is how he wants to play this. I suppose that will give us time to make ourselves look presentable anyhow, if we can find a suitable accommodation."

"That is already arranged, Your Majesty. We are to be set up in a suite of rooms in the east wing of the palace, if you would follow me."

The Seleucids had adapted themselves to Persian luxury as effortlessly as the Ptolemies had absorbed Egyptian trappings, so the rooms we were placed in had a strangely familiar quality to them, even if it was a similarity glimpsed through a distortion. Or in a dream.

We had been traveling long enough that we were a fright to be seen, so much of the intervening day was spent bathing and digging through baggage to find appropriate garments to wear before civilized people. Cleopatra sat rubbing perfume on her wrists while Kharmion interjected herself into my toilette because Mudjet was not tying my hair down tightly enough to suit her.

At the appointed hour, we set off with our escort to join the governor in the main hall. Cleopatra walked with a graceful swing of her hips discreetly calculated to draw attention of a measure not too little nor too much, and all of which belied the swiftness of her gait as I had to hurry to keep up with her while also avoiding appearing ridiculous.

"Remember, you are to be seen and heard as little as possible. I cannot have you blundering your way through this banquet like all the others!" she hissed at me anxiously as we went.

"I do not 'blunder'!" I shot back under my breath.

"And do not mutter as if no one can hear you! Unless you want to go home to be beheaded by our brother or beaten nightly by Salvius, you will keep your tongue in check!"

I rolled my eyes once impatiently, then held my peace as we passed through the gauzy curtains that divided the hallway from our destination.

Metellus Scipio, the governor, came from a long line of illustrious ancestors, the greatest of which had defeated the mighty Hannibal at Zama during the Carthaginian Wars. If any childish part of me had hoped for some trace of the heroic, bull-like Scipio Africanus in his descendant, I was to be disappointed. The Scipio who rose up to meet us as we entered the dining hall had a weaselly, calculating face that attempted to hide behind his enormous, jutting nose and pointed chin.

"Your Majesty!" he called out to my sister. "How magnificent an honor is it to play host to the Queen of Egypt!" He bent over Cleopatra's outstretched hands with an air of oily ingratiation.

"Sir, this banquet is far too much!" my sister answered charmingly. "And a private audience with a man in your position, in the middle of a war, too! I am fairly speechless!"

Scipio waved a hand lazily as we were seated on the couches. They were clustered around tables laden with delicacies we had not seen since we had left home. "Do not mention it, my lady! After all, I know you are a true ally of our noble Pompey in this horrid affair."

My sister's face contracted into a look of penitent concern. "How is General Pompey? We have heard so little in recent weeks. On my way here, I could not help stopping in Heliopolis to offer prayers for his safety as he battles the jackal Caesar."

"All goes as well as can be hoped for at this stage," replied the governor. "Unfortunately for the Republic, Caesar is no fool and the masses still bear him an unaccountable esteem. But even one such as him will fall to the might of our army in the end! It is a certainty!"

My sister lowered her head demurely and murmured, "But of course!"

I tried to do as I was told, though the empty, pompous boasting of Scipio made that alarmingly difficult. All of our intelligence told us that the forces of the Republic's superior numbers were being repeatedly beaten by Caesar's smaller yet intensely loyal legions and that in the provinces, he was overwhelmingly the preferred party. I must have squirmed slightly in my seat because my lower back received a vicious jab from my sister's elbow, out of the governor's sight. Even though he missed this exchange, some latent force drew me to his attention.

"Your maid is rather pretty, my lady! Such unusual eyes!" He gave me a little leer as he took a sip from his wine cup.

I felt Cleopatra stiffen slightly, though her voice remained sweetly engaging. "Oh dear, how thoughtless of me! Here I was so dazzled by our reception that I forgot my manners and forwent introductions! Sir, this is my younger half-sister, Princess Arsinoë."

Scipio threw a hand to his chest. "Forgive my rudeness, dear princess!" he apologized lavishly. "I should have known only the House of Ptolemy could produce two such lovely daughters!"

In my mind I congratulated the Roman on his elegant recovery from both the misstep of mistaking me for a servant and for praising my appearance without initially having done so for my sister. "There is nothing to forgive, sir," I answered. "The Queen is so charming the rest of us are quite in her shadow. To be thought to be worthy of being her lady-in-waiting is reasonably a compliment."

"Ah, see, if the dear princess had spoken earlier, I would have surely known her to be your blood, Your Majesty," the governor said. "Only the wit of the daughters of Ptolemy has a chance of outstripping their beauty!"

This struck me as somewhat backhanded praise, though I knew enough to keep my expression politely interested. Cleopatra gave an extravagant little laugh. "Sir, careful now! Our little Arsinoë is still very young. What will we do with her if you continue in turning her head with such gaudy praise?"

He chuckled. "Oh, what is the point of being a noble young lady if not to be given compliments?"

My sister delicately picked an olive from the plate nearest her and bit into it appreciatively. "Mm! We have been traveling for some time and we have missed delights such as this!"

"Yes, yes! You both must eat! My cooks have done fabulously and we must give them their due!"

The three of us ate in silence for a few minutes. I had no appetite, but Cleopatra kept giving me significant looks over her shoulder when she did not think I was eating with enough enthusiasm.

Finally, Scipio downed a large gulp of wine and clasped his hands in front of him. "Now, Your Majesty, to business! What did you wish to speak with me of?"

Cleopatra dipped her fingers into the waiting water bowls and dried them on an offered cloth before beginning, her voice humble. "Sir, you know I ruled with my father, may the gods bless his memory, for several years before his death. Rome approved of this arrangement."

"Indeed, my lady. It had the blessing of the Senate."

"Upon his death, my father asked the Senate to ratify the co-ruler-ship of my younger brother Ptolemy and myself, and this too received their blessing. My father knew my brother was too young and inexperienced to rule on his own, so he wished me to be there as his guiding hand. He also feared the influence of untrustworthy lords and double-dealing eunuchs controlling my brother and through him, Egypt."

The governor nodded, so she continued. "Sir, I have ever tried to rule Egypt to show we are friends of Rome. I have helped Pompey in his endeavors with ships and corn, even when our harvests failed. I sent Roman men to be given the justice of their own land when my own people bayed for their blood."

"Yes, my lady. Rome is lucky to have a friend such as yourself."

She heaved a pained sigh. "My brother, no doubt counseled by wicked advisors, has driven me and my sister from our kingdom and has robbed me of the throne sanctioned to me by blood and the will of Rome. I come to my Roman friends in the east to lend me troops and supplies so that I might reinstated in my rightful place alongside Ptolemy. Will you assist me, sir? For the love I bear Rome?"

Scipio shook his head slowly. "My lady, I am more sorry than I can say, but the Senate will never divert troops to Egypt while Caesar knocks against the gates of Rome and our provinces."

My sister remained solicitous. "But my brother does not understand the importance of our alliance with Rome — he is so young — he will not keep General Pompey supplied as I have. It will be much harder to fight Caesar without Egypt's help and Egypt will do nothing to aid him without my guidance. It is in your best interest to help me."

"It cannot be done. If you would but wait until we have settled this matter, perhaps the Senate—"

"I cannot wait!" Cleopatra burst in upon Scipio's words. Her face was still smiling, but her voice had taken on a desperate edge. I could feel something almost like a faint wave of heat coming off of her and realized she was trying to manipulate her *heka* to swing the conversation.

"Sir, forgive my passion, but every day I am gone from my kingdom, my brother's scheming lords seek to undo everything my father and I have built with Rome's friendship." She paused and placed her fingertips a hairsbreadth away from the governor's. "If the Senate cannot help me, surely the noble Scipio would not begrudge me just a few men of his legions. You have so many, my lord, and Antioch is far away from Caesar's reach."

The governor had an almost hypnotized appearance as he listened to her speak, so she lowered her voice. Her eyes seemed to grow larger. "Perhaps," she said, her tone minutely seductive, "perhaps, the noble Scipio could lead his troops into Egypt himself. Think of the glory he could win for himself, in Africa, just like his noble ancestor. Pompey made a name for himself as a friend to my father, I am more than my father's daughter. The rewards would be... immense..."

I sat watching in fascination. I could almost feel the tug of her *heka* as it circled the hapless Scipio. She was hitting all of the right notes: the prestige of Africanus that would stroke his vanity, the riches of Egypt that would tempt his greed, the making of a personal alliance with a foreign prince that could elevate his status in Rome. He fumbled for his voice. "My dear lady, I don't know..."

"Come save Egypt, sir. Come save me. Come be the new Roman man in Egypt, the way Aulus Gabinius could never dream of being," she said, her voice almost a whisper.

Something like a whipcrack went off in my brain at the mention of the Gabiniani's general. I knew instantly she had made a mistake.

The governor shook himself alert like someone awakening from a deep sleep. "No, no," he said almost groggily. "No, I mustn't leave Syria while I am posted here. I'll be exiled for treason like Gabinius!"

My sister knew she misstepped and tried to correct her course, but it was too late. "Sir, please! I have no one else to turn to. I will ensure the Senate does not censure you, I give you my word!"

Scipio then began digging in his heels. "Now, my lady, there is no need for a scene."

Cleopatra's amicable mask dropped away as she jumped off the couch angrily. "Truly? After all I have done for Rome, it denies me aid when it has no trouble toppling every other upstart princeling in the east. You say I have no grounds for complaint, sir? You are a coward, Scipio, and I am sure the rebel legion will gut you like a fish before the end! Do not think I will forget this insult! Come, Arsinoë, we are leaving!"

I gaped, too stunned to move, so that my sister had to forcibly drag me behind her until my legs recovered themselves. We burst in upon everyone waiting for us back in the rooms and Cleopatra immediately threw herself into thrusting our belongings into bags and trunks. She shouted orders to everyone in reach as Apollodorus made himself scarce to find us a boat.

"But my lady! The sun is setting!" cried Kharmion as she tied up bundles of clothes.

"It matters not!" my sister barked viciously. "Better to deal with bandits in the desert than the ones who live in spacious palaces!"

Mudjet said nothing as she hurriedly helped my out of my evening clothes and back into the heavier Bedouin layers. I tied the knot at the back of her headscarf and we gathered up baggage to follow the servants out to the camels.

In a flash we were flying out of the palace and back across the southern bridge to where Apollodorus stood waiting for us with a pilot who looked more captive than captain at the helm of his craft. The city watch on the last bridge gate were so cowed by my sister's murderous glare that they opened the way for us without argument, sending us sailing out of Antioch and from whence we had come. Two days' travel and we rejoined my sister's men who were waiting for us on the outskirts of Selucia, gambling amongst themselves but ready to move thanks to a messenger sent ahead by the Sicilian.

"Where are we going?" Mudjet called to me from her camel as our train set out into the desert once more.

I glanced up at the sky. "It appears back to the south, but aside from that I do not know."

Chapter Twelve

Cleopatra kept us moving towards our next destination at the same frenzied pace we took out of Syria until Apollodorus railed at her that it would kill the few horses we possessed. She stared at him uncomprehendingly for several long seconds, and then ordered her camel driver to slow our train to a walk. I tried not to think on how I had seen a similar expression on Berenice's face once upon a time.

After several fruitless days of asking my sister or Apollodorus where we were headed, I sent Mudjet out among the guards to sift for information. At last she reported back that the drivers claimed we were bound for Jerusalem.

"Who rules Judea?" she asked me, as she brushed a lock of hair back into her scarf.

"Ah, now that is the question, my sweet," I said, squinting towards the billowy forms of my sister and Apollodorus ahead of us. "The Hasmoneans have held their kingdom since the revolt against the Seleucids, though everyone knows their line is almost spent. I suspect we travel to Jerusalem to treat with Antipater the Idumaean."

We lived in late times where all of us were ruled by conquerors, and the Jews were no different in this regard. As with everyone else, their conqueror was more concerned with positioning himself in Rome's favor than in that of his subjects. Antipater's people were not born to the faith of the Hebrews and their calculated conversion only two centuries prior meant they were held in silent contempt by those who jealously traced their bloodlines back through their people's captivity in Babylon and perhaps even all the way to the ancient times when they were slaves to the Egyptians.

Antipater had never allowed this to worry him overmuch, as he had cultivated powerful friends in Rome while positioning himself among the feuding Hasmonean dynasty he worked to supplant. He had defeated the troublemaking Prince Aristobulus of that house and controlled Judea through the formerly deposed elder brother of the prince, Hyrcanus, whose weakness of will was rumored to be degenerating into a weakness of the mind. The diminished king still held his other title, high priest of the temple, but most likely this too would be his only until Antipater could rally enough support for himself in the post, or for a candidate of his choosing.

We rode through the parched *wadis* and past Jerusalem's high stone walls, into this other power struggle in Rome's inescapable shadow. Guiding my camel between the crowds in the narrow market streets, I looked ahead at the great temple which dwarfed the palace of the Hasmoneans even in its unfinished state, and was left to meditate upon the fate of the mad Hyrcanus, slowly being driven from his birthright.

The unstable princes of this house were a tragic relic of the rebel Maccabees who had won their independence from the legacy of Alexander, but they had not the stamina to maintain that freedom. Wild and undisciplined in the face of usurpation, I feared it was a fate we were destined to share.

We passed under the shadow of the imposing temple the Jews had built and rebuilt to their faceless god, Yahweh, watching as the holy men milled about on its steps with their heavy beards and long tunics. We had not gone much further than this when a contingent of palace guards intercepted us.

"Greetings from Lord Antipater, Your Majesty," spoke their captain to my sister. "The governor invites you and your party to rest and refresh yourselves at the palace."

"Your master is very kind," Cleopatra replied. "Please lead the way."

As we followed the soldiers, I leaned over to Cleopatra. "How did he know we were here already?"

She shrugged. "Antipater has ears everywhere. I am sure he has known we were coming for days."

"He probably heard of our wild departure from Antioch," muttered Mudjet under her breath, which caused my sister to shoot a look at her though she made no comment in return.

Antipater did not have the appearance of the devout Jews we had seen at the temple. He sported a beard, but it was shorter and meticulously trimmed, which gave him a cosmopolitan air shared by many of his people who lived in our kingdom. His robes were fine, though one suspected he was equally at home in a well-made Roman *tunica*. He was not especially tall or imposing, rather, I suspected his prowess in navigating the difficult waters of politics stemmed from his ability to blend in with a crowd.

He glided over to us and bent over my sister's offered hand. "My lady. Welcome to Jerusalem."

"Thank you for your escort, sir. We are deeply grateful," she answered.

I thought I could feel the rippling pull of her *heka*, but it was different than the soporific haze that had spread across Scipio's table in Antioch. This was subtler, more delicate. Like a jeweled spider strumming a golden thread. Here we were not entering a fog. It was a web.

"This is my younger sister, Arsinoë," she said. "We are honored to meet you in the flesh."

I noticed no change in Antipater's eyes as they moved attentively from Cleopatra to me, where they lingered to accent a minuscule movement of acknowledgment before returning to her with the same level of attentiveness. Here was a master tactician who understood I could not be ignored, and yet was careful to not give me more than my due in the presence of my higher-ranking sibling. My sister could spin her glittering web, but this was not a bumbling oaf who would simply stumble into it blindly. They were both playing a game and it was not clear if either possessed an advantage yet.

Antipater graciously led us towards a fine room where couches were gathered together and musicians plied small lyres.

"I hope you do not mind, Your Majesty," he said with a sweep towards the lyrists. "I have a fond weakness for music."

"As do I," replied my sister. "I find little more soothing than listening to a sweet melody. Music may round the sharpest edge, though I find it most stimulating."

I knew her words were deliberate. She was signaling that she appreciated the refinement on display, though was not lulled by a sweet song into passivity.

Antipater nodded slowly. "Indeed, I confess I do not have the time to devote to it that I once had. Such is the passage of years."

She smiled. "I have trouble envisioning you as a callow youth, Antipater, lazily picking at a string or fingering a lute."

"Ha, perhaps not as far as that, my lady. What can I say? I have always delighted in being in the thick of things."

"And yet you are here in Judea when brave Pompey rides for the glory of Rome," Cleopatra parried lightly, smoothing a fold in her *chiton*.

My sister spoke as if her tongue was dancing on its toes, delicately probing the direction of the conversation. It was hard to say if Antipater was fully aware of this, though he gave off the air of someone who understood there was such a dance taking place, even if some of the movements were hidden to him. He was a connoisseur of this art and he was enjoying the performance of a skilled artist to whom he was well-matched. I felt that he was a bold man and a capable man, but not a man of the golden laurels and the applause of the stage. He was a silent builder of monuments in the shadow of greater men. I wondered what he was building and who it was for.

"The world needs administrators as well as soldiers, my lady," he answered with equal lightness. "If Caesar continues to insist on making a true fight of this, our mutual friend Pompey requires loyal retainers to hold the lines of the Republic in the east from the Parthians and the other barbarians. It does Rome no good if we quash internal strife only to be overrun by external enemies."

"Quite a task that will be to shoulder alone, sir, with only a dullard such as Scipio to assist you."

Antipater expelled an elegant huff. "I might manage along if that useless bastard stays out of my way." He inclined his head to me meekly. "Forgive the roughness of my discourse, my little lady. Some men are worth a bucket of ill words."

"Our Arsinoë is made of sterner stuff than to quail at a few impolite words," Cleopatra said, turning to give me a little smile. "I was not sure she had the stomach for our journey, but she has proven to be equal to it."

In spite of myself, I felt my heart swell up at her words. There was a voice burrowed deep in my brain that warned me to remember we were in a play, that nothing said should be given a feather's weight, and yet I could not help myself. I loved Ptah and I loved Mudjet, but I had always looked for approval if not love from my sister's cool heart. Some part of me searched for it the way I had once chased birds thinking my mother was among them. It seems foolish now perhaps, though it must be remembered how young I was then. In the growing pains of adolescence, whose approval could be more desirous to my coltish awkwardness than an older sister who all praised as refined and intelligent, to whom even the greatest of men lent their ears?

"Indeed then she is truly a daughter of Ptolemy Soter of Macedonia. Strong are their hearts in adversity," replied Antipater kindly.

My sister gave a resigned yet dainty shrug. "We have to be, sir. Our enemies are ever all around us."

He seemed to ignore her attempt to steer the conversation to our current difficulties and studied me briefly. "Do you have a marriage in mind for her? Perhaps you and I could come to an arrangement. My sons are still young men."

My sister snorted. "Young perhaps, but already married. The daughter of a pharaoh should be more than a second wife to a provincial administrator."

"Phasael is governor of Jerusalem, which is hardly a provincial town, as you have seen yourself!" Antipater protested goodnaturedly, waving a hand towards the city beyond. "Though I confess his wife's family is powerful enough to cause trouble in such a negotiation. So what of Herod? I made him governor of Galilee because he is the younger, though he will rise up from that quickly. His instincts are good. His wife has flax for brains and so do her people. I'm sure we could dismiss them with little trouble. The two youngest I am currently making places for, but if they would suit, I'm sure we could manage to elevate them appropriately."

"I wish I could sit with you this day and bandy about such plans, Antipater. However, I have larger problems than my sister's future right now and my time is running short."

He said nothing in reply for a minute as he closed his eyes to listen to the musicians. Finally, he reopened them and leaned forward towards Cleopatra. "I know what you would ask of me, Your Majesty, but I cannot help you."

I flinched waiting for her anger, but my sister remained calm. She was learning. "A gentleman would let me plead my case before rushing to a conclusion," she noted sweetly.

"A gentleman is someone who can afford to gamble on being swept away by your charm, my lady. I have enjoyed my successes here in my homeland, but I can't rally support to ride to your defense. If Rome wasn't at war and Pompey was at your side in Egypt, I would sail with the next tide. I am only a little man, I can't win a civil war for you singlehandedly."

"The Hasmoneans need Egypt as an ally as much as you do. A weak Egypt ruled by a hotheaded boy and his greedy cohorts does you as little good as me."

"True, though as we mentioned earlier, I cannot afford to go to Egypt when Parthia is looking to any advantage to expand its borders while Rome is distracted. I also must deal with the fact that Hyrcanus' wits wander without warning and his cousins endlessly hatch schemes to unseat him that would make the Ptolemies proud."

"So in the end you have only excuses for me, just as Scipio did," Cleopatra said flatly. Her voice had taken on the heft of lead hitting marble and Antipater looked genuinely sorry.

"Fate has been cruel with her timing, my lady. It leaves you with an unfair field that your kingdom must rattle with internal fighting at the same time as Rome. You are a much bigger person in the reckoning of the world than I, though you cannot compete with Rome for attention. The Republic swallows all for itself."

Cleopatra stood up gracefully. "Very well, Antipater. I am most sorry you choose to see events as you do. I hope you are never in need of my help and I pray our friend Pompey can continue his righteous campaign without my assistance, for I know not how I can do anything for his aid when my enemies block me from my rightful inheritance. I shall wait in Jerusalem one more day to give you a chance to change your mind, then I shall consider our alliance breached."

He inclined his head. "I will think over your words carefully, Your Majesty. Don't think I do not value your friendship."

She motioned for me to follow her out, leading me out of Antipater's presence with her head held high and her chin set resolutely.

"What do we do now?" I whispered at her back slightly ahead of me.

"Easy," she replied. "We give him a day to mull over how much he will lose and he will change his mind. We are leading him gently to our conclusions until he sees that we are right after all."

We did not seek rooms in the palace, though I am sure Antipater had offered them to us. My sister must have contacted Origenes at some point in our journey, as he had made arrangements to put us in a villa owned by a wealthy landowner while we awaited Antipater's final decision.

Our small band of soldiers camped out in the courtyard as we sat in the suite of rooms given to us, trying to pass the time. Apollodorus paced the floor restlessly until it was past midday. Nothing but silence came from the palace.

Cleopatra let out a groan. "I do not know how you expect me to think, Apollodorus, if you keep walking back and forth like that. I am being driven to distraction."

"I thought we were simply waiting for the good governor to ignore us for another few hours before we leave," he snapped in return.

I had been holding wool thread for Mudjet while she wound it. We both looked up in surprise, having never heard the Sicilian speak to my sister in such a tone.

Kharmion frowned. "Watch your tongue, Apollodorus."

He shot her an impatient glare, though my sister seemed unconcerned. Cleopatra had always been indulgent towards Apollodorus' rough manners. I had difficulty recalling a time she had ever been truly angry with him.

"I have been thinking, as it happens, that I will go pay my respects to His Majesty, the High Priest," my sister said. "It would be impolite to ignore someone of his standing."

"I do not know what you expect to gain from speaking with a holy fool," grumbled Apollodorus.

"Oh, maybe nothing, though it seems rash to assume so without speaking to him. He may be a bit eccentric, but the Jews still esteem him as a descendant of the Maccabees, which means he has a warrior's pedigree. Also, he is not as shrewd as Antipater; I might be able to convince him to aid us where the more logical man sees only negatives."

"It is a waste of time."

This finally provoked a stronger response from her. "Where else can we turn, Apollodorus?" demanded Cleopatra. "Our list of allies is all but gone. One demoted king will recognize another."

Somewhat cowed, he said quietly, "I am only worried for your safety, my lady."

"That is why you will go with us," she answered, mollified.

Now it was my turn to balk. "Who is this 'us' you speak of, sister?"

She gave a superior shake of her head. "Stop being a ninny. Hyrcanus is harmless, we will be fine. I am only taking Apollodorus with us because he will wear a path in the floor here if I do not."

The Sicilian looked put out, though he made no rejoinder.

We found the former King of Judea in a public wing of the temple, servants posted outside the space ostensibly to serve, yet just as likely to restrain their lord if he grew unmanageable.

He was not so very old, not even of the age of the lead combatants in Rome's great civil war, yet he appeared much older than the portraits I had seen of those other men. His face was carved by deep lines and his long beard was already mostly white. His eyes were dim and had a scattered, unfocused look to them. His skeletal frame was draped in the heavy dark cloth of the order of the Pharisees, with its hood covering his head.

He sat on a threadbare couch rocking back and forth slowly while compulsively stroking the fringe of his prayer shawl. Apollodorus remained poised to strike out like a taut cat as my sister moved with a wariness to the seated priest.

"Greetings unto you, Lord Hyrcanus, Servant of Yahweh," Cleopatra said cautiously.

His head jerked up at the sound of her voice and swiveled to see us properly. "*And the fish that was in the river died; and the river stank, and the Egyptians could not drink of the water of the river; and there was blood throughout all the land of Egypt*," he answered her in a hoarse whisper.

My sister hesitated at these words, then continued firmly. "You were once King of Judea, and though Antipater rules in your stead, you remain high priest in the temple and the people know the quality of your blood."

"*And I will harden Pharaoh's heart, and multiply My signs and wonders in the land of Egypt*," said Hyrcanus, holding his head sideways to look at my sister.

"I have been good to your people who dwell in my kingdom, but my brother will bring a harsh rule upon Egypt and your people along with all of the others."

The priest froze from his intermittent twitching and stared into her eyes. "*Pharaoh's chariots and his host hath he cast into the sea: his chosen captains are also drowned*."

Cleopatra steadied herself under his gaze. "If you help me rally your people to my cause, I will help you regain your status with Rome. You can be king again."

Hyrcanus lowered his head and shook it back and forth in a worried manner over his bony hands. "*The depths have covered them: they sank into the bottom as a stone*."

She edged closer to him, her voice soft and gentle. "Please sir, let me help you help me."

She reached out to touch his arm, when suddenly the priest flew out of his seat with his limbs flailing. *"There was a great cry in Egypt,"* his panicky voice rose, *"for there was not a house where there was not one dead."*

My sister stumbled back, her eyes wide and her breath coming in a gasp. Without warning Hyrcanus lunged forward and grabbed my arm. Too frightened to move, I stared into his darting eyes. *"Against all the gods of Egypt I will execute judgement,"* he said in an exaggerated whisper to me, as he stroked my cheek with the back of his hand, *"for I am the Lord."*

The servants from outside ran in and worked to loosen the king's grip until Apollodorus could wrench me out of his grasp. Hyrcanus shuddered and gave a wild laugh. *"And Pharaoh awoke, and, behold, it was a dream!"* he crowed at us, still trying to track my gaze through the Sicilian's body.

"We should not have come here, my lady," hissed Apollodorus to my sister. "We need to leave. Now."

We fled from the ravings of the deposed King of the Jews as his shouts echoed behind us, even as distance and the muffling heap of men pinning him to the ground distorted his hysterical words. *"So shall Pharaoh lift up thy head from off thee, and shall hang thee on a tree! And birds shall eat thy flesh from off thee!"* he shrieked at our backs before we could make good our escape.

We walked quickly back to the villa, trying to not appear shaken. All the while my sister muttered to herself as the sun began to sink into the desert beyond Jerusalem's walls.

"There are still a few more hours in the day. Antipater will come to us yet," she said to herself as if we could not hear her.

When we reached the villa, Apollodorus bundled Cleopatra into Kharmion's arms and the two of them retreated into the shade of the house. I started to follow them when Apollodorus seized me by the shoulder and pushed me back towards the street. "You, come with me."

I scowled at him as he moved me along. "Where are we going?"

"Back to the palace. We're going to figure out what the Roman toady's intentions are."

"Why do you need me?"

I watched him choke back some angry emotion. I knew the reason, but I wanted to hear him say it aloud. He had humiliated me more than once in the past several months, I felt it was only fair to return the favor. "Because you are a princess and they will allow you to go places I cannot."

I gave him a smug look. "Perhaps I am not so useless after all."

He tightened his grip on me until I was forced to grit my teeth to keep from crying out. "Don't get conceited. You aren't worth half of what your sister is. She is the Pharaoh-Queen of Egypt, and you're a little half-breed brat who is a thorn in everyone's paw."

"At least a thorn is memorable. And what does all of this make you?"

"My own man, Your Highness. I've earned all I have, unlike you."

I glanced around. "That is not much at the moment."

"That is one of the reasons the Queen and I are superior to you, my dear wee lady. We see the greater picture while little people like you are bogged down in your little ways."

I bristled, my pride pricked. "Careful, sir. I am young yet. Maybe I will prove you wrong when I am older."

He smirked. "Doubtful, though it would amuse me to watch you try, Princess."

We reached the palace grounds once more and Apollodorus passed some coins to get us past the gate. "Try to appear as though you know what you are doing," he said to me in a low voice. "Go poke around in the suites and get the ladies or servants to tell you what they know. I'm going to check around the stables. I will find you later."

"Wait, how shall I do that? How will I find you?" I asked.

He gave me a grim smile. "You'll think of something. Even you have a handful of wits to call your own." And with that he walked off in the direction of the stables.

With the Sicilian gone, I had no option but to do as he wanted. I glanced around to find a likely point of entry and decided a portico that opened up into a garden was a place where I would not draw too much attention while I figured out what to do.

The garden was obviously carefully tended, with a lushness absent from the dry lands surrounding the city, those hills scarred with scrubby olive trees and prickly underbrush. I stopped beside a bubbling pool and leaned over the edge to allow the swimming fish to brush by my fingers.

While not altogether cold, the pool felt refreshing after the heat of the day and our unsettling encounter with Hyrcanus. I unwound the cloth from my head until it trailed down my back, and I scooped up a handful of water to splash across my face. I allowed it to run down past my neck into my cloak, which was already damp with sweat. At least this moisture felt invigorating. I stood there with my eyes closed and face uplifted, wishing I could unbind my hair to let the uncertain breeze catch it.

"Princess Arsinoë?"

I jumped up at the sound of my name and opened my eyes to see Antipater coming towards me out from the portico, his face looking genuinely concerned.

"Forgive me, sir. I was just stopping to cool my face," I stammered, cheeks burning.

"It is quite all right, Your Highness. If I had known you were here, I would have offered you proper refreshment. You and your lady sister left before I could do so."

I looked up at him and was still surprised to see nothing that looked like calculation in it. All my life, I had learned to watch for machination behind the courtier's mask and could almost not comprehend someone being both an accomplished politician as well as a person capable of true emotion. "Forgive us that, too. I suspect that was rude."

He sat down on the edge of the pond and motioned for me to sit beside him. "Don't mention it. The Queen of Egypt is under a great deal of pressure, some niceties must inevitably fall by the wayside."

I sat down next to him and he smiled. "You remind me of my daughter as she was not so long ago. How old are you, my lady?"

"Fourteen, my lord."

"Ah, then my Salome is only a few years older. She was married recently and I miss her greatly."

"Has her marriage taken her far away?"

"Not out of Judea, but the palace feels emptier without her." He paused, gazing out at something in the distance before continuing.

"Though I shouldn't bother you with an aging father's ramblings. What were you thinking of when I found you, Princess?"

Part of me was afraid to answer. I did not know if I had the skill to navigate a conversation with Antipater. He was treating me sympathetically, but I also understood that he had his own business to attend to and our concerns may not be the same. Finally I said, "We spoke to Lord Hyrcanus."

He nodded in comprehension. "Then you know that his illness is more progressed than has been said publicly. He did not hurt you, did he?"

"No. We were simply caught unawares. My sister had hoped for his intercession because you were unwilling to help us."

"Not entirely unwilling. I am not unsympathetic to her plight and yours. Egypt is too large to be ruled by a boy king; it always has been. Yet if she is not strong enough to find a way to defeat a boy king, perhaps your lady sister is not the correct choice either."

"Do you think Rome is a better master for Egypt?" I asked, unable to stifle the question as it rose up from the catch of my throat.

The governor looked at me thoughtfully. "You mean am I so much a creature of Rome that I think they should rule all? It is an honest question so I will give you an honest answer, my lady. I might want an independent Judea as I suspect you would prefer an independent Egypt, but that is not the way things are. I recognize the might of Rome and so does Queen Cleopatra, we are simply working to raise our grain above the flood lines while we are able."

"Is the power of Latium so inevitable?"

"Yes and no. Rome has expanded as far as it can while it holds to its traditional ways. If it wishes to truly make lands like Egypt and Parthia bend the knee, it will have to accept change as well."

"Do you mean it must abandon its republican government to grow its empire?"

"It is possible, Your Highness. Only time will tell us for certain. The question is whether any of Rome's notables have come to the same conclusions as your humble servant."

I said nothing for a moment, thinking over what Antipater had said. "General Pompey and the Senate fear Caesar named king and the Republic swept away beneath him. Your reasoning suggests that their fears are at odds with the ambitions they hold for their republic."

"Indeed, so it would seem, my lady," he said rising up from the rim of the pond. "I think you begin to understand the puzzle that is Rome. Be wary, little one, as you walk in their shadow. The wind shifts quickly and the undertow is strong." He made a small bow and departed down the portico back into the folds of the palace.

I considered venturing further into the palace to find the kinds of informants that had been suggested to me, but Antipater had made it fairly clear that he would not offer us the help my sister hoped for. I decided to head towards the stables in search of the Sicilian retainer. I had not made it very far before Apollodorus appeared from behind a feed shed.

"Have you done as I directed, Princess?" he asked sharply.

I nodded. "I have done better. I have spoken with Lord Antipater himself. We can expect no meaningful aid from him."

I was pleased to observe some of the surliness in his face slide into surprise. "You spoke with Antipater alone?"

"Yes, and he dealt with me honestly. I think a part of him wishes he could grasp such an intimate ally as the pharaoh of Egypt, but he knows he does not have the strength here in Judea to do so as of yet."

Apollodorus peered at me in a calculated way, as if he was trying to see me in a new light. Eventually, his expression lapsed into one of resignation. "That's unfortunate, though hardly a surprise. Maybe if the Queen hears that you received this from the governor's lips, she will at last believe it."

As we turned back towards the villa, I asked him, "Were you able to find anything out?"

"As a matter of fact, yes. It seems while we have been treating with cowards and madmen, the all-mighty Pompey has suffered a catastrophic defeat in Pharsalus and is in embarrassing retreat across the sea."

I looked at him openmouthed. "Gods and men! Without him, what will we do?"

"Don't lose heart yet, this defeat might be to your sister's advantage."

"But how? He is her patron, the only person powerful enough to retrieve the throne for her!"

"True, though he has been too distracted and distant to be much use. In such a crushing blow as this loss, he will actually need her help. So now is our chance."

"But we will have to find him!"

Apollodorus smirked. "That is the easy part. If only Egypt can save Pompey, it is obvious where his ships are heading."

My eyes widened. "How can we get to Pompey first when Ptolemy is at home and we are still in Judea?"

"It'll be a few days of hard riding, but we only have to reach Pelusium. The general heads for a fort he can defend from in case Caesar sails hot upon him." The villa was in sight now and Apollodorus quickened his pace. "I will ready the men to leave at first light. I need you to ready the Pharaoh."

I stopped. "What do you mean? I am sure she is already packed and waiting for us to return."

His eyes darkened. "Maybe. I am afraid of her cast when we left her. The lunatic priest frightened her more than I think she showed."

"Why? She is so fearless!"

"She fears madness, though. She knows the seeds of it are in all of you Ptolemies. She saw it take Berenice and how the imbalance turned the dead pharaoh into an obsessive old man before his time." He paused and then stared me down. "She may be unsettled, but you must convince her to go to Pelusium. It is our only choice."

Chapter Thirteen

Apollodorus departed into the courtyard to speak with the soldiers, and I followed the hallway towards our rooms. "I do not think anyone is coming," I said softly as I met Kharmion at the door.

She shuddered. "Best let me tell her."

We walked to the back room of the house where my sister sat waiting for us. The wicks had burned low and a couple had sputtered out. It was then I understood the dread of her servant.

Cleopatra sat with her hair disheveled and her blankly staring eyes blazing as she swayed on the low couch, whispering something unintelligible under her breath. She had her *rw* open on her lap and was flipping through its pages feverishly. Her face jerked up at our approach.

"Where are my men, sister? Kharmion? I must teach Ptolemy a lesson!"

"There are no men to be had from Judea, Your Majesty. We cannot raise a powerful enough rebellion this far from Alexandria," Kharmion replied.

"Nonsense! I am the enchanting Pharaoh-Queen of Egypt! I shall raise an army of the dead with the charm of my voice!" Cleopatra said wildly, and waved the *rw* at us.

Mudjet appeared from outside and gave me a frightened look. "She has been like this since you left," she told me in a low voice.

Kharmion moved forward to try and soothe her mistress. "My lady, you cannot do this. We shall think of some plan or another, but we cannot rely on the gods to help us. They will assist us if we help ourselves."

My sister's wild eyes danced as she shook her head. "No, no, no. Damianus retrieved this *rw* for me from the bowels of the Library, it has never let me down! And this one!" She reached for an even older-looking scroll underneath the first. "This is from the old priests in Heliopolis! It can do more than simple spells and potions I have dabbled my *heka* in! This is how I will rule Egypt! Those strange gods will favor me!"

Kharmion's voice grew increasingly anxious. "My lady, please! Go to Ptolemy. Ask him for forgiveness! We can work to reclaim your position better from within the palace than from without."

As if a veil was lifted, the frenzied appearance of Cleopatra's face was replaced by an expression of coldest contempt. "Ptolemy will choke on his own blood when I am through with him. All who oppose me will be torn apart," she said emphatically, her voice like stone hitting stone.

A wave of nausea washed over me, but I worked to steady myself, "Sister, Kharmion's words are wise. If we could go back to the city, we could surely do more there than here."

Her wooden mask dropped away again. She flew at me as suddenly as Hycarnus had, holding me in place as her nails dug into the skin of my shoulders and her frantic eyes searched mine back and forth. "Why can my *heka* see something in your eyes it cannot penetrate?" she asked feverishly. "The mad king saw it too. What are you hiding, Arsinoë? Tell me!"

Internally I prayed to my Lord to defend our secret. *She will strangle me here in this room if she thinks I have some kind of power to summon the gods. She will think I will use it against her.* I said shakily, "Sister, I do not know of what you speak. I am as I have always been. Just Arsinoë."

She stared into my eyes a moment longer before releasing me and stumbling back to her cot, which she sank onto heavily. Sensing her wildness ebbing, I tried to reach her again. "We have heard a rumor in town that Pompey Magnus is coming to our shores to regroup his men after his latest engagement with Gaius Caesar. He was a friend of our father, may he dance in the Field of Reeds, and you have sent his army assistance whenever he asked it of you. Maybe he would favor us."

She turned at my voice and clearly attended to me, looking more like her usual self, so I continued. "He knows how ably you ruled alongside our father, surely you could persuade him that Ptolemy is too young to rule alone and that you have all the enlightenment necessary to guide him. These lesser men we have spoken with cannot see the wisdom in your words, yet surely he will."

My words worked. My sister asked me calmly, "Do you know where he plans to make landfall?"

"He is not in a position to go to Alexandria. They say he will go to the garrison in Pelusium. But that means our brother will be there shortly as well."

Cleopatra stood up and ran a hand over her tangled hair. "Well, then. We have no time to lose."

I felt a little reassured as she leaned down on the table and began writing quickly, but I could not help noticing her left hand still fingered the edges of the *rw*.

I am sitting between the two massive paws of the great Sphinx with my back against its stone chest. Before me lies Tiperses quietly sleeping under a starless sky. The air is still and sand at my feet rests as heavily as a double-matted carpet.

"The City of Yahweh is a mad place, I find," says the voice of my Lord floating down to me. I clamber to my feet and spy him sitting on the Sphinx's back, leaning against its ponderous head. He glances down at me and I see the flash of a wink. "Do not let his prophets frighten you."

"He has bested you before," I call out wryly.

"True, though there were not many Set-worshippers among his people, so I lost not." He snaps his fingers, and in an instant, I stand before him on the stone beast's back. "The question now is what will your sister do out here in the desert?"

I crouch down at his feet nimbly. "I do not know. She has no one else to go to. We are alone, not even in this desert," I make a motion towards Tiperses, "but rather camped out on Sinai hoping Pompey will swoop in to save us."

"Your sister is weighing her options, such as they are. She is running out of time."

"What should I do, my Lord?"

"You are doing well already, Beloved. You have been keeping your eyes and ears open. Let us see what you have learned. What did you think of the son of the Scipians?"

I make a face. "I am almost glad to not have his help. He is a fool."

"Yes, perhaps it is for the best. His blood is princely, but he is born late and is not worthy of it."

"Many of us share that burden, my Lord."

He grins. "To compare him to you is to speak of a sparrow in the presence of a phoenix. The world forgets sparrows."

I trace a line in the sand gathered on the Sphinx's back with my foot. I am suddenly troubled by the glibness of the desert god. "Maybe it should not."

Lord Set moves his head to a thoughtful position, as if he is trying to see inside of me even more deeply than he already does. This only lasts a moment before he shrugs it off easily. "And you say I speak to you in riddles, *nedjet*. I will think on what you say. But what did you think of the Edomite?"

"They call themselves Idumaeans now, my Lord."

"Is it so? Well, men hold themselves as equal with the gods these days, so perhaps all shall have many names now. What did you think?"

I ponder my response. "He is most cunning. I should not like him as an enemy."

"Do you think he is cowardly?"

"No. He is not easily rattled."

"So why would someone such as he refuse to aid a powerful neighbor such as your sister, particularly when they share a common patron in the son of the Pompeians?"

I cast my mind over all I had learned so far. "Because he thinks Pompey will lose this war," I answer haltingly. "He cannot waste support on Cleopatra when he has to slowly begin changing sides."

Lord Set nods, pleased. "Very good, *nedjet*. This is true."

"But he did not trust her or me enough to tell us this."

"Well, it is hardly noteworthy to be a part of a stampede of turncoats," observes my Lord. "The Edomite must show his new loyalty by being the first to smell a change in the wind."

I thought on this. "He is following in Aulus Gabinius' lead. The general accepted Caesar's summons on the condition he and his men did not have to fight Pompey directly."

"Indeed. In war, it is often better if one can avoid definitively taking one side over the other."

"And in politics, my Lord."

His face lights up as if lit by a black flame. "Exactly! And that is the path you must walk in the coming months. Do not bind your *ka* carelessly to one cause or the other. The way is not a straight one."

"What of the cause of Egypt and its gods?"

"That might be the crookedest path of all, Beloved. That is why I have had to find such a clever princess to travel this labyrinth."

And then I wake up.

We rode out towards Pelusium the next morning. We crossed the desert wrapped up like Bedouin women once more to keep the sun and the sand out of our mouths and eyes. Apollodorus rode out ahead to scout our position, taking one of the precious horses while we sat upon the backs of the more reliable camels.

After a while Mudjet commented vaguely, "I cannot see Apollodorus anymore."

The rest of us craned our necks around, but the Sicilian was nowhere to be seen. We continued on, though his absence clearly troubled my sister. Her head swiveled back and forth under the mantle of fabric shielding her face. I tutted my camel to jog over to hers and reined up at Cleopatra's side.

"Do you want me to ride ahead to look for him?"

Her eyes flashed at me and I was startled by the naked mistrust I saw in them. *She thinks I will ride off.* Nevertheless, she called out, "Kharmion! Ride ahead with Arsinoë and see if you spy Apollodorus!" She met my eyes again as she added, "Mudjet stays here with me."

Kharmion nodded, and seeing that I could not argue with her, the two of us chucked the reins of our mounts. The beasts broke into their jolting trot as we headed over the crest of the next dune. At the top, all that greeted us was more desert, so we cantered down the other side.

As we surged forward, I stood up in the saddle to get a better view. At first I still saw nothing, but then suddenly out of the corner of my eye I saw a small group of horsemen moving toward us. They were a distance off yet, but I could tell they did not move like the desert horsemen. And out here, that could only mean they were my brother's troops.

Kharmion saw them at nearly the same moment as I did. "What should we do?" she asked, her voice edged with fear.

"We must get back to my sister. Whip the camels if you need to."

We wheeled the camels back around and urged them into a gallop. I looked over my shoulder at the horsemen and saw that they had noticed our flight. They began to gallop after us, their faster animals gaining ground. My sister and Mudjet came back into view with our train, though by then it was too late for them to flee and we were quickly surrounded by the small force of soldiers.

"Oh ho, my brothers in arms! Look who we've caught here! The Bitch of Egypt herself!" snickered their leader, whose voice was immediately familiar. He removed his helmet and Salvius' puffy features came into view. "The Queen of Sluts and her viper," looking at Kharmion, "and see here, Lucius!" he said turning to his companion. "We've even snared the little sand-blooded princess! Careful, Arsinoë, my sweet. Too much sun for you and your mongrel blood will turn you as dark as any peasant's wife!"

Cleopatra whipped aside the cloth covering her mouth. "Hold your fat tongue, Salvius! You seem to forget that I am still Queen."

He laughed. "Queen of dust, maybe. What are you all doing tramping around in the wasteland in the heat of the day anyway?" He paused and peered at us. My sister who glared back him, but unexpectedly, he brightened. "Well hazarded, my lord!" he said, slapping Lucius Septimus' back. "This one told His Majesty that there was no chance old Pompey's arrival here would not reach your witch ears! Especially since you consider yourself his great patroness. Does he know you've been living in holes in the desert these past months?"

When Cleopatra did not respond, he frowned. "Well, luckily for you, His Majesty said to bring you to the coast alive if we found you. So come, my ladies, we shall be your gallant escorts to the pharaoh!"

We had no choice but to be led to the garrison under the arms of Salvius and his detachment. We rode through the lands we had left months ago, riding out to find allies and finding only disappointment. The bloody-colored garrison on the sea had not changed, though perhaps we had.

"Look, my lady!" whispered Mudjet. I followed her gaze out past the distant beach towards the sea and saw a Roman warship on the horizon.

We were interrupted by the arrival of Ptolemy and his court contingent. My brother wore his shining golden armor proudly as he looked down his nose at our dirt-stained dresses. Theodotus and Achillas stood on either side of him, the latter catching my eye and giving me a wink.

"Dear sisters, it has been too long!" our brother said sarcastically. "Fortunately, my loyal lords found you when they did. The desert can be such a dangerous place..."

"Still playing at soldier, I see, dearest Brother-Husband," replied Cleopatra, her tone as disingenuous as her smile.

Ptolemy's eyes narrowed. "I've won more battles than you as of late. It is such a shame the Syrians and the Jews have proven to be so fickle. Hoping to try your luck with Pompey?"

"Perhaps, why not? You have been no friend of his, why should he help you?"

"Because I am Pharaoh!" our brother exploded. "You are not! Learn your place!"

Cleopatra smiled. "My place is on the falcon throne. One day you will learn *your* place, little brother."

"We'll see about that!" He motioned to several of his soldiers, who went into the fort and returned with a bound Apollodorus dragged between them. "Cut off his feet and work your way up."

Even my sister turned pale. "Ptolemy!"

Our brother looked up at her, his eyes dancing with malice. "And when you're done, do the same to that one," pointing to Kharmion. "Except start with the breasts."

Two other soldiers grabbed Kharmion, who screamed out to Cleopatra. My sister, whose voice had lost its cool edge, cried out, "No! Ptolemy, please! Take Arsinoë instead!"

All of us turned to her in shock. My mouth went dry as Ptolemy walked over to the flank of Cleopatra's camel. "Even if I said I'd do the same to her?" he asked, his attention rapt and his expression strangely hungry.

"Yes," said my sister quietly, with only the merest beat of hesitation.

I was so stunned I could barely breathe. The warning voice in my head that had called out to me in Jerusalem laughed coldly. Cleopatra's stony words slammed into my heart and a part of it I barely knew I had cracked apart. I stood here in the desert between my brother who would mutilate my body and my sister who did likewise to my spirit, with nowhere to go. My Lord Set spoke to me as if I had a glorious destiny, and yet here I was cast aside by my family as a useless appendage, far away from the only person left of my blood who treated me as if I was worth something. Ptah's bright face swam up out of my memories and nearly reduced me to tears. I clutched my cloak at my throat and shivered as if I was submerged in a lake of ice.

Ptolemy moved his gaze to me. "Well, my same-born sister, at least you know our Cleopatra would trade you for her lapdog without a tear. Shall I press the point with her and find out if she loves her Sicilian more than you, too?"

Theodotus cut in abruptly. "Your Majesty, a small craft approaches."

We all stopped to notice that the warship had anchored itself a *dolichos* or so out from shore. A small boat was bobbing its way towards us with several men abroad.

Ptolemy moved away from us. "Achillas, we will deal with Rome first."

"Of course, Your Majesty," the captain of the guard said with a bow.

"Salvius! Lucius! With me!" barked my brother. He gestured for his soldiers to come to us. "Get them down off the camels! Make sure the Queen's face is visible!"

We were taken from the camels and marched behind the king's entourage. Cleopatra and I were jostled towards the front as soldiers roughly pulled back our face coverings and tied them behind us. I sensed my sister was trying to meet my eye, but I faced steadfastly forward. When we reached the shoreline, we were pushed into place next to our brother.

"We are a happy family," he snarled at both of us, though especially to Cleopatra. "If you say anything that contradicts that, my men have orders to run you through where you stand."

So there we three stood silently grinding our own teeth and waiting until the boat reached us and the general they called Pompey the Great climbed out to meet us. My mind was still reeling from the dark venom of my siblings, and, terrified that Ptolemy would cut my throat if I fainted, I willed myself to focus on our arriving guest.

The celebrated general reminded me of an old Kushite lion we had for many years in our menagerie. One could tell he had been quite magnificent in his prime, but by the time I was showing him to Ptah, he was half toothless and his coat no longer shone in the sun.

Thus it seemed with Pompey. His jawline was set with modest jowls that gave him a tired appearance. His hair, worn shaggily long for someone of his age, still clung to its efforts to recall Alexander's golden mien as it lay heavy and sheenless against his scalp. I wondered whether at this point such a pathetically youthful styling was merely a vain, petty taunt at his adversary's reported baldness.

Everything about this man smelled of defeat and desperation. He was a great person, true, though he ran to our land with his tail between his legs and a cunning wolf on his heels, making no secret of his destination. Even if either of my siblings were still inclined to help him, he brought a dangerous enemy to our doorstep. Pompous old Juba might be willing to throw Numidia into Caesar's teeth, but why should Egypt suffer a Roman argument? Despite his obvious exhaustion, Pompey labored to hold himself with dignity as he walked ashore and inclined his head to us.

"Greetings to you, Your Majesties! You greatly honor me with your personal presence." he said with gracious cheerfulness. "King Ptolemy, you must have grown a foot since last I saw you. Queen Cleopatra! Ever does the beauty of your countenance continue to grow!"

"Thank you, General. We are pleased you have reached us safely," said my sister, as she gestured to me. "Allow us to introduce our youngest sister, Arsinoë."

He looked at me, beaming. "Ah, it is good to meet you again, Princess. I remember you as a tiny toddling thing in Rome during your Honored Father's exile. How fitting it is that one given a name meaning 'to lift the mind' should possess the silver eyes of the Lady of Wisdom."

I gave a nod of my head, though fear clamped my mouth shut. I was too afraid of saying the wrong thing.

"We are saddened to learn of your defeat in Pharsalus, sir," said Ptolemy, attempting to redirect the general's attention back to him.

Pompey's shoulders sagged slightly. "A series of lucky accidents for Caesar, Your Majesty. I still have more men at my disposal, I am confident we can regroup." He turned back to Cleopatra. "Your Majesty has always been generous to the cause of the Republic. If you would be willing once more to loan us ships and corn, I am sure we could crush this rebellion."

My sister began to reply, but was cut off by Ptolemy. "You say victory is almost at hand, General, and yet you come with only one warship. Where are your men? Your allies? You bring the fiend Caesar down upon our heads and offer only words. Why should we risk our kingdom to aid you?"

Pompey blanched. "Egypt and I are old friends, Your Majesty. I saved this kingdom from your mad sister so that you might have a birthright! Don't throw away the freedom of Egypt and of Rome!"

"You are a foolish old man and your time is over," replied my brother. He summoned Achillas, Salvius, and Lucius Septimus forward as two other men shoved pikes into Cleopatra's back and mine. "Anyone with half a wit can see that you are no match for Caesar. We must appease the stronger man." Before Pompey could respond, Salvius and Lucius jammed their swords into the general's chest and Achillas cut off his head. I gave a choked scream and Cleopatra started to step forward, but Theodotus placed a hand on either of our shoulders and held us firm. A few of our soldiers rushed at the boat and killed all the oarsmen but one.

As the general's headless trunk fell to the beach, Achillas kicked the remaining Roman sailor. "Take your comrades back to your ship. Pompey stays with us."

The man began rowing frantically back out to sea as our brother nudged Pompey's head with his toe. "He really does look stupidly surprised, doesn't he?" Salvius chuckled darkly at my brother's words, though no one else laughed. "It is all right, Theodotus, you can let go of them."

"Well, now that you have killed our only ally, little brother, what will you do now?" asked Cleopatra, readjusting her cloak and brushing some sand from its creases.

"You're usually a better strategist, sister-wife. Isn't it obvious? I've killed Caesar's great enemy! When he shows up here in a few days, I'll be a hero and we will be the very best of friends. The Consul will support my rights and you will have nothing. You are finished. Which is why I, in my munificence, am letting you and your pitiful little entourage go." He signaled to his men, who unbound Apollodorus and released Kharmion. "Go rot in the desert, sister. But if I ever catch you in Alexandria again, I will take you apart piece by piece."

I stepped towards Ptolemy. The violence in his nature made me tremble with dread, but I knew I had a better chance of outwitting him than my clever sister. "Please, brother," I begged. "Let me come home to Ptah. You know I did not choose to leave the palace."

He looked at me, and I became alarmed at the abashed gleam I found in his expression. "Sorry, Arsinoë. I know you didn't leave voluntarily, but I need an alliance with Rome and preferably a Roman wife to cement it. If you return, the people will make me marry you and that gets me nowhere."

"You send me away with her?" I whispered fiercely, moving closer to him, not caring that Cleopatra could still hear us as the bile rose from my stomach. "She said you could torture me! I knew she bore me no great love, but how can I live with them now?!"

"I know. I'm sorry. I can't," he muttered, shaking his head.

I stared at him in astonishment until finally Mudjet came over and gently led me to my camel. In my fog, I saw the cruel grin Salvius gave me as I was hoisted up into the saddle. The casual indifference of everyone else to all that had just taken place.

I thought of what hideous creatures we were; we, who had been entrusted with the rule of an entire kingdom. What kind universal powers could allow such a brutal thing? Someone rode past to give my camel a smack with the rod, and we departed the fort in no better position than when we entered it, making our way once again into the callous claws of the desert.

We rode in silence for a long while until Cleopatra brought her camel alongside mine. Mudjet glared at her from my other shoulder, though she was ignored.

"Do not be like this, Arsinoë."

"Like what? You would have abandoned me to Ptolemy's whims. Am I just supposed to forget what you said?" I snapped at her.

"I had to say something! Do you deny that Apollodorus and Kharmion both are much more useful to me? You are only a little girl, another mouth to feed."

"You are the one who demanded my presence on this little adventure. It is not my fault if you have regrets about it," I shot back angrily. "I know that neither you nor Ptolemy are overly invested in my well-being, but you are supposed to be the wiser of the pair of you. It would be expected that you would hide your indifference better."

"And yet you were trying to stay with our brother and his sadists a while ago."

"My choices are limited. At least there is food and water in Alexandria. If I have to die, I would rather not starve in the desert."

"Have a little faith, sister," she said soothingly. "I promise you we at least will not die in the desert."

I sighed. "Where are we going then?"

"Alexandria, naturally."

"What?! And have Ptolemy flay us after all?"

"Hardly. We will go in secret. I have remained in touch with Origenes, he will shelter us in his house. We shall see how things progress between our dear brother and the illustrious Caesar. And then I will figure out what is to be done."

I wanted to scream at her, hurl curses at her. She, who was so intelligent and literate, could she not see what she had done? We might have been truly sisters for the first time, we might have been friends. If she would have let me in, I could have perhaps changed our course, unfurled my dreams to her, and in the partnership of her *heka* that flowed like the Nile itself with me as a vessel for the gods to traverse it, we could have made for Egypt a new golden age.

We had quibbled and bickered through our childhood because we were children. Now we were growing up fast in dangerous times. In the midst of the maelstrom we had been given a chance to start over, but she had taken that precious thing and had stomped it into the dirt.

Somehow even then I understood that her words would leave deeper scars than anything Ptolemy might have lashed into me. Baktka had warned me that mine was a path I must ultimately walk alone. Here in these last months I had fought like a drowning man to see if it there was another way. Cleopatra had fulfilled the words of my nurse, there would be no other champion for the gods than the one they held out as their chosen. As foolhardy as I believed that choice to be.

Mudjet and I looked at each other. I could tell she was against whatever Cleopatra was planning, though we had no other option but to go along with her. We would at last return to Alexandria.

Come what may.

Chapter Fourteen

We arrived home so late that Apollodorus had to increase the bribe to our boatman from Canopus to risk being caught by the city watch. We had traded out our desert clothes for those typical to Egyptian farmers, though all of us ladies aside from Mudjet were careful to keep our potentially damning hair covered up. The boatman might not have fully believed Cleopatra's disguise as a Egyptian landowner's widow coming to handle a legal dispute with her grasping in-laws, told in impeccable colloquial Egyptian, but he believed the coins the Sicilian dropped into his hand.

A coded missive from Origenes warned us that his house was constantly watched by spies from the palace, so he arranged to have his man retrieve us from the gardens of Pan before conveying us to his residence. My sister dispersed her small band of soldiers to the outskirts of Alexandria to await her instructions while she, Apollodorus, Kharmion, Mudjet, and I carefully made our way into the easternmost streets of the Soma district, brushing along the farmost reaches of the palace.

We crept into the pleasure gardens and found a dark corner to hide ourselves in while we waited for our contact. Indistinct sounds from other paths signaled we were not alone in the park's confines, though we prayed the others out flaunting the curfew would not draw too much attention. Every so often, the honeyed words of a courtesan would waft across the silent trees and sleeping flowers, or the tiny clink of coins being dropped in a purse would sound in the enveloping night.

Suddenly, a few muffled voices louder than the others signaled that the watch was moving through the garden paths. Kharmion looked to Cleopatra in alarm. "We need to get out of here, my lady!"

My sister shook her head. "No, it will be fine. You, Arisnoë, and Mudjet lie down on the ground. They will not bother to glance at our feet. I will handle the rest."

The maid started to object, but the tread of footsteps echoed close by and the three of us quickly threw ourselves flat against the tiled stones. As we lay there, I had the curious sensation that something was pressing me on the ground in such a way that I could not have risen even if I had chosen to. I suspected my sister was implementing the *heka* both to mask our presence and to prevent me from using the circumstances to attempt an escape.

When the light of the watchman's torch entered our space, Cleopatra grabbed Apollodorus towards her and locked him in a kiss that caught him so by surprise he nearly yelped. This is what the watchman saw when he gave a small cough of annoyance to announce his presence.

My sister feigned bewilderment. "Oh my! Please excuse us, good sir!"

The watchman observed their country clothes with an urban dweller's distaste. "The city has a curfew, miss," he said curtly.

Cleopatra wagged her head in distress. "Oh dear! Oh dear! I had no idea! My sweetheart and I just arrived this evening and we got lost in all these twisting streets! We finally gave up trying to find our way and came to rest in this breathtaking garden. I confess I have never seen something so lovely!" She paused to blush innocently. "And I was so overcome by this place that I fear my love and I got rather carried away..." She glanced at Apollodorus demurely. "Is that not so, dearest?"

I had to hold a hand over my mouth to keep from laughing at the stupefied mumble that came from Apollodorus. Luckily, the watchman had already lost interest in the pair of them seeing that they were not shady merchants or prostitutes with money weighing down their purses. He shook my sister down for a few coins which she hastily gave over, before moving on in search of more lucrative quarry.

As soon as he was gone, Cleopatra nudged me with her foot. "You may get up if you wish."

"Well played, my lady," said Kharmion, dusting herself off.

"Let us hope that will last us until Origenes' man finds us," she answered, looking about in the garden. "The next watchman might not be so easily dealt with."

Hardly had she spoken when another man came down the path, the light from his lantern filling the darkness once more. He saw us and crept up to where we stood. "Can my lady tell me the direction the eagle flies?" he asked Cleopatra.

"North to the graves of my ancestors, in the ancient hills of Macedonia," she replied firmly.

The man relaxed. "We rejoice in your return, Your Majesty. My master begs you to follow me to the safety of his house."

We were lead carefully through the back alleys of the Soma. Most of the houses were quiet. Only the scuttling of feral cats along the walls interrupted the silence as I strained my ears to hear the lapping of the sea in the distance.

I stole a glance at Apollodorus at my side, who had been dumbstruck since the brush with the city watch. If he was not so unpleasant, I would have nearly pitied him. I had long suspected he had nursed a passion for my sister that went beyond the mere loyalty of a servant. Her kiss might have indeed fulfilled an unspoken desire, and yet undoubtedly not in the way the Sicilian had imagined it coming to pass.

"Is not the house of Lord Origenes the first place your lord brother will look for us?" Mudjet murmured as we crossed over to the street where the lord lived.

"It is risky, yes," admitted Cleopatra softly, overhearing her, "but I trust him to have thought of a plan to thwart Ptolemy's thugs."

The servant took us through a rear door where Origenes stood waiting for us, looking more aged than he had when we left only a few months prior. "My Queen, I am honored to welcome you back to your kingdom," he said, bowing low.

"Thank you, my lord," answered my sister. "Your letters have been a succor to me in these trying months. The Demon of Gaul has not beaten us here has he?"

"No, my lady. The word in port is he will arrive sometime tomorrow, so you should take your rest this evening. Please follow me."

Origenes led us down the hallway from the kitchens until we reached what appeared to be a dead end. He reached out to one of the bricks and pried it loose from the wall, revealing a latch that when he pulled it, moved the entire wall aside, revealing a squat set of stairs.

"Quite ingenious, sir," said my sister, clearly interested.

"The years of your sister's reign were dark ones, Your Majesty," he answered somberly. "My slaves built this in secret over the course of the second year, in case my household needed to flee her madness and the docks were closed." He grabbed a lamp and we followed him down the flight of stairs to a large, surprisingly well-furnished room. Setting the lamp down, he gestured about the space. "There is some food on the shelves over there, but my cook will bring you fresh dishes assuming there are no disturbances. If possible, I will check on you daily and find anything you require."

"You are generous, my lord, and you can be certain you will be handsomely rewarded for it once I sort all of this out," Cleopatra commented as she inspected a cedar chest filled with garments. "However, I do not intend to be outside of the palace long, so we will not trespass on your hospitality excessively."

"It is no trouble, my lady," Origenes said, shaking his head. "Indeed, I wish you would stay here until we can arrange a proper plan."

"Do not look so grave, sir!" my sister answered with an unexpected burst of gaiety. "Arsinoë and I will go out and join the gawkers tomorrow when the Consul comes, and then I will decide how we should proceed."

The lord knew it was pointless to argue against her plans, so he bowed deferentially and left us to ourselves. Kharmion wandered over to the food shelves to assess the jars while Cleopatra dug two long cloaks out of a second chest and studied them appraisingly. "Apollodorus," she called over her shoulder, "I want you to head out into the city, I need my eyes to be in the streets before tomorrow."

The Sicilian inclined his head and left without a word. *Grateful to get away*, I thought.

We bustled about the space, trying to settle into it, when I decided to speak my mind about something Cleopatra had said earlier. "I would rather stay here. I have no interest in seeing Caesar or our brother."

Cleopatra stopped what she was doing and smirked. "I am not giving you a choice, little sister. Just because we are sneaking about here does not mean I am going to leave you off the hook. This is still an official function and you are a princess. Endeavor to behave like one and not a sulky child."

In truth, I did not relish the idea of being alone anywhere with my sister since our falling out in Pelusium. I did not like going out into the city without Mudjet when doing so put our freedom and our lives in jeopardy. Cleopatra knew this, and perhaps even secretly agreed I should be wary, but she was attempting to toss off my concerns as if they were silly.

Realizing that an argument would get me nowhere, I let my objections go. "I just do not see why you are in such a hurry to fight them both. Ptolemy is an imp, but Caesar is another animal altogether. He will not be so easy."

She pulled out a silk *chiton* and held it up against her body experimentally. "You worry too much, sister. Leave it to me. Men are easy, it is fighting women that is hard. You will see so tomorrow."

We rose early the next morning and dressed in the dim light of the secret antechamber. I gave Mudjet a furtive embrace before Cleopatra towed me out into the adjoining alley. She climbed up the ladders leaning against the house, with me scrambling after her until we were on the roof, peering out at the flotilla of warships sitting on the horizon.

Cleopatra shielded her eyes against the glare. "Well, His Lordship the Consul is punctual," she noted sardonically. "Come now, we will have to throw a couple of elbows out if we wish to have a good view."

We climbed back down the ladders and stepped into the streets, weaving our way through the gathering crowds. The sun climbed in the sky and blanketed Alexandria in a growing heat that the winds from the harbor could not disperse in any meaningful way.

Much of the city had come out to see the arrival of the man who was known the length and breadth of the Great Sea as the terror of the Gauls and, now that Ptolemy had butchered Pompey, the de facto ruler of Rome. We ducked behind a larger group of bystanders as our brother swept by in a chariot, flanked by Pothinus and Achillas. Theodotus,

Salvius, Lucius Septimus, and many of the other lords followed a short distance behind him in their own chariots. Ptolemy was dressed richly in a Greek style to assure our coming guest that he was a cultured Western ruler and not an exotic Egyptian one. They reached the city docks and waited with the rest of us for the small fleet to sail into the harbor.

The flagship's sailors threw out lines when they were close enough, several of them leaping to shore to help the Alexandrian seamen secure the ropes. They were rapidly followed by a bevy of armored legionaries that had hardly touched their feet to land before another soldier pulled ashore a fierce-looking Anatolian horse that clattered onto land snorting fiercely.

A murmur of vulgar curiosity shot through the crowd as those close enough to see glimpsed the stallion's famous deformity that made it appear that it had cruel bony toes growing from its fetlocks. Sensing some slackness in form, the beast reared up, bucking out at its handlers while its master pushed past it towards the anticipating Alexandrians and our brother. Cleopatra dragged me through the throng for a closer vantage point as I tried to keep the hood of my cloak from falling back. From our better position, I could see the fear gathering in Ptolemy's copper eyes as Gaius Julius Caesar stopped a few feet in front of his chariot and looked up at him, markedly unimpressed.

I, like most of the people there that sweltering day, found myself gaping — I suspect rather half-wittedly — at this man the way we would have if Zeus himself had suddenly appeared among us. We had known he was coming, and yet to have him there in the flesh was rather shocking all the same. If the Argonauts had climbed out of his ship behind him I doubt we would have batted an eye.

I glanced over at my sister, who wore a hungry expression as she looked out at the scene, her eyes flashing golden. I knew she was concocting some scheme or another. That was the look she had worn when she was planning our course in Syria.

Caesar, for his part, returned our collective stares coolly, his intelligent, cunning features set off by unexpectedly dark, penetrating eyes. He was tall and rather fair-skinned for one who spent so much time in the field, his lighter brown hair shaded with red by the sun, and skillfully arranged to diminish the fact he was rapidly losing it. The combined effect of his hair and skin made the darkness of his eyes all the more unusual. He was not a young man anymore, though he wore his age well enough. Next to him, Ptolemy appeared even more of child as he stepped out of the chariot to speak with the Consul of Rome face to face.

"Welcome to Egypt, Consul Caesar," said my brother, as he tried to match the general's indifference.

Caesar gave a slow incline of his head. "Greetings, Lord Ptolemy Theos Philopator. I am looking for General Gnaeus Pompeius. Be so good as to tell me where I might find him."

Ptolemy sneered and motioned a slave forward with a covered plate. "Oh, I would not worry about General Pompey, sir." With a nod from him, the man uncovered the plate. "We have taken care of him for you."

I smothered a cry of alarm and people in the crowd close enough to see screamed in shock. Sitting on the plate was General Pompey's severed head wearing the look of surprise he had died with, now matched by the faces of the people around us. Cleopatra narrowed her eyes.

Caesar did not appear to share our horror and curled his lip in disgust. "Ignorant boy, do you expect me to congratulate you?" Ptolemy blanched as the Consul ripped the covering out of the servant's hand and placed it back over the plate. "The only reason I don't cut you dead where you stand is because I suspect these old fools advised you to do this thing."

Theodotus hurriedly cut in. "We did this to protect Rome and your glorious person, sir. We..."

The Consul held up a hand. "Spare me. I am fully capable of attending to my safety, not that it or the security of Rome are truly your concern. You just want my help settling your tedious domestic squabble."

Our brother gave an irritated snort. "These are my lands, and I am Pharaoh!" he snapped angrily. Pothinus sensed his pupil was about to say something ill advised and tried to move in, but Ptolemy overran him. "I do not need your permission to execute whoever I please, old man. You're only sullen that I beat you to it and the glory is mine."

Caesar laughed coldly. "You are a client of the people of Rome, boy, and you boast of killing a citizen of the noblest blood to those people's chosen representative. No wonder you are having so much trouble hanging onto your throne, such as it is."

Ptolemy flushed with rage, but Caesar ignored him. He turned to his men and suddenly the face he presented to them was filled with sadness. "Men of Rome, Pompey called Magnus has been brutally slaughtered at the hands of cowards and flatterers. We shall bury him with all honors and I shall personally see to it that his assassins are punished."

The legionaries cheered their general, and Salvius, who had always managed to have even less sense than Ptolemy, stormed over to Caesar. "Imbecile!" he bellowed. "We do you a favor and this is how you repay us?"

Caesar glanced at Salvius. With one fluid motion, he drew his sword and decapitated the young lord, drawing a fresh chorus of screams from the watching throngs. Achillas and Lucius drew their swords, though our brother had finally realized this could go no further and held out an arm to stall them.

The Roman smirked at Ptolemy as our brother tried to steady his trembling lips. "I will find the other murderers, Your Majesty. I promise you." With that he walked past the royal entourage, stepping lightly over Salvius' body towards the palace. A phalanx of soldiers marched in behind him.

Pothinus turned to Lucius Septimus and appeared to hiss, "Get these people out of here!" Lucius vaulted into the nearest chariot and began dispersing the crowds. Cleopatra took my hand as we followed the retreating masses back towards the interior of the city and to Origenes' house.

"What will you do?" I asked Cleopatra when we were alone again in the antechamber, Kharmion and Mudjet having gone upstairs to bring a meal to us.

"Easy," she replied, holding up a bottle of oil to the light for inspection. "It is the same old game: I have to outmaneuver Ptolemy, which should not be too difficult."

"But how? He still has the support of most of the nobles and the army."

"The key there is 'most.' And I can sway the nobles to dance to my tune."

She dabbed some of the oil onto her hands and began lightly massaging it into her shoulders, glancing over at my skeptical expression. "Oh, please, do not be so obtuse. The lords and the army are small fare, even Ptolemy can put on a good showing for them. If I get Caesar on my side, everything else will fall into place."

I raised an eyebrow. "Because that tactic has gotten Ptolemy so far."

She shrugged. "Actually, serving up Pompey's head was a rather shrewd gambit. Which probably means it was Achillas' idea, not our brother's. I will just have to try the other path."

"Other path?"

She sighed at me hopelessly. "You are such a child. Everyone knows the two vices of Caesar: violence and flesh. Ptolemy made the first move with a gory present. I think I will succeed if I simply give him me."

"But you are the Queen of Egypt!" I snorted. "You would lower yourself to be a man's mistress?"

"Not just any man. The man who is winning control of Rome. A woman who aligns herself with him could rule the world."

"He is already married," I reminded her, still disgusted. "You would not be his queen."

"The Romans love divorce," she replied, shrugging. "Such a ninny could easily be dealt with. One way or the other."

I tried to ignore the implication of Cleopatra's last remark. "He is so old," I tried lamely.

"Not hopelessly. At least he seems to remain virile enough."

I wrinkled my nose at the thought. "Indeed. The litany of his conquests nearly defies belief. Why would you not leap at the chance to be his newest whore?"

She gave me a condescending look. "It is probably not that many. Men delight in exaggeration." She paused to admire a cuff she had produced from a jewelry box on the table, then continued. "And despite your apparent distaste, he is not too harsh to look upon for a man of his years.

Besides, you for one should be much more pleasantly disposed towards him, seeing how he has not been here three hours together and already he has taken care of Salvius for you."

I winced at the memory of Salvius' headless neck oozing blood on the sand. "It just seems that if you would go through the trouble of arranging a liaison of your choosing, you might as well aim for someone you might actually have affection for."

Cleopatra barked out a harsh, cold laugh that rang against the walls of our hideout. "I know you are young, little sister, but it quite literally pains me when you act so naively. We women have only the power we take in this world, and there is no use being shy about it. I will be sole ruler of Egypt and the good Consul will make that happen. I do not require his love, only his loyalty, and I certainly do not need to love him. Only simple women waste their time falling in love. It would be useful if Caesar would fall in love with me, but I doubt it will happen even with my *heka*. He is too clever for that. If he is interested enough to hold me over Ptolemy, it is enough. I will simply wait for my opportunity."

Chapter Fifteen

She had to wait two weeks, though since we were back in the city, all she had to do was have Kharmion slip messages to Origenes as he went about his business and he would give her a chance to get back into the palace undetected. This was not difficult, the routines of the palace had been thrown into disarray by the arrival of the legion, and Ptolemy continued to squander his chances to win Caesar to his side with his childishness and his temper. I know the legends say we wrapped my sister up naked in a carpet from Pontus and spirited her into the Consul's bedchamber, but every so often even we Ptolemies are not so dramatic. Besides, cocooned in a rug in the early Alexandrian autumn would have only given Cleopatra sunstroke, not her throne back.

No, the story Kharmion would tell us later was much more mundane. She and her mistress simply walked through the main palace hallway to surprise my brother and the Consul at dinner, fully clothed of course. Ptolemy tried to have her arrested, but Cleopatra very prettily fell to her knees and begged an audience with Caesar, to which he agreed. Granted, what happened during that audience — and after it — seems to align with what people say, and indeed she was gone for enough days together that Mudjet and I thought she had been captured. We had started to discuss what we should do and where we could possibly go when Kharmion at last returned with an escort of several legionaries.

"Kharmion!" I cried, never believing I would see the day where I was relieved to see my sister's sour companion. "What has happened? We thought you both had been thrown into prison!"

She gave me a patronizing look. "Everything is well, my lady. It has all gone according to Her Majesty's plan. She has sent for you to join her at the palace."

"But what about Ptolemy?"

"Hmph, he is fine. Now that he is under the proper guidance of his elders."

"What do you mean?" asked Mudjet in confusion.

131

"The young Pharaoh is under house arrest with us," Kharmion replied slyly. "Queen Cleopatra Thea Philopator has won the support of Rome. Come now, my lady. You belong at the palace."

We had no choice but to go with her, yet there remained an uneasiness in the pit of my stomach as we stepped out boldly into the street for the first time since our flight in the spring. There was a matching unrest in the city as we moved towards the palace, the people stopping their business to glare at the Roman soldiers, though some who recognized me bowed as I passed.

Shops that should have been open were not. The atmosphere bubbled ominously. Some men already appeared to be gathering raw materials for fencing and roadblocks. In the face of all of this, I should not have been so troubled for myself personally. Yet I could not shake the feeling as we climbed the palace's grand staircase that Ptolemy might not be the only one under arrest.

Kharmion walked us to my old rooms, where clean clothes and a full tub awaited me. I looked around at the familiar furnishings, at my disorderly stacks of books tottering over most of the tables and couches. In the golden halls of Antioch or the narrow stone compass of Jerusalem, I would have given anything to return here. Now as I stood amongst my belongings in the rooms I had known since I had known anything, I found myself out of place. These walls were the home of a girl I suspected I might no longer be, a girl whose life I could not slip back into as if nothing had changed. It was like an old dress that no longer fit as it should. I hoped my Lord would come home to my dreams soon, my nights had been empty since our return and I had grown into his presence so that I missed him when he was absent.

"Her Majesty will have you dine with her and the Consul at sunset," she said. As an aside to Mudjet, she added, "See that she is presentable."

Mudjet's purple eyes flashed in annoyance, though she said nothing in return. Kharmion wafted back out of the room, and we were left alone again.

"'Presentable,' indeed! As if you are some street urchin..." Mudjet muttered as she helped me out of my *chiton* and into the tub.

I was not offended, though perhaps I was too preoccupied to be. "I should have asked to see Ptah," I belatedly realized. So long had I pushed the prospect of seeing my brother away from my heart, I had nearly forgotten such a sweet thing was within my grasp.

"I am sure he is fine, my lady," Mudjet answered gently as she scrubbed. "Ask your sister at this dinner."

I sighed. "The command from Kharmion is only because she knows I would excuse myself otherwise."

My Mudjet's eyes grew mischievous and she smiled like her old self. "Do you remember all the banquets we played truant from?"

I returned her wicked grin eagerly. "Every one, my dear. And apparently so does my sister."

When I was dressed, I left Mudjet and headed for the main hall. I wished I could have worn one of my simple dresses, but of course I had a heavy *himation* draped over top of the ornately hemmed *chiton* we had chosen from the lot Kharmion left. The long indigo layers swirled around me as I made my way forward, when suddenly I heard a small voice call out my name from a shadowy wing.

"Arsinoë!"

I turned as Ptah rushed into my arms. "*Nedjes!*" I cried out ecstatically as Ganymedes stepped out behind my brother.

"We heard you were back, but no one would tell me where you were!" he babbled excitedly as he squeezed my hands.

"I was in the dark also," I replied, smiling and kissing his cheek. "Have you been treated well?"

Ptah shrugged. "Everyone's been too busy to worry about me much. Ganymedes is teaching me Latin."

I let go of my brother to embrace my tutor, whose comfortable, familiar softness eased some of my trepidations. "What has been going on here?" I asked, retrieving my seriousness.

He shook his head. "It is hard to say, my lady. One day Ptolemy holds the throne singly despite Caesar's anger about Pompey. Next any-

one knows, the Roman is trying to reconcile your brother and sister back
into co-rulership except with Cleopatra clearly having the upper hand.
The palace factions have been turned on their head once more, and all
are ingratiating themselves with the queen or with Origenes."

"So this banquet is a feast of victory."

"For the moment, it would seem. I will try to uncover more information as rapidly as I can." His frown lifted for a moment as he pulled me
back into his arms. "I cannot give words to my joy to see my *nedjet* well."

I tightened my hold on him instinctively. "I have missed you all so
much," I said softly, these paltry words encompassing the fierce jumble of
emotions spilling out of my heart.

"This feast sounds boring to me," Ptah said sulkily, breaking the moment with the forgivably selfish attention of a child.

I laughed, so pleased to behold the round, merry face of my little
brother once more that I would excuse him anything. "It probably will
be. You shall have to keep me entertained, goose."

We parted from Ganymedes hand and hand, and I pushed the curtains aside as we emerged into the banquet hall. Cleopatra and Caesar sat
together on the raised couch, observing all from above, while the lords
of Alexandria were situated around them chatting. It took me a moment
to notice Ptolemy off to the side glaring murderously into his cups, and
though he raised his head at our entrance, I could not read his expression. It was then that Cleopatra saw us.

"Sister! Dear Ptah! Come here and see us properly!"

The whole room stopped to watch us cross the floor. I tightened my
grip on Ptah's hand. We both instinctively slowed our pace to mask our
fear with sham dignity, as we had so often done walking towards our father in this same room and Ptolemy after him.

I kept my head high and my eyes slightly lowered to avoid the sea
of stares around us, the queen's perhaps most of all. No, not hers, I realized with a start. Tonight my *ba* had found another's gaze it shrank from
more. My Egyptian heart feared the starless midnight eyes of Caesar
more than any terror my sister could summon. The cruel lord of Rome
was the fated war the gods had warned me of. He was the *sha* of my Wak-

ing World, and I doubted I would find him as kindly as the black beast of my dreams, so topsyturvy had my life become.

When we reached our sister's couch, we knelt before her with our heads bowed until she motioned for us to raise them.

"You look well, Arsinoë," Cleopatra conceded brightly. "I thought you would pick the indigo one, though the orange silk dress would have been the nicest."

"I thank Your Majesty for your care," I replied softly. "I am glad you seem to be well."

"I know I should have sent you word," she admitted with an airy tone devoid of any actual remorse, "but there were many things to arrange and you were safe where you were."

"Mudjet and I were fine, though surely Your Majesty is aware that the presence of a Roman legion is creating a great deal of unrest in the city."

She waved a hand dismissively. "Oh, the Alexandrians are always riled about one thing or another. If it was not the Romans, it would be the Numidians, if not them, then the Syrians made fun of their accents."

I was alarmed. My sister was usually much more attuned to the tenor of our city. "My lady sister, they are building barricades in the streets. I think they are quite serious."

"They are just a rabble, Arsinoë. We have the guiding hand of the finest general in the world," she raised a glass to Caesar, acknowledging him for the first time before us, "and a legion of Rome's best fighting men. Things will settle in a few days."

I considered not replying, but my tongue got the better of my finer judgment. The safety of the city and our people was more important, and my fear for my rash Alexandria outweighed my fear of our foreign captor. And if Cleopatra did not see her savior as our captor, she was more foolish than the mobs assembling barriers in the markets.

"Forgive me, sir," I said, turning to look at Caesar for the first time, meeting his dark eyes that moved to study me as my voice drew his attention. "But your men are still worn out from battling Pompey. They will not have the stamina to take on all of Alexandria if the city revolts. Our people will not fight in nice little battlelines for your legion to crush."

Cleopatra opened her mouth to speak, but Caesar gestured for her to let my impudence go. "Don't worry, Your Highness. My men might be tired, but they are soldiers. They will do their duty," he said as his face relaxed into an expression of humoring amusement, as if I would be better served playing with my dolls than meddling in the affairs of the bigger people.

"Besides," my sister interjected, "it will not be your concern. We will handle Egypt, we are sending you and Ptah to Cyprus."

I was not prepared for this. "Cyprus?"

"Yes. The Consul has graciously agreed to give it to you. You both will have your own little dominion to govern and the island will once again be under Egyptian control."

Ptah looked at me with confusion and I frowned at the queen. "I do not understand. Why are you sending us away?"

"Do not be so dramatic!" She gave a hollow laugh that seemed to echo a little against the far stone walls behind us. "I am not sending you away! I need your help while we reestablish order and where I need your help the most is a colony that has been out of our administration for some time now. It is a big responsibility for so young a princess, yet after our trials these past months, I think you can handle it. Really, you could be more grateful!"

I bowed my head and gripped my hands together until my fingers were nearly white. "Forgive me, Your Majesty. I am simply overwhelmed by the generosity of you and Consul Caesar."

Cleopatra softened into a lenient smile. "It is all right, little ones. We will talk more about these arrangements later. Please be seated and enjoy yourselves."

I led Ptah over to an empty couch and stroked his trembling hand as stewards filled our cups.

"I don't want to go to Cyprus!" Ptah whispered in my ear, as I watched our sister while pretending to smell my wine.

I took a long, shaky sip from my cup. "I know. I do not either."

"Why can't we stay here?"

"Because she is afraid of us and what we are capable of, *nedjes*," I answered. I felt someone's eyes on me and turned my head until I saw it was

Ptolemy. His mouth twisted into a rueful smile and he jerked his head as if to say, *See how our clever sister will divide and conquer?*

Late in the evening, when I could at last slip away on the pretext of seeing Ptah off to bed, I left my brother with Mudjet and met back up with Ganymedes in an empty courtyard.

"This is unexpected play on your sister's part," my tutor said when I had finished explaining what had transpired at the banquet.

"Do you think we would be safe if we accepted?"

"Do you think you would be safe?"

My teacher already knew my answer. Even if I could somehow believe my sister's intentions were benign, sending a Ptolemy to Cyprus was a byword in this land for the barbarity of this family. My father had given the governance of Cyprus to one of his younger brothers, seemingly as here, in a gesture of goodwill. When Rome was forced to decrease taxes in Egypt or risk open rebellion from our people, they decided what they could not squeeze from the Egyptians, they would rake from the Cypriots instead. In spite of the island's enviable resources, it could not meet Rome's demands and when pleas to the Pharaoh for assistance went unanswered, my uncle committed suicide rather than bend to them. The Republic annexed Cyprus, took over its lands, and our people never forgave my father for his indifference. This episode was one of the many grievances that chased him and Cleopatra from their throne, and it seemed that my sister was remembering the wrong lessons from the affair.

"No, we would not be," I said quietly, gazing out at the courtyard swathed in humid moonlight. "Especially not Ptah."

Ganymedes nodded. "I think she is hoping Rome will do her dirty work taking care of you two."

"One would think she would have learned from our father's mistakes. The people despised him for abandoning our uncle to the Romans."

"It may be a gamble she is willing to take. You are both still young and if she is seen as being kindly to you, then you might be lulled into believing she has your interests at heart. If you leave these shores happy and meet with misfortune abroad, well, such things happen. She can play act that she did what she could. It might be enough to trick the Egyptians."

"What can we do?"

"We should try to delay such a departure as long as possible while we think up a countermove. Luckily for us, if the city is as restless as you say, the people might give us the time we need."

I am in the stables, the smell of leather and steaming manure greets my nostrils before the slightly subtler scent of horseflesh creeps by me. The stalls are empty, so I walk out into one of courtyards connecting the buildings, past mounds of fresh hay stacked against the walls.

There I find my Lord waiting for me, holding the reins of a pair of black horses with bloody-colored eyes hitched to a chariot. He strokes the nose of the left stallion who snorts into his hand. From somewhere unseen to my right, Lady Sekhmet gallops up on a roan mount who tosses its head against the bit.

"Hello, Ptolemy-daughter," she says in her typical growl, though the timbre of her voice is tinged with a happiness that betrays her obvious love of being on horseback.

I incline my head to her before addressing my Lord. "What are we to do this night?" My eyes no doubt beaming with joy at his reappearance.

Lord Set's eyes glow with green fire, which shows he reciprocates my unspoken feelings. "We are riding into battle, *nedjet*. Climb aboard."

A hum of unease shivers up my spine. "Battle, my Lord?"

Lady Sekhmet reaches down to adjust her horse's girth. "Do not be overly afraid, little princess. This battle is already over in the Waking World. We simply wish for you to understand the task that lies before you, what you are really up against."

I look to the desert god again. "Another journey into the past?"

He tilts his head. "Yes, Beloved. This one will not be as intimate as the last, but just as you must see your family as it truly is, so too must you see war for what it is."

I feel myself go a little pale. "I know it is no child's game."

Lady Sekhmet flexes the fingers of her right hand, which are sheathed in a leather bracer with lion's claws at the fingertips. "Naturally you know this, being a sensible girl. But as a girl, all you know of war you have read in books. That will not do for one chosen to lead an army."

"I still do not see why the gods should want me to command an army, even if such a ridiculous event should come to pass."

Lord Set looks at me in subdued amusement. "As I told you, my dear, even we cannot know for certain the exact shape the future will take. All we can do prepare for potential eventualities."

I know resistance to be useless, so I pull myself up into the chariot and my Lord jumps in behind me. He gently takes my hair and winds it into a knot as he tucks it under the lapis-colored *khepresh*, the royal war crown of Egypt.

The goddess of war gives a curt nod of approval. "You wear it well, child. Nearly as well as Khnumet-Amun Hatshepsut."

My Lord grins sharply at her. "I did not think to bring a false beard for my princess," he says, which causes Lady Sekhmet to glare at him.

"Who is that, my lady?" I ask her to divert the gods from getting into an argument.

"She is the nameless one you know as She Who Is Not Spoken Of. She was a great pharaoh, Princess. I held her in my breast even after her son wiped her memory from the minds of her people."

The memory of the pharaoh-queen the goddess called Hatshepsut was not completely erased. Part of her story was known to even me, but her life was so intertwined with legend even the Egyptians spoke of her as someone who may not have existed. She was held out to royal women as a warning of what happened to ladies who lusted after power. It was a warning the women of the House of Ptolemy seemed to studiously ignore, with mixed results. To have her conjured before me in this time seems especially ill-favored, though the gods do not appear concerned.

My Lord hands me the reins of the chariot. "Driving is not dissimilar from being on their backs, *nedjet*. Your task is to listen to their mouths and tell them how to work as one."

I tighten my hold until I can feel the pressure of the bits on the corners of the horses' mouths and then give a light flick of the leather. The horses leap forward, pulling us away from the palace and into the desert. They pound ahead at a quick canter as Lady Sekhmet rides at our side, keeping pace.

We sweep across the paths around the racecourse to the eastern edge of the city. As we gain momentum, I notice ghostly forms gathering at our side, marching in the same direction. The further we push outward, the more solid they become. They are mostly Roman infantry, moving in tight ranks with sweat from the heat of Egypt starting to pour down their faces making their worn leather armor strangely shiny.

Though moving at a more erratic pace, interspersed among the legionaries are men in the armor of the Egyptian army, twisting and darting. Looking at the men of my own land, I understand they are in some kind of retreat. We are close enough to see the fear in their barely-corporeal eyes.

We reach the edge of the eastern cemeteries and are joined by shades of men on horseback who also slowly begin to take on form as their men do. I know they have achieved their transformation fully when I must pull on the reins to keep my horses from snapping out at those of the riders. The one who appears to be the lead commander holds up a hand and his soldiers come to a halt a little ahead of us even as the ones belonging to his adversary continue to flee.

"Slow the horses, *nedjet*. We will wait," says my Lord in my ear. I bring the chariot to a stop and Lady Sekhmet pulls up alongside of us, watching.

I look at the Roman general as he surveys the land ahead. He is a powerfully built man in his prime years, with a square jaw and proud features that strike me as vaguely familiar. He reaches up to remove his helmet and it is only then that I know who he is, as his brown hair tumbles down in youthful curls. Before I can say as much to the gods, an ice-hard voice I know all too well barks out behind us.

"Pompey! Why have we stopped?"

I turn halfway round in the chariot to see my father fly upon us in his chariot, his bulky armor resting against his paunchy stomach, his eyes as dark and cold as caves.

"Steady, my lord," responds Pompey without ire. "My men are only waiting until your daughter's army retreats a little further so that we might encircle them more easily."

"Just see that you show these traitors no quarter," grumbles the pharaoh. "None of that famous Roman munificence here."

"Only an Egyptian could call the Roman army munificent," chortles a young officer at the general's side. His face is arguably handsomer than his commander, but it is the soft face of a pampered patrician, it lacks the vigor of the elder man's. His voice carries the languorous tone of an indulged young man of privilege, cream on silk.

"Remember your manners, Antony," reprimands another voice I recognize. I crane around the young man's body to see the exacting features of General Gabinius studying the young officer pointedly. "You do a disservice to the noble lineage of the Pharaoh to tar him with the same brush as these desert peasants."

The young Antony looks appropriately contrite. "A thousand pardons, Your Majesty. I did not mean to impugn the blood that fought with Alexander."

The flattery softens my father's expression a touch. "Yes, yes. Well, it will be easier to separate the wheat from the chaff when this is all over. I will see to that."

Gabinius narrows his eyes. "That's not what Lord Kemes and the Lady Ankhetep's family have been saying, my lord. They believe you owe them upon your return."

My father's mouth twitches unnervingly. "As I said, General, I will see to that. If you and the great Pompey give me the victory this day you have promised, no Egyptian vermin will dare oppose me. They are a conquered people. It is time to remind them of that."

I see Lady Sekhmet's mouth tighten into a frown, though she makes no remark. Pompey shifts his focus from the impending battlefield to those around him, giving them all an indulgent look that springs partly from an optimistic nature and partly, I suspect, from the benign largesse he feels knowing he is the superior man in the crowd. One can afford indulgence of one's inferiors. "Very well, my lords. Enough chatter. Let us finish this and bring back His Majesty to his rightful place."

Gabinius clucks his tongue in amusement. "Indeed, sir. We must not detain you in Egypt longer than necessary, we don't want fair Julia to pine away too long."

Pompey grins with a hint of sheepishness, then reaches over to slap the other general on the back. "Laugh if you will, Aulus, but I think it only natural for a husband to long for the embrace of his wife! Especially when she is carrying his son in her belly!"

The Romans give a scattering of encouraging cheers to toast the impending heir as Pompey buckles his helmet on once more. His smile turns predatory and with a quick signal of his hand, his legions descend with astonishing speed upon the enemy below.

The gods and I stand and watch from the high ground as Egyptian pikes are felled beneath Roman shields and are scattered in panic as the foreign army methodically pulls them down as farmers harvest wheat. I stand in the chariot, stunned and breathless, as the infernal Roman machine wheels back and forth across the field. It very nearly has the beauty of a dance, if not for the ceaseless screams of our people rending the air.

"We are difficult gods, *nedjet*," whispers Lord Set as we watch hundreds of men struggle in the burning sand as it grinds mercilessly into their weeping wounds. "War is coming to the Black Land once more, and like the moon growing full again, it is likely to take the terrible shape it did before. Our people are strong in battle, but one or both of the young pharaohs will set these wolves from the north upon the fat of this land, and I fear this time they will glut themselves until there is no more Egypt. I have called you my Beloved, and yet I offer up your slender wrists to the beasts of Latium. Such is the depths of my treachery."

I look at my Lord in surprise at these self-effacing words. I see deep love in the god's eyes, the fierce love I still find so unexpected, but with it is the shadow of genuine pain. To have the love of Set of the Wild Acacias makes my *ka* quiver with a kind of exquisite agony, but to have him be afraid for me? How can one's very blood sing with terror?

Lady Sekhmet tilts her head to observe us both, mostly the desert god as if she has not seen him properly before. "Bah, Set," she growls, "you bring me this child to dress for battle and you are the one to become childishly sentimental! The Princess attends to our lessons faithfully — you in turn must have faith in her."

My Lord is abashed. "You speak truly, Lady of the Slaughter," he admits humbly, before glancing at me with a hint of his usual confidence. "I have abundant trust in our Princess. I will do better to show it."

The goddess bobs her head curtly before speaking to me. "Little princess, we show you this so that you might understand the price you might have to pay to defend our land. Always the price is blood, be wary of how you spend it."

She removes the glove of her right hand and takes mine in hers, which sends violent pulses of pain through my arm until my very teeth chatter. The sensation makes me feel faint, though I do my best to maintain my grip as I meet her gaze with watering eyes. "This is the pain of the army below. This is the pain of Egypt. If you lead Egypt, this is your inheritance. The anguish of your men will always hurt, but when the pain becomes too much to bear, that is when you must think most carefully of your plans."

"I wish it did not come to this," I answer shakily.

Her amber eyes soften and I see the gentle gaze of her other Self steal across them for the briefest of moments. "Even the war gods wish that, child. But ever does Ma'at demand balance. She must have something for her left hand when her right cradles Peace."

And then I wake up.

Chapter Sixteen

I sat in an interior courtyard, playing *senet* with Ptah as Ganymedes perched next to us reading, when Pothinus suddenly materialized from behind a column.

My tutor raised an eyebrow from his papyrus. "Can we help you, Brother Pothinus?"

The other eunuch looked nervously around, his discomfort sitting strangely on his usually proud features. "My lord must speak with Lady Arsinoë. Privately."

Ganymedes was about to object, but I rose up. "It is well, teacher. My brother is still Pharaoh, I will go see what he wants. Stay here with Ptah."

Pothinus let out a puff of breath with relief. "This way, my lady. Follow me."

We moved swiftly through the back hallways, trying not attract too much attention. I should have been worried about being seen with my disgraced brother's tutor, but I found rather that I was strangely calm. The gods had warned me that the war approached on ever-quickening feet, so what was the use of fighting the growing veil that seemed to wrap itself around the palace?

"I apologize for the secrecy, my lady," murmured Pothinus as we hurried along the corridor. "But you know the queen and her wolfhound do not wish His Majesty to have any contact with you or your brother."

The old eunuch's unusual deference made me nearly as ill at ease as he was. "Should they be worried?" I asked pointed.

Pothinus gave an involuntary bark of laughter. "Oh, always, my lady."

We entered a back antechamber in the wing that Ptolemy had been restricted to. He was pacing the floor in agitation, chewing on a fingernail, though he brightened when he saw me.

"Arsinoë! I knew you would come!"

"I have not come for any specific purpose, brother," I replied, frowning. "I have agreed to hear you out. That is all."

Ptolemy was all agreement too, his burnished eyes alight with feverish intensity. "Of course, of course!" he said, far too solicitously. "It's just

I have been so worried about you and Ptah! I couldn't find out what the bitch and her dog were doing to you!"

My eyes narrowed. I could not bring myself to hate Ptolemy, even then, but we had always had too many differences to make us close. Maybe because we were born so soon after one another, this was our fate. It was troubling that he was so newly concerned about my person. I had not forgotten his threats in Pelusium.

"We are fine. Though we are not making trouble for them."

Ptolemy seized my arm impulsively, his words spilling off his tongue. "Exactly! That's what I wanted to speak of! How long d'you think that will last? Eventually they will see trouble even where none exists. You think you can play it safe by lying low, but that won't save you or Ptah in the end. Even if you agree to her ridiculous plan and go to Cyprus. I know you don't want to go — you remember our uncle. Or say you convince her somehow to let you stay, what then? You might not desire to be queen, but what if you grow too fair to look upon in the next year or two for our dear sister to bear?"

"*If...*" I replied archly.

"I know, I know! I'm trying to be helpful!" he whined, panicky that he was losing me. "I would not be bringing it up if I didn't think it was likely. So you become a beauty and that demon of hers starts casting eyes at you — you know he will, lecherous snake that he is. Do you think she'll put up with that? You know she must always be the center of attention. She'll get rid of you as surely as if you had challenged her with an army. And it won't be some cozy island she will send you to!"

I shook my head, unconvinced. "She could simply sell me off to a foreign prince. Cyprus timber would make a handsome dowry. It is not enough of a threat to risk open conflict with her."

"Maybe, but what then about poor Ptah?" Ptolemy countered slyly, pulling the knot on the snare he had set for my objections.

He was right of course. Who would protect Ptah until he was grown? Even if she could ignore me, how old would he be when she began to see rebellion in his eyes?

Ptolemy continued. "I know he doesn't want to be Pharaoh, but she will convince herself he is just another me. Help me and Ptah will be safe."

"Help you do what?"

"Beat her. I need you to get out of the palace. You have a better chance than I do, they only watch you lightly. I am sending Achillas to round up the army to expel the legion. Get to Achillas' camp when the time comes. He'll know you come from me. The force we have isn't large, but it'll hold for a while against what Caesar has at his disposal. The troops will fight better if they have one of us to ride ahead of them."

"I do not know what you expect of me," I answered vaguely, even as the memory of my own laughter at the gods' suggestion of making me a warrior reverberated in my ears. "I do not know how to command an army."

"You don't have to. Achillas will handle everything. But you're clever enough, I bet you and he can come up with a way to get me out of here. And then I will take charge."

"What if they harm Ptah for my disobedience?"

"He'll be fine. He's too valuable to get rid of, plus the people love him. You are our best chance to drive the Romans out."

I hesitated, knowing I could not afford the misstep of appearing too eager to sway under my brother's influence. "I have to consider it," I answered at last.

Ptolemy started to say something, but Pothinus exchanged a glance with him and he reconsidered. "Naturally, naturally. Think it over, sister. Though not for too long, we must act soon."

I nodded distractedly and the eunuch stepped back over. "We should return you before you are missed, Your Highness."

I allowed him to lead me out as Ptolemy watched us depart with a calculating expression.

Pothinus and I parted ways as I returned to my teacher and Ptah engaged in a lesson back in the courtyard. I stopped to listen, leaning against a pillar, rolling Ptolemy's words over in my head while Ganymedes and Ptah's voices flowed by me in the background. Part of me longed to be free to laugh at the reversal of fortune my same-born brother and his arrogant tutor had been reduced to, forced to court and flatter me in such a ludicrous way. Pothinus bowing and scraping before my suddenly royal presence, Ptolemy trying to convince me that I would become captivating enough to draw an experienced man like the Consul away from a woman like our sister. Yes, I would have laughed if only I was more sure of what to do. I had not been afraid to meet with my brother, though only because if we had been discovered, I was confident I would be seen as the mutely unimportant thing I was. But my brother's plan would force me to at last take a side and I was not convinced his was the right one. I worked my mother's bracelet about on my wrist in distraction.

"Now Prince Hektor left the ramparts of Troy to find his wife and son, who their maids said already mourned him as dead. What is the name of Prince Hektor's noble wife?" asked Ganymedes.

"Um, Andromache. Daughter of..." My brother faltered.

"King Eetion, Your Highness."

"Yes! Eetion! King of Boeotian Thebes!"

"No, Cilician Thebes, my lord."

"Oh, right! I get all the Thebeses confused!"

"Where is Cilician Thebes?"

"Ancient Cilicia. Anatolia."

"Very good, yes. And Hektor's princely son?"

"Scamandrius."

"Yes, and what did the people of Troy call the boy?"

"Astyanax."

Ganymedes spoke on of the meeting between the crown prince of Troy and his happy, doomed little family. The tragic events of the entire great war played out in this smaller scale. Truly were families always at the center of any conflict, lest I began to think our own drama was somehow of special note.

My thoughts drifted to Thebes; not the city of Andromache's birth on the ancient Trojan coast, or even our own Egyptian Thebes, the ageless city of kings, but the one Ptah had mistakenly mentioned. Boeotian

Thebes, land of Oedipus and the Seven Against, where family was always one's worst enemy. I knew all of their stories by heart, and yet I felt as though I was being pulled into the same pit of mistakes, equally powerless to change course.

My mind cried out like blind Tiresias to the rest of my being for action, and yet I could not discern what action to take. Siding with one sibling over the other was still treason, and which had the right of it anyhow? Cleopatra was a good administrator and a charismatic leader, yet she was willing to give up Egypt's independent sovereignty for her own power. Ptolemy was the ruler the largest portion of the land would support if forced to choose, which made him the most likely to bring peace to our people, yet my *ka* shrank at the thought of an Egypt ruled by either his unpredictable nature or his duplicitous advisors.

A small voice in my head said *What about you?*, but I shook it away. Like Ptah, I had been content with my life before. The gods spoke of duty to me, yet upsetting the order of our family even more than it had already been seemed like it would be the death of me. And us all.

"Every day Ptah looks so much older to me."

I turned at the new voice as Cleopatra moved to my side. I bowed to her, though she did not acknowledge it.

"Yes, though I still see him as our little lamb," I answered, in part not wishing to highlight Ptah's advancing age to our agitated sister.

"Careful with such thoughts, Arsinoë. I once thought Ptolemy was still my little brother."

"You do not see them as different?"

"Maybe now. But things change. People change." The flatness in her voice made her sound tired. "I think you are too blinded by Ptah's sweetness that you are careless of Ptolemy's treachery. You think I am too suspicious of one because of the other, yet I say you are too trusting of one because of the other."

"Ptolemy is my twin born in another womb. I am well aware of his faults," I answered sharply. "I know he might not be a good king, but he is young, sister. You should show him how he should be. I think we are all too young to be so beyond help and hope. Caesar offers you both the chance to begin again, can you not take it?"

She shook her head fitfully. "I want to be able to sleep in my bed soundly for one night in my life. I will never be able to do that with Ptolemy sharing my throne. You should sleep with one eye open as well."

"Do you think we will have easy rest in a civil war?"

"It is worth the wait. A civil war between Ptolemy and me is no war between Pompey and Caesar. Our brother will fall swiftly and hard. Remember that if he tries to woo you to his cause."

I prayed my face appeared neutral. "I am not a maiden to be wooed to anyone's side. I want what is right for Egypt, not only us."

"And you believe you know what that is, little sister?" Cleopatra asked softly.

"Maybe not. But war and bowing even further under the yoke of Rome than our father did does not seem like the path that will take us where we wish to go."

"No one is bowing," she said firmly. "I am still Queen of the Black Land. I am simply making a prudent alliance."

I should have held my tongue, but I could not manage it. "It must be difficult to say that with conviction to Caesar when you're lying beneath him."

She glared at me. "You think you have grown clever, sister. But I know you are still a little girl with her head full of wool and books. If you tried to walk in my sandals you would be on your knees in the blink of an eye. Keep your nose out of this game if you want to keep Ptah safe. Go to Cyprus and keep your mouth shut."

"If I do not, will you shut it for me as our father did to our uncle?" I shot back stubbornly.

Cleopatra smirked at me. "You are a fool if you think anyone at court who would wish you harm would have to send you as far away as Cyprus to accomplish it."

"Not everyone needs plausible deniability in front of their lover."

"Ha," she said with a cold laugh. "Caesar cares not what I do with my littlest siblings, you are below his notice. I must at least pretend to appease Ptolemy, but no one will lift a finger to save you, Arsinoë. Especially if you continue to needle me in this. My *heka* is stronger than you will ever be. And it is stronger than Rome can comprehend. I know a secret of Caesar's and with it I will rule Egypt and restore it to its ancient glory."

"I find it unlikely that a man such as the Consul has many secrets," I said skeptically.

"There is a rumor abroad that Caesar suffers from an injurious sickness that impedes his health, and at times, his work. I know it to be true. I have told him that I and the physicians of Egypt might have a cure. He is invested enough in that and in maintaining Roman interests here that I am sure he will cooperate."

"If his partnership helps you, it seems unwise to threaten him with the sword of this illness. It is clearly not so dire as to slow him down much."

"Perhaps not. However, when a powerful man such as him manifests any weakness, it is important to take note."

"Do you have this cure among your books?"

"Of course not," she said dismissively. "There is no remedy for this sickness, only concoctions to ease the symptoms. I simply wanted confirmation of the rumor. Information is priceless, sister."

"You are the one who mocked me for my books, Your Majesty."

"That is because you and I are not the same. You can try to get them to tell you what you should do, though it will not help. The only thing worse for you, my dear, than siding with Ptolemy is trying to stand alone against us both. We will crush you."

"Then devour each other like snakes." I paused. "If you had asked me to go to Syria, Cleopatra, I would have. Why did you not trust me then? Maybe if you had we would trust each other now."

She said nothing and started to walk away into the palace. Suddenly she answered, "You have always been too self-contained to be trustworthy, Arsinoë. You might be only half a Ptolemy by birth, but I think there is enough in you to make you dangerous indeed."

I watched her continue on her way, but then Ganymedes' voice cut in as he crossed the courtyard to me.

"I believe there were enough veiled threats in that to get going on," he said quietly.

Ptah took my hand and gazed up at me. The trust in his face wrenched at my heart. "Yes," I replied. "We might be beneath lofty Caesar's notice, but clearly some are most absorbed in our doings."

The day passed into night, and still I wrestled with myself. My tutor was correct naturally, my sister spoke threats against me and Ptah, so how could we live here? Ptolemy's words were honey by comparison, though that was because he spoke from an inferior position. If he were to regain the upper hand surely the same menace would flow from him eventually. Ptah and I were to be the baubles of whichever of them was in power. Kept when useful and disposed of when they tired of us.

I needed to get away. I stepped quietly into Ptah's chamber. He was curled up like a cat with his mouth slightly open and his toes twitching in his sleep. I leaned down and gently kissed his head, and as I stood up to leave again, brushed my fingers gently against his cheek.

In these moments, I missed our mother. Though I had begun to realize that what I truly missed was the comfort of the nursery where the intrigues were among the big people, rather than amongst ourselves. I missed the petty rivalries of thin-armed children, before we learned how to use potions and swords. When Cleopatra recited Sophocles to us doing all of the parts with different voices. When Ptolemy and I used to wrestle like cubs over everything. When Ptah made us all laugh with his easy smiles. So much had already been broken and my heart told me we could never go back. I let a small sigh escape my lips as I slipped out of the main palace toward the temple complex.

The evening air hung heavily as I moved onto the temple peninsula jutting into Cape Lochias, where the waters of the Nile join the sea. The fire from the lighthouse on Pharos burned in the distance and the bustle of the daytime city was slowly being blanketed into the more furtive sounds that kept Alexandria company through the night. The clang of iron in the blacksmiths' shops was the only audible reminder that the city was steeling itself against the future.

I crossed the threshold into the Temple of Isis. It was perched on the near side of the harbor, directly across from a twin sanctuary positioned beneath the glow of the lighthouse. Everywhere the goddess' strong image towered over the other figures, even her pharaoh son Lord Horus and brother-husband, the ghostly Lord Osiris. Low light from a hundred lamps cast across her many forms, allowing her touch to extend even further on the sandstone. She was so many things to her people: sorceress, mother, queen. I understood why she held such power, even for Cleopatra, someone who held herself to be less superstitious than her supposedly simpler subjects.

But I was not there for her, I was looking for someone else.

I walked to a far corner of the public area before I found her. Behind a small altar, a lovely stone woman with a jet-colored jackal at her feet stood in front of another ochre-tinged Isis mural. I made an ablution before her for she was Nephthys, Lady of the Desert, wife of my Lord, and I needed her advice. She was a goddess who knew her way through the dark, who saw what was invisible in moonlight. Baktka used to quote the old Egyptian proverb, *Descend with Nephthys, sink into darkness with the Night-bark. Ascend with Isis, rise with the Day-bark,* when she put me to bed at night. I poured a rivulet of oil from a waiting jar over my head as I knelt, closed my eyes, and let my mind drift towards the image of the goddess.

My Lady, I hope my exchanges with your Lord do not offend your majesty. He came to me and I am a lowly being, bound to be a servant of his will. Kite-Loving Lady, you and I dwell beneath the wings of stronger sisters. How do you protect yourself from her in her power? Or are both of you so one of mind that there is no "her" and "you," only an "Us?" Lady of the House, Basket-Bearer, I am so afraid for Ptah and myself. We are in a dark, dangerous maze, and I don't know how to save us. Your Lord is gracious to me, but he speaks in riddles...

A small noise broke my train of thought. I turned to look behind me and my blood froze. I rose quickly, jerkily to my feet, because even surprise could not prevent me from loathing to kneel before Consul Caesar. His long face was as inscrutable as always, but his deep eyes glowed with a faint air of amusement.

I made a shallow show of deference. "My lord."

He inclined his head to a side, studying the altar. "This goddess is not Isis?"

"No, my lord. She is Lady Nephthys, sister to Lady Isis. She helps to guard the realms of the dead. The Egyptians consider her a protector."

"But I see no temples to her in the city. She is subservient to her sister, no?"

I hesitated. I had not planned to be entangled in a theological debate with the master of Rome tonight. "I do not believe it to be that simple."

He considered this, then shrugged. "Well, her fame is less, to be sure." He kept his gaze on the statue. "A little goddess living in the shadow of a famous sister," he murmured thoughtfully, before giving me a sardonic glance from the corner of his eye. "It would seem unwise to waste prayers for assistance on a shadow."

I felt my cheeks burn. "I do not expect the goddess to assist me. I was asking her for advice." Caesar opened his mouth to interject, but I drew myself up a bit more and pressed my way into the pause. "I have always found her more approachable than Lady Isis. As I said, she is protector and one could hardly say that is a detriment in times such as these. Besides," I added haughtily, setting my chin at him, "I would expect the Consul to understand that sometimes a shadow can accomplish more than the sun."

He closed his mouth, and his gaze became penetrating. It was a stare that rooted me to the hard floor. I was almost afraid to breathe under it. I could feel the grit of the sand as it pressed against the soles of my feet. *Did I really leave my quarters barefoot?*

I stood there, locked in Caesar's eyes, my unease giving way to quiet fury with my own stupidity. I had said more than I meant to, more than I should have. My sister might have solved this puzzle of a man, but one in my position should not be half so presumptuous. After what seemed ages, he raised an eyebrow and arranged his face into a crooked half-grin.

"Well met, Your Highness," he said, a keen flash bolting through his dark eyes. "I bow to your piercing insight. Though even such a clever princess should see that she doesn't stray too far from the palace. Your sister is most anxious for your safety, and as you so helpfully brought to our attention, the city is restless."

He turned on a heel and sauntered out of the sanctuary. Relief flooded my chest, though it was almost immediately replaced by searing dread. My pride had shown my hand to a dangerous adversary.

If I had truly any wit, I would have played the fool in front of Caesar. I should have shown myself to be unimportant, and too dull to be a threat to him or my sister. Instead I had shown enough mettle to draw his notice. I would have even greater difficulty navigating this path, all because some part of me had wanted this hard man from Rome to see that I was a person of consequence.

I returned my eyes to Lady Nephthys, and I could almost see her shake her head at me as if to say that this was why the nearly voiceless kites were dear to her. Because she already knew the value of silence.

Now I knew I may have no choice but to accept Ptolemy's offer of alliance. I could not trust him, though if he was the one who changed his mind and sought my life or Ptah's, at least I would be more likely to see him coming. I had much greater doubts that I was a match for Cleopatra's subtlety combined with her lover's force. Like the goddess she had always tried to claim as her own, she was growing in strength while I would be changed to stone if I did not act soon.

Chapter Seventeen

I spent the next day on needles, fearing what Caesar might be planning in regards to me, or worse, what he may have told my sister about our encounter. She did not trust me, her plans for me and our last meeting made that clear, but so far I had not given her reason to strike out against me as a present threat. Nothing was said, though I had the feeling my activities were watched with a renewed interest. I rarely saw Ptolemy or Pothinus outside of official gatherings; they too could sense the shift and were careful not to be seen approaching me.

I was permitted to ride with Ptah around the racecourse when it was not in use, something we both jumped at as a way to escape the claustrophobia inside the palace. We played galloping games with each other, tossing balls back and forth while our horses flew in opposite directions and I helped my brother practice using a bow on horseback. I used this time to forget the dangers that felt as though they were hemming us in on every side. However, as the days passed and both of the pharaohs' words burned in my ears, my distraction grew.

"What is it, Arsinoë?" Ptah finally asked me, bringing his horse alongside mine after I had missed a third consecutive ball toss.

"Nothing," I said vacantly. "I am only thinking."

"No, I want to know!" The urgency in his voice made me look at him, his golden eyes earnest. "You're worried about something else, not just Cyprus. And if you're worried about something, that means it worries me too. You're my sister!"

"I try not to concern you with the big people problems, usually. Do you really want to know?"

He nodded vigorously, so I told him of what had been exchanged between Ptolemy and me. And then some of what passed between me and Cleopatra. I chose not to mention the Consul. He listened with great concentration until I was finished.

"So you and Ptolemy both think it would not be safe to go to Cyprus?"

"I believe so, though I would accept if you wanted it."

Ptah frowned. "It seems like a trick," he said slowly. "We should not go."

"But what I am worried about is what we should do if we stay. I cannot see how I will protect you."

"Is that why you won't go along with Ptolemy's plan? Because of me?"

"Among other reasons," I admitted. "Though it is my chief reservation."

Ptah was silent for a time. "I think you should do it," he said after a long pause.

"As simple as that, *nedjes*?" I replied fondly.

"What else can we do? If we don't go to Cyprus, we stay here under Cleopatra and the foreigners. I don't like them. They don't care about us or Egypt. You always told me that we get to be princes and princesses and live in a palace because we must serve the people in return for all of our nice things. The people don't like the Romans either, and we have to help the people. But with our sister in cooperation with the enemy, we won't be able to do much in here." He gestured at the palace grounds. "Ptolemy is practically a prisoner and I can't lead an army. But you can. You have to be the one."

"I do not know much about battle either, little brother."

"Sure you do! You know Thucydides and Homer by heart! You remember everything Ganymedes teaches us about Alexander and the Persian wars!"

I smiled ruefully. "Book learning is different from practice."

"But Mudjet told me that the Egyptian gods talk to you!" he exclaimed excitedly, heedless of the many secret ears of the palace. "With their help, how could you fail?"

"Mudjet told you that?" I asked, taken aback.

"Yes, please don't be angry with her. I was scared one night because I had a dream where you were in trouble and I couldn't reach you, and she told me that I should not be afraid because the gods would come to you at night to help you, even if I could not."

"And you believed her?"

"Of course!" Ptah answered. "You're a princess of Egypt, why wouldn't the Egyptian gods talk with you?"

I shook my head. "You are sweet, as always, but one thing I have learned from the gods is that they cannot guarantee anything. You might still be in danger and I do not know if I could forgive myself if something happened to you."

"Do the gods tell you to fight?" he asked pointedly.

"Yes, but I owe a duty to you as well as them."

My brother drew himself up in the saddle. "Your duty is to the people and the will of the gods, and so is mine. I am a prince of Egypt! I must be brave, too. I will help Ptolemy here in the palace, and you will be our general."

I felt tears gather in my eyes as I held out a hand to his warm, pink cheek. "Then my only regret will be how fast you must grow up, my goose."

Despite the atmosphere of tension, Cleopatra seemed determined to show her new ally her Egypt and the court of the Ptolemies in all of its exotic splendor. Feasts and banquets continued nightly, and the days were filled with the many amusements that our land was known for. Fantastical beasts preened while magicians filled the palace rooms with mystery and wonder. I had asked my sister to allow me to spend my days in the Library, to fill the hours, but she had refused. I had even told her she might send an escort of guards with me, as much as I wanted to be alone. She still demurred, saying that it was too risky in the streets and that she needed me at court anyway to represent the royal family. So I remained confined to the palace grounds, the end result of my encounter with Caesar in the Temple of Isis revealed at last. Surely she had asked his opinion and he would have undoubtedly advised against letting me wander.

I was picking listlessly through another assortment of gowns Kharmion had sent over for that evening's festivities when a smooth voice behind me interrupted.

"I would choose the green one, Your Highness."

I jumped at the sound and found Achillas leaning against the wall with his effortless athlete's ease, his polished golden armor glowing in the lamplight.

"General!" fumed Mudjet angrily. "These are the princess' private quarters! How dare you enter without permission?"

"Calm yourself, Mudjet. I mean Lady Arsinoë no harm." Achillas moved towards us, his deep blue eyes full of mischief. "Besides, in this cauldron of deceit, I don't know how else I'd be able to speak with Her Highness unobserved."

I straightened my shoulders, trying to maintain my dignity despite my plain *chiton* and my undone hair trailing down my back. "How can I help you, General?"

He stepped even closer, his muscles taut beneath his suntanned skin. Achillas was a great favorite of the ladies of the court. With his blue eyes and ashy hair, he looked as Greek as Apollo. He had the god's casual confidence to match. "I'm here to give you a warning, my lady. You are running out of time. I am leaving court to rally the mob to His Majesty's banner. No more of the Queen's spectacle. You should come with me if you want to leave this palace alive."

I felt my face pale. "I am not in so much danger as that, sir."

"Perhaps not yet," Achillas conceded with a shrug. "Though I know the secret Cleopatra will announce tonight. Then you'll understand that your days and the little prince's are numbered."

"What secret?" I asked, frowning.

He grinned like a cat. "Oh, that you will see. If I told you now, you wouldn't believe me. The convenience for her staggers the mind. But," he bent over to me conspiratorially, "I will tell you a different secret. Pothinus is planning to poison Caesar at the banquet."

"You endanger the princess' life by making her party to this information!" Mudjet hissed.

"Don't worry, Your Highness," he soothed carelessly, still half-grinning at Mudjet's consternation. "I can tell you because it won't succeed."

"How do you know it will not?"

"Because I let that information get back to Caesar. He knows."

"But why?" I asked.

"Because Pothinus is an old fool and he is only going to get His Majesty killed. He has been using his contacts in the city to urge the continued rootless rioting among the people. Yet he is so indiscreet about it that the Queen and Caesar are moving against him. He made me party to this plan, but I will not be dragged down with him. I went and convinced the Pharaoh that it would fail. So we made some alternate arrangements. A few of which your Revered Brother has already told you."

I looked into his eyes quietly. "What would you have me do?"

He laughed and leaned in to whisper in my ear, his breath tickling my neck. "Come find me when tonight is over, Your Little Highness. We'll take back what is ours from old Caesar." He stood back and made a little bow as he left.

Mudjet glowered after him. "He is not to be trusted, my lady."

I was inclined to agree, though the heat of Achillas' attention had scorched my skin, leaving a trail of fire down into my stomach. I knew he was a shameless flatterer of all women, but he had never paid me much mind before. I began to understand why the other ladies threw eyes at him the way they did. I would have to proceed very cautiously indeed. "Do you agree with his assessment, though?"

"About our situation?"

I sighed, annoyed with myself. "That. And the bit about the dress."

When I made my way into the feast, I was glad Ptah was not there. The hour was late, so his presence was excused. I nervously moved my mother's bracelet around my wrist and kept an eye on Pothinus and my brother. The elderly eunuch appeared serenely calm as was his wont, but Ptolemy's eyes darted everywhere and nowhere. The only person he was studiously not glancing at was me. Achillas was rather conspicuously absent, though maybe only to my eyes.

My sister was in fine looks, her glossy hair intricately arranged about her face with a few artful touches to downplay her more aquiline features. Her sweetened laughter floated across the room in response to something Origenes had said. Apollodorus sat draped on a couch to her left, also laughing, yet only with his mouth, the rest of his expression tensed. Caesar sat on her right intently listening to the exchange, though leaving the unshakable impression that he was hearing more of what was not being said than the obverse.

Cleopatra stood up from her couch suddenly as the servants brought in the main courses. She floated over to Pothinus' side, trailing a rich violet train on her *himation*, and leaned in to smell the fragrant dishes being carefully arranged in front of the court.

"Ah, this all looks divine, does it not, my dear Pothinus?" she said, dipping the tip of her finger in a honeyed yogurt dish and delicately inserting it into her mouth to taste it.

"Indeed, Your Majesty," said the eunuch. "The cooks of Egypt are this land's true sorcerers."

"Such a magnificent meal requires the perfect accompaniment, do you not agree?" She motioned for a servant from the wings to bring over a small flask and poured some wine from it into a cup, placing it before the eunuch.

Pothinus began to grow uneasy. "Your Majesty, I do not deserve such special favor from your hand."

"Oh, but sir!" my sister exclaimed brightly. "You are the tutor of a king! Like Aristotle to Alexander. You do such excellent service to the House of Ptolemy, let us toast your life's work!"

He met the queen's eyes, abruptly cognizant, and replied, "I have only ever done my duty, my lady. To my pupil, the Lord of the Black Land."

Cleopatra snickered, her hazel eyes darkening. "We all do what we can, you miserable old half-man. Now drink."

Pothinus picked up the cup and saluted Caesar with it. "Enjoy being saddled with this harpy-faced succubus, sir," he said, and downed the cup in one gulp.

My sister smiled. "Now that Pothinus has enjoyed his wine, I have an announcement that I am sure will aid his digestion." She strolled back towards the front of the gathering. "They say that the gods hear the prayers of the kings of this loveliest of lands. I have prayed for stability for Egypt and this House, and the gods have taken my supplications into their hearts. I do not know if it was fruit-bringing Demeter or plumed Min who answered, but I am with child and Egypt continues to bless the heirs of Ptolemy Soter."

There was an awkward, stunned silence that was finally broken by our brother. "Are you insane, you shameless whore?!" Ptolemy crowed at her. "You think the people will stand by and let your bastard sit on the throne of their gods?"

"Careful, my dear god-loving sibling," warned Cleopatra unctuously. "You are the firstborn son of a Ptolemy who called himself Auletes, but whom everyone else called Nothos — the Bastard. Perhaps you have no room to judge. Besides, you are my divinely given husband, brother. Would you deny your child and wear the horns before your subjects?"

Ptolemy's face turned an exciting shade of purple, though it was not nearly as interesting a color as the one Pothinus' face took on as he clawed at his throat and pitched forward on the table upsetting several platters as foam began to escape his lips.

Cleopatra peered over at him nonchalantly. "Ah, the wine has settled. Splendid." She waved a hand to the rest of the company. "Do not be alarmed, my lords. Pothinus the eunuch is being punished for attempting the murder of Consul Caesar. He conspired with General Achillas, who I see has failed to appear here tonight, though we shall ferret him out presently. We cannot have traitors in our midst."

For the briefest of moments, I fancied Cleopatra and I made eye contact. The crowd sat uncomfortably counting the time until Pothinus stopped struggling and lay still on the table, blood seeping from his bulging eyes.

To stop from staring at the eunuch's corpse, I looked back at Caesar who had not moved from his couch. His expression was politely neutral, as if all of this was just another set of entertainments like those of the previous evenings. However, there was a crease in the middle of his forehead between his eyes I had not seen before. I was struck with a realization. *He had not known my sister was pregnant, either.* A gamble on her part. What would he do with that information?

I did not have time to pursue the thought further. A legionary burst into the room, breathless. "General Caesar! Achillas has besieged the city with a thousand score men! The mob rises to make his way!"

The room descended into chaos as Caesar called orders to his men, and Cleopatra began shouting to Apollodorus and her other retainers to mobilize whatever was left of the palace guard. In the whirlwind of activity, I looked around the room for a discreet exit, when my eyes fell on Ptolemy standing off to the side of the room in front of a curtain. I knew that it covered a passage that connected to a hallway I could reach my rooms from. My brother inclined his head to me.

"I will do what needs to be done to stop this madness," I said to him quietly as I reached his side.

"Tell Achillas to give no quarter, tell our men to fight for the glory of Egypt," he answered in a fierce whisper.

"You could come with me."

He smiled ruefully. "No, I can't. Not while Caesar still tries to plead my case to our sister from time time."

"Well, do not do anything stupid when I am gone. I do not fancy risking my neck for you if you are going to play games to get us all killed." I wanted to remind him that although I was doing what he had asked of me, I remembered what he was capable of.

He made a little tutting noise with his tongue. "You used to be more trusting, sister, dear. Though I suppose six months in the desert with Cleopatra would cure anyone of that."

"And if any harm comes to Ptah, I will make you sorry you have ever drawn breath."

"I won't let a hair on his head be touched. Go quickly now, Arsinoë." He held up the curtain and I slipped out the side passage, hoping I could find Ganymedes before I was missed.

As soon as I cleared the hall, I sprinted back to my quarters. Mudjet rose up at my entrance. Not pausing to explain, I said hurriedly, "Mudjet! We must go. Now."

She nodded and rushed to grab the packs we had made for this moment. In mine were a linen *tunica*, an old *chiton* or two, leather wrist bracers, boots, a pair of daggers, a few packages of food and bandages.

The contents of Mudjet's were similar. We threw heavy cloaks on, grabbing a spare for Ganymedes, and made our way back out into the hall.

"I need to say goodbye to Ptah and find Ganymedes. Hopefully they are with each other."

"You go to Ptah's quarters, I will be there presently," said Mudjet wheeling around towards another passage.

"Wait! Where are you going?" I called out.

She gave a wave of her hand and was out of sight so quickly I had no choice but to let her go. I hurried down the corridor, dodging behind columns when soldiers came running across. I made it to Ptah's rooms and indeed found him with my tutor, who rushed over to me as I knelt down to embrace my brother.

"Achillas is laying siege to the city. We need to leave now if we are joining him," I said, handing Ganymedes the extra cloak.

He put it on hastily. "Where is Mudjet?"

"I am here," she replied, shifting the weight of her pack as she stepped into the room.

I breathed out in relief. "I cannot convince either of you to stay here and watch over Ptah for me?"

"I'll be fine, sister," he cut in. "Ptolemy and Achillas need you, and you need Mudjet and Teacher. Go, guide our people."

I gave him another quick hug and kissed his cheek before we darted out and began the winding process of escaping the palace. Ganymedes led us through some of the back ways for the servants and eunuchs. They were mercifully empty as everyone was preparing for a direct assault on the complex.

"You do not think Achillas would attack the palace yet, do you?" I asked Ganymedes as we moved through the barren passageways.

"I doubt he is that organized at this point, though it would save the three of us some trouble," he answered ironically.

We made it outside, where the legionaries were already digging trenches and moving fortification walls into place.

"Can we get out through the gates?" Mudjet craned her neck around a corner.

I looked out into the darkness. "Doubtful. That is the one place they are sure to be already guarding."

"We might be able to slip across the race course and into the Jewish quarter, though I suspect Achillas is coming from the southwest. I do not know if he will have penetrated that far east of the city in such short measure," said Ganymedes.

I bit my lip in concentration. "If we can make it out the western walls of the palace, we should head for the catacombs until we can find Achillas. It should be safe with the city in such disarray."

"My lady, I do not see how we can easily scale the walls," replied my tutor.

I too was at a loss until the razor voice of Lady Sekhmet entered my ear. *Remember the source of all life and death in our land, Ptolemy-daughter.* That was it. I grabbed my teacher's arm. "We can swim out through the canal! It cannot be blocked without risking the water supply of the palace!"

Ganymedes nodded. "It is a good plan, *nedjet.* Better wet than caught. If we can swim past the Gate of the Sun, we should be able to return to our feet."

The fresh water in Alexandria comes from the Nile, but brackish estuaries and canals cross the city where the Great Sea and our great river clasp hands, many stemming from Lake Mareotis situated to the back of the southern districts. The water in some of these canals is fresh, some is not, though the semi-salty water has many other uses. It can be taken for bathing and some cooking, and is a home for many of our wonderful perch. Which is why one of the larger canals runs right through the palace.

We moved back along the walls until we found the canal making its way out into the streets. We jumped into the dark water and bobbed silently there for a few agonizing moments to ensure we had not been heard. We were lucky that the sounds of the laboring legion masked our splashes.

Satisfied, we swam out until we reached the iron grate that prevents trespassers from getting in and now attempted to keep us from getting out. Ganymedes planted himself against the grate as best he could without being able to touch the water's bottom while I climbed up onto his shoulders, clinging to the iron bars. Mudjet then scrambled up over both of us, and with that extra height was able to pull herself over the top. She reached back down to pull me up after her, and then we had our combined strength, such as it was, to help my teacher ascend.

Once we were all over the grate, we plunged back into the canal and swam until we passed under the bridge where the Gate of the Sun guards the eastern districts. Tired and wet, we managed to climb out of the canal and began making our way across the ancient neighborhood of Rhakotis towards the catacombs of the western cemetery. Firelight blazed in the streets as people continued to stock barricades across the major streets and back alleys. The swing of axes on wood and steel on iron echoed over the commotion of thousands of infamously loquacious Alexandrians making plans.

We passed in the shadow of the Temple of Serapis when we froze at the sound of approaching soldiers. A dozen light troops marched quickly by us, and seeing they were not legionaries, I took a chance at approaching them.

I stepped out of the cover of the temple and seeing that their leader appeared to be an Egyptian, called out to them, "*Em hetep nefer ahauti taui!*"

The men stopped and their lieutenant answered me, "*Em hetep nefer sherit taui.*" He looked at our wet clothes. "It is not safe for civilians to be in the streets, miss. You and your companions should find shelter in case the Romans push out into the city."

He sounded worried, but his tone to me was kind. He had the shorter, powerful build of the country-dwelling Egyptians and although his squarish features had hard, sharp lines, his deep-set eyes sparkled with easy humor.

"We have just come from the palace, sir, and can report that the Romans are engaged with strengthening their fortifications and will likely make no serious forays on the offensive tonight." I pushed back my hood. "I am Princess Arsinoë, and I come on behalf of His Majesty the Pharaoh. Can you tell me where I will find General Achillas?"

The lieutenant and his men immediately fell to their knees. "*Hezet en iammi, heqet-taui*. Forgive me, Your Highness, I did not know you. I am Tahu, son of Khabek of Memphis. My men and I will escort you to the general."

The soldiers formed a circle around us and we headed towards the northwest corner of the city. "We are encamping near the Gate of the Moon, my lady," Tahu said. "The general has managed to pull much of the army from the palace and has called up reinforcements from garrisons as far away as Thebes. He hopes to have more troops from Nekhen and Ombos within a day or two."

"How many men do we have?"

"Around twelve thousand, my lady, plus another several thousand in cavalry. However, we are confident we can raise that number to twenty."

"How many ships?"

Tahu frowned. "That I do not know. You will have to ask the general."

"Has anything been done to secure Pharos?" asked Ganymedes.

"Unfortunately Caesar had already stationed a sizable portion of his men on the island when he arrived, sir. Missives from the eunuch Pothinus on behalf of His Majesty have directed any efforts organized or otherwise to attempt to retake the island and reclaim the lighthouse, but we have not been successful so far. The good news is that other than the palace and the island, we are in control of the city."

"The city is hardly in control," muttered my teacher as we hurried past people running back and forth with weapons and supplies. "This pandemonium must be contained."

"They have just arrived, teacher," I replied soothingly. "There has been no time to organize the resistance in the city proper. Besides, that seems like a fitting role for a royal personage to assume."

"Indeed, my lady," cut in Tahu. "It is well you are here. The troops are willing to follow Achillas' lead, but the civilians will be better managed by a member of the House."

We entered the main camp and made our way to the tents serving as headquarters. Tahu spoke with one of the guards outside Achillas' tent and he moved aside to let us pass. Once inside, the group of gathered officers stopped their discussion at our appearance. At the center, Achillas raised his head and a wide grin broke across his face.

"Your Highness! You are most welcome here!" he cried out with a low bow. At his address, the other men bowed. "I see you also took my other advice," he said slyly, letting his eyes sweep over my bedraggled green dress.

I ignored his flirting. "I have come to help you and my brother reclaim our homeland, General."

"I am so glad, my lady! The people will be relieved to know that at least one royal remains free of foreign control."

"The city is in riot, Achillas," Ganymedes spoke up sharply. "Why are your men not working to suppress the mob?"

Achillas frowned. "We have been endeavoring to capture strategic streets and push back the Roman advance into the Soma, Ganymedes. The mob can wait. Besides, the disorder will impede the legion, which can only benefit us."

"It will not endear our struggle to the Alexandrians if helpless women and children are trampled in their doorways!"

"And when did you become such a military expert, eunuch?"

I stepped between the two men. "Please, gentlemen. We need time to form a proper strategy. This arguing gets us nowhere."

Achillas immediately looked contrite. "Forgive me, Your Highness. It has taken a great deal of work to reach this point and I am perhaps overwrought. And you are all standing here soaked to the skin. I shall have tents assembled and dry clothes sent to all of you. You should go rest and restore your strength. We have much to do, though we can discuss it in the morning." He motioned Tahu to my side.

I started to follow the Egyptian, but turned back to the general. "We must get Pharos back. If we do not have the harbor, we do not have anything."

He made another bow. "We are in agreement, my lady. I will see it done."

Tahu escorted us back out into the night, surrounded by the glimmer of campfires, when I saw a larger glow of light in the distance back towards the palace.

"What burns so in the distance?" I asked the lieutenant.

"The reports say that Caesar burns his own ships, to keep them from falling into our hands, my lady."

I exchanged a glance with Ganymedes as Mudjet said with a sniff, "Well, I suppose that means he is not going anywhere anytime soon."

Chapter Eighteen

We awoke early the next morning stirred by activity in the camp. As the bustling noises of the army drifted through our tent flap, I pulled on a fresh *chiton* from the mat on which we had spread our wet clothes the night before. Mudjet wound my hair into a long braid that hung down my back, making small noises of frustration as she went.

"Tch, one day I will school my lady's wild hair properly!" she said as she wrestled to get some of the flyaway curls to submit, her adept fingers moving in and out of my hair like a weaver.

I smiled as I listened to the cheerful sounds of fearless Alexandria. One could not guess we were under an invasion, my bright city sounded more likely to break out into a carnival. "Not likely, my sweet."

We made our way back to Achillas' tent, where Ganymedes and several captains had already convened. A few of the men wore Roman-style armor. Those I assumed to be Gabiniani, the others were palace guard Greeks. I looked for the Memphisian Tahu and was troubled to see no Egyptians present. I should not have been surprised, though the presence of the gods nagged at the edges of my thoughts. *We are at war,* I thought to myself. *We cannot afford the snobberies of the past.*

At this moment, Achillas noticed our arrival and broke into my contemplations by hurrying over to kneel at my feet. "Good morning, my lady. I trust you passed a comfortable night."

"If I did not, it will not be the last, I am sure," I replied drily. "Where is the legion?"

"Still around the palace, Your Highness," answered Ganymedes, coming to my side. "Your sister sends out raiding parties into the city, but they have been contained by stone block barricades placed by our army at the major crossroads."

"Can we continue to build up such obstacles in the streets?" I asked.

"We have several detachments constructing them as we speak. We are also rounding up more horses to pull the blocks into position."

"I feel as though I must understand everything we do as you, General," I said to Achillas. "But I do not wish to hamper you as I learn."

"It is well, Your Highness." He motioned one of the Roman-clad soldiers forward, a small, thin man with rumpled hair that appeared nearly as unruly as my own. "This is Quintus Fabianus," explained Achillas. "I have assigned him as an aide for you."

The wiry lieutenant made a little bow. "I am at your service, my lady."

I gestured to his attire. "You are one of the Gabiniani?"

"Yes, my lady. It is an honor to serve the youngest daughter of Ptolemy Auletes. Your mother was always very kind to us and our wives; she gave my wife a set of very fine hairpins when we were married."

"We have sent word through our secret channels to the Pharaoh that you reached us safely," continued Achillas breezily, though something in his eyes seemed to be studying Quintus Fabianus as though he had not seen the soldier properly before. "He is pleased and says he will send instructions for us all when he is able. We have also received word from him that your absence has been generally noticed, Your Highness." He gave me a smirk of pure delight. "Caesar is reportedly most wroth that you escaped undetected."

"He underestimated how clever all of our princesses are in Egypt," my teacher said proudly.

I brush away Ganymedes' praise with a flick of my hand. "Well, perhaps it is advantageous to give him and the Queen something to stew over. What do you need me to do, General?"

"It would be good if you were to speak to the men and the city dwellers who have joined us," admitted Achillas. "Say a few words of encouragement. Your Most Revered brother feels very far away to them."

I gulped back a small fit of nerves and nodded. "I will do so. Allow me to return to my tent first and make sure I look the part."

Achillas bowed again. "As you wish, Your Highness," and in a more intimate tone, one that sounded as if he were comforting a small child, "I'm sure you say what our people need to hear."

Ganymedes ducked out of the tent with us as we retraced our route back to my tent. "Can I trust Quintus Fabianus?" I asked him in an undertone. The Gabiniani lieutenant was not with us, but I could not shake the feeling that there were several sets of eyes that might be watching me on behalf of others.

My teacher was thoughtful. "I believe you can. The Gabiniani do not support your sister's claim and will resist Caesar as long as he does likewise over the claims of your brother. Also, I think that story about your mother was genuine, and furthermore, Achillas did not know it. He probably asked for a volunteer from the Gabiniani to mind you and assumed none of them had any ties that would make them protect you at the cost of keeping him informed. It is a fortuitous stroke for you, my lady."

"Well, we cannot rely so heavily on luck from now on, no doubt. This Gabiniani seems well disposed to me, so let us keep it that way. Also, the Egyptian lieutenant who brought us here I believe is a valuable ally as well. I want to keep him close. I need as many men around me who are trustworthy as possible. He will know how best to manage our native soldiers, I think."

"Achillas will use the Egyptians and the other races because he needs the manpower, but he only trusts the Greeks and the Gabiniani," my teacher observed. "Your job I think will be to keep those out of Achillas' favor loyal to our cause, *nedjet*."

Mudjet worked to strap my breastplate into place while I gathered up the skirt of my *chiton* to allow a little more freedom of movement. She arranged my *himation* over and under my armor, hemming the linen in here and there.

"I hope I can do this," I said, strapping on my left wrist bracer.

"I know you can, my lady," she replied. "Speak to them as you would to me. Or Ptah. The city is already fighting the Romans, all you need do is show them you will fight with them. For them."

I found a small mirror and gazed at myself critically. "I still look like a girl child in her brother's armor. Not a very convincing soldier." I sighed. "Or queen."

Mudjet smiled conspiratorially. "Oh, that I can take care of, my lady." She reached into her pack and removed a bundle of cloth. She gently unwound the linen and held up a glittering object that drank up the sunlight that slipped into our tent like a thief. Or an elusive lover.

I took it in shock, running my fingertips along the intricate feathers beaten into its body of pure gold. "Where did you get this?"

"I decided to... *borrow* it the night we fled the palace," she said simply, as if all was obvious. "I thought you might need it."

It was the crown of Nekhbet, the vulture goddess, Her golden wings spread down in protection of the wearer and her head arched above the forehead. She is the patron goddess of Upper Egypt, the lands of my Lord Set and this crown was the symbol of the old queens of Egypt. Cleopatra wore a version of it when she ascended as co-ruler, and it was the embodiment of anything I had to offer the people of Alexandria. I turned it over in my hands, watching the tiny gold feathers catch the light. After hesitating a moment longer, I lifted it into place on my head.

Mudjet pulled my long loose braid forward so it curled over my shoulder. "Go forth and meet your soldiers, my lady. I shall follow close behind."

We stepped out of the tent and were met by the kind face of Tahu, no doubt summoned by my teacher. When he saw me and the crown upon my head, he and the soldiers with him knelt down so that their foreheads touched the ground. "*Tua netjer heqat-taui*! The gods have smiled upon us on this day, my lady. The Pharaohs of old have sent a true Queen in our midst," he said solemnly.

I helped him back to his feet, a little abashed by this earnest reception. We mounted the horses held for us and spurred them over to the Gate of the Moon, where Achillas had gathered up as many of the troops as could be spared. Civilians from the nearest streets also stood milling about, but the shining beauty of the vulture crown drew all heads towards us as we approached.

Ganymedes beamed at me as we came to a halt and Achillas looked surprised. I reined in my horse and decided I could waste no time before my courage gave out. I drew myself up in the saddle and tried to recall the steady grace of my mother, the crownless queen a thousandfold more regal than me.

"People of Egypt!" I shouted as loud as I could. "I bring you a message of hope from His Majesty Ptolemy Theos Philopator. He has seen your brave actions in rising up to defend our homeland, and he wants you to know his *ka* soars out of the palace where his body is guarded to aid you in this fight!"

A soldier called out, "You wear the vulture crown, Your Highness! Will you fight with us?"

"I also bring tidings from the gods of the Two Egypts!" I answered, inhaling the last tremors of my fear. "They have sent me to you to be their standardbearer! The Ancient Ones go with us, men of Egypt! Do not be afraid!"

The soldiers let out a shout, and the people cheered. I wheeled my mount around. "The Romans are fierce, my people, but let us give them a taste of Alexandrian ingenuity. Let us show them that we are weary of being their plaything!"

Another roar echoed from the crowd. "Let us show Caesar that we will not bend our knees to him without the clash of swords!"

Achillas moved forward and shouted, "Look, Alexandria! The gods give you a new queen in place of the treacherous Cleopatra who would sell you to Rome! It is Lady Arsinoë whom the gods have chosen to lead the kingdom at the side of your Pharaoh!"

I met Achillas' eye and as the people roared in approval, he gave me a nod of encouragement.

"*Tua netjer, heqat-taui!*" the Egyptians cried out as I held up my hand to greet them.

"Hail, Arsinoë Soteria Philoaígyptos!" answered the Greeks.

"I thank you, my people, for your great faith," I called back to them. "I might be a child in your eyes, but I swear on the soul of my mother born of this land that I will endeavor to protect you and this kingdom from our enemies until my last breath!"

The crowd sounded almost jubilant in its cries. I spied a group of sailors to the right and spurred my horse to them. "Oarsmen! Alexandria's proud sea-tamers! The wolves of Latium will send their warships to our midst with haste! Will you help me build a fleet to guard our shores?"

The men yelled their assent. "We shall see it done, Queen of Queens!"

I shouted back to them all, "Have faith in the land of your fathers, Egypt! If we fight together, we shall punish Rome for its arrogance!"

I swallowed the hot wind that blew against us. I carried the momentum of the multitude in my stomach. However, there also dwelled the black knowledge that I had allowed the people to hail me as queen above my sister.

There was no going back.

I stand looking out at the harbor. It is so beautiful, just as it is in the Waking World, but the stars glitter on the ground rather than in the sky so I know I am dreaming. I, who grew up in a palace encrusted with jewels and painted in gold, am still dazzled by the sight. I can trace constellations with my toe and I feel as light as air as I trip across this unearthly carpet that shimmers more intensely than a net of the most brilliant of diamonds.

I am transfixed by this exquisite display, yet I move along, drawn by my heart to the Lighthouse of Pharos. Or at least, the lighthouse as it appears in the Dream World. It is nearly the same with its three strata — square, then octagonal, then circular — but as I traverse the narrow mole that connects the tiny island the lighthouse occupies to larger Pharos, I see hieroglyphs carved into the limestone blocks. Rather than Poseidon crowning the apex, a statue of Lord Amun-Ra presides, his tall plumes reaching toward heaven.

I climb the many steps of the lighthouse, though it is nearly like fly-ing. No sooner do my feet touch a step than am I lifted as if by the wind to the next. When I reach the summit, I enter the cupola where my Lord stands in the glow of the firelight.

"Is all of this for me, my Lord?"

His eyes spark like lightning and his voice rumbles like thunder through my bones. "Nothing is too grand for the Queen of Egypt."

I walk closer to the fire that burns through the night to guide way-ward sailors. Lord Set's golden scars catch the light, and I am pulled to-wards their faint outline against his dark skin that bleeds into the color of the sky around him. I reach out and graze the trail of one that cuts across his clavicle with my fingers.

"I am just one of several Queens of Egypt this year," I say, the contact of my fingers on his smooth skin making the edges of my voice husky. There is a stormy static hanging in the air around us that seems to seep into my blood with a little thrill of pleasure. It makes me restless, but I cannot say it is unwelcome.

"I am one of a hundred gods," he answers in a tone of intensity I have not heard from him before. I suspect it is closer to his god-voice and its timbre makes my knees buzz. "It does not mean that all are equal."

I cannot suppress a smile now from his words or his attention. "My Lord is always the epitome of humility."

"I think we have both earned a little pride, Beloved," he replies with his sharp white grin.

He takes me in his arms and a flood of contentment overtakes my body. There is a languorous, heavy feeling in my limbs, as though he is running his hands all over me without moving them. And yet, I cannot break away completely. Minute needles of anxiety prick at my brain and I know he can sense them. He waits quietly for me to speak.

"I do not know if I can complete the great task the gods have placed before me," I say softly. "Soon the winds from the north will bring more legions to our shores. Already the sure-sighted fishermen of Alexandria struggle to gain time against the advent of the admirals of Rome."

Lord Set runs a palm down my back, sending a loose shiver down to the soles of my feet. "Remember, this is not a war about winning and losing, *nedjet.*"

I look up at him in confusion. "And I still do not understand. You told me this land would be nothing but ashes if I failed."

"No, I said that would come to pass if you did not defend this land. You are its defender, the people hail your name and call you Queen of Egypt. If the wolves from the north get their little victory, that will not change."

"So my worries and preparation are meaningless?"

"Never, Beloved," he says firmly. "We all need you because there must always be a link between heaven and earth. In ordinary times, priests and pharaohs can create this pathway, as my grandfather Shu bridges the divide between my parents even as he keeps them apart. In the times of great change, individuals of stronger mettle are needed to guide our people and keep the ways of this land burning."

He gestures at the lighthouse fire. "Just as this fire burns when the night makes mirrors useless, Egypt must be reminded to remain itself even in chains." He places the flat of his hand against my heart, and his deep voice runs smoothly as water over river stones.

He whispers a piece of an old Egyptian love song in my ear before his mouth finds mine:

I come to the river, its surface shining like jewels
Looking for she who lives in all my thoughts
I see her walking between the reeds,
Her eyes like Sopdet and her endless smiles
She of the slender waist and dancing feet!
She and the river are bright shining, their light
An endless song of joy
Lucky was the year in which we met,
Golden is the hour of our meeting

After a time, I wake up.

Ascetics, prophets, and philosophers have debated for centuries on how we bound to the earth can experience communion with the gods. It has been in fashion for such contact to find all forms of physical and spiritual connection at some time or another. The Jewish slave-prince Moyses may have spoken to Yahweh in a bush of fire and Leda may indeed have loved Zeus as a swan. Perhaps they felt these things in dreams like mine. How thin is the firmament of the divine!

I did not unite with my Lord in this dream in the manner of men and women, and I have spent much of my life trying to articulate what did transpire between us, but despite the many languages I command, I struggle with the words.

The closest I have come is what I told Mudjet the following morning when she awoke next to me, my body drenched in sweat and bleeding. That Set's *ka*, if the gods can be counted on having souls, entered my body and held my own insignificant *ka* in its hands. That we stood together in a place beyond light and time, and glimpsed what it meant to be the other. And when it was over, we could never be wholly separate again. A tiny sliver of him was lodged in me and something of me in him. That I knew even if he vanished from my dreams forever, I would still feel him in the center of myself. Through the love of my people and the love the gods, I was given this transcendent mantle.

I have spent all of my life endeavoring to live up to that breathtaking responsibility.

Chapter Nineteen

"Do you think the you are part goddess now, my lady?" asked Mudjet as she gently sponged the blood from my skin. I felt like I was enveloped in a liquid ache that pulsed from my center. She had set up the small bathing tub behind a reed screen, and we continued to talk of my latest dream as we worked to clean away its physical manifestations.

"I do not think so, at least not in the way you imply. The part of Set in my *ka*, it is divine, but I am still otherwise as I have always been. Though maybe my eyes will be opened wider than they would be by my own endeavors."

"Well, that makes me glad," she said decisively, squeezing out the sponge over a shallow bowl at her side.

"Oh?"

"I do not want to be some priestess chained to a goddess." Mudjet gave a wicked laugh. "How boring that would be!"

"When we are in the thick of this business with a war on Rome in our hands, we shall see if you do not repent of your impiety," I shot back, splashing a little water from the tub on her.

She let out a squeak and splashed me back. "If the gods decide this fight on piety alone, my lady, we shall be at this longer than the Greeks and Trojans!"

Suddenly Tahu's voice came from the entrance to the tent. "My Queen, the general is looking for you. Emissaries from the palace have arrived to negotiate with us."

"I am coming," I answered as Mudjet helped me step into a clean *chiton*. I hurriedly arranged the *himation* and moved from behind the screen to meet my lieutenant. "Are they from my brother?" I asked as I adjusted the seat of the vulture crown on my head and we left in the direction of Achillas' quarters.

"No, my lady. They are lords sent by Caesar." He paused. "Presumably they come to talk sense into us all."

"I do not know what they mean to accomplish by that. Do you know who the lords are?"

"I believe it is Lord Dioscorides and Lord Serapion."

Internally, I groaned. I was not against the idea of some negotiation to end all of this and if there was a settlement to be reached, a man of Caesar's acumen would be the one to find it. But surely there were no two lords less likely to bring about a peace to satisfy all of us than Dioscorides and Serapion. I understood that they had been chosen because they would not defect to our camp as perhaps men like Lucius Septimus or Theodotus might, and they were not my sister's minions like Origenes or some of the lesser nobles, yet I knew the contempt Achillas held for them. He thought they had been weak in my father's service and had not improved with age.

Aloud I remarked, "My sister must not be truly interested in a truce if she sends these two as her diplomats."

"I confess, my lady, I do not hold out much hope for these talks. I do not believe either side is willing to compromise their position enough to make a contract."

I sighed, looking about the camp and beyond to the city. "I would rather have peace than bloodshed if it would save the lives of my people, though I do not think anyone else in the royal family shares my views."

"What of Prince Ptolemy?" asked Tahu.

It had been so many years since anyone in my life had referred to my youngest brother by his given name that for the briefest of moments, I did not understand Tahu's question. "Oh, well, Ptah wishes me to do my duty and force the legion from our shores so he would not support an agreement that would allow Caesar or his men to remain in Egypt for any reason." I smiled, slightly sad. "He is the kindest of us all, but he still has a prince's pride in his kingdom."

"I think there is a similarity of purpose on both sides, my lady. It is just that the parties involved are mismatched in the alignment of that purpose and that is why we are in this untenable position. We have two queens and two generals: your sister wants a war and her general wishes to make a treaty; you look for a treaty while your general has not the slightest interest in a compromise. It is most unfortunate for Egypt that my lady and Caesar cannot meet face to face."

"It is probably for the best. The last time that happened, I did not find myself much of a counterpart for the Consul," I admitted despondently. "I am not as cunning as he is."

He looked at me thoughtfully. "Not yet, but I feel that day is coming, my lady. Already today I was thinking of how each time I meet you, you seem to grow in stature in my eyes and in the eyes of our people. This day is no different."

"That is kind, Tahu. I will try to live up to your version of myself."

He nodded, satisfied, and we walked in silence for a few minutes. As the command tents came into view, he spoke up again. "Do all in truth call the little prince 'Ptah,' my lady?"

"All of us in the palace do. It started out as a joke about him as a swaddling babe, but in a house with two boys of the same name it became helpful to have a way to distinguish them conversationally outside of royal titles."

Tahu grinned. "Ever does the old Egypt seep through the cracks of the Macedonian overlords of this land. May the old gods smile on us through you and your brother, my Queen."

Achillas, Ganymedes, and a contingent of Greek commanders were waiting for us, along with Quintus and a handful of the Gabiniani leaders. As we reached them, Quintus fell in at my side. Dioscorides and Serapion had come with only a single guard each, presumably as a gesture of goodwill. Both bowed at my approach.

"Greetings in the name of the Queen of Egypt, Your Highness," wheezed Dioscorides through his remaining teeth.

Achillas gave a snort of amusement. "She still thinks she is, my lord? Perhaps she has not heard the shouts of the Alexandrians hailing Lady Arsinoë as queen."

"You wear a crown, my lady," noted Serapion, his gaze weaving up to my head, "yet you have not been crowned by the ceremonies of your fathers. You must therefore bend before your sister's superior claim."

"My brother is pharaoh by your own oaths, my lords," I answered firmly. "He has declared my sister a traitor in bed with Rome and holds me out to our people as his representative and partner in this struggle." I gathered my resolve to speak my next thought. "When Rome has left our shores, I will take my place as co-ruler and queen at his side, and then we shall have the formalities that you mention. As of this hour, I have not the time for them."

Dioscorides shook his head fitfully. "You are too prideful, Princess. This conflict will bring destruction to this kingdom and to the house of your bloodline. Stop this now before it goes any further."

"You have always been a quick-witted child," said Serapion carefully. "Surely you can do more to help the reign of your royal siblings through diplomacy than war.

I looked at the lords, surprised. "You still believe my brother and sister can rule as one?"

"Why not?" asked Serapion. "You are all mere children. I know these disagreements seem very present now, but all will be forgotten with a month or two of stability."

I continued to stare at him in disbelief, as did all the men around me, as Dioscorides joined in. "His Excellency, the Consul, thinks as we do. That is why he has sent us, to help mend the breach."

"Does the Consul believe that I am the warmonger here?" I asked, frowning in annoyance.

"No, my lady," Dioscorides soothed. "He thinks you serve your lord brother most faithfully, but he and we need you help to convince the Pharaoh to stop this revolt against your lady sister. To restore the balance your wise lord father created in his foresight."

I was at a loss for words. Did these old men not see the damage my father had done by naming joint heirs, a decision they unironically praised as wisdom? I could not believe that a man as clever as Caesar thought reconciliation was still possible... Perhaps he was using these lords to test the strength of the resistance.

Yes, I thought to myself, that made much more sense. He had so few men at hand, he could not risk simply throwing the bulk of them at us if we would stand our ground. Of course, if Dioscorides and Serapion found us willing to negotiate, so much the better, but I doubted he expected that outcome.

Dioscorides interrupted my musings gently in his wavering voice. "Please, my lady. Be a good girl and come home to us."

"It does not suit to see a girl engaged in such mannish pursuits as these," added Serapion distastefully. "It will bring dishonor on your brother to help him in this way. The people will hold it against him."

Bring dishonor to him among the Greek nobility, they mean. The Macedonians had fixed ideas about the roles well-born women should play in war. Goddesses may hold a spear, but ladies should sit at home by the hearth and weep until the men returned covered in glory. I did not want war any more than they professed to. The difference was that I was sure that there was no avoiding it.

I looked at Achillas and my teacher, both of whom were dressed in frowns.

"I am sorry, sirs, I serve at the request of His Majesty and you come from his enemies in this argument. I cannot stand down without Ptolemy's consent."

The lords' mouths turned down in surprised displeasure. They had clearly not expected such obstinacy from the youngest princess. "Come now, my lady!" scoffed Serapion. "Caesar is not a man to be trifled with. Refuse him now, and he will not easily incline his favor to you again."

I felt Achillas near me, taut as a tight rope and was afraid he had been waiting for some kind of challenging pronouncement from the delegation. This threat of Caesar's wrath, vague as it was, proved enough for him.

Drawing his sword, he glowered. "Vermin! You dare to threaten a lady of the blood royal with the jackal from Rome! If you are such loyal servants of his, you can deliver this message to him!"

They stared at him blankly, and their escorts drew their swords uncertainly. "What message is that, Achillas?" puffed Dioscorides, his mouth growing slack in confusion.

I suddenly understood. "Achillas! No!" I cried out, but it was too late.

He grinned coldly. Taking one step forward, he raised his sword and cut off Dioscorides' head.

"Why, that message, my lord," he said casually.

Serapion screamed and turned to the palace guards for protection, but two of the Greek captains had already run them through. He fell to his knees and crawled to my feet. "Princess! Save me!" he begged, as sweat and tears ran down his face.

"That is enough, General," I said to Achillas. "I think Caesar will understand our position."

"Forgive the impertinence, Your Highness," he responded regretfully as he reached down to grasp the terrified lord by his sparse hair. "But in this I must override you." With that, he grabbed his dagger and sliced through Serapion's throat.

"General! How dare you disobey Her Highness' orders!" my teacher roared at the Greek.

Achillas let go of Serapion's corpse and took off the sash tied about his waist to wipe his hands. As he tidied himself, he turned back to me, his blue eyes full of solicitude.

"My Queen, as I said a moment ago, I deeply regret going against your wishes. I did so because I believe to have not done so would put you in grave personal danger." He motioned to two of his men. "Take the bodies back to the palace. Let us have no more of these feints at peace."

I spent the first several weeks learning everything I could about our men and our defenses. Witty Quintus Fabianus remained a patient instructor, and in fact, rather seemed to enjoy explaining the formations and machinations of our army.

"You must have trained men in these matters before, sir. You are an able teacher," I said to him as I was examining a large catapult the men were building from a Roman blueprint.

"I have a knack for instruction, Your Highness, if I say so myself. I've always enjoyed taking young recruits and teaching them the arts and comradeship of fighting together. Though I also must say I am rarely offered the opportunity to teach such a quick pupil."

I leaned around the catapult and grinned. "Beware, Quintus, or you will quite turn my head with such flattery."

He held up his hand and laughed. "I swear it to be true, my lady!" he protested before lowering his voice. "Indeed I think it is our loss that you were not born a man, so that none would challenge your control of our army."

"We can only be who we are," I answered gently. "The gods must have a reason for all of this, even the absurdity of a princess trying to lead a military operation while her brother the prince is trapped in the palace like a maiden in a story."

"Ah, well, we Romans were always taught that you Egyptians do everything backwards," replied Quintus with a wicked grin.

"Indeed if we wish to stay a step ahead of Caesar, we might have to learn how to walk on our hands," I agreed as we returned our attention back to the builders.

With each passing day, the battle lines in the city grew more entrenched, our army working diligently to hem in that of my sister and her general as close to the palace grounds as possible. Ptolemy remained trapped there with them, though he sent daily messages to the camp to be read aloud to the men.

The style of the writing and the jagged penmanship left no doubt as to the veracity of the author, and therein lay the problem. For even Achillas had to admit these were not the polished missives of a Pompey or a Cicero. My brother veered wildly between gruesome threats towards Cleopatra and angry whining about Rome's unfairness. He would insult Caesar's manhood in one sentence and exhort the city to prove he was a friend to Rome in the next. He would boast about leading our people into battle like Alexander reborn before begging his army to come release him from the palace. And these were the missives I was expected to read to the army, to the city.

I did not trust Achillas to advise me honestly and yet even he agreed with the other officers that no good would come of me doing such a ridiculous thing. The Gabiniani were the first to suggest that I should continue to use my own words with our people since they had already been received so favorably. Achillas was forced to concede the wisdom in this, and I shared a grateful glance with Quintus Fabianus who was clearly my champion among his brother legionaries.

Yet I attempted to incorporate my brother's thoughts into what I said because I wanted to keep my promise to help him, despite knowing he would not have done so for me. All the while, I pretended not to see the private letters he sent for his general's eyes only. Ganymedes was less polite about the situation, leading to several heated confrontations with Achillas, but the latter remained close-fisted about what he and the pharaoh discussed. I saw no other option but to accept it and watch around corners when I was with Achillas.

"Too many more of these, and I might begin to feeling sorry for Cleopatra," I said in frustration on one of these occasions, tossing the latest letter across the table angrily as I sat with Achillas and my tutor. We had been running through supplies lists when the messenger from Ptolemy arrived.

"I never thought His Majesty had much creativity, though the threats he paints with his words prove me incorrect," noted Mudjet, who had been reading over my shoulder while she mended a tear in my *himation*.

Achillas failed to hide his amusement at her barb. "He is frustrated with his position, Mudjet. Have some pity."

"That is a dangerous road," I said warningly to the general as much to Mudjet. "He would have no pity for her or me." I picked up the letter again and reread it. "He threatens her with so much, I am surprised he does not wish you to send assassins and be done with it."

Ganymedes frowned. "Perhaps he is afraid of retaliation from Caesar as long as he is stuck in the palace."

Achillas scribbled something on a loose piece of papyrus. "He is afraid of killing the heir," he said vaguely, lost in the columns of numbers before him. Starting guiltily out of his cloud, he looked up at all of us, stricken. "I mean, His Majesty knows you would not approve of such a ruthless tactic. Even against Cleopatra."

I was at a loss as for why Achillas appeared so upset as to have spoken thusly before us. Surely he knew we were not in a position to stop him if my brother truly wished to kill our sister. And it would be almost refreshing to hear that even Ptolemy might have enough of a heart to forestall the murder our pregnant sister in cold blood. Certainly Achillas' rejoinder about me not approving was not incorrect. We were at war, yet surely we could not devolve into beasts because of it. Then it struck me. Achillas had called the baby the *heir*.

I looked at him, dumbstruck. "Achillas," I said quietly, weighing my words, "does Ptolemy think it is possible our sister's child is his?"

We sat in an uncomfortable silence no one else seemed willing to break. At length, the general replied, his frame sagging slightly, "It is unlikely, Your Highness. But not impossible."

Mudjet's eyes widened as she put a hand to her mouth. I glanced at Ganymedes. "Did the eunuchs know of this?"

He shook his head. "I did not hear it spoken of. Everyone knew Pothinus feared that if the king grew old enough, your lady sister might succeed in trapping him with her charms. That's why he hated her so much, he was afraid she would manage to supplant his place in your brother's council through seduction."

I studied my mother's bracelet. "Their consanguinity does not shock me overly, despite their relation being even closer than usual. We are Ptolemies, after all. They are hardly the first full siblings to come together in such a way in this land. I am simply surprised that either of them could put aside their enmity for even one night of congress. It has been a long time since they have not been enemies."

"His Majesty claims it only happened once or twice," admitted Achillas in a subdued voice. "He says she drugged him."

"That is neither here nor there," said Ganymedes. "Why does the pharaoh not tell this to Caesar? He might not cleave to Cleopatra if he does not think the child she carries is his."

"It explains how she managed to get with child so handily. Caesar has precious few children to show for all of his supposed conquests, but the Ptolemies have always been fertile," said Mudjet.

"Careful, my sweet," I chided. "We have no proof either way. The child may very well be the Consul's."

"That is the reason he cannot tell Caesar," cut in Achillas. "He has no proof."

"But there is doubt!" said Ganymedes.

"Doubt enough?" countered the general. "What grown man, especially one with the alleged prowess of Caesar will believe that a beardless boy impregnated a woman he slept with only a few times when the man has the same woman in his bed every night?"

"I think they have been too busy to be together that much," observed my teacher.

"Well, a skulking eunuch would know!" shot back Achillas. I gave them both a look and the general's anger deflated quickly. "It is simply," he began, addressing me, "I think His Majesty is also ashamed. The marriage customs of this kingdom are not understood by outsiders, especially the prudish Romans. He still needs an alliance with Rome and he will need Caesar's help for that."

"So much for the cutthroat boy pharaoh of our letters," scoffed Ganymedes.

I made a dismissive gesture. "It does not matter. I do not approve of assassinating my sister, and I too have doubts that Caesar will believe our allegations, as they come from the Queen's enemies. Let us not speak of this for now."

We returned to an uneasy silence, all of us occupied by our own thoughts. My own centered on the tiny being floating on the turbulent waters of my sister's womb, my heart full of pity for the unsuspecting little lamb, who knew not the family it was to be born into yet. Or was this a *heka*-grown child, full of knowingness and power? For one must always be wary when another Ptolemy appears on the horizon.

Chapter Twenty

Our focus remained upon the island of Pharos, and many of our schemes centered around how we might steal it back from our foes. I sent Tahu on my behalf to recruit more troops. While my brave people answered my call as best they could, I was unsure if these extra farmers and artisans could shatter the professional lines of the Caesar's legion.

Achillas and I surveyed the extra troops we had managed to add to the forces holding the Heptastadion, the long stone bridge that bound Pharos to the mainland.

"The eastern lines could spare no more, Your Highness," he said, frowning.

"It may be enough," I answered uncertainly. "We have to try. The longer we wait, the more likely Caesar is to reinforce his position. We probably only have a day or two before he notices we pulled some of our men in the east away and then we will be vulnerable to a shock attack there."

"He is already spread thin, maybe he can't do anything about it even if he knows. I can send recruiters down the river to press more farmers into our ranks. I don't want to lose a lot of men in an abortive attack."

"How long would that take?"

"At least a week," he admitted.

I pondered this. I was loath to wait so long to advance, though I agreed with Achillas that it might be equally risky to attack prematurely and suffer major casualties. I looked out towards the sea. "I worry about waiting when we don't know how long it will be until Caesar receives reenforcements. His legion in west Africa is not far enough away for my comfort."

"But it is tied up with Pompey's remaining troops in Numidia, my lady." He gives me a crooked grin. "Remember, the Roman war didn't end simply because I cut off the old fool's head."

I bit my lip, pushing the memory of that awful day from my mind. It reminded me too much that I was now locked in an alliance with the very people who had threatened to dismember me in the desert. "I don't like to leave our security to the responsibility of a leaderless enemy army."

"No, of course not," agreed Achillas. "But we are not friendless in the Republican camp. The Gabiniani have heard from their comrades abroad that the Senate has sent Cato to hold Africa against the rebel legion and you know he'd rather die than surrender a blade of grass to Caesar. Plus, Pompey's youngest son, Sextus, prowls the sea west of Egypt causing all sorts of trouble for Caesar's men as they attempt to reach him. They've started calling the boy 'Neptune' for his unnatural ease as an admiral!"

Lucky for us, but how long can we rely on the unintended aid of our foes? I lost myself in these thoughts until I felt a hand on my arm.

"My lady," said Mudjet, pointing behind us to the south. "Look."

Out of the desert came several dozen columns of men. At their head were a handful of Egyptian men, some on camels, some on horses. They stopped in front of us and dismounted. Standing before us, their posture was impeccable and their bearings proud. Something about them suggested a time long ago, a mysterious region the Greek Ptolemies had brushed only the surface of. These were no peasants and farmers.

"Who are you? Do you come to aid the forces of Ptolemy Theo Philopator or shall we round you up as Rome-lovers?" Achillas barked at them, yet they paid him no mind.

I blinked at them in astonishment, suddenly grasping who they were. "They are the Lost Lords, General."

The Egyptian nobles who had helped to rally the kingdom to my father's cause during his exile had been paid back in false coin by him. He had grudgingly accepted the Egyptian wife they had forced upon him, but he refused to elevate their status when he regained his throne. He had executed a few families to reassert his dominance over them, including all of my mother's relations, and many had fled abroad with what little remained of their wealth, most to the south where they held property. Those few who remained in Egypt when the dust had settled retreated from court never to return, supposedly living in retirement in scattered towns, choosing to preserve their ancient bloodlines rather than destroy themselves trying to gain political ascendancy again. The Alexandrians had called them and their dead comrades the Lost Lords from the moment they left.

The oldest of them smiled at my words. "One cannot lose what was never lost, my Queen." He bowed. "I am Ehoou-hanif, son of Tsillumes. I have left the desert not to fight for the honor of the Greek King, but for the honor of the noble granddaughter of Sesupti, the companion of my boyhood."

I felt my chest constrict with emotion. "I never knew his name," I managed to whisper finally.

"He was a great man, my lady. A man who loved this land so much he gave his favorite child over to a bitter man like your father so that your half-sister might not rule us to the ruin of all."

"I am Amenei, son of Kemes," spoke another younger lord, his sandy-colored eyes sitting deeply in features that were reminiscent of an overeager hound's. "We dance with gladness to see you wear the vulture crown, Your Highness. We have brought as many men as could be immediately spared to aid you."

"We will do what we can to rally any reluctant Egyptians to your side," said a third lord.

"We are few in number and we know we might sever our Houses into the *Duat*, my lady," broke in a fourth. "But we would shame our ancestors if we did not do what we could for the true Queen of Egypt."

I looked to those who had spoken and the others standing by their mounts. "My lords, you are welcome here. This is General Achillas, who is my commander under me and my brother. Those of you able to fight, he will look to you to help him organize my Egyptian troops. We aim to seize back Pharos from the iron core of the legion, and we will need whatever aid you can give. Those of you who are older," I paused to nod respectfully to Lord Ehoou-hanif and several of the others, "I need your help just as dearly. I need you to assist me with the non-combatants. Listen to their problems so that I might hear them, help them understand what we are fighting for. I also need your connections with our southern towns for supply access. Are you willing to aid me, lords of Egypt?"

"It is done, *heqat-taui*!" they said with one voice as they gathered their forces and rode past us into the camp.

Achillas frowned. "I am uneasy about this, Your Highness. These men are an unknown quantity."

"We need fighting men. The Lost Lords will be better recruiters for us in the farther cities and towns. They will be able to keep us supplied with corn as well. I am sorry they are not Greek enough for you."

"That's not what I meant, Your Highness!" he replied hurriedly. "I mean their loyalty is suspect, can we rely on them?"

"You mean their loyalty to my brother is suspect. I agree, but they are loyal to my mother's memory. I will see that they do their duty."

"But what if something — gods forbid — should happen to you, my lady?"

I gave him a piercing look. "Then I suppose you should make sure nothing happens to me, sir."

I find myself on the shores of Lake Mareotis, its waters placid and a pale jade color against a flat horizon that by a trick of the light, appears to be a blushing violet hue. I look for some sign from my Lord or perhaps Sekhmet, but there is only me, the lake, and the strange sky.

I glance down at my right foot as a persistent itch in the arch sends a branching ticklish sensation up my leg. The feeling fills me with an overwhelming desire to step into the lake. Unable to resist, I no sooner place my foot on the surface of the water, preparing to step down, when the top of the lake solidifies and instead of wading into the water, I step aboard a large seafaring ship. The planks of the hull and the keel fold themselves into place around me, the prow sprouting like a fern as the sails stitch themselves up and unfurl majestically. They are beginning to invisibly ink a design on the white canvas when my Lord materializes at the helm and walks over to me.

"Most impressive," I say to him with a little laughter in my eyes.

"Oh, that is not my doing. Blame my lord there." He gestures at a figure that has dexterously materialized to my left. The man holds aloft his finger as he traces in the air the picture forming on the sail, his hooded cloak formed from a menacing Nile crocodile, with the front legs draped over his shoulders hanging down his chest. Despite this fierce clothing, when he turns to face me his expression is inviting. His face is rough and craggy, yet even that jagged exterior could not disguise his divinity.

I incline my head. "Sobek."

He grins with all of his long, pointed teeth. "Ptolemy-daughter."

He finishes his drawing on the sail with a little flourish, which is revealed to be a picture of the *sha* and a crocodile playing *senet*.

"Surprisingly, Sobek has always had a healthy sense of humor," observes my Lord, his emerald eyes sparkling.

"Naturally I do," replies the other god, lord of crocodiles and naval matters, mirth brimming in his own lime-colored eyes. "Why do you think crocodiles smile all the time?"

Set chuckles, then composes himself. "In seriousness, *nedjet*, we are here to teach of watercraft and such."

"I have lived in an aqueous kingdom nearly every hour of my life," I comment, unimpressed. "I do understand boats."

"Ah, but you must know ships of war in these dark times, little princess," says Sobek. He waves a hand at a rope line so that it shifts its position to another more of his liking. "We are going to make you an admiral."

He cups his hands around his mouth and blows air up at the sails that fill with wind. With another wave of his hand towards the prow, the ship springs forward out into the lake. The rows of oars work themselves as we pull away from the shore.

"Well, I already know that my lord has constructed a *quadrireme* for us," I say, placing a hand upon the rail. "They are the flagships of our navy."

Sobek grins again. "Indeed. Very good, Ptolemy-daughter. While not impenetrable, their thicker hulls are good protection from enemy bombardment."

"The trade-off is they are inevitably slower in their maneuverability," remarks my Lord as he too passes his hand over the railing. He looks up at me with a playful expression, and as quick as a flash, he grabs me by the wrist and jumps into the water.

But we do not land beneath the lake, for once more a craft appears beneath our feet. The ship that builds itself below us is smaller than the one we left Sobek in, his hands resting on his hips.

My Lord makes a throwing gesture at the sail of this boat and a picture of him perched on Lord Ra's ship of the sun, spearing the demon Apep, appears in red ink. Wind fills the sail, and we are propelled further out at an even quicker pace than the one we had achieved in the *quadrireme,* in spite of the smaller number of oars present.

"This is the *hemiolia,* Beloved. A warship of such speed and maneuverability that it is the favorite of pirates and raiders all across the Great Sea."

He reaches for the lines and pulls the sail so that it is angled to drift us back towards Sobek, who I can see is adjusting his own trajectory accordingly. We easily reach the *quadrireme* before it has made anything approaching our progress. The Lord of the Pointed Teeth leaps aboard our vessel in an easy, elegant vault over the railing.

"Usually it is considered customary for the hemioliateers to do the boarding," says Set wryly.

"But this is the Dream World, He Who Burns the Sands," answers Sobek. "One must expect the inversion of one's expectations." He returns his attention to me. "The navy of the Black Land has some of these, though not a terribly large number of them because the pharaohs have been wary of their thinner hulls. The important thing for you to know, Ptolemy-daughter, is that the wolves of Latium are fond of these ships inasmuch as such a land-loving people can be. They use them often, especially to transport their soldiers."

"So my lord is saying our time before Caesar receives his reinforcements may be even shorter than I anticipate."

He nods. "It bears considering. If they can outrun the blockade ships of the Pompey-son."

I look back over my shoulder at the *quadrireme* and sigh. "Then we do not have very much time to build such large warships, even if we could procure the materials."

"Perhaps you could, though you would have few vessels at your disposal."

I shake my head. "Our strength continues to be numbers, thus must it be also on the water. However, like my forebearers, I am hesitant to rely solely on the *hemiolias* to fend off men who have much more experience with them than I do."

My Lord steps in and places his hand on my shoulder. "There might be another way." He glances to his left and a third ship appears alongside us. It extends a plank of wood to the *hemiolia,* and the three of us walk across it to the other side. Here the sail that unfurls is marked by a picture of Hapy, the androgynous Nile god, clutching a flail in one hand and holding up the other in a posture of forbearance towards a rearing wolf.

"This is a *trihemiolia,*" says Sobek. "It is larger than a *hemiolia,* so not quite as fast, yet it is much quicker than a *quadrireme.* The navies of our land have found them quite useful in the past."

I lean over the side to touch the hull, giving it a knock. "A thicker base?"

"Yes, that is where most of the extra weight is concentrated."

I pull myself back up and hold onto the rail, thinking. "I should like to have many of this vessel, though I still do not know if we shall be able to get timber thick enough to make that practical."

My Lord ponders this, too. "I believe that is the correct course, though, Beloved. Build as many of these as you are able, with *hemiolias* in support made of timber that is not sturdy enough for *trihemiolias.*"

"What of *quadriremes?*" I ask.

Sobek frowns. "I do not think you have enough time to make them your focus. Though it might be beneficial to have several to build a fleet around, more than that might be an extravagance you cannot afford."

"I thank my lord for his wisdom."

"Oh, I am not wise, Ptolemy-daughter," he replies with a laugh. "I am just thick-skinned. I have seen a great deal."

And then I wake up.

Chapter Twenty-One

Mudjet was brushing my hair a few mornings hence when Quintus Fabianus came to my tent, his helmet tucked under his arm.

"Good morning, sir," I said to him, swiveling about to give him a smile. "You are about early, what news is there in camp?"

"Conditions in camp and in the city proper remain much as they have been, Your Highness. I come to inform you that the general is having a staff meeting to discuss our strategy moving forward now that we have planted ourselves firmly against whatever pushback the legion can offer."

"Has the general requested my attendance?"

Quintus hesitated a beat. "He says that you are of course welcome to attend, though if you would rather not, he completely understands and would be happy to outline the proceedings at your later convenience."

I raised my eyebrows slightly. "I am sure he would. Though I think I can find the time to attend this meeting myself." I turned to Mudjet. "Do you think we can be spared from our womanly duties, my sweet?"

"Oh dear my lady, it will be a great trial, but we shall have to take a break from admiring your finery and elegantly napping to actually attend to the business of the war we are in the middle of," she remarked with an exaggerated yawn.

The Gabiniani lieutenant laughed, relieved. "That is my spirited lady! I had hoped you would not be put off by Achillas' less than enthusiastic invitation."

"You need not worry about that, sir. I know Achillas and my brother hope I am nothing more than a poppet they can hold up as a symbol and place upon a shelf to sit quietly when they have no need of me. Ptolemy should know me better than that."

"Then if you'd be so good as to follow me, my lady, I will show you the way."

I rose up. "Mudjet, would you go find Tahu for me? I would like him with us also, and I suspect the commanders have neglected to extend him

196

notice of this meeting." My companion nodded and trotted off in the direction of the harbor barricades.

We crossed the camp as the sun began to climb its way over our heads, promising to make the day a hot one. I draped my *himation* over my head for shade. Our encampment was relatively empty, as most of our soldiers were along our front lines facing the palace or directing civilians who needed relocating as skirmish markers shifted, but the scattered few that remained near their tents saluted as we passed.

The thump of hoofbeats drew up along our side, and Tahu grinned down at us as Mudjet clung to his back. Quintus reached up and helped her dismount, as my Egyptian lieutenant slid off so he could walk along with us leading the horse.

"You made quick time," I said to Mudjet as she worked to pin my *himation* into place on the move.

"Well, Sir Tahu is always easy to find. One must simply look for a native telling a Greek what to do," she answered with a saucy toss of her head.

Tahu chuckled. "If the young Greek overlords would not go about things so stupidly, Lady Mudjet, I would gladly keep my mouth shut."

"I hope you didn't waste all your wit on those peons," added Quintus with an amused guffaw. "I want to hear you tell the commanders why you know best."

"Only if given leave by Her Majesty," said Tahu, his eyes twinkling at me.

"Nonsense," I said to him. "I want all of my officers to speak freely, not just Achillas and whomever has his ear. If you both remain silent, I shall have to fight alone."

We passed by the soldiers stationed outside the tent into the close heat of the interior, where I could already hear Achillas and Ganymedes arguing about something or another.

"The palace is designed not to be taken! You waste our time and manpower trying to do so!" fumed my teacher angrily.

"Excuse me, Ganymedes, perhaps you forget I am captain of the guard. I am well aware of the defenses of the palace!" growled Achillas in return. "And I have experience with the outer walls and gates, not just with the perfumed eunuchs' quarters!"

The other officers stood awkwardly around my two sniping commanders, until one of the Gabiniani legionaries left in charge by Aulus Gabinius saw our entrance. "Hail, Arsinoë Philoaígyptos!" he said a touch too loudly, in order to drown out the raised voices.

Everyone else turned in the direction of his salutation as the Greeks bowed and the Gabiniani present placed a fist over their chests. My teacher immediately abandoned his discussion with the general and stepped over to take my hands. "May the gods shine their faces on you this day, my lady," he greeted me in a gentle voice completely divorced from the one he had been using to address Achillas.

For his part, Achillas quickly moved to Ganymedes' side and took a knee before me. "Hail, Your Highness. We are pleased to have you among us," he said gallantly.

"Please rise, sir. You need not stand on such ceremony," I answered him.

Achillas stood up apologetically. "Your Highness must forgive the early hour of this meeting, but we have much to organize."

"It is well, I had already risen. Though I fear I am tardy as it would seem conversation has begun without me."

The general had the good sense to appear abashed. "We beg your ladyship's forgiveness for that as well." He paused to glance at Ganymedes. "We are all most passionate about our cause."

I waved my hand. "Wise men may disagree about a great many things, sirs, but we must not allow such disagreements to hinder us. No doubt the Queen and her general rely on the impolitic tongues of Alexandria to undo our work. Let us not give them such satisfaction."

There was a chorus of good-natured assent by the company and we settled into a circle around the main table for a more formal dialogue. Quintus escorted me to one of the waiting couches as I beckoned Mudjet to take a seat beside me and my two lieutenants stood flanking us.

Achillas took the floor. "Would my lady allow me to update her on the positioning of our army?" he asked.

His polite tone seemed impeccable, though its smoothness was worrying to me. Whenever he spoke to me thusly, he did not speak as one general to another. Rather, it was the sweet tone one used to humor a child, and its sugar felt gritty in my ear. Achillas respected me always as a princess of the blood, which is more than could be said for the many that no doubt held my Egyptian ancestors against me, but he did not respect me as a leader. If I was to protect myself from him or my brother, I would have to labor to change that, if that were even possible.

However, I would not accomplish such a thing by throwing a tantrum here over a perceived slight of tone. "Please do, sir. I am most anxious for such news."

He nodded and proceeded. "We continue to hold most of the city in our control, my lady. Caesar and Cleopatra hold the palace along with a few veins of commerce in the Jewish quarter that stretch into the eastern cemeteries and beyond towards Canopus. They also hold the royal harbor inlet, though we control the rest of the coast and they have only a handful of seaworthy ships docked there. Caesar's garrison on Pharos is our nearest problem, though they are hemmed in on the Lighthouse island and the northern half of Pharos itself."

"How much of the island is under our control?"

"We currently hold the southern shore to just past the Heptastadion, as well as the southwestern tip of the island to the Temple of Poseidon. So our inner docks are secure."

"Have they been hindering vessels entering the harbor through their control of the lighthouse?"

"No, my lady. The Romans know how deeply unpopular they are in the city at large and they cannot risk alienating the merchant classes by closing trade access."

"This means we should not have difficulty securing supplies for the foreseeable future, my lady," added Ganymedes.

I held out my hand for the map of the city lying on the table, and Quintus delivered it to me. I studied it for a moment. "It seems to me that we should endeavor to sever the palace from its remaining supply lines in the east. They will be well stocked, so the results will not be immediate, though it may prevent them from regaining a fleet with which to challenge us."

"We are working towards this very goal, Your Highness," answered Achillas. "Your Jewish subjects are more kindly disposed to Rome than most Alexandrians so they block some of our progress."

"Though you mean they are willing to supply the palace, not that they are fighting alongside the legion, correct?"

"Yes, my lady."

"That is because their district is on the doorstep of the palace and they fear the swiftest retribution from my sister if they are as recalcitrant. You all must be cognizant of this as you fight in that quarter. I demand that you deal with my subjects there fairly and see as little harm comes to them as possible. They are in a difficult position, and they are not our enemy, is that understood? They will be even less likely to aid us if we are cruel to them."

There was a murmur of assent from the assembly. "Do we still hold the Heptastadion firmly?" I asked one of the Gabiniani on my right.

"Yes, my lady," he replied, reaching over to trace our movements and those of our enemies on the map in my hands. "The legion has no access to the city from the great causeway. To reach their forces stationed on the northern end of Pharos and the lighthouse, they must sail into the outer harbor in a large arc to avoid us."

"This is good. I believe we should focus our greater energy on taking Pharos back from the garrison rather than taking the palace at this juncture."

Ganymedes smirked in triumph as Achillas looked taken aback. "But my lady, your lord brother is trapped in the palace! Surely we must retrieve him as soon as possible."

I shook my head. "Ptolemy is fine where he is. Caesar would not dare to harm him and will not allow my sister to do so. Assassination is not his way. The palace ironically might be the safest place for the pharaoh; if he were here with us, he would be in much more danger. If we can wrest the island away from the enemy, we will have complete mastery of the harbor and we can form a complete blockade against any reinforcements Caesar can attempt to recall. Once we do this, then we can turn our attention to the palace."

"My lady," Achillas' voice was urgent, "you speak of fighting the hydra's tail when we need to cut off its heads. If we take the palace, we will take Cleopatra and her Roman dog. The legion will surrender without their general."

"But Caesar's best men are on Pharos," observed Quintus Fabianus. "We could cut what strength he has out from under him if we capture the island."

"He is Caesar! As long as he is at liberty, he will be able to summon allies to his side," Achillas argued.

"And there is no guarantee that the legion will capitulate even if we get our hands on him," pointed out Ganymedes, rallying his previous opposition.

"We won't know if we are too craven to try!" barked a young Greek captain.

I held up both hands. "Enough! I will not have this bickering! We must learn to disagree with one another civilly or the legion defeats us without taking the field." The officers all looked at me guiltily. With calm restored, I continued. "Now my Gabiniani, I wish to hear your opinion: if we were to capture Caesar, would Rome rise to save him?"

The men conferred with each other briefly before one of their centurions spoke. "It is difficult to say, Your Highness. The civil war has unsettled many of the old factions and alliances. The people are stout supporters of Caesar, and his retainers in Rome such as Marcus Antonius might be able to whip the Senate into deploying a rescue mission. However, many in the Senate do not trust Caesar or his intentions and might be grateful for an excuse to get rid of him. Cato the Younger is well respected in Rome and he detests Caesar; he might have the clout to rally other opponents while Caesar is away."

"The Senate could probably convince Marcus Cicero to join them. He will always speak against the dictatorship," added another officer and his brother soldiers made noises of agreement.

"What of his other legions? Would they abandon their fight with the Republican armies and fly to Egypt?"

"If they were able, it is likely, Your Highness," says the centurion. "But we are fortunate that we began our struggle when we did." He grins as he wipes the sweat from his brow. "We might burn, but in places other than Egypt, it is winter and the Great Sea is treacherous at this time of year. Sailing here will take time."

"Then it seems to me that it would be more decisive of us to gain control of the capital as opposed to worrying over whether we have Caesar in our thrall."

The Gabiniani considered this. "So it would seem, Your Highness," replied the first officer. "The remainder of the Roman army may or may not come to Caesar's defense were we to take him, and if Caesar were to escape Egypt, he may or may not return. There are arguably too many variables in that course to warrant our slavish devotion to the course of capturing the general."

Achillas huffed impatiently. "Very well, if that is the majority opinion we shall concentrate our efforts on Pharos and keep to holding those stationed at the palace, not mass an attack on the complex yet."

Looking to placate my general, I tried to be gracious in victory. "Sir, if an opportunity presents itself, we shall of course assault the palace and seek out the general and my sister. I only ask you not to attempt to force events in this."

He nodded, somewhat mollified. "As you wish, my lady."

Having gained this point, I felt I held enough confidence within the company to broach the subject of our naval resources. "Sirs, another matter I desired to speak with you of is the state of our fleet. I know our enemy has no navy of consequence at this time, but winter will not hold them back forever and Caesar's reinforcements will come by sea. Even if we do not plan to engage their ships in battle, I feel we must be able to form a line of defense for the coast against their arrival. I would like a sizable amount of our resources to be devoted to this project. My people are a seafaring people, we should utilize this strength in our struggle."

Quintus once more came to my aid. "I believe this to be a sound strategy. The Alexandrians have a tactical advantage in regards to the topography of the immediate sea in addition to their affinity for sailing and water — an affinity we Romans largely do not share."

"Indeed," chimed in Ganymedes. "We will have the upper hand in both skill and numbers on the sea, even if the legion defends its own here on land."

"It would be best if we could prevent additional legions from landing here," agreed another captain.

"In this I concur with Her Highness," said Achillas to the gathering at large. "Though to build a workable fleet, we shall need a reliable source of timber. As of now most of our supply lines are in the east and we share them with the enemy. It will be difficult to avoid raiding parties. We cannot afford to give the palace free building materials."

"Perhaps I may be of service," answered Tahu, speaking for the first time. "If it please my lords, I will make arrangements with our southern cities to send us supplies through the delta tributaries that are west of Canopus. They are not as large, and it may take them longer to reach us because we will have to move overland for a greater distance, but we should avoid interference from the other side."

Achillas made a gesture of assent. "Yes, Lieutenant, make this so."

Now was the truly difficult part for me to explain. *Give me the right words, Sobek.* "Thank you sirs, for listening to my request with open ears even though I am just a simple girl. If I may be permitted another suggestion to men no doubt wiser in the ways of war than I?" Seeing I continued to hold their attention, I screwed up my courage and started in on my plan. "I know that the tradition of my fathers is primarily to stock the fleet of Egypt with *quadriremes* and even *quinqueremes*, built to withstand great bombasts from enemy ships. However, I fear that focusing our efforts on these models above smaller scale warships will injure our cause in several respects.

"Firstly, that these vessels, because of the large number of decks they require and the thickness of their hulls, will consume so many of our resources as to hinder our ability to construct a number of ships that will be helpful to us. Related to this issue is the large collection of men required to effectively pilot these ships; we would need so many sailors at the oars that I fear for the ability of our troops that remain ashore to hold our positions against the legion."

"Your Highness, it is admirable to see the thought you've put into the positioning of our navy," interrupted Achillas, "yet I'm sure your intrepid man here," he motioned to Tahu, "will no doubt find the timber we need. And I shall see to it that we find enough men to row two hundred *quadriremes*!" he finished with a flourish.

This created a pleasant little stir among the younger Greek officers, though my teacher watched them and the general with a deeply skeptical air. Sensing that I was beginning to lose the focus of the room, I as politely as possible ignored this minor tumult and turned once more to engage the Gabiniani.

"Aside from these concerns, I also am unsure of the wisdom of constructing a fleet of such slow ships. Especially in light of the ships our adversaries will have at their disposal. It is not the Roman navy that is coming to us, but rather a legion traveling by sea. Is it not so that your countrymen favor the swifter *hemiolias* for such operations?"

One of the centurions nodded. "This is true, my lady."

"*Hemiolias* are much more nimble than our *quadriremes* and I worry that the incoming legion will simply dance around our tortoise ships unless we have vessels that can match their speed."

Several of the Gabiniani seemed to seriously attend themselves to my argument, and I could very nearly feel the tide reverse once more in my favor.

However, Achillas detected this also and inserted himself back into the discussion. "Your knowledge of seamanship is worthy of a daughter of Alexandria, my lady, though I believe your worries to be premature. We do not need to engage the Romans in an open sea fight if we can hold a decent blockade of the coastline. They will have to come to us, and even if a few of their little skiffs manage to flit around us, they will no doubt run aground on the unfamiliar shoals of the inner harbor. Our goal should be the blockade, not a naval battle, and in that case the larger *quadriremes* with their elephant-hide bellies are the best protection we can offer the city."

Now the muttering of approval swept the tent more strongly, and I knew I was beaten. Witnessing how adverse the Greeks were to bringing our fight into the sea, I dared not press the point for risk of having the officers revoke their consent to build any more ships at all. I knew we would need them dearly, and I would find a way to make do with ships not of my choosing. "Then I shall bow to the expertise of my courageous commanders to build a navy worthy of the Black Land."

Relaxed now that I had conceded the issue, Achillas saluted jauntily. "This shall be the finest fleet Egypt has ever launched, Your Highness!"

"Perhaps I could suggest a small compromise that my general might build me several *trihemiolias* to have in reserve in case of emergency?"

His cheer restored, he was willing to indulge me. "If it would bring my lady pleasure, I will leap to oblige," he said, clouding the expression of my teacher considerably.

"I ask not on a princely whim, only for my peace of mind," I answered curtly, masking my deeper annoyance.

"Then I would be happy to unburden your brow, Your Highness."

I was not about to be swept away by his charm this morning. "I shall carry my burdens until Pharos is ours."

He gestured expansively to the company. "Then we must finish taking Pharos without delay!" he said, which caused the younger officers to cheer.

Having exhausted all of our most pressing arrangements, the meeting broke up soon after so that the junior officers could attend to their various duties. Without a specific destination in mind, I decided to retreat to my tent to study my maps and my books for the rest of the afternoon. My tutor and those who had become my entourage since my arrival — Mudjet, Tahu, and Quintus Fabianus — wordlessly fell into step around me.

"You did well today, *nedjet*," said Ganymedes after a time. "You were very queenly, even though you did not carry every motion."

"From what I have observed, being queenly often necessitates capitulation," I replied, lost in thought as we walked.

"Certainly to be a *good* queen," he retorted with a fond smile.

I looked to Tahu. "Achillas has not put too much upon you, has he? All that I ask is that you try to find us new supply routes."

The Mephisian shrugged cheerfully. "Do not worry, Your Majesty. I shall find what we need. I would not have spoken so if I was at a loss."

Invigorated by Tahu's infectious confidence, I shook off some of the bitterness I felt at not having convinced my commanders to diversify our fleet. "Quintus, was I wrong to back down on the issue of the *quadriremes*?" I was afraid I may have disappointed him by not being aggressive enough.

He smiled. "No, my lady, I think you did well. You stated your arguments concisely and with good logic. I believe many found you persuasive in spite of the majority."

"And you were wise to grasp the opportunity to still get some *trihemiolias* out of Achillas," observed Mudjet.

"This is true, Mudjet!" said Quintus. "An excellent maneuver!"

"I pray it is enough," I said, biting my lip. "My commanders hold fast to the city, where the enemy infantry has the advantage. I agree with a blockade, but naval warfare plays to our strengths. I have much more faith in beating Rome at sea than here in the streets. To not plan for an attack that could force the enemy's hand makes me uneasy."

"I agree with you, my lady," said my tutor. "And I know that everyone present does as well. We shall figure out some contingency."

Quintus nodded. "I will work on my brother soldiers. I think the Gabiniani can be brought to our viewpoint."

"We can consult with the fishermen and our sailors also, my lady," added Tahu. "I am sure amongst us all we can draw up some plans so if the Greeks' predictions fall through we will not be caught flat-footed."

I grinned, pleased. "Excellent. We have much to do then, my friends."

Chapter Twenty-Two

"See how light the construction of these shields are? How they protect the whole of the body?" Sekhmet says to me as she hands over a Roman *scutum*.

I hold the shield in my hands, feeling the weight of it which is indeed lighter than that of the traditional round *aspis* I am used to, though the length makes it also feel unwieldy.

We stand in Roman battle armor, whose stiffness I am trying to adapt to. The designers clearly did not have young girls in mind when they made these. We dispensed with the heavy helmets, though being strapped with plating, daggers, and everything else, I feel I have enough to get going on. I run a hand over the metal *umbo* in the shield's middle.

"Can the *umbo* withstand the force of punching outwards in a defensive maneuver?" I ask the goddess.

"Yes, Ptolemy-daughter. The shields will resist Egyptian pikes at a distance and up close."

I frown as I tap the *umbo* with my knuckles experimentally. "So we must avoid ordered attacks on the legionaries if possible. Covert warfare in the streets and sea battles if we can organize a sizable fleet are our best hope."

Sekhmet nods. "Though shields or no shields, you must understand how the wolves of Latium wield their blades." She hands me a sword from one of the scabbards on her back.

I take the hilt in hand. "This I know. It is a *gladius*." I give it an exploratory swing. "It is heavier than I would like. The blade seems overlong for its purpose."

The goddess pulls out another *gladius* for herself. She too tests the weight, and frowns. "Hm. Yes, I shall have to assume a form better to teach you of this foreign blade." She closes her eyes, whispers a string of spells, and I watch as Sekhmet's form melts away and is replaced instead by that of Caesar's.

I try to remain steady, but I know she sees me flinch. "He is an excellent general, Ptolemy-daughter," she says as my mind works to reconcile the Lady of the Wounding Claws' words spoken with Caesar's voice. "Yet he is still only a man. You will not be able to outsmart him if you continue to be fearful of him. Now, prepare to defend against my attacks. What is the best way?"

She moves forward, and I instinctively block the thrust. "I think this blade is best for stabbing, my lady." I step towards her and jab the sword at her torso. "It can cut and sever, but these are not its strengths."

Sekhmet parries my attack. "Good girl. It is so." She whirls to the side and attacks again to throw me off balance.

I skitter a little, though recover quickly enough to knock her blade downward. "The steel is not particularly stronger than that which we make, it seems to me."

She pulls back to regroup. "Indeed, they are comparable. The *gladii* used by the legionaries here are lighter and not as strong as those the Latins use on their northern frontier." The goddess angles her next move higher to force me to block from above.

I lift my arms and place both hands on the hilt of the *gladius* to stop her downward motion. "I think my lady gives his lordship the Consul too much credit," I remark as I brace myself against her attack. "He might be a fine soldier, though I question whether his reflexes are still as quick as the Lioness of the Nile's."

Sekhmet chuckles in Caesar's ironic laugh. "Perhaps you are right, Ptolemy-daughter." Her face shifts again and a younger Caesar appears. He cannot be more than twenty. His features still bear their angular appearance, but the lines on his face vanish and his cheeks lose their sunkenness. He remains lean, though his limbs show a little more youthful flesh on them, and he looks stronger and more muscular. His light hair is long enough to fall into his eyes, which are the only part of him unchanged. That and his twisted smile, which is still leering at me.

Somehow, this helps. Here is not the great Caesar, master of Rome. This is an arrogant, untested youth like Salvius was. He is not so handsome as to leave me tongue-tied. I can see that, like my sister, it is the spark of his charm and intellect, rather than a face that could launch a thousand ships that draws people to him.

I break the hold of Sekhmet's *gladius* and swing my blade behind me, using the pommel to knock her off balance. She takes a step back to steady herself, and I take my chance to run at her, throwing my whole weight against her and knocking her to the ground. Straddling her middle, I abandon my sword, pull the *pugio* at my waist out of its sheath, and hold it to her throat.

Sekhmet beams at me with the young Caesar's face, which sinks back into the version I know. "Well done, child. I am pleased." She continues. "You can use this to cut a throat, but that is difficult in close combat. Go for the throat if you can, but you can also use this to slash a leg tendon to disable an adversary."

She reaches up and places her hand over mine on the dagger's hilt. "If you are lucky enough to catch an enemy without armor though, this is the best way." Caesar's armor vanishes and the goddess in his form lays under me in a simple *tunica*. She moves the dagger in our hands and points the blade midway down the torso. "Now take your other hand and find the edge of the breastbone."

When I do, seemingly running my fingertips along the chest of my sister's lover until I find the bone's edge, she goes on. "You stick the blade in at this point as hard as you can, then jab it upward under the ribs. The heart is there, as are the lungs, and many veins. This does too much damage for a foe to recover."

I nod mutely, hit once more by the enormity of these lessons. Caesar's form disappears and Sekhmet is herself again.

"Do not be afraid, Ptolemy-daughter. I know you will find your courage when the time comes."

And then I wake up.

"You need to command the civilians to stay in their houses. We cannot execute the maneuvers we require in the streets if they continue to be underfoot," Achillas said to me as we headed to one of our vantage points near the Library.

"It was you and my brother, sir, who asked me to rally the populace to our cause," I answered shortly. "Do not blame me if they go about their tasks enthusiastically. Confusion in the streets favors us since it hampers the movements of the legion."

"War is the province of — soldiers — my lady. Civilians only get in the way."

I smirked to myself, noting he nearly said "men" instead of "soldiers." Poor politic Achillas, trying to maintain the fiction that he believes I am a general at his side. "We are not engaged in a traditional war, Achillas. If the people want to fling rocks at the Romans, I will not be the one to stifle them."

"Even Ganymedes knows the throne is vacant when the mob rules, Your Highness."

I tossed my head. "Fine. What do you propose then?"

He grinned at me conspiratorially. "Organized rebellion, Your Highness. Structured involvement of noncombatants."

"Carefully laid plans rarely prosper in Egypt," I remarked. "This is a floodgate land."

"Trust me on this, my lady. No one has ever defeated a Roman army with schoolboys and housewives. We need the well-applied support of men strategically placed in Alexandrian society to crush Caesar."

I frowned. "Most of the nobles will not help us, even the ones who hate Cleopatra. They are too afraid of Caesar and the more sentimental among them think that they will endanger the pharaoh if they openly aid the rebellion."

He made a kind but dismissive gesture. "Oh yes, those spineless saps are a lost cause. I am talking of those with real power in Alexandria."

I looked at him. "And who are they, sir?"

"Those who sit highest among the merchant class, my lady. They have influence in the city, access to gold, and contacts outside the kingdom; in short, everything we need."

We rode on and I rolled this idea over in my mind. "Why would they help us any more than the lords? Rebellions are risky and bad for business."

"We are still the side of Ptolemy Philopator, the divinely anointed son of your father. He is the best hope for stability in this land."

"I do not think coin-loving men would place heavy bets on a boy king who cannot even shake a woman off his throne."

"Don't be a snob, my lady," cajoled my general. "These men are well-thought of throughout Egypt and some, beyond. They are just another kind of nobility."

"It is not their pedigrees that concern me. I worry for their loyalty. It is not as if they have offered their services to the pharaoh without prompting."

"As you said, Your Highness, they are cautious. They are also men who pride themselves on their manners. It is possible that they didn't want to speak to the House of Ptolemy out of turn."

I gave a little snort. "The fear of causing offense has never slowed the tongue of an Alexandrian."

Achillas reined his horse and took ahold of the reins of mine. "We need powerful allies, my lady. It paints a pretty picture when the people flock around you and cheer, but people as a whole are weak. It is the powerful who wield Fortune's sword. We have good access to troops, but we need gold to keep them. The merchants can secure funds from spheres outside of the Queen's control."

"I agree we need more money for supplies and for the men, I simply think the merchants are too cozy with themselves — and possibly with Rome — to care what happens to us. I worry that courting them will make us appear weak in their eyes."

"Not if we present our case convincingly. And right now we are holding our own with the most venerable of Caesar's legions, that counts for more than a little!"

I rubbed my temple. "If only it did not feel so desperate to go to them. Maybe it would be better to ask Lord Ehoou-hanif and the elder lords to ride south into Nubia to seek aid. Or west to Libya."

Achillas made a quiet sound of impatience. "Forgive me for being blunt, Your Highness, but the power of the Lost Lords is long spent. If they had maintained influence in their desert farmhouses, you can be sure your father would've wiped them out so thoroughly, the bones of their ancestors would be ground from existence. They hold to a sliver of dignity because you yourself, in your lovely graciousness, have returned that sliver of relevance to them. If the young ones can fight, that is well. But that is all they are good for."

I grit my teeth at his words, but knew it would be fruitless to argue with his prejudices. "Very well, sir. If you think the merchants are capable of being convinced, we shall try. Have a message sent, and I will speak with them at their earliest convenience."

The general looked guilty. "Actually, this is not a task Your Highness will have to concern herself with. Some of the officers and I will take care of this." I gave him a quizzical glance, and he cleared his throat apologetically. "It's just, you see my lady, you are very young and these are men of the world..."

"You do not think I can treat with them? I have spoken to lords and great men all my life." *Not to mention the gods themselves,* I added to myself.

"I know this, but these are not lords. They are busy men whose time is valuable. I wish we had the leisure to show them your great worth, but we too are short on time."

I reached down to loosen his fingers from my reins. "If you think this is best, so be it."

He dropped the leather and clasped my hand. "This is about the ways of these men, my lady. It would wound me terribly if you thought I was not your most ardent admirer."

His touch startled me, and I was frozen in his hold for a long moment, locked in his handsome eyes. Gradually, I remembered that we were stopped in the middle of the camp with many eyes upon us. "You forget yourself, General," I said hoarsely.

He immediately let go, yet his eyes danced with mischief. "Let them talk, Your Highness. They hail you as Queen, you may do as you please."

We continued on our way, though my heart was troubled by what had happened. I was worried for a meeting with the merchants that I was being shut out of. I was worried that Achillas attempted to smooth out that wrinkle with flirting. I was afraid I was too young and would fall for his game.

We parted company eventually on our separate business, and I rode over to the docks where Tahu was organizing work gangs for shipbuilding. He bowed with a grin at my approach, though grew serious when he observed my expression. He made a few orders to the men under him and excused himself to my side as I dismounted.

"What is it, my lady?"

I briefly explained Achillas' plan to garner support from the merchants and my exclusion from it, leaving out the last parts. "Am I wrong to be concerned?"

"No, my lady. I do not think it bodes well that they wish to do this without you. At best, it is a slight against your talents."

"And at worst?"

He frowned and dropped his voice. "At worst it shows they, and perhaps the Pharaoh, are jealous of your accomplishments so far and are willing to risk failing to secure the aid of the rich merchants to keep you from having any claim if they succeed."

I shrugged. "I have no need of laurels, Tahu. If they wish a little victory for themselves, it matters not to me."

Tahu shook his head. "No, my lady, no false modesty. You are too clever for that and you know that you are in personal danger if you do not prove your worth to this cause. I also know the general is too cagey not to be aware of that. It worries me heartily that he would keep you from this meeting."

"But it does not surprise me," I answered. "He may pretend other-wise, but he is my brother's creature, not mine. I would have to be very useful indeed for that to change."

He stroked his chin contemplatively. "There may be another path, Your Majesty. Another group, powerful in Alexandria, who may be per-suaded to help us. Though I know not if Sir Ganymedes would approve of you aligning yourself with them."

"Who?"

He hesitated. "Does my lady know of whom I am referring when I speak of the Five?"

By the end of the week, Achillas had arranged the desired meeting with the leading merchants of the city. When the time came, he cheerfully stopped by my tent with his hand-picked delegation before heading out into the city. "Wish us luck, Your Highness, as we go into battle!" he saluted with a deprecating sweep of his cloak.

"Indeed I do, sirs," I replied primly from my couch where I lay buried in my books. "Do not let the merchants sell you a trifling deal."

"Of course not, my lady! We will report faithfully for the cause of this army and our royals!"

"Of that I have no doubt," I said, as I flipped a page and gestured to my left. "For I am sending Quintus Fabianus with you as assurance."

"My lady! Is that really necessary?" Achillas balked, trying to remain merry as my Gabiniani lieutenant and I looked at him with amusement.

"Calm yourself, General," I soothed. "I am simply sending him with you as an observer, he will not interfere with your negotiations."

Achillas struggled to give his practiced shrug of nonchalance. "If that would put your mind at ease, my lady, I would. Alas, I have given the host of our meeting a specific number regarding our attendants and it would put them ill at ease if we came with more men than was promised. Not to mention impolite on our part."

I fixed my jaw firmly. "Then one of your men must stay behind, sir."

He narrowed his eyes at me as minutely as he could, and for a moment seemed to find no words to counter me with. Finally he murmured, "Suspicions among friends are beneath the dignity of those such as us, Your Highness."

I could sense both Mudjet and Quintus tense up at the suggestion that the general and I were equals, but it was not important now. I caught Mudjet's eye to warn her off confronting Achillas over it.

"This is true, General. This is not suspicion. You yourself assigned Quintus Fabianus to have a care for my person and be my lieutenant. We came to an agreement that my presence at this gathering would perhaps hinder a settlement, even though I might personally believe otherwise. However, one of the benefits of having such a faithful aide as Quintus is that he can go places on my behalf when I am unable, for whatever reason. This meeting is a perfect illustration of that."

The general could not argue with my logic when he had been the architect of the situation, even if he now regretted it. So he capitulated as gracefully as he could manage.

"That is a fair assessment, Your Highness." Achillas glanced at Quintus. "And you, sir, have proven to be a loyal man to this cause so I welcome your help in this matter." He spoke quietly to one of the officers who saluted him and departed as the rest of the contingent exited my tent with only the most cursory show of deference.

I gave Quintus a sly grin. "Good luck to you, sir."

"I live to serve, Arsinoë Philoaígyptos," he replied with a wicked little salute and breezed out after Achillas' party.

After they had all departed, Mudjet made an angry noise. "Achillas is too bold with you, my lady."

"We need his help, my sweet. As we are so rarely in agreement, I at least must indulge some overfamiliarity to deflect away from calling attention to how often I contradict him."

"You are Queen in these camps!" she huffed. "The men have said so! Your will should be law."

"We both know that this is an army with several masters."

She crouched down to meet my eyes. "Then you must make yourself the sole master of it, my lady."

"I know this, but now is not the time to whip Achillas or my brother into seeing things from my view. They have their uses to us, remember? And I can only build my allies slowly in their shadow. It is all easier said than done."

What transpired between Achillas and the merchants I only know of through Quintus Fabianus, and even his account is fractured by the Greek general's last attempt to shut me out of the proceedings by conducting most of the discussion privately with several of the lead men away from both delegations. He closed the door on his arrayed show of skill and strength to spite me, and I believe it was one of the reasons he left empty-handed. Suffice to say that the merchants were grieved to be sure, but they could not afford to alienate either royal party in this conflict and they, as high-ranking fathers of the capital, must remain neutral.

Aside from that, I also believe that even if he and I had been of one mind in this venture, it had been doomed to failure. These rich men had the most of anyone to lose in a civil war outside of those who might lose their lives. Their entire world was built on the quest for stability. Trade carries many risks, and yet the men who are most successful at it, the men whose help we sought, were successful at it because they found the safest path in an unpredictable world. These were not men who delighted in plying their own vessels through pirate-infested waters and haggling with peasants and thieves for a snatch of cloth or a handful of spice. No, these were men who had settled into comfortable lives in a civilized city while they hired out others with death wishes to hunt down their merchandise. It mattered not to them who sat on the falcon throne as long as the ships came in on time and tariffs were reasonable.

Though do not suppose I thought myself superior to their situation. My Ptolemy blood had not made my nose so long to look down over as that. Set had cautioned me against committing wholeheartedly to one of my siblings over the other, so how could I berate these men for doing as I had done? We speak of war as glorious, full of high ideals and pride, but at its deepest level it is only a larger vehicle for our personal self-gratification. The God of War's counsel led only to choosing one's self above factions and that is all any can do. It sounds very selfish, but what we fight for is only a mirror of our own desires and values. And there is always dark and light in that mirror.

Once Achillas had returned, I gathered my lead commanders to discuss what was next to be done. The Gabiniani officers drew out barricade maps for me to show our positions throughout the city and several of the Greek lieutenants updated us on the status of our standoff with the members of the legion positioned on Pharos. Meanwhile, Achillas sat morosely off to one side.

I turned to my tutor. "Teacher, how goes our access to shipbuilding materials?"

"Timber remains difficult to come by, especially for the *quadrireme* hulls, but we are managing for now. It would be better if we had better supply lines away from the ones in Canopus and those lines we share with the palace. Tahu's plan has worked as well as we could have hoped, though it is not a permanent solution."

I nodded. "Lord Ehoou-hanif," I said, giving my attention to the old lord, "do you know of anyone else in the south who might be friendly to our needs?"

He bowed. "I will send one of our number to investigate our options at once, Your Majesty. I am certain we can procure the necessary supplies."

Achillas glowered at Ehoou-hanif and I gave my sulking soldier a sympathetic look. "Come now, General. Do not allow the merchants of Alexandria to sour our progress. Our army has done exceedingly well so far, thanks to the steady hands of our fine officers." I nodded encouragingly to those assembled and was pleased to see they seemed to accept the praise gratefully. "You yourself have done much of this. We are bound to suffer some setbacks, but we must not be disheartened by them."

He gave me a pained smile. "Your Highness is kind. However I fear that this failure will deliver allies into the hands of the Queen."

"It is possible, though I think the merchants will choose no side rather than that of our enemy. Either way, we shall deal with the situation as it arises. In the meantime, perhaps we can seek out other allies."

"I do not think we have the strength as of yet to recruit aid from outside the kingdom, my lady," said one of the Gabiniani. "And while it is noble of the populus to assist us, we do require the help of more powerful persons."

"We are coming off of drought years, Your Majesty," added Lord Amenei. "Even if the people want to help us, food and coin are in short supply."

"An army has many needs," I answered meditatively. "Food and gold are among its most pressing, but we also have a great need for information. It has been suggested to me," I paused, careful to avoid glancing at Tahu, "that we might entreat the Five to bring us information they glean in the course of their dealings, in addition to whatever other help they might be able to give as residents of our fair city."

Achillas let out a hoot of laughter. "Ha! Here you were telling me not to despair a moment before, Your Highness, and not two breaths later you believe things to be so dire that we need the feeble assistance of flesh-mongers!"

A smarmy Greek officer leered at his commander. "Maybe they could have their charges exhaust the legion for us!"

"The fop in the northern Soma even has some boys we could send Caesar," barked another. "That would certainly give the Queen a fine fit!"

"I must agree with the general," said Ganymedes with a frown. "Though for my part it is because not only do I think those people have nothing of value to offer us, but also because it would be unseemly for a lady of your status to be seen in their company."

"I am a highborn lady leading an army against another highborn lady leading another army, teacher," I countered wryly. "I would argue seemliness is already somewhat compromised in the eyes of many."

"You have been addressed not only as a queen among your supporters, Your Highness," answered my tutor sternly, "but as a goddess among many of your people. These are titles your sister lays claim to also, though with much less demonstrative evidence from outside the palace walls. Her reputation has already been compromised by her dalliance with Rome, yours has not. I do not want your good name associated with people of that character. It is important for you to maintain this moral advantage."

I fancied I saw Ganymedes give a pointed look at Achillas when he uttered his last remark, but the general's expression remained passive.

"I believe the Five would have information useful to us and would be more likely to align themselves with the mood of the city than with the palace, especially if we did them the honor of asking directly. Gentlemen, we need allies in Egypt more than allies abroad. If we can harness the energy of the people, I believe that our cause will prosper. However, if you all are of the opinion that this would be a misstep, I will close the matter." I looked around the assembly and was met by dissenting grumbles and shaking heads. Only Tahu and Quintus Fabianus remained silent. "So be it. We will not discuss it further. You may go about your business, sirs."

Everyone filed out into the camp until only those two men and Mudjet remained. "You did not do much to my defense, sir," I said to Quintus, pretending to be cross.

"I too have some concerns about enlisting the help of the Five, Your Majesty," he answered. "Though unlike the others, I am clever enough to know when you will do what you will without our approval."

I laughed. "Well then, I appreciate you keeping my secret."

He grinned and turned to Tahu. "I assume that it was you, sir, who put this naughty idea in our lady's head."

"It is true," said Tahu. "Not without reservations, though I will stand behind it as a plan with rewards for our cause."

Quintus nodded. "I know Tahu would never do anything to bring harm to Your Majesty, so if he is willing to follow you on this, you will have my support also."

"It is settled then," I said. "Tahu, can you arrange this meeting for us?"

He bowed. "It will be done, my lady."

"Good. Quintus, when the time comes, I will need you here running interference so that our absence will not be noticed."

"Of course, Your Majesty."

Mudjet smirked. "It has been too many weeks since we have slunk through the streets of Alexandria like thieves, my lady."

"We are getting rather proficient at it, are we not?" I answered in amusement.

Three days hence, I was with the quartermasters, checking over our weapons stores so that they might take appropriate orders of our needs to the smiths in town, when Tahu appeared and beckoned me to his side.

"It is done, my lady. Tonight at midnight we meet with the Five."

"Thank you for this. Mudjet and I will be ready when you call."

Chapter Twenty-Three

When we felt we could leave unobserved, Mudjet and I threw on some plain clothes and scurried out into the descending robe of night. We left Quintus Fabianus at my tent to deflect inquiries, and then met with Tahu near the edge of our encampment.

The three of us continued on our way through the city until we reached the back streets of the Rhakotis district. There were more people around than I would have liked, but Alexandria has always been a restless sleeper. The siege only added to its insomnia. We moved as purposely as we could manage until we came to a house with the sign of a mirror above its door. I knocked and the door was answered by a servant woman.

"Who sent you to this door?" she asked.

I had been told in advance of the password requirement. "She who is the Queen of Joy and the Mistress of Music, She Who Beats the Drum," I replied.

The woman bowed. "Enter and be glad, Queen of the Moon Gate."

We entered the house and were met by the heady scent of perfume and oils. Curtains as fleeting as cobwebs hung over the doorways that opened up on either side and as we were led towards the back rooms, the flash of jewel-bright eyes flickered here and there behind the them. We reached the farthest room and the servant knocked on the red door. A brittle voice said, "Enter!" and we were taken inside.

The room smelled of myrrh and the faintest hint of sweat. We trod on heavy carpets imported from Pontus and were greeted by five figures seated on couches circled about a round table set with several jugs of wine. The tarnished brass oil lamps flickered on their chains suspended from the thickly plastered ceiling.

"Welcome, Your Royal Highness." said the woman who had spoken with the brittle voice, as she stood up to meet me. She was a thin, elderly woman who barely came to my shoulders. She wore a thick black wig in the old Egyptian style with a scarlet ribbon wrapped around her forehead. The matching silk robe she wore was shot through with gold and silver thread and cut in a fashion from the East. Her thin fingers wore a cacophony of rings and her small eyes were ringed with thick layers of kohl.

"Thank you, *mu-ti*." I turned my attention to the others. "Thank you all for agreeing to meet with me."

"We are honored to be worthy of the attention of a princess of Egypt. But first, I believe some brief introductions are necessary. We flatter ourselves that our names may be known to Your Highness, though I doubt our faces are." She motioned to the middle-aged women to her right. "This woman has the honor to be the Sail and the other, the Palm Fruit." She turned to her left and singled out the younger woman. "This woman is the Sweet Harp." Lastly, she gestured to the only man amongst them. "And as you might have deduced, this gentleman is the Leopard."

I nodded to each in turn. Naturally these were only their names of business, yet all were famous in Alexandria and abroad. The old lady lowered her head. "And if it please Your Highness, I have the honor to be the Mirror."

I handed her a bag of gold that I took from Mudjet. "Thank you again for arranging all of this, madam. I hope this will cover some of the detriment of closing your house this night."

"It is well, my lady. Please be seated." She guided me towards the vacant couch in the circle. I sat down and the servant placed a cup of wine in my hand before departing, shutting the door behind her.

"Now," said the Mirror with a wave of her hand, "to business. What would Your Highness wish to discuss with us?"

I took a sip of wine before I began. "I do not think I have to elaborately delineate my position to you, so I will be brief. I know you have eyes and ears everywhere and nowhere. You know I oppose the influence of Rome in our city on behalf of my brother the Pharaoh. We currently enjoy some advantage in strength of position and manpower, though this will be nothing but a memory when Caesar is able to retrieve the rest of his legions. Even without their numbers, the legion he has right now has cut its teeth in the very mouth of Hades. So I am endeavoring to find ways to use our current control of the city to our benefit."

"You have come to the wrong people if you are looking for more men, Princess," said the Sweet Harp, her perfect Cupid's bow lips pursing into an impish smile. "Though the Leopard might have a few you could borrow."

The Leopard twirled the end of his beard on his thin forefinger, amused. "I do, but they cost me a fortune and I would be hard pressed to part with them."

The Mirror gave the two of them an admonishing look. "Enough. Your Highness, please continue."

"I also know that all of your houses have more contact with the Roman soldiers than any others in Alexandria."

"But not with Caesar himself, to our dear Harp's endless despair," interrupted the Leopard again with a predatory grin in his companion's direction.

The Sweet Harp pulled a languishing face, and turned to me. "It is intolerably unfair that your lady sister keep a man of his formidable — *reputation* — all to herself."

The round-faced Palm Fruit cut in. "Oh, stop your prattling, both of you! Princess," she said turning to me, "you cannot ask us to forgo the business of the legion in the name of civic duty. Their coin is as good as anyone's."

"When they don't haggle endlessly over prices!" sniffed the Sweet Harp. "You'd think some of their members were made of gold!"

"It's easy for you to be choosy, Harp," said the Leopard in a gentler tone. "You're further out in the Soma than Palm and I. Her Highness' excellent barricades make it difficult for many of the Romans to even make it as far as your house." He raised his cup to salute me.

"I could never ask any of you to forswear your business with the legion," I replied, trying to regain control of the conversation. "If you did bar your doors to them of course, it would be injurious to their morale and for that I would be eternally grateful. However, I mainly came here to ask that you and your charges keep your ears open to the wine-talk of the soldiers and to see if you might be willing to keep me informed. All I ask is for you to give us any help you feel able to."

A new voice, subtler and lower than the others spoke up. "Why do you come to ask of us these things in the heart of the night, Princess?"

I turned to the sound of the voice and meet the stately gaze of the Sail, who leaned forward and waited patiently for my response. "Because my high officers would have tried to stop me from coming in the daylight. They disagree with my plan to harness the many talents of this city to aid us. They believe we can succeed with troops alone."

"And you do not, my lady?" Her pale blue eyes flickered like the light of the lamps.

I hesitated. "No."

"Why not?"

"Because I have looked Caesar in the eye."

The Sail nodded slowly and leaned back on her couch. "This one sees things for how they are. The only wise thing our boy king has done is to send this sister out to lead the people." She then spoke to the group at large. "We cannot hold ourselves separate from the city, sisters and brother. Without us, Alexandria has no pulse in its veins and it will wither if we do not do what we can to assist the Princess Arsinoë. She has shown herself to be far-sighted and not too proud to ask even whoresellers for aid for the sake of our land. She has come here herself — no wonder our kingdom's weakest fly to her tender arms."

"We are honored naturally, Sister Sail, yet I'm sure the princess has held a dozen meetings with the merchants filled with the same innocent bleating," the Palm Fruit said huffily.

"Do you make the same request of our merchants, my lady?" asked the Mirror, her old papyrus voice carrying the note of sweetness that no doubt led her to help me call this meeting in the first place.

"The merchants powerful enough to equal the reach of you assembled here I cannot hope to win over, just as I cannot hope to be a general equal to the master of Rome," I replied truthfully. "They are foreigners to this land and pragmatists, whose fortunes are tied to stability and continuity. They will never support a third daughter who rallies the natives to her banner. I know some of you are not Egyptian by birth any more than they are or any more purely than I could claim, but I know you love this city and this land. I know you all have worked together for years to protect your courtesans and keep undesirable elements from flourishing, when it might have been more profitable to simply compete with one another in depravity. You, Madam Palm Fruit, pretend to scoff at the notion that you and your associates are civic-minded, though I see much evidence that those gathered here might be the strongest defenders of the true Alexandria."

The Five sat in silence for a few minutes, until the Leopard broke it abruptly. "Marvelous, Your Highness!" he crowed with a clap of his hands. "With a tongue as silver as your eyes, the Queen should be wary indeed! How can I close my ears to such eloquence! What say you, Palm? Has the Princess won you to her cause?"

The Palm Fruit sighed heavily. "Yes, yes... You know I bear no love for the Romans, but my house is the closest to the palace, so I dare not shut my door." She looked at me. "I will keep you informed of anything I hear, Your Highness. You have my word."

The Sweet Harp giggled. "I for one can't wait to have a little fun with our Latin guests. Don't worry, Princess. Your sister isn't the only one who has a few potions up her sleeve..."

"I already have nightly brawls between our sailors and the legionaries, maybe I will simply stop holding the Alexandrians back," said the Sail with an ironic smile.

"And I," rasped the Mirror, "I will shut my door to all Romans. This is my city, my home. We are not simply another Roman colony. We stand with you, my child. Even if we are hiding in the shadows."

"I thank you all. This is more than I could have wished for. I am sorry if this brings hardships to your doors."

"Bah. As you say, Princess, we are at war," commented the Leopard with a shrug. "The hardships will come regardless. Better to make some of them of our own choosing." He leaned his head down at me sympathetically. "Though you understand we cannot win this war for you. This will not last."

"I know. This is not a traditional war. All my strategies are only meant to buy us a little more time. This is no different."

It was nearly dawn when we crept back into camp with Tahu, parting ways with him when our tent was in sight. Quintus greeted us in hushed relief and parted the front flap as we ducked back inside. Mudjet helped me undress and then sank down on her own couch with a satisfied sigh before almost instantly drifting off to sleep. I knew I should have been tired as well, but my mind was too awake.

"My lady should try to sleep for a few hours," Quintus' voice drifted softly over to me from outside the tent flap.

I rolled over onto my side. "My mind is fixed on too many things."

"Permission to enter, my lady?"

"Of course."

My Gabiniani lieutenant bent into the tent and walked over to my couch. "May I?" he asked, gesturing to the corner by my feet. I nodded, curling them up to make room for him. "Now," he said, "tell me what the Five had to say."

Keeping my voice low so as not to wake Mudjet, I recounted all that had happened at the Mirror's house. Quintus listened until I was finished, only nodding his head occasionally to let me know I held his attention.

"It would seem my Queen was most successful on her mission," he observed with a triumphant grin. "These were not naivë folk she spoke with."

"I do not know how much good it will do. I hope I do not disappoint Ganymedes for nothing."

"He only worries for you, my lady. As we all do. Yet I think this was the bold plan of a true general. You could not have better placed spies in all the city." He paused to look at me with pride. "I wish my wife could have met Your Majesty. She would've appreciated my lady's quiet streak of daring."

"You must miss her a great deal," I said, tucking my hand under my cheek.

"I do. But I feel blessed for the time we were given together. I fell in love with Egypt as I fell in love with her, and that love gave me three sons and a place to call home. Many are given much less in life."

I met his gaze. "It is indeed my loss to not have known the woman so respected by one such as you, Quintus."

"It might be too bold to say, my lady, but I think my wife would have enjoyed caring for you as a daughter. She loved our boys, though I believe she had always wished to have a little girl as well."

I smiled. "I have been a girl in search of a mother for half of my life. I think I would have liked that."

He returned my smile fondly before letting his mouth assume a mischievous twist. "I believe this coming day I shall have to find something complicated to occupy Your Majesty's engineering corps. Master Tychon keeps threatening to send a battalion of Nubians south to procure war elephants."

I smothered a laugh at this, imagining my army trying to maneuver elephants through the crowded streets of Alexandria. "Gods defend us, my engineers are quite mad! Achillas is already annoyed with the interference of the rank-and-file Alexandrians — he will be beside himself if I unleash elephants on the city!"

Quintus let out a chortle. "The general would be fit to be tied. Especially if Your Majesty came before the men galloping astride an elephant, no doubt he being envious to have not thought of such an ostentatious display himself!"

I wiped a tear from my eye. "It would be quite the contest to see which of us would be more ridiculous to be sure."

"The young engineers wish my lady to be hailed as a great general like Hannibal."

I shook my head. "They know elephants did not help the illustrious general much with Rome either?"

"I believe them to be operating in the spirit of the law rather than the letter, my lady."

"Hmph, let us hope so. We shall need more luck than Hannibal if we do not want to come to the same grief as Carthage."

"Strange reports are reaching me, Your Majesty," Ganymedes said to me as he, Mudjet, and I toured our barricade lines in the Soma on horseback about two weeks later.

"Oh?" I said in return, pulling my attention from the stone block I had leaned down to test the positioning of. "Is it cause for concern?"

"Honestly, my lady, I am not sure. It has been brought to my attention that the soldiers of the legion are telling peculiar tales about certain people Your Majesty mentioned in my presence some weeks ago."

I feigned ignorance as I sat up and adjusted my footing against the saddle. "I prattle on about a great many people, teacher. Of whom are you speaking?"

"Those known as the Five, my lady. It is being said around the city that courtesan-masters may have taken a tack against our enemy."

"That hardly seems likely. The legion are a thousand men far away from their wives. It would be poor business to stir trouble up with paying customers," I said.

"That is what I thought, and yet it is rumored that the Old Lady of Rhakotis has refused to let the Romans pass under her door. And there is another jade who lives here in the back streets of this district whom Caesar has forbidden his men to visit because they keep returning to the palace under some Eastern drug or another that renders them unfit for duty for hours on end. And it is said he will have to prohibit another whorehouse soon as half of the legion keeps getting into nightly brawls with the merchants' sailors."

Mudjet raised her eyebrows dramatically. "Dear me, what a mess!"

I lowered my eyelids to remind her not to overdo it. "Indeed. Though I see no cause for our alarm. The activities of the Five do not seem to involve us. Perhaps it is the intervention of the Lady of the Sweet Words on our behalf."

Ganymedes studied me skeptically for a moment. I met his scrutiny with an innocent expression that eventually made him relent. "As you say, *nedjet*. It is a fortunate distraction. I have also heard rumors that the people are beginning to believe that you are a favorite of their gods, perhaps they have in truth bent events to your will."

I demurred politely, and we resumed our inspections until Ganymedes was called away to assist a battalion of the Gabiniani with their fortifications. "I do feel sorry for deflecting him," I said to Mudjet, who sat on her horse smirking at me when he left. "But there are several parts of this he will not understand."

"It is as Kharmion told your sister once, my lady. The gods help those who help themselves."

I glanced around us. "Do you think we can risk a meeting with the Mirror? I am worried my new allies might be going about their tasks too enthusiastically. It might cause more trouble than aid."

"If we can, now is the moment. Though we should go on foot and make sure to put our hoods up."

We dismounted, leaving the horses with a detachment of our soldiers and cutting through the back alleys until we came to the back door of The Mirror's residence. Mudjet rapped out a prearranged knock and a kitchen slave admitted us. We were taken up a back stairway to the old mistress' private quarters. We entered and found the Mirror reclining on her large couch.

I made a deferential gesture as she began to rise. "Do not trouble yourself to get up. Forgive our intrusion on your resting hours, *mu-ti*."

She waved a hand, causing her rings and bracelets to jangle. "It is nothing, Your Highness. I always have an ear for you. Please, sit! It is positively scandalous that I lounge here in my dressing robes while a *heqet* stands in my presence!"

We settled ourselves on another waiting couch. "My tutor has heard wind of your collective work. It sounds as if everyone has been very effective."

"It is also rather scandalous how much we are enjoying this game the Princess of Egypt has set us on," she said in her fragile voice. "We begin to see why the city at large has joined it so readily. Has our information been finding my lady's Memphisian?"

"Yes, it has been extremely helpful. I am most grateful. I am only worried that the zeal of the Five might cause the Romans to shun you all completely and we might lose access to the enemy. Not to mention endanger you and the lives of your *hetaerae*."

The Mirror gave me a smile that carried a drop of condescension for my politesse. "Your Highness is kind to use such a forgiving word for our girls. And I understand your concerns. Sister Harp has been very cheeky, though she and her girls have been sure not to go too far. And all of us have been rotating our best charges into her house for insurance. Caesar can bluster all he wants, his men will not be able to forgo the best flesh in Alexandria on the word of a leader who cannot resist similar pleasures himself."

I grinned. "That is indeed very clever. I hope Madam Sail has not been too wind-tossed by the activities of the legion at her residence."

"Ah, Sister Sail has given herself a breezy name, but my lady knows she should be called the Iron Gate. She is quite capable of handling herself. Besides, it is only for a time. Our goals remain twofold: use the houses of Sister Sail and Sister Harp to tie up as many of the enemy's lower men as possible, while using that chaos to drive the officers into the houses of Sister Palm and Brother Leopard so that we can harvest information, with my house coordinating our efforts."

"So dividing up all of the courtesans in Alexandria, the Sail gets the fearless girls, the Sweet Harp gets the prettiest, and the Palm Fruit and the Leopard get the sly ones," observed Mujet, ticking off our allies on her fingers. "What does that leave you, *mu-ti*?"

"Ooh, those Ptolemies do raise such saucy ladies!" the Mirror said to her with an amused cackle. "Do not worry for me, *sherit*. I have the girls we can count on to organize. The ones that are friends with our neighbors and know every hovel in this city. The ones who can navigate a strange partisan war such as this."

I threw up my hands playfully. "I have been tricked, my sweet. The Five told me they could field no army, and here they have such an army I would bargain my *ka* for!"

The Mirror's lined face crinkled up. "Do not fret, dear Princess. We *are* your army as much as your archers or horsemen. Only do not say so to Sister Harp or she will demand the rank of general from you!"

So my secret army continued its covert war while my other army built stronger barricades and taller siege towers. Cleopatra tried to find courtesans from outside the city to serve the legion safely, but even in the southern towns, houses of comfort seemed to vanish every time Apollodorus arrived there.

The Queen began to truly comprehend the reach the Five had within her kingdom. My men would stand on the roofs of Alexandria and yell to her that she would have to open her legs to the whole legion to keep them happy. Women in the markets would sashay past the enemy guards gossiping loudly that the Romans loved their republican ways so much that it was only fair that the queen should give to the common soldier what she freely gave to the general.

The Sweet Harp had her girls distribute messages all around the city and to the legion to give to Caesar, laughingly enticing him to sample the delights of her house before rushing to his harsh judgements. Mudjet would bring the latest offers to me so we could giggle over the florid prose describing Gallic snow maidens and sleek Nubian goddesses.

Ganymedes disapproved of us howling over the promises of exotic Eastern dances and tricks, though he did not forbid us our fun until the Harp started circulating a pamphlet promising Caesar she would find him a girl who looked like the renegade princess so that he could finally get the better of the little minx for once. My men loved it and hooted the taunt towards the palace exuberantly, but my tutor was livid and barked at anyone who mentioned it in his presence.

"It is meant to be a compliment, Ganymedes," Achillas noted, equally amused, with a grin in my direction.

"It is disgraceful for such things to be implied about a princess royal in the streets like she is a common fishwife!" my teacher fumed. "It should not be encouraged!"

"But it is not me in truth, Teacher," I said mildly. "Just someone who looks like me." I had thought the barb a stroke of genius and had sent a message to the Harp telling her as much. She replied jokingly that she was sure she could deliver if the Consul proved interested, though she was afraid the girl might have to keep her eyes closed because my eyes were a color hard to come by in this kingdom.

"It is the principle, *nedjet*," he answered angrily. "These are people who are not fit to speak of anything to a lady of your rank, let alone suggest a foreign adventurer take liberties with you." He glared at Mudjet, who was struggling to maintain her composure. "And you are supposed to have a care for Her Majesty's person, Mudjet! Not go along with the filthy ideas of the city!"

She coughed. "Yes, sir. Forgive me."

Chapter Twenty-Four

Quintus Fabianus was standing with me in the Soma, explaining to some of our engineers how to make our copied siege towers more effective, when a richly dressed man rushed up to us. He had the gaudy ostentation of the city's merchant class, along with their heavy stature, and a bevy of retainers bobbing in a long train behind him. When he reached us, a sickly wave of perfume doused us, making the Gabiniani lieutenant wrinkle his nose.

"Are you Princess Arsinoë?" the man asked, squinting at me doubtfully.

"She is Queen in these camps," answered Quintus coldly while several of the engineers made disdainful faces as the merchant's perfume wafted over to them.

I waved my lieutenant silent. "I am."

"I am Prokopios of Crete, and I have come to you, Your Highness, to report the theft of my property!"

I raised my eyebrows. "Forgive me, sir, but we are not the city watch. What has been stolen?"

"My Nubian slave has run off and is hiding out amongst your army. I demand his immediate return. I have had reports that he is working in your docks."

Quintus looked at me in exasperation. "Do you want me to go sort this out, Your Majesty?"

I shook my head. "No, you stay here and finish with the engineers." I turned to them. "Listen carefully to Quintus Fabianus. We need as many of these towers built as strongly as you can manage. Even if we cannot bring them to bear directly on the palace, I want our archers to be placed in range of the legion. Is that understood?"

The engineers saluted and returned their attention to the lieutenant's descriptions. I followed Prokopios down to the harbor as he gesticulated wildly.

"... and he cost me a fortune, Your Highness! I haven't gotten a thing properly done in days! I will have to chain his ankles when he comes home!"

We reached the docks where my men were scrambling to build the ships we would need if we wanted to forestall a naval blockade. I found one of the overseers and called him over.

"This man says one of his slaves is working for you down here, is that possible?"

The overseer shrugged. "Certainly, Your Majesty. If men appear willing to work, we don't turn them away. We assume you sent them."

I turned back to Prokopios. "What is your slave's name?"

"He's called Atlas."

"Do you have anyone with that name working on your team?" I asked the overseer.

"No, Your Majesty."

I was about to give my apologies to Prokopios so I could return to my business, when he waved his finger in the direction of what would be, with luck, one day the ship's stern. "There he is! That man belongs to me!"

We all whirled around as one of the worker stopped and slowly stood up. The Nubians are a slender, well-built people, so the sheer size of the man who obediently traversed the length of the ship's hull to where we were gathered astounded me. He was very tall, as was common, but he was also nearly the width of two men together. His expression was calm though proud, and he seemed to be waiting politely for one of us to say something.

His master was the first to regain his bearings. "Atlas! How dare you run off! I will have beaten until you forget what it is to not feel the lash upon you!"

The man said nothing to this tirade and merely looked at me. He met my gaze, then slowly knelt down before me. I was embarrassed that I still had to look up to him even on his knees. "Are you Nubian?" I asked him in that language, belatedly grateful that Cleopatra's foresight had ensured we had always employed tutors in the tongue of our southern neighbors.

"My mother was Amharan, Your Majesty," he answered in Nubian, his voice deep and even.

"Forgive me, I know only a little of Amharic, so I must continue in this tongue if we wish to keep our privacy. What is your name?"

"Dejen, Your Majesty."

"Are you this man's slave as he claims?"

"Yes, Your Majesty."

"But you ran away to join the army?"

He cracked a grin full of large teeth. "I was out doing chores for that one, and I heard you speak to the city. I said to myself that this one is a queen of iron. She has come to set all of Alexandria free. So I wait for my chance, and then I run."

"You are as strong as an elephant, Dejen, why not run home and be truly free?"

"If such a little queen stays and fights, Your Majesty, what honor is there in going home for this one?"

This brought a smile to my face. "I assume you do not want to return to your master?"

"He is a small man, Your Majesty. He preens with the other merchants in the city and they think they are better than everyone. Even the House of Ptolemy. They laughed when Achillas the Greek came to them, begging in the dirt. They laugh at the little princess who plays the general. They are fools. I will stay with you if it is your will."

"Well, I knew I would never have the support of the merchants anyway," I answered with a gesture of playful defeat. I returned my attention to Prokopios and switched back to Greek. "I am sorry, sir, but this man's name is Dejen, not Atlas. You must have mistaken him for your missing slave."

The merchant was apoplectic. "I don't care what he says his name is! He is my slave and I am taking him!"

"And I am issuing a royal command in the presence of a witness," I nodded to my overseer, " that this man is now free. He is not yours to take."

"You can't do that!" squeaked Prokopios of Crete in disbelief. "What about my money?"

"I am the representative of Ptolemy Theo Philopator," I replied loftily. "I am a princess of the royal blood, and you and your brother merchants have refused to aid us in our fight to save your city and livelihoods. This is war and sacrifices must be made for the greater good."

Prokopios realized he had lost and knew he had no recourse against an aristocrat, but he got in one last tirade before he left. "Fine! Keep the treacherous beggar. He'll abandon you too when it suits him! You'll be sorry, Princess! We'll never help you now!"

As he stormed off, the shipbuilders burst into laughter and catcalls at the portly merchant and his nervous entourage until the overseer rushed over to get them back to work.

I looked up at Dejen, who had returned to his feet. "I think your talents might be wasted as a laborer, sir. I have many men from the south who I might be able to organize more effectively under a commander of their own land. Would that suit you?"

He nodded. "My Queen gives me my freedom and prestige back in a single instant. Whatever task she assigns me will be to my liking."

"I did nothing, Dejen. One such as you can never have your freedom or your prestige taken from you."

Dejen smiled and then looked back out over the harbor around us. "You know, there are others like me, Your Majesty. Slaves who have heard your voice."

"Will they fight with us?"

"You have only to ask."

I was pleased none of my fastidious Greek commanders were around to preach caution at me. "If they will fight for me, I will fight for them," I said to him firmly.

He grinned again. "Leave it to me, my Queen. I will bring you an army."

"This cannot continue, Your Highness."

I was in my tent pouring over Thucydides some time later, attempting to glean what I could from the text about Athenian naval strategy, when Achillas' voice cut across my thoughts. I gave him a questioning look.

"You can't keep accepting runaway slaves into the ranks, it'll upset the free population too much."

"A soldier should not care who stands next to him as long as that man is true," I answered, barely raising my head from the scroll on my lap.

"It's not so much that, it's their former masters. They'll not look kindly on us stealing from them."

I looked up from the page at him. "We still need men, General. If the civilian population wants protection from the legion they might have to part with a few slaves. I am not breaking into their houses and spiriting them away in the night. I will not turn down the help of those who offer me their lives willingly, slave or free. Our enemy's numbers remain small, for now, but they are almost infinitely more trained than our troops. So we need to hem them in with a greater force."

"We have the Gabiniani..." Achillas began to say.

I waved my hand impatiently. "Five hundred of the most experienced of which departed with their general and are now off sparring in Hispania. Yes, we have the Gabiniani. They do not like my sister, true, but is that grudge enough to keep them on our side when they fight one of their own? Aulus Gabinius agreed to fight for Caesar in spite of his ties to Pompey, we cannot be sure his men will not do the same. I want men in place who are loyal to us in case we lose them. We are not made of infinite coin with which to bribe Latin mercenaries."

"I will ensure the loyalty of the Gabiniani, my lady."

I shrugged, irritated. "I trust you to do what you can, sir. But it is my job to prepare for all contingencies."

Achillas looked as though there was more he wished to say, yet he decided against it. Hesitatingly, he moved closer towards my couch and crouched down at my feet. "I wish you did not have to take on all these burdens, my lady. It is not right for one as delicate as yourself."

I gave a little huff of amusement as I turned over the scroll to the other side. "I have been called many things, General. 'Delicate' has never been one of them."

"Oh, of course children are made of bendable stuff, but you are becoming a woman now, Your Highness." His sapphire eyes swept over me until they pulled mine from my reading and arrested them. "You should not have to be so embroiled in this dirty business."

I could feel myself blushing despite my best efforts. "A queen is different from an ordinary woman. We have different cares."

"I know, but your sister does not have to ride the lines from morning to night. She does not have to wrinkle her head about strategy." He placed one hand on the arm of the couch and with the other reached into my lap to withdraw the scroll. "If you would just let me help you..."

"General Achillas! What is going on here?" We both jumped at the voice of Ganymedes, who was standing at the entrance to the tent.

"Nothing, sir," answered Achillas politely, returning to his feet. "I was simply discussing the implementation of some plans with the queen. But I have much to do, so if you are in need of an audience with Her Highness, she is at your disposal." He sauntered past my tutor who continued to glare at him until he was gone. Ganymedes turned back to me, his eyes still full of displeasure.

"Teacher, I..."

"Your Majesty must remember her place," he cut me off coldly. "She should not be entertaining men alone in her tent."

I bristled. "I am commanding this army, teacher! I cannot wait to give orders until an appropriate chaperone is found!"

"Is that what that was?"

I blushed again. "I do not know what you are saying."

Ganymedes sighed heavily and came over to take my hands in his. "I do not wish to scold you, *nedjet*. But Achillas serves your brother's interests, not yours. And just as your brother cannot be trusted to have your interests in his heart, so too must you be wary of Achillas."

"I know that!" I could not help but reply indignantly. "I am not so much a child anymore."

My teacher looked down at my small hands in his large, fleshy ones with a sad smile. "I know this, Your Majesty. That is why I am afraid for you."

I am in the desert. The sun beats down on the sand making mirage mist rise in the distance. I feel the lurid heat, though I do not sweat and burn. The sky above me is full of dark clouds as I walk towards Set, who sits on a rocky outcropping. When I reach him, I see in his eyes a dark menace I have never witnessed before.

He conjures up desert wasps in his hands and methodically crushes them into dust. I kneel at his feet and wait for him to acknowledge me.

"I am displeased," he growls finally, rolling a crawling wasp over his long fingers.

"So it would seem, my Lord. I am sorry if I have offended you. I know we have made little progress, yet holding a veteran Roman legion in stalemate is still an accomplishment."

"Not with that." He gives an impatient bark that causes the wasp to twitch its wings in agitation. "You have done well. But I do not approve of the schemes of the Greek imp."

"Who? Achillas?"

Set crushes the wasp in his fist and smacks it against the rock face, making the whole earth tremble. "He dares to look upon you with lustful eyes and a forked tongue! I will not allow him to corrupt you for his base purposes!"

I am wary if only because Set's anger burns hotter than I have ever seen. This is not the mere disgust he showed towards Salvius, this is something much deeper. I know I should proceed cautiously, but I also know that I can navigate the temper of the desert god through levity more easily than with bowing and scraping. "I did not realize my Lord had forbidden me mortal men," I remark flippantly. "I will be sure to lock myself away, then, to please you."

His green eyes smoulder dangerously. "Do not be pert with me, child! I am most serious."

I keep my gaze steady. "And so am I. I do not favor General Achillas especially, my Lord. I need him as a soldier who can command the respect of my troops and his cooperation to control the flow of ruinous ideas coming from my brother. I must make do with what is available to me."

"You blush under his gaze," the god points out sharply.

I lower my head. "Your Lordship must forgive me that. I am still a young girl who is not used to the attentions of men."

This coaxes the smallest of smiles from him. "You are bold enough with me, *nedjet.*"

"You give me that boldness, my Lord. I have known you nearly all my life. Besides," I say, holding my palm over my heart, "you have given me a piece of you. We are One."

He stands and takes me in his arms. "You are right, Beloved. Forgive me."

"There is nothing to forgive, my Lord."

He gently strokes my hair. "I am still worried for you. The warring city is a dangerous place."

"I know. But we must not falter now."

He frowns. "There is a saying among the horse-taming people. About the Greeks..."

'The horse-taming people' is the name by which the Egyptian gods call the Trojans. "Do you mean the old adage *Beware Greeks bearing gifts,* my Lord?"

He meets my eyes directly. "Yes, Beloved. It is so. And never was there a Greek to be warier of than your Achillas. He is not to be trusted. Guard yourself."

And then I wake up.

After my dream, I could not sleep. The air was hot and thunder rolled ominously towards the city from the desert at our backs. My Lord was agitated indeed if such a storm threatened here in the Waking World.

I left my tent, signaling to the guard on duty that I needed no escort. I walked to the edge of our camp until I reached the furthest house on this picket line. I climbed up the ladder to the roof and walked to the ledge to look out at the glow of my men's campfires.

Those of my sister's burned in the distance. I wondered what she was thinking. Was she awake too, vainly chasing sleep as her child swam in her womb? Did she think of me? Or had Kharmion made a potion for her to fall into nothingness? Perhaps she slept on untroubled by the uncertainties that plagued me. Maybe that was the true power of her *heka*.

I was joined by Tahu, who moved from the shadows to my side. "How can I serve you, Your Majesty?"

"With nothing, my friend. Unless you know a remedy for troubling dreams."

He smiled. "My father used to take me into his arms and tell me the old stories until I drowsed off again."

"My nurse would do the same for me. I miss her often."

"May I ask about your dream, my lady?"

"You may, though I fear you might think me delusional if I acquiesced. A state most alarming for the commander of an army."

"I doubt it, Your Majesty. You have always shown yourself to be of a clear-eyed and judicious mind. Besides," he grinned, teeth gleaming in the blackness, "a little delusion is good in a pharaoh. How else could one mortal man decree the building of the Great Pyramid for himself alone?"

"Very well. My kingly delusion is that I believe the gods speak to me in my dreams."

"But that is the most fortuitous and kingly delusion of them all, my lady! How can we help but prosper if the gods favor you?"

I laughed a little. "I fear you jest with me, sir."

He grew serious. "I do not, my Queen. Which gods speak to you?"

"The gods of the Black Land. The Lord of the Red Land particularly holds me in his thrall."

"Lord Set does not deign to speak with us mortals lightly. Blessed are you, my lady, to gain the Red Lord's favor. We need the God of War in these perilous times."

"He has been my companion for many years now, and I still feel shy about revealing him."

"The Red Lord is a secretive god as well, Your Majesty. You suit one another. You are more than our Queen, our general. You are a *hemet-net-jer*, a god's wife. A title many in the royal palaces have claimed in the past, with little proof. Long have we waited for the gods to speak to us again. May they continue to bless us with your guidance and theirs."

I bit my lip. "My Lord detests Achillas. He believes him to be false and a danger to me."

"The general is an ambitious man, my lady. Such men are always dangerous."

I touched his shoulder. "If you believe in our cause, will you discover how dangerous he truly is?"

"I will see it done, my Pharaoh."

"My brother is Pharaoh, Tahu."

"Not to me, my Pharaoh." He bowed and descended the ladder into the house.

Chapter Twenty-Five

I am on the athletic field once more, and Sekhmet sits cross-legged in the turned dirt waiting for me. Her head is held aloft and her eyes are closed, yet she radiates her energy in such a way that she appears as alert as if she was about to pounce on a foe. I settle myself down next to her and await her instruction. The eyes of her lioness hood remain open, staring endlessly towards the horizon.

"Do you know why we are seemingly at rest this night, Ptolemy-daughter?" she asks at length, her eyes remaining closed.

"Tell me, O Sword of Egypt."

"Because combat of arms is only one half of war, Princess," she says. "The other part is knowing your enemy. Do this, and then you can anticipate what he will do. Correct anticipation eliminates unnecessary wastes of resources. What does your enemy have?"

"The greatest living general of men, and a single legion of steady, battle-hardened troops."

"What have you, Ptolemy-daughter?"

"More people with which to fight, but people who are either untested soldiers, or excitable, terrified subjects who are defending their homes and families. And," I make a gesture to myself, "novice commanders."

"You have the Greek. He is no novice."

"Set says he is not to be trusted."

She tilts her head to the side. "Trusted, no. Yet he is still useful to you at this time. Even a chipped blade may still cut."

"My lady takes a more practical view than my Lord."

Sekhmet makes a little purr deep in her throat. "Set thinks he is carved of stone, yet always he has been ruled by his emotions." She looks at me, her fireheart eyes glowing with amusement. "He does not always see clearly when it comes to you. That is why we appointed him your guardian but did not leave you solely to his instruction." Her gravelly laugh saws through the air and she gives a clap of her hands. "Enough of the Lord of the Stinging Tongue's foolishness. Tell me, what weakness can you discover about your northern wolf?"

"My sister said his weaknesses are violence and flesh."

"What say you?"

I hesitate, and the night in the Temple of Isis rushes back upon me unbidden, making my face hot. "I do not think it is that simple."

She nods. "Good. Tell me more."

I think on this. "She called them vices, and they are not the pursuits of a gentleman, though to call them vices brings to mind a man ruled by impulse. Caesar does not strike me as such a man."

"Indeed, Ptolemy-daughter. So what do you think is his true weakness?"

I meet her eye. "He hates to lose. Violence and lust are simply means to an end."

"Bravo, Princess! Now you are thinking as a general!"

I flush again, this time with pleasure at having earned such unguarded praise from the stern goddess. "But how does this help me? He is well-versed in avoiding the thing he hates and I do not know if I have the skill or resources to challenge that."

"You may not, child, but that is besides the point. The point is how he will react given what you know. Now, this man comes to the Two Egypts with control in his *ib*, and wielding the weapons of violence and lust. Who stands in the way of his desire for control of our realm?"

"The heirs of Ptolemy."

"Yes. How can he use the weapons at his disposal to achieve his aims?"

As if a lamp were lit in a darkened room, I see Caesar's path illuminated. "My sister presents him with an opportunity to use flesh to bring one half of the falcon throne under his control. Caesar is notorious for his affairs, but he rarely uses rapine for pleasure alone. He sleeps with rivals' wives and captive noblewomen because they have information. Lust is easier than rampage, and Cleopatra offers him the path of less resistance."

"So you know what weapon faces those who oppose the pair of them."

I shiver, thinking of the bloody portion left for me. Perhaps my sister had been right to offer up her body when she had the opportunity. Despite these dark thoughts, I continue to roll the goddess' instruction over in my mind. "You agree that the general is not a man driven by bloodlust," I say slowly to her.

"This is so," she agrees.

I bite my lip as I follow the meandering path of this idea. "Then he will not lash out at us unless he is driven to it, because he does not love war for its own sake."

She does not contradict me. "And what will drive him to this pass, child?"

I stop to ponder. "Pride in his own ability. Or my sister's *heka*, if she can."

"Ah, the *heka* is unavoidable," says Sekhmet thoughtfully. "Though do not despair, and focus instead on what you know of your sister. For the *heka* cannot not change who she is, only bring forth what is already inside. What are your sister's weaknesses?"

"She is quick to anger and it clouds her vision when it takes her," I admit. "Sometimes, also, her quick mind makes her overconfident."

"Yes, so you must remember this as you go against her."

"Unless Caesar is strong enough to check these faults, which he may be. They are not flaws he shares."

"That makes them well-matched, but it also means they will perhaps be at odds of purpose. Use that to your advantage."

I sigh. "Ptolemy and I are also at cross-purpose often, and we are the weaker pair. Though if Egypt is to remain free, I must stay with him and weather the violence that will come down on our heads for opposing Cleopatra. Unless Caesar secretly harbors a taste for skinny princesses."

Sekhmet gives a shake of her head. "That is not your path, Ptolemy-daughter. It is not for those who wear the mantle of the gods' favor to bend in supplication. We are fashioning you so that others will bow to you, not the reverse."

"I do not feel worthy of that, Lady of the Strong Spear. Yet I will endeavor to be obedient."

For a single instant, her expression softens. "That is all we can ask of you." Then she returns to her lesson. "There is a third person to consider in this train of thought, child. Do you know who it is?"

I think of Ptolemy, Achillas, even Apollodorus. "Who, my lady?"

Her gaze becomes a long needle piercing my chest and revealing my *ka* to the open air. "What are *your* weaknesses, little princess?"

I should be afraid, though in truth I am not. The gods see all, they already know the feebleness of their servant. Nothing I could say would shock the bloody goddess because confession is not what she is seeking. She is asking me to look inward and show her that I understand the knotted threads of my own *ba* that will attempt to ensnare me as I labor in this fight. Part of me is very nearly relieved; this is a test I can do much more easily than swinging a sword or tacking a sail. I have precious few illusions about my own worth.

"That is simple, my lady," I answer promptly. "I think over-long about everything except in the governance of my tongue, and I am stubborn when I should be sweet. My confidence is only as wide as spider's silk, yet somehow I have enough arrogance to be defiant to all when it suits my fancy. I have more weaknesses than my opponents combined, yet I believe myself to know better than they."

Sekhmet lifts my chin like a firm mother who loves her children as fiercely as she corrects them. "Self-knowledge is an uncertain gift from the gods, child. It brings great strength, though often only through great pain. However, to know one's self is a more potent weapon than all of the machines of war and all of the intelligence that can be gathered about an enemy. When all else abandons you, look inside your heart to find your way."

And then I wake up.

I was perched on the skeleton of an unfinished railing aboard one of my new *trihemiolia*, drawing my knees up to my chest, conversing with Dejen as he worked a plane along the wood's edge and directed the shipwrights raising planks to form the hull.

"Ah, now this pleases me, Queen of Queens," Dejen said. "Prokopios bought me to pull loads like an ox, but my father's family have ever been craftsmen. I have been whittling at this and that since I was deemed trustworthy enough to hold a knife."

I reached over to run a hand over the smoothed wood, rubbing away the fine coat of sawdust. "I have not much experience with skills of the hands." I giggled at myself. "Mudjet barely trusts me to help her wind wool."

He studied me playfully. "Ah, well, that might make you an unfortunate housewife, my Iron Queen, though the old gods seem to have intended you for more than weaving and sweeping."

"You have not seen my handiwork, sir. We shall have to hope they have done so, otherwise I shall be twice-cursed," I answered with a grin.

We were then interrupted by the approach of Ganymedes and a small contingent of native soldiers. Dejen helped me down from the railing and I ran over to meet them.

"*Nedjet*, Achillas and the Gabiniani are making their move on Pharos," Ganymedes called out, his voice full of concern.

"Why was I not informed?" I asked, regretting the foolish words the moment they left my lips. "Has he at least had the sense to take the native troops of the Lost Lords with him?"

"Yes, but the lords themselves have been left behind as well. I prevented them from coming with me because I wished them to take care of any civilians who are caught in the middle. They are livid at the insult to Your Majesty's command."

I held the back of my neck distractedly. "That is our problem. My command is so fractured I cannot even be sure that Achillas necessarily should have told me of this. He will say that it had my brother's blessing and that is enough." I paused, glancing about. "Teacher, have you seen Tahu?"

"I have not since this morning. I know he is on your business, but I have no other information."

"Does my Queen wish me to find her Memphisian?" the deep voice of Dejen came from behind me.

I shook my head. "No, no. It is simply that I feel as though the general noticed his absence and used the opportunity to make this attack. Achillas must know that Tahu keeps me informed of everything that happens in the camp and in the city."

"I am sure he will return when he hears of all of this. We should find high ground from which Your Highness can watch the proceedings," said my teacher.

I agreed and all of us departed at once to a nearby roof to watch Achillas' grand strategy unfold. Like many of our previous skirmishes, it was not a battle full of grand military art — only the grinding, grunting give and take of two armies trying to gain the upper hand in a relatively confined space, neither making much progress. Each side would grasp a few more feet of ground, then the other would agonizingly claw it back. The monotony had a hypnotic effect on those of us who were only spectators and it was only when I felt Quintus appear next to me and drape a swath of linen over my head and around my shoulders that I realized that I was almost entirely drenched in sweat from the afternoon heat.

"Thank you," I said. "How does it look below?"

"About the same," he answered. "I think this will end up being another stalemate. We were the only people caught unawares by this attack, I'm afraid. You will have to forgive your loyal servants for not preventing these events, Your Majesty."

"It cannot be helped now. We shall have to do better in the future."

Quintus proved right. As night descended, my army had taken a small chunk of the enemy's position on the island, but it had not been the decisive push my general had wanted. So it was with decidedly less pomp than he had bargained for that Achillas met us on the roof, looking dirty and exhausted.

He held up his hands defensively. "I know what you would say, Ganymedes, but I needed the element of surprise to challenge the legion."

My teacher was not impressed. "Nothing involving engagements should be kept secret from Her Majesty. What if she had been with the troops on Pharos and had been caught in the crossfire?"

Achillas' conciliatory attitude evaporated. "It is patently unfair for you to suggest I would not have secured the safety of the princess before beginning the attack." He appealed to me directly. "My lady cannot believe I would do such a thing."

"Before today, I would have agreed, sir, though I cannot overlook the fact that the number of secrets you and my brother are keeping from me continues to grow. I do not know what to believe."

He tamped down his anger and tried to be placating. "My lady must not listen to my detractors," he said, glaring at Ganymedes. "They love you very much, but they forget that others care for you as well. All the Pharaoh and I do is for your protection. You have become the palace's symbol to the people, we would not let any harm come to you."

It would do no good to argue with him, yet as usual I could not control my tongue in favor of being queenly. "I do not need protection, that I have plenty of!" I snapped. "What I need is to be treated as a true partner in an endeavor that I have worked just as diligently in as you or Ptolemy!"

"Of course, Your Highness. You have done everything we have asked of you and more. But you are only a young woman, we simply wish to lighten your load..."

I cut him off, furious. "Our opponent is a young woman! I know we talk day and night of Caesar, yet do not think for a minute that Cleopatra is not in charge here! She... she has weapons you cannot even fathom!"

I did not wait for the general's reply, but instead stormed off to my tents. Mudjet rose as I entered, though I waved her off angrily and threw myself down on my couch.

My companion ignored me and came over to stand at my side. "What can I do for you, my lady?"

I held my head as I shook it. "I do not know. Nothing. I do not see how I can continue to lock horns with Achillas over everything. I cannot lead my own head without his interference. I am fighting with shadows."

She began to reply when a voice from outside the tent flap interrupted her. "My Pharoah, may I enter?"

"*Tua netjer*, I have been worried about you, Tahu. Of course." He came inside and I motioned him forward. "What news have you?"

My burly Egyptian lieutenant came to my feet and knelt down, resisting my attempts to raise him. Then I knew what he had to say was serious. "I beg my Pharoah's pardon for failing to know of the attack against Pharos in advance. It will not happen again."

"You cannot be everywhere, do not be troubled. I know you devote the last of your strength to me."

He grimaced. "The Leopard had sent a message to me to warn me of it, but I was away and did not receive the information until it was too late."

"It does not matter. The attack was not entirely unsuccessful and we had few losses. My involvement or lack thereof was likely immaterial."

Tahu's face lit up with uncharacteristic anger. "No! The information I have for my lady proves that if Your Majesty allows this repeated disrespect from her officers, she will be lost!"

"What have you heard?" I asked, trying to keep my voice even.

"I have done as my Pharaoh asked of me. I have found out the plots of Achillas and your lord brother."

I blanched at his tone. "What are their intentions?"

"Lord Ptolemy has no intention of escaping the palace to join our forces. The general and he are in agreement that he should await events rather than running to the defense of his own people," Tahu said, unable to hide the disgust in his voice.

I sighed. "This is not shocking. I had hoped that circumstances would raise my brother's character, but he has always been lazy. If he does not have to lift a finger, he will not do so. I suspect our chances are improved without him here with us anyway; I will trust my own instincts over his help."

"That is not the whole of it, my lady. Your lord brother harbors this complacency because Achillas is tasked with providing a ransom to Caesar for the young king's release. They expect Lord Ptolemy to be able to walk out of the palace unmolested rather than bear the indignity of flight."

My cheeks colored at the memory of my own bedraggled escape from the palace. Naturally Ptolemy would demand the smoother path as always. I quickly set aside these thoughts, though, when I realized I would have larger problems on my hands than embarrassment if my brother was given attendant authority over our forces.

"What is the amount of ransom with which the general seeks to tempt Caesar with?" I asked, trying to calculate how we could match a sum to block their offer.

Tahu looked at me gravely. "It is no sum of coin, my Pharaoh. It is you."

I heard Mudjet let out a gasp at my side as ice froze around my heart. "I do not understand," I said dumbly. "Even if they wish to be rid of me, which would not be the most absurd of ideas, why would they expect Caesar to accept such an exchange? He is still Pharaoh and to them I am only a princess. What use would I be to him?"

"You are modest as usual, my lady. You are the face of our army, only you could have rallied so many different factions together into a coherent rebellion. Even if the Consul is foolish enough to believe you are only the figurehead of our struggle, he might see it as a prudent trade to demoralize our men and give them an untested boy in return."

I swallowed thickly against my dry throat. "Has their offer been met positively?"

He shook his head. "Achillas dares not raise the issue to the enemy without ensuring that he has enough support for this plan in our own camp. Otherwise, he risks a mutiny. He has hinted here and there amongst the Greeks and the Gabiniani, but no one of consequence has been receptive whilst we are holding our own against the legion. The Gabiniani in particular are not impressed with Lord Ptolemy's leadership since they placed their allegiance behind him in opposition to your sister."

I breathed out weakly. "Well, I suppose we must be grateful Achillas has been unsuccessful as of yet. Though this places his actions of today in a darker light. I will be on my guard. Thank you for this, Tahu."

He placed a hand over his heart. "I live to protect you, my lady. As do many. The general will not find his task an easy one."

He took his leave and I sunk into my own thoughts once more, twisting my mother's bracelet around my wrist.

"What are you thinking of, my lady? asked Mudjet after a time.

"Oh, of how worthy of Hephaestus my snares are. To protect myself, I must of course continue to lead the army in such a way that they will hold to my cause despite Achillas' designs to surrender me to our enemies." I grimaced, then continued. "But such excellent generalship will only make that enemy more enticed by Achillas' offer should he manage to convey it to them."

Chapter Twenty-Six

I sat in my tent, rubbing my temples as I read over the stack of letters I had from Ptolemy. In spite of what I had learned from Tahu about my brother's intentions, I was not entirely in a position to reveal my awareness of these hidden plans, so I persevered in searching vainly for some kind of overall strategy in his erratic advice, even though I knew it was hopeless, to mask my knowledge. I had long suspected that the absurdity of his instructions was what kept them reaching me despite his sequestering in the palace. My sister no doubt hoped I would try to follow his nonsensical advice.

Once I had reached this conclusion, I next tried to envision what Caesar would hope to gain from me beyond the disorder it would cause among our army. I relaxed my mind as Sekhmet had shown me and thought. I imagined the organization of a Roman legion, the nature of the Romans themselves. Men born to certain freedoms and privileges in their world, trained to fight as one body, one will.

That was it. The legionaries were allowed to be vocal in their dissents and even challenge their commanders because it was up to the commanders to win the loyalty of the men. If that was done, the men would never back down. Caesar was relying on the divisions of loyalty in my troops — those loyal to my brother, those loyal to me, those loyal to Achillas, even those loyal only to themselves — to destroy our resistance from within. That was the true reason he was waiting for his other legions, despite their slow progress on the winter seas and difficulty abandoning their fight with what remained of Pompey's forces. There was a chance we would crumble from within without him having to dirty his hands much.

I mused on how I could change this. I was not overly worried about Ptolemy's influence. The troops had little respect for a pharaoh who was not on the battlefield; he might think his capture, such as it was, enough of an excuse, but many of the men did not see it that way. The ones out for themselves could be bribed with coin, though I would have to stay ahead of anything Achillas might offer them behind my back.

If he was doing so, that is. I knew not his intentions in this regard. So far he had done nothing openly disloyal to my brother and little except nettle me, but his mind was veiled from everyone and that was very dangerous. So there it was: if I hoped to bind my men to me as Caesar's were to him, I had to realize that my rival for sole command was Achillas, not my brother, and proceed accordingly.

The enormity of that task was settling on my shoulders when Mudjet stepped into our tent carrying a pitcher of water. "My lady, do you have a moment to spare to Lord Ehoou-hanif in his tent?"

I pushed aside Ptolemy's letter and sighed. "Yes, yes. I will come. I should try to soothe the lords after the snub Achillas gave them anyway." I stood and started towards the tent flap.

"Oh no, my lady," she said with a giggle. "Not like that! You are not fit to be seen!"

I ran a hand over my hair. "Is it as bad as that?"

Mudjet led me over to the basin in the corner and filled it with water from the pitcher. "Not so much, perhaps. Though I think we should take a moment to make you more suitable."

I rinsed my face and wiped myself down with a damp cloth. Mudjet went over to my trunks and produced a white linen shift dress in an Egyptian cut. "Where did you get such a thing?" I asked in surprise.

"Oh, somewhere or another. I cannot recall. I thought it might do for a clean dress when you were not riding around on horseback. It will please the Lost Lords, too."

I dabbed a little perfume in the hollows of my neck and stepped into the dress as Mudjet smoothed a few of its pleats. "It fits well, though I do not have the jewelry to set it off properly," I said, turning to look at it from behind.

"It looks well enough, my lady. I think I shall let your hair down with it, though."

"Not too scandalous?"

"Maybe, but it is more in keeping with the style," she answered with a grin as she undid my braids.

Thus arranged, I reached for the vulture crown, but Mudjet picked it up for me. "I shall take it with us, but I thought your head might enjoy a few minutes of breeze."

The beautiful crown was heavy, so I did not object. Maybe more time away from its weight would stir a plan on how to deal with Achillas and my brother into my brain. We walked through the cool moonlight across the nearly sleeping camp until we reached the desert tents of the Lost Lords. We entered the tent of Ehoou-hanif, and I was greeted with the sight of all of the Egyptian lords gathered there, along with my teacher, Tahu, Dejen, Quintus, and a handful of my other retainers, all with large smiles on their faces.

I looked at Mudjet, whose face echoed their happy expressions. "What is the meaning of all of this?"

Ganymedes came to me and took my hand. "Forgive the subterfuge, *nedjet*, but we wished this to be a surprise."

Ehoou-hanif moved forward and bowed. "Your Majesty, your subjects wish to formally acknowledge you as our Pharaoh."

"I do not know what to say," I whispered, stunned. "You offer me a gift I cannot repay."

"It is our gift to give, Queen of Queens," said the deep voice of Dejen. "It has been spoken of amongst us — those of us who would follow you even unto death. We are in agreement."

"You have ruled among us too long without your proper dues, Your Majesty," added Amenei. "Let us bring you the honor you deserve."

Ehoou-hanif guided me towards his couch, set up in the center of the tent. "Please excuse the humbleness of the seat we enthrone you upon, my Queen."

"I think it is a fitting remark upon the reign you set me on, my lord," I answered. "My circumstances are humble but my purpose is in the heat of action, full of the lofty hope against hope of my kingdom."

"Well spoken, Your Majesty," he rejoined and received a flat box from one of his servants. Opening it, he continued. "If it please Your Majesty, I and the blood of my ancestors offer you this *menat* to wear as befitting a lady of your exalted status."

The large *menat* necklace was indeed very old and made with exquisite craftsmanship. Its beads were of faience, ivory, and cinnabar inlaid with gold. The beads from which its large half-moon shape hung were in the shape of Sekhmet, as was the counterpoise bead that would hang down my back. The old lord carefully arranged the necklace around my neck as a shaven-headed priest stepped forward with a tray of small dishes. "This priest has served my family for a lifetime. He holds the proper rituals in his hands."

The priest gave a bob of his head to me and handing the tray to an assistant, began. "The Black Land and its People have already called this Woman, Blessed by the Gods, as their Pharaoh, Daughter of Lord Ra. We come tonight to consecrate her in her Five Names so that even in the *Duat* they will call her *Taui*-Pharaoh."

He took the first dish, filled with a white paste, which he placed on his fingers and spread across my forehead. "White is the blinding light of Father Ra's radiance, strong as His eternal Reign. So too shall be the reign of this Pharaoh, whose First Name we name as *Akhuiakhutre*, Light and Renown of Ra."

He next took the second dish filled with oil and touched my chest along my breastbone. "As we enter this world, we are named by the Gods through the mouths of our parents. The Birth Name the Gods call the Pharaoh by is *Tjesiib*, in the language of the Greeks — Arsinoë — She Who Raises the Mind. So it has been, so it shall remain."

He then reached for the dish that held a single falcon feather, and touched the feather to my lips. "Horus is the Father of all Pharaohs, but the Gods in Their wisdom know that just as there are two Egypts, so too are there two Gods who rule our land. We know Lord Horus stands with us this night, but He has given the care of this Pharaoh to the Lord Who Brings the Thunder in these perilous times. So we call upon an ancient custom and cede this Name to Lord Set. The Pharaoh shall be known by the *serekh* of *Meretkaset*, Beloved of the Ka of Set."

He reached for the final two dishes filled with sand and, taking a handful of each, sprinkled them over my head and in a circle around my person. "Our land is the child of Two Kingdoms. Nekhbet is the Queen of Upper Egypt and Her Sister, Iaret, Queen of Lower Egypt. They are our mothers and our protectors. May They spread Their wings and raise up Their Heads in defense of the Pharaoh whose *nebty* shall be *Iaitrwedja*, She of the Two Ladies to Whom the Gods Open Their Mouths."

Lastly, he took the vulture crown from Mudjet and lowered it onto my head. "Lord Horus also grants a golden Name to His children, the Pharaohs, that will go with them into the eternal land of the Gods. It will blaze in the darkness where there are no other lights, where the Dream World stretches to the ends of the universe. May this Pharaoh be known in the *Duat* as *Khaiwadjet-Merettaui*, She Who is Like the Shining Eye of Horus, beloved of the Two Egypts. It is so written, so it shall be."

All around me knelt down with bowed heads. The priest held a hand out towards me. "We hail Thee, Pharaoh Tjesiib-Arsinoë Akhuiakhutre Meretkaset Iaitrwedja Khaiwadjet-Merettaui. May Thy reign be blessed."

In that night, surrounded by those I loved and those who loved me, I became the fourth woman of my name to hold a claim on the throne of Egypt. My brother had spoken words to the effect that I was his co-ruler in our sister's place, though it was the love of Egypt that made those empty words flesh and bone.

We were happy that night, laughing and celebrating in a moment where the weight of our impossible task melted off of us and we danced in a flitting scene that smelled like freedom. The day would come soon enough, with all of its schemes and cares, yet we lived in that night as if we were the masters of our destinies. This is how I like best to remember my faithful friends, lords by birth and lords by their own aristocracy of worth, with me and so happy. This memory always tastes to me of honey.

Chapter Twenty-Seven

It was early morning as I traversed the harbor on horseback with Mudjet, speaking with my shipwrights as they continued to labor on my fleet, when a runner from our camp approached.

"Forgive the interruption, Your Majesty. There is an old woman waiting to speak with you in your tent." He opened a small box to reveal an exquisite old hand mirror. "She says it is urgent."

I exchanged a look with my companion. "I am coming directly. Make sure she is comfortable."

We rode back to the Gate of the Moon and entered my tent, where my visitor sat heavily cloaked on one of the couches. She rose at our appearance and knelt at my feet. "*Hai heqat-taui, a'a meret en akhmui-remthu,*" said the Mirror as she removed the hood of her cloak.

"You are most welcome here, *mu-ti,*" I said to her, gesturing that she should not kneel. "Please be seated again."

"There is no time, Your Majesty. You are in grave danger."

"What is this danger?"

"Your Greek general has been gathering strength to cement his own status as the ruler of this land. He plans to seduce you into marriage and stage a coup over your brother. He knows Ptolemy's rule carries little weight with this army, he is no obstacle. If he gets you, though, he secures ties to the blood royal and the loyalty of the native Egyptians, as well as the non-Greek foreigners."

"He would dare this?" cried Mudjet, aghast.

"This and more, *sherit,*" answered the Mirror as she met my gaze and held it deeply.

I understood. "Achillas only requires me for the success of the coup. After that, I am nothing but a rival for authority over the army."

She nodded, pleased at my adeptness. "It is so, Your Majesty. He is as jealous of your popularity as your brother and sister. He is embarrassed that it is you who command with such acclaim against the mighty Caesar."

"How did you come to know this?"

"I closed my doors to the Romans, my lady remembers," she replied with a cynical smile. "Therefore, it is a good place for your men to gather where they know they will not be overheard by the enemy. Because you so wisely kept your pact with us secret, they also assume they will not be overheard by you. My girls have the eyes of antelopes and the ears of foxes."

"Do you know how deep this conspiracy runs?" I asked, studying my hands with such intensity I marveled I could not see my bones in the daylight.

"I do not for certain. Though I am reasonably confident it is confined to the Greeks and furthermore to their higher officers."

I closed my eyes. "That is enough. I will have to make an example of him or I will have an insurrection in my ranks."

Mudjet wrung her hands. "You must find Tahu or Quintus at once, my lady! They will consult with Ganymedes and decide what is to be done. This must be dealt with swiftly."

I looked to the Mirror. "I have sent Tahu to bring more recruits and supplies from Memphis, and he will not return before morning. Quintus is supervising the engineers building replacement siege towers in Rhakotis and Ganymedes is engaged containing skirmishes near the Jewish Quarter."

"Then send for Dejen!" wailed Mudjet frantically.

"Dejen is building my ships, I can spare him even less than the others. How long can this wait, *mu-ti*?"

"Not long, Your Majesty. Achillas will strike soon. The longer he delays, the more likely you are to discover the conspiracy. It appears he is only looking for an opportunity to get you away from your tutor."

"Then we shall give it to him," I decided. "He is at the battlements in the northern Soma. I shall send him a message to dine with me this evening, should the fighting be contained. He will know that my guardians are detained elsewhere. We shall see how determined he is in this plan."

"May the gods protect you, Your Majesty." The Mirror peered at me sympathetically from her narrow eyes.

I slowly breathed out. *There is no other way. You cannot wait for Ganymedes or the others.* Mudjet had left the meal prepared for us. She had begged me to let her stay, but I had refused.

"Please, my lady," she had murmured as she brushed eye paint across my lids, her lips nearly white. "What if something goes wrong? He is strong, what if he defends himself or overpowers you?"

I had shook my head vehemently, interrupting her task. "No, it must be this way. If we are alone, he will not suspect a trap."

Now I wished I had bowed to her entreaties as I worked hard to steady my hands. I checked the lay of the nearly sheer violet-colored *chiton* Mudjet had borrowed and altered in haste from the Sweet Harp, to see that the dagger at my waist was concealed. That was my only protection. I caught my reflection in a bowl of water on the table. I prayed I did not look as pale as I felt.

Darkness had settled uneasily over the city when Achillas entered the room at the appointed hour. I had received his elegant reply hardly an hour after I had sent it. He would consider it a great honor to dine with me that evening, he wrote in his loose, flowing hand. As if acceptance had ever been in doubt.

The general wore a loose embroidered tunic dyed a rich shade of vermilion and I could smell the ground lotus perfume he wore in his curling golden hair as he strode towards me. He was as handsome as ever, his days in war making him appear even more powerful and commanding. I felt very small again, like the child he had surprised in her rooms at the palace. Was that merely a few months ago? It seemed like a lifetime.

"Your Highness," he bowed with the grace that had made him captain of my image-conscious father's personal guard.

Thinking of my father was not the waking nightmare it usually was. Rather, remembering his fatal pride drew iron into my shivering breast. Ptolemy Auletes would have been inconsolable in his fury to imagine that an upstart noble such as Achillas would dare to aim for the throne of our ancestors. On any other night, such willful arrogance could only blind me to the Waking World as it was. But tonight, tonight it might be the only thing that could save me and Egypt.

"General Achillas." I held out my hand which he bent over. I tried not to flinch as his lips brushed my knuckles. It was the daring gesture of a confident man, to actually kiss the hand of an Egyptian queen, but I could not show my anger. Not yet.

"My lady shows me immense favor to permit me to join her for her evening meal," he said, his smile as sweet as poisoned berries. "I confess I have cherished dear hopes that she might grant me such an invitation, though I had begun to despair of it as a vain wish."

"I did not want to make myself a nuisance," I replied in what I hoped was a light voice. "I know my general is terribly busy night and day pursuing our interests. We do not have the luxury of leisure that we might have possessed in the palace."

His smile widened. "Your Highness is as conscientious as she is kind. But a request from your lips is never a nuisance."

I felt a blush spread across my cheeks and I raced to find a better pretext for it. "There is also my teacher," I said softly, allowing my eyes to drop to the side as if in embarrassment. "He has taken such a set against you."

"Ah, my lady must not worry herself too much over that," he soothed. He reached out for my hand and applied the merest pressure to the fingertips, making my pulse leap uncomfortably. "I know our disagreements are simply the result of eunuch-meddling. Another reason I have longed for us to meet separately."

My face was red as I fumblingly pulled my fingers from his unresisting hold. "Then we are in agreement, sir. I am pleased you are here," I said with a sweeping gesture meant to be welcoming.

He grinned and casually sat himself down on a couch before I could seat myself, so I chose instead to pour him a cup of wine. He took the cup from me and drank deeply as he boldly gazed into my eyes over the rim.

This man had risen a long way to casually accept service from me and I wondered just how much he was willing to dare. The Mirror had said he already held himself out to his most loyal men as Pharaoh in name, clearly he was in a gambling mood. There was no place in this path of his that would be safe for me.

He watched me carefully as I sat down, and I was pleased to see his eyes trail over my dress with interest. The Harp's gown was doing its work.

"You look dazzling, Your Highness," he said, his voice warm with appreciation. "You were a comely enough child when you arrived in my camp, but Mars must have spoken to his lover to give you grace in the crucible of battle. Cleopatra will be green the next time she sees you, especially if you spend a little more time out of the sun to lighten your complexion."

My mouth twisted above my cup at the two-faced compliment. "It would be difficult to lead my men if I stayed inside attending to my face, sir."

He made a flippant gesture. "I have told you to leave that to me. You are their symbol, their goddess. I will do the grunt work of leading the troops."

"That might be the way the Greeks do it now, but it is not the way to lead Egyptians," I remarked gently. "Great Ramses and his father Seti, and Thutmose, and my Macedonian grandsires always marched at the head of the column. Egyptians will march into the Lake of Fire and back for their Pharaoh. Generals are only mortal." I sipped out of my own cup carefully.

I saw something flash across Achillas' eyes that he quickly hid. "Of course, my lady. Though their Pharaoh is Ptolemy, not you."

You may both think that if you wish, you did not see my consecration in my Names. "Naturally, though my brother is an enemy captive. They follow me because I am of the blood, because I fight for him."

"Ptolemy is a weakling and a fool," he replied baldly. "You and they would be better off without him."

I frowned, mildly unnerved by how quickly Achillas made his move. *He is afraid of being interrupted by Ganymedes or someone else, I must remember he has been planning this for a long time. Longer than me.* "Careful, sir," I answered quietly. "You speak treasonously."

He reached over and grasped my wrist with impulsive fingers. "I don't care," he said emphatically. "I don't want to see you tied to him when we are victorious. You deserve more than that. Do you really want to marry your own brother? To one day do as your sister has done?"

Although I moved to pull away from his hold, I could not hide my distaste at being joined to Ptolemy, even symbolically. "That is my duty to my people. There is no other option."

"There is!" he said urgently. "Marry me. Make me your husband, and I'll lead us to greatness."

I managed to pull my wrist out of his hand. "Marry you?" I repeated, pretending to be bewildered.

"Yes, dearest Arsinoë, Queen of Egypt," Achillas said, his lips curling up into a fond smile that seemed to pat my incredulous head. "I am your most willing slave."

I arranged my face into an expression of naive skepticism. "You have flirted with me at a distance, yet these bold words of love are new."

"I have been afraid to let you see my devotion. I didn't think Ganymedes would approve, either," he pleaded.

I gave him a shy smile. "Indeed. Though you have been abrupt as of late, I thought you had tired of my presence."

He frowned and shook his head. "Never yours, my queen. I was angry because of the influence of Ganymedes when he has not the experience or skill I have. If you would only grant me your hand, I would have the power to fight with a free rein and chase Caesar all the way back to Latium."

I got up and moved across the room. "You mean make you Pharaoh," I said to the night air. I needed to hear him speak the words my spies had whispered of.

He followed me to where I stood and turned me around to face him. "Yes, but that's beside the point. We'll rule together. I'll be there to guide you, to keep you safe. You can have a life of ease and luxury again. The life a royal lady should have. And I will make Egypt a new empire."

I tried to shrug off his grip, but he held my shoulders tightly.

"You aspire to be my Caesar, like that man is to my sister," I accused him in the finicky tone of a child-bride. The little girl Achillas aspired to marry. "I do not play her games."

"Of course," he scoffed at the thought. "You are no harlot like her. That's why we shall marry." He lowered a hand to stroke my waist as he leaned in towards my neck, his breath warm with wine. "I still have much to teach you, my sweetheart."

I knew this was my moment. With my free arm I grabbed my dagger and thrust it as hard as I could into Achillas' chest at the point Sekhmet had shown me. Just as he registered the blade's entry, I yanked it up through the cavity and back into my hand. He stumbled away from me clutching the ragged wound as thick blood gushed through his fingers, his sapphire eyes wide with surprise.

I struggled to control the tremor in my voice. "You underestimate me, sir. Just as you have from the moment I first came to you. You also assume your army, as you think of it, has no loyalty to me. I know you mean to give me over to Caesar to ransom Ptolemy."

Achillas tried to speak, but the blood filling his mouth made him choke. He staggered towards me, moaning and reaching out with his free hand. I danced sideways to stay out of his arm's reach and held up a hand. "You would try to tell me that the deal was a clever ruse against the Consul. I know that it is. I know your real object is to marry me and be crowned my consort, so you might murder me at your convenience to reign alone. You come to me with sweet words so that you might have your way with me for a little while, so that I might love you and be blind to your ambitions."

He stumbled again and his throat gagged on the endless wellspring bubbling up from his pierced chest.

"I am not so easily deceived or won," I continued haughtily. "You fancy yourself Caesar's better in all things, and yet you cannot even seduce a guileless girl such as me to fall for your charms."

I watched as my general sank to his knees and gently fell on his side. I walked over and knelt beside him as the light ebbed from his eyes.

"I did not want to do this," I said softly. "Though in my heart I knew long ago that if I did not strike first, you would slit my throat as I slept.

I know by doing this, I lose an accomplished commander and I might end up in the hands of my sister anyway. If that comes to pass, it will be through my own abilities or lack thereof, not because an arrogant snake like you deceived me." I leaned down so I now whispered in his ear. "I do not need the help of Mars. I am beloved of the Lord of the Red Land and your lies are dust beneath his feet."

Those were the bold words I spoke to the corpse of my leading general. By the time Ganymedes and Quintus found me, several hours later at the time I had arranged with Mudjet, I was curled up on a couch I had dragged like a madwoman to the opposite side of my tent from where Achillas lay, retching nothing into a bowl. It would be many nights before I could sleep again, and many more before Mudjet did not hold a watchful vigil over me.

However, this was all behind the veil. In public, I had no time to wallow in what I had done. The next morning, I sent out a runner with a missive explaining events to Ptolemy as vaguely as I dared, knowing even if I claimed proof of Achillas' treason, my brother would not be pleased that I had killed his foremost remaining retainer. I hoped it would reach him even if it passed through the attention of several other gazes ahead of his. It mattered not if the enemy discovered the contents — they would know soon enough anyhow.

After this, I had no choice but to call together my commanding officers and show them the body of Achillas. I watched them carefully from behind the general's bier the men filed in, at first orderly, but then in a growing astonishment as they beheld the corpse lying in the middle of my quarters. The Greeks appeared shocked, but I noticed the Gabiniani present did not. I took heart that the higher Latin officers looked to me with polite attention. They were prepared to listen to my explanation.

"Sirs," I began calmly, letting my voice carry clearly across the stuffy interior of my tent. It was going to be a hot day. "General Achillas is dead. He conspired to marry me and supplant His Majesty the Pharaoh, and for this grievous treason I had no alternative other than to swiftly exe-

cute him. We are in a dangerous fight, gentlemen, and we must not un-
dermine our alliances with such treachery."

Several of the soldiers' eyes registered horror, though it was unclear
if it was because of Achillas' actions or his death.

One of the Greeks spoke up. "Who carried out this deed, Your
Majesty?" he asked, his small eyes searching about for the culprit.

Ganymedes answered before I could. "Captain, I executed the general," he said without emotion. "For the safety of the Queen."

"This should have been done in the light of day, Ganymedes," said
one of the Gabiniani generals, but his tone was not overly censorious.

"I concede this is true, sir," admitted my tutor. "But I discovered the
intrigue only last night, and hurried to her Majesty to inform her. I entered this tent to find the general admitting to this blasphemy with his
own lips while attempting to seduce the queen with lying promises. I
could not stand by and allow her reputation to suffer in the eyes of our
people and the Pharaoh when she was innocent of wrongdoing."

I kept my face neutral as my teacher fabricated these events. I glanced
from face to face, trying to read the officers. I was confident of the loyalty
of my Egyptians and the foreigners, but the remaining men were more
problematic. I hoped that my Gabiniani commanders would be willing
to accept events as they were told, knowing my quality and knowing their
dissatisfaction with my brother's feeble absence. As for the Greek men, I
relied on some of them no doubt knowing that there was enough truth
in Achillas' intentions to accept Ganymedes' version of events as at least
partially truthful. That they had enough involvement in this plot to not
voice any serious opposition lest they be openly implicated.

At length, the first officer spoke once more. "I am glad you have come
to no harm, Your Majesty," he said slowly, almost grudgingly. "Achillas is
dead, so the gods must have judged him guilty. Who do wish to hold his
position for you in the field?"

"Ganymedes has proven his ability to carry out my orders and he is
familiar with our current strategies," I replied, meeting the eyes of the
group at large. "He will be my head general in the field."

I knew this was a difficult medicine for many of the Greek officers to
swallow, men who did not want to serve under a eunuch and especially

one whom Achillas had clashed with. Because I needed them as surely as I needed the others, I attempted to soften the blow.

"However," I told them, allowing a drop of honey to soften my tone, "I will continue to be the supreme commander as His Majesty's representative. Therefore if you have concerns or disagreements, you may bring them to me and I vow to give you a fair hearing. Is this acceptable?"

I could tell that a few wished to further object, yet they realized my word was now truly law and that I had offered them a fair deal. It had been a risk to assume that they would not have an organized candidate to name as my dead general's replacement who could boast more experience than my teacher, but the general assent of agreement signaled that I had gambled wisely.

"Very good. Achillas served the House of Ptolemy well prior to his mistake and he was perhaps deluded by the upheaval of our world. He will be properly buried with full rites in the catacombs. I pray that no one else shall succumb to his folly," I added, and dismissed the officers, who bowed and returned to their divisions leaving me with Ganymedes, Mudjet, Quintus, and Tahu.

I let out a heavy breath and collapsed back onto the couch behind me. "Well, at least there was no mutiny."

Ganymedes grinned. "Your Majesty handled that excellently. You maneuvered the Greeks into a corner they could not back out of without exposing how deeply they were in Achillas' counsel." He glanced down at the body, permitting a look of pity to cross his round face that he never would have given the same man in life. "It was a wise decision to allow the general a proper burial."

"Why did you not let me own my role in his death?" I asked abruptly.

"I thought it best that I was blamed in case his execution sparked a more fervent response. The Egyptians might have accepted you as the mouth of their gods, but the Greeks are ingrained to be wary of a powerful woman. I do not want them to turn on you as they have on your sister. I am only sorry that my promotion may cause discontent in their ranks."

I smiled, touching his arm. "You are the best person for the job, teacher. I know I put my cause in capable hands. If the Greeks are so riled by it as to abandon us, they were never ours to begin with."

Tahu took a step forward. "These are wise words, my Pharaoh. Yet if the Greeks stay, you must remain vigilant to their schemes."

"Will the Egyptians and the others accept these events, Tahu?" I asked.

He nodded. "My men and those of the Scattered bore no great love for Achillas, who always treated us high-handedly." He turned to Ganymedes. "We know that Sir Ganymedes does all to serve our beloved *hemet-netjer*. For her sake, we will follow him into the Lake of Fire. The Scattered and the slaves whom my lady has protected will follow anyone who fights for their Queen of Queens."

"Thank the gods for my natives. Quintus, will the Gabiniani cleave to me?"

The lieutenant waved a dismissive hand. "Never fear, my lady. Most prefer you, their lady of action, to your cowering brother, and the rest will come around. They have to put on their stoic airs in front of the surly Greeks, though I suspect they are secretly impressed by your decisive solution to this problem. It's very Roman."

I nodded to him as regally as I could, but I knew he saw how my my eyes shone. "This is good. Now that I have rid us of an enemy in our midst, we must look to our defenses and move forward as best we can. We must expect Caesar to strike us soon — he will undoubtedly assume we will be disorganized without Achillas."

"We should strike him first and show him Achillas was not our leader, my Pharaoh," said Tahu. "What should be our next move?"

"We need another delaying action, my lady," my teacher contended. "We have to get the men Tahu has brought from Memphis into battalions and Dejen says our builders still require more time to expand your fleet."

"We are building siege defenses as quickly as possible, my Pharaoh," added Quintus, "though must share resources with the shipwrights, which is slowing our progress. As are our daily skirmishes with the legion's attempts at sabotage."

"I will continue to attempt to arrest the corn supply from reaching the legion, though I do not think it can be halted entirely to starve them out," Ganymedes said with regret.

I considered our many problems, but the one voiced by my teacher about the legion's supply lines caught in my teeth. *Sekhmet would tell me that food is an illusion in the desert. It is all about water...* I sat bolt upright, my mind cleared. "Teacher! The corn does not matter, we must cut off the water supply!"

He frowned. "But how? We are surrounded by water."

"But only some it is drinkable," I pointed out, leaping from my couch and beginning to pace around the bier. "And we control the fresh water through the majority of the canals. If we can introduce seawater into the legion's supply, they will be helpless!"

"We would have to keep our own water supply clear," remarked Tahu, thinking over the idea carefully.

"We could divert some of the canals to keep us and the city supplied," said Quintus, walking over to the map table to trace invisible lines across the city.

I broke off my pacing and darted over to look over his angular shoulder. "Do you think we would be able to engineer mechanisms to pull the saltwater into the remaining water?" I asked him urgently.

Quintus thought for a moment. "I believe a sort of water wheel would suffice. But, my lady, the stone we stand upon is porous. Eventually, the water will clear itself and there will be more fresh water running under it beneath the canals."

I nodded. "I know this. We will find out if Caesar does. As Ganymedes said, we need a delaying action. The other legions of the enemy are nearly upon us. This will, with luck, buy us some more time to finish the fleet we need to meet them."

"I think it is a clever plan," said Mudjet, smoothing out a corner of the map while she studied it. "It will show the enemy that my lady is capable of leading us without the traitor Achillas."

"The horse quivers in the desert where the camel is calm," intoned Tahu quietly. "These men of Rome, they are afraid of the desert. They will be frightened if they think their water is tainted."

"It is the only thing we have thought of so far that could even potentially shake the legion," admitted Ganymedes. "I will make the necessary arrangements at once, Your Majesty."

"I will go with you, teacher, and speak to the engineers," I volunteered, feeling lighthearted for the first time since the previous afternoon. Even the corpse in my tent could not haunt me properly in this moment where my mind and those of my companions raced with plans.

Just then, a boy in ragged clothing appeared with a piece of papyrus folded and marked with the hieroglyph of an eagle. I took the paper in my hand and opened it to read Ptolemy's response scrawled in his usual sloppy script. I could read his rage in every letter, and yet I had to suppress the desire to laugh at his childish threats:

Sister, you are a fool and you've doomed us all! I don't care what Achillas did, we need him now! I could have killed him later! How dare you order this without my leave? This is treason too! You are on your own, you will have no help from me on this folly of a course you've set!

- Πτολεμαῖος

"Well at least we are finally free of his interference," Ganymedes remarked drily. "Perhaps my lady should have killed the Greek sooner."

"He does not care that if you had spared Achillas, he would have assassinated you and him," said Tahu with a frown.

A bitter laugh escaped the confines in my throat. "That is hardly shocking. That he will have to figure out how to do it himself later is probably a grave disappointment," I answered with a toss of my head. I could imagine the hysterics Ptolemy had thrown himself into when he received my report. My mouth began to twitch into a smile, but then I saw the small postscript hiding at the bottom of the page. It was clearly written by someone else in an elegant, careful hand:

A bold move, Your Highness. Let us see now how you play the game of war alone.

It was unsigned, though the author was obvious. I pointed it out to my teacher. "We are also spared the uncertainty of knowing whether the Consul is in my brother's confidence on this matter."

My tutor frowned at the neat Greek letters as if he was correcting my old worksheets. "Then our way is clear. I will have our engineers building by nightfall, my child."

I looked to the boy who had brought the message. "Did they give you any money to deliver this?" I asked gently.

He reached into his pocket and produced a single copper coin. I went over to my own purse and pulled out four silver coins. I returned to him and placed them in his hand, causing his large eyes to widen in surprise.

"Have you had anything to eat today?" The boy shook his head and I gestured to Mudjet. "Follow this lady, she will find you something to eat."

The boy's thin face cracked into a grin that would have melted stone. He happily took Mudjet's hand as she led him out of the tent. I watched them leave, unable to pull my eyes away from the boy until I felt a hand on my shoulder.

"I am sure the Prince is well, my lady," said Ganymedes kindly.

"Was I arrogant to trade Cyprus for this?"

"You chose to accept the world as it is, not to settle for a fable spun by your sister. You know there are no guarantees for Ptah's safety in these days. Better to understand that and try than to shut your eyes and grope blindly into the future."

"If this was indeed the correct course," I murmured wistfully. "I wish that it felt that way in my heart. All that I feel is doubt."

"Ah my child, this is the way of the world. You are growing up so quickly." He squeezed my shoulder sadly.

Chapter Twenty-Eight

I went out with my teacher and Quintus Fabianus to speak of our needs to the engineers. The siege had afforded them many opportunities to display their talents, but they had grown bored with copying Roman siege towers and constructing new battlements. When we described what we wished to accomplish with the canals, their faces lit up and they immediately began conferring with one another on how it best could be done.

"Would it be possible to introduce the saltwater slowly, to add to the confusion?" I asked Hieronymos, my chief engineer, whose people originally hailed from Samothrace.

I might have doubted my Greek officers' loyalty, but never the ordinary Alexandrians and never my engineers. I made sure to compensate them well, and they had developed a rapport with my Gabiniani lieutenant which had in turn given them direct access to my ear. Knowing how respected they were in our camp, they were not eager to trade that away for the privilege of being harried about by the Roman tacticians they would be working for on the other side of the palace walls.

"I'm sure it could be done, Your Majesty," he replied. "We could start with some of the canals, and then slowly close in on the supply line until they were cut off. That would also give us a little more time to build additional wheels."

"This would be ideal. Do you have the men you need?"

He made an equivocal gesture. "We would be able to work more efficiently with an extra battalion more to handle the unskilled tasks. And we will require more timber for the wheels."

I nodded. "I shall get Tahu to send you some of the new men from Memphis, they will be fresh. And I will speak to one of the quartermasters to divert the supplies to you."

"Then we will begin at once, my lady."

"Don't fret, Your Majesty," said Tychon, one of the other engineers, with a cheeky grin. "We shall send the Romans a salty puzzle."

While my engineers worked, I redistributed my troops along our front lines. I sent Ganymedes and as many reinforcements as I dared to the Soma to replace Achillas, thinking Caesar might think us weaker there now. Tahu replaced Ganymedes in command of my men in the Jewish quarter. Leaving Quintus with my engineering corps, I still nursed a desire to send more troops against the lighthouse, yet I knew we were not in a position to challenge that stronghold after our previous attempts.

Within a day, the first water wheel was completed and set up at a far point near Lake Mareotis. There is a point where a large canal ditch from the lake splits into two branches that cut through the city in separate directions. The western branch is the one that all of the tributary canals in Rhakotis and the western Soma spring from; the eastern branch is the starting point for the canals that feed the eastern Soma, the Jewish quarter, and the palace.

I pored over maps of the city with Hieronymos and Quintus for hours while my men sawed planks and split wood. "I do not want to block the tributary of the eastern canal that leads to Canopus," I told Hieronymos, pointing to the map in front of us. "We are receiving supplies from there and we cannot cut ourselves off from the Nile, so we must start blocking the canal just past that fork in the waterway."

The engineer bent down to study the lines closely. "Your Majesty, if we do this we shall have to dig a tributary canal to the east to keep your troops stationed there and the people of the district supplied with fresh water."

I considered the lay of the street along the canal side, tried to remember how close the houses were to the banks. "Should we do this? Or is it more efficient to move the wheels and canal locks further north?"

"It would be more efficient to build in the north," he admitted. "But the closer our mechanisms are to the palace, the more likely they will be sabotaged."

"Better to keep them firmly behind our lines then," remarked Quintus.

I agreed. "Then we will get you the extra men to dig the new water-way. If possible, we should create two forks in it so the army and the city are not all clamoring for water in the same spot."

"It shall be done, my lady."

"There are tributaries to the west of the palace too, those will also have to be salted. Where do you think the dividing line for our own supply should be?"

Hieronymos frowned at the map. "Here," he pointed. "Where the Soma meets Rhakotis. Your Majesty's men hold the Library and that is a good landmark for reference. The point where the districts meet is a spot a little further back and should be protected."

"Very well, that is what you shall do. This project holds my full attention. If there is anything else you require, speak to my lieutenant here and I will see that it is granted."

"Thank you, my lady," he said, inclining his head. "We should be fully operational within the next couple of days. Once the machines are in place, we will start manipulating the locks and adding the seawater."

"And I will make sure our canal boats begin transporting it from the harbor immediately."

Quintus and Hieronymos bowed before returning their attention to the plans. Mudjet and I made our way out of the tent to return to the dusty noise of the streets.

"My sweet," I said, turning to her, "I need you to send messengers to Palm and the Sail. Explain to them the rudiments of this plan and where they and the people of their districts will be able to find water. Tell them they have permission to pass along that information to any civilian leaders. I do not want my people in the Jewish quarter and at the docks to think I care not for their welfare."

Mudjet nodded. "It will be done at once, my lady."

While she went off in search of runners, I returned to our encampment and began organizing sailors to barrel seawater from the harbor. The first full barrels that would fill our boats I sent off towards the engineers' camp near the lake, but any extra were set out in the sun to bake off the water so that on later trips, the boats would only have to contend with the weight of the salt.

Having set these men upon this task, I set off towards the Heptas-tadion to inspect our lines. At the edge of the causeway, I found Dejen supervising our fortifications facing the long bridge towards Pharos. The Amharan's face split into his large-toothed grin as he jumped down from a sea wall to meet me.

"Sir, are things well here?" I asked, returning the salutes of the men.

He nodded. "Yes, my Queen. I know you fear an assault from the gar-rison at the lighthouse, so I left my work in the harbor in my men's hands for a while so I might check on our resources here."

"What is your assessment?"

"I think Caesar is too afraid to lose his best advantage over us by lead-ing his men out for the time being. We should be safe and I will go back to the docks."

"Good," I said, agreeing with him. "Without Achillas to interfere, I would like to begin building lighter ships for our fleet. Your men may finish the *quadriremes* already begun, but any new warships should be of smaller make. *Triremes, trihemiolias,* and *hemiolias* mostly."

Dejen grinned in understanding. "My Pharaoh wishes to be able to attack like a lioness as well as defend her home like a cobra."

I returned his smile. "We cannot let the Romans have all of the fun, sir."

"Indeed not, Queen of Queens. Would Your Majesty also like a *bireme* or several for scouting?"

"That would be perfect, Dejen. Thank you."

He bowed. "We shall begin reallocating timber immediately, my la-dy."

We stood surveying the labor of the workmen for some minutes. "I received a letter from the Pharaoh," I said, breaking our contemplation. "He is very wroth with me for dealing with Achillas as I did. Will the Scattered be unwilling to follow my lead if my brother starts withholding his support of our work?"

He snorted scornfully. "The Scattered and the Egyptians alike follow Your Majesty because you walk among them and treat them kindly. Your brother is like a god, above them but his words are like droplets of rain on the wind. He is distant god and not a very powerful one at that. The men of this army will put their trust in you, the goddess they can see."

"What of the Greeks?"

"The Greeks, my Queen, are difficult to understand," he replied with the peculiar shrug Africans always reserved for the eccentricities of the northern folk. "Some will follow you regardless because you have shown them your quality."

"And the others?"

He looked at me seriously. "The others will follow you until a better offer is presented."

I touched the barricades in thought. "These battlements are strong. Thank these men for their fine work."

"Of course, my Pharaoh," he said with another small bow. "They build walls like iron for our iron-made Queen."

Once everything was in place, we began adding saltwater to the canals and waited to see what would happen. My engineers drew up a schedule and used it to carefully increase the salinity of the water. I met with them each day observe their progress and was always offered a sample of what the men had begun referring to as "Roman wine."

On the fifth day, I spat it out. "I think there is no mistaking it now."

"The Palm Fruit sent word that there has been some concern creeping among the *miles* of the legion for a day or two now," reported Quintus, making a face while he rinsed the salty water from his mouth. "We will see what transpires when this batch hits their lines."

I was awoken from an empty, dreamless sleep by a rumbling in the distance early the next morning. Blinking my eyes slowly to get my bearings, I rooted around for my dagger and had begun to assemble decent attire when Mudjet burst into my tent.

"Hurry, my lady!" she cried, rushing over to help me pull on my *chiton*, her face flushed and her violet eyes sparkling. "You must see this!"

I was still alarmed by the sudden flurry of noise and activity, but there was excitement in my companion's voice rather than fear. I dressed in a hurry and threw the vulture crown on my head before following Mudjet by the hand out of the camp and into the city.

"Where are we going?" I called out to her, trotting to keep up, as my men saluted and cheered our progress.

Mudjet let out her high, buoyant laugh as a response and led on until we arrived at the house of the Sail, its door marked by a sketch of a splendid ship. Mudjet took us around to a back door and knocked until we were let in.

I cast my glance about, probing the shadowy corners of the alley. "This is not our ground alone, are we safe here?"

"Do not worry, my lady," she answered. "We are quite safe and besides, we are expected."

A servant escorted us down a back hall to a ladder that led to the roof. I scrambled up the rungs after Mudjet until we surfaced on the brightly colored parapet. The Sail stood there facing northward, her pale blue silk *himation* trailing in the wind.

She turned slowly at our arrival. "The gods smile upon the wits of our Moon Gate Queen," she said, her regal features glowing as she gestured out in the direction she had been looking.

I followed her indication and was amazed. The entire Roman camp was in disarray. Men had abandoned their tents and were marching in disorderly phalanxes towards the palace. The noise from their angry shouts had pulled me from sleep.

"What are they going to do?" I puzzled aloud.

"With any luck, they are going to attack the palace," said Ganymedes, who joined us on the roof along with Tahu. Despite not knowing of our arrangements, he still gave the Sail a cross look, but Tahu had rightly convinced him that this was the best vantage point.

"They've been in revolt all night because they have no water," added my Egyptian lieutenant. "We have fortified our positions, but Quintus Fabianus says the legion has not made any new formations since yesterday morning. They have been low on water for nearly a week and all that was drinkable is gone. And now they are surrounded by the desert and the sea."

"Should we attack them now that they are in panic?" I asked my teacher, my voice catching on my own excitement.

He shook his head. "No, if they are this furious, perhaps they will take care of your sister and Caesar for us. We should wait," he said firmly.

"But what about Pharos?" I pressed. "Now is the time to strike there if nowhere else!"

"We need all of our men to hold the lines against the city, my Queen. If we move them to concentrate on Pharos, the legion will break through and reach our water supplies. We must stick to our plan and use this solely as a diversion."

Despite my elation over our plan's success, I felt a sting of disappointment that we could not use the momentum of this minor victory to go on the offensive. However, the enemy's disorganization would most likely last a short while until they realized they could dig for wells through our rocky coast. I bit my tongue in frustration even though my teacher was likely correct.

"If my commanding general believes we should take the safer position, that is what we shall do," I said. "We are engaged in a defensive campaign, after all. Send a message to Quintus in the engineers' camp to leave enough men to manage the wheels and have all others report to the docks. Any man who can be spared from the front lines should also be sent there to work on the ships. Our time is precious."

Ganymedes and Tahu vanished to make the arrangements, while Mudjet, the Sail, and I went back to watching the enraged legionaries slashing *gladii* and *pila* against the golden gates of the palace while the royal guards stood waiting for orders as to what was to be done.

I caught myself looking for the silhouette of Cleopatra passing between the painted columns on the foremost veranda, her pregnant form soft in the middle of this razor-toothed war. How would my proud sister deal with such a threatening insurrection? Would she send out her *he-ka* over the legion like a comforting spring rainfall? Or would it be a vengeful torrent, cruel and devouring? She needed this army, but she had needed the Gabiniani once upon a time, too, and that had not quieted her stony wrath against them. Then again, perhaps she had learned from her errors, as I was endeavoring to do. And always there was Caesar looming in the background like Moros, watching us all with his canny raven's eyes.

"My lady must be the true daughter of Pallas Athena and Odysseus to have managed such a bit of trickery," remarked the Sail, breaking into my thoughts with a wry smile.

"I doubt the virgin goddess will bless such an insinuation," I answered with chuckle of amusement.

"Ah, well, everyone knows goddesses will have their secrets," she countered with a knowing look that felt as though the courtesan mistress saw right through me into my dreams, though she made no further comment.

The roars of the legion continued into the night, ebbing and flowing like the waves in the harbor. After a particularly long interval of violent shouting, there suddenly was an eerie silence the city had not known in days. The unexpected quiet grew and, with it, my concern, even though we could still observe from the roof of the Sail that the bulk of the legion remained camped on the stairs of the palace.

My lieutenants and I had begun to discuss what our strategy should be if the enemy's soldiers broke into the city in a frenzy of thirst or other madness, when a note from the Palm Fruit brought an explanation.

Your Majesty –

The riots in the legion continued through yesterday, despite the efforts of the tribunes and centurions to calm the panic. At last, Caesar was forced to speak to the men himself. He told the legion that he understood their concerns and he was working on a solution. A few ranked men suggested they should pull out of Pharos and throw the full weight of the legion at the Western Soma line to get at fresh water, which your forces must have. Caesar said to them such a foolhardy maneuver would be exactly to the rebel princess' liking and would play right into your hands. He then admonished them for being so easily cowed by the tricks of a child, a girl-child no less. Because the Romans insist on their republican ways, another soldier dared to say to Caesar that Your Majesty might be a girl-child, but that you had outfoxed a trained soldier like Achillas and now you held the Dictator of Rome by the tail. Someone else volunteered that the city thought you the incarnation of a goddess, and Fortune would not favor your opposition. Another voice told him to abandon the Queen and make an alliance with you instead, before he and his men were the laughingstock of Rome. Eventually, the Consul controlled the tumult, but he will have to figure out the riddle of our limestone quickly or even his word might not be enough. My eyes at this scene say that Caesar spoke calmly and easily to the legion, though when he turned his back to them to return to the palace, he was furious. Be careful, my lady. A snake who is trod upon still has fangs.

- Palm

Despite the Palm's sage advice, I could not resist sending the finest cup I had filled with clean water to the Consul as a belated response to his earlier message. My runner said he merely stared at it when it was placed in front of him. And that my sister eventually threw it at the wall in a rage.

It took a week for Caesar to learn how to plumb our limestone for fresh well water and another two to dig enough wells to supply his men. This may sound like a very transient sort of victory for us, but those were three weeks that the legion did not harass my lines were three weeks I could move several thousand more men into shipbuilding instead of having them tied up in skirmishes with the Romans.

I still struggled with the insomnia Achillas' blood had purchased, so in a rare moment of inactivity several days after Caesar's men regained their water, I sank into sleep as the sun was setting. It was a black, dreamless sleep that had no beginning or end and was only broken by the gentle shake of my shoulder.

"Forgive me, my lady, but there are fishermen who have come to speak with you," said Mudjet kindly.

Too groggy to inquire further, I stood up and smoothed down my hair as Mudjet replaced the vulture crown on my head. In the gathering dusk, I stepped out of my tent to find Ganymedes and a small cluster of men waiting for me.

The sailors made signs of obeisance to me. "Hail thee, *heqat-taui.*"

I nodded to them. "What have you heard, sirs?"

Their captain raised his head and looked me in the eye. "The Thirty-Seventh Legion is in the wind, Your Majesty. They will be here by tomorrow."

I made a gesture over my heart. "Thank you for this warning, men of Alexandria." I had a soldier hand them each a bag of gold. "May this small token signal my gratitude and feed your families in place of the fish you might have caught."

"Thank you, Your Majesty. May we offer our services to your fleet? The waves grow bold and all of my men are good navigators."

"I accept your offer gladly, sir," I replied, truly grateful. "I shall need all I can muster to hold the Thirty-Seventh at bay."

Ganymedes had the sailors escorted out before turning to me grimly. "Now it comes to it, my lady. I shall ready the fleet to sail at sunrise to intercept the legion."

"Thank you, Teacher. Find Quintus, he will help you. And send word to Tahu to hold our lines as they are."

He departed and Mujet took my hand. "Do you wish for me to find a potion to help you sleep?" she asked softly.

I knew what she meant. She was asking if I should go seek one last scrap of advice from the gods in the Dream World, but I knew they had told me all they could. They would do what they were able and so would I. "No, there is no time. Bring me a lamp, though. I am going to offer a prayer."

She walked over to the table and returned with one of the lamps, as I picked up a bottle of perfume from a cask over by my couch. "Who are we praying to, my lady?"

I sat down on the ground and placed the lamp in front of me. "We ask the help of all of the gods to shield the Black Land in this hour of need, but the fishermen who brought me these tidings have already signaled the name of he whom we must ask specifically." I unstopped the bottle and sprinkled out droplets of the perfume as the smell of cloves began to fill the air. Quietly, I intoned:

Lord Shu, He of the Sweet Breath, Lord of Cloud and Fog. The sea sends us men who wish to make your children the chattel of wolves, slaves in their own land. King of the Sea Winds, as you hold out your arms to hold up the sky, so too throw out your arms to save your children from the soldiers who come to put your land to the sword. Accept our prayers and we will sing of your mighty deeds to the people and they will know you are with them.

With no more hope of bridling sleep again, we sat on the carpet on the floor of the tent and listened to the night bloom into a dark pomegranate that broke open to release star seeds into the sky.

I might have openly prayed to Shu, though in my *ka* I whispered to the heart of Set as well. With him there was no need to speak aloud, for he knew the desires of my soul before I did. He knew that I felt the energy of my army rushing headlong towards the enemy, burning with the will to meet them in battle. And yet he also knew I feared we were still so green, so possibly, fatally unready. We might never be ready, and still I prayed to the gods. Not for victory, but rather for them to turn their faces to their children in this moment as we stood on the edge of the abyss. If they could not save us, that they might show us we were not alone.

I prayed for a storm.

Chapter Twenty-Nine

Billowing black clouds raced along the horizon as day broke over us and the *hemiolias* of the Thirty-Seventh Legion appeared in the distance. The sea turned from sparkling aquamarine to an angry slate blue. It had cruel sickle edges and the wind tore through everything in its wake, churning up bladed sand that slapped our faces raw.

"We cannot hope to launch the fleet in this weather!" Quintus called to me over the hoarse shout of the wind as my servants worked to double-anchor my tent. "The sailors say it is too risky!"

"It is well!" I yelled back. "The storm will prevent the legion from advancing, we do not need to set sail yet! The waves have made it too dark to navigate the shoals and they do not know the safe way across the harbor! And they will drown their men if they try to set out too many in smaller craft! Have Ganymedes keep the ships at the ready and we will launch only when we must!"

He nodded and waved as he turned back into the storm holding his cloak over his face. Mudjet wrapped a blanket around us both as we huddled together, bracing against the flying air which bolted through the tent in spite of our efforts.

I wished there was some task I could attend to, but my teacher had told me to wait until our course of action was decided. After so many weeks of activity, sloth came even less naturally to me than it ever had before and I struggled not to fidget against Mudjet's shoulder.

"Perhaps the Lord of the Swelling Breaths opened his ears to my lady too well," she said in my ear.

I smiled. "Indeed. However, we must be grateful to him and the others. Even if we are blown away by his generosity."

She giggled. "Yes, the largesse of the gods always takes one's breath away."

"Tsk. Blasphemer."

"*Hemet-netjer.*"

We tittered at our own amusement, when another cloaked figure carrying a bundle appeared in my tent. "Tahu!" I called out, recognizing the shape of my lieutenant even before he pulled back his hood.

He knelt close to us so he did not have to yell. "Is my Pharaoh well?"

"Yes, we are fine. Is the army protected from the storm?"

"Yes, my lady. All are in their tents awaiting orders. They praise the holy gods for their aid." He looked at me slyly. "And their Pharaoh who speaks to them on their behalf."

I waved a hand. "I do not know what you are talking of."

He shrugged, keeping his happy grin. "As you wish, Your Majesty. Though you should be kind to me and my fancies, for I have come to release you from Sir Ganymedes' injunction to remain here."

I sat up, not bothering to hide my eagerness. "What are we to do?"

"Nothing if my lady is not willing, though I thought you might be in search of an errand. Would you like to come with me and a dozen guards to survey the coast?"

"Yes! I cannot bear to sit here for the duration of this tempest!"

"Very well, though if you and Lady Mudjet are to accompany us, I think it best if you dress as soldiers." He gestured to the bundle he had brought. "These should be of an acceptable size." He turned his back to us as we hurriedly disrobed and pulled on the clothes and armor in the bag. "The helmets are a little big because I thought you could then hide your hair in them."

It was a prudent suggestion and we helped each other gather up our braids, tying them as flatly around our heads as we could manage. Once that was done, we fitted the helmets on, which now sat snugly on our heads.

"You may face us again, sir," I said, fastening my cloak over the armor.

He surveyed us, pleased. "That will do nicely, Your Majesty. Please, follow me."

We braced ourselves as we left the tent and bent over against the dust and wind. "I assume my tutor does not know we do this!" I shouted to Tahu as we pushed into the gusting air.

"No! But I think it is important for our general to see how things stand as they are!" he hollered back.

We met up with the soldiers Tahu had selected to come with us, who were facing our horses facing away from the wind's fury. We mounted up and rode out towards the coastline, which was blessedly in the direction where the wind shifted to our backs and urged us on.

Closer to the water there was less sand to kick up into our lungs, though it also brought the roar of the waves nearer. The Roman ships could be seen rocking back and forth further out, their sails stowed and the individual craft spaced far enough apart to prevent them from colliding. We trotted along the beach with some caution in case the original legion attempted to move their lines in the confusion of the storm. Nothing unusual confronted us until we rounded a coastal wall and found two beached boats resting on the shore.

Tahu held up his hand to bring our group to a halt as he and I climbed down to investigate. The boats were empty and appeared abandoned aside from a dozen large barrels between them.

I lifted a barrel lid. "They are empty."

Tahu frowned as he inspected another, until his thoughtful look suddenly lifted. "Of course. They have come for water. The palace legion is not the only army that has been deprived of water recently. The Thirty-Seventh has been at sea for several weeks, they must be low and sent scouts in spite of the storm to find a supply."

I glanced down at the ground where there was a brief trail of footprints that had not blown away yet. "They cannot have gotten far in this weather. We must find them," I said, indicating the marks.

"Indeed, my lady," Tahu agreed. "Stay close to me."

"Should we leave the horses and go on foot?"

He thought. "No, I think it is better to stay on horseback. We will be faster that way." He gave me a leg up before returning to his own horse. "We must track these scouts!" he called to the men. "Keep your eyes open, they must not make it to the city!"

We moved along swiftly but cautiously as we searched for the enemy sailors. I looked up at the sky and hoped it did not grow much darker. We had not bothered to bring torches that would both give away our position and struggle to stay lit in the gale.

"How many do you think there are?" I leaned towards Tahu to make myself heard.

"Not more than half a dozen, judging by the boats. They probably wanted as much room for the barrels as possible and did not want to lose too many men if the boats failed to reach the shore."

"What kind of weaponry are they likely to have?"

"Again, nothing very heavy, my lady. Swords and daggers, probably. Arrows and spears are bulky and would not do them much good in this wind anyhow."

We traveled in silence until we saw movement up ahead. We halted and watched the small huddle picking its way across the beach, fighting the wind. Tahu looked to me and nodded. He raised his arm noiselessly to our soldiers, curling his fingers into the shape of a circle. With no other direction, we spurred the horses to a gallop and within minutes overtook our quarry, encircling them with the horses while our men raised arrows at their heads.

The sailors threw their hands in the air. "Don't shoot! Don't shoot!" cried their leader in Greek.

"We will not if you stay as you are," I answered in kind. "Move and you will die where you stand!"

The cornered men looked from one of our faces to the next, still shaking. "We will not move, but please! Don't kill us! We are friends!"

This took me by surprise and I looked to Mudjet, who frowned quizzically. "What did they say?" asked Tahu, thinking he had misheard.

"They say they are our friends," I said to him incredulously.

"We are your allies!" pleaded the leader again. "We are from the Thirty-Seventh Legion! We were sent for water and to let your mistress know that the general has made it safely aboard the flagship, and we are only waiting for this storm to end to attack!"

We received this statement in stunned silence until Mudjet broke the spell in a gleeful crow of laughter. "Gods defend us! They think we are your sister's soldiers, my lady!" she cried out in Egyptian to let our soldiers in on the farce. They chortled in response.

The imploring faces of the sailors grew even paler.

"Cleopatra Philopator did not send you, sir?" their leader asked me haltingly.

I shook my head. "I am afraid not, sir." As laughable as the mix-up was, I could not afford to waste any more time with it. In their confusion, the Romans had dropped a crucial piece of intelligence into my lap. I pulled my horse back from the circle. "Tahu," I called out, "take these men back to camp and keep them under guard, but see they are well-treated."

"Yes, my lady. But where are you going?"

I wheeled my horse around to face them all. "To the shipyard. Storm or no storm, if Caesar is with the fleet, then we must strike now!"

I did not wait for him to respond as I kicked my horse back down the beach, its mane lashing out at my arms as we pounded across the sand. I felt too unbalanced with the extra weight on my head, so I impatiently ripped off my helmet and tossed it aside. My braid uncoiled itself from my head and trailed behind me like a banner in the storm that continued to rage around us. *Lords of* Taui, I prayed, *grant us passage to the sea.* Beneath the sound of the wind I could hear hoofbeats gaining on my own, and I glanced over my shoulder to see Mudjet galloping to catch up with me. Glad that it was her, I gave my horse more rein and asked it to increase its pace, knowing my companion would have no difficulty catching up with us.

We were neck and neck as we rode into the shipyard, where the troops were wrapping sails and making minor structural repairs amid the general commotion of battle preparations. The soldiers who saw me called out titles of respect, which I acknowledged with a hand as I scanned the docks for my commanders. At last I saw the back of a towering man directing the loading of weapons onto one of the *quadriremes*.

"Dejen!" I shouted. "Where is Ganymedes?"

He turned, smiling with recognition as he gave a salute. "I think you will find him conferring with the engineers to the west, Queen of Queens. Does my Pharaoh have news from Tahu the Memphisian?"

"Yes! Keep loading these ships, I want them at the ready immediately!"

"It shall be done, Your Majesty!"

We rode on as quickly as we dared in such a crowded location until I saw my teacher and Quintus sketching out plans on a map as several other soldiers pinned the papyrus to the table. The Gabiniani officer lifted his head at the sound of our approach and with an eager grin rushed over to grab the reins of our horses.

"Have you been riding about in this weather, *nedjet*?" asked Ganymedes with a cursory glance at our outfits. He decided to pass over them without remark.

"We have, Teacher, but it is all worth it," I answered as Quintus carefully helped me from the saddle. "We have captured scouts sent by the Thirty-Seventh and they have informed us that Caesar has sailed out and joined the legion personally."

I knew my teacher would immediately grasp the significance of this news. "We will ready the fleet at once, my lady. With the wind at our backs, we should have the advantage of maneuverability. We will cut the head off the snake before it has a chance to bite our heel. Quintus, I will need you to be in command of one of the lead *quadriremes*. Go alert the other vessel captains; all ships capable of being floated should raise sail."

He nodded, with a little wink to me. "Of course, sir."

I held his arm. "Be careful. I still have need of you."

"For you, my Pharaoh, always." He bowed and departed down the line towards the far end of the docks.

I looked out over our ships. "We need fewer *quadriremes* and more *triremes*," I said absently to Ganymedes.

"I know, my lady. We have worked hard to make up for all the time Achillas wasted building these heavier warships. It may yet be enough. After all, the *quadriremes* should do a good job of blockading the coast from infiltration."

"We must not let the Roman *hemiolias* work their way behind our blockade line," I said. "I will see to it that Tahu and the Gabiniani remaining onshore arrange our archers and siege towers seaward to demonstrate against the legion onshore so that Cleopatra is not tempted to send out reinforcements from our rear."

"Where would you like me to send Dejen the Nubian?"

"Give him admiralty over a coterie of our *hemiolias* and see to it that those ships are staffed with our best Phoenician sailors, along with at least one local fisherman who has the topography of our waters in his blood. We can use them to hem in the Roman fleet from spreading out and looking for weak spots along the coast."

"It will be as you say. Is there anything else, my lady?"

"I wish I could sail out with you," I admitted quietly.

Ganymedes patted my shoulder. "We need you here, *nedjet*. We need you to direct the infantry onshore. Let us handle whatever passes for a Roman sailor."

I smiled. "The ones we captured thought we were my sister's soldiers."

He chuckled. "Did they now? Well, perhaps they had last spring's information."

"Perhaps. We are a watery people and our alliances are fluid."

"Let us go see if the Roman ships are faster than their intellects."

Father Ra's solar disc was already high in the sky as I watched my fleet sail out of the harbor. The long line of *quadriremes* was not the force I had hoped for when I had chased the wind with Set and Sobek in my dreams, but they were still the children born of that dream and I felt as much their mother in that moment.

I left the bulk of the Gabiniani to hold our positions along the Heptastadion with orders to take any part of Pharos not already under our control, if it were practical. These Roman soldiers of mine were excellent combatants though they were not sailors, which is why I did not send them out with the fleet. Instead I sent my water-dwelling Alexandrians and Greeks to greet our sea-arriving foes.

Tahu and I arranged our eastern lines to pin as much of the landed legion as possible so they could not scramble to their commander's defense out in the bay. Here I used native troops familiar with the layout of these streets and the interiors of the buildings to prevent them from maneuvering behind us. On the ground we set our pike-bearing infantry, while my lieutenant and I positioned ourselves on the roofs with my archers.

The bowmen and those from the palace traded a handful of volleys without much enthusiasm, the lack of urgency on both sides no doubt owing to the everyone's attention being drawn irresistibly towards the water.

"*Pedjeti*, let us send a volley of incendiary arrows to the boats in the royal harbor," I said to my archers. "It will give them something to do aside from bothering us or helping Caesar."

The men dipped their arrows in pitch and took turns lighting the tips with a torch passed between them. Once they were ready, Tahu gave the signal and they released towards the royal docks, managing to set several structures ablaze. Most of the palace infantry were then diverted to trying to douse the rising flames while my men put their shields up to deflect the fiery volley the enemy archers sent us in response. Because in our forefathers' wisdom they had built so little of the city with wood, my men had little difficulty in containing the few spots where the flaming arrows struck true.

"We must be careful to keep the fighting away from the Library if possible, my Pharaoh," said Tahu as he stamped out a cinder. "It is one of the few places in our control that has enough flammability to set off an inferno in the city."

I agreed and sent a runner to Lord Amenei, who led the troops stationed closest to the Library, to request that he keep his lines deep there to prevent such an accident. That dispatched, we reverted our attention to the sea battle unfolding on the horizon.

"Caesar cannot want this fight," observed Tahu as our ships moved to break the line held by the Thirty-Seventh Legion. "He is severely undermanned and night will be upon us in a few short hours. He will not be able to navigate in the dark like our sailors."

"How many crafts do you count against us, sir?" I called over to one of my captains perched on a siege tower between our roof and the next.

"No more than fifty, *heqat-taui*. We outnumber them nearly two to one."

"I do not count even that many, Queen of Queens," chimed in a Libyan archer. "There are less than forty."

My mouth dried as I clung to the hope that Ganymedes could at least draw out the battle until nightfall. Despite our superior numbers, I feared the slowness of our fleet in the face of the faster Roman ships. Several of the opposing craft appeared to also be *quadriremes*, which might even our chances, though the bulk were various smaller vessels, mainly *hemiolias* and *biremes*. We needed the aid of the Night-bark for surety.

The legion's fleet seemed to sense this, keeping close to one another as protection from both our advance and the choppy waters churned up by the storm. I began to fear all we might be able to accomplish this day was to picket in the enemy, when part of Caesar's right flank broke away from the rest of the fleet and appeared to make a run for the coast. The impasse broken, my main line of *quadriremes* swung into pursuit, their large sails grabbing the blowing wind hungrily.

"What a bold attempt by the *ahat-kheftyew*," commented one of my sergeants-at-arms. "Who pilots those ships for the enemy?"

"The sails are Rhodian," I answered vaguely as my vanguard ships surrounded the separated Roman vessels.

"Will Caesar save them?" asked Tahu, frowning.

I opened my inner ears to Sobek's wisdom. I listened to the swell and slap of the sea, and watched the battle with my mind's eye. As the ships moved to and fro like *senet* pawns, Sekhmet prowled into my thoughts. *What will one who hates to lose do, little princess?* The question startled my mind into an automatic retort. *It is not that he hates to lose that matters here...*

Aloud to my lieutenant I finished the thought, "He cannot afford to lose those ships. He will have to sail to their defense."

Indeed, I had hardly spoken the words when the rest of the legion's fleet swung around to engage ours. Soon, the wind brought the roar of battle and the acrid smell of smoke as two ships engaged with one another were set ablaze. Fueled by the whirling air, the billows spread until they covered much of the fleet lines and made our eyes sting. The clang of metal on metal rang out closer to where we stood as the palace men tested our street formations under the lowered visibility.

"Hold the lines!" Tahu called down to them. "Allow no soldier to pass!" My soldiers braced themselves between walls and behind the rubble barricades, a few of them picking up smaller rocks and using slings to whip them at the enemy. A few pikes found their mark and my sister's troops sidled back once more to regroup.

A loud crack from the bay hit the air like a thunderclap. I whirled around to try to see what was happening, though the haze rising from the north made it nearly impossible.

"That sounded like a ship foundering, my Queen!" hollered an archer.

"Pray to Lord Sobek that it was one of Rome's!" sang out another. Their comrades gave a hoarse, smoke-tinged call of approval and they sent a round of arrows towards the palace gates.

I did not share my men's confidence. Something in my heart fluttered uncomfortably as it strained towards the battle lines out in the harbor. If we were to rout the legion, I felt we would have accomplished it by now. The longer they held out against us, the less likely our victory became. Ur-hekau, I murmured to Set, *I need to see what has become of us.* I felt the wind shift, dispersing the smoke and the storm clouds, revealing the harbor below.

"*Iammi a'a pheti,*" said Tahu in a low tone.

At first, it was not as bad as I thought it would be. Our ships appeared to be pulling back from the fight, and I could see remains from two sunken vessels, only one of which was ours. Another *quadrireme* had been towed behind the legion's lines, though I doubted one more ship would seriously advance the enemy's position. It was only once I stopped counting masts and began looking more closely at the debris floating in the water that I comprehended Tahu's horrified malediction.

The harbor of Alexandria was choked with corpses. Their slick seal bodies rocked back and forth by the waves that ponderously delivered them to the shore and stacked them on the beach like kindling. My hand flew to my mouth, and my lieutenant asked no permission to take hold of my shoulders because, in moments such as those, propriety is meaningless.

The troops of both sides forgot about one another, and all stared vacantly towards the sea. Eventually a few cheers went up from the legionaries, but the palace's own men were silent, subdued by the ghoulish flotilla drifting to their docks.

Finally I managed to whisper, "Tahu, I must return to the harbor."

He nodded and left command instructions with one of the captains, who bowed to me with a determined set to his mouth. "Do not worry, Your Majesty," the soldier said firmly. "We know our *hemet-netjer* will bring us victory from defeat."

I longed to feel as confident as my troops as I struggled to find my footing down the ladders and stairs of the house. In a fog I stumbled through the streets, wondering how I could find a way to appear sober, let alone queenly as the enormity of our situation steeped itself in my veins and pooled in the pit of my stomach. It was as Sekhmet had promised in my dreams as we had watched Pompey destroy Berenice's army: all I could feel was the pain of Egypt wrapping itself around my heart like a noose. We followed a winding route behind our lines to pass to the harbor, so we had not yet reached the shore when I saw the willowy form of Mudjet running to meet us, her face ashen. As I rushed up to her, she looked back to the beach before meeting my eyes again.

"My lady, Quintus Fabianus—"

She did not need to finish her sentence. I bolted past her, past my army regrouping itself along the sea walls, in the direction of my beloved companion's backwards glance.

Chapter Thirty

We had lost so many men, so many brave soldiers, but — may the gods forgive me — all I could think of was my Gabiniani lieutenant as I tore across the harbor to where the wounded who had not drowned had been placed on mats in long rows in the sand.

I cared not if Mudjet or Tahu kept pace with me as my mind fastened itself to this one small disaster to cope with the looming, monstrous one that spread from the sea into the hearts of my army. I saw where my teacher stood over one of the prone bodies and I ran until I was close enough to throw myself down next to Quintus' gasping form. He was breathing, though only barely. My stomach retched at the blood-soaked rags covering what could only be a devastating wound in his abdomen. I glanced up at Ganymedes whose expression told me that the bandages were fresh and the bleeding could not be staunched.

I reached over and took Quintus' hand in mine, the pressure from my grip forcing his eyelids open. When he saw me, he smiled weakly. "Ah, my Pharaoh... I wondered what physician could have such slender fingers..."

"Shh, do not speak," I admonished him. "We are finding a physician to tend you; you must save your strength."

"It is unnecessary, my lady. No physician can mend this." He inclined his head slightly in the direction of his torso. Mudjet had caught up to us. She found a skin of water and eased a few drops down Quintus' throat, making him sigh in gratitude. "Thank you, Mudjet. It is good."

My throat thickened as I tried not to betray my distress. "What can I do to help you, sir?"

He smiled again as he took a shuddering breath. "My Queen and General holds my hand and asks after my comfort. What more could I ask of above this singular honor?"

I lowered my head. "We are defeated this day and so many pay the price for me. I would suggest the honor belongs to you."

"All generals suffer defeats, my lady. Even Alexander, who might have never otherwise lost a battle, lost India to the near mutiny of his men.

Just because the enemy carries the day does not mean you have failed. A commander —" he stopped to catch his breath. "— a commander who could hold out as long as this against the Roman army under one of its most brilliant tacticians and suffer virtually no casualties until now is a general to be envied by the most illustrious names in history. To fall in the service of such a general is glorious."

There would be a day in the future where I could reflect upon Quintus' words with pride, though in that hour, even the heartfelt praise of a legionary could not assuage my grief in this sea of blood.

"I am so sorry," I whispered, no longer able to hold back the tears that began to run down my cheeks. "I have brought us all to this moment."

He squeezed my hand, though the pressure from the gesture was slight and fading. "Fate brought us here, Your Majesty. She rules the gods and men alike. Do not weep for what must be my destiny. I have been a soldier all my life, a good death in battle is pleasing to me." With his other arm he shakily reached up and brushed away some of my tears with the back of his fingers. "However, when I meet Caesar in the halls of Dis, I will strike him for bringing such anguish to the heart of my Pharaoh."

I choked out a small smile. "I should like to see that."

He attempted to to laugh, but the movement caused him to wince in pain. I tightened my grip on his hand as Mudjet dabbed away the blood from his mouth. His straining muscles relaxed again and he turned his attention back to me. "Though because my Queen has availed herself to this humble soldier, I will make two requests of her."

"Anything, sir."

"The first is that she must swear on the hearts of her gods that she will not allow herself to succumb to despair upon this day. Her strange gods have clearly marked her for more than this and it would be blasphemy for her to throw such a destiny away."

I took a wavering breath to steady myself. "It shall be so."

He nodded, pleased. "The second..." He struggled with his breath for a minute and rested briefly when it passed. "The second I confess I am somewhat ashamed to ask for."

"You have fought bravely, Lieutenant. No request should you be ashamed to ask. There is nothing I would not grant."

He gazed into my eyes and for the first time, I saw the sheen of tears in them. "Will Your Majesty stay with me until it is over?"

I took my other hand and slipped it under his so that I cradled his larger hand in my two smaller ones. "Not the gods themselves have the strength to move me from your side, Quintus Fabianus."

His face relaxed once more and he closed his eyes with a contented sigh. My teacher murmured that he would see to the realignment of our troops and departed without a sound. Tahu sent a runner to Dejen to assess the damage to what remained of the fleet and to have crews in place to make what repairs could be managed.

With that done, he took a position guarding over us where we sat facing out towards the city. His face on the surface was expressionless, though if one knew him, the sadness in his eyes told all.

All four of us waited silently as the minutes rushed past and Quintus' breathing became more erratic. Mudjet eventually went off in search of a lamp, and its flame cast uncertain shadows over us and the dead army encamped on the beach. As the night sky deepened and the stars answered the flickering light of our lamp, my lieutenant gave one last spasmed squeeze of my hand before his body went still. I let go of his hand to wiped some of the grime from his brow and probably would have continued to do so through the night had not Tahu gently picked me up from where I sat and carried me back to my tent.

The moon still pierced the sky as Mudjet and I sat waiting for the fragile thread of dawn to stitch its way through the fading storm clouds. I had not moved from where Tahu had placed me down.

I again thought of the grip of Sekhmet, though I could not tell where Egypt's pain ended and mine began. And then there was the relentless dawn that would rise up to cast light upon my crippled army before the eyes of the city. The vulture crown lay heavily against my skull, yet I could not exert myself to remove it from my brow.

"Ganymedes will no doubt be looking for us soon," observed Mudjet, her own voice weary and bitter. "We will need to regroup."

"Yes. Somehow we must not despair. The Thirty-Seventh remains offshore, we should take comfort in the fact they have not made landfall," I said, twisting my mother's bangle automatically.

"Quintus Fabianus made you promise not to give up, my lady," my companion whispered, her words tinged with her own uncertainty.

She was right, I had promised my loyal Gabiniani that I would not lose heart. I knew not how I would face the coming day or my people, though I knew that I would have to. I had taught Ptah long ago that to rule was to serve the people. I could not disappear in the moment they needed me the most. How could Ganymedes hope to rally our troops if I refused to leave my tent?

I took a shuddering breath. "We can not falter now. I must be faithful to my people." I removed the vulture crown and turned it over in my hands. "However, before I meet my men, there is something I must do."

We walked hand in hand across the camp until we entered the boundaries of the western cemetery. Here the shadows were long, and we followed them until we reached the cavernous entrance to the catacombs.

Torches lit the dim halls continually now as many in the northernmost streets of the Soma took refuge here to protect their families from the fighting. Despite so many unexpectedly living residents, the catacombs retained their hushed atmosphere couched in the dying light of uncountable *ka*s.

Many of my dead soldiers had arrived before me, their relatives attending to the last rites amid the dank claustrophobic air. Corpses were tenderly bathed with water and oil, their limbs gently lifted while loving fingers wrapped them in linen strips. More care could not have been taken if their charges had merely been wounded and sleeping. As we passed, wan mothers and wives paused to whisper, "*Tua netjer heqat-taui,*" and the compassion in their voices brought fresh tears to my eyes.

I found the body of my lieutenant with his mother-in-law and his youngest son, both of whom to my embarrassment knelt at my feet before I could prevent them.

"Please, *mewet*, you give me too much honor. It is I who should be bowing to you. You cannot know how sorry I am for your loss."

The old woman gave me a sad smile. "My lady's face tells all. It was this family's greatest honor to serve the Black Land and our *heqat*. Long will our humble descendants speak of the esteem Queen Arsinoë Philoaígyptos heaped upon us."

I looked over at the curly-haired boy barely younger than myself. "Your father was a good and brave man. It was my privilege to have his service." The boy lowered his gaze and nodded mutely. I turned back to his grandmother. "I am also grieved that words of condolence are empty air in this hour."

"It is well, Your Majesty. I feel the song of your love for our grief flowing from your *ka*. That is all we can offer one another. I feared for my daughter's happiness when she returned the love of the Gabiniani, but Quintus Fabianus was true to her until her dying breath." She motioned to her grandson. "I am glad to have this one here with me, though I confess I feel it is a blessing the other two are away at sea during these turbulent days and that my flower did not live to hold her husband in his winding sheets."

I nodded to these words as she took Quintus' bound arms and gently crossed them over his chest. She then placed her thickly veined hand on his covered forehead, and her voice rasped out an old song I had once heard Baktka singing to herself as she sat alone holding the hand of my dying mother:

Carry me in your arms, O Lord Who Loves the Dead
May your hands gently wrap me in the waiting cloth
As my mother once did when I was a helpless babe
Like my mother you bend over my bed, like a faithful dog
You await my awakening into my new life
May You take me by the hand and lead me to the Halls of the
Living
May You tell the Lord of the West of my faithfulness
May you touch my rib and release my ka *in the Blessed Field*
Like a songbird freed from a cage.

We left the catacombs and made our way to the tents of my teacher. The cacophony of noises through our camp gave me hope that our men had not yet given into despair as I had nearly done. I would speak to them soon, though first I knew I would have to rally my officers who would be more pessimistic in outlook. As we passed by the Gate of the Moon, the towering figure of Dejen met us coming from the docks.

"Hail, my Pharaoh," he said, his face full of concern. "Your Majesty has not let fear into her heart this day, has she?"

"No, sir," I answered steadily, preparing inwardly for the much more skeptical audience to come. "These are the wages of war and I am She of the Five Names. I do not quake for mere Romans."

He clapped his massive hands together. "Good! Good! Our Pharaoh walks with the tread of a she-leopard. She cannot be broken!"

"Have repairs begun on the fleet?" I asked as he fell into step with us.

"Yes, Queen of Queens, though we have diverted much of our supplies towards building a shoreline barricade to prevent the legion from landing."

"That is a good idea, did Ganymedes order that?"

"Yes, my lady. He thought you would approve even though it would slow our repairs on our ships."

"He was correct, that is the best plan available to us." I stopped to crane my head over my shoulder. "Though I cannot see our progress."

Dejen held out his arms. "If it please Your Majesty."

I nodded and he grasped my waist and lifted me up until I was perched on his right shoulder. From that vantage point, I could see the large wooden boards being lifted into place with ropes directed by my harbormasters.

"We also have the fishermen out beyond the shoreline setting up breakers to keep the boats further out than even the shoals," he added, gesturing beyond the barricade.

"Excellent. Thank you, Dejen."

He carefully placed me back on the ground and we continued on our way until we reached Ganymedes' tent. A guard pushed back the flap and we ducked into the room where what remained of my officers were gathered around the map table, heads bent low in discussion until my teacher saw us approach.

"*Nedjet*," he said to me gently, forgoing my more proper appellations. "We are glad you are here."

I nodded and addressed the room. "Forgive my tardiness, gentlemen. I am most pleased with the arrangements for our defenses that have been made in my absence."

The praise managed to elicit several small smiles from my officers, who in addition to being somewhat understandably disheartened were no doubt exhausted. Ganymedes moved a map of the city in front of me on which the proposed layout of the harbor barricade was sketched.

"We think this line should be enough to keep the legion at bay, Your Majesty," he said. "We also believe the mood in the city has been lifted by building the barricade before attending to the ships. It has shown Your Majesty's concern for her subjects is in the forefront of her mind."

"As it is. Thank you, Teacher, for anticipating my will so clearly."

"We will have to be vigilant in regards to Pharos, Your Majesty," remarked Lord Amenei. "We hold all of the close shoreline, but the legion could still land on the northern coast of the island."

"Thank you, my lord, that is very much so." I glanced to the Gabiniani centurion across the table. "Sir, how much of Pharos do we continue to hold?"

"Our position is intact, Your Majesty. We still hold the southwestern leg of the island as well as the entire south side up to the Heptastadion."

"Excellent, sir. I shall personally commend the Gabiniani for their exemplary defense of our lines."

"That will please the men, my lady. Thank you."

I frowned at the map. "We still have civilians in those areas, how are they holding up?"

Unexpectedly, the centurion's eyes brightened. "Feistily, my lady. They are even more incensed about the Romans' enduring presence than perhaps we are," he said with a wry grin.

"Good. Make sure we are maintaining any support they require of us."

"Of course. They ask us to invite Your Majesty to the Temple of Isis as soon as they retake it."

"With pleasure," I agreed, letting loose a short laugh. Growing serious again, I looked to another of my Greek commanders who I knew held battalions in the east. "Sir, are we steady in the Jewish quarter?"

Before he could answer, Tahu appeared and quietly took a place to my left in our circle. I briefly acknowledged him before turning back to the other officer.

"Our lines are holding, Your Majesty," the Greek replied, "but I am not convinced that the barricade will protect us from the Thirty-Seventh landing in the royal harbor if given the chance. I do not know if we have the strength in infantry alone to prevent them."

There was a murmur of assent from the group. "So far we've held the high ground, my lady," said another. "If the Romans gain even a couple of rooftops from us by landing the new legion, we could be overrun."

"The barricade in the harbor has taken much of our building supplies also, as Dejen no doubt told you," added my teacher.

I meditated on these words while my mind turned over the thought of our strategic roofs. They were made of good, strong materials which is why we had been able to do so much from them. I hit upon an idea, but it was one for my people, not my soldiers. I would bring it to them later.

Aloud, I said, "My thoughts continue to be inclined with attempting another engagement with the Thirty-Seventh at sea, is that against the will of you, sirs?"

A Greek officer sighed heavily. "After today, part of my mind says no, my lady. We thought we had an easy advantage over the Romans and to our dismay they held steady in the face of our assault. We may be no match for them." He paused. "However, what other choice lies before us? How can we simply lay down our arms and surrender to the Republic?"

"My house is Spartan, Your Majesty," spoke up another commander. "If this is our Thermopylae, then we must stand our ground."

I was pleased that it was several of my Greek officers who had spoke up first. I gave them an encouraging nod. "Teacher, will you lead my ships into the teeth of war again for the glory of Egypt?"

Ganymedes smiled and pressed his palms together. "I would sail a rowboat into the legion if it were the will of my Pharaoh."

"What of you, my Gabiniani?" I said to the gang of Romans in the room. "The gods have claimed your brother Quintus Fabianus for their halls of glory, so I must appeal to you directly. Will you stand with us?"

"We hold not to the vicious queen or the enslaver of free Rome, Your Majesty," answered one. "We are yours to command, as ever."

One of the centurions chuckled. "Indeed, my lady, perhaps it is better to call us the 'Arsiniani' now."

The company huzzahed their assent to this and my spirits were lifted once more by the indefatigable swagger of the Gabiniani. "I thank you all for such a vote of confidence. It gladdens my heart that my commanders are by my side. For I shall need to address our men and our people this day, and they will be full of sadness and fear. We must show them that we still have hope. This was our first major battle with Rome and we live to fight another day. We must remember that not all who arm themselves against the wolves of the north are so lucky. Yet we have much to do, good sirs. Our coastal barricade must be built up strong and our fleet repaired. I believe that if I ask, the city will help us in all they can, but we are still short of materials."

Tahu stepped forward. "My Pharaoh, I may have a plan to alleviate some of our need."

"Tell us of this plan, Lieutenant," said Amenei eagerly.

Tahu looked at the Greeks. "You, sirs, uphold the belief that we should have a defensive line of vessels covering the harbor mouth in front of the immobile fortifications in addition to the movable fleet, correct?" Several men nodded, so he continued. "It would be wasteful to use our resources on ships we do not intend to sail. Luckily, I know of somewhere we can get an anchored navy."

"What navy is this, Tahu?" asked Ganymedes.

He grinned. "At the mouth of the Nile in Canopus sit our tariff guard ships. They are not exactly seaworthy, but they are *quadriremes*. If we only need them to float as they have all these years, I think they would be most useful to us."

One of the Gabiniani lit up. "Well done, Memphisian! If we commandeer these vessels, we will also prevent the palace from gathering revenue."

I looked to Dejen. "Interested in leading some of my sailors in a bit of piracy?"

The Nubian let loose his booming laugh and clapped Tahu on the shoulder. "Of course, though I demand the wiliest of all Egyptians accompanies me!"

"Can my sister effectively keep us from taking the guard ships?" I inquired of the Egyptian lieutenant.

He shook his head. "Not likely, my lady. If Dejen and I take a couple of *hemiolias,* we should have little difficulty. Two *quinquereme* to tow the customs ships will be adequate."

"Does everyone agree to give Tahu and Dejen these supplies and the men to capture these ships?" I posed to the tent at large. There was a vote of assent. "Teacher, I will put you in charge of finishing the coastal parapets while they are gone."

Ganymedes bowed. "It will be done, Your Majesty."

"Everyone else I need focused on rebuilding the fleet. Any damaged ships should be repaired if feasible; if they are not, they must be salvaged for materials. If we continue to build mostly smaller vessels, we should have an easier time increasing our numbers. Our lines in the city must also be held, though I do not think we are in immediate danger of a serious Roman offensive at this time."

"It will be done, Pharaoh!" my officers answered in unison.

"This gladdens my heart, sirs. Now, let us go to the people and show them we are unbowed."

We departed together while runners were sent to gather all those who would agree to listen to my words.

The decided meeting point was the steps of the Temple of Serapis, tucked back in Rhakotis far from the front lines but in a location accessible to most in the city. By the time we arrived on horseback, a large crowd of soldiers and residents had convened before the steps, and I tried to see such a sizable crowd as evidence of support. At the very least, support to the proposition of hearing me out, which was indeed something.

Tahu helped me dismount, and together with my officers I climbed the temple steps to a height where my people could see me. The afternoon sun was hot and caught the sheen of the vulture crown as it sat upon my head, setting its delicately carved feathers aglow. I prayed I would not sweat too profusely under its weight before those assembled, lest it be seen as a sign of weakness. Ambient noise meandered through the crowd as we ascended until Ganymedes held up his hands for silence and an eerie quiet settled on us all.

"My friends," I began slowly, calmly. "Egyptians, Greeks, Nubians, Libyans, Kushites, Hebrews, Persians," I paused to smile at the assembled Gabiniani, "even Romans," which coaxed a subdued bubble of laughter from the crowd. "All of you who have been born to this land and those who have taken it into your breasts as your own, I come before you this day with all of the anguish you hold within you inside my own *ka*. I know you are weary with sorrow for those we have lost, I know you are afraid for all we have left. I know it would be easy to surrender now and gamble on the supposed great mercy of Consul Caesar to save our friends and families, and protect us from the queen's anger."

I paused again to let them absorb this, to let them understand that I was not insensible to their worries. "But my friends," I continued gently, "we have all known my sister, Cleopatra Thea Philopator, since she was a little girl. We know that the gods have made her clever and strong, but we also know that they have made her quick to anger and slow to forgive." I watched as a ripple of nods flowed through the people. "She holds Caesar out as her partner in kingship, yet he is an important man in Rome. He cannot and will not stay here forever, and who will protect us from the queen's revenge when he is gone?"

"The Romans are strong, *heqat-taui*," called out a voice from the crowd. "Can we beat them?"

"I do not know, my friends," I answered truthfully. "If I said yes, I would be false before you and that is beneath the dignity of us all. I do not know if we can defeat Rome. However, for my part, as long as I have life in me, I will serve you and Egypt against your enemies. If I do so alone, that must be my *shai-t*."

"What say the holy gods, *hemet-netjer*?" asked another voice.

"The gods have not abandoned us, my friends. Witness how Lord Shu and the Lord of Storms shielded us from the fleet of our foes. How Lord Sobek crushed a *quadrireme* of the enemy. How the Lady of the Long Teeth guided the arrows of the archers who protected your homes. I too wish we had destroyed the warships of the Romans, but it was not our *shai*. Yet we still hold the city, our city..." A tide of agreement swept over my listeners. "The fairest city in all the world. Alexandria, the jewel in the mouth of the Nile."

The sound of assent grew louder. "This home of ours is such a precious place, my people," I said, agreeing with their abiding love of our Alexandria. "I flatter myself to call you 'my people' because I believe the *iait*, the old gods, have brought us together in this moment. I do not call you 'my people' because they have made me your queen, I call you this because I believe we are all *ta-meriu*, that we are all children of this glorious land, Egyptian and non-Egyptian alike. Those words have always been used to divide us by virtue of our birth. If you have ever loved me as your *heqat*, I ask you to embrace one another as brothers and call each other by this name. Let Rome see we will stand together, even in the face of the death they bring us."

The crowd erupted in cheers and from the corner of my eye I saw my teacher's face radiating with pride. "What would the Queen have us do?" shouted those closest to the front.

"*Ta-meriu*, to have a chance to defeat the legion at sea, we must repair and expand our fleet with all possible speed!" I called back. "If anyone, soldier or civilian, can assist us in the building, they shall have my eternal thanks!" A roar of approval responded. "To do this, however, we are in great need of timber! Does clever Alexandria know where we can find what we need?" My early idea sat patiently waiting in my head, though I trusted both the generosity and ingenuity of my people to supply it without my asking.

I was not disappointed. I caught sight of the Leopard in the crowd and with a minute bow to me he addressed Hieronymos next to him loud enough for everyone to hear. "Sir Engineer! The roof of my house and those in the Soma are strong and their timber is sound. Could this timber be used to build the Queen of Egypt the ships she requires?"

"My men could make such an offering work, sir," replied my chief engineer.

The Leopard stroked his beard and turned to face the gathering. "What say you, people of the Soma? Rhakotis? Would you rather give up your roofs for your Queen or see them burnt by Rome?"

Another man called out, "Come, Alexandria! The rains will not come again for months! Let us remind the enemy that there is no puzzle too difficult for such as us to solve!"

With the crowd in agreement, I spoke out. "A thousand thanks for this precious gift, Alexandria!" I sought out the faces of the Lost Lords. "My lords, elders of Egypt! Will you help my people get these materials to the engineers?"

"We shall see it done, *heqat-taui*!" Ehoou-hanif and the others cried back.

I placed my hand over my chest. "Then let us depart from this holy place, *ta-meriu*, for we have much to do. I hold all of you in my heart. Do not lose hope, my brave friends. Let it not be said of us that we gave up our home to Rome without a fight."

I waved to the crowd who clamored loudly in response. Not with the noise of a broken people, but with the determined boom of a proud army of men, women, and children who loved their land and would defend it as long as they were able. That they did so under my star is the honor of my life.

Chapter Thirty-One

My army and my people worked night and day for a week to rebuild our navy. The intemperate weather that had harried the Thirty-Seventh Legion since its arrival persisted in fluctuating intensity keeping them from charging the coast while we proceeded with repairs. The storms were no help to our labors, though we thanked my Lord for keeping half the enemy at bay.

This might appear to have been the perfect opportunity for my sister's forces to attempt to turn the tide in her favor, but her army remained much smaller than ours. Caesar was forced to use this time to entrench his positions rather than going on the offensive. I kept my lines near the palace and along our posts on Pharos heavily enforced, both to keep the legion from gaining ground and from sabotaging our docks between the two arms of Caesar's soldiers.

While we were thus occupied, Tahu and Dejen sailed to mouth of the Nile just beyond Canopus and easily captured the customs ships from their officials, not in small part because the staff aboard each vessel eagerly joined the conquering crews. So they returned to Alexandria with the ships we needed for our blockade, more men to help in our defense, and a bare minimum of recalcitrant prisoners to be put under watch. I was so pleased I gave a banquet for the city in their honor where we happily toasted them and the aid of crafty Sobek to our endeavors.

As evening descended on us and the next week poised itself to begin, Hieronymos came to the tent that served as our military headquarters. "My lady, I have been consulting with young Aniketos and he believes the weather will break tomorrow. And a Phoenician is never wrong about the weather."

I looked to Ganymedes, who nodded wearily. "Then we will mass for another attack with the tide, Your Majesty."

"How many ships have we completed?" I asked Dejen to my right.

"We have repaired thirteen *quadriremes*, three *quinqueremes*, and about a dozen *hemiolias*, my Pharaoh. We have also constructed three new *trihemiolias* and five *biremes* from scratch."

"There are also the five *quadriremes* and two *quinqueremes* we retrieved from Canopus, my Pharaoh," added Tahu.

I sucked on my teeth. "And we have nine *quadriremes* that did not need repairs, so our total number of *quadriremes* is twenty-seven. With five *quinqueremes*, twelve *trihemiolias*, twenty *hemiolias*, and eight *biremes*, correct?"

"Yes, my lady."

"Do we have a final count on Caesar's ships?"

"Our scouts say thirty-five, Your Majesty," answered one of the Gabiniani.

"Should that not be thirty-four?" cut in Lord Amenei. "We did sink one of the Rhodian ships."

"But they captured one of our *quadriremes* in return," said a Greek officer.

"One ship is immaterial." I held up a hand. "What kind of craft are we speaking of?"

"Ten *quadriremes*, my lady. The rest are *hemiolias* and *biremes*," said the Gabiniani legionary.

I turned to one of the Rhodian Greek captains. "Can you guess how Admiral Euphranor will arrange such a fleet?"

"Euphranor will have to array the majority of his *quadriremes* in his front line, though I doubt he can have a front line of more than twenty ships, Your Majesty," he said. "So I would wager he will place eight *quadriremes* in his front line with two in reserve, along with twelve *hemiolias* in the front line and the other thirteen ships in reserve."

"Teacher, how should we array our lines?"

Ganymedes frowned. "Based on our numbers, I think we should have two lines of nearly equal strength, one behind another, rather than risk spreading our ships too thin. Perhaps twenty-two in the front line, with twenty in reserve, with a third line ten or fifteen behind that."

I rubbed my eyes. "We have seven of the tariff ships from Canopus to blockade the harbor and I would like at least that many smaller mobile craft to stay with them in support. Would your layout permit that?"

"Yes, Your Majesty, we should have no trouble doing that."

I took some ink and a sheet of papyrus to hastily sketch out my tutor's lines, dividing up our fleet. Then I drew out the fleet of the Thirty-Seventh as my captain had described and studied it briefly. "It seems to me that we will want to draw the enemy's ships as far away from the legion at the palace as possible. How can we trick them into chasing us, though?"

Tahu answered my question first. "If we threaten western Pharos with our full fleet, they will have to come to us, my Pharaoh."

"That is potentially risky, Sir Tahu," said a Greek commander. "The far side of Pharos is on our camp's doorstep. If we — gods forbid — are overrun, there will be no retreat."

The officer brought up a valid argument. I did not want to lose our encampment and my navy in one fell swoop. As I pondered this, a Gabiniani sergeant spoke up. "Your Majesty, I believe if my brothers and I were placed on Pharos, we could defend our position on land to prevent such a calamitous outcome."

I looked to the Gabiniani commanders present. "Are you all in agreement with this?" They made noises of assent. "Do the rest of you think luring the legion's fleet to the far side of Pharos is the best plan?" Everyone else nodded. "Very well, that shall be our course."

"Where would you like your servants, Your Majesty?" asked Ganymedes.

"Ganymedes will lead the fleet, with most of you with him. Teacher, I will leave it to you to assign everyone to their ships. Dejen, I want you to lead the blockade fleet in the harbor. Just let Ganymedes know what men you require. Hieronymos, I wish you to have full rein in the eastern districts protecting our position near the palace so I am giving you command with Lord Amenei to aid you. We will place all the men we can spare from the ships with you. I will take command of our forces on the Heptastadion and Pharos, with the core of the Gabiniani and Tahu with me. Any questions?"

The room shook their heads, and I found myself staring out at them all fondly. The last battle had taught me well, and I understood it might be the last time we all stood here together. "I thank you all. Be valiant in battle, calm in the storm. *Shai nefer, ta-meriu.*"

My officers murmured words of thanks and good luck in a cascade of languages. We stepped out of the tent and into the light of the burgeoning day that would perhaps decide the future of our treasured city and our beloved homeland.

In our tent, Mudjet and I donned our armor before joining our troops on Pharos. She laced on my cuirass before I reached around to secure hers, working in subdued silence as we navigated the waters of our own thoughts.

"I am frightened, my lady," she whispered I quickly braided her hair into a long plait while she tied her sandals.

I tied off her plait and started strapping on my bracers. "Do not be afraid. Stay close to me and I will keep you safe."

She let out a little cry that was half laugh, half sob. "No, my lady, not that," she said, stopping to pull me down beside her and grabbing my face between her hands. "The gods made me a survivor. That is why they gifted me to a daughter of the treacherous House of Ptolemy, so I might protect you. Your lady mother, may she dance in the Field of Reeds, trusted me to keep *you* safe. I am frightened that I am about to fail in that charge."

I wound my hands around her outstretched wrists. "I have taken my destiny from the very palms of the gods, the toddling thing that entered the royal palace when I was still in my swaddles could not have guarded against that. I would leave you here in the safety of the camp if I could, but I am a selfish wretch and I cannot do without she whom I trust the most at my side this day."

This made her smile. "A chain of iron could not hold me here if you ride into battle."

"Then no more tears. Let us go meet our fate together."

I mounted horses with Mudjet, Tahu, and the Gabiniani officers to ride out across the Heptastadion. Our men on the bridge saluted and shouted words of encouragement as we traversed the causeway to our encampment on Pharos. As we stepped out onto the island, I was surprised to see how many civilians remained among the armored ranks of my soldiers.

"We cannot make them leave, Your Majesty," a Gabiniani explained. "Most of the women and children have departed, but the men stay to hold their homes. The priest of Poseidon has been ministering to the sick and wounded for us."

"I should go thank him for that." I spurred my horse towards the temple grounds at the southwestern-most corner of the island. As we approached, the elderly priest came down the steps to meet us.

"Hail, Arsinoë Soteria Philoaígyptos!" he called out.

"Greetings, Your Grace! I have apparently been long in your debt, forgive the lateness of my thanks."

He gave a dismissive wave of his hand. "Poseidon favors the sea-loving Egyptians over the dirt-coddling Romans. And this temple favors the bold Egyptian queen over her skulking brother and traitorous sister."

"Is there anything you require?"

"We are well-stocked mostly, my lady, though we perhaps need a reinforcement of medicines if you think it likely this watery battle might spill over onto our island."

"I shall send over whatever supplies I can." I motioned to a captain. "Please see to the priest's requests." He rode off and I turned my company northward again to begin repositioning our men.

As the morning tide swelled, Tahu pulled Mudjet and me onto a remaining rooftop so we could watch the fleet sail out of the harbor and begin the maneuvers that would swing them out around the island.

"Alas that I have lived to see this scene repeat itself," I sighed. "May the outcome be more favorable."

"Much of the ways of the world are cyclical, my Pharaoh," said Tahu as he turned to meet my gaze. "Praise the gods when you live to see the wheel turn round again."

"Look," said Mudjet, pointing towards the sea. "The legion agrees to chase us."

The ships of the Thirty-Seventh had begun to raise their sails as the oarsmen struggled to change the direction many of them were facing.

"How far west will Sir Ganymedes lead the legion?" asked a Gabiniani lieutenant.

"I believe the commander plans to use the shoals on the western inlet as a natural barrier," said Tahu. "Our sailors will know how to navigate around them and they will perhaps catch the enemy off guard." He glanced at the soldiers around him. "Though that means the enemy might be pinned close to the northwestern shore. We will have to be cautious that they do not make landfall there as a diversion." The troops nodded and he relaxed briefly.

Euphranor's swift *hemiolias* quickly made up ground to where my front line of ships waited for them, and I could hear the shouts of the *quadrireme* masters calling for more speed. As Tahu had predicted, I saw my flagships take up positions behind where nefarious shoals lurked just beneath the surface like unquiet ghosts. The legion massed its best ships from Rhodes on the right, no doubt to keep my navy from attempting to flank their fleet and make a run for the palace. The left flank closer to the island coast appeared to be Pontian vessels, which were slower but better suited for disembarking troops.

"I do not recognize some of the sails in the middle," I said to Tahu. "Do you?"

"I see Lydian sails, but the others seem to be various Asiatic craft, my lady. I do not know the nations of origin."

Mudjet touched my shoulder and indicated towards Alexandria. "The *ta-meriu* stand with their Pharaoh."

From our distance, I could still make out the shapes of hundreds of people standing on the roofs that remained in the city observing the coming cataclysm as anxiously as we did. Women's scarves rippled like flags in the breeze and the endless clang of the blacksmiths and weapon-fashioners who had filled the air with noise these past long months had fallen uncannily silent. The city and I held our breath as one, for there was nothing else for us to do.

"My lady!" cried out a guard. "The Rhodians move to challenge the shoals!"

We all whirled about as four *hemiolias* on the right darted forward like swallows and my front line vessels swung out to surround the attacking enemy.

This is the part where I am supposed to tell of how my rallied men flew to their oars and sailed out to smash the enemy's line. How my teacher brought Caesar's best admiral to heel and our superior numbers made the Roman fleet tremble in fear. How I vindicated the trust my people and our gods had placed in me. But even at my most brazen, I have never claimed to be all of what I have sometimes been held out to be, so the truth must win out over illusion.

Alexandria and I saw the ships made of our houses and very bones hammer against the hulls of the Roman vessels to no effect. We saw our seafaring men, born to this aqueous life, driven to grief by Roman steel. I saw too late that my people were a people of the storm and flood, but nothing had prepared them for the flash of battle on the waters they revered as a mother. That the fish who had fed us would now be fed on the flesh of their hunters. I forced myself to fight the urge to look away when the third of my ships splintered and sank to the harbor floor.

Ganymedes did all that he was able, but we were beaten again by the fleet of the Thirty-Seventh Legion. This battle was not even as close as the first one. We lost the element of surprise and Caesar wisely returned to shore, leaving Euphranor to handle us.

I had learned enough in my military education to be like my adversary and understand when it was best to delegate, but my admiral was a palace eunuch and his was a man who had the Great Sea's water in his veins. My teacher had faithfully paid back my trust in him with admirable administration of our army and greater success than his detractors had dreamed possible. Yet at the end of the day, he was not a soldier any more than I was. And our luck appeared to be at last wearing thin.

I watched, agonized, as our ships began falling back once more towards the shore. I motioned to Tahu. "Get rowers out to the ships that make it back. I want half of them to join the custom ships in the blockade, the faster ships must come here and help us reinforce Pharos."

He nodded and took off down the line selecting men to convey the messages. I turned to the Gabiniani. "With no sea battle to distract them, the legion will come here and try to take the island once and for all. We cannot let this happen. Someone send a runner to the Soma, ask the commanders to give us all men that can be spared. I have lost one fight today, I shall not lose another!"

"I will go, my lady," said Mudjet, already halfway down the ladder and grabbing the reins of the nearest horse.

I nodded. "Quickly, my sweet. Be careful."

With Mudjet sent off, I rode to the settlement part of the island, where a contingent of civilian fighters met me. "What are your orders, *hemet-netjer*?" asked the forwardmost man.

"Caesar is bringing more men to take the rest of the island, sirs. If any of you still have women or children here, send them across the Heptastadion to catacombs. If any man wishes to join them, there will be no blame from me."

"Never, *heqat-taui*! We would never give the bastard Caesar the satisfaction!" shouted a man from the middle as the group rumbled in agreement.

"Then I give you a thousand thanks, *ta-meriu*. I want half of you to take any high ground offered by the buildings with my archers and armament towers, take pikes or whatever weapons you can lay your hands on. The legion still holds the lighthouse, we must keep them from gaining any other vantage point here. The other half will help the army keep the enemy from scaling the shoreline wherever possible. We must limit Caesar's points of entry."

I saw the rear line of my fleet reach the shore of the island and the ships empty of what troops remained aboard them. I rode out to meet the disembarking men calling out as I passed, "Stay with your battalions, *ta-meriu*! Stay together! The day is not lost yet!" I found an officer and shouted to him, "Where is Sir Ganymedes?"

"He is coming, my lady," answered the captain. "The flagship is un-harmed, he is simply directing the retreat of the navy so we are not lost in detail."

"Good. Get your men organized to meet the legion, for they are as-suredly coming."

The commanders who had gathered around us as we talked gave quick salutes and rushed off to corral their soldiers.

I found Tahu again directing archers arriving from the Soma to the rooftops. "Tahu! Where should we concentrate the army?"

"Caesar will want to take the whole island if possible, my Pharaoh, but what he needs above all else is the Heptastadion. He has troops al-ready on part of the northwestern shore and to the north of the Temple of Isis. I think he will use the landing force to pull those two camps to-gether to strangle us down until they can reach the bridge."

"So, we should have a minimal force in the south as a backstop, but we should mass around the north of the causeway?" I asked, closing my eyes to envision our deployment.

He nodded. "Yes, my lady. That is our best chance."

"Very well. See it done."

Mudjet galloped up to us, her mount's sides streaming with sweat. "Thank you, my sweet," I said. "We have already seen reinforcements making there way here."

"I have also spoken to the Sail and the Leopard, my lady. They say that a *hemiolia* of the enemy has already picked up Caesar and a detach-ment of the landed legion to take Pharos."

"What is he coming with?" asked Tahu.

"Light infantry and a cavalry unit from Gaul."

He scoffed. "The horses will be a waste of time. There will not be enough space for a proper charge."

"But the Gallic soldiers will be formidable even if they are dismount-ed," I said. "He is bringing shock troops to scare the civilians who remain. Send out word to the local leaders, I do not want them caught by surprise when these soldiers arrive."

"They have also had word from the Palm Fruit that Caesar knows you hold personal command here on the island, my lady," said Mudjet. "He hopes to capture you before Ganymedes can get to us."

"Well, we shall try to disappoint the Consul," I remarked.

Lord Amenei appeared at our side, reining in his horse as it tossed its head amongst the noise of our soldiers' preparations. "*Hai heqat-taui, iqer sekhri*! Sir Hieronymos is pleased to report our eastern position is holding secure, so he sends me to aid our glorious *hemet-netjer*."

"Excellent, my lord. We are pleased to have you here. Tahu will know where you can best serve our cause."

Tahu nodded. "My lord, the Gabiniani are protecting the Heptastadion and our lines north of the bridge, though I could use a commander to lead our soldier holding in the Romans on the northwest coast. Can you do this?"

Amenei placed his hand over his heart. "Consider it done, Your Majesty." He cantered off in that direction.

As we watched him depart, a voice rang out from the Gabiniani. "Latin sails approaching, Your Majesty!" We turned north to see several *hemiolias* coming in for docking against the rocks of Pharos.

"Everyone form up the lines," yelled Tahu. "Be ready for the legion to rush into an assault from the boats!" To me he said, "Your Majesty should take her position up with the archers."

"*Shai nefer*, my friend," I said, placing a hand on his shoulder. "Keep yourself safe."

"The same to you, my Pharaoh," he answered. "May the Lioness of War guide your arrows."

Mudjet and I rushed off to the collection of rooftops where our archers were arrayed, climbing up ladders to reach them until several captains leaned down to help our ascent.

Straightening myself, I walked to the edge of the roof where I could see the gangplanks of the Roman *hemiolias* hit the rocks of Pharos with a bang as a lieutenant handed me a bow and quiver.

"*Pedjeti*, aim for their legs and necks to bring them down," I called to the men around me as I slung the quiver over my shoulder. "We must thin the advance. Shoot for armored spots only as a last resort, the Romans make their armor thick."

The archers shouted their assent and set their arrows back in their bows. We waited until the first wave of legionaries poured out of the ships with a primal scream where Amenei's lines were positioned to meet them. I drew back my own bow and listened for the moment where they would almost be upon my army. As calmly as I could, I drew air into my lungs.

"Fire!" I shouted, and a glittering shower of arrows descended to greet the legions of Rome as they slammed into the waiting pikes of my army.

The sound of the battle grew to a deafening cacophony as we sent volley after volley down towards our attackers in an attempt to relieve the pressure on my infantry. Mudjet organized a group of civilians behind our array to run back forth with fresh arrows, so that every so often I felt a tug on my quiver as more arrows were dropped in its hold. As the hours wore on, my arms groaned from the strain, though I dared not show fatigue to my men who held their position so stoutly. My presence seemed to cheer them and they joked with me through their exhaustion as they would any other comrade.

"An excellent shot, my lady!" a soldier sang out as one of my arrows brought down a Gallic charger.

"Our Pharaoh should be called the Queen of Archers," shouted another.

I laughed, then spotted a row of infantrymen forming up with bows angling in our direction. "*Pedjeti*! Enemy bows! Shields up!"

My men in a single practiced motion slung their bows over their shoulders and lifted up the shields at their feet. We braced ourselves as the Roman arrows smacked into our upraised shields. As soon as the volley was over, the archers dropped their shields and notched fresh arrows in their bows to return the favor.

In the midst of this melee, where the crush of my army and those of our opponents met in a dull roar of men and metal, I spied Caesar. He stood with his troops, though pulled far enough away from the next man that in the mob he was virtually alone, helmet shining in the blazing sun. He did not see me.

Unthinkingly, I reached into my quiver and notched an arrow against my bow. The deadly will of Sekhmet seemed to take over my senses, blinding me to everything else in this moment. Dark voices swirled in my brain, calling on me to fulfill my destiny as a Ptolemy, reminding me that I was already a bloody princess who had killed before. The voices tamped down any feelings of guilt I still harbored for the death of Achillas, screamed that the men I may have felled in these last hours did not matter, that their *ka*s were weak in the light of my glory. I could almost feel my eyes roll back in my head like a predator giving the death blow, the taste of Berenice's blood lolling from my tongue.

I should have been terrified of myself in this moment, I shudder to recall it, but some force had released all the ropes of my *ba* and I gave myself over to the commands of the gods who bathe in destruction. I surrendered, however briefly, to the full power of Sekhmet the Unappeased and Set the Fiend. I took stony aim at Caesar's neck and pulled back my bow.

However, before I could take the shot, a sound hit my ear and cut through the voices in my head like a knife. The sound was one I had never truly heard before in life, only in imitation, and a memory filled my head, chasing out the murderous voices.

In the memory, I sat in a courtyard with Baktka, Mudjet, and a young slave from the mews. I was even younger and the slave was making bird calls, to the delight of my companion and me.

Having gone through numerous iterations of songbirds, wading birds, falcons, and hawks, the slave leaned in conspiratorially and made a quick piercing whistle followed by a soft, undulating whinny. It was a lonely and beautiful call that spoke of the endless desert, of careful, gliding flight. That day had been the first time I heard the cry of the stealthy kite.

Now in the heat of battle, I heard the cry again. The elegant bird swooped down in front of me, whistling as as it arced back up to a roof ledge on the Temple of Isis ahead of me. I lowered my bow to watch it pass. From its perch above me it whinnied again once, and then darted off towards the south. Back into the wild. I whirled around to where Caesar had been, but he was gone and my chance had evaporated.

I stood dumbly trying to recall my thoughts before the kite's appearance, though I could grasp them no more firmly than a half-remembered nightmare. I wondered if the kite was a messenger from the Daughters of Nut, perhaps they had decided this was not the Consul's time. Or that I was not to be his killer.

Tahu appeared behind me as I tried to collect myself. "My Pharaoh, we have the legion falling back! Should we keep up the attack and attempt to push them off the island?"

His voice brought me back to the present. "Can we sustain it?"

"Not without significant casualties, though this might be our best chance."

Amenei appeared at my side, huffing. "My lord, Tahu wishes to try one last push to rid the island of the legion. What do you think?"

"Caesar's numbers here are the smallest they have been. If we are to do it, now is the time," he said catching his breath.

"Are the people willing?"

"They will go where you lead, Your Majesty."

"Than let us mass for one more push. I wish to touch the stones of the lighthouse." I pursed my lips together and gave the piercing whistle of a falcon.

Even in the din, I saw many of the Gabiniani turn towards my call, knowing they would catch the light gleaming off the vulture crown. One of the archers raised a banner overhead and brought it down in a sweeping motion the Gabiniani would not mistake. A hoarse, raucous cheer went up from the men and they charged full long into the legion's ranks, which receded before their fury. After a few determined pushes, much of the legion turned in full flight towards their ships, even as a few clumps of determined veterans dug in before my infantry.

Mudjet stared at the scene openmouthed. "Can we stop them from reaching the ships?"

"Probably not," answered Tahu as he gave directions to those signaling with our banners. "Though a retreat is still a retreat."

"We have them on the run past the Temple of Isis, my lady!" a captain cheered.

"If we could only catch Caesar in all this," said another soldier wistfully.

A local man shrugged. "Bah, I'm sure the old dog is already safely aboard the ship."

The press from the fleeing legion seemed to reach the closest *hemiolia* all at once as men desperately clawed their way onto the waiting vessel. In the mad dash, I noticed the near side had begun to list dangerously towards the shore.

"Gods defend us!" I murmured breathlessly. "They are going to founder the boat!"

Indeed, no sooner had I said the words aloud than the vessel started to buckle under the weight of too many men. We could hear the furious shouts of the officers warning the troops from climbing aboard, but the panicked men obeyed only their instincts to be free of Pharos. A last leap of soldiers proved to be the tipping point and the *hemiolia* jerked angrily to one side, spilling out the legion as it sank to the sea floor. A few men were able to jump free of the vortex of the sinking ship but many were either caught up in the wreck or grabbed by the immediate undertow. Another of the Thirty-Seventh's *hemiolias* came about and sent rowers out to pick up those who were not drowned.

"Should we try to get a ship out to challenge the *hemiolia*, my lady?" asked Tahu.

I looked out at the scene below us. As much as my troops had accomplished in this latest assault, I realized that to continue it while the navy was in full retreat and reinforcements for the legion were close by would be catastrophic. Even if we could clear Pharos proper, and I had grave doubts that we could do so without devastating mortality, I could see we were not strong enough to storm the lighthouse this day.

With a disappointed huff, I said, "No, I think that is a lost effort. We continue to hold the Heptastadion and have gained the eastern coast up to the temple. That is enough. We are not organized sufficiently to sustain this attack without potentially losing what we have gained. The legion will need to regroup as well. Get our troops to hold their lines where they are."

He nodded. "I think that is wise, my Pharaoh. The sun is setting, at any rate."

I faced my men at my side. "*Ta-meriu*, you have fought bravely! Our fleet was defeated, but thanks to your efforts, all was not lost this day! Stand firm and we will have another day tomorrow!"

The men responded with words of encouragement as I climbed down from the roof so that I might cross the Heptastadion to assess our damages. I had nearly reached the causeway when a runner found me.

"Your Majesty! Sir Ganymedes is looking for you! He is in the inner harbor with Sir Dejen."

Mudjet and Tahu followed me as I hurried across the bridge on foot until I saw my teacher and Dejen outlined against the sinking sun. Abandoning propriety, I cried out, "Teacher!" as I ran into his waiting arms. "I am so glad to see you well!"

"And I you, *nedjet*," he answered in a relieved voice, as his expression fell. "Forgive your servant for failing to carry the contest for you."

I shook my head. "It is all right. We will try again. We still have the causeway and part of Pharos."

"Thanks to you, Queen of Queens," said Dejen, grinning. "The legion found you harder to manage than they anticipated."

"Indeed," said Ganymedes ruefully. "Your Majesty sunk more Roman ships on land than her poor admiral was able to at sea!"

"We thought Caesar might have been aboard that ship," said Tahu. "Has there been any word of him?"

My teacher nodded. "Yes, unfortunately for us, Caesar was able to escape the ship before it was swamped. It appears he leapt clear so that his other vessels could retrieve him."

"Though my Pharaoh did succeed in giving the general an embarrassing dunking," chuckled Dejen.

"Well, I suppose we must be content with that," I answered. "Is our eastern perimeter secure?"

"Yes, my lady," replied Ganymedes. "Hieronymos has done an admirable job. I do not think we are in too much danger from the legion there. Caesar wants the Heptastadion too badly to waste time with our forces by the palace."

"Then we will keep bringing reinforcements to our encampments on Pharos. I thought we might achieve a swift victory at sea, but it appears we must prepare for a grinding one on land. We simply need enough force to take the island, we must find it somehow. Otherwise this war will drag on forever and I cannot wish such a fate upon my people and Alexandria the Shining. Let us do what we can this evening, then give the army time to sleep and care for the dead. We will construct a new plan in the morning."

Chapter Thirty-Two

I opened my eyes in the light of a clear dawn, our first in nearly two weeks. For the briefest of moments, I thought I was back in my bed at the palace. I thought I had awoken from a long dream where I had run away from home to be a general in the army and fight against Rome and my sister. The *sha* had been there, and it had turned into Lord Set the Lurking One, and he had called me his beloved. Plots had been hatched and battles fought, and I had nearly slain Gaius Julius Caesar while my brother beheaded Pompey the Great.

Without rolling over, I could hear the even breathing of Mudjet in her sleep and I give a little snuff of amusement. It had been the strangest of dreams. Soon, servants would come to shake open the curtains and offer us plates of fruit for breakfast. Ganymedes would bring a pile of scrolls for my lessons and Ptah would search for an excuse to leave off our studies early so that I might take him down to the harbor to watch the ships come in.

I drowsily closed my lids against the light with a slow smile, content to drift back to sleep for a few minutes more. But then my memory caught up to the rest of my mind and I jolted awake in my tent in the shadow of the Gate of the Moon.

I swallowed my heart down into my chest as I worked to slow my shallow gasping breaths. My eyes darted around the tent as I acclimated myself once more to my surroundings. My waking mind relearned its place, and as it did, a beautiful sliver of glass was born in its wake. As perfect as crystal and as sharp as shame, it slid down the middle of my insides and left tiny drops of uncertainty behind it. Each drop became a torrent filling every corner in my body, down to the farthest reaches of my fingertips.

I laid down again, instinctively clutching my stomach for comfort. The remembrance of yesterday flooded my body like hot oil and I fought its powerful waves of fear.

Do not panic, I told myself, *there is nothing to be gained from it. You told the others today would come with new opportunities. Believe your own words. Think as you have been taught to. What choices lie in front of you?*

My brain seized on phantasms of surrender and execution and death until I grit my teeth and forced it into rationality. I remembered in the midst of my embarrassment and feelings of dishonor that the gods were still with us. I could rest in this knowledge not because of my dreams, but because they had created options for me that were not available to my adversaries. If we had carried the day, we would have achieved total mastery of Alexandria and our enemies would have been utterly defeated.

That had not happened, and yet our losses were not measured on the same scale as Caesar's would be had our positions been reversed. We had lost our battle at sea, but because we held so much of the city, we could choose other battlegrounds. Caesar could only win this fight through complete victory, while I could gain ground by halves.

Mudjet interrupted my thoughts. "Are you awake, my lady?"

"Yes. I am rising presently."

She sat up and rubbed her neck distractedly. "I cannot believe the Trojan War went on for a decade. I am exhausted after six months of this!"

I gave a little laugh. "Maybe that was the true reason Achilles refused to leave his tent at the beginning of *The Iliad*."

"Indeed, that seems altogether more plausible in this moment than notions like honor or the possession of a girl he had just met." She smothered a yawn. "What will you do this day, my lady?"

I shrugged. "All that we can do. We will attempt to reinforce our lines on Pharos and hope Caesar does not feel inclined to make a push for the island today. We pulled many of his men away from there yesterday, it may take some time to reinstate them."

"What of the fleet?"

I laid my arm over my eyes. "I think we shall leave it as is for a time. My aspirations to admiralty are apparently not to be, and I am not even sure if we have the materials to achieve any meaningful repairs."

She rose to light a lamp. "Well then, as usual, we have much to do. Come here, my lady, and I will help you dress."

We left my tent in search of my officers. I could feel my men's fatigue as we passed, though they did not appear unduly disheartened. All inclined their heads with kind words to us as we went. Near our smaller docks, we found Tahu making notes of supplies.

He greeted us cheerfully. "A pleasant morning to you, my Pharaoh. I hope that you slept well."

"I have done better, but I appreciate your solicitousness, sir."

"Today will be better than yesterday, my lady," he said. "I am sure of it."

"I hope so. What needs my attention?"

"I think at this time we are well in hand. Sir Ganymedes is checking our position in the Soma, and I am having him call on Madam Palm Fruit to see if there is anything we should be aware of."

I gave him a wry look. "So you told him at last?"

He grinned. "You know he always had his suspicions, especially after I led him to Madam Sail's, though my Pharaoh maintained her innocent airs most convincingly. I thought it was time to lay all of our weapons bare. He took it with good grace; probably because you have been so successful with our spies."

"I was bound to have a few successes in this endeavor by luck if nothing else," I answered, amused.

"We have more than luck on our side, my lady," said Tahu stoutly.

"It remains to be seen, my friend. Mudjet, would you go to the Mirror and see if she requires anything of us?"

She pulled up the hood of her cloak. "Of course, my lady. I will return soon."

Tahu bowed to Mudjet as she left before turning back to me. "I dispatched Lord Ehoou-hanif and Lord Amenei to the catacombs to handle any difficulties the people there might be experiencing. And Sir Ganymedes also sent Hieronymos and Dejen to the island to manage with the Gabiniani before he left. Unless you would rather have them recalled here to work on shipbuilding?"

"No, no. We are of one mind on this. We will resume work on the fleet if the proper materials can be obtained. Let us focus on reinforcing the city."

As the morning wore on, Tahu and I retreated to one of the nearby tents to study our maps out of the sun's glare. I had expected Mudjet to return more swiftly than she did, though Tahu assured me she no doubt had become entangled in some business or another for me. I had nearly reached the decision to go find her when Ganymedes arrived unexpectedly, his shoulders heaving as he tried to catch his breath. I motioned for someone to get him water, but he held up his hand.

"There is no time, my lady. We are betrayed. The merchants and Greek nobles have struck a bargain with Caesar: they will find a way to give him you for the release of Ptolemy. We have to get you out of here."

I felt the blood drain from my face. "So the hopes of my brother and his dead general come to pass in spite of my efforts. My price has been met."

"Not in the eyes of your army, my child. It is telling that in the face of our setbacks, the enemy had to strike this bargain with those outside your circle."

"It seems that Caesar maintains hope that he can convince Lord Ptolemy to speak to the people and stop the rebellion," said Tahu at my elbow.

"Possibly. Though I believe that the general has been trying to get anyone to give you up to him for months because he has greater faith in beating the young Pharaoh than you, my lady," said Ganymedes. "Although our betrayal does not come from within, our camp is the city, and that is impossible to defend from noncombatant infiltration. The merchants and nobles will send men to kidnap you because they know where you are. You must leave now."

I looked to Tahu dizzily. "Will you help me?"

He nodded. "We will be as shadows, Your Majesty."

A panic grabbed at my heart. "Wait! I cannot leave without Mudjet! Where is she?"

"I know not, but you cannot wait until we find her. You must leave immediately, child. I will send her after you if I can," replied my teacher as he opened chests to dig out clothing for me.

Ganymedes found a plain cloak and threw it around my shoulders. I lifted the vulture crown off my head, it was too heavy and too bright to take with me. The heaviness in my chest was another matter. I bowed my head. *Forgive my failure, Sekhmet.* I felt a hand on my shoulder and Ganymedes gathered me in his arms.

"The crown resides in your heart, *nedjet*. No one can take that from you. You have been an Amazon queen out of legend. I tell you true, Caesar comes to capture you because you have met him squarely at every turn. He cannot face the Romans if he continues to be so ignobly harried by a child princess and her army of slaves and renegade Egyptians," he said with a wink at Tahu, who returned it with a little bow.

"Will you keep my men going?"

He grinned. "Do not worry, we will give Caesar all he can handle. And do not despair if those cowards trap you in their nets. I will always come for you."

I held onto my teacher for an instant longer, then I draped the hood of my cloak over my head. Tahu and I slipped out into burning sun. I did not look back.

We walked swiftly and silently along the nearest backstreet, keeping watch for anyone who might be connected with the lords who were hunting me.

"Where are we going?" I asked as we went.

"I think if we can get you to the Temple of Isis on Pharos we might be able to claim sanctuary. Though if you are safe, it matters not where we go."

"What about the garrison at the lighthouse?"

"Caesar remains short on reinforcements, he has had to remove most of the men there to fight in the city. Those that are there are being harassed by our own troops. That should be enough of a diversion for us."

Cutting through the crowds, I saw a few people look at me out of the corner of their eyes but no one impeded us. We rounded a harbor wall, stepping out into the vast open space of the coast. There were many people and no hiding places.

And then I saw Ptolemy.

He was with a set of Roman guards, no doubt to keep him from slipping away before I was retrieved. We both froze in place, and for the first time, I was truly afraid of my brother. Recognition lit his features, but there was not even a hint of warmth. There was only a mechanical coldness, a barren streak of some dark emotion I could not grasp.

I understood that the lords of the city had not hatched this plan on their own. He had wheedled it into our sister's ear, and she had accepted. Why? And then I saw the truth: she had accepted because she had planted the seed in him first.

It was as clear as a cloudless day. She must have spoke admiringly of my victories, filled Ptolemy's head with visions of my supposed glory. How mighty a swath I cut as a pharaoh in my own right. That was the dagger thrust for my brother, his vanity would not have allowed him to cede so much to me. Better to get rid of me at last and possibly lose than to see me eclipse him in the hearts of our people. Especially since he had already lost so much face to Cleopatra. And she, like Caesar, she was more confident of beating him than me, and had worked to undo what little shreds remained of our alliance. Lost in my role as general, I had forgotten my political skin. I had been so focused on my need to outwit Caesar and the legions that I forgot that having her Roman chimera meant she had a free hand to exercise her talents in the palace alone. That a soft bed at night was not her only indulgence over me.

I felt as if I had not drawn breath in hours. I could hear the ragged breathing of Tahu at my side, yet none of us seemed capable of movement.

At last, it was Ptolemy who broke the spell. "Arsinoë!" he howled at me across the harbor.

I heard Tahu unsheathe his sword, and with a raspy whisper of, "Run, Your Majesty!" he gave me a small shove to get me going. I bolted into the crowd like a runaway horse and I pushed myself not to glance back as I heard the clatter of armored men coming after me.

As I ran, I knotted the train of my dress above my knees to give my legs more freedom. As if through a heavy curtain, I could hear the commotion of the masses around me. I leapt over jars and crates, sidestepped goats and chickens, and was immeasurably grateful that no Alexandrian seemed to be trying to thwart me. On the contrary, the frequent sounds of crashing and angry shouting suggested that many of them were throwing up obstacles to my pursuers.

Thank you, ta-meriu, I said silently.

I cast around through eyes stinging with dust to get my bearings. I had no better plan than Tahu's, so I changed my course slightly towards the Heptastadion. I hoped the contingent of our soldiers remained there as he said and that they still held our lines close enough to the temple to cover my escape. Or that they would at least be able to slow down the men at my back.

The clatter of hooves told me that several had found horses in an attempt to catch up to me, but luckily the harbor was too crowded and the chaos was terrifying for the animals who were only city beasts, not battle steeds. I felt a freeing sensation in my otherwise constricted chest. At the least I was confident Ptolemy himself could not catch me. I had always been quicker, even before I had received the favor of the gods. I let myself savor a glimpse of triumph in that what I did on my own, my brother continued to make others do for him. *That is why Cleopatra and I will forever be greater kings than he.*

I made it onto the island and could glimpse the temple in the distance. My lungs were burning and I could feel a trickle of blood dripping from my nose as the sand had ripped its way into my nostrils. I forced myself to keep moving forward, even as my brain began to register the unaccountable absence of my men on the Heptastadion and of almost any other people on Pharos. It sent a creeping sense of dread through my spent limbs.

Just as the temple entrance came into focus, I finally understood. There, standing before the graceful columns of Isis, surrounded by piles of dead Egyptian soldiers, was Caesar. I stopped in my tracks with my breath coming labored gasps, as much from the sight of the corpses and their author as from exhaustion.

"It's all right, Your Highness. None of my men will harm you if you come with us quietly," Caesar called out to me.

"I am not concerned about your men," I spat back at him, despite the aching rawness of my throat. "I am concerned about your whore."

I saw the flash of a smile from Caesar. "At the moment, you do not have the luxury of worrying about the future, my lady," he said. He took a step towards me, hand on the hilt of his sword.

At my back, a clamor suggested my other pursuers were catching up. My body reacted without my instruction — I darted to my right and took a running leap into the sea.

As the water closed over my head, I began to assess my situation. I thought about staying under and letting the harbor take me. I tried to calculate how long it would take the Romans to find bows among the remains of my soldiers. I wondered if they would jump in after me.

But my heart had already decided what I was to do. My arms pulled me back to the surface, and I swam as swiftly I could manage towards the lighthouse. As the water rushed by my ears, I could hear the soldiers shouting at each other. Their haste told me that gambling on Tahu's information was correct. My brave dead troops had pulled the garrison out from the tower by the sea.

I worked hard to increase my head start; they would have no choice but to gather boats or to take time to remove their weighty armor to swim after me. There was the narrow mole to the far island from Pharos, but it would hardly be faster unless these men had also had the reflexes of cats. I pulled myself along even faster still, knowing Caesar would divide his force and attempt all methods.

I reached the shore and crawled out of the water, coughing up blood and seawater. Still on my knees, I turned my head to look out over the harbor. The waves peaked against the hulls of the ships as their sails and flags fluttered like bright insects. I could pick out screams from the direction of the city, but that was so far away. Here there was only the sea, the ships, and me. My happy, beautiful Egypt.

I knew that my next moves were my last, and I tried to hold onto those ships even as I stood again and compelled my wasted legs to climb the lighthouse steps. The winding staircase filled me with despair, though I forced one foot in front of the other as quickly as I could manage. Every flight or so, I paused to retch on the punishing stones before the echoing shouts of the soldiers would push me on.

I reached the top in haze of sweat and vertigo, my arms trembling as I pulled myself onto the railing's edge and gazed upon the ships once more. I steadied my equilibrium as the droplets of water clinging to my frame shining like the purest of jewels dripped down and fell on the side of the lighthouse. I closed my eyes and let one foot test the hot blowing air. I watched the birds cry to one another as the sun caught the crest of their wings and made them glitter. I took a deep breath and prepared to let go of the column. The silky voice of my Lord suddenly drifted into my ear like a wayward messenger. *Be brave,* nedjet, it whispered.

As my fingertips brushed off the salt-grit rock, a damp hand grabbed my wrist to pull me back towards the floor. Wobbling in my balance, I whirled around until I saw I was truly in Caesar's grip at last. Because I was still wet from my flight, it took some time for me to notice the water pooling at his feet, his own shortness of breath.

I tried to back off the edge of the railing, and he threw his weight in the other direction to keep me from jumping. I looked into his dark eyes and fancied for a brief moment I saw something akin to fear in them. The thought of it made me want to burst out laughing. *This arrogant old man is afraid I will dash my brains out on the rocks of Pharos, that I will escape him and my spiteful sister. Then he will have swam after me like a fool for nothing. Little does he know my* ka *is a kite he could not have caught if he had a thousand snares.* I was so amused that I let loose a wild giggle. I jerked up on my slippery arm to free it just as the smell of smoke hit my nose.

Pure animal instinct made me lift my head until I was looking over Caesar, beyond him, and back to Alexandria. Fear convulsed through my body as I saw a towering wall of fire flaying the ancient backbone of the city. Tears sprang to my eyes as I watched the panicked masses flee the inferno, trampling everything that was not already burnt to ash. I realized this was Ptolemy's doing. Unable to outrun me, he had done what he always did. When he could not win, he destroyed. And it was then that I also knew where the heart of the blaze was. In growing terror, I looked to the southeast and beheld the Library engulfed in flames.

I felt as if I too was on fire. The feeling emanated from my chest and I understood that what I was experiencing was not simply the pain of seeing our transcendent library sacrificed to the winds of war. Egypt burned and the piece of my Lord I carried in my *ka* writhed at the destruction. I felt the agony of the gods as their land was ripped apart. I felt as if it would rend my bones from my body as wave after wave of misery lashed at my brain.

I know I screamed my life away in that moment. I know Caesar pulled me down from the ledge because I no longer offered any resistance. I know I was bundled off into the arms of one of his tribunes still wailing uncontrollably. Save this, I have been stripped of any other memories of this day.

Chapter Thirty-Three

I had not stopped shaking since we left Pharos. I curled myself into the corner of my cell, where I clamped my mouth against my chattering teeth. My thoughts raced around my head like spooked horses, eyes rolling back, mouths frothing. Gone was the girl crowned queen in her Five Names, lost were the light-winged victories and scattered joys of the last half-year. My dreams were full of fire and blood and the gods were silent.

It reached such a pass that my guards were instructed to force me to eat. They took turns holding me down and pushing a thin gruel into my throat. The tribune named Titus pitied me, I felt it in his grip when it was his turn to hold me. I felt it in the way he held my mouth open when that was his place. I felt it in the slight measuring way he coaxed the gruel into my stomach. He was the soldier whom Caesar handed me off to once I was off the ledge. He had seen all my shame.

I rarely responded to his kindly words, but I knew I was not hidden from him as much as I tried to draw into myself. Slowly, slowly the animal panic in my heart died away, and I was left with only an ironclad numbness. Then I waited for the blade in the night. For the queen's retribution.

I had been in the bare cell a week at the most, though it felt like whole years strung together, when the door opened one morning and Cleopatra walked in. Nausea rose in my stomach as the waves of *heka* pushed into the confined space and filled every corner in a suffocating layer of pure presence. It slunk around me like a mad dog, sniffing and probing. Looking to her, I could not tell how much of this she could observe.

She reached behind her and harshly thrust someone forward. The young woman lost her balance in the motion and stumbled onto her knees. Her clothes were dirty and her hair was caked in unwashed bunches, but her familiar tear-stained face bloomed with joy when she saw me, reigniting the light in her lifeless violet eyes.

333

"My lady! My lady!" my sweet Mudjet murmured as she crawled over to me and took me into her arms. I could find no words to express my elation that she was alive, so I clung to her in silence while a few tears wetted her soiled dress.

Cleopatra watched us with contempt as if we were two filthy beasts. "You know that you have brought this upon yourself," she said. "I would have been happy to leave you and Ptah alone," I raised my swollen eyes to her as she continued, "but you were just so sure you could beat me."

She stalked over and pushed Mudjet away from me. She bent down like an ibis in spite of her pregnant stomach to roughly lift my chin so we could see one another face to face. "How could you be so foolish, Arsinoë?" she asked, a small, aggrieved note clinging to the edge of her anger. "Ptolemy was set to hand you over in exchange for his sorry hide, did you think you could win against him? Let alone me? Do you think I enjoy all of this?"

I remained silent, I could not think of any more words for her. I could have buried my face in the dirt and begged her to protect Ptah; I would have done that once. But nothing I could say would be the luck I needed for such a request. I had failed Ptah as surely as I had failed Egypt and my Lord. The black god had sought out a champion and had found only a child. Now I would die for my mistakes and there was no spell I could cast against my sister that would wipe our history clean. I would be cut down by my family like so many Ptolemies before me. My father had forbidden anyone to weep for Berenice. I found myself wondering if Ptah would be kept alive long enough to weep for me.

She inclined her head to the side and frowned. "No words for me? Is your hatred as deep as that?"

I watched her eyes narrow into a saner version of the look she gave me that night almost a year ago in Judea, as if she were trying to see me through a veil. She searched my face, seemingly both unable to see what she wished and seeing too much that she did not.

"Or are you some holy woman now?" she hissed with surprising malice. "The peasants whisper that the Egyptian gods love you, that you are their *hemet-netjer.*"

The Egyptian words rolled easily from her practiced tongue, though in her mouth they turned sour and ugly. The title I treasured above all others, except perhaps when Set called me *nedjet*, ruined before my eyes by my embittered sister. "If that sorry little tale is so, it proves their day is done and you with them. I could splatter you and your pride all over this room with my *heka* alone if I pleased, I know you feel it all around you. Have you really any concept of its might? I could show you, you know." She waited to let the threat hang in the air with an unexpected delicacy, savoring its sweet venom. "However, I have a more exquisite punishment in store for you, sister-dear."

I responded dully, "Some new poison?"

This made her snort in derision. "Oh no, my wee false queen. What I have planned is much more excruciating than any poison in my book. Once Caesar takes care of Ptolemy for me, which should be short work seeing how your troops now hate him, we shall rest on our laurels briefly and then we shall take you to Rome. And after the good citizens have had their fill of hurling garbage at you and you have been humbled enough to lick my sandals in front of them, I will graciously allow you to be strangled to toast my victory."

I stared at her. I would not have thought she was capable of astonishing me anymore and yet this proclamation stunned me to my core. "You will put me through the shame of a triumph? You would bring such dishonor to the blood of Ptolemy Soter before barbarians? Your own blood?" I whispered, my throat nearly refusing to say the words.

Cleopatra gave a cruel shrug. "You have some of my blood, but you are also a half-Egyptian mongrel and a traitor, and I will have an example made of you before the people of the Black Land. I will make them wish they were under the stony hand of She Who Is Not Spoken Of. And Rome will see I am not to be trifled with."

"Why me? Why not Ptolemy?"

"Because Ptolemy would be no fun," she replied, her mouth twisting into a malicious grin. "I want you to know just how much I can humiliate you before I kill you, little sister."

Cleopatra was correct, of course. Too many of my men knew that Ptolemy and his allies had sold me to the enemy to save themselves, and they despised him for it. They were not nobles, many were not Greek; they knew they had lost a champion for their Egypt and were now only involved in a bickering fight between rival conquerors. The Gabiniani were so disgusted with my brother that they nearly revolted for brokering a deal with the woman they hated for the most temporary of advantages.

In my broken heart I sighed for those brave soldiers who would now die for a cause that was not their own. I felt the restless bones of the old pharaohs clatter in their plundered tombs. The last death rattle of the old Egypt.

And then Caesar's ally Mithridates came overland from the east, joining the legions wily Antipater at last deigned to send my sister from the north. Caesar then had twenty thousand men at his disposal, finally enough to match our forces. No more siege, now the Romans went truly on the offensive. As much as it must have galled him, Ganymedes agreed to help Ptolemy defend Alexandria, because a victory was his only chance to gain my freedom. Not that I think it would have mattered in the end. Even if our army had carried the day, Cleopatra would have killed me before she fled our forces. She and I had reached an impasse, our breach could not be healed. We were two sharp-eyed hawks locked in deadly combat. Only one of us would be able to fly away.

My men fought courageously, yet their mettle and their pikes were not enough. The legions were led by lords of war who had fought a hundred battles. Many of my soldiers were farmers and children.

The so-called Battle of the Nile was the last war of Egyptian Egypt. Like the dreamy lotus eaters, too late did this ancient land rise up against the yoke of the Greeks. Now they would wear the chains of the people who had risen to take Alexander's place. The Romans overran Ptolemy's camp as soon as they broke the Egyptian line. My ever-changing brother fled like his soldiers, scattered to the dust of history, and in the end, the ancient Egypt he had always scorned had its final revenge. The primordial Nile — Egypt's Mother, Father, Lover, Foe — its Everything and All Things, dashed his ship against her waves and pulled him down into her silty lap. He burned her land and she fed him to her crocodiles. Such has always been the violence of her love and hatred.

The defeat of my army also killed my beloved teacher. He was found with a Roman *pilum* in his back still in the confines of the camp, surrounded by the bodies of dozens of his soldiers.

I could see it so clearly in my mind, Ganymedes trying to rally a counterattack long after Ptolemy had abandoned the field. Convincing a detachment of men to keep fighting to allow more of the troops to reach safety and regroup. The relentless push of the legionaries, the exhaustion and fear of my soldiers, one by one being cut down. My tutor at last realizing they too must fall back, and the spear piercing him as they turned to run. Cleopatra ordered his corpse decapitated and the headless trunk hung from an obelisk in front of the palace. The head she threw at my feet and left there so I could watch it rot and be devoured by rats in the moonless night.

With Ptolemy dead, my sister placated her inconstant lords by marrying Ptah and crowning him as her new co-ruler. He had to leave his toys and his nickname and take his place in our family's house, where there must always be a Ptolemy. Ptolemy is dead, long live Ptolemy. Ptolemy Of No Ruling Epithet, the Fourteenth of His Name, was nine years old when the double crown was placed on his head. I begged my mute Lord to protect him.

After my sister's visit to me, the forced feedings stopped. In their place was a single small bowl of gruel a day no longer delivered by sympathetic Roman guards, but by Apollodorus or one of his minions. Mudjet and I would sit reciting poetry to one another and pretend not see him or how watery the gruel grew each day.

"You think you can ignore me forever, Princess. You are very mistaken," he said one day, slamming our bowls down.

I slowly turned to him. We might have been prisoners, but I had come too far to acquiesce to his barbarous attitude. "I did not realize you had grown so insecure, Apollodorus, as to need my attentions," I shrugged his presence away while tipping the bowl of gruel towards me with my toe to inspect the contents like fine wine. "I am sorry if my sister is spending so much time stroking Caesar's... *ego*... that she is neglecting you."

In a flash he picked me off the floor and slammed me against the wall. Mudjet shrieked. "Both of you can scream all you want, no one will hear you," he hissed, inches from my face. "I told you that you weren't your glorious sister's equal, do you still not understand this as you sit in a cell in your own filth? You act like you are still a Ptolemy. You are nothing. If you are lucky, your corpse will be thrown into the Tiber."

"And you are still a brute masquerading as a gentleman," I replied disdainfully. "I have wielded a sword and an army, and held both in the face of Gaius Caesar. I am not afraid of you anymore, Apollodorus."

He pushed me harder into the wall and I tried not to wince in pain. "I'll call in a few of my men and we'll see how long you keep that whorish tongue in your head. If I am feeling generous, they will only use their fists." He glanced over his shoulder. "Or should I have them start with Mudjet?"

I repressed a shudder. "If my sister allows you to do this, you are correct. I am not her equal. I am her superior."

He let go of me angrily and I fell onto my knees. "Still a delusional little girl after all. Let's see if you can hold such a high opinion of yourself when you're too feeble to protest." He stalked out of our cell, pausing only to kick Ganymedes' skull into the far wall.

I waited until he was gone before crawling over to what remained of my teacher's head. It was still unpleasant to face, but our midnight scavengers had cleaned up much of the viscera. I picked it up and ran a finger along the angry crack the Sicilian had kicked into the bone.

"Forgive me, Teacher. Though you know Apollodorus has always been ill-mannered."

Then our gruel began arriving every other day. It did not take long for the constant gnawing presence of hunger to squeeze our bellies like a vise. I began to await Apollodorus' men eagerly, barely able to contain my poise until they departed before falling on the meager gruel in a snarling spasm of animal need. Only the last shreds of my dignity prevented me from snatching Mudjet's portion for myself, and I could see a matching thread of decorum dangling in her eyes. We waited and dreamed only of food, the longer days only made time pass more leadenly.

"You are growing too thin, my lady."

I ran a restless hand along my jutting collarbones and glanced back at Mudjet's hollowed cheeks. "It cannot be helped," I answered listlessly. Perhaps we shall be granted the mercy of starving at home rather than being murdered in Rome."

"I would have thought the Queen would feed you well to prevent such an escape." She looked at me with a wan ghost of her usual saucy smile. "Such as it is," she added with a rueful little giggle.

"She is distracted. She has her child's future to plan, a kingdom to manage, and a lover to entice to stay abroad as long as possible despite his commitments. She might be forced to forgo some attention to a sister she is only going to kill when it is convenient anyway."

Mudjet gave me a thoughtful look. "I think it is as Achillas told you. She was surprised how lovely and grown-up you were when you came back. She is willing to risk having you die from lack of food to have you appear more plain before the Romans."

It was my turn to try to remember how to laugh. "Now I know our end is imminent, my dear, if Cleopatra Thea Philopator has found something to be envious of me for," I replied, grinning weakly and holding out my ugly, wasted arms for her approval.

"That, and how long so many of her own people resisted her rule for you. How even here in the bowels of despair, we hear whispers that the people still look for you. You are no longer a weak child before her prowess, my lady."

"No more a child, true. She might succeed in making me weak again," I replied, closing my eyes against the vertiginous wave flooding my head.

Mudjet did not reply for several minutes. Finally she said, "Have the gods abandoned you, my lady?"

I could yet feel the pressure of Set's hand over my heart, the glimmer of him that lived in my *ka,* but how to explain even to Mudjet how light the feeling had grown? How what once was a firm embrace had become as fleeting as the brush of lips? The stark chasm the gods left inside me with their silence. How truly alone I felt. How part of me feared that my failures meant they had surrendered me to whatever fate my future decreed.

"I know not, my sweet," I said to her, unable to hide my sadness as I did my pensive thoughts. "The gods are quiet, though mysterious are their ways. Perhaps I am being tested."

She frowned. "It seems unfair for the holy gods to test you at this late hour. I think you have sufficiently proven yourself to them."

"Ah, but Ma'at has never promised fairness, dearest. Only balance."

The weeks dragged on. I began to lose track of time, of place, even of who I was. Every day, Mudjet and I would rise when the first sliver of daylight crawled up our wall like a lazy spider. We would rise and she would make me recite the same words every morning through our hunger and our growing disorientation like a talisman:

I am Arsinoë, Third-Born of Her Father; Princess of the House of Ptolemy Soter; Queen of Upper and Lower Egypt as the Fourth of Her Name; Beloved of Set, Lord of the Red Land, He Who Thunders; Sister to Ptolemy the Fourteenth of His Name, Pharaoh of the Black Land, Incarnate of Horus the Wadjet-Eyed.

"What are your Five Names, my lady?"

Arsinoë, Light and Renown of Ra; Beloved of the Ka of Set; She of the Two Ladies to Whom the Gods Open Their Mouths; She Who is Like the Shining Eye of Horus, beloved of the Two Egypts.

As the ever-lengthening days blazed on and the ceaseless moans of our empty stomachs robbed me of sleep and the ability to think deeply of anything, I began to almost wish I could see Caesar again. I wished I could throw myself at his demon's feet and beg him to soothe Cleopatra's savage temper. I remembered that despite his own beastly reputation, he was also known to be merciful to his defeated adversaries. It was because of this I told myself he was ignorant of our treatment.

Or maybe that was a foolish fancy of my exhausted mind. Maybe I had wounded his pride too deeply for pity. Maybe they conspired together in each other's arms just as was said and my wasting body was his revenge as well. I could no longer tell. I ceased to dream of food, and I began to dream of death.

Chapter Thirty-Four

I stand before an enormous gate lit with torches. It is on a scale that would laugh at the works of Ramses the Great's feeble attempts to cow the weak. It makes the pyramids feel intimate. I feel my *ka* shrink in my chest, it does not want to pass through this gate. I do not know what is on the other side. I do not want to know.

"But your *ka* knows, Ptolemy-daughter," says a jaunty, adept voice in the darkness behind me.

I turn, and a young man steps out of the darkness towards me. Young is a relative term; my Lord is young in face, as are many of the gods. Only their eyes show their true age. This young man is younger than my Lord, though he shares some of Set's clever features. His deep bronze skin glows softly against the blackness he emerges from, his tawny eyes move with the practiced quickness of a predator and peek out at me playfully from under his black jackal-headed hood.

I bow my head. "My Lord Anubis. Your appearance seems to remove any doubt."

"Oh, do not be afraid," he says, his eyes still dancing. "You are not entering the *Duat* with the dead. You are here on a special assignment."

"What assignment is that?"

"Your final training exercise, child," speaks another voice, a soft growl emerging from the dark. Sekhmet joins us at the gate, holding an oil lamp. She looks me over. "You have done well, Ptolemy-daughter, but you must be prepared to survive all you shall have to endure in the Waking World. Therefore, we are sending you through one last challenge in the Dream World to steel your *ka*."

"What do you wish me to do, my lady?"

"It is not me, Ptolemy-daughter. It is He of the Desert Winds who will guide you through this last training. You will help him with his nightly battle."

My stomach buzzes uncomfortably. "But how? I am mortal!"

Sekhmet gently places two fingers over my heart. "Not entirely, little princess."

"How will I do this?"

She smiles with all of her teeth. "With our help. Never fear, you are ready for this." She waves a hand and I am suited up in well-fitting leather armor.

Anubis conjures into his hands a woven basket, which he carefully balances on top of my head. "You must not think that because you believe you have not heard my lady mother's song that she does not care for you. You know she speaks with a kite's voice."

I reach up and touch the basket wonderingly. "She is very kind to spread her wings over my humble person."

He smiles encouragingly. "She wishes nothing more than your safety. Anything you desire, simply think of it and it will appear in the basket."

"I will descend into the Night-bark with the help of Nephthys-Singer of the Songs of the Dead," I answer in as strong a voice as I could manage.

"As I told you, do not be afraid. I shall guide you on your journey, Ptolemy-daughter." With that, Anubis transforms into his jackal self. He flicks his ears forward and wags his tail in a friendly manner.

Sekhmet walks up to the stone gate and places her right palm against it. "Remember to trust your *ka* and not your eyes, child."

"I pray that I will prove worthy of your tutelage, Lady of the Sharpened Sword."

She flashes a smile that speaks of laughter and not carnage as she hands me the lamp. "Here at the edge of the world, we are our other Selves, Ptolemy-daughter. I am the Lady of the West, the Queen of Joy, and you shall be Pharaoh *Tjesiib*-Arsinoë of Egypt, the Red Lord's *hemet-netjer*. Do not forget who you are."

She pushes against the gate and it slowly pulls open. I bow to her as Anubis and I enter into the realm beyond.

The most noticeable thing is the silence. I can feel a breeze against my cheek that darts and hovers about us, but it makes no sound. As we walk, we are surrounded by the company of uncountable pale lights that move through the air like fireflies. They flutter up to my face and dance around the lamplight. Anubis every so often jumps up at one or the other and prances after them in a movement that is so dog-like I nearly forget I am traversing the *Duat*.

He stops and turns to me. "It is no game, Ptolemy-daughter," he says, his voice appearing inside my head without him moving his mouth, "I must remind these *ka*s that I am not always at their beck and call. All must wait their turn."

It is then that I realize the lights that surround us are the dead, traveling their way across the *Duat*. They are following us because they are begging Anubis to lead them, and listening hard, I can hear their frail voices whispering the words of the Book of Going Forth in what I had thought was only silence. The prayers the dead are to use to help them on their journey, to take them to the Field of Reeds.

Anubis tilts his head in understanding at my look of dismay. "I am not hurting them, they will be fine. And they will not hurt you. Look," he gestures towards me with his nose, "they think you are one of them and are simply curious." I look down at my chest and see that my own *ka* burns through my skin with a deep golden glow cut by a thin red vein cutting across it. "The *ka*s of the living are always brighter," he adds. I do not need to ask him the meaning of the pulsing scarlet scar.

We continue on until we reach a long pier leading out into the waters of a lake so immense I imagine this is what the waters at the end of the world look like. The Nubians and the Kushites speak of the vast sea that leads to India; so big as to dwarf the Great Sea. I wonder if this sea is even bigger. The waves ripple across to us, yet they too make no sound. As we head out onto the pier, the dead do not follow us. They disperse as if they had suddenly remembered a pressing appointment. We walk to the end of the pier without them and Anubis sits down, his tail slowly whisking from side to side.

"What are we waiting for?" I ask.

"The Ship of the Sun," he answers. "Reach up into the basket."

I do and pull out a long white silk ribbon. The Ptolemy diadem. I gently place the lamp at my feet. In the night world, the ghostly ribbon seems to carry its own light and I hold it as if it were a cobra.

"Tie it over yours eyes, Ptolemy-daughter. They will not be able to withstand the Gaze of Father Ra."

I do as I am told and now I wait in an even more complete darkness. I am just beginning to wonder how long we will have to wait, when I hear the rhythm of paddles in the water and a tremendous light appears to my right. It radiates such a fierce heat I fear that side of me will be scorched. Even under my blindfold I squeeze my eyes shut.

The light moves ponderously until it stops so that I can tell it now is before me full in the face. Anubis gives a little bark and I hear him leap into the boat that must be resting before me. I worry for a instant about how I will follow him without my eyes when a strong hand takes mine. I relax in its familiar grip.

"Do not be afraid, Beloved. I will not let you fall."

Set takes my other hand and carefully guides me into the boat. The warmth the light generates remains powerful, but I feel my skin becoming accustomed to it as if it were a very hot day. My Lord says something in an unknown tongue and the boat moves forward as the paddles splash back into the water.

I feel Set stroke my head. "Are your eyes closed?" he asks me gently.

"Yes," I practically gasp.

His touch is like a potion coursing through my veins with such intensity that I feel dizzy. My heart rejoiced at the appearance of Anubis and Sekhmet in my dreams because their presence had taken away the fear I had held in their absence. Only now in my reunion with my Lord do I understand how terrified my *ka* has been in the last weeks.

"Then I am going to turn you so you may greet He Who Shines on All."

He brings me towards the source of the light and the rays touch my face, almost as if they were probing me. For the first time in all of my dreams, I kneel down before a god of Egypt until my nose is against the warm wood planks of the hull.

"Hail the King of All, He Who Burns the Darkness," I murmur to the ship's floor.

I can feel the Eyes of Lord Ra upon me. When he speaks, his charcoal voice crackles like wood in a fire. "Greetings, young Ptolemy-daughter. We are pleased you are here. Many of My heavenly family speak well of you. Especially My fiery Lioness, and her praise is hard won."

"The gods are kind to their servant, Your Radiance. I do not know if I shall be much help against the beast You face, but I shall serve You as best I can."

The light bobs in a way that suggests a nod and Set helps me to my feet, leading me further towards the ship's prow so that the heat may be less intense.

"Why am I here, my Lord?" I ask him.

"Because I am jealous of the many battles you have fought without me, *nedjet*," he replies smoothly. "I long to have us fight side by side."

I frown. I cannot see my Lord's face, but I do not need to. I know that he is lying to me. Something in his voice snags on this fact and unravels his words before me. Now the fear I had been swallowing lances at my heart and makes me truly afraid. At last I say softly, "It is hard for us when the gods hide their faces from us. Long are the inky nights of their silence."

Set understands me. I feel him close his eyes as if in pain before he answers me. "It has not been our choice, Arsinoë. Your sister's *heka* has engulfed so much, we have not even been able to penetrate the walls of your prison until this night. You have not met us in the Dream World in many nights, yet we have been trying to reach you from the start. Why do you think this night you have met so many of us? My sisters have used powerful magic to break through, but we believed only by drawing you into the *Duat* could we sustain contact."

I touch the basket on my head. "I am humbled by the love of the gods, yet it seems like a great deal of trouble for one princess."

"You have fought valiantly for our people, Beloved. The gods are grateful, and they know when to show their thanks."

I pause to feel for the god's meaning hidden behind his words. He is still not being fully honest with me. "That is not all."

Set hesitates, then speaks. "You are dying, my lovely one. This is the last plan I have to save you. I know not if it will succeed."

I startle. "I am weakened, I know, but surely not dying? Cleopatra wants me for the triumph in Rome, she would not have me die in Egypt."

"In her anger, she has miscalculated. Her fury with you and all you have achieved has blinded her. You will die of her accidental neglect soon if we cannot stop it. The only reason you are still alive is because my *ka* sustains yours," he says placing his black hand over my heart. "But the *he-ka* insulates it from me and it is weakening as well."

I take a deep, shuddering breath. "What is your plan, my Lord?"

"I have brought you here to help me defeat the Snake tonight. Battle should reinvigorate the part of my *ka* that lives in you and that should keep you alive."

"Well, if you are fighting beside me, I am not afraid of defeat."

"It is not as easy as the clash of swords, *nedjet*. There is that, yes, though there is another part that is much more dangerous." He pauses for a moment before continuing. "The beast must be fought with arms, though also in the mind."

I nod slowly in understanding. "To defeat Chaos, one must allow it inside and defeat it there. This is what I must do tonight if I am to live."

"Yes. This is what must be done."

We stand at the prow listening to the paddles cut into the waves. "Will my Lord promise me something?"

"All that I am master of, Beloved."

"That you will remember your duty and let the Serpent kill me if Lord Ra is threatened."

"Hmph, the clever princess has grown very confident if she thinks she wields such power over me," he quips.

"I know you can be stubbornly single-minded about things."

He reaches out to me and squeezes my hand. "Like all of my favorite companions. But I will do as you ask."

It is then I hear something other than the paddles break through the water. It lands with a heavy thunk upon the boat and it makes a deep hissing sound as it saws its body heavily across the wooden floor. I feel Set's fingers reflexively tighten around mine, and I am filled with the certainty that the strength of his grip will not avail me. Against all the instincts of my body, my mind forces me to kneel down as the creature approaches. Its scaly skin brushes mine instantly turning all beyond my blindfold dark, and my Lord's hand vanishes from my grip.

I slowly undo my blindfold and am confronted by a total void. There is nothing around me anywhere, except Apep. It is truly a monstrously large serpent, terrifying to behold yet also strangely beautiful. It has the appearance of a common desert viper, pale as sand rock with darker, impenetrable eyes. The only thing that distinguishes it from a common asp, other than its size, is the long pattern of hieroglyphs that trail down its coiled sides. From what I can see, it is a litany of the beast's epithets, for names give us power always. I suspect part of the impermeability of its hide came from the spell these names cast.

I watch Apep sit up and test the air with its tongue several times. In a low hissing voice, it finally speaks.

"You are not Set Bloodslayer."

"No."

It flicks its tongue in and out as it slithers around me at all angles. Apparently satisfied with its inspection, it returns to my line of vision and rears up to my height so we are looking at each other.

"You are *Khaiwadjet-Merettaui*," it says. It is not a question.

I do not respond, so the serpent speaks again. "It is foolish of the Set Kin-Defiler to send a pharaoh to face me. Especially a woman-pharaoh."

"I may be a woman-pharaoh, but you know I bear a piece of Lord Set's *ka* and that *ka* defeats you every night, Creature. My arms have been molded by Lady Sekhmet of a Thousand Battles."

Its tongue flicks out in a movement that conveys amusement. "We shall see, Pharaoh. We shall see."

It backs away as it plans its first move, and instinctively I reach up into the basket. My hand returns with a piece of papyrus and a *menat*. It is the *menat* Ehoou-hanif gifted to me on the night of my name ceremony, still as beautiful as it was that night. When we were all still together and whole.

My eyes are drawn to the Sekhmet-shaped beads and I recall her words to me as I entered the *Duat*. *Trust your* ka, *not your eyes, do not forget who you are.* I must be ready for Apep's trickery, I must remember the power of my Names. I tie the *menat* around my neck and adjust the counterpoise.

I then turn my attention to the papyrus. It contains a drawing of a priest holding up a scroll in front of Apep, with Lord Ra in His cat form menacing the snake with a knife. It is then the words of the Book of Overthrowing Apep come back to me. This is the key to defeating the monster. I close my eyes and remember the first step. *Spitting Upon Apep.*

I open my eyes and the serpent has vanished. In its place stands Caesar, his dark eyes flashing and his mouth twisted into a leering grin.

I very nearly laugh, for the serpent has miscalculated if it intends to frighten me with my old fear. It searched my mind and found the man who defeated me in battle and stole my freedom, and made the assumption I must be afraid of him. But I have not feared the wolf of Rome since we met on Pharos. Even ignoring that, Sekhmet has already prepared me for this battle in her wisdom. Caesar produces a *gladius* and strides forward to meet me. I pull a *gladius* of my own out of Nephthys' basket and easily block his first parry. When I do so a second and a third time, I see a flicker of confusion in the monster's eyes.

"I told you, Serpent, I have been well trained," I say as it fails to catch me from behind.

"I do not understand. This one has defeated you in the Waking World," Caesar hisses angrily.

Now I do laugh. "Yes, with an army and the treachery of my enemies. Not all battles in the Waking World are fought one to one as the fight in which you nightly fail to best my great Lord."

In frustration, Apep in Caesar's form charges me to try to throw me off balance, but in doing so it gets too close to me. Taking a moment to aim, I spit directly on its face. Caesar growls and turns back into Apep, who retreats to regroup. I keep my grip on my sword while I think of the second step. *Oppressing Apep with the Left Foot.*

Apep exhales a breath of black smoke that obscures it from view. I tense up and wait for the smoke to dissipate. When it does, Achillas lunges at me from the right. This shade catches me by surprise, but I ward off its attack and attempt to keep it to my left side. Seeing what I was doing, Achillas tries to stay to my right.

"You are very desperate indeed, Serpent, if you try to fight me with someone I have already defeated personally. This is worse than your last choice!" I taunt the creature to confuse it as well as keep up my own spirits. I am not afraid of Achillas, though I do not like seeing him standing before me again.

"All fear the dead, especially those they slay by their own hand," Achillas snarls as he thrusts his sword at my torso.

"Ah, but I am a Ptolemy and a pupil of Lord Set besides, Monster," I reply as I counter forward and hit it with the flat of my sword. "Perhaps I have no shame when it comes to murder."

Achillas laughs harshly. "You are foolish, Mortal, if you believe Set Kin-Cursed is not afraid of the slain dead. What else do you think we speak of all these many nights?"

I am startled by this thought. Achillas takes advantage of my distraction by trying to knock me down with the pommel of its sword. I throw forward my weight to catch myself and stumble onto Achillas' foot with my own left foot. It howls angrily as Apep in its own form returns and slinks to the other side of the void in a puff of dark smoke. I drop the sword as the next step comes to me — *Smiting Apep with the Lance* — and I reach up in the basket to pull out a pike.

When the smoke clears, my father is walking towards me with his cold eyes peering out over his beaky nose. The snake has been faithful to his slight paunch, so at least I do not have to worry about being quicker than this shade.

"Now Arsinoë," my father warns. The creature is doing a faithful impression of him, the only tell a small tinny echo at the back of the throat. "You would not harm your father, would you?"

"It depends," I answer. "What has my father done this day?" I move towards him, pike outstretched.

It throws out its arms. "But my sweet child, I am unarmed!"

"Wrong, Beast," I say with a rueful laugh. I strike out with the pike and it jumps back. "The first rule of the House of Ptolemy: everyone is always armed. And my father has never called me his sweet child."

I have caught it flat-footed. It seems unable to think of a weapon to use against me, and instead grabs me roughly by the arm to overpower me by strength. I jab with the pike as best I can in such close proximity, but the tip fails to penetrate and my father manages to wrench it from my hands. As it turns to me, its sharp grin lolling in triumph, I swiftly produce another pike from the basket and throw it as hard as I can at the shade. It lodges in my father's breast and drops it to its knees as it morphs back into Apep.

I hear its furious hiss as the cloud of smoke envelops the snake. I cannot pretend I am not a little perturbed at having to skewer the image of my father, even though we were not as close as Apep assumed. I rush forward through the heavy smoke before it vanishes pulling out of the basket the manacles I will need for the next step: *Fettering Apep*. I feel an urgency to move quickly, imagining it will be difficult to shackle the monster. I stumble blindly into the haze and stop short when I see the shade sitting in the center of the slowly disappearing fog.

"Well, you did not think it would be as easy as all that, my lady?" sneers Mudjet, appraising me icily.

It is not real, I tell myself, *it is not her. It is Apep*. But my mind is revolting at the sight of my sunny Mudjet sitting there looking at me with a somewhat superior air, and her face full of disdain.

She stretches languorously. "Oh, so my lady comes to fetter me in chains? Is that not a bit redundant? I am wasting away in prison because of you, my Princess. You have already shackled me to your life, go ahead and mark me for the slave I am," she holds out her arms with the taunt.

"I have never thought of you as my slave," I answer hoarsely.

"Then what am I, my dear, dear lady?" Her eyes light up in gleeful amusement. "Oh my! You do not believe we are truly *friends*?" she mocks. "Oh no, Princess. Friendship is for equals and you do not hold us as equals. I have no more choice in being your friend than you had being your sister's ally in the desert. It is only a matter of survival."

I am shaken, but the words Mudjet speaks begin to wake me up. "No. No. My Mudjet is a person of endless resourcefulness. Just like her mother. If I died tomorrow, she would always find a way in this world. I know she is not so dependent on me."

Mudjet's lip curls. "That only proves you do not *really* care about me. I will get by, but by the heavens! Do not leave you to fend for yourself for two moments together!"

I sit down slowly next to her, keeping my posture bent. "I have failed you, my sweet, as surely as I have failed everyone else. I am not the lady a person of your immeasurable worth deserves, indeed, I should probably be the one serving you."

I can feel the greedy gaze of her hard purple eyes upon me so I let out a heavy sigh, and in one swift motion I spring the fetters on her wrists.

Apep roars and I hold onto the chains for an instant so that the reappeared creature and I are looking at each other. "You fail, Serpent, because your demon heart does not understand friendship. Mudjet and I are friends because we are equals of the mind and of the *ka*, even where the gods have decreed us unequals in the status of the world. And that equality will survive the endless ages of the world."

I release the chain and Apep rears back as the smoke gathers around it again. I reach again into the basket and retrieve an excellent dagger. The fifth step: *Taking the Knife to Apep*. I wait tensely as the smoke clears, but when it is gone Apep is nowhere to be seen.

A small voice behind me says sadly, "I always knew you would do this one day, Arsinoë," and it is all I can do to keep my knees from buckling. Full of dread, I turn around and face the pained eyes of Ptah gazing up at me.

He glances down at my dagger. "I used to think you'd be different. That maybe you really did love me. But I know now you're just like all the others. Blood counts for nothing when there is an advantage to be gained."

I steady myself. "You are not my brother. My brother knows the undying love I bear him."

"Do I?" the monster in my brother's skin asks slyly. "Long months have passed since you gave me anything other than hollow words to that effect. Why should I believe that you still care about me at all?"

"I have done everything I can to return to him!" I cry out.

"All I know is you said you'd come back for me," he answers. "You didn't. You lied. You have forgotten me."

"Ptah's love for me is not changeable any more than mine is for him. He knows my heart," I retort, trying to keep my limbs from trembling.

"Are you so very sure of that? he whispers conspiratorially. "I am all alone in a house full of treachery. All alone with *her*. What has she said about you to me? Maybe I am not so innocent to your promises anymore."

"I do not believe you."

"Oh yes, you do," he says smoothly. "I see the fear in your eyes. I don't think you have it in you to raise a knife to me."

The mention of the dagger snaps me from my growing panic. I have to smite Ptah here, otherwise I have no hope of saving the real Ptah. With a shuddering sob I drive the knife into the shade's chest, crumpling on the black ground even as I hear the moan Apep is able to make in my brother's voice before it transforms back into itself. I expect to see the black smoke, but it does not appear. I raise my head and see that the wounded snake has not changed back to itself.

It has changed into my mother.

She is as beautiful as I remember, with her long black hair cascading over her shoulders nearly down to her waist and her lustrous dark eyes set in her sculpted features. She seems to float rather than walk and she looks untouchably elegant, especially as I glance down at my own disheveled appearance.

My mind is screaming at me to ignore her, that she is a demon trying to destroy my sanity, but it sounds like a warning shouted by someone a thousand leagues away. I cannot stop myself from reaching out to her wordlessly. She glides over to nearly within my grasp and as she turns her attention to me, her noble expression changes to one of revulsion as she kicks me away with her foot.

"Do not touch me, wretched thing!" she spits at me.

I cannot stop the words before they fly from my mouth. "*Mewet*, I—"

She shudders in distaste. "Do not call me that! I had no choice but to bear you to that monster, your father. Every day I lived in that life was torture. I must have been cursed by the gods."

I feel as though I am being smothered by the void around me. My vision blurs on the edges. "We were a little happy once, though, Mother," I say softly.

"Hardly, foolish child. You and your brother were daily reminders of the bondage my family sold me into for their own chance at power."

"Your family was trying to save Egypt, to save our people!" I protest.

She laughs coldly. "Ha! Is that the lie those old beggars told you?" Her eyes narrowed contemptuously. "I am sorry. I forget that is the same lie you have told yourself about your own pathetic exploits. You tell yourself you were trying to save your precious people, but you are just another demonic Ptolemy. You loved the killing, the chaos."

"No!"

"Killing Achillas brought you more pleasure than he would have in your bed! You delighted in competing in power with your siblings! All of you would raze your kingdom to ground and bathe in its blood like it was wine!"

I shake my head back forth, unable to speak. My mother glides to the other side of me, and by some invisible force, compels me to look into her eyes. The eyes I know so well, drained of their gentle warmth as if they were dry wells. "You are an abomination, Arsinoë. It would have been better if I had strangled you the hour you were born than to let you grow old enough to call me 'Mother.'"

I reel back so suddenly in horror I stumble over my own feet and fall hard against the ground. I curse it for not swallowing me up and ending all of this. Not even on Pharos did I so desperately wish to die.

I can feel my mother feasting on my pain. I do not even want to raise my head again, except that something catches my attention out of the corner of my eye. I crawl over to it and pick it up. It is one of the Sekhmet faience beads, it must have broken off of my *menat* when I fell. I hold it in my hand, cool upon my palm. It shows Lady Sekhmet holding a flame, for she is the daughter of Lord Ra and the goddess of fire, as well as war.

The word "fire" lights a path in the darkness of my mind. The final step. *Putting a Fire Upon Apep.*

As soon as the thought comes to me, I feel the loose bow lying across the top of the basket. I take it in my one hand and with the other carefully grasp an arrow with an incendiary pitch tip. I notch it, aim, and it flies through the void before the gloating serpent has understood what I have done. The arrow does not stay fast, but the lighted pitch easily sets the beast ablaze. I barely have time to make sure the fire found its mark before I jolt awake in Anubis' arms.

He has changed back to his human form and although I am blindfolded again, I can tell he is grinning at me. A baleful shriek makes me jump, but he holds me down.

"It is well, Ptolemy-daughter. My father is finishing off the demon."

I hear something weighty crash into the water, and in an instant I feel Set's strong arms around me. "You have done marvelously, Beloved. I am so proud."

I have a hundred questions for my Lord, I want to know of his battles with Apep that the serpent alluded to. I want to understand what happened to me this night. But I settle for one. "Is this enough?"

He understands what I mean. "Yes, *nedjet.* Though you are very weak, you will not die in this prison."

"How can you be sure? We do not know how long my sister will keep me here."

"The forces of *ma'at* cannot ignore that you have battled Apep and won. I might not be able to save you from death coming to claim you, but you will not die forgotten in a cell. If you must die, it will be in the glory of a goddess."

He reaches to undo my blindfold and as I am about to protest, I wake up.

I heard someone crying softly. I slowly opened my eyes to see that my head was in Mudjet's lap and that it was her sobs I could hear. I tried to say her name, though my mouth was dry and all I could muster was a tiny groan.

The noise was enough to get her attention. She nearly choked on her tears. "Gods be praised! Oh my lady, I thought I had lost you!"

"What happened?" I asked hoarsely.

"You started running a terrible fever in the night, my lady. I called to our guards to send for a physician, but no one heeded me. I.. I did not think you would last until morning in your state."

I tried to sit up, but the exertion left me giddy. "I do not know how much longer we can go on like this, no matter what my Lord says."

Mudjet's eyes flashed. "Did you dream of Lord Set? What happened? What did he say?"

"Many things occurred, which I will tell you about sometime, my sweet. The short of it is he says I will not die in here."

"Well then," she said briskly. "At least we know we must be getting out of here quite soon."

We laughed a little as my Mudjet wiped some of the sweat from my face, and then we settled back into the business of surviving the coming day.

Chapter Thirty-Five

The spring reeds had put forth their shoots weeks and weeks ago by the time that our cell door opened and a cheerful, sunburnt Titus stepped in with our gruel. However, his happy grin vanished when he saw us. It had been a week since my battle with Apep in the Dream World, but three days since our last meal.

The night before, in spite of the assurances of the gods, we had lain on the dirt floor side by side with our hands clasped. We had begun to recite the Book of Going Forth to one another, certain the end was surely coming for us by morning or the next evening. We no longer had the strength to fight our foodless days. Now, even with a friendly face before us, we were too weak to see anything but the looming horizon of the Lands of the West.

Mudjet gave Titus an anemic smile but could not lift her head from the wall she rested it against. I gathered what felt like the last of my will to raise my own head from her lap.

"Welcome back, sir. Has Apollodorus wearied of our company already?" I managed to gasp out before laying back down glassy-eyed.

I do not know how much time passed after he left. I weaved in and out of consciousness, occasionally stirred by Mudjet's erratic breathing. It was dark enough for torches when he returned, though I did not bother to open my eyes. I knew the measure of his footfalls. I could sense the presence of others, and I attempted to care, but I could not summon the strength to do so. None of it mattered because I was going home to be with the gods.

There was a cool hand on my forehead and a sharp, clever voice near me muttered in disgust, "Gods defend us..."

The voice made me open my eyes. I blinked the cell back into focus and found Caesar's angular face looking into mine, his deep eyes glittering in the low light.

"I'm going to take you to the palace so a physician can examine you," he said steadily, to make sure I followed his words. I had expected him to speak in the same stinging tone he had used to swear at the gods, but instead his voice was gentle. "Do you think you can hold onto me, Your Highness?"

I nodded, and made a feeble gesture to Mudjet.

"Titus Manlius will take care of your maidservant," he assured me. "Come, my lady."

I raised my arms like a sleepy child and clasped them around Caesar's neck. He slid his arms under me and tensed himself against the ground before picking me up off the floor. The abrupt altitude disoriented me, though I worked to keep my head from spinning as I craned about to see Titus hoist up Mudjet. Assured she was safe, I laid my head against the Consul's chest and closed my eyes again in resignation. I listened to the thump of his heart through his *tunica*, almost smiling at my surprise that it beat just the same as any other man's. For all the months he had been here, ostensibly in the luxury of our land, he still smelled faintly of sweat and horses, like a general in the field. It was comforting. The smell of him, and the fact he had found me were signs he was not so entirely in my sister's thrall.

We walked briskly out into the evening air and I was overwhelmed by the cacophony of familiar scents that floated towards me. I had almost forgot what the air outside our cell smelled like. When the scent of incense wafted to us, I knew we had made it into the palace. However, with the perfume was mixed a sour note I could not quite place. A slight disharmony that ingratiated itself into the very stones of the complex, unaccountable to everyone inside, manifesting to the multitudes of slaves and servants as a slight sense of unease. But I recognized the footprints of the *heka* for what they were.

I heard a worried voice rush upon us. "Consul Caesar, what are you doing? Does the—"

"Never mind that," he said, the sharp voice of command returning, vibrating from his chest into my ear. "Go find me a physician."

The feet scurried away.

We kept moving through the main portico, the men's feet echoing on the sandstone floors. We turned several corners, eventually stopping in an unoccupied chamber where Caesar lowered me gingerly onto a couch. I thought I would be completely engulfed, so deep and soft the cushions felt. Titus set Mudjet onto another couch and I watched him carefully drape a silk shawl over her. Satisfied, I raised my eyes up to Caesar, who stood scrutinizing me with an expression drawn in anger, though who was the target of his displeasure was uncertain.

"Thank you," I whispered, still far too exhausted to be apprehensive in my homecoming.

"I think we both know that's probably a bit premature, my lady," he answered, the lines in his face softening somewhat.

The physician arrived and began his inspection. He listened to the fluttering of my pulse and peered in my mouth while Caesar stood to the side watching, arms crossed. The physician pulled out some vessels and had started mixing liquids when my sister stormed into the room, her hazel eyes flashing. Through my half-opened gaze, I saw how heavily her pregnancy hung on her now. She still maintained her heady air of authority, and on the surface, she remained fair to look upon in her characteristic way. And yet there was a tightness around her mouth and glint of something I could not name in her eyes. She must have been straining her *heka* to keep up appearances.

"What do think you are doing?" she demanded, her face flushed in anger, her *heka* giving the atmosphere of the room a leaden feel. Underneath the foreboding, there was also a cruel kind of levity in the air, as if the *heka* was savoring its mastery of the Black Land.

"Trying to keep the girl alive long enough to get her to Rome as something other than a corpse," Caesar replied with annoyance. "Did you think I would not find out about this?" he added.

I could sense the *heka* trying to press itself upon him, yet it was as if Caesar carried an invisible shield to deflect its advances. Lost in the fog of my sister's magic, I did not have the presence of mind to be rightly afraid of one who could hold against a *heka* alone that the gods of Egypt had struggled to overcome for a single night.

"She is my sister, she is my concern! Not yours!" Cleopatra shot back, her voice surrendering the bare amount of restraint she had possessed when she had entered. The air in the room stilled to the weight of a boulder.

"Gods and men, woman! If you don't want her for the triumph, that's fine by me. It matters not. But if that's so, just cut her throat and be done with it," Caesar remarked coldly. "The northern barbarians wouldn't drag their kin through an end like this. At this rate, I will have to delay my departure until she is even capable of standing!"

"She is a traitor!" my sister shrieked, balling her fists in frustration. "I will not coddle her simply because you feel pity for anything with breasts and pretty eyes!"

"We have barely wrestled control of the city back," he ignored her taunt, his voice full of dark anger. "I will not jeopardize that because you want to torture the child. Can you imagine what the people will do if they find out you've been starving their so-called goddess? They'll ransack the palace and string you up to be food for the vultures!"

My sister glared down at me, our eyes meeting. I thought about how easy it would be for her to kill me with her bare hands, that very instant. I imagined her slim fingers — so like my own — closing themselves around my neck. Or perhaps she would take the Consul's suggestion and cut my throat with the dagger I knew she had carried in her bodice since Damianus' murder.

We looked at one another, her eyes alive with anger and power, and mine? Mine lit only with the flickering light of indifference. She could do as she pleased because I could no longer resist her, and perhaps that is what stayed her hand as we watched each other beneath the fiery attention of Caesar. Her mouth twitched in repugnance at my frailty and growled with displeasure as she flounced out of the room.

With her departure, the air in the room grew sweeter once more, though the ominous hint of malice remained. For a moment, Caesar's burning eyes followed her trail, impatience pulling the muscles of his face rigid. But then without warning, he looked back to me. I was startled to see his displeasure ebb away to reveal an emotion I could not put a name to at first, though I recognized the slight confident turn of his mouth that showed he understood that he had carried the argument with my sister and he, as usual, relished the victory.

The physician at my side hesitated. "Am I treating these women, sir?" he asked.

His question drew back the Consul's attention from my face and he nodded curtly. "Do what you must. If the palace servants won't grant any requests you might have as you work, seek out one of my men. They will assist you." He then turned on his heel and stalked out the way Cleopatra had gone.

"Do not alarm yourself, my lady. We shall have you well again soon enough," the physician said to me solicitously, though with a nervous glance toward the hall outside of the room.

I smiled painfully. "Oh, that? We are the House of Ptolemy, sir. That is nothing to us." My discomfiture stemmed not only from my weakened state, but also because I had belatedly identified the sentiment in Caesar's eyes. Had it truly been affection, or were my weary eyes deceiving me?

For another half-month, Mudjet and I were like infants again, learning to eat, learning to walk. We had been imprisoned for only a couple of months, but we had been allowed no exercise and our muscles were deteriorated as much from captivity as from poor diet. Every day, we were given a little more to eat, and bit by bit, our stomachs remembered how to consume it. We practiced hobbling back and forth, one on either arm of Titus until like newborn colts we remembered how to run. Once our strength began to return, we spent many afternoons tossing balls to one another and more than a few times we were admonished by various passing eunuchs to soften our laughter.

"Just as in the old days, my lady," observed Mudjet with a gleeful lob of the ball.

I pushed myself into the air and caught her throw handily. "Indeed. Except now instead of being reproved for being unladylike, everyone deplores our gallows humor. We are abidingly creatures out of joint with our circumstances, dear." I threw the ball back.

Mudjet sidestepped quickly to retrieve it, and paused. "Are you afraid?"

"Yes," I admitted. "But waiting is worse. I have probably built it all up so much in my dreams that nothing they actually do is going to be all that shocking. I only wish they would allow me to see Ptah one last time."

She nodded. "Better our untempered hearts on our sleeves than cowering in the dirt again."

"No more cowering. We take the lessons of Sekhmet into our *kas* and meet the Fates straight-backed."

Even once we regained our health, Titus remained at our side, undoubtedly to keep away my sister's malevolent retainers and lackeys. He became an easy friend, his naturally buoyant personality lifted by the adventure of being a young patrician on his first campaign away from home in a land as enticing as Egypt.

I found myself looking for my other Roman friend, Quintus, in the young Titus, but the latter was younger in more ways than one and more earnest. Less ironical than my Gabiniani lieutenant. Mudjet and I had seen things that would make the pleasant tribune's hair curl. I had done things that would chase his spritely courtesy to me from his face. And yet we were comradely with each other all the same.

"I used to scoff at the tales told of the Gabiniani back home," he said to us as Mudjet sat massaging my calf muscles to build their resistance up once more. "What land could be as wonderful as that of Romulus and Remus? But now that I have seen Egypt, I think I begin to understand."

"The Black Land is lovely," answered my companion, "but — I know, my lady, it will hurt a bit—" she said, interrupting her own thought at the mewl of pain I had made at one of her exertions, "—but I think what has really captured the heart of our dear Sir Titus is the company of Egypt," she finished with a wink in his direction.

"Naturally, Lady Mudjet," Titus said with a laugh. "I should be envied by all my brothers for passing my days here in such excellent company! Because of the queen's rumors, they think I mind a bratty child,

when in fact I enjoy the conversation of the finest lady in the East and her equally noble companion!"

I wiped a bead of sweat from my temple as Mudjet changed the direction of her manipulations. "Oh dear, do not let the Queen hear you say as such, sir!" I said, smothering the small gasp of pain that flew up from my stomach. "She would still not need very much poison to finish me off presently."

"I don't know, my lady, the peasants say that you are a goddess. Even a weakened deity might prove very difficult to kill," he answered.

I made a dismissive gesture. "I thought the Romans had more sense than to listen to idle gossip."

"Hardly, Your Highness. There is nothing my people love more than a juicy rumor. We mock the Alexandrians for their loose tongues, but secretly we are no better."

"We shall have to remember that when we leave for Rome," said Mudjet pretending to make a note of his information.

The tribune had learned to adapt himself to our morbid humor, so he chuckled along with us. "I live to be your cultural ambassador to Rome, dear Mudjet."

"Indeed, there is much you can tell us, sir," I said imperiously, while laughter leaked from my eyes. "We should hate to appear like bumpkins before the cosmopolitans in the capital."

"Yes!" chimed in Mudjet. "I would simply *die* if the cut of my *tunica* was wrong while I burned at the stake!"

"Or if my hair was not done up in the latest knot," I countered. "After all, all of Rome will see it."

"Little demons," said Titus affectionately in return. "It is a wonder we ever got the better of you, Your Highness. I doubt the immortals are as fearless as you."

"Oh, I am afraid of everything, Titus," I answered, stretching out my legs as Mudjet finished working on them. "I have simply taught myself to not spend what little time I have left fretting over a fate that cannot be changed."

He grew serious. "You think there is no hope, then?"

I gave him a sardonic glance in return. "Do you know of any vanquished general who has survived a triumph?"

"I suppose not," he replied guiltily. "Yet it is unnatural to see one so young submit to death so easily."

"I do not want to die, but this is also Egypt. All the Greek rulers in the world cannot change the preoccupation this land has with death. I have lived all my life in the shadow of the afterlife."

"I confess this is something I still find unnerving about the Egyptians."

"Foreigners think we are in love with death," Mudjet answered him thoughtfully. "It is not like that. We simply know that death is only a journey to another part of life. The journey is arduous and dangerous, yet life is often those things as well. In death, we are reborn into just another life, yet it is a life reunited with those we love in the light of the love of the gods. How can we be afraid of such a destination?"

"That is why there are always tears at a funeral here, but there is also always dancing," I finished.

He nodded, then his face lit up. "Now dancing I understand! Come, Your Highness! I must teach you some Roman dances to show off when you arrive!"

He pulled me to me feet and spun me through a country dance until I was gasping for breath from laughing rather than pain. Making sure I was steady enough on my feet, he twirled me from one side to the other, and as I turned I thought I caught a figure out of the corner of my eye. I whipped my head around violently enough to cause me to momentarily stumble into Titus.

"I'm sorry, my lady!" he cried, immediately contrite. "I shouldn't have moved so quickly! Are you all right?"

I did not answer at first, my eyes straining to see through the shadows under the portico. But if there had been someone there, they had gone.

I gave my attention back to the concerned Titus. "No, I am fine. That was mere clumsiness on my part." To break the moment, I pulled Mudjet to me and handed her off to the young tribune. "You should take Mudjet instead. She has always been the more admirable dancer."

I pushed them together playfully and the pair spun off in the same wild little dance, their laughter echoing around the courtyard. I walked over to the portico and peered behind the long row of columns. Naturally, they were empty. I shook my head, angry with myself. *If I was going to hear the voices of the gods, I might as well be mad enough to see things that were not there as well,* I thought as I turned to rejoin Mudjet and Titus.

One night in the earliest blush of summer, we sat in our room, Mudjet mending the thong of a sandal and I with a scroll on my lap, reading. It was then that Caesar reappeared in our doorway. The last weeks had left me with the impression he had been avoiding us since he had rescued us from prison, most likely because Cleopatra wished it so and he was too busy to pick a fight with her over a condemned prisoner.

I glanced up from my lap and gave him a bob of my head. "You honor us, Caesar."

He looked back at me with his inscrutable expression. I wondered what he was thinking of. Mudjet's eyes met mine questioningly and I gave her a minute shrug.

I decided to try again. "How may we serve you, sir?"

This seemed to prod him back to the physical room. "I am taking you down to the harbor before first light. We shall raise sail for Rome with the tide," he said quietly, his tone diffident. "You and your maidservant may take a small bundle of personal effects each. It will be searched."

Mudjet had gone a shade paler, though I did not feel afraid. Not yet anyhow.

"Shall Her Majesty be joining our party?" I asked, folding up the papyrus on my lap.

He shook his head. "No. She is staying here to stabilize the kingdom before entering into her confinement. I am leaving you in Rome for the time being while I attend to some business in the east."

"I suppose one cannot put the Parthian cart before the Pontic horse," I remarked to my scroll as I tied up its bindings, before glancing up at him pointedly.

He smirked. "You are a quick study, Your Highness."

"I live up to my name, my lord. We shall be ready to leave at your call."

He nodded vaguely and went to leave, but stopped. He almost appeared to hesitate, then he brusquely motioned to me. "Come. Quickly, now."

I threw a glance at Mudjet as I followed Caesar out into the hallway. He took long strides that I jogged to keep up with as we moved through the palace. I attempted to guess at our destination, though I was completely at a loss. The path he chose was an obscure one, even for this unused part of the palace, and halls were deserted. Suddenly his pace slowed and he steered me by the shoulder to an antechamber. I walked into the room and saw a small figure standing at the far wall tracing with a finger the hieroglyphics carved there.

A lump nearly trapped my voice in my throat. "Ptah!"

My brother whirled around and sprinted into my waiting arms. I held his face between my hands and we searched each other with our eyes as if to record every detail of the other.

He trembled with emotion under my touch. "I wanted to see you, but she..."

"Shh, I know, *nedjes*. I am so very glad, I have been brought low with worry about you."

"And me about you! I heard them whispering that you were nearly dead when they brought you out of prison. I thought you would die without me seeing you!"

"It was not so dire as all that," I murmured. "I am better now, at any rate. Mudjet takes good care of me."

Ptah's face flushed with excitement as he gripped my shoulders. "You were so close, Arsinoë!" His eyes darted to Caesar, who stood a decent distance away studying his fingernails, pretending that he could not hear us. "Even *he* was worried!" Ptah continued, dropping his voice a notch. "He raged at our sister for not being able to persuade the city to give you over. And that trick you pulled with the water— I thought the legion was going to sack the palace! You were so clever that he was always thinking of you — I thought Cleopatra would go mad!"

I could not help but smile at my brother's enthusiasm. "It is a shame I could not do more. I am sorry I could not come for you." I reached up to touch his face again. "I cannot believe how much you have grown. You look as regal as Lord Horus."

He frowned. "I do not want to be Pharaoh," he said, almost petulantly.

"But you must, *nedjes*," I replied gently. "Our people need you. You are the embodiment of the love the gods hold for them, they need to know the gods hold them close even in these difficult times. They look to their King to lead them, not Cleopatra. Who will speak for Egypt to the men of Rome if not their Pharaoh?"

"I do not want to talk about tariffs and legislation with my sister's murderers," he argued, his tawny eyes glassy with hurt.

I sighed and squeezed his hands. "You must not think on that too much. I will be strong for you and Egypt there if you will be strong for me here. It will break my heart if I think you will surrender to despair when I am gone."

The sadness in him was almost more than I can bear, but at length he said quietly, "I will be a good king, so that you will be proud of me."

I leaned forward to press my head to his. "I will always be proud of you, Ptah. Pray for me in the *Duat*. We will dance again together in the Field of Reeds."

He threw his arms around me again and I held his feverishly warm body to mine. At last I let go and walked quickly out of the room before I could be tempted to go back. As I returned to my quarters, it was Caesar this time who had to try to keep up with me.

I paused at the threshold and without looking at him said, "I know you did not have to do that. You have my gratitude."

"I needed to make sure the boy knows his place while we are gone. I gambled on you being too attached to him to preach rebellion," he replied, with a careless shrug I saw in my periphery.

"I also know you are under no obligation to take me with you when you leave here. I am appreciative of your concern, fleeting though it may be."

The indifference in his voice was replaced by a softer tone. "And I know all you Egyptians think I'm a demon sent from the very bowels of Dis to torment you. But I am not a monster, Your Highness. The least I can promise you is a swifter death in Rome than the perverse affair it appears it will be if you remain in Egypt."

We said no more to one another.

Chapter Thirty-Six

In the hours just before dawn, Mudjet and I readied ourselves to leave. We each had a small pack with some extra clothing, that was all. It seemed silly to bring anything else. I left behind any jewelry I might have bribed a servant to steal from my old rooms and contented myself only with my mother's bracelet. When Titus appeared with a contingent of legionaries, we were prepared.

The ship was moored at the royal harbor, only a short distance from the palace steps. There, several other vessels were being loaded with captured soldiers from my army and local animals to entertain the people of Rome. Standing on Titus' arm looking out over the onyx waves, I did not see Caesar come up from the docks to meet us, only the slap of the tribune's salute against his breastplate caught my drifting attention.

Wrapped in his traveling cloak, the Consul gave me his characteristic wry smile and a somewhat unseriously gallant bow as he held out his hand to me. I hesitated for a moment, then let go of Titus' arm and allowed Caesar's long fingers to arrest mine. He held my hand while I descended the worn stairs to him as if he still harbored concern for my health. Once I reached his side, he gave me a satisfied tilt of his head before smoothly tucking my hand in the crook of his elbow to lead us to our ship.

As we walked across the long dock, I returned inward to my own thoughts until Mudjet tapped my shoulder and drew my gaze to the south towards the city. I turned my head and stopped in my tracks as if bewitched, dragging Caesar to halt at my side. Normally at this hour Alexandria was still asleep, even the bakers had not risen yet. But on this morning, from dozens of windows and even from some of the few scattered rooftops that survive my rebellion, the flickering light of oil lamps burned in the nascent morning. The flitting shadows brought a faint glow against the wounded buildings still scarred by Ptolemy's fire. As my eyes adjusted to the play of the light, I glimpsed the outline of people standing by the lamps. They remained silent as they stood and slowly, I could make out that they raised a hand each toward the harbor.

369

Mudjet took my free hand and squeezed it. "The farewell of kings, my lady," she whispered reverently.

I knew this, and that was why my *ka* ached. Alexandria had awoken early to see me off as if I was a pharaoh on my funeral sledge. I questioned whether a defeated queen had earned such an honor, but I brought it inside of my heart to keep me warm in the long nights to come. I glanced in the palace's direction and wondered if Cleopatra was awake to witness this. Afraid of her anger that already rested heavily on the city, I did not dare signal to my people in return, though I knew they and I understood each other without word or gesture. Instead, I closed my eyes and said a prayer in my *ka* for this ancient, luminous land and its courageous inhabitants. I prayed for them and the difficult days ahead of us all.

I opened my eyes again and turned to apologize to the Consul, but he was not looking at me. His enigmatic eyes were fixed on the lamps in the distance, his face drawn into a frown of contemplation. I understood him enough now to know he was not angry, only thoughtful. Though of what he was thinking I could not guess. A vain corner of my heart wanted to ask him if he was not in fact impressed, but I smiled to myself at my own foolishness. Caesar knew Alexandria thought me a goddess, yet what kind of Roman would he be to believe such a story?

I lowered my head deferentially. "The tide comes for us, my lord," I said.

My voice recalled him with a start and his watchful eyes studied me rather than Alexandria. After a long moment, he nodded. "Indeed. The morning must nearly be upon us, seeing how the city is wakeful."

I made no reply, even though I was hardly deceived by his nonchalant tone, nor by the studious indifference of his men as they helped us aboard the ship and began to stow the last of our cargo. We stood to the side as the sailors shook out the sails and began loosening the ropes. Once the helmsman steered the boat out into the greater waters of the harbor, we were taken into the hull where we settled in for the voyage north.

I find myself back in my prison cell. I sit with my back against the cool wall and watch as the dimmest light of early morning peeks through. I am lost in thought contemplating how I shall have to see the last handful of mornings I have before me like this, through prison bars, when I feel a tug on the hem of my shift. I look down at my feet and see a large scarab beetle pulling at the linen as he ambles haphazardly across its folds.

I pick him up and hold him in the palm of my hand so we may look at one another face to face, his glossy black shell gleaming even in the dim light.

"Hello, Ptolemy-daughter," he says to me, waggling his antennae in a friendly way.

"Greetings to You, Lord of Daybreak," I reply, for I hold Khepri in my hand. He is small but mighty, for he is one of Father Ra's many forms. As the god of sunrise, he takes the form of a scarab to roll the sun across the sky, to banish the night once more to the underworld.

"I come to remind you that you are not alone as you leave our shores," the small god says, lifting his shell to flutter the wings beneath it. "We go with you to the land of wolves. Even if you cannot see us."

"I am sorry I failed to secure victory for the holy gods of Egypt, my lord."

"Mountains have birthed themselves from the sea, rose, and crumbled into dust in the blink of our Eye, Ptolemy-daughter. We shall endure because we have no end. Yet that does not mean we value not your courage. I climb into the sky every morning to bring hope to our people because duplicitous Set defeats the beast Apep every night. He can be treacherous and our savior, just as you can be defeated and still victorious."

"I wish I could wear you in my hair for strength my Lord, until all is over," I confess, the kindly little beetle's attention drawing this admission from me.

Khepri clicks his mandibles sympathetically. "I would, child, but I am not a god of death. I am here to create you from the ashes of your resurrection. Be who you were destined to be and be reborn before the eyes of the Latins."

And then I wake up.

We sat below decks until we gained our sea legs and then walked the length of the under-galley back and forth to pass the days. We chattered in Egyptian, and I tried to improve my Latin by conjugating with Titus when he was free. We lay atop our bedding in the summer's growing heat, and huddled under our blankets when errant storms blew up.

One clearer evening, we received permission to go above deck for some fresher air. The breeze felt heavy with salt as it brushed by us to fill the sails flapping over our heads. We were too far out to see any islands, so there was nothing around the fleet except the seemingly endless blue of the sea. Mudjet busied herself airing out some of our linens and I stood at the rail listening to the lapping of the waves against our boat and the distant sounds of work from the other ships. Someone somewhere was singing an old sea song.

"It goes without saying that you are not permitted to throw yourself overboard," said Caesar's voice casually, cutting through the melody of the distant singer.

I looked back at him, standing a little ways behind me. "I suppose it does not speak highly of me that I had not even considered that," I answered with a resigned shrug.

He grinned like a wolf and moved forward to join me at the rail. We stood silently staring out at the opaque water. After a time he asked, "Would you have done it?"

In the light of his last statement, I did not need to ask what he meant. "I do not know. Pharos already feels like another life. A dream. We do many things in dreams we would not dare in the Waking World."

"I'm not sure I believe there is much that you would not dare if pressed, Your Highness," he said, meeting my eye; his, as usual, difficult to read.

I shrugged again. "Perhaps that is true. Perhaps our dreams only reveal the people we are meant to be."

"If one believes in one's dreams," he pointed out, a trace of skepticism hanging on his words.

I glanced off in the other direction, smiling to myself before returning his gaze. "Oh, one must always be watchful of those who believe in their dreams, my lord," I replied, my eyes no doubt full of the saucy mischief that used to earn me such censure from Pothinus. "They are the most dangerous of beings, for what could they not be capable of?"

Not waiting for his answer, I tucked a loose curl of hair behind my ear and left Caesar in my wake as I went to help Mudjet with our sundries.

Latium was in full thrall to summer when we docked in the town of Ostia. The balmy lands of Rome were gripped by heat and humidity nearly as strong as those in an Egyptian summer. The marshy inlets that surrounded the port bred stench and disease in the hot months, but it was here that the river of the Romans, the ancient Tiber, came to embrace the sea.

Caesar did not wish to create a spectacle by keeping me in Rome proper, so we were placed in a small country house in Ostia's outskirts with a small contingent of guards and a few slaves to handle the domestic chores, making the board and fare much improved from our confinement back home. Titus was among those allowed to remain with us and we prodded him for news while we tried to assist him with his suit for the hand of a local *nobile*'s daughter.

A few weeks after our departure, the Queen of Egypt gave birth to a boy, my nephew. He was anointed Ptolemy Caesar, Prince of Egypt, but it did not take long for everyone to call him Caesarion — little Caesar. Cleopatra was equally quick to illustrate any way, large or small, where the infant prince resembled his alleged father, though Caesar appeared to remain aloof. He allowed the boy to use his name, yet he made no attempt to formally recognize him. Nor did he seem to be in any hurry to return to Egypt to see the child. We puzzled about this state of affairs, conveyed to us by Titus.

"Is it because Caesarion would not be recognized as a Roman citizen?" I asked him, carding wool for Mudjet to wind.

"I don't think so," Titus replied while rolling a pear between his palms. "That might be the case, but Caesar would probably have the power to grant the prince citizenship if he desired to."

"Does the Queen know that?" Mudjet joined in, looking up from the wool strand she was twisting into thread. "Also, would your fiancée like a shawl dyed in blue or red? I should be able to manage either."

"Most assuredly," he answered her. "They say she is most displeased that Caesar is not exerting himself to rectify the situation. And she is not my fiancée yet, Mudjet."

"Tosh! She will be once you tell her of your exploits and present her with this shawl made by an exotic Egyptian handmaiden," Mudjet answered before turning her attention to me abruptly. "The Consul is a man with no sons, no living heirs at all. He is not a young man. Why would he not do this? It makes no sense!"

I thought the question over. I thought of the secret Achillas had revealed to us so many months ago. "Because he does not trust her," I replied slowly. "He cannot trust her and therefore he cannot trust this child of hers belongs to him."

Titus nods. "I think you are right, Princess. To risk his *dignitas* in Rome for a foreign queen, my general would have to be much more sure of the character of the lady. He approves of Cleopatra because she is a sort of female mirror of himself, but that also means he knows she is capable of any deception to press an advantage."

"This much is certain, though that irony will irritate her if he is in truth the boy's father," I remarked with a cool toss of my head.

"I think it would be wise for the Consul to make himself scarce in Egypt if he continues to be reluctant," remarked Mudjet.

"Indeed, Mudjet. I suspect that is his plan for the immediate future," agreed Titus. "Also, I believe a shade of red would be be very pretty against my fiancée's complexion," he added sheepishly.

Eventually, as Titus had predicted, Caesar left Rome again on campaign, taking our tribune and the rest of his men eastward across the sea. Without the kindly Titus, we were more isolated, though we could not grudge him the opportunity to earn the glory in war that we were certain would surely impress the family of his betrothed.

We continued to hear snatches of gossip from the outside regardless, for Rome has never been a city of kept secrets and Ostia followed suit; how Caesar obliterated the vast holdings of the King of Pontus, how rapturous crowds fêted him in Tarsus, how my sister wrote him love letters and threw murderous tantrums if he did not respond. Which was often.

As for us, Mudjet cajoled our slaves to teach us about local herbs while we tended the small garden surrounding the house and spent countless hours in the kitchen with them, improving our Latin while they prepared our food. I tried not to cast wistful looks in the direction of the theater, knowing better than to even ask. I schemed to obtain the occasional book and we watched as the longest year of my life slowly died and was replaced by the new year.

We were helping the slaves with the weeding in the garden one early spring day when I spied a man making his way up to the house from the winding path below. The farmhand who delivered our supplies had come hardly two days previous, and we received no other visitors, so all of us stopped our work to watch the lone figure slowly progress towards the house curiously.

"Is it Caesar?" asked Mudjet, half-rising to get a better view.

I squinted, shading my eyes with a hand. "No, that is not the way he walks. And even we would have heard that he had returned to Rome."

"Should we be concerned, do you think?"

"I do not see the point," I sighed, shrugging. "If this man means to murder us, presumably the guards at the door will stop him. If the guards are bought, we cannot stop him anyway." I took a rag and wiped my hands. "But I think we are safe. His gait is an old one for a assassin."

The man appeared under the portico with one of our guards, and was led over to us. As I had thought, he was an older man with a prominent nose in the style of the Romans, dressed in an expertly cut *tunica* and *toga* made with very fine fabric and skill.

I realized that Mujet had perhaps been looking at his head when she mistook him for Caesar, for he had a similarly receding hairline and appeared to be of a comparable age, although the shape of their features were different upon closer inspection. His skin hung on his frame more heavily than the Consul's and he bore the marks of a city life in Rome as Caesar did the marks of a life in war. Yet his expressive face and intelligent eyes spoke of a sort of bottled energy that he could command at will. And I was surprised to find myself sure I knew who he was, though he spoke first.

"Which of you maidens do I have the honor of addressing as the Princess of Egypt?" he asked in a mellow, solicitous voice.

I rose and brushed my unruly hair back with a hand. "I am she, sir. May I offer you a stool and some refreshments?" I motioned to some of the slaves with us to move seating into place while the others went to retrieve food and drink from the kitchen.

He made a small, elegant bow. "My lady. I am honored to make your acquaintance."

"The honor is mine, sir," I replied, touching a hand to my chest and gesturing with the other for the gentleman to make himself comfortable.

The slaves returned with several plates of olives, bread, and cheese, accompanied by a cask of wine. Mudjet poured out two cups of wine for us and made a question with her expression as to whether I wished her to stay. I returned her unspoken query with a small inclination of my head

that said I would call for her if needed, so she nodded and retreated into the villa behind the slaves, while the guard settled himself a few feet
away.

I turned my attention back to my guest with a smile. "Forgive the
simplicity of our offerings, sir. If I had known I would be so esteemed as
to enjoy the company of such an eminent scholar, I would have demanded the Consul leave me enough provisions to toast you in the Egyptian
style."

"Your Highness knows who I am?" he asked, surprised.

I nodded. "My kingdom has—" I faltered momentarily. "—*had* the
greatest library in the world and basks in the warmth of Athens' glow.
I was raised in the pursuits of the mind your people reserve solely for
boys and if I am allowed some conceit, I was not an inferior pupil. The
face and achievements of the distinguished former consul Cicero are well
known to me." I paused to give him a mischievous look. "Indeed, you
are fortunate I have not already ransacked your person to see if you have
books I may commandeer."

Marcus Tullius Cicero chuckled appreciatively. "I am deeply gratified, Your Highness, though you embarrass me with such lavish praise. I
had assumed I came to you as an anonymous Roman citizen."

"An anonymous Roman citizen I would have deemed far too busy to
grant me so much of his time," I replied deprecatingly.

"You are humble, my dear," he noted disbelievingly, shaking his head.
"Not at all like what we have heard of your sister, I might add. But you
are overly kind to an old man who has outlived his usefulness. I have very
little to occupy my time now that Caesar has brought down the Republic." The last he said with a tone of deep sadness, as if he had lost a revered
family member.

I did not wish to see the great orator depressed in my company, so I
searched for something to say that would cheer him. "Even if I had been
ignorant of you before my arrival, sir, I have been here some months now
and all in Ostia sing of the excellent consul who rebuilt their city by the
sea when the pirates razed it to the ground."

"Ach, that was nothing," he said with a dismissive wave of his hand,
though I saw the hint of stroked vanity in his eyes. "There would have

been nothing to rebuild if Pompey hadn't so expertly decimated the sea rats." His eyes grew distant, remembering. "I cannot believe that was twenty years ago. You, little princess, not even born yet and Pompey now dead."

"I am sorry for that," I said truthfully. "I had no part in the plot that took his life, but I regret that I was there and could not spare him. A man such as he did not deserve such an ignoble end."

"Few receive the ends they deserve in this world, Your Highness. We do not live in the Age of Heroes where at least occasionally we obtained our just desserts from the hand of the gods. Pompey, for all of his faults, did not deserve to be slain by those he held as friends any more than you deserve to be executed for standing against two tyrants in your own land."

I tilted my head, interested. "You hold Caesar to be a tyrant?"

He sighed. "It is difficult to say, my lady. He raises the undisciplined mob above our institutions. He may yet be turned back to the virtues of our fathers, though he carries the seeds of tyranny in his heart. With him in dictatorship, I fear for the future of our liberty."

"You wish him to be like Cincinnatus and live for a country life rather than glory," I observed.

"Ha, perhaps that is a fair assessment. Your Highness is well-versed in our history."

"I had a good tutor, sir." Now it was my turn to sound melancholy.

"Yes, and a good general so I've heard. I am sorry for your loss," he remarked kindly.

I gave a movement to show I was impatient with myself. "It is the way of war. I cannot fault Caesar when Fortune has favored him. Even to a sympathetic audience," I added with a smile. "For there are many kinds of admirable men, and I would be lying if I said I could find nothing worth admiring in the Consul."

"That is a charitable sentiment towards the author of your present circumstances, my lady."

"My sister is the architect of my present circumstances, Caesar is merely an instrument. One does not curse the arrow shot by the bow-man."

He looked at me cleverly. "Do not think I failed to notice that you changed adjectives when you spoke of the Queen of Egypt, Your Highness."

"I would expect nothing less from you, sir."

"Why?"

"I modified your statement to better reflect the truth," I explained, motioning to the garden around us. "Cleopatra's genius constructed the prison that my life has become. But I am the author of it."

He nodded thoughtfully. "An interesting point. However, it concerns me that you still deem Caesar an admirable man. Young people such as yourself should look to good men to admire, not those who make such questionable choices in pursuit of their own gratifications."

"But I think you would agree all men — even those who are good — are not exactly the same," I countered, considering my words carefully. "Just look at you and your friend Cato. I believe you both to be men of integrity, yet you are very different."

"This is true, my lady," he admitted with a small chuckle. "And he never failed to remind me of what a deplorable Stoic I would have made."

"He certainly would have disapproved of you sitting here with me," I noted drily.

"Yes, though at the same time, Cato was a young man once too, despite his old man's brain." He glanced at me impishly. "Did you know he once lost the hand of an heiress to Metellus Scipio?"

I laughed. "Cato might have been too serious a husband for me, and yet I suspect the heiress wishes she had chosen him over Scipio. There are two men who could not be more different."

Cicero let out a hearty laugh of his own. "He wrote some very questionable verse over the affair and eventually convinced himself that it had not been of great importance to him either way. The way one does in those situations." He paused. "He was a relentless thorn, though I do miss him. Every day. He would scoff at me sitting here with you not because of who you are, dear Princess, but because I sit here and rail against Caesar when I do not have the courage to sacrifice myself for the principle of the Republic as he did."

My mind flashes back to standing on the ledge of the lighthouse. "I am the greater coward than you, sir. I was once presented with the opportunity that Cato was and I could not follow through."

He studied my face gently. "There are things in this world worth dying for, my lady, but that does not mean you should rejoice in throwing your life away. Death absolved my dear friend of any other stake in our struggle. He might have made a glorious personal stand, though the Republic lives only as long as living men defend it. Our opposition is weaker because of his choice."

I bit my lip. "In the end, this I cannot speak of. I hold many complaints against the Queen of Egypt and Rome's Consul in my kingdom, but our ways are different than yours. I too might have been Egypt's tyrant in your eyes."

"You fought for the liberation of your people from a foreign power. There is always nobility in that pursuit, Your Highness, even if the cause was not in my people's interest." He grinned at me, gesturing expansively. "Why do you think I have so longed to see you for myself? How could I not set eyes upon the little girl who single-handedly kept Julius Caesar at heel for so long? Our people speak of you as a second Penthesilea!"

"Now it is you who embarrass me with lavish praise, sir," I replied with a self-conscious shrug. "I am still no warrior, and I had the help of many hands in my work. Though the mistakes and the ultimate result I will take responsibility for."

"Pompey was a statesman and general his whole life, and he was not so effective at running a campaign against Caesar as you were, my lady," he argued stoutly. "We saw you stymie the hardest legion in Italy for six months and only fail because you were betrayed by allies, just as Pompey was. Rome will not forget that the great Caesar was nearly outwitted by a child. Your people will not let your cursed sister forget."

I looked at him quietly. "Nobility and daring did not save Penthesilea either."

"No," he conceded, "and yet there is something to be said for the regret of Achilles, child." He glanced at me and hesitated. "If you were not condemned to the riotous rituals we sate the plebs on," he added slowly, "I would beg the presumption of giving you advice."

"Doom or no, I would hear the advice of a wise man such as you, Master Cicero."

I was startled to see a sort of watchful concern bloom on the orator's previously cheerful face. "I would tell you to be on your guard, Your Highness, for no lady who bears such charming and clever mind could have possibly escaped our intrepid Consul's notice. The Egyptian Queen may think she is his Briseís because she claims to have borne his child, but he will never respect her as he will the Amazon queen who met him in battle."

I shifted uncomfortably beneath his words, and I was reminded of my arguments with Ganymedes over Achillas. "This too is beyond my ken, sir," I said to set my guest at ease. "There is much about the Consul that is a mystery to me. I have fought him for months and I feel I know little of the man behind the general."

"That is because while I do not hold him to be good, even I will admit he is too complicated to be a stock villain," Cicero said with bitterness in his voice. "We would all not be in such a state if he was." I looked at him sympathetically, which made him cough gruffly. "Bah, do not mind me, little one. I should let you enjoy what sunshine remains to you without the cloud of my regrets or those of Rome. Your way is difficult enough without your captors bleating for your commiseration."

He rose up and I accompanied him back through the villa to the front door. "It has been a pleasure to meet you in the flesh, my lady," he said, turning to bow over the hand I offered to him. "I sincerely wish that Caesar would pour out some of his famous mercy and spare you."

"That is very kind of you, sir, but my sister would never allow that. Besides," I answered, growing playful again, "Cato always believed mercy to be sinful. Perhaps the Consul is turning Stoic."

Cicero burst out laughing. "That will be the day I know my city must be doomed by the gods!" He continued to let out a few more guffaws before growing serious once more. He briefly hesitated before taking my hand in his again impulsively and I did not resist. "However, I cannot help but believe that is one of the many things the Stoics are wrong about. May the gods keep you, Your Highness."

"And you, sir."

Chapter Thirty-Seven

Mudjet and I continued to keep ourselves occupied as best we were able as we passed into a sultry, languorous spring so very far from home. I had been a year without my freedom, a year since I had rode ahead of my people wearing the vulture crown, nearly a year without seeing Ptah. With each passing day, that past grew more indistinct, less finite in my mind. I began to wonder whether all of it had been a long, frenzied dream. Especially the dreams.

A week after Cicero visited us, a freedman of his appeared with a crate of scrolls and books, with his compliments. I devoured as many as I could, uncertain of how long I would have to enjoy them, reading aloud to Mudjet while she sewed and leaving the lamp by my bed burning late into the night. I would send them back weekly to the old orator with notes full of fragmented thoughts and scattered observations, which he would in turn acknowledge or dispute with his next shipment. We debated the Greek masters and critiqued the Alexandrian poets, and he commended me for being a more faithful literary pen friend than Caesar was. Naturally, I replied, for the Consul was a busy man and I found myself at last the woman of leisure Achillas had promised to make me. The irony was that my days were both too long and too short all at once.

While Cicero and I dawdled on the fringes of Rome, Caesar had returned to Africa to quell the last of the men clinging to Pompey's memory. The fight was costly but he prevailed as he always did, and when messengers from the south rode through Ostia on their way to deliver the good news to Rome, mine were the only eyes that did not follow their lathered horses.

I drifted away from them to the gently sloping ridges that curved down to the pebbly banks of the harbor, and I looked to the south from whence the riders had come. I looked towards the horizon and to Africa beyond it, where Caesar stood in Carthage or Iol, readying his ships to sail not north yet, but east. East to the city of my heart, east to my glorious Alexandria because he might be demon and a fiend, but he was a man who kept his promises. And he had promised my sister to return to Egypt. He had promised that she would be in Rome to see my end.

Once my sister's flotilla had left Egypt, we were moved up the river to Rome and placed in a proper prison again on the Capitoline mount. We were hoisted through the cracked stone streets in a borrowed chair, peering at the crowds through the faded curtains that were there to protect the citizens of Rome from us as much as us from them.

Mudjet and I watched Rome in the eyeful silence of novice travelers and I thought on how being in the capital of Latium was more of a homecoming than an arrival. I had lived here once already, driven from Egypt as a small child fleeing a revolution with my parents and Cleopatra. Ptah had been born under the watchful gaze of the Seven Hills. My mother had first sung the songs of her people to me here, where the Black Land sounded like a place as distant as Atlantis. Now I had returned, now I was the revolution. Perhaps I had always been destined to retrace this thread of history, despite my Greek face and Egyptian heart. Perhaps Rome had placed a secret mark upon my brow that let her call me back to her cobbled alleys and houses of brick. The chains I wore to do so were just a surety that I would come. Now that the final wheels were in motion, I began to prepare myself for what was ahead of me.

She arrived in Rome in late summer, a year behind us. Naturally Cleopatra caused a commotion everywhere she went from the moment she came ashore, draped in gold and escorted by her full entourage. She told anyone who would listen that she was a simple visiting dignitary and would keep to herself. Not that anyone believe her in her embroidered silks and her lavish equipage. Though if she had secretly hoped to be honored and celebrated, she would be disappointed. The flinty, fickle Romans loved their republic and had an inborn distrust for royalty, especially the monarchs of the east. Strong men and spectacle were one thing, but kings and queens were quite another. True, many had started to look to Caesar for nearly unfettered leadership, yet there was a reason even he proceeded among them so cautiously. These were a people whose ancestors had murdered their own founder Romulus when he had supposedly grown too kingly.

And then there was the matter of Lady Calpurnia Pisonis. The typical Roman aristocrat was hardly faithful to his wife, though the general understanding was that the lady could rely on a certain amount of discretion about these matters, particularly in intrigues carried on in the city in the midst of neighbors and acquaintances. As she earlier had expressed to me, my sister did not give a fig for any embarrassment her lover's wife might feel by her presence and set out to publicly demonstrate that the poor young woman was a nonentity beneath notice or comment.

As I sat in my new cell awaiting the haughty Queen of Egypt's pleasure, even a naïf in such matters as myself questioned the wisdom of my sister's conduct. I knew Cleopatra saw herself as a Macedonian Hellene who ruled Egyptians, but I doubted whether our hosts would make such a fine distinction. The citizens loved their Consul, though they obviously feared his being led by the nose, or perhaps something more valuable, by a woman they saw as nothing more than a scheming courtesan.

I understood their unease. My sister was not be taken lightly, and yet in the end I found their fears unlikely. I had seen them argue, I had seen the *heka* reach for Caesar and I had seen him repulse it. True, canny Antipater had also eluded its grasp, but my sister had been learning then and the Judean governor had been touched enough to regret his inaction. There had been no weakness in Caesar when Cleopatra aimed for his *ka* with a *heka* nearing the zenith of its powers. He had not flung me back into its ghost claws when it bayed at him for my life. So Rome chattered maliciously behind Cleopatra's back and Caesar gave her the run of his villa across the Tiber so she was at least sometimes out of the city and public eye, even if her name continued to be on every tongue.

Caesar spent most of his time during this period shoring up his power base in the Senate and preparing for the unprecedented four triumphs they were allowing him to hold to commemorate his great victories. Because he continued to be a man of varied interests, he was also completing a reform of the Roman calendar and overseeing the final months of building for the grand temple of Venus he was dedicating to his lovely alleged ancestress. My sister convinced him to add a statue of herself as Isis made out of gold for the sanctuary, and then feigned indifference when the Romans studiously ignored the idol even as they left offerings scattered about the still unfinished structure. The Latins had been guardedly fascinated by the moon-eyed goddess, so it was a mark of their dislike for the Queen of Egypt that they shunned such a richly appointed portrait.

More distressing to us than Cleopatra's presence in Rome was a long series of delays that kept pushing back the holding of the triumphs, so Mudjet and I went back to waiting through our second summer in captivity. After a great deal of wrangling, the first triumph was held in early September. The defeat of Egypt's rebellion was achieved before the subduing of Pontus, so we at least did not have the longest wait.

Eventually, as the harvest month came to a close, Cleopatra appeared in the early hours at our cell door again as she had a year and half ago. Her waspish waist had returned, and she moved as easily as a snake on water. She was flanked on either side by several young women holding a variety of baskets. The *heka* curled around her feet like an obedient pet, but it did not have the crushing force it had displayed in Alexandria. Perhaps it knew my sister was not the master of the city it now found itself in.

I bowed my head with a sardonic twist of my lips. I had been waiting for this morning for far too many months to be fearful of her or the day to come. "Greetings, Your Majesty."

She scowled, her eyes flashing. "Oh, so you deign to speak with me now? One would expect more time locked up would make you less uppity, not more."

I shrugged. "Blame the barbarians. They feed me too much."

"You are fortunate Caesar took pity on you when he did," she spat out. "I could have dragged that out much longer."

"That is not what the physicians said, but no matter. A small miscalculation and poof!" I waved a hand in the air. "You would not be in this position of victory over me that you have coveted so deeply. Today you have your revenge."

"You had better believe that," she snarled. "We shall see how flippant you are when the rabble of Rome drag your name through the mud."

"You have survived months of that," I replied. "I think I will manage an afternoon."

Quick as lightning, she slapped me across the face. "You know nothing!" she snapped, kneeling down to glare furiously at my indifference and Rome's disregard. "Do you think I care that these peasants do not love me? I do not need them to love me! They have their jests now, but they will fear me in the end. I will break them later just as I break you today, sister."

We stared icily at one another. I felt the *heka* rear up on its haunches, bristling angrily without striking. Was she holding it at bay? Or could my sister's magic sense what she could not, that I had battled the Dark Serpent and won. That I was not as defenseless as I might seem on the surface.

Rising, Cleopatra turned her back to me, and for a brief moment, I almost thought I saw a small sag in her shoulders. As if a tiny part of her might regret some of this. The emotion appeared to pass quickly.

"Anyway, it is all too late," she said to the outer hall beyond the doorway, gesturing back to her companions. "These girls are going to wash and dress you for the triumphal procession. It does Caesar and I no good if we lead you through the streets looking like something we fished out of the Nile."

I could not help the small snort of laughter that escaped me. "Like Ptolemy..." I sniggered.

My sister moved her head enough for me to see her disapproving frown at my joke, before she glided imperiously out of the doorway without another word.

Some of the women laid down their baskets and began pulling out clothing and jewels, while others poured water into a shallow basin. Mudjet took control of the basin and helped me wash.

I studied the outfit that had been chosen for me to die in. It was deliberately, completely Egyptian: I would wear a traditional white linen shift with a hundred expertly folded pleats and an elaborate ebony wig with another hundred intricate braids. A large collar of gold and lapis lazuli, with matching cuffs, and painted sandals. One of the servant girls was arranging pots filled with kohl, eye color, and rouge. I must look the part of a captured foreign queen for the people of Rome. With such adornments, I would have the honor of looking more Egyptian for a Roman triumph than my siblings had appeared at their coronation.

The girl with the makeup stepped forward to paint my face, but Mudjet swiftly moved to intercept her. "No, I will do this," she said sternly. "You Roman children will not do it properly. My lady is a queen, not a *hetaera*. If the Queen of Egypt and her jackal want Egyptian, then they shall have it."

Mudjet swirled the sapphire-colored eye paint with a practiced hand and lightly ran the brush over my eyelids. She flicked the rouge in a streak across each cheek, and then with a steady hand drew the heavy lines of kohl encircling my eyes ending with the long kite-tails at the corners. Lastly, she took the smallest pot filled with lip paint and colored in my mouth with as much care as the priests lavished on the noblest of mummies. She retreated a step back to check her work and nodded with satisfaction.

As we finished, one of the girls bent down to tie the sandals on my feet and Mudjet smoothed a plait of hair on the side of my head.

"I wish I could share this journey with you, my lady," she said, fussing with the lay of the gold collar around my neck even though it was properly in place.

"I know," I replied, arresting her wrists gently. "But it is better this way. I am glad you will not have to see this."

The mask of her composure slipped down and she pulled me fiercely into her arms. "Do not let them see you cry," she whispered in my ear.

I squeezed her thin shoulders. "Never, dearest." We pulled back from one another and I gave her a small smile before turning to address one of the servants. I inhaled deeply, taking in all the sense memory of this moment, before saying in the steadiest voice I could manage, "You may tell them I am ready."

She bowed and walked out to find our guards. She returned a few minutes later with Titus, who could not help but raise an eyebrow at my elaborate appearance.

"Are you sure you are the Lady Arsinoë?" he asked, pretending to glance behind me. "For there seems to be a courtesan with a bearskin on her head in her place."

His brave attempt to make me laugh succeeded in bringing a grin to my face. "Better to think that Arsinoë leapt into the sea on her way to Rome since you, sir, may be the one who must strangle the courtesan this evening."

He grew sober and looked at me thoughtfully. "It may be so, though the word is that the city is unsettled by the outcome in Egypt. The citizens do not cleave to your sister or her ambitions. My advice is to hold your head up and remind them you are yet a princess. Perhaps this is not your last day, my lady."

With that, I reached back to press Mujet's hand one more time and then followed him out of my cell to our marshalling point on the edge of the Campus Martius. I heard scattered cheers go up from the crowd in the distance. My *ka* bled as captive soldiers who had fought for me and Ptolemy were led out in chains behind the native beasts brought as exotic curios. To my surprise, many who saw me still bowed in my presence. I opened my mouth to apologize for their suffering, when I recognized Tahu.

His eyes found mine, and he nudged the man next him, pointing. "See? Though we leave this life for the next, we can die knowing our cause was a righteous one for we fought for the Lady of Heaven."

I was startled, never had I been compared to Isis, and yet now multiple soldiers made signs of reverence to me usually reserved for the Excellent Goddess. I felt more dizzy than divine, but if this was the comfort I could give the brave men who had fought for me, so be it. I returned their gazes and gave a short, regal nod of my head to indicate my approval. A few even smiled at this.

Tahu's eyes shone. "May the Lord of the Red Land keep you, my Pharaoh."

When a quiet chorus from the captives echoed his words, my heart was momentarily too full to speak, so I simply laid a hand across my chest. I swayed against my own dread and prayed to my Lord to help me find the words my people needed to hear. One last time.

"*Ta-meriu*," I began quietly. "It is the most glorious privilege to lead you into our final battle. You have fought with honor and bravery and because of this, I shall walk without fear into the Lake of Fire if that is what is required of me. Our people do not fear death, so we shall go before the young gods of the Romans with our heads held high because we belong to the gods who raised the pyramids and flood the Nile. Pray for me in the *Duat* as I will pray for every one of you."

"Pray for us, *heqat-taui, hemet-netjer*," spoke my soldiers in unison. "We shall meet again in the Field of Reeds."

Reluctantly, Titus murmured, "We must go."

He took a set of heavy iron chains from a hook on the nearest wall and gently locked my ankles into my manacles and wrapped a linking chain about my waist before enclosing my wrists. Securing the second wrist lock, he paused to look at me, his eyes sad and his hands unable to let go of mine.

"Thank you," I said softly. "For everything."

He inclined his head. "You are an extraordinary person, Your Highness. It has been my privilege."

I lifted my right hand from his and laid it across my chest. The manacle was warm from the heat of the day.

He accepted my gesture and reluctantly let go of my other hand to take his position in front of all of us.

I turned to Tahu for one last piece of intelligence. "Tell me of Dejen," I whispered hurriedly.

My faithful Mephisian shook his head. "The Lion of Amhara drowned with your brother when the royal flagship was destroyed."

"He was with Ptolemy?" I asked.

Tahu gave me a loving, sad smile. "He hated Lord Ptolemy, but he knew it would be the wish of our Pharaoh that her brother be spared from harm if possible. He gave his life for your will, my lady, not the boy's, and he did so with the joy of an Egyptian."

Love for my comrades stole my speech again, but I knew Tahu saw my gratitude threatening to spill from eyes and make me break my promise to Mudjet. I lifted my iron-wrapped wrists to dab away my tears and signaled to the waiting Titus that we were ready, which he acknowledged with a small nod. I took one final breath and stepped out into the blazing light, the sound of my chains scraping together carving itself into the deepest corners of my ears.

As we shuffled out onto the route, I was taken aback by the relative quiet of the crowd. There was a busy, buzzy hum from many conversations — no raucous cheers or angry hissing. I kept my gaze forward and my step as firm as my shackles would allow, but out of the sides of my eyes I could see people stop their tongues to watch me pass. A few leaned in to speak to a neighbor, though as they did, their eyes slid from me to some point behind us.

I hobbled along in confusion, this was not the horror that I was told of. It was demeaning, to be sure, to be dragged around so that the masses might gawk at me, and yet, the citizens of Rome did not fling rotten fruit at me either. They did not hurl disgusting epithets towards me and my men, no one spat at my passing. They did not seem to know what to make of me any more than I did of them. We clattered along to the rising sound of a thousand mutterings, which made me feel alternatingly terrified and foolish.

Finally we approached the end of the route, where the Clivus Capitolinus loomed menacingly, waiting to lead us to the Temple of Jupiter. Upon reaching the temple steps, where members of the Senate stood off to the sides observing the parade, Titus carefully pulled me aside. I kept my head pulled so high I was afraid the muscles in my neck would snap, but I could not watch my men marched back to the nooses waiting for them without losing all my composure. To honor their sacrifice for me, I had to deny myself a final goodbye glance.

Above the thousand mutterings, I heard Tahu's strong voice ring out above the fray in one final parting shot to our wardens, "*Hai heqat-taui, a'a meret en akhmui-remthu!*"

"*Hai, heqat Iaitrwedja!*" answered half of my men.

"Hail, Arsinoë Soteria Philoaígyptos!" said the others, before their guards beat them into silence. The people of Rome gaped at this last Egyptian insurrection, and I bit into my cheek to hold my tears at bay.

The disquieting unease of the crowd was abruptly shattered by cheers emanating from where we had come on the Campus Martius. They swept through the lingering masses like a brushfire. I turned my head reluctantly and watched as Caesar and Cleopatra made their way down the road I had just dragged myself across like a beggar, their golden chariots gleaming in the bright sunlight. They seemed to fly through the milling throngs too entranced by their beloved general to hiss at my sister.

As they bore down on us, I could see Caesar wore his red-hemmed senatorial robes stitched with golden palmettes and a mantle of purple sewn with elaborate designs in golden thread. He seemed to be looking off at something in the distance, his expression calculating under the laurels resting on his brow even as he occasionally gave a polite acknowledgement to the adoring crowds.

Cleopatra, following in her chariot a scant few lengths behind him, had carefully dressed herself in a Roman *stola*, though naturally the most luxurious she could manage, the tails of her dove-colored diadem fluttering behind like a banner. The precious silk of the dress had been dyed with expensive saffron, with the *instita* and *limbus* in that reddish violet the Romans are so fond of. She had the look of power that she so loved to cultivate, and yet I doubted as to whether that was how she should have come before the people gathered here. People who already mistrusted her, who did not like to see her sit beside Caesar as an equal, who might misconstrue her appearance meant to impress as presumptuous in a land where only properly married women and Vestal virgins wore costly yellow dyes. A richly dressed Kharmion stood in a third chariot drawn alongside that of my sister's, holding Caesarion, to complete the family portrait.

Despite their speed, I stood in what felt like eternal agony waiting for them to arrive at the feet of Jupiter. When they finally stopped the chariots at the bottom of the steps, soldiers materialized to help my sister and Kharmion from their transports. With Caesar at the lead, they climbed to the top of the stairs to a prepared dais so that the crowd might have full view of them. A centurion grabbed the back of my head to push it forward into a bow as they passed me halfway up.

Upon reaching the dais, Kharmion and Caesarion faded to the rear and my sister sidled up to where Caesar stood, her hand resting lightly on his wrist, a quiet gesture of possession meant to defy the local aristocracy and presumably the Lady Calpurnia.

As I was yanked forward to their feet by the rough centurion, I paused to wonder where the shy Calpurnia was. Was she saddened by my sister's presence? Jealous? Or simply resigned, as her husband's affairs were many, infamous, and predated her? My chains rattled noisily on the marble steps as I limped towards them, forced by the manacles into waiting for my back foot to catch up with the one in front.

At the foot of the dais my escort stopped me, Titus moving forward to stand on my left and the rough soldier on my right. This unknown man was the one who addressed Caesar and the crowd:

"Glory unto you, Great Caesar, and unto your towering victory over the rebels to Rome's authority in Egypt and to that of Cleopatra Thea Philopator, friend of Rome!"

Cleopatra smirked at this, even as the multitude was swept by another wave of murmuring. The centurion continued, unfazed. "Citizens of the Republic, we are victorious! Dead is Achillas, assassin of noble Pompey! Dead is Ganymedes, the plotting eunuch!"

I closed my eyes briefly at the names of both these men, my teacher and the brazen soldier I had never quite figured out. I found myself praying for them both, despite Achillas' treachery. Many steps had brought me here, to where I stood with cold sweat gathering beneath my voluminous wig, Achillas was only one of many.

"Dead is Ptolemy, the usurper to whom the largesse of Rome and his lady sister was not enough!"

This was the hard part to give to the Romans, surely. In a world where women had few practical political powers, how to tell them that my father's firstborn son was not Egypt's rightful ruler? I was certain that they had been told Ptolemy was a troublemaker who wanted independence and that Cleopatra would dutifully bend her knee to their superiority, but would the citizenry believe that tale?

I felt my face flush slightly and I realized that this lie angered me. My pride, that I thought had been burned from my heart in Alexandria, flared up at the idea that my slithery brother be given so much credit. Ptolemy would have licked the dust from Caesar's sandals if it meant he could be the only pharaoh in Egypt. Cleopatra had won by virtue of being cleverer than him, and because she got to Caesar first. I wanted to roar at the crowd that I was the one who wanted independence, I was their troublemaker. I stopped myself, though Cleopatra noticed my agitation and looked at me askance. I met her gaze to remind her that I was not taken in by Roman propaganda and she turned from me back to the centurion.

"And here is Arsinoë, sister of Cleopatra, who seduced the people of Egypt to abandon their anointed queen and the gods so that she might wear a crown as well!"

I saw a furrow in my sister's brow. She never liked to hear of other women being seductive. I pressed my lips together to suppress a smile, even here in this moment I must be less than her. Though it was an interesting choice of words, I wondered who wrote this speech. I glanced at Caesar, who remained sphinx-like and did not see me.

"She has been brought here to be humbled before you and to face the judgment of the gods. Kneel before the Consul of the Republic, wretch!"

The centurion finished speaking, and I knew what I must do, but I could not will my knees to bend. Fear clenched my teeth, though it was something deep within me that placed steel in my legs. I had a flicker of hope that my Lord had traveled across the sea to be with me as I waited to be sacrificed to the enemies of my people. He told me to be brave, perhaps this is what he meant.

I felt the energy of the multitude swell behind me, they saw my defiance. The sound of the crowd at my back bloomed like a storm, but their voices were not angry. They spoke to one another without drawing breath as if they were afraid to disturb me, standing stoically before their Consul and their gods.

I also felt the rising rage of Cleopatra, her *heka* radiating a fury so intense it was a marvel she did not burst into flames. Though my heart told me not to look at her, that she was not important here.

So, instinctively, I met Caesar's eyes instead. He and I looked at one another for what could only have been a handful of moments, yet they were seconds that stretched on until I began to truly see the man that lived behind those incalculable eyes. The ambitious boy of a diminished house, the fearless young man who scribbled poetry even as he ruthlessly cut down Rome's enemies, the confident dictator whose full attention I now held in my hand like a delicate piece of glass. Soon it would shatter, surely never to return, though in this small sand-grain of time it belonged to me.

In the distance, I heard the muffled shouting of the centurion, the gathering noise from the spectators, but they were so far away. Caesar and I stood somewhere beyond them, the man who could be king of Rome and the girl who was almost queen of Egypt. For just that moment, he might have truly seen me as I was, for good and ill, as I once was afraid he had that night in the Temple of Isis, a lifetime ago.

I was drawn back into the fray by the rough hand of the centurion on my shoulder and the *pilum* of Titus gently pressed against the back of my knees, which at last sunk me to the ground. I was grateful that Titus allowed me some dignity, rather than a blow I probably deserved that would have no doubt sent me sprawling. On my knees, I broke my eye contact with Caesar and lowered my head slightly to prevent being forced to do so by the centurion. The surly soldier huffed in relief, pleased to have the proceedings back as they should be.

The centurion undid the chain around my waist to produce an iron leash I could be led by. "I now hand this conquered rebel queen over to you, Consul, as the benefactor of the citizenry."

He handed one end of my chain to Caesar who took it as the centurion and Titus turned me around still kneeling so that I faced the crowd. Without invitation, Cleopatra came forward and took the other end of the chain in her hands. I tried not to recoil as she pulled it taut enough so I could feel her grip. The last of my energy drained out of me through my chains and I found I could not lift my head to look out at the people who stared at me like nervous animals. I stole a glance upward at my sister, who coolly surveyed them with the detachment of a lioness looking at an anthill. Caesar's expression was equally magisterial, though I could spy a tightness in his jawline that makes his pulse visible. I did not have more time to ponder this as I was unceremoniously dragged off the dais and scooped up into a cart that transported me back to my cell to await my execution when night fell.

Another wave of calm overtook me as the gold-streaked sky faded into twilight. I removed the heavy wig and jewelry, and set them aside for someone else to gather up. I shook out my hair and removed the golden sandals. I wished for water to wash my face with, but none was forthcoming.

As Mudjet and I sat in silent contemplation, I turned my memories to the happiest I could think of. Sitting under a canopy to escape the oppressive heat of a dying day like this one, writing compositions while Ganymedes lectured to me about Alexander's invasion of India; Baktka telling me old folk stories as she brushed my hair before bed; dancing with Mudjet in an abandoned courtyard during some feast or another, giggling with too much wine; teaching Ptah how to ride. The last I can see so clearly: Ptah trembling before the fine-boned desert mare with the blazing coat who kept tossing her head in the teasing wind.

Will she be gentle? Ptah turned to me with pleading eyes.

Just like riding on the back of your puppy, nedjes, I had said, with a smile of encouragement. *Do not be afraid to remind her who is the rider here, like Alexander did with Bucephalus!*

Ptah grimaced weakly. *I'm just glad you're not making me start out on Erebus.*

Erebus, black as pitch, flicked his ears forward at his name and let out a snort before laying them back against his head.

Oh, ignore Ptolemy, I answered flippantly. *He has never forgiven Erebus for nipping his backside that one time. He has perfectly lovely manners as long as you as give him his respect.* I reached up to stroke my horse on his favorite spot, the space where his brow and mane met behind the ear. The dark stallion shut his eyes and gave himself over to my fingers working his rippling flesh.

But how can I give her respect when I'm supposed to be the master? Ptah asked.

Ah, that is the difficult bit, my love. That is why riders are made, not born.

I lost myself in my well of memories as if I had years of time left to examine them. As if pitied by the Night-bark, the evening passed. I continued to dream, and no one arrived. The stars began to fade from the sky and we still sat in our cell. Waiting.

As the morning arrived, Mudjet at last whispered, "Why has no one come for us?"

I stood up and went to the door to peer down the hallway to see if any of our guards were there, but the hall was empty.

"I do not know. Something is wrong, though."

We sat there all day, beyond all notice and any news. No one brought us food, let alone information. Every couple of hours, one of us would attempt to sleep while the other kept watch. My heart pounded in my chest, though I clung to the serenity of the night before as best I could. Maybe this was my sister's doing, her last chance to drive me mad with expectation before the end. She knew me about as well as I knew myself — surely by now she had discovered that I was not afraid of dying, and only the delay of the inevitable caused me any true discomfort.

I was startled out of these thoughts by the opening of the bolt on the door. The light from Titus' torch made him fill the doorway, though I could still make out the presence of several men behind him. Their shadows rushed forward on the floor towards me.

"Welcome, sirs," I said to them, gathering every last scrap of calm I could muster from the depths of my *ka*. "I pray you make this quick, I do not wish to suffer much more."

Chapter Thirty-Eight

Titus shook his head and knelt down to take my hand. "What did I tell you, Your Highness? You were very brave and this is not your last day."

Mudjet gaped. "What do you mean? No captured leader survives a Roman triumph!"

"Well, let us not be too upset if that proves untrue, dearest," I said mildly. I was equally astonished, but my choices were either to quip with my Mudjet or faint, and I wished to keep my feet.

"You did well, my lady. You have won the plebs to your cause and Caesar dares not execute you without risking a riot," Titus explained, trying to hold his composure in front of the other soldiers even as his eyes creased with joy.

"But how?" I made a gesture to the thick layers of makeup still clinging to my face. "Your people bear little love for mine and I am not sure anyone has come to them looking more like an Egyptian harlot."

Titus gave me a grin. "Yes, but as a result, your sister pressed her advantage too strongly. She wanted to make you look as Egyptian as possible to mark you as the enemy — but in whose image did she make my general erect a statue of her in the temple of Venus Genetrix?"

I began to understand. "To Isis."

"Exactly, and you've looked a great deal more like the great goddess of Egypt since your arrival than your *stola*-wearing sister. The people have a wary respect for the sorceress goddess from the Nile. The city has been ignoring that statue for a month, and suddenly this night it is flooded with offerings and votives? The pious fear the wrath of Isis if the princess who bears her likeness is killed by Rome."

"And the impious?"

"I believe that many others were startled to remember how young you are, Your Highness," he admitted. "To condone the death of a girl hardly old enough to have left her family's hearth in our world... it gave many pause. They resent the Queen of Egypt trying to bloody the hands of Rome with the murder of a child. And despite the whole ordeal, you are a young woman — a child — who did not cry or beg for mercy.

Grown men have done that, my lady. But not you. No one knows whether to weep for you, pray to you, or be completely terrified by you. The only growing consensus is we cannot kill you."

Mudjet beamed, though I remained uneasy. "Has my sister been told this?"

Titus' grin faded a little. "Yes."

"I can infer that she took it as one would expect."

"Her wrath continues to be terrible to behold. She has been threatening to storm the walls here and strangle you herself if 'the Romans are so cowed by the defiance of a stripling girl.'"

"She did have her chance before," Mudjet noted in her practical way.

"That's what the Consul told her," Titus agreed. "But now we are here, and the citizens of Rome — and he as their representative — are the arbiters of your fate. And she as a friend and client of Rome must abide by their decision."

"Assuredly that was received with good grace," I added drily.

"I thought she would lose her wits completely."

Titus' remark reminded me of what Ptah had said to me at our last meeting. I realized that part of her anger stemmed from jealousy, rather than only the frustration of my commuted execution. She was beside herself that she had defeated me and yet I was the one receiving praise and protection while the city continued to loathe her very name. She could not fathom how she was unable to charm her way into Rome's heart while I was hailed as a goddess incarnate by yet another group of people. Deep in my breast, I was inclined to agree with her confusion.

There was another thing troubling me, though I was at a loss at how to express it. For Cleopatra should not be the only one exceedingly angry with me and my performance.

Finally in a low voice I said, "I know that the Consul's actions are bound at least in part to the will of the people and sometimes he does not have freedom of choice in certain matters. I hope he knows that I did not plan to embarrass him so in front of the city now that they speak to save me and besmirch his triumph. He has shown me mercy several times, and I do not want him to think I am complacent because of it. I understand how important a patrician's *dignitas* is to his person."

"Don't worry about that, Your Highness," Titus said. "You puzzle him greatly at times, but he is rarely angry at you. And he is not now."

"*Rarely.*"

He chuckled. "Only when you slipped through our nets at the first. After all, it is difficult not to commend your continuing deftness in the face of the adversities thrown in your path."

This made me smile, though I quickly grew somber. "So what is to become of us now?" I asked.

"You will be sent into exile, my lady. Somewhere far enough away to assure your sister you will not meddle in Egyptian affairs and so that you will have some protection from her, no doubt."

My spirits sank a little. I knew that I should be endlessly thankful for my deliverance, but now I was faced with the prospect of living and still never gazing upon my home again. I was banished from the Black Land as long as my sister drew breath and probably beyond as Caesarion grew up. Ptah would grow up, too, but would he do so soon enough to gain the upper hand over Cleopatra?

However, I knew this was not the time express these thoughts aloud, certainly not with the other guards present and possibly not as discreet as Titus. I had to remind myself I was still on stage as surely as I had been at the triumph.

I bent my head to them. "Great is the mercy of the free citizens of Rome, and of their honored Consul. The world will sing of their compassion. May the gods shower their good deeds with many blessings."

Titus understood my words and bowed at the waist as he rose. "When I have any news for you, I will return. I don't think you will have to wait much, they cannot risk keeping you in the city too long."

As he and the others left, I said to Mudjet, "Indeed, they have seen the price Alexandria paid for keeping more than one Ptolemy at a time."

She shook her head with a smile. "Oh, my lady, it is not that. The old men of the Senate already had to worry about the plebeians crowning Caesar king. Now they have to send you away lest the mob crown *you* instead."

Within the week, my new fate was decided. It was arranged that the great temple of Artemis in Ephesus would offer me sanctuary. The high priestess and her college of *megabyzoi*, the eunuch priests who served under her, had apparently petitioned Caesar and the Senate for my deliverance prior to the triumph, so all that remained was to tardily answer their letter in the affirmative. I made a request for maps, which was granted, and spent the intervening afternoons lying on my stomach tracing the sea path between Rome and the Asian coast. My finger would occasionally trail down towards the south, but I pulled it back abruptly before it made landfall at the small notation at the mouth of the Nile. I struggled at night to not dream of the little map city labeled Ἀλεξάνδρεια.

A few days before our departure, Titus and another guard came carrying a chest between them that they set down at my feet.

"What is this? I asked, perplexed, as Mudjet lifted the lid.

"Oh, it is new garments, my lady!" she said, pulling a light blue *stola* out of the chest for me to see. "This is very beautiful silk, it will suit you perfectly!"

I smiled at her enthusiasm as I picked up a second *stola* folded beneath the first. "Excellent, there is one here for you also."

"I could not, my lady," she protested. "These are both for you, they are too fine for me."

"Nonsense," I said with a click of my tongue as I held it up to her. "This one is not even dyed, though it has a cunning pattern running along the hem. I will not carry an extra dress on my back when you must wear the same clothes you have been imprisoned in." I glanced over at Titus. "Do you know who sent this?"

He shook his head. "No, my lady."

I frowned. "I would have thought we both might be considered young for *stolas*."

"Perhaps it is a gesture of rank as opposed to age," suggested Mudjet as she spread out the garments.

I found a pair of *fibulae* pinned along the hem of the undyed dress, delicate bronze creations with small glass beads that I fingered gently.

Mudjet looked over my shoulder. "Those brooches are pretty also." She felt along the edge of the blue *stola*. "There are no pins for this dress," she said, puzzled.

I peered back into the chest and pulled out a small pouch sitting on top of a pile of manuscripts. I wanted to abandon the pouch to dig through the books, though I resisted, choosing instead to loosen the ties and emptied the bag into my palm. Out tumbled a pair of silver *fibulae*, the metal braided in and out with scalloped gilt and a cluster of small jewels, along with a folded bit of paper.

"Oh, now *these* are pins worthy of my lady!" beamed Mudjet, taking one in her hand.

I placed the other *fibula* on the ground and unfolded the paper:

A humble gift to Penthesilea, Princess of Egypt and Queen of the hearts of Rome. May the gods go with her on her journey.

(Cato would have laughed, my dear. And I did. Bless you, brave girl, and be glad we send you away. He's not worthy of you.)

I smiled to myself, then passed the paper to Mudjet. She made a little hum of amusement. "And here I thought there were no gentlemen in Rome."

Titus pretended to pout. "Now I am indeed wounded, Mudjet!"

She grinned. "You are our gallant Sir Titus, my lord. You are in a class above mere gentlemen."

Once again we found ourselves boarding a ship at dawn, preparing to sail out into the unknown. I felt somehow more fearful of this voyage than the last. When we came to Rome, the path was clear, the end within our grasp. Now I moved towards a point somewhere in the distance that I could not see.

Exile was open-ended, indefinite. There was a reason that some chose death over it. It was prison with invisible bars, where pain and longing would haunt my every thought, my every step. We are creatures of our seat of place, no matter how solitary we might be as individuals. Egypt was a land of anguish and blood for me, but I could not let it fall away from me like a snake shedding its skin. I no longer wore the linen gown and flowing ebony braids, but I was still one with Egypt in my heart.

I could not fault Cleopatra for forcing those trappings on me. Perhaps she understood she was only showing the world my true colors, the secret self that lived behind my foreign-colored eyes. And having exposed me for who I really was, she could cast me out of the home cherished in my *ka*. If she was angry with this outcome rather than my execution, I believed that in time she would grow to appreciate it as the crueler punishment. Banishment was an executioner as surely as the sword and the noose, he only killed his victims slower. And now I sailed towards the embrace of a permanent severance with all I had ever known to await the hangman of time.

We arrived in Ephesus late in the evening. As we neared the Ionian coast, I could make out the rocky hills in the distance by the torches on the wall of the city burning in the low light.

"The captain dares not bring the ship any closer to the coast in this light, my lady," said Titus, approaching us at the rail. "We shall have to go out in one of the boats."

The crew helped hand us into the small boat as two sailors began the task of rowing us to shore.

As we bobbed in the surf, drawn from the sea by the River Kaystros towards the inlaid city harbor, I found myself trying to imagine being back on the Nile, on one of those so rare outings where we were all together. The whole House of Ptolemy enjoying a brief glimpse of what ordinary families do. Ptolemy and Salvius towed lines in the water, while Ptah giggled with delight at the antics of several of the hunting dogs from our mother's lap. My father with an arm around Cleopatra and the other around me, pointed out the different crops growing along the river bank. The scene was so peaceful, I very nearly thought I had conjured it from thin air.

But then I thought on it too long and the telltale scars rose up from the picture, like old stains on a tapestry. Gazing beneath the surface, the absence of my stepmother and Berenice moaned beneath the glittering, lazy river waves. Ptolemy and Salvius kicked and pinched each other, along with the nearest rower. My mother's face was wan and her hands trembled. My sister's eyes were alight with an adoration my father hardly registered. I looked out at the workers on the field, having long ceased searching for my father's undivided attention. We were revealed to be nothing more than bad actors in a play, using zeal to mask our mediocrity. Our hidden malice made me shudder and shook the memory from my mind as the harbor came into view.

We reached the docks and our rowers jumped out to bring the boat in. Titus helped us disembark and we walked forward to meet the small delegation waiting for us, lamps in hand. At their head was an older man with sea-green eyes and olive skin. If his robes had not given him away as a priest, his gently rounded form and features were familiar to me from years of living in a palace as the signs of those made eunuchs at a young age. His face broke into a wide grin as he motioned all those with him to kneel before me.

"Greetings unto you, Your Majesty! I am Xenos, chief *megabyos* of the Temple of Our Lady of Ephesus. We are honored to receive you, valiant Queen of Egypt!"

I blanched slightly. "Good sir, please rise. I thank you, but fear greatly should my sister hear that you have addressed me thusly. It is she who bears that title."

The priest stood back up, yet his good-natured face continued to smile at us unconcerned. "Oh, tosh, my lady. Everyone from Hispania to India knows that Cleopatra may hold Egypt in name, but that you have won the throne of the people's hearts. Even the proud Romans have fallen in love you!" he said, and gave Titus a wink.

The tribune laughed. "Don't worry, priest. Your transgression is safe with me. Though I doubt I can say the same for the sailors."

"Well, come what may!" the *megabyos* replied, with a dismissive wave. "The gods know I speak the truth. I am sorry if the so-called Queen of Egypt cannot bear to hear it. Anyway, we are pleased to receive you, my lady. A cart awaits us, allow me to take you to your new home. If you can forgive the crudeness of the transport."

"Of course," I replied. I turned to Titus. "I fear this time, we truly say goodbye."

"Alas, I suspect it is so, my lady," he answered. "Though if I thought I could succeed in a petition to remain in your service, I would make it."

I shook my head. "That is kind, but it would be a dull station for a man of your talents. This is a far-flung post to force your young bride to accept. Remember me fondly, when it comes to your mind, sir. My best wishes for your success and happiness go with you."

Titus bent over my hand. "May the gods keep you," he raised his head and met my eyes with a twinkle, "Your Majesty." He straightened and saluted. "Farewell, Mudjet, Queen of Companions!"

She gave a mocking, playful wave. "Bah! Be gone with you, Sir Titus and your Roman flatteries!"

He laughed again and gracefully leapt into the boat as the sailors pushed it off from the shore. He waved once more and we watched him recede towards the west until the boat was a black speck against the darkening sky. We then followed the priest into the cart and the driver started us towards the city.

Ephesus was very old city that had watched many a king and queen come and go, yet I was touched that despite the late hour and our route that only skirted its built and rebuilt walls, many of the inhabitants had come out to see our arrival. Their children placed wildflowers in our path and their old people passed blessings to me in their mellow-tongued Greek. I smiled shyly at them, and they responded with open, toothy grins.

"I did not expect this," I said to the *megabyos*.

"Your fame is wider than you give yourself credit for, my lady," the priest answered. "This has always been a proud, free city. Not unlike your

Alexandria. We have never enjoyed living under the hand of foreign conquerors, and Rome is no different. The people here applaud anyone who
has fought for their independence so fiercely."

I opened my mouth to respond, but at that moment was struck
dumb by the sight of the Great Temple as it loomed before us in all its
splendor. Its towering columns and enormous friezes were lit by torches
so that even in the night, their cascade of color and skill was clearly visible.

"If my lady is not too fatigued by her long journey, the High Priestess
would beg an audience with Your Highness."

Still unable to tear my gaze from the temple, I nodded. "It is I who
should be begging an audience with Her Grace." With a motion to the
driver, we altered course towards the steps of the temple where the cart
came to a halting stop and the priest helped me and Mudjet down to the
ground.

The rest of our delegation dispersed into the night as the three of us
made our way up the cool marble steps. The cypress trees swayed mildly
in the night breeze. From behind one of the columns appeared a slight,
dark-haired girl with large brown eyes in a heart-shaped face and skin
the color of bronze. She wore the pale *chiton* of a priestess and carried
a lamp in her small hands. Its light quivered against the tiny, nervous
movements of its bearer.

"Ah, Nuray! Do you come looking for us?" said the priest.

"I was hoping you would have come back soon, master, but I did not
know when to expect you," replied the girl in a low, gentle voice, her large
eyes fixed on Mudjet and me.

"Well, the sea-wolves made good time. Dear one, this is the Queen of
Egypt. Show her you have not forgot your manners."

She started and bowed her head, embarrassed. "Forgive my impertinence, Your Majesty."

I could not repress a smile. I suspected this priestess was only a few
years younger than me, and her wide-eyed ways reminded me of Ptah. "It
is quite all right. I would stare at us too — we probably look as though
we have been set upon by wild animals. This is my companion, Mudjet,
and we are pleased to meet you."

Mudjet smiled at the girl, and she blushed very prettily. "Your Majesty is very kind. If it please you, my lady, my name is Nuray and I serve the Lady Artemis here in the temple."

"Nuray's family is from the settlements in Illium, but she has lived here for several years now. I am sure she will be happy to lend you any assistance she is able," Xenos explained with a fond look at little Nuray.

We followed the swaying light of the young priestess as we passed into the main sanctuary. Here we met Artemis of Ephesus, with her eastern headdress and her outstretched hands, her slim-fitting dress decorated with animals and pulled away from her torso to reveal her many breasts that bedecked her like an exotic necklace.

She was not the cool virgin of Athens; she was older, more terrible. I would not wish to face her in battle, she had something of the predatory look of Sekhmet. She spoke in the language of those who came before, when the Cretans first vaulted on the backs of their bulls and and sung to their ancient snake goddess. I felt she had lived long enough to meet the gods of the Black Land.

We continued beyond the altar, and stopped before a set of beautiful doors of carved ivory. I could not resist running my hand down the panels, touching the grooves as they twisted across the doors.

"They are lovely, are they not, my lady?" Nuray murmured at my elbow.

"Indeed. Though I should hope so. It took Nubia nearly two years to procure the ivory my father demanded for this princely offering."

"And another year to complete the carving," added Mudjet.

I held my hand against the ivory, which managed to hold a faint living warmth in spite of the shade of the temple. I had not been taken into the presence of my father's body when he died, and now I stroked the horn-bone of elephants and rhinoceroses as if I touched the bones of my father. Was his immortality confined to the extravagant gift he once gave to a goddess I had never heard him invoke? Long are the arms of dead, soft are their fading voices.

The priest gently took my hands in one of his. "The way of life is always scattered with the bones of the past. The Huntress of Ephesus knows this," he said as he pushed open the doors to allow me to pass.

Chapter Thirty-Nine

I stepped into the indifferent light of the inner sanctum alone, the others waiting for me outside. The high priestess sat on a stool meditating. She was very old, which somehow I had not expected. Her long white hair hung down past her waist under the *himation*, which was pulled over her head. Age had paled her skin so now age spots littered her face like wine-colored freckles. When she turned at my approach, I was equally surprised by her milky, opaque eyes. No one had told me the priestess was blind.

"Greetings, Pharaoh of Egypt," she said, her clipped tone at odds with her helpless appearance.

"I am not Pharaoh any longer, Your Grace."

"No, but that title belongs rightfully to those who rule the Egyptians. Cleopatra Philopator rules Egypt, but not the Egyptians. Or," she asked cleverly, "would the Girl-Pharaoh prefer her other title of God's Wife?"

I lowered my head. "That is also a title I do not take up lightly."

"Hm. They said you were cautious child. I see that it is true."

"I have narrowly escaped death to be banished across the sea after leading a failed revolution, Your Grace. One might argue I should adhere to some caution for once in my life."

"Ha!" she cackled. "They also said you had an unruly tongue. That is apparently also true."

"Your Grace will forgive me, it is one of my many faults. Though I thank you for offering your home to me in my exile."

"Our city was founded by the Amazons in the Age of Heroes, Arsinoë Philoaígyptos," she said with a shrug. "We are the natural sanctuary for a warrior queen. Besides, it is destiny. We have known Alexander's generals and their descendants since the beginning. Do you know, child, the name Lysimachus of Macedon gave our city when we had to abandon the old walls because of the marsh plagues?"

I did, though I had not thought of it until that moment. "Arsinoëa — Arsinoë's City. For Ptolemy Soter's eldest daughter."

She cackled again. "Never say the gods lack a sense of humor." Then she grew serious. "You are now a long way from your heart's gods, my lady. You must learn to stand again without them in case they cannot swim."

"They have struggled to reach me since I lost my freedom, Your Grace. My sister... she is very powerful. But I shall endure."

She cocked her head to one side. "We shall see. Do not think I cannot see the shadows you hold in your breast. If you despair, there will be no hope for the little Pharaoh."

"Is there any hope now?"

The priestess looked thoughtful. "A hairsbreadth, perhaps more. Or less. However, you burying yourself alive here would accomplish nothing."

"Surely Your Grace would not suggest scheming against the rightful Queen of Egypt?" I said pointedly.

"Not in some open, foolish way," she answered. "You are a queen now, no longer a lost child. Just remember to live enough to take an opportunity when it presents itself."

"How does one 'live enough,' Your Grace?"

"That is for you to decide, Your Majesty. Your African gods and mine have seen fit to resurrect you from your death sentence. If little Princess Arsinoë was not killed in the fires of Alexandria, she most certainly died in Rome. What will Queen Arsinoë do with her life? If the girl risked everything she knew for Egypt, what could the woman be capable of?"

Here my interview with the high priestess ended and I rejoined Mudjet and the others. We returned to the cart and began following a sandy road beyond the temple into the rugged country at its back. The priestess Nuray peered at me out of the corner of her eye, trying to discern what the high priestess might have said to me. Or perhaps simply trying to understand what kind of person I might be. The *megabyos* sat in a pleasant silence as we rolled beyond the torchlight and into the burgeoning countryside. Set back among the hills, we wound our way up a tilting path until we arrived at the door of a small house facing the sea in the distance.

"It is not very spacious, my lady, but we hope it serves," said Xenos.

"Beggars can hardly be choosers, sir," I answered with a smile. "I pray we have not turned someone out of their home to accommodate us."

"Not at all. The temple owns several, let us say as the Romans do, villas, to provide important persons hospitality during their pilgrimages. This one is not as grand as some of the others, though it is the most secluded. We thought Your Majesty would prefer the privacy over luxury."

"I do, the *megabyzoi* have been most thoughtful."

"And there is such a fine view from here," added Mujet.

"Indeed. The view is perhaps the best," returned the priest. "The larders are stocked with food, and you will find lamp oil and wool for thread in the closets. I will leave a clay pass with your companion to show to the merchants in town when you need more. They will charge our treasury directly."

"Thank you. I am touched by your generosity."

"And for when you do want an idle moment or two, Your Majesty has free rein within our library," Xenos said with a playful glance. "It is not as grand as Alexandria's, though you are welcome to what we have."

"Oh dear," I said with a laugh, "I see all of my reputations precede me."

He chuckled. "We will leave you to settle yourselves. I am always at your disposal."

"Thank you again." I turned to Nuray. "I hope you will visit us as often as your duties may allow. We shall need someone to teach us about our new home."

The priestess blushed again and smiled. "If Your Highness wishes it, I would be happy to offer my help. Such as it is."

"Excellent. For now though, I should allow you both to return to your beds before sunrise."

Xenos helped Nuray back into the cart and we waved to them as they began the descent back towards the temple.

We crossed the threshold into our new home and began to look around. The doorway opened up onto a small open courtyard with an atrium through which we passed to reach a receiving room with a few couches and tables.

"Is this the only dining area?" asked Mudjet.

"I believe so, unless through here... no. This is the kitchen."

We surveyed the kitchen and then went down the hallway that led away from the receiving room, where several rooms branched off of the hall.

"How many bedrooms are there?" I said, glancing in one.

"Three, I believe, if you count this tiny room over here. This must be for servants."

"I think this room is meant as a study, not a bedroom. The main bedroom is surely large enough I cannot imagine also needing a study. Would you like your own room?"

Mudjet walked into the second room. "It is a cheerful space. Though I will need to get another bed unless I plan to sleep on this table. My lady will be well in the bedroom by herself?"

"I can probably manage. I just supposed that you might value a place of your own after all these years."

"That is most tempting," she answered as we made our way to the main bedroom. We took a narrow back stairway to the house's raised second floor which was comprised solely of this room.

"Well, if you are too good to sleep on that table from the study, we will move it in here and I will find a use for it," I teased.

She threw me a saucy look before leaning out the window. "One can see the garden below from here. I wager there is a passage out there from the kitchen."

We returned to the kitchen and stepped back outside through the side door into the garden. By the door came the savory scent of cooking herbs, though as I followed the path further out, the sweetness of the planted flowers danced out towards the river and beyond it, the green Aegean.

As we stopped to observe our view, I said, "You were learning to cook in Ostia, but I should learn some skill or another also. We will have some time at our disposal."

She considered this. "I could teach my lady to spin and weave," she answered after a moment. "It would be something useful."

"I like the sound of that. We shall need a loom then, though."

"I am sure we could procure one. Where should we put it?"

I thought. "The only room with enough space and light is the main bedroom. The trick will be getting something like that up the stairs."

"I am sure we can arrange it."

I gave an amused shake of my head. "One night in Ephesus and we are already hopelessly domestic, my dear. Give us a year, and we will be so matronly we might be mistaken for respectable women."

"Goodness, my lady. Let us pray it does not come to that!"

In the next month or two, we established ourselves in our newest life. We lured Nuray out of the temple to the point that she spent a day with us entirely every midweek and ate a late meal with us at least one evening a week, often with Xenos the High Priest.

"How was it that you came to the temple, Nuray?" I asked her one day as we spun wool.

"Well, naturally, my parents will say that they hold such love for the Lady of the Woods that they dedicated their most precious daughter to her name."

"And if the Great Goddess stood before them and they could utter no falsehoods?"

She sighed. "They would say that I was a fourth daughter and a sixth mouth in a house just noble enough to allow them to send a child into religious service."

"Ah, that is an old tale indeed," remarked Mudjet with a little smile in my direction as she twirled the spindle in her hand.

"Except your mother sent you into service with the bloody Ptolemies, my sweet. You should have been so fortunate to have been given to a deity," I said with a laugh. "I am sure Nuray finds her life tedious at times, but at least she is not likely to awaken some morning to a knife at her throat... oh dear, I have snapped my thread."

"The people of Egypt say I was given in service to a deity, my lady," she answered with a waggle of her head as she worked mend the broken thread.

"Then you should curse the Fates for making it a sharp-tongued harpy and not some flowery nymph," I returned sportively.

"Now that much is certainly true," she shot back. "All the tales my mother told me suggested princesses were all honey, and yet the only princesses I have known are as tart as sour apples!"

Nuray looked slightly aghast at our exchange, which made me take her hand gently. "I know Mudjet speaks to me as few supposed servants should speak to their mistresses. But we have known each other since before we could speak at all, and I have never enjoyed lording over her very much."

"Huh! As if you could force much upon me against my will!" Mudjet smirked with a wink.

"It would be like commanding one's shadow," I continued. "One would simply look foolish."

"Do not fret overmuch, Nuray," said Mudjet. "Our queen is still my lady and the fact that I sit here before you shows the depths of my love for her. We just choose not to use empty courtesies to appease others."

"I think it's nice," the younger girl answered. "I've had few friends since I left home. We priestesses are pleasant to one another, but we aren't, well, you know."

I squeezed her hand. "That is why you are perfect with us. We have always been out of joint, too. The Fates do make good decisions, also."

Chapter Forty

Time passed slowly in Ephesus. There were the daily rhythms of life to be sure, but nothing like the rhythms of the Nile. The droughts that swept through the land, filling your mouth with dust, cutting down the weak like the blade of a scythe. And then the floods, when Hapy returned to his people and the river beasts grew sleek once more.

I was learning every day that I was a Greek-less Greek, that while I thought I was a Hellene in Egyptian clothing I had more in common with the mountain goats on the hill passes here than with the other peoples of the Aegean. Or perhaps I had simply become the strange lady who was paraded in Rome.

Mudjet and Nuray tried to keep my spirits up, but as the summer folded itself in a restive autumn, I found myself wandering off to take aimless walks alone on the coast with only my thoughts for company. I watched the waves roll against each other as they raced for the beach. Much as I tried to give up my old life, Ptah kept me tethered to Egypt, as did the evil eye I knew Cleopatra cast against me. I believed she meant to grind me down with an exile's life lived in the shadow of her sword. Though I was not stone, she would find this a more difficult task than she anticipated. I could wait a long time. She had always underestimated me. However, this weak courage was not always enough to chase away the dwindling days and steeping, darker nights where the past prowled behind every bend in the hill paths and swayed rhythmically with the lonely trees.

"What song is that you are singing, Your Majesty?" Nuray had paused from tying bundles of herbs together to look up at me.

I had hardly noticed I had been murmuring in a low tone as I had been cutting stalks for her, so it required a moment to remember. "A very old song. My nurse used to sing it to me when I was small."

"What does it mean?"

413

I ran over the Egyptian lyrics from the verse I had been singing in my mind and crudely translated them into Greek:

Love sent me away
To where the lotus grows
Where sun fills the day
And the mighty river flows
The king is a god they say
He calls me his sweet rose
Yet my long hours are gray
Without he whom my heart chose

"It's pretty, though very sad," she remarked.

"It is a sad story, full of misunderstanding. Like many stories."

"Who is the maiden who sings it?"

This brings a small smile to my face. "No maiden, and you know her well. The Egyptians have a legend that when Aphrodite promised Paris that she would give him Helen of Sparta as his bride, she was not altogether truthful with him." Nuray's eyes widen as she listened to me, so I continued. "My people say the goddess only let him abduct a shade of the beautiful Helen and while the Greek world tore itself apart over the theft, Aphrodite placed the real Helen in Egypt for safekeeping."

Nuray frowned. "But how could that help? The war was still fought and in that case over nothing!"

"Indeed. I believe the Egyptians see that as a meditation on the immutability of one's fate and the illusion of life in the Waking World."

"So what did Helen do in Egypt during all those long years?" she asked.

"The stories say mostly a lot of weeping for her husband and child and about the cruelty of being a pawn of the gods. Some of which is very similar to things she utters on the walls of Troy in the *Iliad*. Naturally all the while the Egyptians marvel at her unearthly beauty, and Pharaoh Ramses falls hopelessly in love with her, though she remains chaste to his advances and he gallantly relents."

"The events of the Trojan War took place during King Ramses' reign?"

"Oh, who can say?" I replied with a little shrug. "He is the most famous of pharaohs so naturally he must have consorted with all heroes
and dabbled in all great events. The Egyptians have never let the truth get
in the way of a good story."

We worked in silence once more until Nuray spoke again, "It is twice-
over sad. That song."

"How so?"

"Helen is sad in Egypt, homesick for Greece while you are sad in
Greece, homesick for Egypt."

"That is also a meditation on the immutability of one's fate, my dear.
We mortals are always looking off in some direction from which we
came. It is our destiny to not be content with where we are and with what
we have."

"I think you have a right to be discontent, my lady."

I sighed. "No more so than anyone else, perhaps indeed less right.
Many people have suffered more than I have, though I doubt few have
caused more suffering. And for that I deserve my sadness."

She looked at me seriously. "No one deserves sadness. Any more than
we deserve happiness. Though I believe what we do when we are given
one or the other is what makes us, for better or worse."

"These are wise words, Nuray. Maybe one day I will be wise enough
to follow them."

I am pleased to find myself drifting along the Nile in a reed boat. I sit
with my knees drawn up to my chin and my hair unbound, fluttering behind me as the boat slowly pushes forward. I look over towards the bank
where a rippling crocodile slips into the water. He glides towards me, and
I reach out a hand to caress his snout when he surfaces next to my craft.

"Hello, Ptolemy-daughter," he says in his familiar gritty voice.

I smile as the crocodile's face transforms into the rough features of Sobek, easily treading water at my side. "Did you call me here, my lord?" I ask him.

"No, The Red Lord cometh. I simply could not pass up an opportunity to see you again, Arsinoë Apep-Slayer." He flashes me a large grin of dozens of razor teeth and flicks back under the water. I look to the other bank and see the hippopotamus goddess Taweret sunning herself. She opens a eye at my passing, but yawns and turns her large body to better capture the light.

Ahead, I finally glimpse Set. He steps off the shore and wades through the river to reach me. He touches the side of my boat and is transported aboard so we are sitting facing one another.

"Greetings, Beloved."

I incline my head. "My Lord."

"How is Ephesus?"

"Far away, my Lord."

He sighs. "I know. But your sister is in ascendence and her arm is long."

"This I know. Is that what you come to tell me?"

Set gives me an indulgent look. "Hardly. I am sending you a consort."

My eyes widen. "Pardon, my Lord?" I stammer foolishly.

He chuckles, his emerald eyes dancing. "He will come to you tomorrow. I wish you to receive him as you would me."

"But I do not want a husband!" I blurt out, flustered.

He waves his hand airily, full of mischief. "You are too young to know what you want. You used to not want me either."

I sniff haughtily. "Not exactly surprising when the *sha* invades your dreams as a child."

Set smirks, changing into the *sha,* and steps into my lap. He settles there like the overgrown saluki he is and nudges his head under my hand. "This man is a gift for you," he explains, passing this thought to me without moving his mouth. "All gifts in the Waking World are fleeting. I do this because he is one who sees you as I see you. I would not bring anyone to you who was less."

"What about Achillas?" I retort, still nettled.

My Lord does not rise to my bait tonight. "You know very well that I did not summon that dragon-seed to you. And I did not approve of his designs. Though it is hardly surprising he was drawn to your star."

"It seems over-praise that you think that he was enticed by anything other than my crown."

"Heart, however concealed, is a power, *nedjet*. One day you will learn to remember this."

I sigh, mostly in resignation. "Very well, I see you have already made up your mind."

The *sha* licks my hand and vanishes.

And then I wake up.

The early dawn light was already creeping through my room. I shivered slightly. I still did not want my Lord's gift. Another person in my life made me uneasy, seemed like an unnecessary danger. But Set was not to be denied lightly. My sister was finding this out slowly, as she had won the battle for Alexandria, and yet she was not Queen of Rome and the world as she thought she would be. She could bind me, yet the Lord of the Wild Acacias would continue fighting her influence.

I rose and walked down to the servant's room where we had placed a small tub for washing. I began to fill the tub with water from a basin Mudjet must have left for me last night. She wandered in when she heard the sound of the water.

"Do you want me to help you, my lady?"

"No, it is well. You should try and sleep a little longer."

She lingered for a moment, though she sensed my desire to be alone and retreated. I stepped into the tub and washed absentmindedly. I dressed in a clean *chiton*, though I bound up my hair in an indifferent manner. I only had my mother's bracelet for adornment, so at least I

would not draw too much attention for being especially decorative today.

I went through the motions of my routines in a daze. If Mudjet and
Nuray noticed, they remained silent. Mudjet knew I was often secretive
if I had met the gods in the Dream World, so she might have excused my
behavior to the young priestess in some fashion. As for herself, she also
knew I had difficulty articulating these encounters quickly, and as a result, had learned not to pry. This was a blessing, how to explain my Lord's
ridiculous scheme to them? I looked around corners suspiciously all day,
but I did not even encounter any of the eunuch priests, let alone a strange
man.

At long last, the sun began to dip into the sea, and as it descended,
I began to feel abundantly foolish. Perhaps my Lord had meant to tease
me out of my melancholy, though while he was capable of being playful,
it was unlike him to toy with me in the Waking World. Eventually Nuray
returned to the temple grounds, Mudjet began moving around earthen-
ware to prepare our supper, and I in a fit of temper stalked out to the garden to walk off my restlessness.

The garden always smelled of blossoms and the salty tang of the sea.
I wandered the path somewhat indecisively, thinking of the scolding I
would give my Lord for his little joke when I looked up suddenly and my
stomach lurched. The sun was setting in earnest now and I was not alone.

There was a man standing with his back to me, looking out at the distant
waves. He made no attempt to hide himself from view, but even if he had
wished to it would have mattered not. I would have known the particular
weave of his cloak in a legion. I arrested my step silently, though I could
have barked out with bitter laughter at Set. Baktka always said that the
gods who tread the underworld have mercurial senses of humor. With a
slight shake of my head, I cleared my throat lightly.

"You honor us, Caesar."

Chapter Forty-One

Caesar turned at the sound of my voice, and for a fleeting moment, I saw for once he was the one caught off guard. But as one would expect, he recovered quickly.

"Your Highness," he replied, returning my greeting with a small bow and a gesture towards the cliffs. "Your view is very fine."

I raised my eyebrows. "I do not know if it is wise to call me such, Your Excellency. I doubt the Queen of Egypt would appreciate hearing me still addressed as a member of the royal family. We have heard she was informed of my *regal* reception here in Ephesus and is deeply unhappy about it."

He grinned and walked over to me. "It is usually considered wise to mention you as little as possible around the Queen," he said, his mouth twitching.

Caesar offered me his arm, which I took, though not with some lingering trepidation. "Have you come to slay me as an offering to the Lady of the Moon, my lord?" I asked as we fell into step with one another.

"If that could grant me a victory over the Parthians, I'd consider it, Iphigenia. Alas, I think what I really need is more horsemen, not the blood of virgins."

"Never has a Roman been so quick to assume the virginity of a Ptolemaic princess," I remarked drily.

Caesar let out a chuckle at that. "Your sister is so quick to heap abuse on you that it's safe to deduce that at least *some* of it must be untrue. That is my advice to you this evening, Your Highness: all know that slander often contains a grain of truth. Learn to sift for it among the lies."

I nodded sagely in his direction, yet I knew he could also see the laughter in my eyes.

He continued. "When she's not describing your dead brother as a military mastermind, she's busy telling anyone who'll listen that you have summoned the gods of Egypt against her. I think she would pull down every temple from Alexandria to Ombos if she thought the peasants wouldn't riot."

I was surprised by this, but tried not to show it. "She has been known to call on the Egyptian gods herself."

"Not lately. Cleopatra spends a great deal of time giving offerings to Juno and Venus."

I was tempted to suggest that those goddesses were little help to the Trojans in war, but I knew how proud the Romans were of their Trojan roots and that Caesar himself claimed Venus as an ancestress so I tread gently. "It is good to receive help from family members," I answered.

He pretended to be put out with me. "Scoff all you like, my dear, but you're the one who is hailed in the streets of Alexandria as the consort of demons."

"My sister, Beloved of Our Father, wears the double crown. Who am I to argue with her wise judgment in these matters?"

"Oh, don't try to grovel," Caesar snorted, though not angrily. "You've proven many times you are utterly hopeless at it." He gave me that wry look of his. "Is there a decent meal to be had in this backwater, or must I go back to my ship for battle rations?"

"I am sure we can provide a simple repast, though I should send a messenger to the chief *megabyzos*. The high priest should be present when we are hosting such an eminent guest."

Caesar rolled his eyes. "Very well, I suppose you must. Though it has been a long trip and I am in no mood for eunuch-chatter."

"Of course not, sir," I replied in a humoring tone. "The high priest is a man of circumspection, he will not overstep himself."

Circumspection was also one of Mudjet's many talents, so a slight raise of the eyebrows was all the comment we received when we entered my house.

"Mudjet, would you go tell Xenos that we are entertaining a guest this evening and we invite him to join our party?"

"Of course, my lady. I am sure His Grace would be delighted."

As she walked past me, I leaned towards her and added, "It would be best if only the high priest was aware of who is dining with us."

She nodded. "Naturally, my lady."

A thought struck me. "We do have enough food?"

Mudjet smiled. "Never fear, I can make do. Will you be all right until I return?"

"Thank you, I am confident I can manage."

She slipped out the door, and I motioned for Caesar to make himself comfortable. I retrieved a vessel of wine and several cups from the kitchen, still fighting the prickly sensation climbing the base of my spine. I felt like a housewife who had invited a leopard through her door.

I handed him a cup and resolved to stop dissembling. "Why are you here, my lord?"

Caesar studied me briefly before he answered, his black eyes glittering. "I'm not exactly sure myself — no official capacity, if that's what is worrying you. Arguably, this is a good vantage to observe Parthia from, but I shall have to deal with some matters in Rome before I can turn my attentions eastward. So perhaps I was just curious to see how you were getting on. Does that intrigue you?"

I shrugged off his question as I poured wine into my own cup. "I do not have much experience with intrigue, sir."

"Your Highness doesn't hold my intellect in very lofty regard if she thinks I'll believe that of the girl who spun a revolution from a courtiers' scuffle," he scoffed.

"And Your Excellency does not hold my intellect in any kinder estimation if you think I will believe you would travel so far if you were content to only inquire after my welfare. Your reputation precedes you."

Something in his gaze shifts and I realize the glimmer I had seen earlier was partially meant to hide that he was indeed looking at me carefully as men look at women. "What if I confessed to being the mercenary scoundrel you so coldly make me out to be, my lady?"

"I would say it is a long way to come for a seduction, my lord."

He laughed. "It's comforting to know that as old as I am, young women might yet fear falling under my spell. Or is the quick little princess as mercenary as I am, and she thinks I am in a position to improve her lot?"

"You might believe you are Fortune's favorite sir, but, I am not so naïve as perhaps I once was. You have spared my life when it was in your power to do so and for that I am grateful. Though any dreams I have left are not in your power to grant and I do not waste my time."

Caesar raised his cup sardonically. "I salute you, Your Highness. I cannot remember the last time a woman asked nothing of me."

I bristled a little at his mockery. "I may not be Cleopatra, but I am not just anyone."

"Indeed it would appear not," he replied, growing serious. "And it has been quite some time since I believed otherwise."

I opened my mouth to respond, but then Mudjet reappeared with Xenos and the moment passed.

The *megabyos* bowed to me and kissed my hand before turning to show obeisance to Caesar. Mudjet retreated to the kitchen to finish preparing refreshments while we seated ourselves on the couches and began cycling through the usual social blandishments.

I tried to remember all my years of training in presiding over sparkling royal dinners, though I had to inwardly protest that none of that could have prepared me for entertaining a man whose story with me was such a bundle of contradictions. We were supposedly foes, yet he had three times saved my life, like a friendly spirit in the old stories. He had placed the yoke of slavery upon the necks of my people, yet he somehow had my Lord's blessing to be here. Sometimes I was able to keep the conversation light, remembering how to bandy like an Alexandrian, but I struggled not to lapse into distracted fits of reserve, pushing the food around my plate.

Xenos and Caesar were discussing temple levies in Ephesus, when Caesar paused mid-sentence. I looked up from my barely touched dinner and was alarmed at the ashen shade his face had taken. He met my gaze with wild, dilating pupils.

He began, "Forgive me, my lady, but I believe I am about to terribly inconven—" before his eyes rolled back in his head and he started to slump off of his couch.

The high priest and I leapt to our feet simultaneously, though in the midst of our alarm, I felt strangely calm. I darted to Caesar's side and caught his slipping frame as the convulsions began to course through his body.

"Xenos, help me get him on the floor so he does not hurt himself." The priest and I lifted the Consul's shaking form to the ground and I knelt with Caesar's head in my lap so I could keep it as still as possible. The end of his sentence was still caught in the back of his throat, and he sounded like a man in a dream who is trying to call out but cannot make himself heard. Drawn by the commotion, Mudjet reappeared from the kitchen and nearly dropped the bowl in her hands.

"Mudjet, get me some damp cloths and make up my bed when you can. I want to move the Consul there as soon as it is prudent." She nodded and darted back out of the room.

I took the edge of my *chiton* and wiped some of the sweat beading on Caesar's brow. His body was still jerking against my light restraint, though I could feel each wave becoming perceptively less intense.

Xenos glanced at me. "I had heard whispers that Caesar suffered from the falling sickness. I confess I assumed it to be a malicious lie concocted by his enemies."

Mudjet returned with a cloth that I took from her and placed on Caesar's head. "I knew he suffered from some malady or another. My sister told me long ago that she had told him she possessed the means to cure him of an illness he carried, but that she did not actually wish to heal him, even if she had been able, because she would lose power over him in the process. Now that I see it is the falling sickness, I understand her reasoning. A Caesar who might occasionally be incapacitated would be very useful to her."

The minutes crawled by. Gradually, Caesar became quiet and his breathing slowed to a deeper pace. He remained pale, but the color began returning to his face. His eyelids fluttered open, and he looked up at me and grimaced.

"I usually plan a more gallant design for getting into a lady's lap," he said weakly, which made Xenos knit his eyebrows together.

"Well, it is difficult to argue with the results, sir," I commented tartly, which made Caesar cough out a small laugh. "Do you feel strong enough to moved to somewhere more comfortable?"

He nodded, and the high priest and I helped him to his feet. Between us we shouldered Caesar to my quarters where we slowly lowered him into the bed.

"Should I get assistance, my lady?" Xenos asked me. I slid my gaze over to our charge, who gave me a nearly imperceptible shake of his head.

"No, I believe we shall be calm now. Unless the Consul experiences multiple attacks in quick succession?"

Caesar shook his head more pronouncedly this time. "I don't think I've ever had more than one at any given time, thank the gods. I don't wish to detain you any longer than I already have, sir, though perhaps you would be good enough to send a runner to my ship to tell my captain that I will spend the night in town and that they should not expect me." He paused and looked to me. "If I may intrude upon your hospitality a little longer, my lady."

"Of course. This house is yours, Consul."

The high priest's expression suggested he wished to say something to me, but he decided against it. "Very well. I shall send a message to your ship, sir." To me, he added, "Do not hesitate to send Mudjet to me if you need anything." I inclined my head. "Then good evening to you both."

As Xenos left, I felt a heaviness settle in my limbs as the excitement of the night fled my body. I was exhausted to my bones, though far too agitated for sleep. I stood at loose ends in my own room, lost in my own distracted thoughts.

After a moment, his voice drifted across to me quietly. "You don't have to stay up if you are tired."

"No, my lord, I am not ready to sleep yet. I will stay and keep an eye on you until I am. Do you mind if I weave while I do?"

Caesar gave a wave of his hand to indicate he did not as I settled on my stool. "I didn't know you could use a loom."

I picked up the shuttle and fingered the end of my thread. "Arguably I cannot, but I am endeavoring to learn. Mudjet and one of the young priestesses are trying to teach me. It passes the time."

We sat in silence for a few minutes, only the clacking of the loom chattering in the low light. The darkness was likely wreaking havoc on my design, but I felt better having my hands occupied and so I picked through my rows mostly by memory.

Caesar sighed from the other wall. "I wish it were true. What you said."

I paused. "What did I say?"

"That this was my house."

I made a disbelieving noise at this and resumed my threading. "It is too quiet here for you, sir. You would weary of it very quickly."

"Maybe you're right. Though I feel a calmness in me that I haven't felt in a long time. It isn't unpleasant. And you seem to be managing."

I snapped a thread and wound a new color in. "I would live on the moon cheerfully if I knew Ptah was safe," I explained, to dispel any remaining misunderstandings the Consul might have about my motivations. Or those of my sister. "But that is the one thing I cannot have. He is my sister's security against my misbehavior. She knows as long as he is with her, I will do whatever she asks. She fails to understand that if he was with me, we would not challenge her. We would live modestly, somewhere like here." I paused to glance in his direction and found him looking at me attentively. "I did not refuse to go to Cyprus because I delight in power. I felt it was my duty to protect my people from invasion and ultimately, from her. She does not understand the difference because she sees the world through eyes dissimilar from mine. She assumes I am like her and our brothers are twin-minded. Ptah is not Ptolemy. They might share a name, but they have always been like night and day. She forgets this. Ptah has never wanted to be Pharaoh. He is our baby, our better part. He only ever wanted us to be a family."

"A happy family might be more illusive than a crown," he observed.

"Indeed, and yet it does not seem to stop you trading one for the other."

Caesar snorted dismissively. "You think I misuse my wife. It's not that simple."

I shot him a look. "I think Roman women are taught to put up with a great deal from their men."

He sighed again. "I did not want to remarry, you know. I didn't even want to marry Pompeia after Cornelia's death. I married both Pompeia and Calpurnia because it was expected of me. There was no grand love between Pompeia and me, but I only divorced her to salvage my *dignitas*. It wasn't personal. I wasn't always as powerful as I am now. As for Calpurnia, perhaps there was a part of me that hoped she would be the love of my maturity, the way Cornelia had been the love of my youth. And she is good. Good and gentle and sweet. A perfect Roman wife."

"I sense a caveat."

"I think we both know I've gone beyond Rome at this point. What I need is not a retiring Roman lady, but a queen among women. A woman who can lead an army and make foreign princes kneel at her feet. And mine."

"Ah, this is where my sister comes into your plans. It will please her that you do take your... political arrangement... with her seriously."

Caesar pulled himself up so that he rested on his elbow facing me. "Only the shortsighted would think Cleopatra is the woman for such an undertaking. I meant you."

I dropped the shuttle as I whirled around, springing to my feet. "Do not mock me, sir," I said. I was not ready yet to accept his words simply because Set had forewarned me of them.

"I would do no such thing," he answered calmly. I found myself as unnerved by the seriousness in his eyes as I had been confronted by the taunting mockery in them once upon a time.

"If you had such a high opinion of me, you would have supported my claim to Egypt over my sister's," I argued pointedly.

"Not necessarily. When I arrived in Egypt, the choice was between Ptolemy and Cleopatra. You were barely in the picture. She was the more capable ruler and the more willing to accept Egypt's status as a client of

Rome's—" he made a motion to cut off my interruption, "—long-term. Based on the information at hand, I made my decision. Once your brother engineered your escape as his ally in the field, I did have some concern because I had by then observed you to be more intelligent than him, but I challenge anyone to have made the prediction that such a slip of a girl would make a passable military strategist and such a shrewd galvanizer of popular support."

"*Passable...*"

He smirked at me. "I am giving you honesty, my lady. A rarity between the sexes."

"And yet you come to me acting as though you would trade horses not midstream, but once you were already successfully on the other river bank. To what possible purpose?"

"I brought unruly Egypt under control as I was supposed to," he explained as carefully as I had laid out my mind to him. "Cleopatra was, and is, the right ruler in Egypt for Rome's interests. Our alliance for that undertaking was mutually beneficial. She is not the right woman to help me further Rome's greatness beyond Egypt. For that, I need you."

Now I snorted. "I cannot decide who would make the bigger fool, you for coming all this way with such a ridiculous story or me if I were to believe you."

He sidestepped my derision. "Cleopatra is many things: proud, intriguing, fiercely intelligent. But she is a hopeless diplomat — you know this. She was raised to rule and therefore has hardly a wisp of humility with which to navigate a political scene where she is not the master. You were born a princess, yes, but the youngest of three with two brothers besides so you have a patience she will never have. You said it yourself once, you know the value of shadows."

"I have no desire to rule the world."

"Perhaps not, though I think you'd be surprisingly good at it."

"I do not particularly care for you."

He cocked his head to one side, his ink-colored eyes amused. "You don't love me yet, but I think you could. You at least *like* me more than you want to let on."

I ignored him. "I once sneered at my sister for stooping to be your mistress when she had no hope of being your wife or your equal. It seems ill-advised for me to make the same mistake. You talk of ruling the world with me, where would poor Lady Calpurnia fit into this?"

"I would divorce her and see that she is married to someone who will treasure her many fine qualities," he admitted with a shrug. "I'm probably in a position to give her more as a matchmaker than a husband anyway." He broke off to give my haughty expression a raised eyebrow. "Don't look at me as though it'll break her heart so badly. She's young, and I'd see her with a kind boy her own age, which is the secret, elusive dream of all Roman girls. And Cal isn't ambitious, so it won't ruin some grand plan of hers. I think she's rather embarrassed to find herself the first lady in Rome, actually."

"Even if that were true, I fail to see why such a partnership as the one you are proposing would require such drastic steps as those. Perhaps I have no interest in putting you in my bed, even if you are not used to hearing that."

Caesar's expression became wolfish. "Luckily for me, I'm already in your bed, my dear. And I didn't actually put that on the table, *you* made the assumption earlier before dinner. I'm only gratefully seizing on an opportunity to follow your lead."

I rolled my eyes. "I think most people who have met you would have made the assumption. Even Ptolemy had enough imagination to presume we would end up in this position."

"Mea culpa," he replied, relenting, though he continued to gaze at me warmly. "But just because I also wish to ravish you senseless doesn't mean I'm not deadly serious about making you queen of the world."

"I think you are a little old to play the lecher with me."

"And I know you're not so superficial as to let that trouble you overly," he replied with infuriating confidence. "Also, I assure you I am much more worth your while than that dolt Achillas."

I glared. "Achillas was my general, nothing more. No matter what he thought."

"I know that, too. I just wanted confirmation — which that terribly black look from you did admirably."

I bent my head towards the wall next to me, sighing. "I will admit you are very clever and capable of being rather charming, my lord. I am not too proud to own that. However, there is a dark violence in your heart I have every right to mistrust..."

I trailed off, staring at the cracks and grooves in the stone as if they were a map to help me navigate this strange conversation. When my voice returned to me, I was unable to wholly excise the fear from it. "I have lived so long without a shred of safety," I whispered as much to the wall as Caesar. "What I have here is not much, but how could I give it up to face the precarious world with only the protection of a man who brings destruction in his wake?"

I could feel him incline his head in acknowledgment. "I have filled the rivers of Europa with blood, it's true. I have a need to dominate everything on earth because it is my destiny to do so. Sometimes I cannot control it. Cleopatra and I are too much alike, we will tear apart everything we build. Calpurnia isn't strong enough to stop me from doing so. You have more compassion than your sister, but you're not afraid to defy me. You did so in chains in Rome where no woman and precious few men would dare to unbound. The people were won to your cause so completely in that moment I couldn't have executed you even if I had wanted to. Cleopatra has been there over a year and is still a pariah. She stalks and plots in my villa and I have been consumed by you since you left."

"Most flattering," I said skeptically. "Though since you are a man who delights in the chase, forgive me for thinking I will have little to show for it in the morning if I swoon into your arms for a handful of pretty words."

"Arsinoë."

I turned back towards him and watched as he pulled himself up from my bed and crossed the room to me. He gently lifted my chin so we were looking each other in the eye.

"You're right," he said. "I may be a fool and a rather old one at that to be here. But I've been haunted by a vision of a new Rome, free of its tired provincial ways, since I was a boy. I've known that I was the one to lead them there as long as I've known my name. I wouldn't risk the dream of my life that I am so wonderfully close to achieving if I wasn't certain you were meant to be at my side when I succeeded."

"Careful, sir," I answered, clinging to the last of my composure, pretending I had felt nothing when he said my name. The first time I had heard him say it. "They always claimed the only reason you gained the upper hand on Pompey is that your daughter nearly charmed him into wanting nothing except a private retirement."

He smiled. "It's a risk I'm willing to take. Are you?"

"I think you are forgetting a dangerous obstacle."

"Let me worry about Cleopatra for once. I'm rather brilliant, you know."

"Hmph. You are a rogue and brigand."

"And if I can manage to tease a fraction of the affection I have for you out of your incredulous heart in return, we'll be masters of Parthia by summer next."

There have been times in the intervening years when I have wondered how my life would have diverged if I had not let him kiss me that night. But life is a game of *senet* where Fate may have as many moves as we do.

Chapter Forty-Two

Two weeks is not an especially long time. I am no different from most, in that I have watched many weeks slip by without note or worry. We move through this life on the unthought-of assumption that time is a commodity we purchase from the gods, easily bought, but just as easily wasted. We are terrible spendthrifts when it comes to time, though our consolation is that even lost time can be savored preciously.

Two weeks was the amount of time Caesar could spare to me before he would be missed in Rome. On the outside that may seem like very little, but I had begun to realize on the first night that the large unspoken enormity that had hung between this man and me was none of the things I had always feared it was: it was simply fate. Not the dreadful goddess Fate or the iron will of Set even, merely the idea that in this very particular place and in this moment we were meant to be with each other.

The greater plans we had spoken of that first night were not important — we forgot Parthia, Rome, even Egypt, and instead rebuilt each other into new casts of ourselves for the pleasure of the other person. He set aside the bloody general and the impatiently superior politician I knew, and became instead the keen intellectual, witty and kind. I in my turn set aside the willful child and the proud captive he knew, and instead became the thoughtful young woman who recited poetry and laughed at his jokes. We spent our time together comfortably, where he eased my heart by treating me as a person worthy of his regard and I eased his by demanding nothing other than what he was able to give. Neither being states we were accustomed to.

Mudjet did not take this well in the beginning. That first morning after, when she entered my room to find me cross-legged in my shift on my bed conversing with Caesar in his *tunica* at my small table, she said nothing, though I saw the baleful look she cast in his direction. She set a small tray of food in front of him perfunctorily, and met me at my dressing table to arrange my hair. As she began combing out the tangles — the snarls admittedly worse than usual I realized with some self-consciousness — she was not harsh, yet I could feel the agitation in her fingers.

"You should not worry," I said in Egyptian in a low voice, brushing away my embarrassment. "I can handle myself."

Picking out a few strands and beginning to rapidly braid them, she responded sardonically, "I am more concerned about him handling you, than the other way around."

"Maybe that would be good for me. Cleopatra always said I should not be so priggish," I retorted lightly.

Mudjet sighed. "I know you do not leap unheedingly into much, my lady. I just do not want to see your heart bruised after everything else that has happened."

I turned and touched her arm. "I know. You care for me when no one else does, do not think I hold that thoughtlessly. I am not afraid because my Lord told me this would come to pass, and though I did not believe him, everything has happened as he said it would. Perhaps because he always seems to know me better than I know myself."

"The Red Lord has no right to thrust you into such a position."

"Ah my dear, when has he ever placed me in a sensible position?"

She did not answer, her mouth still gathered in a frown, yet some of the creases in her forehead smoothed themselves out and we spoke no more of it directly.

I continued to practice my weaving during the day while Caesar would work on legislative drafts and occasionally verse if he was temporarily stymied by a political question, punctuating our more idle talk with a pointed diplomatic query or discussion on meter. At these times Mudjet would often sit with us for the sake of propriety should we receive any visitors and work on mending or correct my pattern lines if they got too out of hand.

"My lady, your line is crooked."

"Is it? Oh yes, I see it now," I ripped out the thread and started to rethread the row. "I blame the Consul. He is distracting me."

Caesar pulled a virtuous face. "Not I, my dear. I simply asked you if you thought the Egyptians would throw up serious objections if Rome increased the import tariff we have on the linen they're sending us. If Mudjet feels your genius is only in women's work like weaving, I'll bow to her judgment and not worry you with all this political talk."

Mudjet snorted. "My lady hardly needs any tutelage in those matters from you, my lord. There is a reason she has worn a crown before she learned to use a loom."

He laughed. "Well met, my lady. Indeed I am surprised you had to even teach her that, with her Minerva eyes," he made me a japing bow from his seat.

Then it was my turn to scoff. "Pfft, you have done us in now, Mudjet. The Consul will no doubt bombard us with pithy epithets meant to extol my supposed wiles."

"I have a reputation to uphold, Your Highness!" protested Caesar. "I cannot be heard making any courtesies to a lady that could be described as 'pithy.' It is hardly my fault in any event," he circled his attention back to Mudjet, "that your mistress has the eyes of Minerva, the mold of Diana, and the lips of audacious Venus Herself."

I groaned and returned to my thread row, as Mudjet giggled at me in spite of herself. Out of the corner of my eye I saw Caesar cast me a saucy look before reverting to pages in front of him. Mudjet remained wary, though he managed to melt some of her reservations as the week wore on.

In the indistinct light of evening when we were less likely to be observed, we stole across the rocky plains on borrowed horses to walk along the coast. In the nights, we belonged to ourselves. As we went, we alternated conversation and silence. I marveled that I could so easily become accustomed to the presence of a man whose manifestation used to fill me with such dread. Somehow despite our many faults and apparent dissimilarities, in many ways we suited each other well.

"I wanted to ask you something the first night," I said to him, "but—"

"But we got a little off-topic," Caesar finished with a deadpan leer. "I lay the fault at your perfect little feet, sweet one. However, I can refuse you nothing. Ask away."

"Why did you follow me to the Temple of Isis that night?"

He grew thoughtful. "I don't know for sure. I think at first I was simply trying to keep an eye on you." He paused. "Which given the events that followed, showed some prescience on my part." He continued, his grin fading. "However, I stood there watching you, and I was transfixed by the realization I knew nothing about you. I stood there that night and in the many days that followed, trying to gain some kind of understanding about who you were, only to have you constantly slip through my fingers. Part of me kept expecting one thing from you and yet every time you spoke to me, your words surprised me. And it was a tactical disadvantage I have struggled with, nearly to this moment."

"I have been told men appreciate women who are mysterious."

"That may be true, but you are so contradictory as to be confounding, Your Highness. It's rather vexing."

"What would be the point of making anything easy for someone of your many talents?" I asked with a smile. "Is that why you were watching us with Titus Manlius that day in the courtyard?"

"So you did see me? I was afraid you had."

"I saw someone. I confess I did not think it was you at the time. I thought you were avoiding us."

"I was, for the obvious reasons. It is dangerous to grow to interested in you, my lady, I think," he said with an adventurous wink. "Luckily, I have solved your riddling ways."

"Oh?" I arched an eyebrow.

He beckoned me closer and murmured in my ear, "I think your subjects had the right of it and you are some kind of goddess secretly consorting with us poor mortals."

I pushed myself away from him lightly. "And you must have had too much wine this evening, sir!"

He dismissed my protests with a gesture. "You can deny it all you wish, but you are obviously some kind of falcon goddess, the way you have escaped all snares as if you had wings!"

"All the snares except the one that binds me here," I observed.

"Perhaps, though considering you should be dead, that is still quite the accomplishment."

"I attempt every morning to avoid waking up dead," I noted acerbically.

"My goddess' tongue has always been one of my favorite parts of her," Caesar laughed, giving me a glance that made the heart of even one such as me flutter out several beats. "She thinks she knows me inside and out, yet little does she realize I've been hatching a plan," he said as we walked on.

"I assume you are always doing thus, and I would be foolish indeed to assume I know every corner of you."

"You may hide under your veil of false modesty, my lady, but I know you see more than you let on. As your remark as to my perpetual planning reveals. Yet you are correct: a plan within a plan, then. You told me you longed to live with your brother somewhere quiet, but could you manage to bear a location not as retiring?"

"What do you mean?"

"Well, Cleopatra doesn't really want the boy underfoot anyway, so what better offer could I make to her than to arrange to take him on the Parthian campaign with me?"

I stopped in my tracks. "You could do that?"

He shrugged breezily. "I don't see why not. Cleopatra will have the free rein she desires and her lords should be satisfied that the Pharaoh is out getting a proper military education. We'll leave out the bit about me absconding with the exiled princess, naturally."

I could not help but throw my arms around his neck. "Nothing would please me more than this!"

Caesar gave me an indulgent smile as he clasped his hands around my waist. "I am pleased when you are, my dear. Though I see I still have work to do if you think this is the apex of your happiness."

Now it was my turn to grow serious. "I realize that it sounds disingenuous to claim that I am a person of small desires, considering how much trouble I went through to be queen of Egypt, yet it is the truth. I have always found greater contentment in small moments like these than moments of high glory. Though I suspect you might disagree."

"Not entirely. I understand how you feel. You know that I love a good show and I rarely feel more alive anywhere above a battlefield, but it doesn't mean there aren't times when I'm sitting in some miserable tent in a damp forest at the back of beyond that I don't feel the pull of the smaller moments, as you call them."

I disengaged myself from his embrace so that we could resume walking. "What do you think of then?"

"My daughter, mostly. It is one of the few regrets of all my undertakings that so many of them took me so far away from her, especially during her childhood. She never upbraided me over it, even as I probably deserved."

"Maybe she understood the touch of destiny that rules your life and accepted it."

"If anyone did, it was no doubt her." He paused and sighed. "I am glad she did not live to see the final unraveling between me and Pompey. It would've broken her heart."

"All speak of Lady Julia as a woman of singular grace and strength. I think she might have surprised you both."

"It is certainly possible," he replied with a low chuckle. "Certain women in my life have a habit of turning my expectations on their head."

Late one night, I wandered out of bed to my window and looked out over the dark hills and the whispering sea. The stars glowed, and the new moon hid her face from view so that the waves could be heard murmuring in the black expanse, yet their movement could not be discerned. A choked breeze, churned up by its travels wafted over my exposed skin. Soon, the nights would become colder as the year of my banishment would turn into another. It had gone slowly, then quickly, though I could not imagine the rest of my life like this.

I tried to picture it, but the future gaped back at me with no detail, no design. With Caesar, without him, it did not matter. I could not see us together in the distance because I could not see him as anything but as he was now. The young man once shown to me in a dream was nothing more than that, and Caesar as a truly old man? I could not see that, either. My heart warned he would overreach himself long before he succumbed to the ravages of time. And I could only imagine myself as a sibylline hag, twisted and alone, listening to the voices in my head and in my dreams.

"What are you thinking about?"

I looked back over my shoulder to where Caesar was watching me from the bed. His voice was kind, his face alert and calculating as he tried to discern me in the sheltering darkness. He had not been asleep as I had thought, and I wondered if war had taught him to sleep at halves like a charger.

I gave a noncommittal shrug. "The future, I suppose. I am trying to see it, but it is hidden from me."

"Don't let it concern you overly," he held out his hand to guide me back to bed. "There are few certainties in the future so it is better to move ahead with eyes open, but few plans because things can change at any hour. Flexibility is much more valuable than foresight."

I let myself be pulled back down into his arms. I studied him as my finger gently outlined the contours of his face.

"You do not have the appearance of a man who is content to lend things to chance."

He arrested my hand and kissed its fingertips while he considered my words. "Of course not. However, the wise general is constantly making adjustments as he moves so he isn't frozen into inaction by the unexpected. That is where the flexibility comes from."

"But you cannot always guard against the unexpected. As you alluded to several days ago, you did not intend to suffer a falling fit in my presence, for example."

"Granted. I do tend to avoid exposing myself thusly in a position of weakness, as it is assuredly unmasculine. Though it ended up having some advantage to me."

"Well, I suppose it did present you with access to my bedchamber," I admitted, grinning.

"Tosh, my lady. I'm not so ungallant as to crow over that temporary advantage. I was referring to the fact I learned by virtue of the evidence that I revived with no injuries and little distress. That is, despite events unfolding without warning, you must have reacted coolly and sensibly. Which is no small thing — I can't tell you how many times I've come to with bruises and cuts because the legionaries around me were at a complete loss."

"Surely it is not so unique a skill."

"You'd be surprised," he said. "We've tried having dedicated aides to me in the past, but it never works out. So we make do."

"At least when you are home it must be easier."

"Actually I rarely have them when not on campaign. The attacks come more frequently under stress and fatigue. Yet another reason you will be invaluable on our little adventure; I've seen I can trust you when I am vulnerable. Again, no small thing."

"It does not solve all of your vulnerabilities," I murmured, lapsing back into my melancholy. "I cannot keep you safe from your Roman detractors. Are you not worried about what they will do in Rome while you engage Parthia?"

"Not unduly. I plan to have all the men I need in place before we depart, and because some of the Republic's old guard are intent on making the people uneasy about my dictatorship, some distance from the situation for a time might be prudent anyway. Also, I confess I'm having trouble caring either way. I'm tired of Rome and its politics. Once I'm back on the battlefield I'll feel like myself again."

I could not help but run my eyes over the scars and sinews of Caesar's body. He was still remarkably fit for a man of his years, age had taken away flesh but not yet muscle. And yet, I wondered if this was one more fight too many. The physical remains of many close calls illustrated how lucky he had been up until now. Could his health hold on through as arduous a task as quelling the Parthian Empire? And then there was the falling sickness, could his body absorb the punishment of a long contest without succumbing?

Caesar interrupted my thoughts. "I'm aware that you are inspecting me with a critical eye to my fitness for my grand designs, and I should probably be a bit provoked by it. Though I confess I enjoy the attention from you too exceedingly to be put out."

"So I am reprieved for my impudence?"

"For the moment," he said with a laugh as he deftly maneuvered himself on top of me. "Though much more scrutiny and I will demonstrate to you again just how capable I still am."

Chapter Forty-Three

During an afternoon when Caesar had returned to his ship to handle some of his own arrangements, I spent my time catching up on household tasks. I was out in the garden selecting some fresh flowers for my room when Mudjet came out looking for me.

"I have finished with some dyes I promised to give to Nuray, do you mind if I take them to her?" she asked.

"Not at all. Here, take her some of these mulleins too. I know the temple grows their own, but ours look especially nice this year," I answered.

Mudjet took the flowers from me. "I should not be gone long."

"Take your time. Visit with Nuray, she is so fond of you. It is a fine day. What will they say of me in Ephesus if you tell them I made you hurry back to attend on me?"

She made a face. "Probably that I am the worst of chaperones in that I am going to dally about in town when I should be using this opportunity to bar the door against Caesar."

"You should try that," I replied, eyeing the remaining flowers in my hand critically. "He enjoys a challenge."

Mudjet gave me a playful shove. "Try not to get into all of the trouble while I am gone, my lady."

"Heavens, no!" I exclaimed dramatically. "If I do that, how will I fill the rest of this indeterminate exile?"

Her high laughter floated back to me as she trotted down the hill.

I went back inside with the flowers I had cut and filled a small vase with water from the cistern. I placed the vase on my dressing table and began straightening things that were out of place. I walked over towards the window to shake out a curtain when I was diverted by the stacks of Caesar's papers all over my other table. I leafed through several vapidly, since my Latin remained rather deficient.

I would have moved on had not one page on the pile caught my eye. Even in my relative ignorance, I understood the words *de bello Alexandrino.*

I should not be surprised, I told myself. Everyone spoke of Caesar's erudite commentaries on the Gallic wars, and people assumed he would write of the conflicts with Pompey. It was only natural that the events of the last several years would figure into the narrative of the larger civil war. I shuffled through the pages, attempting to process any of the words written in Caesar's neat hand until I reached the last sentence on the last page. It trailed off into the empty void of the past and my suspect Latin, though like the words that had led me here, even I could see by fragments.

Here was written of the nameless youngest daughter of Ptolemy Auletes, who saw an empty throne in Egypt and escaped to the rebel camps of Achillas the Greek, to wage war against her siblings. She quarrels with the commander and two of them are left suspended in time circling one another, waiting for Caesar to come and tell them of their ultimate fates like the Pythia sailing from Delphi. I passed a finger over her description, wondering if this princess of ink and reeds could weave her own story.

"Looking for something, curious kitten?"

I looked up at Caesar leaning in the doorway. "Oh, just seeing what the gossips in Rome will be saying about all of us next year," I gave a small flick of the papers in my hand.

He came over and examined them over my shoulder. "Ah, yes, well this one is still a work in progress."

"Clearly. You have not even covered the actual siege yet. Or the fact that you eventually prevailed. No Roman is going to want read a book where the ending is a cheeky adolescent princess dancing past a disorganized legion," I said in amusement.

He pretended to be annoyed. "I haven't had the leisure to get past that point because the cheeky adolescent princess in question kept me too busy fighting a full-scale rebellion she orchestrated." He reached over to pull me to him. "And now the audacious child dares to upbraid me for my sloth in the matter when she keeps me a slave to her desires day and night!"

I smirked. "You are a free man, sir. Go find a brothel in town where you can write your memoirs in peace. I am sure that is where you told your men you were anyway."

"Ha! It is true. My captain jested with me that I must have found an uncommon whore indeed that kept me so engaged. I told him I would've invited him to join me, but this brothel had no pretty young men for him."

"What did he say?"

"Oh, he said he was astonished that I could bear the establishment then," replied Caesar with a wicked grin.

I shook my head, laughing. "Perhaps Mudjet is right. I should have barred the door."

"It is precious that either of you think that could stop me at this point," he said pressing his teeth into my neck gently.

"That is what I told her."

He raised his head to study the manuscript in his hand. "I don't know, I rather like a version of this story where you slip your traces like the falcon you are and sail off in the clouds of history."

I slid out of his grasp and shot him a playful look. "Ah, except then you would not be able to come catch me, my lord!"

"Never fear, I would catch you, sweet one. But that story is one for myself, not for bored men in Rome." He sat down on my couch and motioned to me with mock command. "Come now and let me tell you about the time I was kidnapped by pirates."

"Everyone knows of that. Though if you wish to recount the tale all the same, I will try to become giddy at your cleverness at the appropriate moments."

"Hmph, saucy thing. Now come over here and listen. It really is a good story."

I went over to him and curled myself into the crook of his arm as he began to tell of the great battle of wits between him and the pirates who had taken his ship hostage so many years ago, when he was a renegade boy outrunning the anger of ruthless Sulla. Resting my head on his shoulder, I smiled quietly as the young Caesar berated the pirates for setting such a paltry ransom for him, but began to grow drowsy as he forced

his captors to cater to his whims while he awaited the arrival of his payment and his revenge. Not because Caesar was not an engaging story-
teller, indeed, even my poor friend Cicero praised his adversary's orato-
ry. But rather because I was being granted a moment of the rarest sort in
these years of my life — a moment where I felt safe enough to lay aside
the vigilance that hung on the edges of my days and steeped the darkness of my nights. Caesar was no doubt still the leopard I thought he was
when he arrived, yet being in his arms was the closest I had come to the
embrace of my Lord in the Waking World. For whatever that might au-
gur.

"I fear I'm boring my falcon goddess," he remarked.

"No, I am listening. Go on."

"But now I am distracted. I must know what that smile of yours
means. I think you are laughing at an old man, Your Highness."

I shook my head. "No, I am simply happy."

"Is that what that looks like? I don't know if I have ever seen you wear
it before."

"Is it any wonder?" I asked.

"No, but I wonder if I should ever tire of looking at it."

"Hm. Roman flatteries."

"You may think that if you want to, but I have sworn to convince you
otherwise if I can. Do not underestimate me, my lady."

"Hardly. One could argue that is the lesson of this little escapade of
yours amongst the pirates."

"Only an Egyptian would mistake a swashbuckling tale of adventure
for some kind of sermon!" he said, exasperated.

"What can I say, sir? We have meticulous standards for our entertain-
ment and we can smell a stealthy parable far before it arrives. You shall
have to give up your grand ambitions and become a scraping tutor, lec-
turing as your people would say, ad nauseum."

He groaned. "Gods forbid! I want to convince blithering old Marcus
Tullius to go back to Athens to do that sort of thing, but I have no intention of joining him."

I pulled my mouth into a haughty frown while my eyes sparkled. "Ah,
now you have gone and offended me greatly, my lord. For Sir Marcus is

a friend of mine and if you have any care for my person, I will not allow you to send him away against his will."

Caesar scoffed. "A friend, indeed! I'll have you know, my little scholar, that you can't believe everything they say about that puffed-up blabber mouth."

"I can form my own opinions, if you please," I replied. "It is not hearsay I am relying on. Sir Marcus paid me the great honor of a visit once, as well as presenting me with traveling clothes fit for a queen when I left Rome." I looked at him sideways. "Which is more than I can say for other supposedly noble Romans."

"I am agog. When was this, you minx?"

"Oh, when you were off in Africa or Pontus or some such. Certainly not somewhere paying me half so much court as you do now."

He shook his head, amused. "Cicero the secret monarchist. Who would have known? Though I suppose since it was by your charms he was so seduced, I can't blame him."

I rose up and went over to my dressing table where I opened the small box I kept my mother's bracelet and the silver *fibulae*, my only bits of jewelry. The latter I took and placed in Caesar's hand.

He turned them over one by one, studying them and then meeting my eyes above their pale shine. "I shall have to be careful indeed when I bring you back to Rome, my goddess. I knew the plebs were fond of you, though I had no idea I might have rivals for my suit!"

"Rivals, indeed!" I pretended to be insulted. "Do not make such sordid insinuations about what was a lovely *respectful* conversation. You should try something like it sometime."

"I do, my sweet, but I get very distracted when you huffily toss your head like that. It's quite beguiling and suddenly being respectful doesn't have much appeal. What did you talk about, fussy Marcus and you?"

"Oh, many things," I said. "Cato and Stoicism and the Republic. And your own person, which should please you."

"I am torn between deep gratification that you might have been thinking of me even a little back then and dismay that your companion in that conversation was a man with such a set against me. You shouldn't listen to all of his tall tales — he has always been fond of exaggerating."

"Says the man telling me pirate stories," I snickered. I paused. "He warned me about you."

He rolled his eyes. "I miss the days when Cato was our pet Cassandra — at least he was born that way. Cicero used to be more diverting."

"He was not incorrect," I pointed out. "The pity is that I am too foolish to heed him, apparently."

Caesar frowned thoughtfully, deepening the creases on his face. "No, my love. He is the fool for having met you and not recognizing that you are more than a match for me. Or any man. He and I, our collection of years flows largely behind us. But you, you have not yet reached your crowning years and look at all you have managed. Any man who meets you and does not fly after you as I have done is more the fool for letting you get away."

I went out to work in the garden as another day wound itself towards night while Caesar napped in my room. After a time, Mudjet left the kitchen to join me, settling herself against the trunk of one of the olive trees.

"Do you need my help, my lady?"

I wrenched out a weed. "No, I am fine. I simply figured I should expend some effort on our weeds if we do not wish to be overrun." I looked up at her with a smile. "Though I would be pleased to have you stay and converse with me as I do. The aromas from the house smell heavenly, I am enthralled by the thought of dinner."

She gave me a gratified look. "I am trying some new herbs with the lamb shank. I hope you and the Consul are pleased by it."

"I am sure I will find it mouth-watering. As for the Consul, he is welcome to go elsewhere if he is unhappy."

Mudjet scoffed. "I could serve him twigs, my lady, and he would declare them ambrosia as long as I do not try to keep you from him. If he were a beardless boy, it would be rather sweet."

"And because he is not?"

Her mouth twitched with impatience. "I am only sorry that the gods have sent my peerless queen a Jason when I wished a Leander for her."

I chuckled as I dug around the base of a particularly stubborn weed. It may have not been the Hellespontos, but I could not say the Lord of Rome had not swam for love of me. "I do not know, being Medea has always sounded like much more fun than being Hero, wasting away her nights with waiting."

My companion's face clouded slightly. "I am more worried that my lady is Creusa in this story. And if that is so, we know who Medea is."

"Ha, if my sister had had a chariot of winged snakes, you would think it would have come up before now."

My joke restored some of her good spirits. "It certainly would have changed the complexion of our war somewhat," she said. "Though if we had all known my lady possessed the talents to exhaust Caesar so, we probably would have overrode Ganymedes' defenses of Your Majesty's virtues in the interest of shortening the whole affair."

"Dear me, that would have been wicked of you all," I replied. "Though I once offered as such to Sekhmet, but she said it was not my path."

"It would seem the gods changed their minds," Mudjet noted drily.

I thought about her words. "Not exactly. I believe what she meant was it was not for me to come to Caesar as a supplicant as my sister did. That it was their will that he come to me after I showed myself to be his equal. Though that sounds unduly pretentious on my part."

"No, you have the right of it. It is exactly as Sir Marcus told you in Rome. You are his Penthesilea, not his Briseís."

I tossed my head to shake a tendril of hair out of my eye. "That might remain to be seen, my sweet."

Mudjet was about answer me with some retort or another, but the sportive expression on her face fell into one of mild dismay instead. I started to question her when a cheery voice called out, "My lady! Mudjet!" I turned to see Nuray crossing the gate with a wave.

I gave Mudjet a small shrug and waved back. "Hello, my dear! How are you?"

She reached us and smiled. "Well, my lady, thank you. And you? I'm sorry I've missed our suppers together recently, but Master Xenos has been in a strange mood for nearly a fortnight. He has kept me so busy I could barely slip away to return this shawl Mudjet left by mistake with me," she said, pulling the garment out of her basket.

"Thank you, *kharsheret*," said Mudjet, reaching out to take the veil while looking at me pointedly, "though I am sure the *megabyos* has his reasons for his actions."

I arched an eyebrow at her. "Never mind that, we are very glad to see you. You must tell us all the news from town."

"Oh, there is not that much to tell, Your Highness. All the old stories and quarrels, though there is a rumor that the high priestess means to step down next spring. All of the priestesses are in a froth over who will be her successor."

"Can we speak to the *megabyzoi* on behalf of your candidacy?"

"What an idea, my lady!" laughed Nuray. "You can, if you wish the college to think that your exile has addled your wits!"

The three of us giggled. "I suspect the city already sees us as mildly eccentric," Mudjet said. "Why not go full hock into pleasant capriciousness?"

I began to reply when another voice interrupted me. "The smells wafting from the kitchen are exceptional, Mudjet! What are you making?"

We all twisted around to see Caesar standing in the doorway with his head buried in a handful of papers. Our collective muddled silence pulled his eyes from the pages and he registered Nuray's additional presence for the first time. "Ah, forgive me, my falconess, I didn't realize you were entertaining."

Truthfully, I had hoped Caesar might remain asleep while Nuray was there. Not because I did not trust her discretion, but rather because I felt responsible for her in my way. She was not so much younger than I, yet we were at those ages when a few years made a difference in how we approached the world. I knew intellectually that she was no doe-eyed naïf, yet she maintained an innocence that I often found strangely enviable. Part of me nursed an urge to protect her from the world outside of tranquil Ephesus, maybe because I saw in her a mirror of myself. An Arsinoë that had experienced a peaceful life, or something approaching one. This same part of me was afraid of hurting my friend if too much of my former life seeped into this place. Caesar offered her no harm, but I knew the unintentional damage the likes of us could do to others.

Aside from these flights of my own fancy, it was obvious that Xenos disapproved of our guest and I did not want to intentionally cause her to be disobedient to his wishes that his priestesses keep a low profile until Caesar left the city. Though at this point it was too late for that, so I made a dismissive gesture nonchalantly. "There is nothing to forgive. Nuray has been our friend since our arrival, we are not bound to formalities."

"It is only lamb, sir," said Mudjet, answering his initial question. "The merchants in town had some new spices I wanted to try."

"I'm surprised you have to go all the way to town for such things, my dear, when you have this wonderful garden right here," Caesar said with a sweep of his arm. "Indeed, I feel it must be enchanted, for every time I step into it there are more lovely girls growing here."

Nuray went scarlet, and I gave him a waggish look of reprimand. "Careful, sir, this one belongs to the Lady of the Moon."

He laughed and held up his hands. "It is a statement of fact, Your Highness, nothing more. Do not tell Artemis Far-Sighted that I meant offense!"

The little priestess found her voice again. "I am very sorry, my lady," she whispered. "I didn't realize *you* were entertaining."

I gave her a pat on the hand. "Nonsense, do not pay him any mind. He is not even supposed to be here. Ask anyone."

"Where *are* you supposed to be, sir?" asked Mudjet, her eyes dancing.

Caesar shrugged. "Rhodes? Hispania? Who knows? I can assure you wherever it is, it is infinitely less enjoyable."

"Roman flatteries!" muttered Mudjet, with a crooked grin.

I gave a little huff of laughter at them both, before I realized Nuray sat rigidly pale, her eyes afraid both to leave Caesar's and to keep their stare. "Really, dearest, it is quite all right. You are safe with me, his lordship is not altogether as bad as his reputation suggests," I said to her gently, ducking Caesar's wolfish smirk in my direction.

Nuray relaxed enough to break her pose, gripping my hand. "I just don't understand why your lady sister need send one of her Roman lackeys to spy on you," she said, her face earnest. "You have done nothing wrong and I do not like the way this old centurion speaks to you." She delivered the last bit with her courage screwed up so that she did not appear to care whether she was overheard or not.

I was so taken aback by her fierce defense of me that it was Mudjet who put together their meaning first. Throwing her hands over her mouth to control her laughter, she failed to hold back a shriek of amusement as she spun to look at Caesar. "Ah, your fame does not proceed you here to the feet of Artemis of the Hoof and Claw, sir! How tragic for your famous Roman *dignitas*!"

"You wound me more with your hilarity, Mudjet. So cruel are the ladies of Egypt!" he pouted.

Realizing that I had not been punctual with introductions, so long had it been since I had been with anyone who had not known the Consul on sight, I tried to think of a way to correct the oversight without putting poor Nuray in any more of an awkward position. "Sir, do you have a *denarius* on you?" I asked Caesar, breaking up his sparring with Mudjet.

He reached into the purse at his waist and produced a coin, pretending to be exasperated. "Alas, once they get their talons in one, always do women start looking for money!" He tossed the *denarius* to me with a wink.

I reached out, catching it and passing it to Nuray face up. She took it from me puzzled, until Mudjet caught her eye gave her a significant look towards Caesar and then down to the coin. Nuray studied it for several moments before her eyes went wide and darted to me, panic-struck.

I smiled to put her at ease as I raised a finger to my lips. "As I said, my friend, it is quite all right and you should not be afraid, but we should probably not speak too loudly of it."

"Indeed little one, Her Majesty is a subtle creature who affects an air that I am far too beneath her to be spoken of in the same sentence," Caesar said.

I rolled my eyes at him as I returned my attention to the priestess. "The Consul is here on a reconnaissance assignment because he is planning to campaign in Parthia next year, and I am showing him hospitality as is my duty as a subject of my sister and of Rome's ally, Egypt."

Mudjet snorted unhelpfully, though Nuray did not seem to hear her. "That's rather unfair of the Queen, isn't it? I mean, you were his prisoner, and now you have to pretend that you're friends?"

"You do not know my sister, dearest. This is the kind of punishment she will hate herself for not thinking of for me, but this is not her doing. The Consul asked of me this favor and I freely consented."

"But why?"

With a small frown of thought, I looked past her to Caesar, meeting his eyes. "The path he and I have walked together is not a simple one, yet he has been honorable to me when given the opportunity. I have little to offer here in return for any such kindnesses, so doing this does not seem unduly burdensome."

"It is so, wee moon priestess," agreed Caesar, the jesting tone in his voice ebbing away. "As you know, Princess Arsinoë is a fine lady with few equals. It has been a blight on my fortunes to so often been forced to be her adversary. It pleases me that we may meet the future as friends."

Nuray did not appear completely convinced, though I saw Mudjet studying me acutely from where she stood.

On our last night, we did our best to push the morning back. I fought with myself not to cling too tightly, lest I lose the last tatters of my resistance, even though I knew it was futile.

Caesar ran his fingers through my hair. "Don't be sad, my love. This the beginning, not the end."

I blinked back a tear. "I almost believe you."

"Ah, then I've made good on my promise to win you over. I am delighted," he said, unable to hide the triumph in his voice.

"And I am still a silly girl. I do not have my sister's art, I cannot hold my heart back in anything. That is why I shall always be her subordinate in all things. Even in our dealings with you."

Caesar stopped his hand's meandering and held fast the back of my head. "That's not true. It is an honor to win your heart, Arsinoë. You are loving, but you were raised in a hard house that taught you not to trust unthinkingly. To have come through that fire and not be cold because of it is a gift, not a curse. It means you still have the ability to find happiness. It is why I need you; I need your strength, but I need your heart more. I told you my wife Cornelia was the love of my youth, I fought for her when Sulla ordered me to divorce her. I want to feel that again, and I have begun to remember with you."

"I am not so virtuous," I said, turning away. "Lady Cornelia deserves such adulation. Remember I am a Ptolemy, I have spilled blood and blood has been spilled for me."

"You did what needed to be done. Your soldiers fought for you until the end because they believed you were worth fighting for. That is rare."

"I brought death to the man who might have defeated you, I did so out of fear and pride like a child rather than a queen."

"Achillas was a braggart and a fool, and he would have come to a sticky end anyway. You were right to have Ganymedes kill him when he did."

I winced, dropping my gaze. "Ganymedes did not kill Achillas. I did."

Caesar's eyes narrowed. "You killed him?"

Saying the words aloud brought back the enormity of my guilt. There might have been women who would have been proud to admit such a feat of blood to a man like Caesar, though I was not one of them. I remembered my brother serving up Pompey's head to him that first day in Alexandria. He might not be easily shocked, but he was capable of being disgusted. I held back a shudder.

"Yes. There was no time and I had to have it done before he suspected that I knew he was at best going to sell me to you and Cleopatra for some temporary advantage or another."

"And at worst?"

"He was going to steal the throne of Egypt from Ptolemy by tricking me into marrying him and proclaiming him Pharaoh."

He nodded in understanding. "He would have had you killed as soon as he secured his position." His brow furrowed as he searched his memory. "I was told he was stabbed to death — you stabbed him?"

"I had no time to brew a poison. As I said, I do not have the foresight of my sister."

He touched my shoulder and I tried not to shrink from his hand. "You tell me this with shame, though this just confirms all I admire in you. I have seen and done too much to be a good husband to a sheltered gentlewoman. But you have seen what I have seen and you have not let it harden you. You feel pity for killing a man who would've fed your entrails to his dogs if it suited him. I know you still care for siblings that are the biggest nest of vipers I have ever encountered outside of a Greek play. This is your strength."

I was comforted by his confidence in me, though any relief I might have felt in my admission was clouded by a seeping sadness. "I am still angry at him. And Ptolemy. And probably my father for raising us to fight amongst ourselves. Perhaps he thought that through competition the best prince would rise, but in the end all it has accomplished is the eclipse of his line."

Caesar looked at me seriously. "Do not waste anger on the dead, my love. They are far from us and we only end up injuring ourselves. People assumed I wept crocodile tears for Pompey when he was killed, but in death, I forgot our differences. They didn't matter anymore."

I cast a sidelong glance at him. "You are crafty, sir. You come to me on bended knee with your flatteries about how much you require my assistance, then you complete your seduction so you might lecture me once more with your vast experience."

Caesar's expression lightened. "A little contempt is worth the price to see the ghost of a smile from you again. I don't want to think of leaving you so melancholy tomorrow. You persist in thinking that I have had my fill of you, when the only reason I am departing with such haste is to keep you safe from your enemies until I can shield you myself at my side. If you cannot have faith in me, at least have faith in my intentions."

"Hm, you told me when you arrived that you had no intentions."

"I was unsure. Remember, I still felt I barely knew you. What I had glimpsed in Egypt and in Rome intrigued me, but what if exile had broken you? Instead I found a queen remained: sad yet dignified, witty yet kind, cautious yet unafraid. I am supposed to be the most jaded of men, and yet here I lie practically begging you to trust me."

I sighed heavily. "I do trust you, as much folly as that might be. I have fallen in love with you unwisely, but not carelessly. Do not forget that."

He grinned. "Never. The gods gave me Cornelia to tame my impetuous youth; they gave me you to tame my prideful dotage, poor pet."

I cast my eyes upward helplessly. "May they protect me. First they spur me to liberate Egypt from the mightiest army in the world, then failing that, they task me with bridling Gaius Caesar. At least I know if I am sent to the land of the damned in the next life they will be hard pressed to create more exacting punishments for me."

He chuckled and gave me a long kiss. "It might not be as arduous as you think. If I hear my name from your lips again, I will be hard pressed to meet the tide."

It was barely dawn when he began dressing. I watched from the bed, existing in that moment as much as possible. Finally, I rose and loosely put on my shift as I walked over to him.

Caesar bent over among his belongings and retrieved a small gold ring strung on a leather strap. He took my hand and placed it in my palm. "I will have you believe I am coming back."

I had seen the ring many times before, though I had not studied it closely. I cast my mind back to the first time I had ever seen Caesar in Alexandria and I could remember the strap peeking out of his armor. I turned it over in my hands and read the inscription on the inside of the plain band. *Ivlia Caesaris.*

I looked up at him, startled. "You cannot give me this."

"Of course I can. I gave it to Julia just before her wedding. When she died, I took it back to remember her by. It is a simple ring because she was a woman who needed no adornment. I loved her as my daughter, but I admired her as a woman. I have had the good fortune to have known many remarkable women, but very few whom I truly respect. She was one, so are you. I will ask her to seek the gods' protection for you, and when I return, I will replace this ring with something you can call your own."

I slipped the thong over my head. "I would tell you to keep yourself safe, but I know you will not heed me."

"I'll be fine. Let me wrangle those old men in Rome, and I will be back at your door before you know it. Dream of riding across the Tigris with me."

We walked to the outer doorway of my house and stopped on the threshold, Caesar on the outside, me on the inside. Our hands held those of the other and words no longer seemed necessary.

At last I said softly, "May sweet winds fill your sails."

He leaned down and kissed my forehead. "Don't be afraid. I hold you fast in my heart."

Caesar turned away and started down the hill towards town. He looked back once and neither of us moved. After a long moment, he continued down the hill. With his back receding from me, I rested against the doorpost. I finally stepped away when I began to fear I would be changed to stone. I wandered back into the house, stopping in the doorway of Mudjet's room.

She looked up from the wool skeins she was counting. "Is he gone?"

I nodded.

She held my gaze, and I was surprised to see a kind of hesitation in her violet eyes. "May I ask my lady a rather impertinent question?"

"When have I ever asked you to curb your tongue for me, my sweet?"

Mudjet bit her lip. "He took so much from you, my precious friend. Your home, your crown, your people, many of those who held you dear. Then he came across the sea with the boldness of Theseus and helped himself to all you had left. How does your heart find its way out of such a forest of pain to love him?"

I crossed the room to where she sat and knelt down at her feet, taking her hands in mine. "I know how foolish it sounds, I know how traitorous to those whose memories I bind in my very *ka* it seems. My defense to them is no doubt weak, and that is something the Lord of the West will judge me on one day. All I can say to you, most perfect of all friends, is that my heart forgives the things he did because, unlike everyone else who has ever raised a hand to me, he did all without malice. His war with me was political, not personal. My own blood sought my life, but he never did. That I can forgive."

She nodded solemnly. "Then that is that, my lady. Such clemency of spirit is worthy of a *hemet-netjer*. May the wolf of Roman prove himself worthy to touch even the hem of the gown of such a *heqat* as mine."

I leaned down to kiss her hands. "In generosity of spirit, I have had no nobler teacher than you, Mudjet. You allow for all my shortcomings and yet you love me anyway without reservation."

She wrapped her arms around me. "The Lady of Heavenly Affection laced our *ka*s together before we knew her name, my lady. We have no reservations between each other."

As I sat down with Mudjet that evening, we ate quietly and I believed that I was at bottom lucky. At best, I had the love of a fascinating salamander of a man who said he wanted to lay the world at my feet and reunite me with my brother. At worst, I had enjoyed a few days of sunshine in my life far from my home with no serious consequences.

Though, a few weeks later when I was weak with nausea and unable to even bear the thought of food, let alone empire, I remembered that there are always consequences.

Chapter Forty-Four

"We should tell Xenos."

I removed the damp cloth over my eyes and turned to the sound of Mudjet's voice. She sat next to my bed mending a cloak. She had been silent for a while, perhaps hoping I would sleep, but had apparently given up.

I tamped down a spasm of vertigo before I answered. "I am not convinced there is anything he can do about the situation. Unless he can exorcise a demon," I replied weakly.

"He might be able to," Mudjet said with a smile. "Though you will feel better once you can keep more broth down."

I made a noncommittal noise, then breathed out heavily. "I suppose we must. It will be apparent soon enough anyway."

"We should invite him to dinner tonight. And Nuray, she should come also."

"Very well, but you will eat with us. I need your clear head in this, too."

She nodded, pleased that I was agreeing with her. "I will try to make up something to tempt your appetite."

"A lost cause!" I groaned.

"Ach, so little faith!" Mudjet clucked in amusement.

The *megabyos* responded that he would be enchanted to accept our invitation and arrived promptly at the appointed hour with Nuray whose face shone with delight to see us. As we settled before our meal, I tried to fight off another wave of nausea rising from the pit of my stomach.

"Ah, this looks excellent, Mudjet! Happy are the times I can spend in such agreeable company! And my lady, I am so pleased to see you up and about. We've missed you during your illness, I hope you are feeling better?"

I thought it best not to put off the topic since it had been so helpfully raised. "I am better today, sir. It is kind of you show such concern. But

456

I confess my recent indisposition is in part why we have asked you here, for I need your advice."

"I am yours to command, Your Majesty. I have lamented that you have not sent for a physician, I would be gratified to do so for you."

I shook my head. "No, I do not need a physician to diagnose me, my friend. And neither will you in another few months."

Xenos sat in stunned silence. Nuray looked at Mudjet and me in astonishment. I bent down to try the soup in front of me. "This is quite good, my dear," I said to my companion. "Well done."

Finally the priest recovered himself enough to respond. "I thought of saying something to you that night, my child. To warn..."

I waved my hand. "I know. But I was fully aware of the position I was putting myself in and I can plead no ignorance. I am no innocent and what has happened has happened. It is the will of the gods."

"Careful, my lady. It appears there are at least a couple more wills at play here than those of the gods," he replied archly, though his expression remained indulgent.

"Fairly put. Though as I said, I would like your counsel on how I should proceed. I know I do not live in temple precincts, though I feel I have played loosely with the protection offered to me here by Lady Artemis. Would she accept any offering I would make in amends?"

"She will be pleased by your sentiments, Your Majesty. I'm sure we can find a suitable token to give to her. Though I believe your more pressing issues are temporal in nature."

"I agree, Your Grace."

"Does the Consul know?"

"No," I admitted. "I have relayed no message."

"Has he given any assurances of regard to you?"

I felt an uncalled-for blush rising in my cheeks. I realized that I had since been trying to put things Caesar had said to me out of my mind to shield myself.

"Yes," I at length answered, "though if I search my feelings, I discover that I have been placing as little weight on them as possible as a precaution."

He nodded approvingly. "That is probably wise. Nonetheless, I think it important to find out his intentions on the matter, so we must contact him immediately."

"It would have to be in strictest secrecy. If it was told to my sister..." My voice trailed off.

"Of course. I will find a priest to send who can be entrusted with discretion and for whom we can concoct a plausible cover. It would be best if you could think of a manner of cipher to put the message in that would be discernible to the Consul and not obvious to anyone else, to be safe.

I bit my lip. "I will think of something."

"Good. If you can manage by the morning, we will send our messenger with the first tide. And Nuray," he turned to the young priestess, "I wish you to stay here and tend to her ladyship for the next few months. Mudjet will need your help."

"Yes, sir. It will be my pleasure," Nuray remained discombobulated, but met my eye and smiled encouragingly.

I sighed appreciatively. "I thank you all from the bottom of my heart. I am truly blessed to have friends such as you to guide me."

Xenos grinned. "It is our honor to assist the Queen of Egypt, my lady." He clapped his hands together in amusement. "Well, for the home of a royal lady living in remote exile, I must say I have most stimulating meals here! Truly the Egyptians are blessed with a talent for the sensational!"

That night I sat at my table and worked to compose my message. For a long time I simply stared at the sheet, unable to think of what to say. I remembered the face Caesar had made when my sister announced the impending birth of my nephew, did I have any right to expect any more than she received from him? Would he think this had been my scheme all along as it had been hers? How would I tell him how afraid I was? I wracked my brain until nearly dawn, then Euripides came to my rescue. I dipped my pen in ink and called on captive Andromache to speak the words I could not:

Now aforetime for all my misery,
I ever had a hope to lead me on, that if my child were safe,

I might find some help and protection from my woes.

I prayed that the words would be true.

It was not the most pleasant time of year to be traveling across the sea to Rome, but Xenos thought it best to allow for no delay. Part of me wondered if I should have simply waited until spring when Caesar said he would return. However, a smaller, lonelier voice told me to not hold him to his word. My proofs were little, and Cleopatra still kept court in Latium. All I could do was watch the ship carrying my message drift out of the harbor and disappear into the horizon. And hope.

Nearly two month had passed in this way since the priest had left. The days grew warmer again as spring flushed against the last of winter's touch. I had managed to successfully weave a new *himation* that I worked on embroidering while Mudjet and Nuray stitched together a pillowy mountain of small *tunicas*. We dried herbs and told old stories.

Then at last, as we were sitting outdoors winding wool between ourselves, Nuray spotted a figure coming up the path. The young priest looked exhausted by the time he reached us, so Mudjet flew inside to fetch him some wine. She returned and motioned to Nuray that they should withdraw and leave me with the messenger.

The priest drank deeply. "Forgive my poor manners, my lady. I know you must be in haste."

"No, no. Please drink. You have made an arduous journey on my behalf. The very least I can do is show you a little patience and hospitality. Though when you are refreshed, I beg you to tell me everything."

He took another sip and began. "When we reached Rome, I knew I would have to spend a few days observing to find the most expedient way to reach Consul Caesar. I saw that whenever he left his villa, crowds would mob him and his retainers with written petitions. The *megabyos* and I assumed this would be the case and he warned me not to try to throw your letter in with that lot, where it might be missed or worse, read by someone other than the Consul's eyes. So I hung back around the villa and in the marketplace, talking with merchants and slaves until I was pointed in the direction of a young girl working in Caesar's kitchen. I gained her confidences by gifting her with a few amulets from our temple, since young maidens are always in need of Lady Artemis' protection. I probed her to see if it was possible to get an audience with her master under the guise of having business from the high priest of a private nature."

"Not entirely false."

The priest smiled. "Exactly, my lady. Part of a truth works much better than an elaborate lie."

He continued, "This young woman was very helpful. She told me I would need a way to persuade the house steward to allow me that kind of access since he ultimately controlled the flow of people in the villa. I asked her if there was any help the steward might need of Artemis that I could provide him. She looked doubtful for a moment and then brightened, remembering that the steward's son had a wife who was soon to deliver her first child. Master Xenos had of course made sure I left with many amulets blessed with Our Lady in her power as Artemis Eileithyia, Goddess of Childbed, so I produced several to smooth our path with the steward. She told me that her master was having a small dinner party at the house three nights hence and she would see to it that I would get a chance to speak with the steward."

"You must have been successful," I observed, holding back my impatience to hear what the priest had learned.

"Indeed, my lady. The steward was a gruff older man, as you might expect, but that meant he had proper reverence for our temple and agreed to look for a moment where Caesar was relatively alone so I might place the letter with him.

"I was permitted to wait in the kitchens where I was also most generously fed. Finally the steward fetched me, saying that his master was sitting with Decimus Albinus, an old friend, and that was probably as good an opportunity as I was likely to get. I was ushered into the presence of the men and the steward told the Consul my name and that I traveled on business from the temple in Ephesus.

"Caesar seemed to give me his attention and asked if indeed I came on temple business. I responded that my elder, the *megabyos* had sent me. His lordship was very quick to pick up the difference and he took the message as I held it out to him. He read it impassively, paused briefly, and then turned to the other gentleman, asking him to excuse us for a moment while he answered this letter. The gentleman agreed and laughed at his commander for always working.

"Caesar then escorted me into his *tablinum*. He motioned for me to take a seat as he pulled out a piece of paper, and asked me if I knew the contents of your letter. I told him that I knew the information, but not its manner of delivery. He then asked if you were well when I had seen you last, and I said that you had been a bit distempered in body, but lively in spirit. He chuckled at that and called you a clever girl who plays the pretty dove but is secretly a falcon goddess. 'But I must show the exiled Queen of Egypt that she isn't the only one who knows her Euripides,' he said."

The priest handed me a letter. "He wrote this, and told me that it was imperative that it reach you, my lady."

I took the letter in my hand and tried not to appear too apprehensive as I broke the seal. I also tried not to feel too ridiculously pleased when I read his reply:

> *But with all that I would ask about these times,*
> *I now know not where I may first begin...*
> *I to thee, and thou to me. And after these long, long years*
> *I have at last discovered the tricks of the gods.*
> *But these tears, in gladness shed,*
> *are tears of thankfulness rather than sorrow.*

(You're a marvel, my love. Look for my sails on the horizon, I am flying to fetch you both.)

I rested and waited mostly after this. The draining sickness of early pregnancy ebbed out of me like a low tide, and I made practical plans about traveling. I cherished the hope that Caesar would indeed manage to bring Ptah with him.

The thought of holding my brother again in my arms again was such a delirious dream that I could barely envision what it would be like. I wondered how much taller he would be, how the sound of his voice would be changed. Though it was not just for my own gratification that I wished this opportunity for Ptah. To fight with Caesar, to learn how to handle an army from the most astute of generals, this was the proper school for the Pharaoh of Egypt. Cleopatra might hold authority now, but the people of the Nile would always look to their king to lead them, especially into battle. I remembered how the lords rallied to Ptolemy, even as I won them victories and Cleopatra had the most stable power base. I reached into the past and thought of Hatshepsut, the noble Queen-Pharaoh who built Djeser-Djeseru, who fueled the greatness of Thutmose. Surely this could be Ptah's destiny as well.

I am wandering the halls of a palace by a black lake. I make my way down a columned veranda that opens onto a large airy portico. There is a figure wearing the *hedjet*, the tall white crown of Upper Egypt, seated with his back to me as I step out into the night air. There is also a creature sitting at attention by his side, a small, oddly-shaped beast that rears its head back in my direction as I approach, its long teeth gleaming in the moonlight. The figure reaches down to stroke the head of the creature, an action which seems to calm it. I falter in my advance, for I see that it is not the *hedjet* crown the figure wears, but the *Atef*, its ostrich feathers fluttering in the soft breeze as it blows off the lake.

"Hello, Ptolemy-daughter," says the figure in a melodious voice whose edges have been worn smooth by centuries of time.

"My lord," I whisper. "You are most unexpected."

I walk until I am standing next to him at the portico's edge. The figure turns to look at me and smiles gently, his deep eyes glowing slightly against the dark green cast of his skin. Bound in his white wrappings, Osiris — Lord of the Western Lands of the Dead, Judger of Souls, the Slain God — offers me a seat by his side with one partially wound arm.

As I lower myself onto the bench, he nods approvingly, then returns his gaze to the lake. We sit like this for a time. The moon reaches down to touch the rippling surface of the water. The thought that I am dead crosses my mind.

"You are not dead, Ptolemy-daughter."

I turn back towards Osiris, who is studying me kindly. "Well, that is reassuring," I answer. "Especially in *her* presence." I gesture to the beast, its red eyes blazing like rubies in the otherwise soft darkness. She makes a low growl, though the sound carries a distinct note of indifference.

"Ammit will not harm you," says the dead god. "As you can see, this is not the Lake of Fire."

We lapse into another thoughtful silence. The reason for which the Lord of the Reborn has chosen to appear to me seems not to be one he is in a hurry to divulge. But then again, time works strangely for the gods of the Underworld. And it is difficult to imagine the mummy-wound Osiris rushing to do anything.

I decide to be the impetuous one. "How may I serve you, my lord?"

He slowly turns to me again. "There are only two paths in the Land of the Dead. One is the path of Right which leads to the Field of Reeds and immortality. The other is the path of the Damned, and you know where that leads..." He glances down to Ammit who yawns widely and stretches her long front limbs. "There is little in the way of choice."

I nod, though I choose to remain silent. I expect that Osiris is not finished.

He continues. "You face difficult choices ahead of you, Ptolemy-daughter."

"Much of life is difficult choices, my lord."

He nods. "Indeed. But soon you will hold several lives in your hand and you will be the arbiter of who will live and who will come to me. Because the scales of Ma'at demand balance. Some will live, though others must die in their place. This is the cosmic order. This is the way of the living."

I shudder involuntarily, placing a hand on my stomach. "Why are you telling me of this?"

Osiris' closed-lipped smile widens slightly. "My younger brother is afraid you are prone to noble sacrifices. He wants me to dissuade you from laying down your life hastily."

"I do not want any others to die for me," I reply, shaking my head.

"I know, your heart is brave. But this matter also touches this one," he says as he carefully puts his hand over mine at my waist.

I feel panic rising in my throat. "I *will* do whatever needs to be done to protect my child."

"Whatever needs to be done can encompass many things, Ptolemy-daughter," he warns me in a calm voice. "Be careful of your words."

"What else can I do, my lord?" I demand quietly. "The Lord of the Red Land insisted on sending me a gift possessed of its own will and path. He and Caesar avow they will protect us, yet despite what they both think, neither is invincible. I know by now not to rely completely on the designs of men or gods."

"This is so, Ptolemy-daughter, though my younger brother is bending all of his will to protect her."

Her, flutters my *ka* at Osiris' words.

"But the power of your sister's *heka* remains strong." He shakes his head at the fear in my eyes. "No, do not be alarmed, she does not know. Yet her *heka* works to undo you, and this child is part of you. Also," he pauses with a slightly amused air, "it is unfair to you, Princess, to suggest that it was only my brother's influence that called the son of the Julians to you."

I do not want flattery, however well-meaning, to cloud the matter at hand. "If I died, would my child be safe?"

The Lord of the Dead's brow furrows. "The future is problematic to read. Sacrifices must be made, who makes those sacrifices is changeable.

It may come to pass that my brother's desires are thwarted and I will shortly meet your *ka* in my Hall. However, remember it often takes more courage to live than to die."

I do not know what to say to this. The moon is submerging itself into the lake in earnest now.

"Set is your murderer, my lord," I murmur at last, looking up into his dark eyes. "Why help him or me?"

Osiris smiles again. "Set is my brother, Ptolemy-daughter. We knew each other in the womb before the Nile took water. We embraced each other before there were stars in the sky. Love carves its name into the Book of Life more deeply than Hate is able. Take comfort in that."

And then I wake up.

Chapter Forty-Five

Several more weeks passed and I began to look to the west as the days continued to lengthen. I prayed against delay because despite Caesar's bravado, it would take most of the summer to mount an effective campaign in Parthia. Simply landing an army of the size needed would take time. I was sitting in the garden perched over maps calculating how quickly the legions could march inland, starting from Issus or maybe Tarsus, when I heard hurried voices from inside the house.

I went in and found Xenos, Mudjet, and Nuray huddled together in the hall. They abruptly stopped their conversation at my approach. The priest looked grave and my friends stricken.

"What is it?" I asked warily, even as my heart hammered and I was sure I did not want to know.

They glanced at one another and finally Xenos spoke, "My wretched Queen, we've had merchants from the west in port. The news is all over town... Caesar was murdered in the halls of the Senate and the Republic has been thrown into civil war once more."

I could think of nothing to say to this. The others stood watching me apprehensively, but I did nothing. I could not cry or scream because I could not breathe. My staggering mind groped for something to hold onto in the midst of its numbed shock, so I began to assess how another war in Rome would affect my exile, how it would affect Egypt.

"Is my sister still in Rome?" I inquired at last, breaking the weighty silence.

The priest was clearly surprised by my question. "No, my lady. She stayed until the funerary games, trying to get Mark Antony to endorse Caesarion as Caesar's heir. But his will designated his sister's grandson Octavian as the adoptive heir of his estate with no provisions for your nephew, so Cleopatra could not hope for any political cache for an unrecognized half-foreign son. She returned to Egypt to mobilize her fleet to fight the so-called Liberatores. It does her no good if the assassins win."

"It would if she were serious about an independent Egypt," I muttered. "A more republican Rome will have difficulty maintaining an empire."

"I believe she does not think the Liberatore faction can win, because apparently they did not manage to buy off Caesar's biggest power base."

"The army."

"Yes," said Xenos. "So the army will put its support behind Antony and the boy Octavian. The assassins will try to carry the day, though it is doubtful they can succeed."

I rolled my sister's options about in my mind. "So she is hoping to secure the patronage of either Antony or Octavian to maintain her own position."

"Or both," agreed the priest.

"No," I said slowly, shaking my head. "She cannot hope to have them both. They are allies in a common cause now, but Mark Antony has been by Caesar for years. He is ambitious enough that he must have hoped to gain more by the will than he did. If he has a chance to throw over an untested youth like Octavian, he will do so. Antony is the known quantity, she will go to him. Either way, we must continue to lie low here. The longer it is that my sister is distracted from thinking about me in these uncertain days, the better."

Mudjet moved towards me, but I stopped her. "I am fine, Mudjet," I said sharply. More sharply than I had intended. "However, I am tired and will go lie down for a while."

I returned to my room and laid down on the bed. I waited to feel something — anything — yet all I could feel was a leaden weight that pressed on my chest until I felt buried alive.

Eventually one emotion surfaced. Shame. I could not shake the thought that somehow I had brought this to pass. I reached beneath the neckline of my *chiton* to hold Julia's ring and thought of her. How she, as I had teased her father on that first night, had nearly cured Pompey of his love of glory. How she probably would have succeeded had she not died.

And then there was me, cursed bloodthirsty creature, who had gone along with Caesar's dreams of empire, agreed to help him. Knowing how unpopular those dreams were among men of his own kind who could hurt him. After seeing his old scars, knowing he was not invulnerable.

He had blazed through our lives like a hero out of myth, and I, as much a monstrous Ptolemy as any in my line, had destroyed him. Nothing in our path was ever spared. Even a whirlwind such as him could not withstand our poisonous touch.

Time dripped by as I laid there in my roiling thoughts. I heard footsteps pause by the doorway and then after a while move on. Slowly, I sank into a fitful sleep.

I am sitting on a dais in an empty vaulted room. I turn my head and Sekhmet appears at my side. She sits down next to me and gently folds back her lion's head hood. Her lovely face glows with an inner light and her sharp eyes warm like a stoked brazier.

I look away from her cow-eyed gaze to watch as long, graceful horns rise through her flowing jet hair. She is no longer Sekhmet Blood-Drinker, she has changed into her other Self. She has become Hathor, Lady of the Loving Ways. Without a word, she reaches for me and gathers me into her lap like a child. As warmth emanating from the core of her being wraps around my body, the growl in her voice softens to a purr.

"It is all right, Ptolemy-daughter. It is not your fault. Though you must let it out."

Her words seep through my veins and unstop my heart. In my life I keep believing that I have reached the summit of all of the grief my being can hold, but I am retaught by experience that there are always new sorrows in this world and they are adept at opening old wounds while they cut their own. Aching, silent sobs wrack my body as bitter tears pour down my face buried in the goddess' fragrant embrace. She murmurs wordlessly to me as I hold on to her for what might be a lifetime.

Eventually, I wake up.

When I opened my eyes, it was still dark. I pulled myself up, descended the stairs, and crossed the courtyard to the kitchen where I filled a bowl with grain. I grabbed a small jar of oil and poured a measure of beer into an empty carafe. I floated out of the house like a wraith, the collection of vessels the only things weighing me down. I walked the long, bladed path from the low cliffs until I reached the shore, where I placed my burdens on the rocky ground and began to gather up medium-sized stones. I balanced several flattish ones on top of one another, then picked up some smaller, prettier rocks and scattered then around the base of the pile. I put the bowl on the stones with the carafe next to it, then knelt before them and started to pour the oil into the grain. I did not need to think of the words that flowed out of my mouth from the depths of my memory:

"May his name be given to him in the Great House, and may he remember his name in the House of Fire on the night of counting the years and of telling the number of the months. He is with the Divine One, and he sits on the eastern side of heaven. If any god whatsoever should advance unto him, let him be able to proclaim his name forthwith."

I stirred the grain and oil together with one hand and reached over to take the carafe with the other, but my hand groped the empty air. I opened my eyes and saw Mudjet kneeling on the other side of the stones, the carafe in her hands. I scooped up part of the mixture in the bowl and she poured the beer out over my outstretched hands. She added:

"May his ib *be with him in the House of Hearts. May his heart be with him, and may it rest there, or we shall not eat of the cakes of Osiris on the eastern side of the Lake of Flowers, neither shall we have a boat wherein to go down the Nile, nor another wherein to go up, nor shall we be able to sail down the Nile with thee."*

I returned the mixed grain to the bowl:

"May his mouth be given to him that he may speak forthwith, and his two legs to walk therewith, and his two hands and arms to overthrow his foe. May the doors of heaven open unto him. His soul shall not be fettered to his body at the gates of the underworld; but he shall enter in peace and he shall come forth in peace."

We sat in silence as the very first light of dawn crept across the sky. I sighed and wiped my hands on the hem of my shift. "Tahu once reminded me that all of life is cyclical. I agreed, yet in my haste to outrun the past belonging to my family it seems I have fallen into the fate of your poor mother instead, my sweet."

"My mother's lot was a hard one," said Mudjet slowly, "yet she lived her life with no regrets, trusting always that the gods would light her way in the darkest hour. If a simple woman such as her could believe that, surely my *hemet-netjer* will keep her courage."

"You are right, as usual," I answered, shaking the last of my dream-grief and the rituals of The Book of Going Forth from my mind. "We should go back. We have left poor Nuray on her own. And we should start seriously attending to preparations for the coming months. It will be easier since we know we will be here."

Mudjet nodded and took my hand as we walked slowly back towards the house. As we rounded the hill and the house came into view, she said, "I think your sister's *heka* wrought this."

"It sounds like a great many daggers wrought this," I replied.

"No, I mean, your sister sends her *heka* against you in all things. Even if she does not know that the Consul was yours, her power would have pushed to crush him unwittingly because he would have fought for you."

"If that is so, it also means she is losing control of it. She should have been able to sense such a thing. She has stretched it too thin and now it burns unrelentingly."

Mudjet squeezed my hand. "It also means he did love you."

I gave a hopeless shrug. "It is a comforting thought, dearest. But it helps us little. You must help me learn to be a fortress for this child." I touched my stomach. "We are her fine generals now."

I set myself against this newest test put before me. I was on my own, although not alone, and I would have to prove myself equal to the task. As I had disciplined my body and my mind during my rebellion, I disciplined my heart as my body waxed heavy into the heat of summer. This coming little one was a gift from the gods to me and I would have to be as strong as they for her sake because she and I were not destined to live under the protection of her tenacious father. I prepared as best as I could and when she was placed in my arms at last in the dying days of the month the Romans had named for Caesar, my eyes welled up for joy at this precious jewel I had been entrusted with. This fleecy lamb with an iron grip and bold, curious eyes.

"The gods are merciful and grant another child to the line of Ptolemy Soter of Macedonia, Lord of the Black Land, Incarnate of Amun-Ra. We welcome you, Princess of Egypt, Daughter of Kings. May you be as noble as the Macedonians, as wise as the Egyptians, and as dauntless as the Romans." Mudjet paused to lower her head to speak to me. "How shall we address thy lady daughter, Your Majesty?"

I gazed into the face I had waited so long to see, running my fingers against her silky cheek. "Her name will be Aetia, for eagles are the badge of the House of Ptolemy and of the Legions of Rome. May her wings carry the strength of both."

Nuray and I were sitting out in the garden, enjoying the last few summer days before the coolness would make port in Ephesus. I had worked diligently to absorb myself in my infant daughter's world and tried to banish ghostly thoughts of Caesar and Parthia.

Mostly, it was not difficult, for Aetia burrowed herself in every fiber and sinew in my body and I was helpless before the incredible miracle of her existence. Yet still did the web of the past spin itself in the lonely watches, catching me unawares, its power woven from the threads of my *ka*. In those hours, my memories became spiders that crawled along the inner walls of my head, watching me with their hundred, hundred eyes.

We had spread a blanket on the ground and Nuray was weaving flowers together while I rocked Aetia into sleep. The song I had been murmuring in Egyptian died on my lips as I saw Mudjet running up the hill. She had gone into town for food and had returned without even the basket she left with. I placed my daughter down on the blanket and told Nuray to wait where she was. I hobbled off as best I could to meet my friend. I could feel my body groaning against the strictures of my still-healing muscles and the unaccustomed weight it was still carrying. Mudjet saw me coming and increased her speed. When we reached one another, she collapsed with a moan into my arms.

"What is it? What has happened? Is it my sister?" Panic filled my brain to see my unflappable Mudjet brought to such a state.

"Oh my lady, I cannot! I cannot!" she gasped. "Oh, why do the gods make you suffer so for obeying them?!"

My heart froze. I realized what Mudjet had run so far to tell me before someone else did.

We knelt down where we were and I found myself comforting her as she sobbed against me. I was enveloped once again in the numbness that had wrapped me in its deadening embrace when I was told of Caesar, and yet, this was different. There the paralysis that struck me was shock, now it was the muffled thump of a drum that had been beating in my brain since I had looked back over my shoulder at the oil lamps of Alexandria. We sat there without speaking, preserving these last few moments before the words would need to be said aloud and we could no longer pretend it was some other catastrophe. I looked up at Nuray, who had ignored my directions and stood over us holding Aetia.

"What has happened, Your Majesty?" she asked, alarmed at Mudjet's uncontrolled weeping.

I stroked Mudjet's head gently. "Mudjet has come to tell us that my brother is dead, my dear."

Nuray went white and clutched at my daughter's small form, while Mudjet made a wounded animal noise before lapsing back into tears.

I sighed and a few tears escaped my eyes to fall down on my faithful companion's head, but I said nothing else. I had no defense, Osiris had told me that the scales of Ma'at would demand their share. I should have known a perfect creature like Aetia would require a heavy price. Perhaps I had been foolish and assumed the murder of her father would sate the Just Goddess. I almost had to smile at the thought. As if Caesar had been tied enough to anything except his own fiery light to ransom anyone, even one knit of his own flesh. No, Osiris had warned me of the weight my words could carry and now I would walk the ways of my *ka* with that knowledge always. Every day, my Ptolemy fangs grew longer.

"What do they say in town, my sweet?" I prodded Mudjet after a few minutes.

She coughed a little to regain some authority over her throat. "They say that it had been months since anyone had seen His Majesty in public. No one thought very much of that though since he had been confined to the palace grounds since the rebellion and only allowed out into Alexandria with the queen. Then at the start of the month, Caesarion was crowned as co-ruler with your sister as Ptolemy the Fifteenth of His Name. No one has seen the body, but the rumors from the palace servants in the city is that she poisoned him and had Apollodorus bury him in the desert."

May my Lord preserve his body in his lands and send his son to guide him in the Duat. "Ptah was as brave as he was honey-sweet. It is a testament to this that he survived this long and so many months after Caesar's death has had Cleopatra's back against a wall. I will pray for his *ka* to one day forgive me for all my failures."

"There is nothing for him to forgive, my lady," Mudjet said gripping my shoulders. "Ptah was so proud of you. He knows you did everything you could. Perhaps more than you could."

I looked out over the garden wall towards the sea with a rueful smile. "I had almost let myself believe that he would be at my side, riding across Parthia with Caesar and me. It seems like a very foolish dream now."

"Hardly, my lady." Nuray spoke up. "It is a dream of the heart. Those are the dreams we must hold on to. They make us who we are."

Mudjet smiled. "And our lady knows the importance of holding onto dreams, even once we wake."

I let go of Mudjet and reached up for Aetia, as Nuray lowered her into my arms. "Shall we ask Mudjet how we are to formally address your

brother-cousin, my star?" My daughter's dark eyes widened as she made a
small trilling noise, pleased to be allowed into the conversation.

"He is hailed as Ptolemy Philopator Philometor Caesar, my wee lady," answered Mudjet leaning in to kiss the tiny fingers waving out towards her.

"Quite a mouthful, even for our House," I pondered, giving my attentive daughter's face a quizzical look. "Alas, *nedjet*, I think we shall look to the fine example of your Uncle Ptah and forego the laborious titles. I have never found them to be true to life anyway."

I am in the catacombs, the torchlight inert in the lack of wind. The halls of the dead are quiet, their shelves draped in cobwebs and the dust laying on their bodies like shrouds. Through the spiraling years of grime and decay, wooden boards with faces painted in life watch me from the shadows. Egyptian faces, Greek faces, Roman faces, Jewish faces, Nubian faces, Gallic faces. The catacombs have always been welcoming to all who meet death in our land. All are equal here, the rivalries and alliances forgotten as much as the empty shells they leave behind.

I reach out to a portrait of a young Egyptian woman to brush the dust from her eyes as I would chase the sleep from my own in the morning. I observe the dust on my fingertips and realize I am waiting for it to turn into blood.

"Death is not so easily erased, *nedjet*." My Lord sits in an empty alcove to my left, his head bent away from me until he knows he has my attention. When he turns to me, I am startled by the expression on his face, for I have never seen the like on him before. His whole frame is cramped as if in agony, even though he is gamely attempting to hide it. His green eyes are full of painful surprise and tears of blood seep from them, trailing down his dark cheeks. His normally golden scars are scarlet, pulsing with every movement.

I rush over to him and take his elegant hands in mine. "What has happened, my Lord? Who has done this to you?"

He winces and pulls his lips back into a grimace of a smile. "You have done this to me, my Beloved. Your *ka* claws at my *ib* as if it had teeth."

I drop his hand and stumble back in horror. I sink to my knees and moan. "Why is this my burden to bear in this world? Why must everything I touch turn to ash?"

Set climbs down out of the alcove and gingerly sits down next to me on the dirty floor of the catacombs. "Shh, my child. It is not as hopeless as that. Your fluttering little honeybee of a *ka* cannot kill me. It stings me because it is in pain, just as a bee might to an elephant."

I reach out and sweep away some of the blood tears from his face. "This seems more dire than a bee sting, my Lord."

"It is cumulative," he says with another wincing smile. "I have been swallowing your *ka's* pain ever since we were Joined. I was startled to feel such mortal pain in my breast, but I learned to live with it. I tasted the bitter fruit born of the death of your Latin servant and your Greek teacher and your mottled army. I ate your fear and loneliness these past years through the part of your *ka* you left with me and they sharpened the earlier pains, though I adapted to that as well. And then still more pain came. Why do you think I sent Hathor to you when the son of the Julians was slaughtered? I was writhing as if on fire in my House. That is when these turned color." He gestured to his scars. "And now, now because I could not save the little Pharaoh, I can hardly breathe without anguish. My eyes do not cease to weep."

I took his hand once more. "I understand now. I am heartbroken again beyond what I would have assumed my endurance, yet I have found myself able to comfort Mudjet and even the Lord Who Shakes The Lightning. The piece of your *ka* you graciously left with me feeds me strength and my piece in you gives you a window into my anguish."

Set casts an imploring look to me, as if he were a hurt child. "Is this what mortals feel? How do you endure it?"

"It is not easy, my Lord. It hurts a great deal at first, and you wonder how you manage to rise from your bed, let alone go on with the business of living. You learn to imbibe memory, the happy memories as well as the sad, and that hurts as well but there is a sweetness mixed in with pain so you continue to do it. Slowly, slowly, the sharp pain dulls to an ache that can sometimes burn like a fresh wound, but it becomes a scar that you carry forth into the world. And if you wish not to be consumed by despair, you teach yourself that it is you, yet does not define you."

He shakes his head. "I do not see how it can be better."

"It feels that way in the beginning. Yet somehow it always does. You suffer this much because I have lost a great deal in such a short time. I will heal in time and so will you." I placed my hand over his god-heart. "We shall have golden scars in here instead of on our bodies."

"You have grown wise, Beloved," he says solemnly. "I shall learn to be strong again for you for I have your *ka* to guide me."

And then I wake up.

Chapter Forty-Six

After this, the feathery touch of Ma'at seemed to take pity on the endless turmoil of my storm-swept life and I was granted a few scattered halcyon days. I lived in the present ever so briefly with my daughter and my friends, released from the shadows of my same-born brother enveloped in the mud of the Nile, from my airy sprite of a younger brother whose *ka* the gods had set free, from the caustic reach of my rapacious sister.

And yet, the smouldering ruins of Alexandria's inferno burned far longer than the physical manifestation of the fire we had collectively set, the ashes burning away Sekhmet the Ender of Days until Hathor the Honey-Voiced emerged, their charred flecks flying in the eyes of Set Who Weeps Not until blood poured down his dark cheeks. They blew across the Great Sea, igniting the funeral pyre of the greatest mortal of our age. Turning him into a god among the people he left behind, before traveling east to settle in the nostrils of a forgotten princess in exile whose dreams still smelled of smoke.

From my remote parapet, I watched the movements of our game's remaining players with the detached attention of a theatergoer. In the middle of a story I would be telling Aetia or as Mudjet and I aired out linens in our courtyard would come snatches of news about Cleopatra and her ongoing exploits with her new dear friend Mark Antony.

Though it was only as the trickle of gossip became a torrent telling of the grand passion between my sister and her latest Roman paramour did I realize the deceptively lovely Hathor had not been mindlessly comforting me the night I clung to her in anguish. That the Egyptians once more showed their perceptive wisdom in grasping that love and war were two faces of the same goddess. My sister might have robbed her of her fangs, but the goddesses of love are never weaponless. Like the suddenly remembered lyrics of an old song, proud Hathor's words whispered in my waking ears with unbidden clarity:

Do not weep, little princess. I will make the arrogant Queen of Egypt kneel in the dirt of my acolytes. She will forget everything in the face of her heart's desires. She took everything from us and now I will destroy her with the very weapon she used falsely. You are the Red Lord's hemet-netjer, *but you have been my most faithful student in fourteen hundred years, I claim you as my own, Queen of Swords and Hearts. All the pain she visits on you will be returned to her tenfold. I swear it on the heart of my Father.*

I shrank from the goddess' curse, as I had long ago learned that the wounds of war are finite, but the wounds of love are dizzying in their clever variety. I could not recall such a curse from Hathor's lips, even if I had wished to, and her blazing anger reminded me that although the dread goddess had been humbled and Cleopatra had chosen to turn her eye from me for now, my sister and I would remain at war as long as we both drew breath. That the idyl my *imi-ib* and I enjoyed was a fleeting one.

The warmth of late summer spilled over us once more, and the anniversary of Ptah's death came and went, leaving me to trail about in its rooted memories while Aetia took her first steps away from the tenuous safety of my arms and into the world she would grasp as her own through her indomitable spirit. We watched her full of fierce pride and fiercer love, and I sometimes can barely recall those days when she was kept earthbound by untutored feet.

"*Mewet, mewet!*" she demanded of me one afternoon, squirming in Mudjet's arms as I sat holding wool for Nuray while she wound it into spindles.

"Ach! What, what, *imi-ib*?" I laughed, putting down the spindle and holding out my arms to her. "If you wish my attention, you must claim it on your own!"

Mudjet chuckled and put my darling on her feet so she might toddle over to my waiting fingers, waving her tiny hands excitedly. "Careful now, *kharsheret*," she said, still stifling her giggles. "Even a Caesar must place one foot in front of the other."

I scooped up Aetia from my knees and pressed her warm little body to mine. "How is this, my love?"

Aetia chattered to me in a pleasant stream of ambiguous Egyptian and Greek words while I stroked her curling hair, her bright, flashing black eyes alight with the fire of her father's *ka.*

"Such a lamb, our wee lady," gushed Nuray, reaching over to kiss Aetia's fingers.

"Indeed," agreed Mudjet. "An enchantress of the highest order of her Ptolemy kin. Our people will adore her."

"And you tell our star to place only one foot in front of the other!" I scolded her with a smile. "Our people might never learn of our precious secret."

Mudjet made a cluck with her tongue. "As if such a thing can be kept from Egyptians!" She was about to continue, when her mouth fell into a frown. "There is a man coming up the path."

For only a moment, I imagined it was him. My heart leapt up in my chest and my lips parted into the suggestion of a happy smile. He was here as he had promised and he would sweep me up into his wiry arms as if I were an empty-headed girl who had not seen or done such terrible things. He would crouch down and take up our daughter, he would laugh his jackal's laugh and lose himself in her eyes — his eyes — and we would ride down to his flagship, his men readying the sails for the east. My brother waving from the rail, his tawny hair tousled by the wild wind. The tide would be with us and the world would rise up to meet our oars.

But then I shook my head in irritation at my own foolishness. I must remember to cease living in a lost future as much as in my altered past. "Who is it, sweet?"

My tall Mudjet stood up on her toes. "I don't know, but the cloak is Roman."

Gods, what if my sister?... I looked up at her concerned eyes. "Why don't you take our eaglet for a visit to Master Xenos? Just in case."

She nodded. "What of you, my lady? I cannot leave you."

"I will be fine. You say it is only one man and there has been no news of warships from the west in port. Nuray will stay with me, will you not, dearest?"

"Of course, my lady," the little priestess replied, her expression equally worried, but her fingers laced together to keep them still.

"Very well," sighed Mudjet before she threw out a hand to my daughter. "Come, *imi-ib*, do you want to visit town with me?"

Aetia, who loved being in the port bustle of Ephesus, tumbled out of my embrace and lunged for her outstretched fingers eagerly. Her rapturous smile faltered when she glanced back at me.

I waved her off breezily. "Go on, *nedjet*. I will be here when you return. Bring us something interesting."

"*Medjat!*" she announced after a thoughtful pause.

"If you wish. Now, go with Mudjet like a good girl."

Nuray and I watched pensively as the two of them went off, taking the long back path down to the river to circumvent our visitor.

I told myself to be calm. This person did not lead an army to my door, surely they offered no more than the polite interest that others had brought before him. We did not receive many visitors in our seclusion, but they were not wholly absent from our life, and this was a pantomime we had completed many times before. When a person unknown to us came to call, Mudjet or Nuray would lead Aetia down to the muttering Kaystros or over to the temple, and my daughter would happily follow them in the steps of what she only saw as a delightful outing. We made her safety a game, to shield both her life and her innocence. I worried for the day when she must discover she was a Caesar and a Ptolemy. I worried for that burden heaped upon her slight shoulders.

"Perhaps we should go inside, my lady," said Nuray softly.

Her voice broke through my thoughts and I turned to give her an encouraging smile. "You are right, my friend. Let us go through the kitchens and retrieve wine as we pass."

We returned to the pleasant, worn front courtyard of the house and Nuray placed cups and a jug of wine on a small stone ledge against the wall flecked with moss and sea salt. She handed me our wool and we resumed our winding until after a while, a thin man in a Roman traveling cloak and armor stepped through the columned entryway, walking staff in hand.

He was not as tall as Caesar, and while they shared a similar spare build, this man's face was not as long, his nose more arched and hooked. His eyes were narrow and intelligent, though lacking the other's infernal spark, and his mouth had a pinched appearance above a pointed chin. A not wholly unpleasant-looking man, but one who so filled the archetype we foreigners have of weedy Roman patricians that I nearly laughed aloud. This was the kind of man Caesar poked fun at for my amusement on our night-veiled walks along the beach below.

"Forgive the impertinence, Your Highness," he said in a smooth, slightly nasal Greek, giving me a polite bow. "But you have no porter."

"There is nothing to forgive, sir," I answered. "We live simply here. But you must be weary from your climb. Nuray, would you pour our guest some wine?"

Nuray rose silently and proceeded to arrange the cups while I motioned to the stone bench at my right. "Please be seated, sir. To what do we owe your attendance? Do you come from Rome?"

"By way of Syria, my lady," he replied, giving me a smile as he accepted the bench gratefully. "But I am being most rude by forcing an audience from you without properly presenting myself. If it please Your Highness, I am Gaius Cassius Longinus."

The sound of glass smashing against the marble floor meant Nuray must have dropped the cup in her hand. Years of hard practice in my family's cruel *lykeion* meant not a muscle on my body betrayed me in such an obvious way, and yet I had not drawn breath. My mind raced with frantic thoughts as to how I could warn Mudjet without giving ourselves away. *Gods defend us, they know of my daughter and they've come to throw her from the city walls like Astyanax.* The shadow of the thought made my blood run cold.

"It would seem your reputation precedes you, Master Longinus," I remarked with a tranquillity I certainly did not feel.

"I regret to have alarmed the priestess of Artemis," replied Cassius with surprising sincerity. "Your Highness has nothing to fear from me — I come as a friend."

"That is a rare thing indeed in these unsettled times," I said, giving him a pleasant smile before looking over my shoulder at Nuray, whose distraught face was torn between terror at our visitor and embarrassment at the shattered remains of the glass. "It is all right, dearest. Cups are easily found. Perhaps you would instead go into town for me and tell our friend that she may keep my eaglet overnight at the temple, may it please the Lady of Ephesus and her servants. I will be quite well until she returns."

"Yes, my lady," murmured Nuray miserably and hurried past us towards the front door, where she would no doubt run as fast as her legs could carry her to Mudjet and Xenos.

When she had left, I turned my attention back to my guest. "You must forgive us," I said, rising up to bring one of the remaining wine cups over to him. "The priestesses are young and the sailors in port love to fill their heads with the most fantastic tales."

His mouth pulled up into an aristocratic smirk as he took the glass with a nod of thanks. "It is completely understandable, Your Highness. We are well aware of how baffling the East finds Roman politics."

I laughed in a way that I prayed sounded careless. "Hardly, sir. Senates and rotating consulships are baffling to us. Assassinations are not."

Cassius chuckled. "You are as astute and as charming as your reputation, my lady. No wonder your brazen whore of a sister is so afraid of you."

"Be warned, my sister is never more dangerous to her enemies than when she is afraid," I said. "Now, what possible service could an exiled princess perform for the Lord of the Liberatores?"

"You flatter me, Your Highness—"

Gods above, I hope so.

"—but my dear brother in law Brutus is our leader, not I—"

Yes, but the whole world knows you put the dagger in his hand. You were the monster who planned it all. I would be with my brother in Ktesiphon by now save for you.

"What's more, I don't come solely seeking favors. I believe we may be of service to one another."

This does surprise me enough to raise my eyebrows. "Indeed, sir?"

He leaned forward with a manner that passed for eager. "We have a mutual friend, Your Highness. Marcus Tullius speaks very highly of you, and he is sympathetic to our cause."

"Though not your methods, I have heard," I cannot resist pointing out. *My kindly, vain once-benefactor is not a murderer.*

"Fairly put, my lady," he conceded. "That is why we didn't invite him into our plans. But now Cicero holds blockheaded Antony and the Octavii brat in check for us in Rome, and I have secured our position in the east with my late victory over Dolabella, for which Syria has declared for me as governor."

"I congratulate you, sir."

"Syria is secure and Brutus is hailed as a savior in Greece, my lady. I have twelve legions behind me and I am sailing next for Egypt."

I looked at him wide-eyed, allowing alarm to pass over my face for the first time. "Egypt?" I said rather stupidly.

Cassius nodded. "Yes, and I'm here to take you with me if you'll agree to it."

Now I was gaping at him as guilelessly as Nuray. "I beg your pardon?" I finally managed to choke out.

"I have the legions to overtake Cleopatra's troops," he said, smiling at my surprise. "I'll take Egypt, with your help to rally the people against your sister. The queen is a danger to Rome, I will see to it that Cicero speaks for your rule as pharaoh to the Senate. You can go home, Your Highness."

Home. We could go home... My mind filled with the sting of the sand, the pungent smell of life bursting forth from the Nile and my heart swelled up in my chest with undreamt-of expectation. I would see the light of Pharos and touch the ancient altars of my gods with my waking fingers. I would see the happy faces of the *ta-meriu* again, hear their glad voices...

The ta-meriu... The thought of my people conjured up a wholly different set of sensations. The legions of Cassius cutting down my bravely resisting people while I watched their second destruction. I saw myself sitting in an empty palace, a hollow crown upon my head while a pair of Roman tribunes flanked my throne on both side, whispering in my ears. The people and the gods weeping at my betrayal. I saw the feverish eyes of Hyrcanus becoming mine.

And then there was my daughter. At first I gazed into this blighted future and saw her beautiful face nowhere. Then I saw my life, my *imi-ib*, in chains beside her brother Caesarion and the young Octavian, dragged from my arms into new triumphs and cautiously preventive death by my Roman overlords. I saw myself half-wild with grief, begging Cicero for his aid and the apologetic impotence of his face.

Amidst all of these emotions, I willed my flailing heart to slow its beat and remember that I was no longer the child forlorn in the glittering palace of the Seleucids and the courtyards of Jerusalem. I was Arsinoë Philoaígyptos and a queen must not be ruled solely by her heart. An errant piece of advice passed through my mind — *a good general knows his enemy* — and I considered the man looking encouragingly at me. I nearly sighed aloud in gratitude. *Thank you for lighting the way, my love.*

Cassius was a fine general, yet not cut of the same cloth as Caesar and Pompey. He was bold, but he had little vision. That was why he had only thought of killing Caesar, not what was to be done when his hated adversary was no more. Also there was Brutus, who was honorable, but incapable of inspiring the sort of loyalty that made the legions of Gaul and Spain fight for Caesar like demons born out of the Lake of Fire.

And this reminded me of what I had said to Xenos that terrible day. The Liberatores had not bought off the army. Once this was remembered, the twelve legions standing behind us on the shores of Alexandria vanished from the docks as if they were the ghost armies of my dreams. I followed their wispy trail and saw them gather around a sharp-faced young man who appeared sickly but who looked every legionary directly in the eye. The boy Octavian. Octavian Caesar. I had fought Apep, I knew the power of names and that name was worth more than the ethereal promise of liberty Cassius and Brutus held out to them.

I was suddenly as certain as stone — they would lose. It was as if the gods had decreed it. I was also certain that if he could remain strong in body, Octavian would be the master of Rome in the end. I wondered if my sister had the wit to see that.

I slowly shook my head. "I am sorry, Master Longinus. I cannot risk bringing more death to my people by condoning the landing of another foreign army amongst them, even if it would allow me to return to the place I love above all others."

He pulled back, slightly bemused. "You think you can save them by sacrificing yourself?"

"I don't know," I admitted. "But I do not think your invasion will save them, and I do not think you can save me from Cleopatra. That is a great deal of uncertainty to sail off into." *I might risk everything again for the love of the warrior-poet who called me his falcon goddess and my brother who would have followed me under any star. But both of them are dead and you are not fit to tie the sandals of either.*

Cassius frowned, and after a long moment shrugged. "As you wish, Your Highness. I'm sure the Senate will find a suitable Roman to sit upon the falcon throne in your absence." He paused to grin coldly. "Perhaps it will be me."

"Perhaps, sir." *Never.*

He stood up, and I rose at his side. "I won't keep you any longer then, my lady. If you change your mind, a letter from Cicero will always find me. Though don't expect much in return if it reaches me in Alexandria."

"I understand," I said and held out my hand to him. "Thank you for your consideration. I appreciate you were under no obligations to present me with any deference."

"Of course, Your Highness. I'm always pleased to meet someone who has earned Marcus Tullius' rare adulation," he replied, bending over my hand respectfully. He straightened himself and went to leave, but turned back to peer at me as if trying, yet failing, to see into my heart. "You know you're not safe here," he stated as if it was no great concern of his. "She'll come one day and that will be that."

"I have known my sister longer than you, sir," I answered, drawing myself up. "I know my risks. I pray for your sake that you know yours."

He looked at me a long moment, his lean face drawn into lines of deep puzzlement. I could tell he was recalling the stories my people tell of me and struggling to decide if I knew something he did not. Finally he shook himself as if from a dream and bowed hastily to show himself out.

I stood frozen in the middle of the courtyard, the humming of the cicadas reverberating from the garden. I stood there long enough to be sure he was gone and then I sank down to my knees, uncontrollable sobs shuddering through my body. I wept as I had in the arms of Hathor, as though I would die of it. I cried for my people, who I could not protect. I cried for my daughter, for whom I feared I was little protection, even if this time she remained safe. I cried for myself, given another chance to escape my dark future and forced to watch it slip from my grasp.

And I cried for Caesar. I held my hands to my eyes so I could wash the touch of his murderer from my fingers. I cried because he had known I was not my sister, who would have married Cassius if she believed it would help her, and he had left me all alone to repel the advances of his enemies for love of him. I cried because I missed him.

Finally, as the sun began to pull back from the skylight above my head, I reined in my tears and smoothed out the folds of my *chiton*, pre-occupied. Cassius was right, one day soon my sister would come for me and our great struggle would be at an end. He had said it to frighten me, but I was not afraid. It was the triumph all over again, and when the time came, I would be ready. As a queen.

Chapter Forty-Seven

We were given an amnesty of another two years before I saw Roman war sails on the horizon. Mudjet and I stood watching the small fleet drift towards the harbor. Neither of us pretended that these ships came to us in peace. Once upon a time, in those early days, I lived in fear of this sight. Later on, if they had come flying the Taurus standard of Caesar's legions, I would have run across the city to meet them. Now, they were simply a manifestation of inevitability. This had always been my sister's final move, certain as death itself.

"Where can we go, my lady?"

"There is nowhere to go. If we tried to conceal ourselves in Ephesus, they would only burn every building down. We will go to the temple and hope Great Artemis' protection is enough. You and Aetia will hide. Your duty is to save her, if possible."

My faithful companion nodded. Quietly we linked arms and leaned our heads against one another.

Xenos was waiting for us when we arrived at the temple. He bowed over my extended hand as he always had, but then he gathered me up into his arms.

"We will fight for you, my lady," he said fiercely.

"No, sir," I replied, shaking my head. "That is not a fight your people can win. I will not rain destruction down upon those who have been so generous with me. I only ask that the temple hides my child and Mudjet. I will sit with the Lady of the Silver Bow and pray for her mercy. I do not know if the emissaries of my sister will have the gall to drag me from this sacred space, but I hope that if they do, my blood will be enough."

The old man had tears in his eyes as he led us into the presence of Artemis of Ephesus. All of us bowed to the venerable lady with her far-gazing eyes. We sent Mudjet and Aetia behind her towering figure, and then Xenos and I returned to stand out on the temple steps. Nuray ap-

peared beside us, white in the lips, but she grasped my hand firmly. We
did not have to wait long.

The party was smaller than I expected, but what truly surprised me was
their captain, striding before the centurions like the graceful aristocrat I
had once seen laugh at my father in my dreams. Mark Antony himself
had come on my sister's behalf, and I wondered what she was so afraid of
that she sent a lion to kill a sparrow.

Perhaps she had anticipated the *megabyzos*' offer and thought I was
heartless enough to force Ephesus to die for me as well. Perhaps she trusted no one in Egypt to do her bidding. My pulse quickened at the thought
of my *ta-meriu* clinging to my memory as surely as I clung to theirs.

This thought of home, driven from my mind lately by the Unblink-
ing Goddess, rushed upon me in a deluge. In the face of my own doom,
coming towards me in Roman sandals, my *ka* made wild bargains for
the chance to dip my fingers in the Nile once more. Vain, silly plans I
brushed aside like the tentacles of a daydream.

I had never met Antony. He had been with Pompey when the old
general came to my father's assistance, though I was too young to remember it outside of the dreams I shared with the gods. He had a gladiator's
build, stocky and muscular, but there were hints of age creeping into his
body as it tried to ward off wrinkles and weight.

The latter I suspected came from a love affair with Egypt as much
as with my sister. My forebearers had been fit military men too before
falling under the Black Land's spells and indulgences, and as Caesar's face
came upon me unasked for, I was reminded again how unusual he had
been for resisting the lures of so many powerful *heka*s.

Antony's head still had its fair tumbling curls and his face had the
ruddy complexion of a man used to being outdoors. The general claimed
descent from Heracles and Dionysus, and in him I saw the brute strength
of one and the relish for extravagance of the other. In short, I doubted
Cleopatra had ever met a man quite like him — part bodyguard, part
pet. It was an unusual combination that she had found pleasing.

In his defense, Antony looked somewhat uncomfortable as he and his men approached us. He stopped at the bottom of the stairs and shielded his eyes against the sun to look up at me.

"Welcome to Ephesus, Consul Antony," I called down to him, attempting to sound cheerful.

"I'm not a consul anymore, Your Highness," he answered, also measuring out his tone warily, trying to feel me out.

I feigned embarrassment. "Forgive me. Of course. But I have always found Roman politics so confusing, and news is slow to reach us here." I did not know what this man knew of me, so I decided to err on the side of appearing ignorant. I had gained a little wisdom since that night on Cape Lochias when I had picked a fight with a much craftier adversary.

Antony coughed awkwardly. "My lady, you must know why I'm here."

I made an exaggerated frown. "Surely my loving sister, Queen of all Egypt, is not still mad at me? She has everything she has ever wanted!"

"She knows you still plot against her."

That might be fair, but not how she imagines.

"She knows Cassius Longinus came to you before he fell on his sword at Philippi."

True, though she was not lucky enough that I should challenge her outright by falling for him.

"She knows you still lust after her throne."

It probably does me no good to explain that I planned to cede her the throne of Egypt for a time while I went off to conquer the world with her blood-and-smoke lover. That perhaps there were other things of hers I have lusted over.

"My sister is so suspicious!" I exclaimed aloud. "I have given her no trouble for nearly five years and yet she makes a man as important as you, sir, come and spy on me!"

I could feel Xenos and Nuray glancing at me curiously, and I prayed that they did not look too shocked by the role I was playing. I needed them to be convincing.

I reached over for the priest's arm. "Tell them, Sir *Megabyzos*! Am I not simply a humble girl living quietly in great Lady Artemis' city? I can plot nothing. How can I hurt her from out here?"

Xenos looked to Antony and spluttered, "Her Highness lives in a discreet retirement here, sir. We are the only ones who have done any plotting, and that was only to convince the princess to become an acolyte of our dear Lady."

I giggled fatuously at this. "Oh, I keep telling them I am not holy enough for such service! To give up the few pretty things I have left, why that would torture!"

Antony cleared his throat again. "My lady, your illustrious sister and I must fight that whelp Octavian. We cannot afford to have him follow Cassius' example by coming here to strike an alliance with you behind our back. I'm sorry, but you live here on the sufferance of Cleopatra Thea Philopator and she has ordered your execution."

I wiped the ingratiating smile from my face. "I live here on the sufferance of the People of Rome, who showed me a clemency the Queen of Egypt never has," I said. "You and she have no authority here."

"The people of Rome cannot save you and we shall soon enough have the victory to show it," he answered, unimpressed.

"The people will revolt when they hear that you have executed a young woman on the steps of a temple. You will be reviled by the gods for such hubris."

He shrugged, though I could see the flash of discomfort that passed through his eyes. "The people have short memories and the gods favor the bold. Now come down here, my lady. Don't make this any more difficult than it needs to be."

"Apparently my sister told you I was a child to be scolded. I am a blooded princess of Egypt and I have faced greater demons than you, sir," I answered.

I stood firm and gave Antony the same imperious look I gave the Romans in the triumph. I did not bend willingly then, I would not meekly submit to this slaughter now.

Antony shook his head and pulled a dagger from his belt as he strode up several stairs towards me in impatience. His sudden movement startled Nuray, who let out a scream which was quickly answered by a smaller wail from within the temple. At the sound, everyone froze and I felt as though my breath was snatched from my body. Antony gestured to his men to go investigate and I then clung to Xenos so I might keep my feet under me. The soldiers returned and thrust Mudjet out into view, with Aetia clasped in her arms. My daughter cried out to me with searching arms, and I could not resist taking her into mine one last time. I took her with my back to my executioner and buried my face in her sweet-smelling neck.

"I am sorry, *imi-ib*," I murmured in her ear. "I had hoped you would not have to see this. Remember you are the sun of my life and my love will follow you always. To the very ends of creation."

I turned to face Antony again, and if the situation had not been so serious, I would have burst out laughing. Antony gaped at us like a man bewitched. Slowly he knelt down and sheathed his dagger. Frozen in this singular moment, we would have made a strange sight for anyone happening upon us.

He looked up at me. "May I see her?"

I knew I was not in a position to refuse with two centurions behind me, so I placed Aetia on her feet.

Antony motioned gently to her. "Come here, *puella*. Let us meet properly."

Aetia, bone of my bone, yet born as fearless as a lioness, tripped lightly down to where Antony knelt and calmly allowed this bearish man to take her by the arm and hold his palm against her face.

"Oh sweet one, you look so much like your sister. And she was the very best of women."

I blinked speechlessly, watching Antony stare transfixed by my daughter. Finally I recovered my voice and said softly, "Is it as obvious as that?"

Still gazing at Aetia he replied, "I always wondered what Julia's child would have looked like. Now I know." He moved his attention back to me, "And I would know these eyes anywhere. If Caesarion had half as many inheritances, the people would be falling at the boy's feet unquestioningly."

My nephew's name brought panic back into my heart. "My sister cannot know," I croaked hoarsely.

Antony peered at me. "No, no... she would go insane. She can never know..."

"Please, I do not care if you have to kill me," I pressed urgently. "Just let her live. No one needs to know. If not for her sake, for her father's memory."

Antony stroked Aetia's hair distractedly. "Her father's memory... did he know?"

I nodded. "I was able to get a message to him, he told me he was happy. He did not get to meet her."

"Did you love him?"

I took a shaky breath. "Yes. In spite of everything."

He smiled sadly. "Those are the words of all of us who really did." He sighed. "Sometimes I can't believe he is truly gone. In those last days he seemed so preoccupied, even as we planned the Parthian campaign. I thought he was just lost in his mind on that course, he was like that sometimes. But maybe he was thinking of you and her."

"Perhaps. It would be pleasant to believe we were in his heart, even a small corner." I reached around my neck and lifted the loop of leather over my head and handed it to Antony.

His eyes widened. "He gave you this?"

I nodded.

Antony touched the small gold ring hanging from it wonderingly. "We couldn't find it after... we thought it had been taken. Or cut off and lost. He must have been sincere if he entrusted this to you."

We continued to hold ourselves in silence for a time until I at last asked, "What is to be done, my lord?"

Antony lowered his gaze from my daughter and shook his head in distress. "I cannot go back empty-handed, my lady. She... she is all I can think about. I am a slave to her happiness. I don't see how I can leave my task undone and not have her find out."

I almost felt pity for him. He was a lovesick boy mooning over a woman he believed really was a goddess. A goddess who could grant his every desire, his every ambition. It was hard to see the battle-hardened general who helped bind all of Gaul in servitude reduced to such a state.

"My lady."

I turned toward the voice and saw Mudjet looking at me. With our captors in some disarray, she pulled me aside close to Xenos and Nuray.

"There might be another way. Let them kill me in your place."

I had thought I was afraid when Antony heard Aetia's cry. I thought nothing in this world or the next could terrify me more than that. But my Mudjet's words stole the very ground from beneath my feet. "No!" I whispered, my voice coming in a strangled gasp. "I cannot let you do that."

My sweet, my dearest Mudjet continued to look at me unmoved. Her beautiful eyes full of the loving fire she had wielded all these long years of my life to protect me from the many harms summoned to me by men and Fate. "Please, my lady. We are both half-Egyptian, all anyone will remember is that some half-breed was killed here. Aetia needs you to live if there is any chance of convincing Lord Antony of letting you go."

"No, I told you to keep Aetia safe," I argued in a rising tone of panic. "If you are with her, she will be fine." I looked away, full of shame. "Better with you than her Ptolemy mother," I added softly.

She smoothed a loose lock of my hair in that manner she always did. "She is a Ptolemy too. And she needs her mother."

I felt the tears running down my cheeks. "I do not deserve such a sacrifice from anyone. Especially you."

She shook her head. "Let me be the judge of that, my lady."

"How will I live without you?" I asked, unable to curb the galloping fear in my voice.

Mudjet reached out and wiped my face. "I am only a servant, my lady, a small person in the world. But you have always been my friend and you have treated me more as a sister than a slave. It is my honor to protect you and your child. Besides," she lowered her voice, "your Lord came to me in a dream and asked it. I see why you find him hard to deny."

My head shook of its own volition. "You do not need to listen to him. I will tell him so."

"It is well. This is my choice. Lord Set said there was a chance if I did this, it would break the power of the Queen's *heka* over you."

"I do not want you to throw away your life on a chance!"

She ignored my protests. "He said if I offered myself willingly and you met me with a blood sacrifice of your own, her *heka* could no longer touch you."

Antony cut in suddenly. "I don't know what you are talking about, but I do know if I don't kill you my lady, I will have to have some proof that makes it look as if I did."

Mudjet took my arm. "A blood sacrifice that he could take back to her," she said urgently.

Antony looked slightly green, but I realized as reluctant as I was, this might be the only way. I ran through my mind trying to think of something I could give him. Something I could live without, but something my sister would assume I could not survive. Something she would know was mine. And then it came to me. I had to believe it was the dark genius of my Lord at work, for it was a tactic he had used before. My heart recoiled, but it was perfect. The gesture would be full of the theatricality she loved, dramatic enough to mask its potentially non-lethal nature.

I whispered my plan to Xenos, and he gazed at me in horror. "You cannot ask me to do such a thing, my lady!"

"But you could do it?" I searched his eyes.

"I could find an appropriate instrument, but the risk—"

I gripped his arm. "You must help me do this. I need your help to save my daughter. And me."

The priest let out a low moan, though he nodded tearfully.

"It seems to me the proof I will give should negate the sacrifice you offer, my dear," I begged Mudjet, "yet I sense that you will tell me I am wrong."

She shook her head again. "This is about the *heka*, not just concealing your escape, my lady," she explained patiently, as if I was still a child failing to properly attend to a lesson. "Besides, we will need a body here in Ephesus in case she ever decides to affirm the deed for Lord Antony's sake."

"It cannot be some unfortunate girl who dies in town a month or two from now placed in a tomb?"

My feeble protests rang in my ears and I blushed in mortification at my own weakness. But I would make any barter, no matter how callous, to avert this impending disaster. If I in my disgusting frailty could not move Mudjet from her course, then the gods could take all of Ephesus if they wished, if they would spare her.

"Your sister's *heka* makes her bold to offend the sanctuary of the holy gods by spilling your blood in their midst. She demands this grand gesture. For credulity, we must give it to her."

I reverted back to Antony. "Will you accept this arrangement?" I murmur, my head bowed.

"If you can give me the proof I need, then for the sake of Caesar's blood and in respect to the gods, I will agree to this plan." He paused. "You won't cause trouble for us?"

"No," I said, forcing myself to stand up and address him with the firmness I had when he arrived. If this was to be, I could not throw our position away on my own anguish. "Once you see the lengths I am willing to go to escape the blade of her anger, I think you will take my word as bond. Can you take us away from here?"

"Where do you want to go?"

I did not have to think. "Egypt."

Antony balked. "You can't be serious! She'll find you in two hours!"

I willed myself to believe in the plan of Mujet and my Lord. That there would be no *heka* hanging over my head. "No, she will not. We shall go south and she will not find us."

Clearly uneasy, he sighed. "I cannot dissuade you?"

I shook my head. "I swear on the blood of my daughter that if we are caught, I will not expose you. You had never seen me before you arrived here, you killed my maid by mistake."

Mudjet set her jaw. "Then it is settled." She then spoke to Nuray. "I cannot leave my ladies unattended. Can your heart renounce the service of Lady Artemis so that you may take my place and go with them?"

Nuray looked to Xenos, who said, "You must follow your heart, my child. The Lady of Ephesus will accept whatever path you choose. Service to her has many forms."

She breathed deeply. "It will be my honor to serve Lady Arsinoë and Lady Aetia in your place, Mudjet."

The two young women embraced, and Mudjet whispered something in Nuray's ear.

Xenos patted the young priestess gently. "Then you must stay and endure the first test of your service by helping an old man in the terrible task the Queen has set before me." To Mudjet, he added, "You will rest in a place of honor on these grounds, my brave girl. Our Lady places great esteem on such bonds of loyalty."

I asked one of the soldiers to stay with Aetia outside, and watched as this battle-hewn man tenderly gathered her up in his arms with a curt nod. My daughter leaned her head against the breastplate of his armor and contentedly closed her eyes. The rest of us entered the temple and bowed again to Artemis.

Without consulting each other, Mudjet and I methodically began to remove our outer clothing. We moved in the rhythm of participants in a sacred dance where the choreography was so rooted in our being, it need not be thought upon. And indeed, we had performed the dance of dressing and undressing with each other so many times before, perhaps in this last time, it was only natural that we needed no words. Mudjet removed her pins, stepped out of her *chiton*, and held it over her arm while I handed mine to Nuray. In a careful, practiced motion, she helped me pull her garment up and drape myself in her waiting *himation*. She gave me a smile as she fixed the hem edges. Then I reached back to Nuray to retrieve my *chiton* and dressed Mudjet in mine. When I was finished, we held each other briefly and kissed the other's cheek.

"You are far too good to me," I said to her softly, my lips quivering as we pulled apart to look at one another. "I wish there was another way."

"Once, when we stood on the lines in Alexandria, during the siege, I was struck by a feeling down to my very marrow that I would die for you, my lady," she answered calmly. "And I was surprised by how unafraid of that thought I was. It is the will of the gods that I should do this."

The smooth edges of her gentle voice, the curve of sound that hinted at the clear ring of her high laughter, tore into my heart. I was pulled back into haunting echo of the *Duat* and the form of Apep in my sweet's guise. The serpent was evil, but not untruthful, and at last I began to see the grim accusations it could carve into the black skin of my Lord. That I was heir to the same terrible kingdom of loneliness and despair. The cry that the hot wind of Pharos snared from my throat escaped its bindings again and I threw myself into her arms that trembled ever so slightly as they wrapped themselves around me.

"You must let me do this quickly," she pleaded in my ear with the same tone she once used to urge me to bed. "I am not afraid but your pain has always been more than I can bear. Do not make this harder."

"I am One with the Lord of Ending," I sobbed quietly into her shoulder. "How can I go on, knowing I scatter such destruction all around me?"

"You will, my love, because destruction and creation are links in the same chain forged by the gods and my *heqat* is a lady so great that the holy ones invite her into that deepest of mysteries." She shifted so that her forehead rested against mine. "May the sweet balm of Lady Nephthys pour forth upon my *ka*, and may the eyes of Lady Iaret and the wings of Lady Nekhbet always shield you from harm. For you are a Queen of Egypt, my dearest Arsinoë. Be brave and live."

With reluctance, I turned to face Antony and handed him my mother's bracelet. "I will send this with you as well to give to the Queen. She will recognize it and know I would not part with it lightly."

He placed it in a small purse at his waist. He motioned for Mudjet to take her place in front of the altar as I shakily climbed onto it and rested my head against the cold, hard marble as if I were preparing to sleep. Xenos had returned from an anteroom with a tightly twisted piece of cloth and a cunning little dagger. Even in the shadowy light, it gleamed with its own radiance.

He instructed Nuray how she must hold me down and placed the bit of cloth between my teeth. I gripped it as tightly as I could, and all I could think of was the legends of my childhood. I felt the gaze of the capricious Greek gods upon me, full of the complacent justice of the Greek Ptolemies finally paying the appropriate price for their ready adoption of Egyptian practices abhorrent to the sensibilities of the divine Olympians. I watched Antony place his arm across Mudjet's chest and signal to Xenos.

So the last thing on Earth that my left eye saw was my sister's lover cut my unwavering Mudjet's throat before the stony face of the Ephesian goddess. Her mercy to me was that the pain ripping through my skull made me lose consciousness before I could cry out.

Chapter Forty-Eight

I awoke slowly. I was in a dark room and it took me some time to understand the swaying motion I felt was the rhythm of the sea. I was in the hull of a ship. As I rose up on my elbows, I tried to remember how I had arrived at my present state, though my mind was blank. My head throbbed, and as I reached up to touch my forehead, I was greeted by a heavy wrapper of linen strips. My memory came flooding back and I held my palm over my left eye. Or rather, my left eye socket. *Oh, Mudjet...*

Nuray walked in at that moment and broke out into a hesitant smile. "Oh, my lady, I am so glad you've woken!"

My stupor was quickly overcome by alarm. "Where is Aetia? Where are we? What happened after the temple?"

The young priestess swept over and gently pushed me back down onto the cot. "Shh, all is well, my lady. Lady Aetia is sleeping right over there," she gestured to our left and I swiveled my head so that I could see her. My daughter lay sprawled on her cot with a corner of blanket balled up in her fist.

"She has greatly enjoyed her first sea voyage so far and has quite charmed Lord Antony's men. She is a born leader indeed," Nuray added.

"How long have I been asleep?" I asked.

"About two days. You half woke several times, but we simply gave you medicine for the pain and to make you sleep."

"Thank you. Is Antony a man of his word? Is he taking us to Egypt?"

"Yes, though he remains deeply troubled about it."

"Better that than he be too sure of us, I think," I replied. "Were you able to save—" I made a motion to the left side of my face.

Nuray nodded. "Master Xenos placed it in a cask of spirits so it should be preserved until we reach Alexandria. He did well with the cut, the eye was mostly unblemished and we were able to staunch the bleeding in good order. Your face remains a little swollen, though that will pass."

I put a hand on her arm. "I am sorry to have made you a part of something so gruesome."

"I understand it was the only way. It was a brilliant idea, much more shocking than something else."

"It will be worth it if Set is correct and this frees me and Aetia from my sister's thrall."

She smiled mysteriously. "I know it will, my lady."

"Oh?"

"Mudjet told me so," she explained. "When she spoke in my ear on the steps. She said that your Set told her that her sacrifice or yours would be enough to break the Queen of Egypt's power over you."

"Then why did she insist on both?" I interrupted, stricken.

"Because he told her that together, both offerings would destroy her sorcery completely."

I gazed at her shocked. "Her *heka* will be destroyed?"

She nodded. "Mudjet once long ago explained the *heka* to me, and though I confess I still don't quite understand it, I believe it means as her creative life-force, it won't be eradicated. But it will be like an ordinary person's again, without its special power."

I sat there looking at my hands. "And she goes out to fight Octavian Caesar and Rome. She cannot win now."

"No, probably not, my lady," Nuray admitted. "Naturally, Mudjet did not want to say this in front of Lord Antony. She needed him to agree to the plan."

I felt my right eye welling up, and my left was full of phantom tears. "That, and she did not tell me because she did not trust me to agree either if I realized that our actions would most likely lead to the death of my sister. My fearless Mudjet tried to spare me the burden of having the blood of a sibling on my hands." I sighed heavily. "I once accused Caesar of leaving nothing except destruction in his wake. As if I was any better. I hope you do not regret leaving your life in Ephesus for my sake."

"No, not ever," she answered with a newfound firmness I had not heard before. "I love Artemis and I have generally been content with the life of a priestess. Yet my parents dedicated me to that world when I was a child, I've never known anything else. You and Mudjet became my first grown friends, you opened up another path to me. I will never regret that."

I smiled at her gratefully, and turned to watch my daughter thrash one of her arms about in sleep, a determined frown on her pale little face. I thought of the many nights Mudjet and I would stand over her while she dreamed. I did not know how Aetia and I would continue on without the girl who was my other self. "I pray that the gods will forgive me for leading Mudjet into exile and death, and then abandoning her corpse in a far off land," I said quietly.

My dear Nuray placed her hand on mine. "Do not weep for Mudjet, my lady. She might have been born lowly, but she wrested her destiny from the hands of the gods as if she had been the highest born of women. Even at the end. Her soul is strong and will find its way to the lands of peace."

In the cooler evening air a few days later, I stumbled onto the ship's deck with Nuray's help. I did not feel strong enough to stand long, so I found a coil of rope to sit upon as I gripped the railing. At length, Antony came over and stood with me.

"I am glad to see you well, Your Highness," he said, his voice sincere.

I smiled skeptically. "I doubt that is strictly true, sir, though I appreciate the sentiment."

"Are you in much pain?"

I shrugged. "Some. It is tolerable."

Antony seemed as though there was something he wished to say to me, yet he did not know how to begin. Long years of dreams with the gods had taught me patience in the face of silence, so I sat quietly while he found his footing. He reached into his waist purse and pulled out my mother's bracelet.

"It is a fine thing," he remarked, turning it over in his hand.

"It is very old. It was passed down among the women in my mother's family when they married. My nurse gave it to me on her deathbed because she knew neither she nor obviously my mother would see such a day for me."

"I'm sorry you cannot keep it."

"It is for the best. My mother died afraid for my safety among the royal family. If a trinket of hers could shield me one more time, she would never have me hold onto it for sentimental reasons."

He placed it back in the purse and pulled out Julia's ring. "I do think you should keep this," he said, putting it in my hand.

"It is amusing that I feel no more worthy of it the second time it is given to me," I replied, holding it in my outstretched palm.

"I don't feel more qualified to judge the recipient than my commander," Antony answered simply.

I put the leather loop around my neck. "I am truly sorry that I have put you in such an awkward position. I will not molest you or my sister when we reach Egypt, I give you my word again."

I could not tell him of the damage already done by Mudjet with my unwitting assistance, and even if I tried, would he believe me? He and all of Rome spoke of the enchantments of Cleopatra, yet they made these claims in a metaphorical way. The confusion on Antony's face when Mudjet spoke of the *heka* made that clear. Even if I warned him of the dangers he now faced with her, why would he take the word of an exiled girl so far away from action and information? Surely he would tell me that he was the veteran of a hundred battles who did not need magic to defeat an inexperienced child like Octavian. The fact that my sister sent Antony to kill me before Caesar's heir could recruit my help suggested that she was much more afraid of me than him. I, however, felt she was making the same mistake with the Roman boy that she made with me at first. She was underestimating him and the Roman people the way she had me and our own subjects.

Antony made a small shrug. "I love your sister more than life itself, though I did not want to risk offending the gods when we need their help more than ever. She said that with you dead we could rely on the Egyptian gods for aid, but the gods of your land are strange to me, my lady. I don't trust them in the thick of a fight."

I was confused by this. Cleopatra had told me she believed like our people that I was beloved of the gods, why would she assume that they would help her if she murdered their acolyte? Then it came to me. She no longer believed that the gods loved me more than her, she had convinced herself that I was using my own *heka* to block their access to her. Once I was gone, my *heka* would lift like a veil and the Egyptian gods would awaken as if from a dream and remember the duties they owed to her as the Queen of Egypt. In her mind, it was I who had incurred the wrath of the gods with my hubris, not her. It also showed that she still thought of me as more Egyptian than Greek, because she was not concerned about offending the Greek gods like Antony was. She assumed as an Egyptian, the other gods would not rise to my defense.

"It seems a bold risk on her part, but then she has always been like that where I have usually been accused of being over-cautious. Though seeing how she is Queen of the Black Land and I am an exile presumed dead, she would appear to have the right of it," I answered.

We lapsed back into silence until Antony spoke again. "My lady, I came over here because I feel there is something you should know before we arrive in Alexandria."

I turned my head away from him sharply. "If it about my brother, I already know."

"I thought you would. I just want you to know that I think it troubles Cleopatra a great deal. She felt she had to secure the throne with no more opposition after Caesar's murder, she needed to protect Caesarion. I know you and her do not see eye to eye..." He cut off guiltily, averting his gaze from my face.

Even in such a grim conversation, I wanted to laugh at Antony's floundering embarrassment. I thought of how much I needed Mudjet or Caesar with me so we could make appalling jests at my situation rather than the dolorous long faces I was likely to have to endure. "I shall have to get used to that kind of thing sooner rather than later, sir," I said with an ironic twist in my voice. "Today is as good as any to start. Please continue."

"I just don't want you to think she took pleasure in killing him."

The dark levity in me dissipated. I gazed out at the water as we cut through it gliding like dolphins, fingering the silver *fibula* on my left shoulder in agitation. I might be in Mujet's *chiton*, but my clever friend had craftily substituted Cicero's pins for her own in my inattention. Her last loving gesture.

I was not interested in my sister's regrets, yet again I was reminded that Osiris had warned me that the Just Goddess would demand payment for my child's life. Aetia had been born and nurtured in such safety that she had disarmed an iron-made soldier seeking my life with a glance of her eye. The gods held her dear because I had asked it of them, yet they had taken Ptah from me nearly as soon as my daughter had drawn her first breath to achieve that protection.

It had been an impossible choice, and though I had made it blindly, I could not say that it was not perhaps in part a willful blindness that I made in my heart. And how could I rage against Cleopatra who had arguably made the same choice in protection of her child?

My poor Ptah, born under such a cheerful, unlucky star. A sweet boy in a family that devoured such people. We were probably all born too late in our line to thrive, but as the youngest, he had been born the latest of all and was disproportionately punished for the sins of our House. That was the guilt on my *ka* I would have to answer for in the *Duat* above all others.

"Do you know if he suffered?" I asked finally.

"I don't believe so. The servants whisper that she used a large dose of wolfsbane. If that is so, death would have come quickly."

"If the Queen of Egypt agreed to be merciful for once in her life, I am glad she spent it on Ptah," I said quietly as Antony and I watched our progress across the rolling sea.

At last one morning, Nuray roused me from my sleep. "My lady! The coast is visible!"

We scrambled above board and I gazed hungrily at the shore I thought I would never see again. My stomach fluttered as I could just make out the flash of the mirror of the Lighthouse, the crumbling shoreline of Pharos. Oh, how I had missed my glorious Egypt! I longed to feel the rough touch of sand again, smell the lotuses blooming on the Nile, the burn of the desert wind. I had been taken away so many years ago —

not much more than a child — and was returning still perhaps young in age, though I wondered how much of the girl Arsinoë remained.

I came home to Egypt the same age my sister had been when she sent me away, what was the meaning in that? I was afraid of her discovering us, yet I wanted to see her with my own eyes. *Really just your own eye, love,* said Caesar in my head. Was she as I remembered her? Was I the same to her?

"I'm sure the royal barge will come out to meet us, my lady. You should hide below decks until we dock. I will have one of my men alert you when it is safe for you to disembark," said Antony, interrupting my thoughts.

I nodded and reluctantly returned below with Nuray to stow ourselves behind the stacks of provisions, taking turns whispering lullabies to Aetia. We could hear feet board our ship. I did not fear Cleopatra coming below decks, but what of someone like Apollodorus? I willed my body to be still as Nuray stroked Aetia's flyaway curls.

"I have always hated the waiting," I murmured to Nuray, rubbing my wrist in absence of my bracelet.

She smiled. "Patience, my lady. Surely we will be able to leave soon."

I returned her grin. "You have not been to Egyptian ceremonies. If we are lucky, you will not have gray hair by the time my sister is finished."

"Speaking of the queen," said Nuray, finding an even lower voice with which to speak, "do we even need to hide like this? With her magic supposedly destroyed?"

"Possibly not, but this is not the venue where I would like to test the success of our counterspell." I paused with a wicked glint. "And unlike some Egyptian royalty, my sister still has eyes in her head with which to spy us traipsing about in front of her."

Nuray threw her hands over her mouth to stifle her guilty laughter. "My lady is an imp!" she squeaked. "I suppose we can say we are showing deference to Lord Antony's feelings by staying hidden and not giving him an ulcer in return for his generosity."

As time wore on my daughter grew restive and crawled back into my lap.

"Story!" she demanded of me.

"Shh, my love. What kind of story would you like?" I whispered back.

Aetia dropped her voice a little. "One with animals!"

"Hmm, a story with animals... What about a princess who was turned into an animal?"

My daughter nodded eagerly so I began. "Once upon a time, there was a princess who lived in a faraway land. She lived an ordinary life for a princess until one day Zeus saw her and fell madly in love with her. He tried to hide this love from Hera, but the queen of the gods was not fooled, not even when Zeus turned the princess into a lovely cow to protect her."

"What color was the cow princess?"

"I know not, *nedjet*. What color do you think she was?

She frowned in thought. "Zeus is king in the sky. He would make her blue like the sky."

"A wise answer. Then it was so. The cow princess was the color of the bluest sky on a summer day."

"What happened next?"

"Well, Hera cleverly asked Zeus for the beautiful sky cow as a present and he could not refuse her. So the queen of the gods took the cow princess and tied her to an olive tree."

"Do cows like olives?"

"I am not sure, my star. If not, maybe she would like to eat the leaves."

"Then what?"

"Now Hera, knowing that this was no ordinary cow, was afraid that the cow princess would escape. So she sent her favorite servant to guard the cow princess. He was a giant named Argus and he had a hundred eyes to watch the cow princess with."

My daughter's own eyes grew wide at such an incomprehensible number. "How could he have so many? Were they on his head?"

"Even the ancients were not sure. Some say he had them all over his body; on his cheeks," I playfully kissed Aetia's cheeks, "arms... hands... stomach... knees... feet... toes..." She gave a little squeal at each of these.

"Or, some say he had eyes like a bee or spider, with many many small eyes where you have yours. Either way, with so many eyes, he could sleep with some of them closed, but some would always be watching. That is why he was a perfect guard."

"Was the cow princess sad?"

"She was very sad, *imi-ib*. She was far away from her home and she was all alone."

"Did she cry?"

"Yes, but not with her princess voice. Do you remember when we were in the market and the baby calves were being taken away from their mothers?" She nodded. "Do you remember the sound the mother cows made?"

"Yes. It was sad."

"Indeed. That is what the cow princess sounded like."

"Why didn't Zeus help the cow princess?"

"He did. He sent Hermes to rescue the cow princess, because Hermes is the cleverest of the gods. He disguised himself as a shepherd and began to tell Argus a story in which he wove a magic spell to put all of the guard's eyes to sleep."

"What story was it?"

"The ancients do not say. What story do you think it was?"

"Umm... The Princess and the Jar!"

"The story about Pandora? It is possible. Let us say that was the story. Anyway, once Argus was asleep, Hermes untied the cow princess, but he was afraid Argus would wake up and chase her, so he killed the giant while he was sleeping."

"I wish the giant didn't get killed," Aetia said, frowning seriously. "He didn't hurt the cow princess."

"It is true. Sometimes even the gods make mistakes, *kharsheret*."

"Did the cow princess get to go home?"

"No, she ran away from Hera's house and wandered the earth lost."

"She was probably scared because Hermes hurt Argus."

"Perhaps she was, my sweet. So the cow princess was lost and she wandered all over the world. She was still sad because Hera sent a fly to sting her and it hurt her a great deal."

"She should have used her tail like cows do."

"She did, but this was a magic fly so it always came back."

"What did she do then?"

"Finally she swam across the sea and used the water to escape the fly."

"Flies don't like water."

"Exactly. She swam and swam and swam until she reached the other side of the sea. She climbed onto dry land and shook herself off. She wandered into this new land looking for someone to tell her where she was, when she met the strangest creature she had ever seen floating in the river. It was similar to a cow, though this animal was much bigger and heavier. It had a wide head and a large mouth with tiny ears that flicked back and forth.

"'Excuse me, Mister Swimming Cow,' said the cow princess. 'I am lost, where am I?'

"The animal replied, 'I am no cow, I am a hippopotamus. I live in this river and sun myself on this sand. This land is called Egypt, and you are welcome here, Miss Cow, but do not come any closer to the water, for it is full of hungry crocodiles and they will eat you up!'"

My daughter's face lit up. "Egypt! That's where we are!"

"Or will be soon," said Nuray with a smile and a glance around our hiding place.

"The cow princess thanked the hippopotamus for his help and she decided to find the nearest city," I continued. "When she arrived in the city, the people were amazed to see a blue cow coming out of the desert. Knowing her to be special, they were very nice to her and told everyone they knew about the beautiful cow. Zeus, who had been looking for her all over, heard of the Egyptians talking about the strange cow so he came to Egypt and turned the cow princess back into a maiden."

"Did the princess stay with Zeus?"

"No, it was too dangerous because Hera was still very, very angry. So Zeus left the princess with the Egyptians who promised to take care of her."

"Do they have cows in Egypt?"

"Yes. They even have a cow goddess, remember?"

"Hathor!" said Aetia, glowing proudly.

"That is right! Now, the king of Egypt had heard about this magical maiden so he came to see her. When he arrived, the pharaoh fell instantly in love with the princess and married her as quickly as possible."

"Did they live happily ever after?"

"I think they must have, my love."

"Will we be happy in Egypt like the cow princess?"

"I hope so, *nedjet*. Do you think we will?"

She thought for a moment. "Yes. We'll be happy."

I pulled her close in my arms. "Then it is settled."

As the day drew to a close, one of Antony's centurions came at last to release us. We gathered up our few belongings and I carefully wrapped Aetia's hair in cloth before tying the end over her face so that only her eyes showed.

"It should be safe for you to leave now, Your Highness. I was instructed by General Antony to give you some coin to ease your passage south," he said as I tied cloth across my own face and pulled the heavy hood of my cloak so that it hung over my eyes.

Eye, my lady, said Mudjet in my head.

"Thank you, sir," I replied taking the offered bag. "The general is very generous. I thank you all for your assistance and courage. I am sorry I have nothing to give any of you in return."

"The thanks of Arsinoë of Egypt is enough, my lady. I saw you when you were marched in Caesar's triumph. Such bravery should not be snuffed out by the jealous Queen of Egypt." Nuray picked up Aetia, and the centurion saluted her. "Goodbye, *puella*. You too were very brave crossing the big sea. Your father would've been proud of you."

The corners of my daughter's eyes pulled up so that in spite of her wrapped face one could tell she was smiling.

We returned to the deck of the ship and slowly made our way down the gangplank. As my feet touched land, I felt dizzy knowing the dust of my home lay beneath my sandals. We made our way through the streets I had once known so well, where everything was the same and different all at once. We crossed under the Gate of the Sun and walked along the banks of the canal I had used to swim out of the palace so many years ago.

I realized with a jolt that it was not really so long ago, only the length of a child's life, but here I was still running from my sister. Soon, I told myself, soon I could stop running. We came to a confluence of the canals and paid a boatman to take us to Canopus, where we could then arrange passage down the Nile. It was by now dark, but the men who plied the waters of the canals knew no hours and with an extra copper for lamp oil, asked few questions. We were not the first people to slip out of Alexandria under the cover of night.

Chapter Forty-Nine

I am back in Heliopolis, in my Lord's temple. I realize my vision is unimpaired, which causes me to reflexively touch the left side of my face. I find it to be whole. I look down at the floor to see the old hand glass the Mirror once sent me as her calling card and I cannot resist picking it up to see my reflection.

My unblemished face gazes back at me, though around my intact left eye are the markings of *wadjet* tattooed in brilliant turquoise. I silently thank Thoth as I place the mirror back down and turn my attention to the space around me. The sanctuary is still in its neglected state, but the fire I lit on his altar continues to burn.

As I step into the light it casts, Set appears on the other side. He has lost the wounded look he had the last time we met in the Dream World and is as he appeared when he found me in the desert palace, sleek as a panther, with endless fire in his effulgent eyes. "It is good to have you back where you belong, *nedjet*. I am sorry you have such a long journey southward still before you."

"It is not so very far. I have made longer journeys."

He moves around the altar to my side and takes me in his arms as he reaches up to cradle the left side of my face. "I am sorry I could not spare your courageous Mudjet."

"As am I." I place a hand over one of the scars on his arm. "Does it pain you much?"

"Yes, though I try to follow your advice on mortal grief, so it is not as it was. The other gods have taken to calling me Set the Compassionate."

This makes me laugh. "Late is the hour of the world indeed if I have wreaked such havoc on your reputation."

"No, Beloved, you have saved me," he says simply. "Before you came, few spoke to me in the Black Land. Now the people see what you have done and they know you held yourself out as *Meretkaset*, they remember

I hold out my hands to protect them as much as my nephew does. It is good."

My heart grows heavy again. "I wish you had not convinced Mudjet to sacrifice herself for your plan."

"I would not have forced her to do anything had she been unwilling. It was she who told me you must not be told everything until it was over. She is one who knows you as I do."

Set had used that turn of phrase to me before. It reminds me of a question I had held in my *ka* for him for some time. "You have said thus similarly to me before, my Lord, and I have always meant to ask you. Why did you let Caesar come to me?"

Set's expression grows clever. "That reason is not enough? You have always had the bloom of a hidden flower, Beloved. Rare are those who know you as I do."

"It is a reason, though I do not think it is enough for Him Whose Form is Unknowable to show such special favor to an enemy," I reply with a smirk.

My Lord's face grows contemplative. "Yes and no, Beloved. The son of the Julians kept the double crown from your head, which does still displease me."

"But?"

He smiles. "But every time he was given an opportunity to harm your person, he did not. At the cost of convenience, at the cost of enraging your sister who was at least his ally if not his beloved, at the cost of showing his might before his own people. He built for himself a reputation for mercy for those he had defeated, yet to no one else did he demonstrate such repeated clemency. There was no one whom I trusted more in the Waking World to keep you safe."

"It is unfortunate that I could not do the same for him."

"The likes of him were not built for safety, *nedjet*. Your destinies were intertwined, though you were both made to follow your own paths. Just as your daughter will, with her queenly *ka* and her warrior's heart."

"For now our paths lead to you, my Lord."

"Indeed. I anxiously await your arrival in my city, Arsinoë, Queen of Queens."

And then I wake up.

In the old city of Canopus, where strangers to our land thought panderers and dicers ruled the merchant ships and traders' stalls, we haggled for our passage south with the quick-witted river pilots. I had let Nuray speak for us in Alexandria, but here it was I who dealt with the captains who hired out their crafts, speaking in the colloquial Egyptian I had picked up from servants to mask my more aristocratic upbringing. Though even when I mistakenly used a more formal word here and there, we were protected by the fact that the men I was bargaining with would more likely assume I was a higher-born Egyptian lady, not a Greek noble, whose general disdain for the native tongue of this land was well known. Cleopatra and I had always been atypical in that regard.

After coming to acceptable terms with our captain, we went to leave an offering at the city's famous Temple of Osiris to bless our journey. He might be the Lord of the Dead, but he was also the Lord of the Sacred Fire in the city whose hieroglyph is a burning vase. Here even in this den of sin did people pray to He Who Lights the Paths of the Dead.

We stood in the muted light of a hundred lamps and placed our small votive amongst the others. Around us, supplicants lined up to have priests write out prayers to be burnt into heavenly smoke in the fires of the temple.

I approached one of priests and said to him, "So many prayers, good sir. The fervor of your worshippers makes me fear for my travels."

"Fear not for your travels, good lady," replied the priest. He hesitated, studying us carefully and then he continued in a low voice. "The people fear for the *ka* of the slain princess so cruelly murdered in the house of the gods and buried without the proper rites of the dead. They are asking

Lord Osiris to send out Lord Anubis into the *Duat* to help her find her way to the fields of our ancestors."

I could not find the words to respond to the boundless love of my people. It was Nuray who answered the priest. Giving him a coin, she said, "I too would like to ask the Lord Osiris to guide the Princess of Egypt on her journey."

"Bless you, Daughter of Anatolia. May the gods reward your generosity." The priest bent his head and wrote out the prayer before handing the papyrus off to an acolyte to throw into the fire.

As we stepped back out into the bustle of the street, Nuray squeezed my arm. "I trust the noble Osiris to understand of which journey I speak," she said with shining eyes.

We traveled down the shifting, ageless Nile for nearly a week.

The further south we traveled, the lighter my spirit became. Touching the sand of home reopened the scar on my heart left by my brother's death and my *ka* still wept in the lonely hours for Ptah, though it was the sluggish inspissate flow of an old wound, not a fresh one. I had mourned for my brother as dead from afar ever since I had set foot on the Roman warship over seven years earlier. I had prayed for him every day with the prayers for peace one only speaks when the object of your thoughts is living on borrowed time. My only regret was that his path was not one I walked with him, as vain a hope as that was. We all travel our own paths and the sphinxes we meet at the crossroads can only ever be our own demons, not someone else's, no matter how close we hold those whose burdens we long to bear.

I wept also for Mudjet, though there I tried harder to check my grief because I knew she would have disapproved. There my tears were mostly for the loss of her companionship, its price beyond pearls. She had been my mother when mine died, my sister when mine pushed me away, my advisor when all others were taken from me, and my friend in a world where they were hard to come by. She had been the twin of my childhood and sharer of all my days, and I knew a part of me would always be looking for her fleet-winged laughter just beyond my sight.

We watched as the wading birds dipped their curving beaks into the river. The waterfowl chattered to one another as we passed. Blankets of songbirds took wing together as the deep heat of the desert sun placed a sheen on the surface of the water beneath us, though all of this I observed under the shield of my heavy hood. Our boatmen seemed simple, honest men, but we did not want them to think of us later if word of the trophy my sister gathered from me was widely known. Nuray explained to them that I had weak eyes that were damaged by too much light, a common enough malady in this land of nearly horizonless illumination. My daughter took in all we saw with the overflowing rapture of the very young. Sleep would only overtake her when she would gently trip into it unawares.

At last we made dock at the small town on the banks of Nile known as Ombos. Once upon a time, there were larger, more elegant cities here, though now it was just one of many out-of-the-way places that dipped their feet in the river's edge. Tombs from before even the Egyptians' long memories begin dotted the surrounding desert, ones of massive scale said to be made when the gods were young and humble burrows in the sand where the old ones buried their dead before Anubis came and taught them mummification.

The streets were small and the people led small lives. That was exactly what my daughter and I needed. We needed a small nest in a faraway tree where my *imi-ib* could fledge her wings in safety. Far from the bloody intentions of my family and hostile Roman factions.

We walked through the streets, slowly because I was still healing, still learning how to hold my balance in a world I only saw by halves now. I held the hand of Aetia while leaning on the arm of Nuray. They did not know where we were going, but I did. I had chosen this particular remote Egyptian town because if we were to remain in Egypt while my sister reigned, we must retreat to a position of strength. I had come to Ombos because my Lord had called me here. This was his earthly home, this was my true sanctuary.

The Temple of Set in Ombos was grand enough in appearance, though it had a rough shabbiness on its edges. This form of it was built more than a thousand years ago and my Lord's good reputation in the Black Land had not been high in the millennia since, where the cults of his siblings held sway and endlessly recited the tales of his treachery. It was only here, where the past lived quietly and time passed without much comment, that the people of Egypt still whispered prayers to the King of the Desert Winds, the solar shipwright who battled darkness for mankind.

We entered the outer sanctum, and I motioned for Nuray to take Aetia. She picked up my girl as I sank to my knees and lowered myself forward until my forehead grazed the hot sand.

Thank you for calling me home, my Lord. We have traversed the great river in its desert form and traveled the blinding sands of your domain because you have held out your hand to protect us. We are grateful for your favor as always.

My thoughts were going to continue, but just then a middle-aged man appeared from the interior of the temple flanked by several others. By his dress I could tell he must be the high priest and I sat up to make a gesture of respect. However, as he approached me he knelt down opposite me and reached out gently to push back my hood. A wide smile deepened the creases in his face and he and his companions bowed their heads.

"Welcome, my lady. I am Renni, High Priest of the Temple of Set Serpent-Slayer. We are so glad you are here."

I was surprised. "You know who I am?"

The priest's smile widened again. "Yes, my lady. I was told you were coming."

I was in the temple, my lady, Renni says, *sweeping dust and sand from one of the inner courtyards when I suddenly felt a presence just out of my sight to my left. I turned that way and saw two men in animal hoods standing there. I fell to my knees in fear for I knew them to be gods. I confess that I longed to raise my eyes in spite of my terror for I also knew that one of them was my beloved Lord and I had wished to be in his true presence all my life.*

"It is well, Ludim-son, We will not harm you," spoke my dread Lord.

"Oh my Lord, Prince of the Desert, Speaker of Storms, how may I serve you?" I said, slowly raising my head. When I did, I was startled to look upon the face of my Lord's companion. For above his beaked hood he wore the double crown and beneath it he gazed on me with his golden right eye pierced with the light of the zenith sun and with his unknowable left Eye ringed in green in the *wadjet* pattern. For he was Horus, Lord of the Black Land, He of the Outstretched Wings. Though my Lord had comforted me, I trembled anew for I could not imagine the circumstances that would bring the falcon-god and his uncle before me hand in hand.

My Lord continued. "Faithful have been the works of your hands in my house, my child, and so I am entrusting you with a most important duty."

"My Lord, I have dedicated my life to you since I was a boy. Any task you put before me, I will expend the last of my strength to fulfill."

He nodded, pleased. "Ludim-son, there is one who walks in the Waking World who is my beloved above all others. She like you has been faithful to me in all things, and she has shown herself worthy to wear the double crown. But it is not the will of the Lord Who Shines On All that this shall come to pass, so I am sending her to you so that we may keep her safe."

"Safe from who, my Lord?"

"She has been hunted by the Queen of Egypt and the wolves of Latium. She has passed through many trials to escape their snares. We bring her to Ombos, my city, so her enemies might lose her scent."

"We shall honor this lady above all others, as the Beloved of our Lord."

"You will know her as a cloaked figure traveling with a small girl-child with the eyes of a raven and a daughter of Illium. She hides her face because she has given her left eye to break a powerful spell of the Queen of Egypt."

Lord Horus moved his head to the side like a lanner, as if to see me better. "Set-priest, I have come because this lady has been hailed as pharaoh in my lands by the people of my blood and given the Five Names. I owe her my protection, even from another pharaoh. The Pharaoh-Queen of Egypt has given my lands to the wolves of Latium, so I spread my wings to shield the younger Ptolemy-daughter from the eyes of Alexandria until the *heka* of the elder burns itself into the *Duat*."

I was again startled. "My Lords, you say the younger Ptolemy-daughter? Princess Arsinoë lives?"

My Lord spoke thus, "Yes, she is who I send to your care, Ludim-son. Though I wished better things for her, I give her an honored place in my house where she will be safe. Where she can outlive her House and die as a queen in Egypt."

Lord Horus held up his *was*-scepter. "I am blessing the cloth and gold thread that your priests have been sewing for robes. These robes will be infused with the grace of the gods if you take a piece and make a covering for the eye of the younger Ptolemy-daughter. This covering shall be stitched with my *wadjet*, so I may give her my protection. She is a child of dualities. Her destiny is to hold the will of me and my uncle in balance. She will carry the Eye of Horus in the House of Set."

I awoke at this point, my lady.

Renni, High Priest of Set, moved forward again and began to carefully unwind the linen strips around my head. When they lay in a heap at our side, he cast his hand in blessing over the empty socket of my left eye. He then reached into a pouch at his side and produced an indigo-colored patch embroidered with the *wadjet*, the magical eye of Horus created for him by clever Thoth to replace the one stolen by my Lord. He took the strap and adjusted it over my eyelid. When he was finished he sat back and held his palms together.

"Four are the paths of Horus, the Far Flying: protection, sacrifice, healing, and restoration. All of these have brought you here, my Honored Lady. All of these have brought you home."

I held my palms together. "I have come home to be the conduit of the gods to their people. Long may I serve them and the people."

Renni beamed. "We hail thee, *heqat-taui*. Welcome home."

Chapter Fifty

I rise every morning bathed in sunlight and greet my Lord with congratulations for his nightly triumph over the darkness. He rarely speaks to me in the open fashion he assumed when I was younger, we know each other too well at this point for that. We are simply a part of one another now. I feel him deep in my bones the way the old feel the weather. Though as the years fly by so breathlessly, I suspect I might start feeling that too soon enough.

Renni laughs at me when I talk of being old, saying that only a dustbones like him may speak of age and that I must hold my tongue in the presence of my elders. He is joking kind to me in the way of a fond guardian uncle, not that I had much experience with that among my blood family. He reminds of the graciousness of Xenos, whose wisdom and gaiety I miss daily.

My sister reached out to Ephesus one last time to crush him for the honor he showed me every hour I lived in his city, but she had Mudjet's blood and my eye in her hands, and she sat in her empty palace wondering why her *heka* seemed to evaporate from her fingers. I long to write to my friends on that faraway coast, though I know it would be madness to attempt. Perhaps soon the winds will change and things will be different. I still have a fondness for looking backwards into the past that I have not broken myself of yet. I have always been a lover of stories and they spring from who we have been, rather than who we are. My daughter is my instructor in this, she has always dwelled in the present more successfully than I. She does not let the ropes of the past bind her shimmering wings.

I am sitting in one of the temple courtyards with some of the village girls, a copy of Vergilius Maro's *Eclogues* on my lap that I am translating from Latin into Egyptian while they sort dried herbs for the priests, when I hear the sound of hooves and commotion somewhere in the town square. I assume it is a local dispute until I can hear Renni's voice above the fray. I cannot hear what he is saying, but I can tell he is not speaking in Ombos' dialect. Then I know what has happened. I bid the girls to stay here, and to not be afraid. That I will go sort this out. I am not afraid either. I have been awaiting this day.

I wrap a shawl loosely over my head as I step out into the light and make my way towards where the crowd has gathered. People have stopped their work to watch, and those I pass bow out of my way as I go. The crowd at the edge parts at my approach until the young man arguing with Renni from his horse can see me. He stops talking and climbs down, throwing the reins to the centurion closest to him.

Renni is ashen. "My lady, you must go back inside, I will—"

I raise a hand to silence him, though I do not move my gaze from the young man. And oh, he is so young. We are very nearly the same age, it is true, but I have lived a thousand years compared to him. He is slenderer than I expected, and not as tall. They say he is often ill — and he is rather pale — yet that has not held him back from much. Not from beating an old warhorse like Mark Antony at his own game. Not from besting the canniest woman I have ever known.

I bow to him. "You honor us, Caesar."

He appraises me from head to foot. "Are you who they say you are, madam?"

I have not walked out into the midday heat to dissemble with the boy they call Octavian. "Probably, my lord, though people say a great many things."

He snorts sardonically. "Antony did always have a sentimental streak." A pause. "You don't look much like the whore."

"We never did. Our different mothers left their separate marks upon us."

"You know that she is dead, then?"

I incline my head. "We had heard rumors to that effect, my lord. I know that not having her for your triumph must be a grave disappointment, but you know she had a terrible fear of captivity. Particularly in Rome."

No crowd in Rome would threaten riot to give her a stay of execution, sniffs Mudjet in my head.

Octavian shakes his head as if bothered by a troublesome insect. "I specifically placed a guard on her to prevent any such... accidents... and she still managed to sneak poison past me."

I almost smile. "Poison and the Queen of Egypt are old friends. If anyone could perform one last act of sorcery, it would be my sister."

For the first time, I can feel him staring at my eye patch. I realize what he wants and does not want at the same time, what he does not want to ask. I oblige him and remove it. I feel some in the crowd lower their gaze, though Octavian does not. I let him stare at my empty socket, at the thin red scar that trails from the outer edge of the lid like the kitetail of kohl I wear on my right.

"You know, they say she ate it on a golden platter," he says after a few moments.

I would have picked different parts of you to devour, my falcon goddess, says Caesar in my head.

"That sounds like Roman gossip to me, but if that was so, that was her business," I answer as I place the patch back over my eyelid, adjusting it until it is comfortable. "The wild tribes are said to ingest their enemies to gain their power. Though eating an adversary's eye seems to open one's self to internal scrutiny. Perhaps it has allowed me to see her *ka* more clearly."

"You seem to bear her surprisingly little malice, under the circumstances," he observes.

"Our relationship has improved somewhat since she believed in my demise." I look at the boy, he is unamused. Clearly humor is not among his inheritance from his great uncle. "In any case, as you have confirmed, she is dead. A shrewd man once told me that only fools try to revenge themselves upon the dead. Our rage cannot touch them, and in the end, we will only feast on our own bile."

He appears to be unconvinced, though such is the lot of the inexperienced.

"However, I suspect you have not come all the way to Ombos to tell me of Cleopatra's defeat, my lord. I also sense that if you had come here to complete the task Antony left undone, you would not have suffered me to ramble on so."

This does catch him a bit off guard. He raises an eyebrow at me. *There it is.* "I don't like leaving things to chance, but I don't think you have the strength to rally the Egyptians to your cause."

"Doubtful indeed. I am comfortable with my life here and see no need to ride to Alexandria to convince the people of this land to trade a new conqueror for an old one."

"A refreshing stance for you." I see in his pale eyes that he believes my words, and yet he disbelieves that one such as me could relinquish my power so carelessly. He has had his first taste of it, and because he is in the end blood of my love, he cannot conceive of life without it. He will learn that not all power wears the triumphal golden laurels. He will learn — or perish by it as the world supposes I have.

I shrug, unprovoked. "I was greener in judgment then. I gambled once and lost nearly everything. I have little desire to repeat myself."

"But you know what I do want."

"I believe so."

He walks up so there is only a bare amount of space between us. "Where is she?" he asks in a low voice.

Now I cannot suppress a smile. "She is not here, Caesar."

He frowns and narrows his eyes. "What do you mean?"

I make a fluttery gesture with my hand. "My daughter is the daughter of eagles, my lord." He flinches slightly. "I might be content to circle the edge of the desert for the rest of my days, but she needed to soar towards the horizon as soon as she had the strength to carry her there. She was born with noble, restless blood in her veins."

I pause to let this sink in. I have told him the truth, because I realize little will protect Aetia if the ruler of Rome decides to hunt her to the ends of the earth. The man who defeated Cleopatra will find a way. They say he is prowling in the east to discover where my sister sent Caesarion off to and that the younger children are already his captive guests in Rome. My girl and Selene might be safer than the boys, though this Caesar seems to dislike too many loose ends.

Octavian's already pale face blanches with anger. Mostly the impotent fury of a child who cannot believe he has been outmaneuvered by yet another one of the wretched Ptolemies. To his credit, he does not change his mind and have one of his men throttle me where I stand.

Finally, mastering his rage, he asks, "Is she a threat to me?"

Again, I offer him the olive branch of peace. "No. She is high-spirited, but hers is the love of an explorer, not a king. She has no desire for empire, I doubt she would wish to inherit Egypt even if I were queen outright. And truly, sir, can you imagine a Rome that would accept a female ruler? Even one that claims the Divine Caesar as her father?"

I can see him internally scoff at the notion. "Very well, my lady," he concedes. "If you continue to live here quietly and I hear no stirrings of dissent from you or your daughter, you will receive no molestation from me. Though see that you do not begin to boast of the girl's alleged parentage, not that any but the most empty-headed fools would believe such an outlandish tale."

I bow. "Of course, Caesar. Who indeed would believe it?"

APPENDIX A: EGYPTIAN WORDS and PHRASES

Below is a list of Egyptian words and phrases used in *The God's Wife*. Egyptian language studies is a complicated field and I have chosen to use Middle Egyptian, rather than later appearing dialects like Coptic, because many of the words and phrases I've utilized are titles, oaths, and words about the gods — in short, words I feel might have survived from an older language.

Egyptologists use a virtually vowel-less transliteration alphabet to translate hieroglyphics into the Roman alphabet. For a more readable text, I used the much less formal transcription guidelines: the result of which is easier to read, but arguably somewhat less accurate. Where possible, I have chosen traditional vowel usage or attempted to abide by what passes for scholarly consensus.

I am indebted to Raymond O. Faulkner's *Concise Dictionary of Middle Egyptian* (Griffith Institute, 1962), which remains a gold standard in the field, Bill Petty's *English to Middle Egyptian Dictionary* (Museum Tours Press, 2016), and James Allen's linguistic study *Middle Egyptian* (Cambridge University Press, 2000) for an excellent overview of contemporary Egyptian language study, though any errors of interpretation or grammar are mine alone. I am also grateful to E.A. Wallis Budge, whose scholarship and *Dictionary of Egyptian Hieroglyphics* (John Murray, 1920; Dover 1978) are considered flawed and passé, but whose work gave me an invaluable jumping off point for this part of my research.

Ahat-kheftyew - Enemy warships

Akhuiakhutre - "Light and Renown of Ra"

Atef - The crown of Osiris; it resembles the hedjet, but with ostrich plumes.

Ba - The part of a person's soul believed to contain their personality.

Deshret - The red crown symbolizing Lower Egypt, one half of the double crown. Also used as a proper noun to denote the Red Land.

Duat - The Egyptian realm of the dead, ruled by Osiris.

Hai heqat-taui, a'a meret en akhmui-remthu - "Hail, Queen of the Two Lands, greatly beloved of the two gods [Horus and Set] who weep not."

Hedjet - The white crown symbolizing Upper Egypt, one half of the double crown.

Heka - The deified concept of magic in the Egyptian world, literally "activate the ka." The Egyptians believed that magic was performed through the power of a person's soul, using the appropriate spells and rituals. This power could also be used to connect the practitioner with the heka wielded by the kas of the gods. Heka more broadly could also mean to hold great power or influence.

Hemet-netjer – God's wife

Heqat - Ruler (female)

Heqet - Princess/daughter of the pharaoh

Hezet en iammi, heqet-taui - "Blessings of the gracious gods, Princess of Egypt."

Iammi a'a pheti - "The gracious gods of great strength."

Ib – Heart

Imi-ib - "Heart's desire," a term of endearment

Iqer sekhri - "Excellent of plans"

Ka - The part of a person's soul believed to contain their life force, believed to survive death and travel to the underworld.

Kemet - The Black Land/Lower Egypt

Khaiwadjet-Merettaui - "She who is like the shining Eye of Horus, beloved of the Two Egypts"

Kharsheret - Child (female)

Khepresh – The blue war crown of the pharoahs of Egypt, traditionally worn into battle.

Medjat - Book

Menat - A large amulet worn as a necklace, associated with the goddess Hathor.

Meret - Beloved (feminine suffix)

Meretkaset - "Beloved of the Ka of Set"

Mewet - Mother

Mu-ti - Grandmother

Nebty iaitrwedja - "She of the Two Ladies [Iaret and Nekhbet], to whom the old gods open their mouths"

Nedjes - Little/smallest god

Nedjet - Little/smallest goddess

Pedjeti - Archers

Rw - The sacred texts used by practitioners of heka.

Senet - An Egyptian board game where two players take turns moving pawns across a grid of thirty squares, divided into three rows of ten. Believed to simulate the journey of the *ka* through the *Duat*, it bears a passing resemblance to the modern game of backgammon.

Seshaw - The rituals performed by the practitioners of heka.

Sha - A mythical animal used to represent the god Set. Also called the Set Animal.

Shai (-t) - Fortune/fate (feminine suffix)

Shai nefer - Good luck

Sharm' ha hetep - Peaceful greetings

Sherit - Maiden

Ta-meriu - "People of the land of the Nile flood" (the Egyptians)

Taui - "The Two Lands" (a traditional name for Egypt)

Tjesiib - "Raise the Mind"

Tua netjer heqat-taui - "Thank god for the ruler of the Two Lands"

Ur-hekau - "He Who is Great in Words of Power [Heka]" (a title of Set)

Wadjet - The magical eye of Horus, created by Thoth to replace the eye taken from the god by Set. Often used by the Egyptians in amulets as a symbol of protection against evil.

APPENDIX B: THE GODS OF EGYPT

As befitting a civilization as long-lived as ancient Egypt, the number and cosmogony of the deities worshipped is dizzying as well as often redundant and contradictory. Below is a brief guide to those mentioned in *The God's Wife*.

Ammit - "The Devourer"; a female demon with the head of a crocodile, the front half of a lion, and the back end of a hippopotamus. A deity of the *Duat*, she eats the hearts of those judged unworthy of immortality in the afterlife.

Anubis - God of mummification and funerary rites, also a guide to the dead in the *Duat*; depicted as a man with the head of a jackal. Son of Set and Nephthys.

Apep - Demon representing chaos; depicted as a giant serpent. An agent of darkness who must be defeated by the gods nightly to prevent him from swallowing the sun.

Geb - God of the earth; depicted as a man with a goose on his head. Son of Shu and Tefnut; brother-husband of Nut; father of Osiris, Set, Isis, and Nephthys.

Hapy - God of the Nile, particularly the life-giving river floods; depicted as an androgynous man with blue skin and breasts.

Hathor - Goddess of love, beauty, fertility, and music; depicted as a woman with the head of a cow or cow's horns. Her other side is Sekhmet.

Horus - God of Egypt, the pharaohs, and the sun; depicted as a man with the head of a falcon wearing the double crown. Son of Osiris and Isis. Often paired with Ra as a solar deity.

Isis - Goddess of wisdom, marriage, and magic; depicted as a woman with a throne hieroglyph on her head. The sister of Set and Nephthys; the sister-wife of Osiris and the mother of Horus.

Khepri - God of sunrise and rebirth; an aspect of Ra. Depicted as a man with a scarab beetle for a head.

Ma'at - Goddess of truth, justice, and cosmic order; depicted as a woman with an ostrich feather on her head, signifying Truth. Wife of Thoth.

Mafdet - Goddess of protection against venomous bites, also of executions and legal justice; depicted as a mongoose or cat.

Nephthys - Goddess of night and death; depicted as a woman with a house hieroglyph and basket on her head. The sister of Osiris and Isis; the sister-wife of Set and mother of Anubis.

Nut - Goddess of the sky and heaven; depicted as a woman with a water pot on her head. Daughter of Shu and Tefnut; sister-wife of Geb; mother of Osiris, Set, Isis, and Nephthys.

Osiris - God of the afterlife and resurrection, king of the dead; depicted as a pharaoh partially wrapped like a mummy, usually with green skin and wearing the Atef crown. The brother of Set and Nephthys; brother-husband of Isis and father of Horus.

Ptah - God of creation, the arts, and craftsmen; depicted as a mummified man with green skin.

Ra - God of the sun and creation; sometimes depicted as a man with the head of a falcon or as a cat. As arguably the supreme Egyptian deity, he has many names and forms, often differentiating the sun at different points of the day. Khepri is the sun in the morning, Ra the midday sun, and the setting sun is identified with the creator god Khnum. As Amun, he is also king of the gods and wind.

Sekhmet - Goddess of war, fire, and vengeance; depicted as a woman with the head of a lioness. Her other side is Hathor.

Set - God of the desert, storms, chaos, and war; depicted as a man with the head of the *sha*. The brother of Osiris and Isis; the brother-husband of Nephthys, and the father of Anubis.

Shu - God of air and wind; depicted as a man with a crown of feathers on his head. Son of Ra, brother-husband of Tefnut, father of Geb and Nut.

Sobek - God of the Nile, crocodiles, and the Egyptian military; depicted as a man with the head of a crocodile.

Taweret - Goddess of fertility and childbirth; depicted as a hippopotamus.

Tefnut - Goddess of rain and moisture; depicted as a snake with a lion's head or as a woman with the head of a lioness. Daughter of Ra, sister-wife of Shu, mother of Geb and Nut.

Thoth - God of knowledge and invention; depicted as a man with the head of an ibis or as a baboon. Husband of Ma'at.

A Note on the Text

The quotations from Euripides' *Andromache* and *Helen* were adapted from the Edward Coleridge prose translation (1913), but I am grateful for the additional translative insight from John Frederick Nims' and Richmond Lattimore's respective translations through the University of Chicago Press (1956). The quotations from *The Book of Going Forth By Day* (*The Egyptian Book of the Dead*) are from the E.A. Wallis Budge translation (1901), with additional elucidation from the Raymond O. Faulkner/ Ogden Goelet translation (Chronicle Books, 2015). The biblical quotations are taken from the King James Version.

The epigraph texts were adapted from the Andrew P. Peabody translation of *de Officiis* (1887) and the Richard C. Jebb prose translation of *Antigone* (1904). With respect to the latter, I again relied on additional interpretation from Elizabeth Wyckoff's translation of the play, also through the University of Chicago Press (1954).

Acknowledgements

Writing can be a solitary business, less so perhaps when you have daily conversations with Egyptian queens and Roman generals, but producing a book certainly takes an army and being inexperienced in that arena, I am indebted to everyone who helped me make this novel even a fraction of what it is. Especially the following:

To Stephanie Weiss, for her help in navigating the world of self-publishing for someone who knew how to write a story, but didn't have a clue about how to turn a manuscript into an actual book. Thank you for lighting the way.

To my amazing editor, Jessica Hatch, for both taking on such a demanding project from a novice author and for becoming such a believer in my story. Her judicious eye and warm advocacy were a godsend for which I will forever be grateful.

To FrinaArt for her beautiful cover design, which was more than I could have hoped for and for the staff of SelfPubBookCovers for their coordinating help.

To my wonderful coworkers, who have been on my side over this book since Day One and whose frequent encouragement and requests for progress reports helped keep me on track.

To my family and friends, who provided all of that intangible support that makes anything doable and probably, whether they know it or not, lost me more than once to a plot train or flurry of research. Thank you for putting up with my inattention and long disgressions into the finer points of Egyptian mythology. It has always been appreciated.

On the subject of research, endless thanks to the librarians and pages of the Carnegie Libraries of Pittsburgh for their assistance via dozens of trips in the back stacks to find me nearly every esoteric treatise imaginable touching on the time period of this story. Your invisible hand is all over this book and I would be less enlightened without your hard work.

And to my mother – my first reader *par excellence*, my second editor, my endless sounding board – I can't even begin to express my gratitude. She's read this manuscript almost as many times as I have and still comes back for more. It sounds self-indulgent to lean back on the praise of a parent, but I know what a sharp literary eye she has and her faith in this book has fueled me through all the hours of doubt. *Je t'aime.*

And lastly to Steve, whose technical assistance pales in the shadow of his boundless support of every aspect of this project and of me. You are my everything and none of this could have happened without you.

About the Author

Sarah Holz is a native of Buffalo, NY and she now lives in Pittsburgh, PA with her doting husband and three petulant cats. She reads far too much when she should be writing. This is her first novel.

Read more at https://blog.sarahholz.com.

Made in the USA
San Bernardino, CA
19 February 2019